# Expeditionary Force
# Mavericks
# Book 2:

# FREEFALL

## By
## Craig Alanson

Contact the author
craigalanson@gmail.com

Cover Design By
Alexandre Rito

Table of Contents

# CHAPTER ONE

"Well, this is just *freakin'* wonderful," Derek Bonsu grimaced as he deactivated the Buzzard's rack of missiles. The weapons would not be needed, because they couldn't risk firing on the target, a small Kristang village that had been the team's objective for that morning. Now the Legion soldiers in the Buzzard's cabin were grumbling and bitching to each other. The flight from their base had been ninety minutes of bouncing through a raging blizzard, and it had all been for nothing. "I *knew* this day would turn to shit."

Despite the seriousness of the situation, Irene had to smile. "You knew that, because you stubbed your toe?"

"Because the *first* thing that happened when I got out of bed, was bashing my toe on the leg of the cot. That's a bad way to start the day, you know?"

Irene didn't reply, she knew the reason Derek had run his toe into the cot that morning was he had tried to avoid the pile of clothes she left on the floor. Plus her gear bag. Plus he first had to awkwardly crawl over her to get out of bed, because his side of the cot was up against the wall of the shelter. "You need to tell Em."

"*Me?*" Derek protested. "I told her the bad news *last* time, when we were on Fresno."

"See?" She reached across the Buzzard's center console and patted his face affectionately. "She already thinks of you as the bearer of bad news, so it won't hurt."

"Nuh-uh," he shook his head. "Not this time."

"Fine," she relented. "Your aircraft?"

"My aircraft," Derek affirmed, keeping the Buzzard in a lazy circle, orbiting a control point ninety kilometers from the objective. Or the place that *had* been that day's objective, before everything turned to shit. The only good news was they had flown through and out of the blizzard, and the sky was mostly clear all the way to the objective. That would have been good if the Legion troops were landing to 'assist' the evacuation of the village's residents. As it was, the only practical effect of the better weather was to provide a view of snow, frozen mud and the tough fir-like trees that covered the unwelcoming landscape. Since the Legion landed nine days ago, Derek had seen the sun mostly when they flew above the ever-present thick layer of clouds. Not for the first time, he wished he had never seen that world.

The mission was supposed to be quick, simple and easy: monitor the Kristang as they left a planet recently surrendered to the Ruhar. The world was called Jellaxico, and the humans of the Alien Legion had only half-heartedly given it the nickname 'Jellybean'. The planet was just not important enough to merit an official nickname, and hopefully the Legion wouldn't be there long enough to remember it. Jellaxico was an Earth-like planet, if Earth's crust had significantly more rare metals, was larger, had thirteen percent higher gravity, and circled the local orange dwarf star on an elliptical orbit that took it from the middle to the outer edge of the habitable 'Goldilocks' zone. Also if the level of free oxygen was eight percent less than Earth normal.

Jellaxico had been settled by the Kristang for mining rare metals, though that justification for the expense of traveling there had been rendered moot three hundred years ago, when robotic mining began in the rich asteroid belt of a star system much closer to the core worlds of Kristang territory. Since mining became unprofitable, the remaining inhabitants of Jellaxico hung on mostly out of stubbornness, or because they couldn't afford to pay for passage on the one ship per year that swung by to deliver supplies, and take aboard anyone fortunate enough to get off the miserable world. Jellaxico might have continued its slumber forever, with a slowly declining population, except the most recent wormhole shift had given the Ruhar easy access. The Ruhar needed certain rare metals, especially palladium, lanthanum and yttrium, to make their jump drives function properly. The clan that owned Jellaxico actually had no official presence there, and the seven thousand Kristang of various squabbling subclans did not like being sold out by their leaders. Accordingly, the Ruhar had assigned the Alien Legion to handle the task of kicking the lizards off the planet. It was a test, with the Legion force under the command of Emily Perkins. She had one under-strength battalion of six hundred fifty humans and eighty Verd-kris, plus two transport ships and one destroyer. She wasn't happy with the force structure and she also knew the hamsters didn't care. If the Legion could not manage the evacuation of seven thousand lizards who were living in isolated villages, then the whole concept of the Alien Legion needed to be reviewed.

The evac had gone well for the first eight days, with most of the warrior caste and almost all of the civilians happy to get off the frozen ball of mud they called home. Then Irene and Derek approached a village early that morning, and the local leader had a message for the platoon leader. They knew it was trouble immediately, though Major Chan had been trying to handle the problem on her own. Derek and Irene knew that Perkins would want to know what was going on, so they only felt mildly uncomfortable about going behind Chan's back. Sometimes, officers had to be protected from themselves.

Instead of calling Emily Perkins directly, Irene sent a request up to the destroyer *Wyl Chidah*, a Ruhar vessel the humans referred to as the *Wild Child*. After a brief back-and-forth with the destroyer's communications department and then the ship's executive officer, Irene was connected to Perkins. "Ma'am," Irene took a breath before continuing. "We have a problem."

Emily Perkins's own morning had been rather splendid, a fact that had her anticipating bad news. She had slept well considering that only four hours elapsed between closing her eyes and swing her legs onto the deck when the alarm woke her. The coffee, made from beans the Ruhar grew in a lab, was hot and delicious. Breakfast had been biscuits and gravy that tasted, if not like her mother used to make, as good as any diner in her hometown. The destroyer's crew had greeted her cheerily while they ate whatever food hamsters ate for breakfast. When she arrived in the *Wild Child's* Combat Operations Center, the overnight status reports had all been positive. Objectives secured, no casualties on either side, the overall plan was proceeding two hours ahead of schedule.

The relentless good news had her on edge when Irene called. "Striebich, are you going to ruin my day?"

"No, Ma'am."

"Excellent. That is good-"

"I think the lizards have done that all by themselves," Irene explained.

Perkins lowered her voice, a gesture that had no practical value. The ship's Ruhar crew had excellent hearing, and the flight data recorder could pick up the softest whisper. "Why am I not hearing this from Major Chan?"

There was the slightest hesitation before Irene responded. "She is trying to contain the situation."

"Is she going to succeed?"

"No," Irene conceded.

Perkins suppressed a groan. There were two options when a problem was encountered. Try to take care of it yourself without adding to the burden of your superior officer. Or notify your superior right away, hopefully with a plan to deal with the situation. Chan was taking the first option, figuring she could resolve the issue without Perkins needing to become involved.

Choosing Option One was walking a fine line. If the situation got significantly worse before the information inevitably did go up the chain of command, then Chan's choice of the Do-It-Yourself option could backfire on her. Perkins typically got pissed when her subordinates tried to hide bad news from her, but she had learned that she needed to balance the need for information with the need to trust her people in the field. There was a status call with Chan scheduled in two hours, so she could wait until then.

She might have waited, except the Ruhar were closely monitoring all communications, and they were looking for any sign that the human Expeditionary Force could not handle the mission. "I'll contact Chan. Give me a quick summary of the problem."

Irene told her.

Perkins swore, and didn't care that the Ruhar in the destroyer's Combat Operations Center all looked at her with interest. "Ok, Striebich, hold where you are." She keyed the access code for Chan's personal zPhone, bypassing the major's communications staff. "Major Chan? How's it going down there?"

Chan knew she was busted, and there wasn't any point to concealing the problem. "We've got a group of lizards who are refusing to cooperate, Ma'am."

"Refusing like, dragging their feet on turning over their weapons, or like using those weapons against us?"

"Uh, neither of those?"

Perkins raised an eyebrow. "Oh?"

"They're threatening to use weapons, but not against us or the hamst- Against us or the Ruhar. They um, they have Keepers."

"*Shit!*" Perkins pretended she hadn't already heard that from Striebich.

"I've been trying to negotiate with the leader of the local subclan in the village, a lizard called Ashkallah. He plans a messy public execution of the four Keepers he has, unless we pull back out of his province."

"Damn it," Perkins knew the Ruhar in the COC were all listening intently to the conversation. "What about the lizard Administrator of the planet?"

"I contacted his staff, they told me that enforcing the cease fire and withdrawal agreement is *our* responsibility, Ma'am. The Administrator will not step in unless the Ashkallah guy directly violates the ceasefire, or does something against the interests of the major clan. The Keepers are considered personal property, Ashkallah can do whatever he wants with them. Basically, the Administrator told me this is not his problem."

"*Basically,*" Perkins spat. "The Administrator is happy to let Ashkallah take a shot at screwing up the whole mission for us. If it works, the major clan benefits. If not, the Administrator doesn't lose anything."

"Basically," Chan concluded. "Yes."

"Ok, Major," Perkins took a breath. "Good initiative."

"But bad judgment, Ma'am?"

"No. You saved me the trouble of another *delightful* conversation with my counterpart," she meant the Kristang Administrator of the planet. The lizards had, of course, thrown up every roadblock they could to cause problems for the Legion. The Legion, knowing their opponent, had planned for roadblocks and delays. She didn't blame Chan for attempting to resolve the situation on her own. She also knew that the major's plan, to try reaching a compromise with the lizards, did not have a prayer of working. Ending the call with Chan, she turned to the technician at the destroyer's communications console. "Connect me with this asshole lizard."

"Which asshole lizard, Ma'am?" The ship's executive officer asked.

Keeping a flash of irritation from showing on her face, Perkins did not take the bait. "You know damned well which lizard. Don't play games with me, I haven't got the time."

The exec gave a curt head nod, and the technician pressed buttons while Perkins watched. "I'm in contact, Ma'am," the technician announced. "They're telling me that Grand Warrior Ashkallah will call you shortly, at his convenience."

The lizard was making her wait as a ploy, and Perkins was not going to allow that to affect her. While she waited for the Grand Asshole to decide he had sufficiently shown his disdain, she walked over to the weapons console, gesturing the exec to follow. "Colonel Perkins," executive officer Feelax said quietly. "We received a standard request from Major Chan to stand by to provide fire support over the target village, about two hours ago. I tasked two GBU-35s," he referred to a type of Ruhar missile equipped with fragmentation warheads. They were typically used in antipersonnel strikes, against relatively soft targets on the ground. "Also, we have a railgun locked on the target."

"A railgun?" Perkin's eyebrow got more exercise. "Isn't that overkill? The objective is just a tiny village. This Grand Asshole Ashkallah commands, what, thirty troops, maybe less?"

"It's a precaution," Feelax explained.

"Sensible," she agreed.

"We will automatically safe the railgun, if any of your troops are within forty-five kilometers of the potential blast radius."

"Got it." She knew Chan had pulled her team back from the starting line, when the major learned there were Keepers in the village.

They made small talk while Perkins waited for the Grand Jerkoff to grant her an audience. She liked the executive officer of the destroyer and the feeling seemed to be mutual, Feelax saw the Alien Legion as a net positive for the Ruhar military and their society overall, so he was eager to help the Legion succeed in what was supposed to be an easy and simple mission on Jellaxico.

The delay gave her time to think about what, if anything, she could do. The Kristang could be bluffing about publicly executing the Keepers, but she didn't think that was the case. There wasn't any reason to bluff, and since Ashkallah had announced his intentions to the Administrator, he and his subclan would lose face if he backed down. Unless Ashkallah was exceptionally stupid, he could not hope to actually stop the Legion from taking the planet. The world was too remote, too unimportant for his people to put up a major fight against the takeover, especially as the major clans had agreed to cede the planet without a fight. No, Ashkallah likely had more realistic goals. Boosting his own standing, and dealing a humiliating blow to the Alien Legion. If the mission schedule was delayed significantly by publicly torturing and killing four humans, that would prove the strategy the Kristang attempted on Fresno was valid, and demonstrate the weakness of the human side of the Legion.

Maybe, she considered, she could adjust the schedule so that Ashkallah and his people would be the last to leave the planet, in exchange for not slaughtering the Keepers. That would give the Grand Asshole the ego boost he craved, while maintaining the overall schedule.

It would also show future opponents how to get what they wanted from the Legion. Let the camel's nose under the tent, so the saying went, and the camel would soon be sleeping in your bed. She couldn't be seen as giving concessions to preserve the lives of four people. She didn't see how to avoid that.

"The lizard is ready to talk," Feelax interrupted her thoughts.

"Put him through," Perkins ordered, mentally steeling herself for a difficult conversation.

"Am I speaking with the commander of the enemy force?" The voice was harsh but had a lisp that made it sound like 'thpeaking' even through the translation software.

Perkins had to tamp down a giggle before she answered. Ashkallah sounded like a vampire in a low-budget movie. "This is Colonel Emily Perkins, of the human Expeditionary Force. Do I have the honor of speaking with Grand Warrior Ashkallah, of the Yellow Fang clan?" Technically the Yellow Fangs were a subclan, but she figured it didn't hurt to puff up the asshole's ego.

"You do have such an honor. I am Ashkallah of the Yellow Fang. Grand Warrior, Keeper of the Sacred Chalice of Reen, Holder of the Nine-"

"Wanker of great frequency," Perkins muttered under her breath and made a jerking-off gesture with one hand, as the Kristang went on naming his titles, real or imaginary.

"*What?*" The lizard screeched as the *Wild Child's* crew laughed when they got the translation of her remark.

"My apologies, Grand Warrior," Perkins said quickly. "The Ruhar communications equipment is experiencing difficulties."

"Ah," that seemed to satisfy him. "The Ruhar are widely known as incompetent in their use of the technology they have stolen from other species. My time is important. What do you wish to speak about?"

"It is my understanding that you are planning a," she paused. A what? She didn't want to use the term 'public execution'. "A spectacle, for the public."

"Oh," the lizard replied. "That? It is of no importance. As we are being forced to leave this world, we must decide what to take with us and what to leave behind. Under the terms of the agreement, I am under no obligation to turn over any of my property in usable condition. To that end, we will be demolishing buildings, disabling vehicles, and destroying our power generation facility."

"Yes," Perkins clenched her teeth. "That is your right. I was referring to the humans you have."

"My Keeper slaves?" He feigned surprise. "It is a waste to transport property of such low value, so we will be discarding them before we leave. Your Legion is being very stingy on allowances for property aboard the transport ships. I thought the Keepers could be at least of some use, in training my warriors how to kill humans. Why do you ask?"

"We consider those humans, the ones we call 'Keepers', to be traitors," she held to the official line from UNEF-HQ. After Fresno, they had debated how to respond if the Kristang again used Keepers as hostages. The plan was to act like the Keepers were not important, and to negotiate to trade or to purchase them. If that plan didn't work, the mission commander was to 'utilize their best judgment'. Meaning, Perkins had to clean up the mess by herself, and she would get criticized no matter what she did. "We would like them brought back to Paradise, the world you call Pradassis, for punishment. I would like to discuss an arrangement that could be to our mutual benefit."

"Ah, but Colonel Perkins, why would I ever want to benefit *you*? Very well, I will indulge your foolishness. Here are my terms: the Alien Legion will withdraw from this world," his voice turned more harsh, spitting words into the microphone. "Or I will *personally* demonstrate just how much abuse a human body can take over several agonizing days, before a horribly painful and public death."

"Ashkallah, there is no need for-"

"Do not interrupt me, human scum! I am done talking with you and your primitive kind. You will give me your answer, with a schedule for withdrawing *your* people from this world, within one hour. If you do not reply in one hour, I will begin my demonstration in a very public fashion. Your primitive people will no doubt enjoy the show."

The transmission cut off. Perkins saw that Feelax was trying to avoid looking at her, embarrassed for the human commander. He expected that she would give in to the Kristang demands, or perhaps declare that the Legion needed to withdraw so the Ruhar military could take direct control of the operation.

It would be the end of the Alien Legion.

"Excuse me," she said, gesturing for Feelax to step aside. The Ruhar did move, with a questioning look.

When he saw that she was walking toward the weapons console, he moved to block her. "Colonel?" He asked softly.

"Is this ship under my command?" She demanded.

"Well, I, surely you-"

"That question requires a 'Yes' or 'No' answer," she stated. "We call that a binary solution set. *Yes*, or *No*?"

He grimaced. "Yes, of course. Emily, think about what you are doing." He added in a whisper.

"I have thought about it. A lot. Comms, get Ashkallah back on the line."

"He's not- Oh!" The technician expressed surprise. "Got him, Ma'am."

Perkins flipped up the cover that guarded the railgun controls. The weapon's guidance system was still locked on target. Hovering her thumb over the firing stud, she forced herself to speak calmly. "Ashkallah?"

"Yes, Perkins?" He skipped her rank as a sign of his disrespect.

"I have an answer for you, *right here.*"

She jabbed her thumb down on the firing stud. The *Wild Child* shuddered as a dart was flung along the rails of the gun that ran two-thirds the length of the destroyer, accelerating the kinetic weapon to twenty four thousand kilometers per second.

Three.

Two.

One.

The overhead view of the village was replaced by a bright flash, then the sooty top of a mushroom cloud, churning with mud and debris that used to be a miserable little village.

"*Holy* sh-" Irene gasped as she turned to look out the cockpit window at the mushroom cloud, boiling up in the mostly clear blue sky. Derek already had the aircraft in a gentle turn away from the village, increasing power and trimming the controls for the best rate of climb. At ninety kilometers away from where the dart struck, the shockwave would not be a danger to the Buzzard, but it always paid to be safe. Plastering her left hand to the inner lining of the cockpit, Irene craned her neck to keep the mushroom cloud in view as the Buzzard swung away. When the aircraft completed the turn and the village site was no longer in view, she slumped in her seat, the straps automatically tightening around her. "I can't *believe* she did that."

"What else could she do? She didn't have a choice," Derek said quietly.

"I know. It's just- I can't believe she actually *did* it."

"Em is tough, we know that. The Rules of Engagement she got from UNEF-HQ were total bullshit. The brass just didn't want to make the decision, they stuck her with it."

"Derek, honey," she patted his forearm. "I know all that. I'm not surprised, I just-"

"Yeah, me too." He kept his hands on the controls. "It's a shock."

She tapped her lips with a finger. "Hmm."

"What?"

"You know what? I'm trying to feel bad for those people. The Keepers, I mean, not the lizards." She knew there had been civilians living in the village, and the deaths of those Kristang were likely to cause more of a headache for Perkins than the loss of four human slaves. "And I got nothing."

"They made their bed, right?"

"It's not that," she shook her head. "Either way, they had nothing to look forward to in their lives. This was a mercy killing."

Derek was not sure the Keepers would have felt that way, but that was above his paygrade. He made an adjustment to the autopilot, and the Buzzard began another turn.

Irene was not in such shock that she missed the aircraft's change of attitude. "What are you doing?"

Derek shrugged. "Setting course for the next objective on the list. We still have a job to do on this rock, right?"

Perkins safed the railgun, taking its energizers offline, and securing the cover over the firing stud. She moved carefully, deliberately, using the time to think through her next move. When she turned away from the weapons console, the entire crew of the COC was staring at her. Most of the faces displayed shock, perhaps horror. But a few, including Feelax, had a different response. It might have been admiration.

She took a breath before addressing the crew. "My people have learned that you can't negotiate with terrorists."

Feelax gave an exaggerated nod, to be sure she understood the gesture. "You may have *saved* human lives, in the long run. The Kristang will see there is no point to using their human slaves as hostages."

"I hope so," Perkins agreed. She knew she hadn't been given a choice, not really. It was either four human lives, or the Alien Legion. The Legion was key to her plan to rescue the billions of humans on Earth, or failing that, to secure a future for humans elsewhere in the galaxy. She had no problem with the logic of her decision.

The *emotional* impact was another issue.

What really bothered her was not knowing what she would have done, if Ashkallah had *forty* Keepers? Or four hundred? At what point would she have been forced to retreat, or at least send a message back to UNEF-HQ on Paradise, asking for orders?

She hoped if the lizards ever tested the Legion by using hundreds of Keepers as hostages, that she was not in command on that mission. "Feelax, contact the planetary Administrator's office."

"Colonel," there was a note of caution in his tone. "I suggest that you do not-"

"Don't worry," she stiffened to suppress a shudder. "I'm not going to take a hard line with the administrator. I am *not* taking any shit from him, but," she sighed. "I need to offer compensation for the property they lost."

"You are offering *compensation*?" Feelax's eyes grew wide. He knew Perkins was not so callous that she actually believed the Keepers were nothing but property. "Colonel, if you did want to play Tough Guy with the lizards, *that* is an excellent way to do it."

# CHAPTER TWO

The Assassin's Guild representative on the Kristang-held planet Kobamik stepped out of the aircraft that had brought him to the checkpoint that guarded entry the tunnel's entrance, which itself was blocked by massive doors. Before he could get to the doors, he would have to pass through three fences, and an energy shield that would disassemble the molecules of his body if it were not deactivated for him to pass. Also, there were well-armed guards who appeared to have itchy trigger fingers and glared at him with suspicion, eager for action. When they saw him step from the vehicle, their first reaction was suspicion, despite his aircraft having been cleared through restricted airspace, plus receiving an escort from two fighter aircraft that still circled overhead.

Their second reaction was a mixture of disgust at seeing the Achakai robe he wore as a member of that reviled group, and fear when they saw the Assassin's Guild patch on his chest. Assassin Emeritus Tingelz Pomanto was retired from the business of direct killings, yet the patch still inspired fear. Even at his advanced age, he was a deadly force and the guards at the tunnel entrance knew it.

"Pomanto," one of the guards said as he scanned the dishonored one, taking a long time to be extra thorough. The guard did not fear for his own life, he feared what would happen to him, his family and everyone associated with him, if the assassin managed to sneak weapons inside the clan compound at the heart of the city. The compound had been attacked before and clan leaders killed, at the start of the civil war that had the city outside partly abandoned and in ruins. It was true that representatives of the Assassin's Guild were banned from taking direct action on their own, but who could trust the word of the dishonored?

Pomanto noted without comment that the guard used his name without any honorifics, which was intended as an insult and bothered him not at all. After a lifetime of enduring insults, he no longer cared. Two other guards scanned him, requiring him to remove his robes and jacket. Getting into the tunnel was a long and tedious process, longer than normal in an attempt to humiliate him. He paid no attention. The Fire Dragon clan leaders inside the compound had requested his presence, if he were late, then *they* would wait for him.

Through the tunnel in a low-slung, open car, he emerged into sunlight again, as the car drove across the courtyard of the compound. Not caring who watched him, he looked up to where the pyramid-shaped central residency tower showed signs of battle damage that had not been repaired. He noted the location, shape and nature of the blast damage that had occurred when missiles struck the tower, as the opening move in the current civil war that was ravaging Kristang society. It was still a mystery how the Black Tree clan had gotten missiles into the secure compound, and as a member of the Assassin's Guild, his examination of the damage was professional curiosity. He did not see how it was possible to have done what the Black Trees, or some other clan as the Black Trees still denied any involvement, had done. Maybe the Achakai could use what he had seen, or maybe it would continue to be a mystery.

Without making eye contact, he strode purposefully across the courtyard, through another series of checkpoints, inside a bunker, and onto an elevator that took him deep below the surface. Automatically, he tracked how long the elevator descended, and estimated how fast he fell based on how the pressure on the bottom of his shoes lessened. It might be useful to know how deep lay the secure quarters of the Fire Dragon clan leaders on Kobamik.

He was mildly surprised to be ushered into a round room that was empty. The guards accompanying him indicated he should walk forward into the center of the space, treading along a cheap-feeling cloth over the rich carpet. The cloth was there, he knew, so the soles of his dishonorable feet did not contaminate the carpet. As soon as he departed, the cloth would be taken away and burned.

He waited, and waited, and waited, without complaint or external sign of annoyance. Finally, a door opened, and a single richly-attired male strode forward, trailed by two females who wore robes of the same colors. They were either wives or concubines, Pomanto was amused to see one of the females raise her eyes from the floor to steal a glance at him. That was a bold act that she might pay for later, her curiosity about a real-life assassin overcoming her justifiable fear.

"Honorless one," the clan leader said, sitting in the only chair, the females kneeling beside him. "I will be brief, for being in your presence disgusts me."

Pomanto only bowed slightly, observing the proper forms and no more.

If the clan leader was irritated at not provoking a reaction, he kept it to himself. "We wish to offer a commission to your people, a target that I am sure will need to be approved by whoever you call your leadership."

Pomanto bowed again and asked the obvious question. "Who is the target, Honored Leader? Will this be an assassination, a kidnapping or some other action?"

"The target is a human named Emily Perkins. We want her dead."


With the Legion battalion having just returned from Jellaxico, those lucky soldiers had the fun task of accounting for all their gear, because the bureaucracy demanded it. Surgun Jates had the dubious honor of conducting the inspection, which was more disorganized than usual, because half of the platoon's gear had been transported on a different ship. Seeing that Jesse was busy helping a clueless soldier get himself sorted out, and Shauna was talking with an officer on the other side of the field, Jates called on another victim. "Czajka!"

"Uh, yes?" Dave had been standing to the side, watching in amusement as the platoon got ready for inspection of their gear. "What is it, Surgun?"

"Get a tarp and lay out your own gear," Jates instructed. "Make a template for the others."

"Oh, sure," Dave said, relieved that he hadn't been asked to do anything difficult. He expected that Jates asking to show the platoon how to lay out their gear was a vote of confidence in him, that he would not have lost any of his assigned personal equipment, that none of it was broken, and that he knew where all of it was. "Be right back." A few minutes later, he jogged over to Jates with most of his worldly possessions in or strapped to a rucksack. His personal gear did not include a combat skinsuit, though he did have one assigned to him. Skinsuits were kept in a separate facility controlled by the Ruhar, where the hamsters maintained equipment that humans were not qualified to screw with.

"Ok," Dave unfolded the tarp and laid it out, getting the corner nearest him lined up with a stripe on the parade field. He had an audience, including Shauna and Jesse, it made him self-conscious. His assigned rifle, ammunition, rockets and grenades were already in a locker in the company armory, so he only needed to account for all the other crap that UNEF had assigned to him in his official role as an infantry-support contractor.

Propping the rucksack up with one hand, he began emptying the side pouches first. Setting down his canteen, he lost his grip on the ruck and it toppled over, spilling the contents of the main compartment. Out tumbled rolled-up shirts, a belt for carrying ammo, socks and-

Among the other items was a curious thing.

An object shaped like, perhaps it would be polite to describe it as resembling a cucumber. The object hit the tarp, bounced and began buzzing so vigorously it flopped around on the tarp. Dave made a desperate grab for the object, missed and sent it spinning across the tarp to buzz against one of Jates's shoes.

There was a moment of stunned silence.

"Czajka?" Jates broke the silence, pursing his lips to keep from laughing.

"That's not mine," Dave protested, scrambling to his feet.

"Of course not," the Verd-kris surgun looked at the object, then at Dave. "Yours is *much* smaller."

The crowd burst into laughter. Even Jates, who was trying his best to scowl, had his shoulders shaking.

Then, because Dave's day was already pretty much going just *wonderfully*, something else happened to make the situation even better, because of course it did.

Lieutenant Colonel Emily Perkins walked over to see what the commotion was about. The crowd parted for her, and suddenly she was standing on the other side of the tarp from Jates. She looked down at the happily buzzing thing that did not belong there, then at Dave.

"Uh, I can explain," he said in a strangled voice.

"Czajka, if *that's* my birthday present," Perkins cocked her head at the civilian consultant. "You need to try harder."

Hours later, in the room they shared, Dave was sitting miserably on his bunk, while Jesse lay on his back, still laughing. "Oh, man, that was *classic*."

"I'm glad you think so," Dave muttered. He had stuffed the offending object in his rucksack and waited for the mirth to die down, but it hadn't. Seeing that there was no point to continuing the demonstration, Jates had dismissed Dave and designated another soldier to lay out a gear template. He hadn't even been able to talk with Emily, who had a car waiting to take her to a meeting with some group of UNEF generals.

"I'm serious," Jesse rolled over to sit up. "You have to admit, I never saw anything so freakin' funny. Damn, I thought Jates was gonna pee in his pants, you know?"

"Yeah," Dave snorted. "*That* would have been funny. Hey, 'Pone," he used his friend's nickname. "It wasn't you who put that in my pack, was it?"

Jesse held up his hands. "Honestly, I *wish* I had thought of it. It wasn't me."

"Ok. Oh hell, the platoon will have a good story to tell for years."

"That's the way to think about it," Jesse agreed. "Hey, one other thing."

"What?"

"Em," he used the Mavericks' private nickname for their commanding officer. "She is *cool*, you know? Like, she could have been pissed about it. Most women would have been embarrassed. She wasn't, she played along with the joke. She's cool, man."

"Yeah," Dave saw the silver lining in the dark cloud hanging over his head. "You're right. She is."

"You're lucky. Like, you are *so* freakin' lucky."

"You're lucky to have Shauna."

"Believe me, brother, I know it. She was cool about it, too."

"She was," Dave agreed. Shauna had been laughing with the others, but she had given him a look of sympathy also.

"So?" Jesse prompted. "When are you going to stop stringing her along?"

Dave looked sharply at his friend. "Me? When are *you* gonna stop stringing Shauna along?"

"That's different," Jesse shook his head. "Me and Shauna are the same rank. The ball's in her court, you know? On Paradise, every day is Sadie Hawkins Day. Girls have all the power."

"You don't think Em has all the power?"

"She's an officer, and you're a civilian. The rules are different."

"Like you said, it's Sadie Hawkins Day. The old rules don't matter."

"All I know is, you can't let her get away. If you don't ask her- You do want to ask her, right? The age difference is not a problem?"

"We don't care about the age thing. It's just, she'll be a general someday, you know that?"

"I do."

"And I'm, what?" He looked down at the logo on his uniform, which read Paradise Security Solutions, the name of the company he technically worked for. "A glorified mall cop?"

"You're the same as me," Jesse was mildly insulted. "Only difference is, the insignia on our uniforms. Plus, hey, you can quit this gig any time you want. You own that brewery."

"I own a *share* in the brewery."

"It's *your* smiling face on the sign," Jesse retorted.

Dave shrugged. "They needed someone famous to be out front when the company was setting up." He was uncomfortable with trading on his military actions for a private venture. That level of discomfort lessened when he resigned from UNEF to be a civilian contractor. "We do brew the best beer on Paradise," he added with pride.

"You're avoiding the subject."

"What do you want me to say?"

"I don't want you to *say*, I want you to *ask*. Ask her, before it's too late."

The intensity with which Jesse pressed the point made Dave pause to think. "Hey, 'Pone, what's up? Why do you care so much?"

"You're my *friend*, dumbass. Plus, oh, hell. If you pop the question to Em, that might clear the way for Shauna to get moving, you know?"

Dave sighed. "I'll tell you what we should do."

"What?"

"Talk with Bonsu. A couple weeks ago, he asked me if I knew a place he could buy a ring, or have one made."

"Whoooo," Jesse whistled. "Shit, that complicates things."

"How?"

"Because, if Derek and Irene," he figured it was acceptable to refer to the officers by their first names in private, and on a personal subject. "Are getting married, Em won't like you popping the question to her."

"What? Why?"

"Man, do you not know *anything* about women? She'll think you're only asking her because you're feeling pressure after Derek proposed to Irene, that's why. Plus, once Irene is engaged, the attention is supposed to be on her. My sister got engaged and a week later, our cousin Doreen announced she was engaged too, and getting married the month before my sister. My sister and my mother were *pissed*. Damn, I never saw my mama so mad about anything. Trust me, you need to ask Em first."

"I'll think about it."

"Don't think too long," Jesse advised. "Whatever your girl is cooking up, we could be offworld again soon."


The Legion was gearing up for something big, Jesse knew that because the force was recruiting heavily on Paradise and adding personnel every day. The operation on Fresno had been conducted on a shoestring, with almost the entire available Legion force dropping onto that world. At the time, the Legion experiment was new and untested, and many billets had been unfilled. Fresno had technically been a success, still most people looked at how close the operation had been to complete disaster, and decided they were better off remaining in civilian jobs on their adopted homeworld.

Jellybean changed that. Not only was that relatively minor operation viewed as an unqualified success by the human population, the Ruhar government had been impressed, and gave the go-ahead for UNEF to expand the Legion. Pay and benefits provided by the Ruhar were a powerful incentive to former soldiers who had not settled well into civilian life. And seeing Legion soldiers returning triumphantly from Jellaxico reminded former soldiers that they had come out to the stars to *fight*, not to become farmers.

The new enthusiasm for the Legion was a double-edged sword, in Jesse's opinion. Adding to the combat power and sustainment capability of the Legion was a good thing. On the other hand, seeing recruits arrive for refresher training reminded him the Expeditionary Force that left Earth had been composed of whatever units the governments of the five nations could scrape together on short notice. Meaning, among the overwhelming number of serious, dedicated people were the usual collection of knuckleheads.

Jesse's personal burden was a former Marine named Marco Santinelli, who had been a corporal when the Force left Earth. The previous year, seeing no prospects for action and wanting to explore the opportunities of civilian life, he had left UNEF and set up a trucking business, transporting goods between human settlements that were scattered throughout the southern half of the continent humans called Lemuria. The business concept had been sound, the execution less so. The business failed within seven months, and Santinelli had recently signed up for the Legion, as much for the steady paycheck as from any sense of patriotism.

To rejoin the Force, Santinelli, like many others, had to accept a demotion. With no new personnel joining, the Force had become top-heavy. There were too many staff sergeants like Jesse, and not enough privates. As an incentive, the lowest rank was equivalent to Specialist. For Santinelli, that meant he unfortunately was recruited in at the rank of Lance Corporal.

Why was that unfortunate? The United States Marine Corps had a legend about a 'Lance Corporal Schmuckatelli', an everyman who stood in for the worst example of screw-ups. Inevitably, Santinelli had been tagged with the nickname '*Schmuckatelli*' during boot camp and it had stuck to him all the way, over a thousand lightyears from Earth. By joining the Legion, he was again a Lance Corporal, and not likely to climb the ladder of promotion.

Jesse had at first felt sorry for Santinelli, until he learned that the nickname was accurate. Marco Santinelli was a screw-up, a walking safety brief, and Jesse was stuck with him. The Mavericks headquarters security detail had somehow along the way become a sort of dumping ground for screw-ups. Either that was UNEF-HQ's way of sticking it to Emily Perkins, or HQ figured that it was best to keep the screw-ups away from frontline combat units.

Whatever.

All Jesse knew was that he had to watch Lance Corporal Schmuckatelli like a hawk, lest the idiot injure himself, or worse, injure a real soldier.

The best example of Santinelli living up to his name was during introductory training for using skinsuits. Each recruit was issued a set of genuine Ruhar flexible powered armor, albeit a suit that was considerably dumbed down for the purpose of training. The suits were designed to protect inexperienced users from harming themselves or anyone around them, and were pretty much idiot-proof. But, the suit computers could not account for the endless inventiveness of idiots.

The training session was on Day Three of the skinsuit familiarization exercise, when new users were supposed to have already gained a measure of both confidence in what a suit could do, and respect for how it could hurt them if they were stupid. The new users had performed easy runs on Day One, then proceeded on to running an obstacle course on Day Two. The afternoon of Day Three was scheduled for weapons training, where rifles were synchronized to the suit computers. The morning was a relatively simple series of balance and jumping drills, intended for users to gain experience in trusting the suit to enhance their natural abilities, anticipate their moves, and protect them.

The drills began easily, with Surgun Jates first climbing a platform that was four meters high, and jumping off to fall onto the dirt surface of the training ground. He showed how to land and roll properly, moving on to jumping off an eight-meter platform. Jesse went next, using the proper technique.

All the soldiers jumped first off the four-meter platform, with various degrees of skill, much laughter from their fellows and no injuries. Then, while Jesse's attention was diverted by helping a soldier adjust a helmet seal, Lance Corporal Schmuckatelli cut ahead in line to get his turn. He insisted on going seventh because that was his 'lucky number', and the other people mostly rolled their eyes and let him go, anticipating a decent chance they could watch him make a fool of himself.

Their wishes were fulfilled beyond expectations. Schmuckatelli climbed to the four-meter platform under the watchful eye of Surgun Jates, then crouched at the edge, to jump up and gain a bit of extra height as he had seen other soldiers do. Only instead of jumping up one meter, he kicked off the platform hard, bounding up to land awkwardly on the eight-meter platform above, where he slipped and fell before Jates could remotely override the idiot's suit and freeze him in place. To make matter worse than an eight-meter fall he was unprepared for, he had to show off by attempting to perform a showy Hollywood three-point landing.

It didn't end well.

"Ow! Ow ow ow, *fuck* that hurts," he moaned as he collapsed, rolling over and shaking as he held his injured wrist with the good one.

"Schmuckatelli!" Jates barked, pissed off at the idiot. "Shut your dick holster and move off the field."

"Oh, crap," Jesse snapped, pushing Schmuckatelli down on his back while he linked to the idiot's suit to check the medical scanner. "I turn my head away for *one* freakin' minute, and-"

"I think my wrist is broken," Santinelli sobbed.

"It is just a sprain," Jates observed with disgust as he sent out a call for a medical team. "You also sprained your right ankle. It is fortunate you didn't tear ligaments in your knees. Colter, help me move him off the practice field."

They easily carried the injured fool to rest on a bench off to the side of the platform, where he could continue to be an object of amusement, and a living safety brief for the others. Jates motioned for the exercise to resume, while Jesse waited for the ambulance.

"I don't understand," Santinelli moaned. "It works when Iron Man does it."

Jesse snorted. "A three-point landing looks cool, but it's stupid. Maybe a Kung-Fu master can do it, but Iron Man is just movie magic. With your legs out like that, you don't have any leverage for balance. You also rolled your wrist under, that's how you sprained it. Next time, do what the instructors tell you to do, that's why we're here."

"Damn. Sorry, Staff Sergeant. It looks so cool, you know?"

"There's a lot of shit that *looks* cool, but is stupid. Like, you know how in movies the cool guys hold their guns sideways?" Jesse pantomimed holding a pistol at arm's length, cocked on its side. "You see how that's a move for morons? If you hold a pistol upright and if it kicks back, it goes over your shoulder. You hold it sideways, it can kick back into your freakin' face. That will knock you down for the count."

Santinelli nodded silently, gritting his teeth against the pain. "I get it."

Jesse doubted that, in fact, the idiot really got the message. He would get the message when the Ruhar medics injected him with nano machines so he could return to training that same afternoon. The tiny machines would stabilize the sprained areas, acting as artificial tendons and muscles while the biological features healed. It all sounded good, except the nerve blockers would only prevent the pain from being debilitating, it would still hurt like hell. Long experience had taught the Ruhar not to completely deaden feeling for injuries, so the affected person didn't aggravate the damage.

With the first round of jump training over, the trainees clustered around Santinelli, asking what the hell he had been thinking.

"You are gonna be *hurting* in the morning," one soldier laughed. "I had that fancy hamster nano medicine once. Works great, but it hurts like hell when it's active."

Jesse stayed out of the conversation, which somehow got to the subject of back when Santinelli joined the Marine Corps. "I had a high school buddy, we were supposed to sign up together."

Several soldiers nodded, knowing what that was like.

Jates had come over to check on the injured Marine, Jesse flashed a thumbs up to the Verd-kris. Injuries sustained in training were the responsibility of the instructor, in that case, Jates. Having a human injured while under the care of a Verd was not good for morale.

"Your friend was supposed to sign up with you?" Jates asked, pleased to see Santinelli was in good spirits. "What happened?"

Santinelli grinned, the grimace of pain momentarily wiped off his face. "My friend went to his girlfriend's house that weekend, Saturday. She was out washing her car in the driveway and the guy next door was chatting her up."

"Oh," Jates nodded. "Your friend was worried this guy would move in while he was at boot camp?"

"He sure as hell did. The neighbor guy? His name was," Santinelli snickered, finding his story enormously funny. "His name was *Jodie*!"

"For real?" A soldier laughed.

"For real, man," Santinelli said seriously.

"Damn! That is a bad omen," the soldier shook his head. "I would have backed out too."

Jates didn't get the joke. "This Jodie person, he has a bad reputation?"

"Oh, I," Santinelli stammered. "I don't know the guy, never met him."

"Then what is the problem?"

"It's not- You gotta understand, Surgun. Jodie is the guy who would bang my girlfriend while I'm away on deployment."

"Ah," Jates nodded. "That is very caring of you, to think of your girlfriend's needs."

"*What*?" Santinelli's mouth gaped open. "No, I-"

"Did you create this arrangement between your girl and Jodie because you are frequently away, or because of your overall sexual inadequacy?"

"Hey, I- It's not *my* girlfriend. Jodie bangs *every* guy's girlfriend when he's away."

"Impressive," Jates nodded with admiration. "I didn't know a human male was capable of such stamina. He must be exhausted. I would like to congratulate this Jodie."

"No, I-" Santinelli looked around for support, but everyone was laughing. "Look, Surgun, every Marine, every soldier, hates Jodie."

"Why the hatred? Based on what I know of *you*," Jates stared down the hapless Lance Corporal. "This Jodie would be performing a public service if he banged your girlfriend."

Santinelli gave up trying to explain, just as the medics arrived to take him away for treatment, the Ruhar sadly shaking their heads at the stupidity of humans. Jesse went back to training up the new people, wondering how many of them would get recycled back to start the refresher course over again. One thing he knew for sure was that, whatever offworld hell-hole the Legion was going to next, he couldn't wait to get there.

# CHAPTER THREE

Major General Jeff Ross was in his office on Paradise, staring off into space as he thought about the best way to compose the official report about the Legion's mission on Jellaxico. Everyone already knew the details, he was documenting the mission because regulations called for an official report, and because he wanted to assure that history had all the facts. *All* the facts, including the full background of the controversial decision made by Emily Perkins. In the future, people whose only knowledge of the incident came from written reports needed to know-

"You busy?" Brigadier General Lynn Bezanson stuck her head through the doorway.

"You're early," Ross looked at the clock on the wall. "Come in. I didn't expect you until this afternoon."

Bezanson sat down heavily in the chair. The clock was showing the local time as 1118. Too early to indulge in a drink, which was probably a good thing. She needed a clear head during her scheduled call with UNEF-HQ in less than an hour.

Ross read her mind, pulling out a drawer on his side of the desk. "You look like you could use a drink."

Waving a hand, she shook her head. "Not now, thanks," she said, wishing she had a glass of her favorite rum and 7UP. Ironically, breweries and distilleries had been established by former UNEF soldiers, so getting rum on Paradise was not the problem. The nearest can of 7UP, however, was over a thousand lightyears away.

With a longing glance at the bottle of gin, Ross closed the drawer. The spirits, made on the planet's southern continent, did not taste exactly like any gin from Earth, because no one had thought to bring a juniper bush from Earth. The gin was good enough, until the earliest batch of bourbon had aged properly and was ready to drink. "What's up?"

"I got called into the Burgermeister's office this morning." Officially, the Ruhar woman in charge of the planet had the title of Administrator, but Baturnah Logellia found the human nickname of 'Burgermeister' to be amusing. UNEF-HQ had banned the use of the nickname in official communications, but everyone used it in casual conversation. "She read me the party line about Jellaxico."

"Oh?" Ross raised an eyebrow. He could guess what the Ruhar Federal government had to say about the actions of the Legion on that world, specifically the actions Perkins had taken to end the attempted extortion by Kristang.

"They are shocked and dismayed, et cetera. I'm getting a copy of the report later, I'll send it along to you. Nothing we didn't expect, no surprises."

"Did the Burgermeister tell you anything other than the party line?"

Bezanson rolled her eyes. "She sure did. She talked long enough I had to drink a second cup of that awful tea her office serves. I swear, I don't know why the hamsters think we like that stuff. It tastes like perfume."

Having been forced to drink the tea out of politeness, Ross could sympathize. He slid a tin of mints across the desk. "These take away the taste."

"Mm," she mumbled with a mint in her mouth. "Thanks. Off the record, some of the Peace Faction officials truly are unhappy about what Perkins did, they are debating whether to issue a formal reprimand. Killing four of our own people is-"

"Bullshit," Ross interrupted. "That's pure bullshit," he thumped a hand on the desk displaying his anger. "According to the Ruhar, Keepers held by the Kristang are not *our* anything. And they are property, not people. The hamsters read that law to us on Fresno. They can't have it both ways."

"That was almost word for word what I told the Burgermeister."

Ross snorted. "We agree on the law, that's something. I get it that the optics aren't great."

"You're wrong about that," Bezanson shook her head and popped another mint in her mouth. "Their military is impressed. And surprised. They didn't think we lowly humans could make decisions based on cold logic. The overwhelming feeling in their government is that humans took care of a human problem. They *like* the optics. Perkins showed the lizards they can't play that card again."

"Maybe," Ross considered. "Unless the next time, the lizards are holding a dozen, or a hundred hostages. What then?"

The question made Lynn Bezanson uncomfortable. "I can tell you what I've heard around HQ, unofficially."

"What?"

"That we can't backslide now. The policy will be, no negotiating with terrorists. If the lizards are using Keepers as hostages again, we hit the site, no hesitation."

"Well, shit," Ross sat back in his chair.

"You disagree?"

"Hell no. I'm surprised HQ is suddenly seeing the light. This Legion initiative, we're either all in," he made a gesture like pushing a pile of poker chips across the table, "or we're out."

"Good. Because off the record, HQ wanted me to find out what you think about the new policy," Bezanson admitted.

"You can tell them I am on onboard, hundred percent. Being in this job is all about knowing what you can do, and accepting what you *can't* do. We can't save those Keepers, they're screwed either way. And, we can't let them distract us on the next op."

Bezanson had not been read in on whatever the Legion was planning next, all she knew was that it was *big*. Before UNEF shipped Perkins off to Jellaxico for what was supposed to be a quick and easy mission, the Mavericks leader had been shuttling back and forth between UNEF headquarters on the southern continent, and the Burgermeister's office in the north. The debate within UNEF-HQ was heated, about whatever crazy scheme Perkins had proposed next.

The one tidbit of information Lynn had learned, was that Perkins had not done herself any favors by proposing the operation to the Ruhar *before* she got approval from UNEF. She had also gotten the impression from the Burgermeister, that the proposal was considered wild, dangerous and bold, perhaps *too* bold. Ruhar strategic planning had become stodgy and unimaginative, and the planners were comfortable with continuing the same course that had caused the war with the Kristang to drag on and on, generation after generation.

Lynn Bezanson was *aching* to know what the hell the Mavericks leader was cooking up this time. "HQ is considering," she added, "backdating the new policy, so the lizards don't think the action on Jellaxico was only the decision of one rogue lieutenant colonel."

That drew a laugh from Ross. "*Rogue* would be accurate, though, right?"

Bezanson twisted her mouth into a wry smile. She did not say that HQ was unhappy with Ross about Perkins, expecting him to reign in the maverick leader of the Mavericks. That expectation was unrealistic and unfair to Ross. UNEF-HQ had created a monster when they set up Perkins as the public face of the human Expeditionary Force, using her popularity with the Ruhar population to bolster the image of all humans on Paradise. It wasn't the fault of Emily Perkins that she was a dynamic, aggressive and innovative officer. UNEF *wanted* officers to have those qualities. If Perkins took the reins and moved the Force in a bold new direction, Bezanson thought that was due to the failure of UNEF-HQ to develop and articulate a plan of their own.

Anyway, Perkins was a problem for Ross. She had enough problems of her own to deal with. "I'm going to withhold comment on that subject, Sir," she said diplomatically.

"Do me a favor, then? If you can get HQ to move along on releasing the policy, sooner would be better than later."

"The Legion has another mission?" She asked, a bit too eagerly. "Rumors are going around."

"We *might* have another mission. It's," he spread his hands on the desk. "It's a hell of a thing, if we get approval."

"I envy you," she admitted.

"Going offworld, you mean, or the action?"

"Both. Making nice with politicians is not why I joined the Army."

"You know, I might have an opening on my team," he said casually.

"Oh?"

"It will involve work spaceside, not planetside. Although you should have an opportunity to get your boots dirty."

"What's the job?"

"Sort of a forward space controller, a spotter for close-space support missions."

That surprised her. She had never worked with artillery, certainly not the big guns of starships. "You need a brigadier for that?"

"The billet is being handled by a major now. We discovered during our time on Fresno that the Ruhar need a Legion soldier on their ships, to coordinate and prioritize fire support. There are always more calls for orbital strikes than the ships available can provide."

"You've got a major doing it, so why me?"

"Because you *are* a brigadier. That star you're wearing gets attention. Our people can talk to the ground and make judgment calls on which targets to hit. I need someone the *hamsters* will listen to. It's their ships that are at risk providing close-space support, and they can be reluctant to move ships from their established orbital tracks. If a fire-support request comes from a major, the hamsters will take it under advisement."

"You mean ignore it."

"Same thing. If the request comes from a *general*, especially a general who is respected by the administrator of the Legion's home planet, that has authority."

Bezanson could not conceal her disappointment. "You want me to be a liaison officer aboard a hamster ship, instead of here?" Repeating the targeting directions of a major was *not* her dream job.

"No. I want you to *take charge* up there," he pointed to the ceiling. "Theoretically, when we've got boots on the ground, the frigates and destroyers tasked with providing close-space support are at our disposal. On Fresno, we found that wasn't quite true. If you sign on, I expect you to *bust heads* until the damned hamsters do what we need them to do."

"Bust heads, huh?"

"Furry heads, preferably. But you bust whichever heads you need, to get us that fire support. Your first task will be to establish a rapport with the captains of the ships involved."

"Establish a rapport?"

Ross chuckled. "That is a code phrase for 'Laying down the law'. Make them understand right from the start that those ships need to take direction from us. Within reason, of course."

"What are the parameters I'll be working with?"

"Oh hell, Lynn, there's a whole freakin' manual for it. Bottom line is, if you get a fire support request to take out something small, like a platoon-size enemy force, and the Ruhar haven't established complete space supremacy, you need to make a judgment call. Lack of timely fire support may cost us dozens of lives on the ground. But if the Ruhar lose a starship to enemy fire, even just a frigate? That is over a *hundred* lives. Plus even a frigate costs," he didn't know how to convert Ruhar currency to dollars, since there was no established exchange rate. "Several billion, something like that."

"Judgment call," she pondered the idea.

"The point is, it has to be *your* call, not the hamsters. Don't take any shit from them, Lynn."

"Busting heads. I like it," she brightened. "Ok, I'm in. Where do I sign?"

"Uh, we're getting ahead of ourselves. I need to clear this with HQ; they may want you to stay in your current post, at least until they can find a replacement. Plus, the op hasn't been approved yet. When, *if* it gets approved, there's a whole lot of shit we need to accomplish, before we have boots dropping dirtside. Forget I said that last part," he added.

"What part?" She checked the clock. She needed to get moving. "Thank you, Sir," she stood, offering a handshake.

Ross clasped her hand. He had not told her that, in addition to her duties spaceside coordinating fire support, he wanted her help with managing Emily Perkins.

If managing Perkins was even possible.

The Legion was going offworld, and soon. Nobody knew where yet, rumors were flying thick and fast. What was certain was that the pace of training had been ramped up, with units consolidated into battalions. All the additional people in camp meant a lot of work for the combat engineers, and everyone had to pitch in to set up facilities.

Naturally, everyone wished to avoid extra work, so they kept their heads down when volunteers were requested for work parties.

Jates stomped over to the group who were cleaning weapons. "I need volunteers," he growled.

Shauna, Jesse, Dave and the others studiously looked away, pretending to suddenly be *very busy* at whatever they were doing.

Nert, somehow, had not gotten the memo. "Volunteers for what?"

Everyone else groaned. "Nert, you *idiot*," Jesse's shoulders slumped.

"What?" The cadet asked innocently. "All I did was ask."

Dave rolled his eyes. "In the military, that is the same as saying 'yes'."

"Oh," Nert was crestfallen. "I am sorry."

"Well," Jates clapped his hands together happily, flashing an evil grin. "Since the four of you so nicely spoke up-"

"Hey!" Jesse protested. "I didn't- *Damn* it!"

"What will we be doing?" Nert asked, with much more curiosity than was healthy.

"Several of the latrine units that were set up yesterday were installed at the wrong site, they need to be moved and set up right," Jates explained.

"Oh," Nert sighed with relief. "That is not so bad."

"You haven't *heard* the bad news yet," Dave wondered if he could fake an excuse, like death. No. Jates wouldn't accept something simple like death as an excuse.

"Those latrines," Jates's face was impassive, though there might have been a twinkle in his eyes. "Have been in use since yesterday."

"Ohhhh," It was Nert's turn to groan. "Now I am *very* sorry."


After they exchanged pleasantries that actually were pleasant for both of them, and sipped cups of tea, the Burgermeister got to the stated purpose of the meeting. Opening a desk drawer, she pulled out a message written on something like paper, and pushed it across the desk to Lieutenant Colonel Perkins. "Emily Perkins, for your actions on Jellaxico, my government has issued an official reprimand. Consider yourself hereby officially reprimanded."

"I am." Perkins picked up the slick document, wondering what she was supposed to do with it. The thing could go in her personnel file at UNEF Headquarters, although that organization didn't keep paper records. Not knowing what else to do, she folded it and tucked it in her pack. "Is that all, Administrator?"

"No. Now that unpleasant business is concluded, we can talk about something that is actually important." Taking a breath for dramatic effect, she raised an eyebrow. "This should be going to your chain of command first, but since it was your initiative, you deserve to know. Your operation has been approved at the highest level."

"Wow," Perkins had to tense her shoulders to prevent a shudder of relief. The sleazy actions of the Ruhar on Fresno had caused the political coalition of their Federal government to fall in disgrace and scandal, bringing to power the party referred to as the Peace Faction. That party had been slowly but steadily expanding in influence over the past three decades, driven by a citizenry that had grown weary of constant back-and-forth warfare. Enough, said the leaders of the Peace Faction. The Federal Army and Navy of the Ruhar would no longer pursue offensive operations, no longer seek to conquer more and more territory.

Although, that sentiment was not quite true, except for a minority of true believers in the Peace Faction. Offensive operations aimed at degrading the enemy's combat power, rather than adding new territory that would have to be defended, could be approved, depending on the circumstances. An operation like, for example, when Perkins had proposed for the Legion to hire itself out to the Achakai.

"I am, surprised," she admitted.

"No more than I," Logellia agreed with the sentiment. "Rumors I have heard are that the Peace Faction approved this operation to keep the military from protesting directly. If your plan works, the Kristang will be less able to threaten us, making it easier for the government to rein in the military."

Good luck with that, Perkins said to herself, while plastering a neutral smile on her face. "Thank you for telling me first."

"You are welcome. Although, Emily," a shadow fell across the Administrator's face. "This time, I am afraid that you might have been a bit *too* ambitious?"


The senior leadership of the Achakai met deep underground, on the homeworld of their people. Technically, they did not lead their entire society, only the Assassin's Guild. And technically, the planet was not theirs to rule. The world belonged to an assembly of Kristang clans, whose warrior castes collectively controlled the world for the benefit of all. Well, all except the Achakai; the warrior caste didn't care whether the dishonored ones benefited. Specifically did *not* want the Achakai to benefit in any way. They were unworthy, without honor, unclean. Mercenaries hired to perform distasteful tasks, and kept as far away from true warriors as possible.

Regardless of their official legal status, the seven men who lead the major Houses of the Assassin's Guild met in a secret chamber, deep under an anonymous building in an industrial district. Above them, citizens of the world went on about their business, whatever that was. Less than nine percent of the Achakai were mercenary soldiers of any sort, and fewer than one third of one percent belonged to the Assassin's Guild. Most of the Achakai, like all of Kristang society, were females without any rights to own property or control their own lives. Of the males, most were ordinary civilians and had been all their lives, as were the lives of their fathers, grandfathers and so on for generations. Whatever incidents that had caused their ancestors to lose honor and be banished to join the Achakai, those events were long forgotten. Among the Achakai, legends spoke of ancestors banished because they or their families had lost political fights, not conflict on any actual battlefield. Declaring someone dishonorable was a time-tested way not only to get rid of a political rival, but to have their property rights declared void. As that meant such property was then available to be dispersed amongst the victors to increase their own power and wealth, few objected when a family who lost a political fight were subject to banishment.

The seven leaders of the Assassin's Guild, who all had survived many political battles within their own Houses and within the Guild overall, knew the history of their people. Knew the true history, resented it to the very core of their being, ached to restore their rightful place in Kristang society. It was true that among the Achakai, on the world above and scattered throughout Kristang territory, were those who truly had behaved in a dishonorable manner. They had been banished to the Achakai, but rarely joined that society. Newcomers were generally shunned until they could prove themselves. Those who truly had shamed themselves by their actions were few in number, and rarely survived long. After all, if their own clan could not trust them, why should the Achakai extend any trust?

Master Tokwindu thumped a stone on the wooden table, to formally call the session to order. It was an ancient tradition, the stone well-worn from being held by generations of rough hands, the origin of that particular stone lost to history. Nonetheless, it was tradition, and the Achakai clung to the comfort of traditions, as they had few other comforts. Tokwindu conducted the proceedings not because he held the most power in the Guild, or because his House was the strongest, but because he had survived the longest. "This meeting will come to order," Tokwindu announced without need, for the others were sitting quietly, each keeping their own thoughts to themselves. "We have all had time to consider the offer from this Alien Legion. The time to decide is now. Now, or *never*. This opportunity will not happen again in our lifetimes, or the lifetimes of our grandson's sons."

"The offer is not from the Legion," Master Karrat objected. "It is from one of their leaders. One *human*."

"No," Master Dollavezhan said. "The humans, and the Legion," he spat the word as it was distasteful in his mouth, "are nothing but pets of the Ruhar. The offer is from *them*."

"Our intelligence sources tell us the Ruhar were as surprised as we were," Tokwindu said quietly, "when the plan was presented to them. Now, their government has approved the operation."

"That matters not," Dollavezhan insisted. "The Legion can do nothing without the approval of the Ruhar. Our enemies would not have allowed this plan to go forward, unless it benefits them. By weakening *us*."

Master Tokwindu sighed to himself, showing no external sign of his weariness with the argument. "Who," he asked, "is *us*?"

"The Kristang!" Dollavezhan roared. "Have you forgotten all sense of honor? You would sell out our people, to gain more power for yourself?"

Karrat leaned forward, resting his elbows on the table. "We do not belong to Kristang society. They have made that clear to us. *My* people are the Achakai."

Dollavezhan knew he had pressed that argument, and lost, many times since the astonishing proposal had been brought back from the failed action at Feznako. He tried a new tactic. "Should we commit treason against our own flesh and blood, to restore our honor? The clans already think we are beneath contempt."

Tokwindu held up a hand to forestall angry words. "Dollavezhan, history is written by the victors. If we are successful, we will *become* a clan, and no one could deny our honor."

Master Bogauwin spoke for the first time. "Dollavezhan, I will speak only for my House, and my family. My ancestors have sought to restore the honor that was *stolen* from them," he paused as agreeing murmurs rolled around the table. "For millennia. This has been our quest, the focus of our existence. That quest is what has kept us from falling into despair. It has kept us *alive*. This is the first time that we have a realistic opportunity, to achieve the dream we have all held for so long."

Dollavezhan nodded, knowing he had to agree. Also, because he did agree. "The consequences, if we fail-"

"Then," Tokwindu stated, "we will *not* fail. The question is; should we *try?*"

"No," Karrat said, to the surprise of everyone. "The question is, can we *win?* Brave words, brave *deeds*, will not win the day, if we are not properly prepared. Can we trust this Legion?"

"Their leader is a *female*," Dollavezhan noted with disgust.

"She is an alien," Karrat observed. "They are different, we cannot judge them by our standards, though our standards are clearly superior. This Lieutenant Colonel Perkins, though a female, has proven herself to be brave and resourceful. On Feznako, she was a formidable opponent. She even overcame the treachery of the Ruhar. We should not forget that. In this proposed operation, *she* trusts the Ruhar."

"She trusted them on Feznako also," Dollavezhan grumbled.

Master Bogauwin smiled, revealing sharpened fangs. "And she has learned from that experience. Do not forget, Dollavezhan, that on Feznako, she *won*." Another round of murmurs rolled around the table.

"This time," Dollavezhan reminded them all, "she will be risking *our* lives, the lives of all Achakai."

Dollavezhan laughed softly. "My life is at risk every moment, not the least from *you*, my esteemed colleagues." That remark drew a knowing laugh from the others. Assassinations of House leaders usually came from within that particular House, but it was not unknown for disputes within the Guild leadership to be settled by means other than calm and rational discussion. What protected each of them were the formal rules for such assassinations, often the burden of meeting the rules was worse than the pain of allowing an enemy to live. "Come, friends. We do not have to decide the fate of our people today, here. This operation is planned in stages, and we can back out with little consequence along the way, until we *are* committed."

The discussion rambled on, in what Tokwindu was pleased to see was a productive fashion, until it was time for a vote on whether to take the first step. For such an important decision, where the lives of not only all House leaders but every member of the Achakai would be at risk, the vote needed to be unanimous. That was not a formal rule, it was the consensus decision when the proposal was first considered.

All eyes turned to Dollavezhan. If he continued to object, the operation would be stalled until either he changed his mind, or the leadership of his House was changed. Dollavezhan took a breath, enjoying the attention.

Karrat spoke again. "Before we proceed, I must inform you all of a complication." All eyes shifted to the leader of House Minchau. "Before we were presented with this opportunity, the Minchau representative on Kobamik was approached by the Fire Dragon clan there, and offered a contract. As the commission is somewhat unusual, he requested time to confer with the sector coordinator, who contacted House leadership here, as is our procedure." Others around the table nodded, their Houses having similar procedures for potential high-profile contracts. "The contract was properly vetted and accepted."

"Why is this an issue? None of us have suggested we stop accepting legitimate contracts, either for assassinations or mercenary support." With the onset of the civil war, the services of the Achakai had been in high demand, with more contracts offered than could be accepted.

Master Tokwindu nodded. "Indeed, to avoid suspicion, we must continue business as usual."

"Yes," Karrat's face took on a pained expression. "The arrangement of the contract is not the problem. The *target* is."

Dollavezhan asked the question. "The target surely is not one of us?" The clans had very rarely interfered with the Houses, mostly because they feared the consequences.

"No. The target is the human, Emily Perkins."

The other six House leaders gasped. Bogauwin was first to regain his voice. "You are only telling us this *now*?"

"It did not affect us, until now," Karrat averted his eyes.

"No matter," Tokwindu said with a weary sigh. "You can revoke the contract, due to changed circumstances that-"

"The contract has been signed, and fully paid in advance," Karrat stared down at the table in front of him.

"You *fool*," Dollavezhan hissed. A contract paid in advance committed not only that House to fulfill the commission, but if that House failed to deliver, the other Houses were expected to assist. "You put all of us at risk. Why would you do such a-"

"Prestige," Bogauwin said before Karrat could answer. "Is that it?"

Karrat looked up defiantly. "Perkins was a threat to *all* Kristang after the debacle at Feznako. It was inevitable that a major clan would offer a contract to eliminate her. We accepted the payment *before* I heard about her plan to involve us. You would have done the same."

"That is true," Tokwindu said before the meeting could dissolve into useless argument. "My own House has been offered a similar contract, by the Black Trees clan."

"This," Dollavezhan chose his words carefully. "*Is* complicated."

"Does it matter?" Bogauwin looked to Karrat. "If the plan is set and approved, do we still need this Perkins person?"

"If the plan works perfectly and nothing changes," Tokwindu did not have to add a note of sarcasm to his tone. "That is not the only issue. She is popular with the Ruhar public. And the traitors," he could not bring himself to say the name 'Verd-kris', "trust her. The operation carries considerable risk for the humans, the traitors and the Ruhar. Momentum might be lost if she were to be eliminated before we achieve our goal. It would be far too easy for any group to back out, if the plan loses its architect."

"And after?" Dollavezhan addressed his question to Master Tokwindu.

"After?"

"After we achieve our goal. As you said, Perkins is resourceful. In this operation, she is using her resourcefulness *for* us. That is unlikely to be true in the future. She could become a threat to our future clan."

"Hmm," Karrat considered. "Perhaps this is not such an issue. We could wait until we have secured a world, then act to fulfill the contract."

"That might be wise," Tokwindu agreed. "My House should also accept a contract, to do otherwise would raise suspicion. You are right, Karrat, any House would naturally seek the prestige of such a commission."

The meeting dragged on, because all meetings must continue long after the point of usefulness, and finally the leaders voted. The decision to undertake the first phase of the mission was unanimous. With the decision made and their fates possibly sealed one way or another, the leaders returned to their Houses. Tokwindu delayed the usual pleasures he engaged in after a tedious meeting, sending away his wives and concubines, and instead called for his chief assassin.

Assassin Prime Baltazaz Revo appeared in Tokwindu's office quickly, having anticipated and hoped that he would be called. The Master of the House had not yet announced what he was planning, but Revo knew it was something big, for even he had not been consulted. That both thrilled and concerned him.

"Revo," Tokwindu gestured for the man to sit. "I have two tasks for you. You personally," he emphasized.

Revo perched lightly on the forward edge of the chair, waiting with well-practiced patience. Waiting silently and motionless, while not losing focus, was a key skill for an assassin. His mind was quiet also, with only a tiny voice in his head wondering if he was to take action against another House. "We have a contract?"

"We will. First, you have an assignment for the House, directly. It involves former admiral Jet-au-bes Kekrando."

Revo understood why someone would want to kill Kekrando, though the failures at Pradassis and Feznako were not entirely the former admiral's fault. At Feznako, Kekrando certainly could not be blamed for the debacle. Yet, someone had to pay for failure, and Kekrando was a convenient person to blame. What Revo could not understand was why the House was stepping in to act. Kekrando was already under a death sentence by his own clan, the actual date awaiting only legal niceties around the matter of who would get Kekrando's property and position in the clan when he was dead. Perhaps that was the answer: the House would somehow benefit if Kekrando were killed now rather than later. Regardless, it was a high-profile assignment for the House, and for himself. "The second task?"

"The target is a human."

"A," Revo's voice skipped a beat, a fault for which he would berate himself later. "A *human*?" How could any human be worth the attention of the House?

"Yes. I will send details to you, this is somewhat unusual. The human's name is Emily Perkins."

"Ah." Revo had of course heard the name. All Kristang knew the name of the primitive human who had defeated both the armed might of the Kristang and the treachery of the Ruhar on Feznako. Targeting a human made sense because *that* human was an enemy of all Kristang.

Revo was not concerned about the difficulty of striking a target who had to be well-protected. He was concerned about access, but not overly concerned. Surely the House had a plan to get him to the planet Pradassis, or they would not have accepted the contract. "I am honored."

"Revo, there is at least one other House contracted to eliminate Perkins. It is vital that *you* get there first. At the appropriate time. You must not act prematurely."

Getting to the human first added a level of complication that might be difficult to overcome in the field. "What level of collateral damage is authorized?" The chief assassin asked.

# CHAPTER FOUR

Former admiral, most recently senior captain, now prisoner under house arrest Jet-au-bes Kekrando bent down to inspect a flower in the walled garden behind his expansive house. The walls on three sides were stone, with the fourth side of the garden formed by the house itself. The land sloped away from the house, providing a view of the valley stretching down to the river and the hills beyond. In better times, the garden was a sanctuary, a respite from endless deployments that, Kekrando now thought, had no purpose whatsoever. If he won or lost a battle, lines changed on a map, until the lines changed back. Thousands died and nothing changed, other than fewer young men being alive.

That, Kekrando was certain, was the real purpose of the endless warfare conducted by Kristang clans, both against each other and against other species. The warrior caste had too many young men, who not only competed for the available females, but also posed a threat to clan leaders. Hotheaded young men, desperate to prove themselves, to acquire the status, power, and wealth that would allow them to set up a household and begin accumulating females. Females who were desired by the elder clan leaders for their own households.

Hotheaded, desperate young males were both a threat and an opportunity. All the clan leaders had to do was point the hotheads in the direction of the enemy and a predictable percentage of those young men would not return from each battle. If a battle was not sufficiently bloody, the young warriors would provide their own bloodshed in the form of fighting each other. The situation assured the clan leaders had one less threat to worry about, and explained why the households of senior leaders typically included dozens of females, both as servants and for more pleasurable activities.

Kekrando studied the flower, which had come into full bloom only the day before. Sadly, that variety, while exceptionally beautiful, was short-lived. Such was life, he considered. Going down on his knees, he pulled from a pocket the blunt-tipped pair of clippers. Seeing the clippers, the kind given to children so they don't hurt themselves, he smiled. His regular clippers had been taken away by his jailers, along with almost every sharp object in the compound. The jailers were not concerned the former admiral would attack them and attempt an escape. The guards wore plates of body armor and were equipped with both stun sticks and rifles. Embedded in his left shin was a tracking device, and other such devices were probably built into his clothing.

No, the jail guards were not concerned about their prisoner making a foolish escape attempt. They were concerned he might harm himself. Kekrando had finally been condemned to die, following the assassination of his uncle. If the disgraced warrior were to die before his uncle's estate was officially settled, then Kekrando's possessions and his power on the clan council would pass to the wrong people. The former admiral would be ritually executed at the appropriate time to meet the formal customs, and power would shift within the clan.

That was the sum of his existence; a pawn to be fought over, powerless to control his fate.

No matter. He had no intention of killing himself. That would give many people too much satisfaction. He would die with dignity, even if without honor.

Kekrando looked up at the pair of guards watching him impassively from one corner of the garden. They had their heads turned slightly toward each other, talking quietly. He actually felt sorry for them, their job was so dull. They watched their prisoner go about his quiet life, wandering around his estate alone. Alone, because his staff and his wives and mistresses had been banished, his children sent away to live in the households of distant relatives who had not suffered complete disgrace. Alone, because former friends did not visit or contact him in any way, afraid of being tainted by his disgrace.

Assassin Prime Baltazaz Revo sighted through the scope of his rifle, waiting for the target to stop moving for a moment, then pressed a stud on the side of the rifle stock. A laser beam, thin, low-powered, invisible, lanced out at the speed of light, striking the back of the target's exposed neck. The target jerked, a hand coming back to slap the point of impact, thinking the pain had come from an insect bite.

Revo shifted the view to scan the fine mist of blood droplets in the air around the target's head, a computer synced to the rifle analyzed the passive sensor data from sunlight passing through the droplets. The display shining in Revo's right eye blinked, indicating the system was processing. A second later, it changed to 'Target confirmed'.

Revo switched the rifle from laser designator to fragmentation rounds. "Confirmed, it is Kekrando," Revo whispered. "Move on my signal."

As the former admiral bent his head to snip the fading flower, there was a soft phut, phut sound. Looking up, he saw the two guards slumping back against the garden wall, their exposed throats blossoming red. Even as the dead guard's knees buckled, three obscured figures in chameleonware vaulted gracefully over the wall, somehow evading the automated maser cannons and electrified razor wire. Two of the figures grasped the dead guards before the helmets could clatter on the flagstones, laying them down gently and making almost no sound.

Curious but not alarmed, Kekrando stood up slowly, tucking the clippers back in a pocket. The flower almost slipped from his hand before he remembered holding it. "If you came for the flowers," he said to the nearest figure, whose clothing blended expertly into the garden wall, "I regret to say you are too late."

The only reaction from the figure was point his rifle in Kekrando's direction.

"Very well," the former admiral sighed. "Would you mind if I take two steps to my left before you shoot? I would not like my corpse crushing the flowers."

"We are not here to kill you, Admiral," a voice said from behind him. From very close behind him. He had not heard any crunching of footsteps, and the center of the garden where he stood was gravel, rather than the flagstones that ran along the walls.

Turning slowly, though he was fairly certain the figure behind him was not worried about a threat, he let the cut flower drop. As he suspected, the figure wore the symbol of the Achakai assassin's cult.

Seeing that feared ancient symbol caused the former admiral's heart rate to increase slightly, a fact he felt certain the assassin had noticed. For someone to contract the elite Achakai meant this was no mere killing. For an extra fee, the Achakai were known to perform other services, such as extracting information from a target.

If the mercenaries intended to torture him, he would prefer a quick and simple death.

"If you are here to get the codes for my uncle's-"

"Codes are not part of our contract."

They were not there to kill him, or get information. Right then, Jet-au-bes Kekrando realized he had no idea what was happening. "We had best speak quickly," Kekrando said, pointing to the garden wall. "These grounds are monitored by camera, drones, possibly satellites."

"Such surveillance devices are no longer a problem," the assassin declared. It was not said as a boast; for to the Achakai, defeating electronic security measures was child's play.

"There is a locator tag in my left leg," Kekrando reported.

"Disabled. As are the tags woven into your clothing. The people watching you will see you quietly working in your garden, nothing more."

"There are eight other guards in my house, plus fourteen in the house to the south."

"All dead."

"Hmm," Kekrando pondered. "No alarm was sent out?" Though the assassin's face was obscured by a chameleonware veil, it seemed to Kekrando that the figure stiffened. Had he insulted the assassin?

"I assure you, we are not amateurs. You must come with us, now."

"A kidnapping?" Kekrando asked hopefully. At least that would be more interesting than tending his garden.

"No," the assassin gestured toward the house. "A rescue."

Six days later, Jet-au-bes Kekrando still had no idea why he had been taken, for what purpose, nor why the assassin described the action as a 'rescue'. He was taken from his estate in the back of a landscaping truck, driven around for less than an hour, then locked in a cabin aboard a spacecraft which wore the logo and registration numbers of a charter operator. Up into orbit and beyond, he had been confined to the small but well-appointed cabin. Meals of excellent nutrition and adequate taste were delivered through a slot twice a day, and he had receive-only access to news feeds and entertainment programs from the planet he had left behind. It was amusing and enlightening to see that, shortly after he left his home, the compound was attacked by drones. The garden area suffered extensive destruction, the house was leveled, as was the adjacent house. For the first two days, it was reported that a body had been found, a body assumed to be the disgraced former admiral. That was a nice touch by the assassins, Kekrando mused. Clan authorities were not looking for him, because they thought he was dead. That was a neat way to facilitate a quiet getaway.

News reports speculated who could have been responsible for the attack, focusing on those who stood to benefit from Kekrando dying before his uncle's estate was settled. Then on the third day, when it was determined the charred body was *not* that of the former admiral, the narrative of the news coverage changed. A massive manhunt was under way, on and around the planet. Speculation shifted, the most popular story line assumed that Kekrando had been taken by people who wanted to assure he did *not* die before his uncle's estate was settled.

At first, it was fascinating, then interesting, then amusing, finally wearying. He was bored, anxious to learn the true purpose of what the Achakai called a 'rescue'.

On the sixth day, the radiation alarm sounded in the cabin, glowing a soft blue to indicate he was safe from whatever the incident was. The brief duration of the alarm told him the radiation source was likely a starship jumping in nearby. His suspicion was confirmed hours later when the dropship maneuvered, then shuddered as clamps attached. Gradually, artificial gravity increased in strength, pulling him to the floor. He quickly washed himself as best he could, straightened his clothes, and waited. He felt the familiar slight feeling of disorientation when a starship jumped, then it was gone. During his career, he had experienced so many jumps, he felt that he could tell which class of ship he was aboard, just by how the jump felt.

That jump had not felt like any ship he had ever served aboard.

Where the hell was he?

The door slid open, and an Achakai gestured for him to follow. Kekrando made a show of patting his pockets. "Sorry, I didn't leave anything for a tip."

To his utter astonishment, the assassin actually *smiled* at the joke, brief as it was. If the former admiral had been interested before, now he was positively intrigued to learn just what the *hell* was going on.

Stepping out the dropship's door and into a spacious, brightly-lit docking bay, he saw two, no, *four* more things that astonished him. Stretching from the dropship's stairs to the airlock that led to the ship's interior was a dark green carpet trimmed with gold braid, the sort of carpet reserved for honoring important people on special occasions. Flanking the carpet were rows of Achakai, three deep on each side. As he stepped to the deck, the assassins all dropped to one knee, heads bowed, thumping their chests in a salute of honor.

In his long career, Kekrando had never been the subject of such a singular honor, even his lofty rank had not merited such a display. In the Kristang warrior caste, such salutes were for very senior-ranking members of the military, or high-cadre clan leaders. Jet-au-bes Kekrando was neither of those, nor had he ever been.

The third thing he saw that set his mind reeling were a pair of *Jeraptha* of all things, and suddenly he understood why he had not recognized the feel of the jump signature. He was aboard a Jeraptha starship! The Achakai were aboard a Jeraptha ship, an *enemy* ship. He halted, frozen in place, trying to understand what could possibly be the reason for the Jeraptha having hired the Achakai cult, to snatch him from his home and bring him there. "Forgive me," he addressed the Jeraptha standing near the airlock. "Perhaps you could enlighten me as to why you contracted the Achakai to-"

"Urk, urk, urk," one of the Jeraptha laughed, a wheezing sound. "You are mistaken, Admiral. The Achakai hired *us*."

It was fortunate that the meeting took place in the docking bay of a starship, rather than on the surface of a living world, for if a leaf or a feather had fallen on Kekrando's shoulder at the moment, it would have knocked him over. His mouth opened, then closed. For the first time in his adult life, he had absolutely *no idea* what was going on.

"Technically," a new voice spoke as a human woman stepped out from behind one of the glossy green Jerapthas. And suddenly Kekrando realized that he not only had no idea what was happening, he *could* not know. The human woman continued. "The Achakai hired the Alien Legion, and we contracted this ship for transport," Emily Perkins pointed at the deck. "Admiral," she nodded, then snapped a human-style salute. "Welcome aboard the Jeraptha independent trading ship *Sure Thing*."

"Lieutenant Colonel Emily Perkins," he shook his head slowly. "You are the last person I expected to meet here."

"The last?" Her face twisted such that one eyebrow lifted. He knew that was human body language for surprise, or skepticism. He was always amazed to find similar body language throughout bipedal species.

"Well," he admitted. "Not the *last*. I saw my brother Tonnexsun get stomped on, torn apart and eaten by a Grikka when we were young. *He* is the last person I would ever expect to meet again."

"My condolences on the loss of your brother."

"No condolence is necessary. As my younger brother, Tonnexsun of course tried several times to assassinate me, because I was ahead of him in the family hierarchy. Obviously, he failed," Kekrando's mouth wrenched upward in a smile, baring his fangs. "Tonnexsun never had any imagination. That is why he carefully inspected his weapons before he faced the Grikka, but he did not expect the beast might have been drugged to make it especially strong and vicious." His face took on a wistful aspect. "I remember, that was the first day our father ever praised me for my clever thinking and ruthlessness."

"Good times, huh?"

He knew the human was being sarcastic. "Quite so. Colonel, I appreciate the gesture of rendering honors to me, but I regret to report that I am no longer an admiral, nor of any rank at all. I am in disgrace again, if you had not heard."

She waved a hand in what he knew was a dismissive gesture. "Would you like to be an admiral again? In command of a clan's entire fleet?"

He blinked, his mind still trying to process the idea of the assassin's cult hiring the Alien Legion. "Excuse me, I, this is all a bit- I do not know of any clan in need of a commanding admiral."

"The *Achakai* have need of such an admiral," she explained.

If it were possible for an organic brain to experience a short-circuit, his would have suffered such a glitch. It took him several moments to respond. The rows of Achakai were still on one knee, still rendering honors to him. No, not to him. To the commanding admiral they wanted him to be. "I see two problems with your offer. The Achakai are a cult, not a *clan*." He was pleased to see none of the assassins flinched when he insulted them. Any one of them could have killed him in the blink of an eye, yet apparently, he held power over them. They *needed* him. For what? "And to my knowledge, they do not *have* a fleet."

"Those two issues," Perkins grinned, "are why they have hired the Alien Legion."

Kekrando rubbed his chin with one hand. "You have me at a disadvantage."

Perkins slapped a button next to the airlock, and the door slid open. "We have much to discuss. Come, it is time to talk."


The shaze was very good. Excellent, in fact. "Ah, this is a fine bottle of-" He had owned a bottle of the same vintage in his home, before he was disgraced and his most valuable possessions taken from-

He almost spat into the glass, so great was the surprise. The bottle. He recognized where the label had been torn by being mishandled at a party, and pasted back on in the upper left corner.

It was *his* bottle.

He lifted the bottle, examining it closely. "Where did you get this? It was taken away from *my* home, before I returned from Feznako. I assumed it was in the collection of a senior clan leader."

Perkins looked up from her tablet, seeming irritated by the distraction. "It was, let's use the polite term 'repossessed'. The Achakai wished to provide you with a token of their esteem."

"Mm. It is nice."

Perkins set down the tablet. "I sense you are not impressed. Would it change your mind to hear that the senior clan leader who stole that bottle from you, did not survive the repossession effort?"

"Zhokantet is dead?" Kekrando took another sip, smacking his lips with satisfaction. "I have changed my mind. This *is* the finest gift I have ever received. Please extend my thanks to the Achakai."

"They do not want your thanks. They want your leadership."

"Colonel Perkins, it would be best if you started at the beginning."

"The beginning is a *very* long time ago," she sat back in her chair. "I will start with when I joined the story. On Feznako, I met with the local representative of the Achakai. As you likely know, the Achakai maintained a small presence on Feznako, and were regularly contracted to provide clandestine services to the various clans there."

"I was aware of that," he confirmed. He also heard the assassins had been hired by the planet's controlling clan, to ensure that none of the knuckleheaded smaller clans broke the ceasefire and gave the Jeraptha an excuse to use the planet for target practice. The highly unusual, unprecedented arrangement to give disgraced Achakai authority over clan members was very controversial, and very effective. Only two subclans protested against the ceasefire. Their local leaders did not survive long enough to actually do anything, unless staining rugs with their blood counts as 'doing something'.

"Good. In the course of discussing with the Achakai their responsibilities to monitor and enforce their side of the ceasefire, I suggested they hire the Legion."

"You said that before. Hire the Legion to do what?" He pretended calm but inside, he was dying to know.

"To help them become a clan."

The heavy glass slipped out of his hand and thudded on the table, spilling a few precious drops and making the ice clatter back and forth. "Become a- That is impossible."

"They have the numbers. They have the strength. The have the finances. They have-"

"Colonel Perkins, you have been sadly misinformed. I am sorry the assassin's cult has used you for nothing. The Achakai have no honor. They cannot-"

"Bullshit," she said in a quiet, matter-of-fact tone.

He blinked once, slowly.

"I know you understood the translation, but I will repeat what I said. *Bullshit*. I researched the requirements for a group to become a clan, or for a minor subclan to break away from the major clan it belongs to. There are formal procedures."

"The Achakai have no *honor*. No amount of-"

"Again, bullshit. Admiral, if you are just going to spout clichés we both know are not true, then we are going to be here a very long time. From what I can see, there are *many* clans that have no honor. Name a clan that has not signed a treaty, then broken it as soon as it is convenient. Just in your current civil war, more energy is devoted to backstabbing within clans, than to fighting other clans. The Achakai have no honor only because your clans refuse to recognize their honor. The assassin's guild has a very strict code of conduct that they enforce on all their members. *Their* agreements are honorable, in all circumstances. Can you say that about any recognized clan?"

The glass of shaze was no longer appealing. He looked at it and set it aside. "Colonel Perkins, if you extend your insult to my own clan, I will be compelled to-"

"To what? Seriously? You feel compelled to defend the honor of people who sent you into battle without adequate support, blamed you for what happened, and sentenced you to execution, so your property could be used in a power play by spoiled clan leaders who already have way more money than they could ever use?"

"It's not that simple."

"Actually, it is, but let's drop the subject for now. The Achakai informed me, to my great dismay, the formal requirements for a group to be awarded the status of clan. First and most importantly, the group must control a habitable planet."

"There are also minimum population levels," he reluctantly joined what he feared was a useful discussion.

"Yes," she waved a hand. "We know all that. The Achakai have the population level, the financing, the resources, the number of warriors. What they do not have is independent control of a planet. Originally, my thought was for the Ruhar to simply give them a world they no longer want to the Achakai. But, *noooo*," she shook her head in disgust. "That would be too easy."

"The rules state, the world must be taken by force of arms," Kekrando observed. "A group seeking to achieve formal clan status must earn the privilege."

"Exactly. Like I said, your rules are a silly pain in the ass."

"Ah," he thought he understood. "That is why the assassin's cult needs the Legion. Colonel, you are proposing to pull the grikka's tail. You have no idea what you are getting into. When the Achakai attack a Kristang world, even the smallest, poorest world, blood will be shed. All of my people will rise up, united against the Achakai. They, and you, will be crushed."

"Yeah, I figured that."

"You, did?" He asked, more confused than ever.

"Uh huh. That's why we're not attacking a Kristang world. We're taking a world from the Wurgalan."

Kekrando sat back in his chair, then leaned forward and picked up the glass of shaze. He downed the liquid in one gulp. "Colonel, if I ever again underestimate your ambition, please remind me of this moment. I am truly astonished."

"This would not be the first time your people have invaded a Wurgalan planet."

"There have been territorial disputes in the past," he acknowledged. "Usually, the Thuranin and Bosphuraq attempt to resolve such disputes peacefully."

"Unless your patrons find it useful for their clients to fight each other."

"True. I must warn you, the Bosphuraq will not accept loss of a Wurgalan world, not in this fashion. They will intervene."

"The Jeraptha will handle the Bosphuraq," she stated with confidence.

"The plan, then, is for the Achakai to invade and conquer a Wurgalan planet, with assistance from your Alien Legion?"

"Basically, yes. The Achakai have the manpower, but not the equipment or experience. They are not trained to fight in groups, except in very small units."

"As your Legion does not possess starships, can I assume that transport will be provided by the Ruhar?"

"Yes. The Ruhar fleet will also be responsible for suppressing enemy defenses and conducting the landing."

"Interesting. You have manpower, equipment, warships. Why do you need *me*?"

"The Achakai need you. Another requirement for achieving clan status is military power. The Achakai have the numbers and they will soon have the equipment."

"Equipment provided by the Ruhar?"

"Correct. The hamsters will be donating Kristang equipment they have captured and have no use for. Admiral, what the Ruhar will *not* provide is a war fleet. After the Achakai capture the planet, they need to hold it on their own. The Ruhar fleet will only be involved in the initial phase of the assault. The Legion, and the Ruhar, will be involved, but the victory must be won by the Achakai for it to be seen as legitimate."

He paused to think. "The Ruhar will not be providing warships, not even ships they have captured from my people?"

She shook her head. "When the Ruhar capture a Kristang warship, the ship is almost always taken apart for analysis, then destroyed. Most of the Kristang ships they have kept are not flightworthy. The hamsters will be transferring only a handful of captured Kristang ships to the Achakai. They need more ships."

He contemplated another glass of shaze and decided it could wait. "Please. No more guessing. What do the Achakai expect me to do, when they do not have any warships?"

"Get a fleet of warships for them, train them to operate those ships, and then command their fleet to defend their new homeworld."

At that moment, he regretted not having another drink. "*Get* a fleet of warships?"

"Yes."

"Just like that? Have humans mastered the technology of magic?"

"No. We have several options, I am reviewing them. We didn't drag you all the way out here, without a plan to get a fleet for you to command."

"A plan. To accomplish the impossible."

"It's not impossible. Besides, the word is way overused. Did you think it was *possible* for my small team to blast your battlegroup out of the sky over Pradassis?" She used the Kristang name for that world, to remind him that his people no longer controlled it. "'Impossible' is a term people use when they don't want to make the effort."

He stared at her, blinking once. "If I am to be working for you, please tell me you will not be performing my annual evaluation. Your standards are too high."

"You won't be working for *me*. Your employers will be the Achakai."

"That is less comforting than you may have intended," he again contemplated the bottle of shaze, and again forced himself to look away.

"They need you."

"They need me *now*." He raised an eyebrow. "My usefulness is likely to have a limited lifespan."

"If you do your job properly, yes. Train up the ninjas to fly starships and fight in squadron formations, and your job will be done."

"What then?"

She shrugged. "Your alternative was a public execution. This has to be better. Maybe the Verds have a place for you."

"The *Verd*-kris," his lips curled downward with distaste. "Such arrogance in the name they have given themselves. Only *they* can be true to our heritage."

"Admiral, I'm not here to argue the internal politics of your species. I don't *care*."

"The only good lizard is a dead lizard?"

She didn't take the bait to get into an argument. "The only good lizard is the one fighting by my side. The bad guys are the ones shooting *at* me."

"It is better that we avoid the subject. Tell me, Colonel: how are the Achakai reacting to you? To a female?"

"I'm a *woman*, not a female."

"My apologies," he nodded graciously. "I am surprised your leadership did not assign a man to negotiate with the Achakai, to reduce tensions. Did you consider that option?"

"I *did* give the ninjas an option: they can deal with me, or they can go fuck themselves," she said with an insincere smile.

"Suddenly, it is clear to me why you did not pursue a career in diplomacy."

That remark drew a genuine smile from her. "If the Achakai have a problem with me, they haven't shown it."

"You are an alien, and from a primitive species. I didn't say that as an insult. It explains why the Achakai did not object, not openly, not *yet*, to dealing with a fe- with a *woman* in authority. I strongly suspect that happy situation will not apply if the Achakai are expected to serve under, or alongside, Verd-kris units. There could be conflict."

"Yeah," she sighed. "We've already had problems there. We'll handle it, that won't be your problem. Admiral, you probably need time to think about this. Take-"

"No."

She felt lump in her stomach. Kekrando was not just the best candidate for the job, he was the *only* candidate. The wheels were moving, there wasn't time to begin at Square One to find a new leader of the Achakai fleet. "*No?*"

"No, I do not need time to think about it. My answer is yes."

He was screwing with her. That was fair, she decided. "That was fast."

"Colonel Perkins, when presented with only one good option, you can agonize about it, or accept the situation and *get on* with the task. Only the weak-minded waste time and energy in wishing reality were different."

"Hmm. I changed my mind."

"About what?"

"I *do* wish you were on my team."

He held out a hand, a gesture he knew humans used as a sign of friendship. Or at least, a sign of agreement. "We can work together. On one condition."

She hesitated, her hand inches from his. "What's that?"

"If there are any secret weapons I don't know about, you promise to tell me. Before they destroy my ships."

"Oh." She took his hand and gripped it firmly. "Agreed. You'll be the first to know."

# CHAPTER FIVE

Nert walked into the building the Mavericks platoon was using as an office, just ahead of Shauna, Dave, Jesse and three other soldiers. He wiped sweat off his face with a towel, looking in the direction of the break room. The whole team needed a break, they had been working sixteen-hour days to get ready for the Legion's next deployment, and there was still an enormous amount of work to be done. The previous day, he had stashed a four-pack of his favorite beverage in the break room fridge and the Slurm would now be deliciously cold, he couldn't wait to guzzle a can. The humans behind him were talking to each other, distracted and not paying attention to the cadet ahead.

"Hey!" Nert clapped his hands and racing forward. "Look! Balloons! It's a party!"

"*No!*" Dave shouted, lunging to grab the cadet's shirt and missing. He stumbled, almost falling on his face, recovering only when he grabbed the wall that opened into the break room.

"And cake!" Nert beamed, pointing happily at a rectangle on a plate. The icing was white, and written on the cake in blue was 'Party Time'. Next to the sheet cake was a smaller, round cake, with 'Party Time' written on it in Ruhar script.

Jesse poked his head in, followed by Shauna, who should have known better. They both groaned when they saw the figure in the corner.

Leaning against the fridge, arms folded across his chest, was Surgun Jates. "It *is* a party, Cadet Dandurf," the Verd-kris confirmed.

"See?" Nert grinned. "I told you that-"

"Welcome to my *work* party," Jates interrupted.

"This *suuuucks*," Jesse slapped a fist into his palm.

"It is *so* nice to see the four of you volunteering," Jates grinned, his sharp teeth glittering.

"Nert," Dave glared at the teenager. "You *seriously* are an idiot."

"But," Nert sputtered, almost in tears. "But, there is *cake!*"


With newly-appointed Admiral Kekrando signed onto the lunatic plan, Perkins next had to somehow follow through on her promise to acquire a fleet for the admiral to work with. To do that, she needed help from a higher power.

"Admiral Tashallo," she bowed to the beetle-like alien commander, as she entered his office. The *Sure Thing* had taken her to a rendezvous with the Jeraptha Mighty 98th Fleet, for a meeting arranged by the admiral. Without support from the Jeraptha, the entire operation would stall just as it got started.

"Loo-ten-ant Cur-oh-nel Perkins," Tashallo pronounced slowly without a translator, the human words being difficult for his voicebox to produce. He then switched back to using the translator so he didn't literally choke on his words. "I am pleased that we meet again."

"The pleasure is mine," she replied with genuine emotion. "I know that coming here to meet me is out of your way."

"It is? Hmm, navigation was never one of my strengths," his carapace shook with mirth. "We are both busy, and I would like to sit down with you and discuss our mutual interests later. Until then, I have reviewed your request, and my superiors have approved us rendering whatever assistance we can provide, without exposing our involvement, of course."

"Of course." She nodded, tilting forward slightly to make the gesture almost another bow. "Will your fleet be-"

"Oh, no," he shook his own head side to side. "For this operation, you will first need to work with our Inspector General's Ethics and Compliance Office."

She blinked, not knowing what to say. "Um, Ethics and Compliance?" Holy shit, she thought. The beetles think I should work with their internal affairs people? That is the last thing she needed, a bunch of rule-enforcement weenies looking over her shoulder. "Admiral Tashallo, while I appreciate your people must ensure that your involvement complies with the terms of the treaty with the Maxolhx, an operation such as we are proposing must take a flexible view of-"

"Unfortunately, you *must* first meet with Captain Scorandum of the EC Office," Tashallo's antennas dipped in a sort of shrug. "I am sorry. This is very delicate matter, you understand? My actions to interfere at Feznako caused a great deal of trouble for my people." He shifted on his couch, uncomfortable. "And for me, personally. While our government ultimately approved of my actions, the enemy protested up their chain of command to the Maxolhx, who sent a formal complaint to the Rindhalu. Our patrons are not quite as lazy as they have been portrayed, but they do not like being bothered with annoying details, and they made it clear to my people that we cannot be allowed to directly interfere in the affairs of lesser species. Not unless *we* are directly threatened, which is unlikely. *That* is why you must meet with the ECO. Ultimately, that office will either approve or disapprove our participation in the next phase."

He waved for an aide to come forward. "Please follow my aide, she will take you to Captain Scorandum. Hopefully, you will have a fruitful meeting, and we can move forward."

She was led through long corridors of the massive battleship, then took a lift down three decks and walked through more corridors. Whenever she encountered a member of the ship's crew, the beetles openly stared at her, and not in surprise or disgust. She interpreted their expressions as admiration, which was odd. The experience made her wish that she knew more about, or cared about, fantasy sports.

Captain Uhtavio 'Big Score' Scorandum invited her into his temporary office, dismissing the aide and waving for her to sit on the couch. "Hey, how you doin', huh?" He greeted her.

"I am, fine?" She didn't know how to respond, and cringed at her answer. "I am well, thank you. Honored to be here."

He waggled a claw at her accusingly. "I am, I believe the expression is, *pissed* at you."

"Excuse me?" Oh shit. This was already not going well. "May I ask why?"

"Ah, we'll get to that later. I do have to thank you humans for bringing fantasy sports to our attention. It is," he closed his eyes and shivered with an ecstasy like religious fervor, "simply incredible. Tell me, do you play?"

"No, sorry," she considered that maybe she should have lied about that. "My sister used to play in a fantasy fashion league, but that was a long time-"

He gaped at her, his mandibles working up and down. "Fantasy *fashion*?"

"Yes. You, um," she tried to recall the details. Her sister had only been in the league casually, and not for long. "You draft fashion designers onto a team, and they score points based on how often they are mentioned in fashion magazines. Um," the Jeraptha might not understand the concept of 'magazines'. "In media related to the fashion industry."

"Interesting, interesting," the beetle tapped something onto a tablet. "I do not think that has been mentioned before. Hmm. The same concept could be applied to many-"

"Captain Scorandum?" She had to get his attention before he got lost in thinking about potential wagering action. "You wished to speak with me about how our proposed operation can comply with treaties and other rules?"

"I do." He pushed his tablet aside. "Are you familiar with my organization?"

"I understand that your office is responsible for ethics and compliance, within the fleet?"

"That is partly correct."

"I can assure you that my team strives to adhere to the highest standard of ethics, and-"

"*Snerk*," he sighed and looked at her sideways. "You're not one of *them*, are you?"

"I'm sorry, what do you mean?"

"One of those nit-picky rule followers. Colonel, my office is concerned more about the *spirit* of rules, rather than the written details."

"So, you take a somewhat," she sought a word that would not offend the alien. "*Flexible* view of compliance?"

"Of course. Finding flexible solutions is what we *do*. Among other things. We might have a misunderstanding, so allow me to explain. My office works with the fleet, to ensure that compliance with the rules does not interfere with our ethical obligations."

"Um." She was lost. "How would-"

"For example," the beetle leaned his carapace forward excitedly. "Let's say someone has a brilliant idea to screw with the enemy and blame it on someone else. It would clearly be unethical to let such a plan go to waste, just because of some pesky *rules*. My office provides assistance to the fleet, to find a way to implement operations without being declared in violation."

"Oh." She had to remind herself that she was dealing with the Jeraptha, who might have a completely different concept of '*Ethics* and *Compliance*'. "So, you do not perform a more *traditional* role of monitoring compliance?"

"Oh, we certainly do. If some idiot is stupid enough to break the rules in a clumsy way that gets *caught*," he spat the word with disgust. "We punish the offender. And we work to ensure they don't get caught the *next* time, through our program of continuing education," he explained with pride. "I am pleased to say that through the diligent efforts of the EC Office, the fleet has gone eighty-six standard days without being declared guilty of a major violation of rules! That the enemy knows about, if you know what I mean."

"I think I know what you mean."

"Of course, we are also responsible for *enforcement*. If some asshole Thuranin out there is desperately in need of a beat-down, we take care of that."

She pursed her lips. The conversation was not going in the direction she expected. "Admiral Tashallo told me that your office will decide whether to participate in the operation."

"Not exactly," his eyes twinkled. "The good Admiral was having fun with you. Our government has already approved the operation. My office has been tasked with developing a plan so we don't get *caught*. Providing cover stories is among our many, many other duties," he shook his head wearily.

Emily Perkins was not sure she wanted to know what other duties fell under the 'Office of Ethics and Compliance'. But, she had to ask. "What other duties?"

"Well, for example, we assist in accident investigations."

"You do?" Perkins asked with a raised eyebrow. "You are engineers?"

"No."

"Oh. Then you are trained in forensics?"

"Not that either."

"Hm. Then how, exactly, do you investigate accidents?"

"We can sometimes provide insight into how an accident might have happened," Scorandum said as vaguely as he could. "If you know what I mean."

"Uh huh," she answered slowly. "These accidents, do they often occur under mysterious and unexplained circumstances?"

"If we're doing our job correctly, yes. Hypothetically, of course."

"Of course. What, sort of *accidents* do you investigate?"

"Oh, for example, some years ago during a brief truce between my people and the Bosphuraq, there was an unfortunate incident where the fusion reactor at a major Bosphuraq military shipyard exploded. Because the reactor suffered a containment failure at the same time that a battleship's magazines were being loaded with missiles, the energy released was substantial. It destroyed the spacedock, three battleships, four cruisers and entire squadron of destroyers. I believe debris is still raining down on that world."

"You assisted with the investigation of that accident?"

"We assisted *unofficially*, because the Bosphuraq did not request our help. Also, our investigation took place before the reactor exploded. We did note potentially serious design flaws with that reactor, but tragically," he shook his head. "Our report was still being compiled when the incident occurred."

"Uh, *huh*," Perkins made a mental note to involve herself with ECO as infrequently as possible. "So, Captain Scorandum. Why are you upset with *me*?"

"Most of our, um, 'accident investigations' occur during peacetime. Relative times of peace, you understand?"

She nodded. "The war can be hot or cold, but it's still a war."

"Quite so. When fleets on both sides are openly shooting at each other, there is less demand for our services. With the victory of Admiral Tashallo's Mighty 98th Fleet over the Thuranin and Bosphuraq at Nubrentia, we expected the Bosphuraq to offer at least a temporary truce. They have been hurt badly, and we know they have repositioned their forces to defend themselves against the Thuranin. The Ethics and Compliance Office geared up for actions we have been carefully planning for years, but then *you* ruined it all."

"Excuse me?"

"This Alien Legion project of yours."

"It's not *my* project."

"You know what I mean. Just when it appeared that our conflict with the Bosphuraq and Thuranin was quieting down temporarily, you stirred things up. The Kristang *had* to react to the threat of the Verd-kris being unleashed on them. When the Kristang failed to crush the Legion on Feznako-" He paused.

"What about it?"

"I thought you were going to say something like 'No thanks to the treacherous Ruhar'."

"I didn't have to *say* it aloud."

"True," his antenna bobbed up and down, showing his amusement. "When the Legion survived the operation at Feznako, and then after you succeeded at Jellaxico, the patrons of the Kristang felt they had to step in."

"Jellaxico was a minor operation, it meant nothing."

"Your assessment is incorrect. We know that the Thuranin decided to take direct action against the Legion after Jellaxico. Now, you are proposing to expand the conflict further by attacking the Wurgalan?"

"With the approval, and assistance, of your people," she noted, leaning forward onto the table.

"You understand that does not mean we actually expect you to *succeed*? Your proposal is so bold, so unexpected, that it provides unique and juicy action. There is no way my people could resist such a tempting offer," he wagged an accusing finger-claw at her.

"Really?" Her voice dripped with sarcasm. "Why, I had *no* idea."

"I do not blame you for manipulating my people for the benefit of your own."

"But, you are not pleased about the Legion keeping this war hot?"

Scorandum's antenna bobbed up and down once, in what she knew was a noncommittal gesture, essentially a shrug. "That is, as you humans say, above my pay grade. Tell me why you need the services of ECO."

"As one requirement to achieve clan status, the Achakai must have a fleet of starships." She held up a finger to forestall a lot of useless questions and suggestions. "The Ruhar will be handing over several captured Kristang ships, but they can't provide any ships of their own. It's an honor thing," she shook her head with a frown. The freakin' complicated and nonsensical rules of Kristang society were a pain in the ass. "The Achakai can't be *given* anything of substantial value. Somehow, using their own warships that were captured is an exception to the rules, don't ask me how. The key is, the Achakai have to build their own ships, buy them, or take them by force."

"EC is not in the business of providing *loans*," he clicked his mandibles skeptically.

"We are not asking for a loan to buy ships. That won't work anyway. With the latest civil war raging, there aren't any ships available for sale. Every hull the lizards have is in service, if it can fly at all."

"That leaves the third option: taking them from a clan."

"That's out. We thought of that, all the targets are too tough. We would have to hit a shipyard. To do that, we have to control space around the planet. To do *that*, we need ships. It's circular logic."

"What is your solution? You would not have approached my superiors without a plan."

"I, that is *we*, do have a plan."

"Please do not make me guess."

"The *Wurgalan* are not experiencing a civil war," she said simply.

"What does that – Oh. The Wurgalan? You plan to steal *Wurgalan* ships? How is that-"

"The rules do not state the Achakai must acquire *Kristang* starships, only that they have a fleet."

Scorandum gaped at her. "Colonel Perkins, if you are ever interested in a change of career, ECO may have an opening for someone of your, creative thinking."

"Thank you," she laughed. "I'm happy where I am now." Tapping her tablet to wake it, she turned it so Scorandum could see it. "The Wurgalan keep several fleets of reserve ships, in various states of readiness."

"You are misinformed," he explained. "Their reserve fleets are located near major military facilities. Any attempt to raid those ships would involve a major battle with active elements of the Wurgalan fleet. My group does not participate in regular warfare. If you intend a smash-and-grab mission, then-"

"We do not intend to raid a reserve shipyard," she explained. "The Wurgalan also have two collections of old and obsolete ships, what navies call a 'boneyard'. Most of those ships are nonfunctional, kept to be stripped for spare parts. But some percentage of ships in the boneyard are capable of flight, to varying degrees."

"Varying degrees? Such as?"

"Such as, ranging from ships that are likely to explode if the reactor starts, to ships that are capable of performing a short jump. We will need to acquire information about the ships in the boneyard, assess which are the best candidates, then decide how many ships we could reasonably take with us."

"Plus additional ships for spare parts," he looked at the tablet, then up at her.

"We plan to cannibalize some ships we take, to make the others flightworthy."

"How many ships do you need?"

"To make a viable fleet for a clan, twenty-four ships are considered the minimum."

"Twenty-four flightworthy ships. With spares, let's say we must take thirty, thirty-two ships from the boneyard." He paused to consider, looking away. "Colonel Perkins, this all sounds very sketchy to me."

"I know it is unusual, that's why-"

"No," he wheezed with amusement. "Sketchy is not a problem. Sketchy is what we *do*," he explained. "In every conflict there is a need for underhanded, sleezy, dirty deeds that people don't want to know about. Someone gets to do it, why not us?"

She tapped her ear, wondering if the translator had glitched. "You mean someone *has* to do it?"

"No," he stared at her. "Why?"

"No reason. Forget what I said."

Leaning back in the chair, he picked up the tablet and studied it. "I *like* it. The last time we screwed with the Wurgalan was," he looked up at the ceiling, gathering his thoughts. "A long time ago. Too long. The squids are not typically worth our time. Also, as you know, the unwritten rules of the game discourage us from taking direct action against client-level species. We must be extra careful about this one. Hmm, I will certainly need plausible deniability."

That was a phrase she had not heard in a while. It usually referred to politicians wanting to avoid responsibility for their decisions. "This operation is known only to a small group of humans and Ruhar, I can't vouch for the information security measures of the Ruhar. If you must be able to deny any involvement, I don't-"

He wheezed with laughter again. "You misunderstand. 'Plausible Deniability' is the name of an ECO ship."

She blinked, unsure the translation had been accurate. "You have a ship called '*Plausible Deniability*'?" There was too much she didn't know about the clandestine Jeraptha group.

He tilted his head quizzically. "Yes, why?"

"No reason. If I may ask, what is the name of *your* ship?"

"I currently command the *Will Do Sketchy Things*."

"For food?" She guessed.

"What?" He looked at her blankly.

"You will do sketchy things, for food," she suggested.

He stared at her like she had grown a second head. "Why would we need food?"

"Oh." That, she thought, explained a lot.

"For a raid on a Wurgalan boneyard, hmm," he tapped the side of his mandibles with a claw. "We would probably need specialized ECO stealth ships like the *It Was Like That When We Got Here*, or the *I'm As Shocked As You Are*. In case of trouble, we should bring heavier warships, I think the *Parole Violation* and the *Out On Bail* are available, depending on their current assignments. Colonel, I will need to consider how best to approach this problem. We have limited information about these boneyards, and the ships in them. Tell me, how did you learn about them?"

"From the Torgalau."

"Er," he wheezed. "The Torgalau undoubtedly got much of their information from *us*. I would not trust their intelligence to be up-to-date."

"But you're in?"

"My superiors wish you to succeed."

She snorted. "They wish to cause trouble for the Thuranin, by weakening Kristang society."

His antennas spread apart in a gesture a human might make by holding their hands apart, palms up. "It is good that you are realistic. In this case," Scorandum said, "the goals of your people and ours are the same. To answer your question, yes, we are in. At least to the point of investigating whether the proposed operation is profitable."

She tapped her right ear, which held the microphone that provided translation. "You mean whether it is *practical*?"

"Hmm? No, why?"

Again, she was reminded that dealing with ECO was different from working with typical allies. "Captain Scorandum, I will leave the details to you."

"That is wise. Colonel, the assistance my people can offer is limited, you understand that? We can help acquire ships, even with minor repairs to get them flightworthy. Possibly some training of crews. But we cannot fly the ships for you."

"We also need transport, star carriers."

"Presumably the Fleet is already prepared to arrange that for you, or we would not be having this discussion."

The Jeraptha had not yet officially committed to anything, that she knew of. Negotiations with the beetles was handled by the Ruhar, a fact that irritated her. The operation was already horribly complicated. Having all decisions go through the Ruhar was a cumbersome and unnecessary step. Someday, she might be able to cut the Ruhar out of operations, but that time was far in the future.

If she ever got that far.

"The Achakai will operate the ships."

"The Achakai?" That surprised him. "The assassins have no experience with the operation of starships, the Kristang warrior caste forbids the Achakai from acquiring or utilizing advanced weapon systems. Also, no Kristang have experience with Wurgalan ships."

"It is true that the Achakai do not have their own ships," she admitted. They actually did already have a handful of ships provided by the Ruhar, Scorandum didn't need to know that. "They do have highly realistic simulators."

"Oh." Scorandum's own people mostly trained with simulators. Depending on the level of sophistication, training in a simulator could be equal to or better than operating a real ship. A simulator allowed crews to perform maneuvers that would be too dangerous for a real ship to attempt. After a crash, a simulator only needed to be reset, and the only damage was to bruised egos. "You have simulators for Wurgalan ships?"

"The Achakai have adapted their equipment to mimic the operation of Wurgalan systems, based on data from the Ruhar. The Ruhar also will be assisting with getting the ships flightworthy."

"Hmm," Scorandum smiled, his mandibles curving. If the Ruhar would be working on ships for use by the Achakai, they undoubtedly would also be installing hidden software to prevent those ships from being used against the Ruhar in the future. The Achakai would expect that, and look for kill-switches buried in the ship computers. The Ruhar would build in code that would fry the computers if anyone tried to disable the kill-switches, and of course the Achakai would anticipate that. In the end, it would be a contest between the cybersecurity teams of the assassins and the Ruhar. If he were the Achakai, he would plan to wipe the existing computers and replace the operating system as soon as possible.

Of course, the Ruhar would have anticipated *that* also.

As none of that was *his* problem, he didn't care.

One of his antennas flopped side to side in a dismissive gesture. "The first step will be to gather more information about these boneyards."

"Of the two ship storage areas, one is-"

"We will make that assessment," he said without rancor.

She nodded. "You are the expert."

"What is the timeline for this operation?"

"As soon as possible. The Kristang have already noted that a significant number of Achakai are unaccounted for. The cover story is that they have been contracted by a major clan, and of course all the clans are denying any knowledge of where the Achakai have gone. Of course, that helps sell the cover story," she smiled. "We have a limited time to act, before all the clans become suspicious that something other than the usual back-stabbing is going on."

"Then," he rose from the couch. "We have work to do."

After a long meeting with Admiral Tashallo, during which he drank too much vintage burgoze and she drank too much from a bottle of genuine Kentucky bourbon, she went back aboard the *Sure Thing*. "Oh," she shaded her eyes from the blinding lights in the ship's docking bay, certain she would have a hangover in the morning. "Captain Gumbano, please take us to jump distance, we're going to-"

The beetle shuffled his feet. "Colonel Perkins, neither of us expected our arrangement to last this long. We wish to renegotiate our incentive structure, if we are to continue to provide transport and other-"

"Renegotiate?" She really did not feel like arguing with a beetle right then. "You want to discuss incentives?"

"Yes, exactly."

"How about this: we continue the current payment structure, and you avoid being thrown into prison. Plus, the Jeraptha Home Fleet continues to protect you from that organized crime group you screwed over in the smuggling job you did on the side after we left Feznako, which you think I didn't know about."

The captain of the *Sure Thing* shuffled his feet more vigorously. "That is indeed a powerful incentive." He looked away, unable to meet her eyes. "We accept your very generous offer," he mumbled.

"I'm glad to hear that. Now, I'm going to get some rest. Wake me when we get to Paradise."

# CHAPTER SIX

Having been provided the dual incentives of avoiding prison and not being slowly taken apart by an outraged gang of criminals, the crew of the *Sure Thing* took Perkins straight back to Paradise for meetings with UNEF-HQ, but she first stopped by the base where the Mavericks were training. Assembling the team, she regretted that Surgun Jates could not be there, as the Verd-kris was not yet approved for a top-level security clearance by UNEF-HQ.

"Are we a 'Go', Colonel?" Shauna asked.

"I am confident we will get a 'Go' order," Perkins replied. "There is another hoop we have to go through; the operation needs final approval from the Jeraptha Ethics and Compliance Office."

"Oh, come *on*," Dave groaned. "Really? We're waiting for a bunch of-"

"Don't worry," Perkins said with a twinkle in her eyes. "Remember, these are the *Jeraptha*."

Irene had very limited experience with the beetles, so she asked the question. "What does that mean?"

Perkins laughed. "It means their idea of 'Ethics and Compliance' is finding ways to get *around* the rules, so we don't get caught."

"*Cool*," Jesse shared a high-five with Dave. "You gotta love those beetles."


The human with the odd name of 'Emily Perkins' implied that she had a plan for stealing Wurgalan ships from a fleet boneyard, but that was not really true. She had a vague notion, really a *goal*, but not a workable *plan*.

That was fine for Captain Scorandum, who preferred to have his team develop their own plans. A relatively simple operation, like stealing obsolete junk warships from a comparatively low-tech species, would be good practice for his team. They quickly threw together a wide variety of plans that were all practical, and provided acceptable levels of cover to conceal involvement of the Jeraptha, but Scorandum rejected all of them, because they simply weren't any *fun*. Most of the operations lacked the essential *sleaziness* of a signature Ethics and Compliance operation. The key to a truly successful operation was for the enemy to know they had been thoroughly screwed over by ECO, but they weren't able to *prove* anything.

To do anything else would be unethical.

In the end, Scorandum himself led development of the plan, demonstrating why he had earned the nickname of 'Big Score'.

The genius of the final plan was that it relied on the Wurgalan screwing themselves.


For the Wurgalan assigned to duty at the Urskigandia Fleet Reserve Component Training Area, otherwise known as Boneyard Site Two, life was dull. No. The word 'dull' did not adequately describe the insufferable, mind-deadening boredom of being assigned to a place where literally *nothing* ever happened. The

Training Area, where no training had or ever would occur, was in orbit around a gas giant planet on the edge of a remote star system that was accessed by one Elder wormhole, making the star system a dead-end in terms of both navigation and careers. Ships were brought there at the end of their useful lives, to be stored and slowly stripped for spare parts, as they degraded from the icy cold of space and the eroding effects of micrometeorite impacts. Personnel assigned to the Boneyard knew they had reached a point in their careers from which they could hope to go sideways, or nowhere, or maybe down, but certainly never *up*.

Thus, it might seem surprising that command of the Wurgalan Fleet Security contingent at the Boneyard was a highly sought-after assignment, and significant funds changed hands under the table before most new commanders were appointed. The reason was simple: spare warship components could be worth a *lot* of money.

The current commander of Boneyard Site Two was an officer with a rank roughly equivalent to Major, named Osgooth Fornilfonn. The unlucky, or lucky depending how you looked at it, Fornilfonn was previously one step higher in rank, until he failed to anticipate a change of command above him in the organization, and uselessly directed a cut of ill-gotten earnings to the wrong officer. The correct officer punished Fornilfonn's lack of foresight by busting him down one grade, then rewarded Fornilfonn's creative abilities by getting him assigned to a Boneyard, where he could exercise his talents. And, of course, share the earnings with the right people above him in the chain of command.

The first four months of Fornilfonn's tenure were disappointing, for with the Bosphuraq getting knocked on their asses by the Jeraptha, the asshole patrons of the Wurgalan had been forced to freeze offensive operations, leaving little for their client's military to do. Less activity by warships meant less wear-and-tear on vital components. Fewer battles meant less battle damage to be repaired. Overall, there was less demand for spare parts, both legitimate and somewhat-less-than-legitimate. The situation was deeply troubling, because Fornilfonn still had to make monthly payments on the money he borrowed to buy into the assignment, when not much money was coming in.

It seemed like a miracle when he received a clandestine message from an unexpected source claiming to be the Kristang Swift Arrow clan. The Kristang were widely considered to be assholes even by species who acknowledged their own innate assholeishness, but these lizards offered payment upfront, and on generous terms. It seemed that, with a civil war raging across Kristang society, every available hull had been pressed into service, leaving no ships available to be stripped for parts, and creating a desperate shortage of vital components. The representative of the Swift Arrows offered a deal; they wanted all the spare parts they could get. Since the Kristang and Wurgalan had been stealing and copying each other's technology forever, many parts from Wurgalan ships could be made to fit Kristang ships, especially if you weren't real picky about how well the components worked or how long they lasted.

Without the risk of a face-to-face meeting, the Swift Arrow clan representative transferred a tantalizing sum into a secret account controlled by Fornilfonn, and in turn he agreed to look the other way while the Swift Arrows sent bots aboard the ships of the Boneyard, inspecting the condition of the mostly derelict ships and creating a shopping list. When the Swift Arrows had their wish list completed and a price was agreed, the plan was for Fornilfonn to pretend he didn't see anything while the Kristang filled their shopping baskets and flew away.

What the Kristang did not know was that Fornilfonn planned to screw his new business partners by doubling or even tripling the price at the last minute, when the Swift Arrows had no choice but to cough up the extra money.

What Osgooth Fornilfonn did not know was that the Kristang had absolutely no knowledge of, or involvement in, the operation they would get blamed for.

When the drones completed their survey of likely candidate ships in Boneyard Two, the ECO team identified thirty-nine ships in decent enough condition to be worth taking, plus seven others that were stuffed full of useful parts. The operation needed only thirty or so ships, but Captain Scorandum decided to take forty-three because he had plenty of room on the racks of the waiting star carriers, and, why not?

With the shopping list completed, the next phase was to move ships of the Ethics and Compliance fleet into position, inside tightly-wrapped stealth fields. Though the plan did not anticipate any need for violence, the big warships *Parole Violation* and *Out On Bail* were standing by to jump in if needed, but most of the action was performed by small, specialized stealth frigates like Scorandum's own *Will Do Sketchy Things*, and the aptly-named *We Were Never Here*.

Not even the sophisticated stealth fields of an ECO ship could conceal the dent made in the fabric of spacetime by the mass of a warship, and the Boneyard was covered by gravimetric sensors. Scorandum's team took the easy route to fooling the Wurgalan sensors, by hacking into the central computer that monitored the Boneyard. Cybersecurity technology of the Wurgalan was so poor that the Ethics and Compliance Office team charged with cracking the alien system were insulted by being assigned a task that did not in any way challenge them, they grumbled their discontent while they did their jobs. To make the task somewhat less irritating, they planted viruses and worms and a myriad of other hostile software in the alien system, to be triggered at a later date. It would serve the Wurgalan right for providing such shockingly poor cybersecurity. Certainly, it would be unethical to allow such sloppiness to go unpunished.

With the mass-detection system being told to ignore signals from the gravimetric sensors, ships of the ECO squadron maneuvered close to their targets, extending thin power cables to provide a partial charge to the jump drive capacitors of the Wurgalan ships on the shopping list. The jump drive system of each ship was tested under a trickle of power, temporary repairs were made, then the Jeraptha ship moved on to hook up power cables to the next ship on the list. Only three Wurgalan ships failed the testing and had to be replaced by other ships, a result that was much more than acceptable.

When power cables were disconnected from the last ship on the shopping list, the ECO ships backed away and accelerated at a leisurely rate, getting clear of the Boneyard.

Osgooth Fornilfonn would have rubbed his tentacles together with a gleeful laugh, except that was not a common body language of his species. Instead, he checked the amount in his secret bank account yet again, wincing when he saw how depleted it had become, but dreaming of much larger sums appearing there soon. Showing shrewd business sense, he had recently offered his superiors a higher monthly payment in exchange for them taking a smaller cut of the future graft. Not knowing what he knew, they jumped at the opportunity for a guaranteed increase of income in the current low-action environment.

That day, he had cleared his schedule, so he could take a dropship across the Boneyard to meet face to face with the representative of the Swift Arrow clan. That foolish Kristang was going to get a rude surprise when he tried to negotiate a low-ball deal with Fornilfonn. After all, there were many other Kristang clans. He would tell the Swift Arrows that they could meet his outrageous price, or he would deal with another clan. The prospect of seeing shock on the ugly face of the Kristang was almost better than the money imagined-

"Sir?" The pilot of the dropship called through the open door. "There is something odd going on."

"Eh?" Fornilfonn shook his thoughts back to the present. "What?"

"It appears," the pilot checked his instruments again, fearing to deliver bad news. "The jump drives of several ships are powering up. Are we conducting an unscheduled test?" If so, the pilot was *pissed* to be flying through a navigation hazard he hadn't been notified about.

"What?" Fornilfonn pulled himself into the cockpit with his tentacles and hung there in the zero gravity. "No, we are not- NO!"

All over the Boneyard, obsolete ships were powering up their jump drives and disappearing in brief flashes of gamma radiation.


With the little fleet of old, obsolete and barely-flightworthy former Wurgalan ships under the command of Admiral Kekrando, and under the watchful eyes of both the Ruhar and Jeraptha, Perkins took her team back aboard the *Sure Thing*.

"You wish to return to Paradise?" Captain Gumbano asked with a resigned shrug. Being under contract to the Alien Legion ensured steady pay, with opportunities for side jobs that the Legion didn't need to know about. More importantly, working for the Legion kept the Jeraptha authorities from seizing the *Sure Thing* and its crew. While they had been forgiven their past transgressions, the authorities knew it was only a matter of time before the *Sure Thing* did something extra-sleazy, and Gumbano knew things the authorities only suspected. He needed to keep the steady job, even if it could be tedious.

At least, with Perkins, the work was often unpredictable.

"No," she dropped her duffel bag on the deck, for a bot to carry for her. "We're going to the Turnanbey system."

"Turnanbey?" He frowned, partly because he had just lost a wager about where the ship would go next. "That is a Ruhar system." He tried to recall details, and failed because that star system was so unimportant.

"It is *nominally* a Ruhar system. The Kristang have not pulled all their people out yet," she explained. With the Ruhar Federal government under control of the Peace Faction, expansion plans had been put on hold, leaving recently-captured places like Turnanbey in an awkward spot. The Kristang had been slow to leave because their ongoing civil war was taking up most transport capacity, and the Jeraptha were willing to divert one of their star carriers only when there were enough transport ships to fill all the docking platforms. There was also the consideration that, when overloaded transport ships of multiple clans were waiting in orbit for a Jeraptha star carrier, it was quite likely that some jackass from Clan A would be tempted to hit a transport ship of Clan B. As the controlling entity in the star system, the Ruhar would be responsible for any violence suffered by evacuees, so they had to keep transport ships far apart and constantly patrol the area. It was a *huge* pain in the ass for everyone, especially for the Ruhar.

So, until they could be sure that a sufficient number of transport ships would be in the system, the Ruhar were content to allow the Kristang on the surface to carry on about their business, and if that business included killing each other, then, well, that meant fewer lizards to worry about. Being on the surface also meant the Kristang were legally responsible for feeding themselves, and that reduced the supply burden on the Ruhar. The bottom line for star systems like Turnanbey was that while the Ruhar no longer actually wanted the place, they could not simply change their minds without appearing dangerously weak. Their occupation of Turnanbey, and a dozen other marginal star systems taken in the recent offensive, limped along with a minimal number of warships to discourage reckless adventures by the local population. The crews of ships assigned to such systems grew increasingly angry and frustrated while they waited for their government to make a damned decision one way or another.

"Why are we going there?" Gumbano asked in a casual manner, trusting the translator to convey just how disinterested he was, which he very much was *not*.

"Training," Perkins said as she walked past, following the bot that was carrying her duffel bag.

"*Training*," the ship's captain muttered to himself. The human's answer was bullshit, but there wasn't much he could do about it.

Before the *Sure Thing* arrived at the outskirts of the Turnanbey system, it performed a series of maneuvers requested by the human commander. While deep in interstellar space, the ship decelerated and changed course, until it was oriented with the plane in which the planets around Turanbey orbited. Captain Gumbano noted that the speed his ship was requested to travel was slower than needed for achieving a stable orbit around the only inhabited world there. He also noted that the requested jump coordinates were just outside the system's asteroid belt. "Course and speed are nominal," he announced only two hours late, the delay caused by needing to shut down one of the ship's engines before it overheated.

"Thank you," Perkins replied. "We can still jump on schedule?"

"Yes. How long will we be here? I only ask because my engineer would like to tear down one of the fuel pumps." That was a lie.

She knew the ship's captain was lying. He wanted an opportunity to use the ship for smuggling, or some other activity that she would rather not know about. She also knew that he knew *she* was lying about a training mission. They both had to play along to make their arrangement work. "*We* will not be staying here," Perkins explained. "My crew will be taking a dropship out for an extended training mission. I will remain aboard, and the ship will jump to," she tapped her tablet. "These coordinates."

"I see," Vinny Gumbano quelled his disappointment. The coordinates were a point more than a lightmonth beyond the far side of the star system. There was no reason to take the ship there, other than to make sure the crew of the *Sure Thing* did not see whatever the Mavericks were really doing. The reason Perkins was staying aboard the ship was to ensure the crew didn't go somewhere to spy on the dropship. They were both lying, and both knew each other were lying, and they pretended not to know. It was better than most relationships he had. "How long will we be away? I am concerned, because at that distance, we will not hear a distress call from the dropship until it is too late. An asteroid field can be a dangerous place," he hinted.

"Six days. My pilots have experience navigating asteroid fields. Do not worry, you will have plenty of time to work on the engines."

Vinny bowed his head, burning with curiosity. He would love to attach a surveillance device to the dropship, or even a simple flight monitor that would track where the little spacecraft went. But he was smarter than that, he knew that his own military had provided Perkins with sophisticated equipment to secure her against clandestine monitoring, and he did not want to taint his already-strained standing with his government. The *Sure Thing* was not the only beat-up freelance Jeraptha ship available to carry the Alien Legion from star to star. Besides, whatever Perkins was doing, he would see eventually.

In the meantime, he and his crew would have wonderous opportunities to wager guesses about why the Mavericks had really come back to Turnanbey.

The *Sure Thing* jumped in beyond the outer edge of the asteroid belt, moving only slightly faster than the nearest large floating rocks. The dropship launched from the far side with only a puff of thrusters and immediately engaged stealth, moving away at minimum power. Engaging its normal-space engines, the former star carrier accelerated at a moderate thrust and transmitted a recognition signal toward the closest Ruhar sensor satellite, giving the authorization code that allowed Emily Perkins to go pretty much any place in Ruhar territory. Two hours later, a signal was received, acknowledging the *Sure Thing*'s authority to be there and requesting to be notified in advance of any change of course.

By the time the Ruhar received the reply message, the *Sure Thing* had jumped out to the middle of nowhere.

The dropship, a Dodo that was newer and nicer than most of the junk the Ruhar provided to the Legion, coasted through space for thirteen hours before engaging its engines for a gradual deceleration that lasted another nine hours. During most of the time, the five people aboard caught up on sleep as best they could in the zero gravity, or played games on their tablets, or did any of the myriad things that soldiers did to combat the boredom of waiting for something to happen. Nothing was *expected* to happen; the *Sure Thing* had authority to enter the star system, the Ruhar did not know about the presence of the stealthed Dodo, and there were only four Ruhar starships in the entire system. Two frigates and a destroyer orbited the only inhabited planet, keeping a watch on the lizards below and preventing any mischief from striking the slowly-growing number of Kristang transport ships that were gathering within three lightminutes of the world. The other frigate was, according to sensor data that was more than two hours old, patrolling the other side of the star. The odds were very much against the Ruhar caring enough to send a frigate out to investigate the asteroid belt, and the Dodo was long gone from where the *Sure Thing* had jumped in. Unless they somehow had to burn the engines hard to escape an emergency, the Dodo would never be detected.

"All right," Derek called from the cockpit. "It's time for the show."

"Cool," Shauna shut off her tablet and secured it in a pouch, so it didn't float away. Aboard ships, whether starships or the smallest of dropship landing craft, soldiers had to constantly remind themselves to *stow their gear*. Any object adrift could become a deadly projectile if the ship had to maneuver violently or was struck by enemy fire.

"Damn," Jesse said as he floated on the ceiling upside down, looking through the doorway to the cockpit. They all could see the ship's external sensor feed through their tablets or phones, but they all wanted to be part of the action, to *see* what the pilots were seeing. "I should have made popcorn for this show."

"No way," Dave groaned as he held on to the left side of the cockpit doorway. "Last time you made popcorn, you burned it."

"Hey," Jesse pushed himself away toward the alcove that served as a galley. "I'll watch it this time. That oven-"

"*No* popcorn!" Irene ordered. "Colter, the last time, it took a whole freakin' *day* to get that smell out of the cabin. We only have three spare sets of air filters."

"Yeah, besides," Shauna patted Jesse's leg, gently tugging him back near her. "We won't have time before we get into suits and go outside. Right, Sir?"

"Should be," Derek replied, distracted. Irene was flying the ship while he scanned the area with passive sensors. The object they were looking for was tiny, a chunk of dull gray, lifeless metallic rock roughly four meters long by three meters wide. It would have been difficult to find, except they knew exactly where it was. Exactly where it was supposed to be. The rock had been selected for being dense, high in elements like iron, for being anonymous, and for being nothing anyone would care about. A chunk had been cut away, then the inside hollowed out to make room for an Elder power tap, cushioning to protect the rugged but priceless object, and a layer of shielding to prevent casual scanners from seeing what was at the heart of the rock.

The target rock had been pushed away at a precise speed that was calculated to avoid coming near any significant asteroids for at least seventy years, the longest time a dropship's navigation system was able to project.

"Shouldn't we *see* it already?" Jesse asked, already getting bored with watching Derek watch a console display. "We know exactly where it is, right? It's just," he waved a hand. "Math and stuff."

"Math and *stuff*?" Shauna raised an eyebrow. Jesse too often pretended to be dumber than he was, a trait that irritated her. He wasn't in high school anymore, she didn't understand why he still acted like having knowledge and the ability to use it meant he couldn't be one of the cool kids.

"You know what I mean," he was instantly on the defensive, knowing why she was upset with him. "Orbital mechanics."

"Orbital mechanics isn't all *that* simple," Derek said without taking his eyes off the display. "Objects out here interact through the local gravity field in complex patterns. The rock we're looking for may be small, but it has mass that acts on-"

Irene interrupted, to avoid a nerdy lecture from Derek. "The answer is we should see it soon. It's dull, remember? We selected that rock partly because it doesn't reflect much sunlight."

"Just enough," Derek reminded everyone, "to avoid being suspicious, or a navigation hazard." The Ruhar had a practice of tagging objects that were difficult to see on passive sensors. They usually only bothered to do that in star systems with heavy traffic, but ships with nothing much else to do were sometimes given busywork by making them catalog and tag asteroids. Five minutes later, with the other four growing impatient, he looked away from the display. "Shit."

"Shit?" Irene repeated. "Have you got it located or not? If we're going to match course with it, I need to initiate the rendezvous maneuver soon."

"That's the problem," he explained. "No. I don't see it."

"Let me try," Irene suggested, pulling up the detailed sensor feed on her console.

"Go ahead," Derek returned to his console, fiddling with the controls.

"It has to be there, right?" Dave asked, a hint of anxiety creeping into his voice.

"Yeah, unless," Derek muttered.

"Unless what?" Shauna prompted the pilot.

"Hmm? Oh, unless the hamsters somehow knew what we were doing out here the first time."

"*Know*?" Jesse asked. "How could they know? We didn't tell anybody."

"Yeah," Dave added. "You wiped the Dodo's flight logs, before you gave that ship back to the hamsters. You did wipe the flight log, Sir?"

"Yes," Derek said, annoyed. "We scrambled the whole system. Caught hell about it from the Ruhar crew chief. No way did they discover what we were doing from that Dodo's memory. Still," he let his voice trail off.

"What?" Shauna asked.

"They wouldn't have to know *what* we were doing, to be suspicious that we were doing something out here," Derek mused. "The cruiser was monitoring the whole sector, it tracked every move we made. Maybe something about the pattern we flew got them thinking something was hinky out here."

"Come on," Irene scoffed. "The hamsters had better things to do than watch us twenty-four-seven."

"They didn't have to," Derek defended himself. "The cruiser's AI watched everything."

"Yeah, but," Dave didn't want the two pilots arguing. "We thought of that. Everything we did that might look suspicious, we had an asteroid between us and the cruiser, and we were careful not to be line-of-sight to sensor satellites. Sensor coverage out here was thin."

"It still is," Irene said. "Let's not get into speculation, Ok? We should find the rock any second now."

Ten minutes later, she was forced to admit she was wrong. "Son of a *bitch*," she exclaimed. "It's not here. Somebody took it."

# CHAPTER SEVEN

Lynn Bezanson arrived early for her meeting with Major General Ross, prepared to wait, so she was pleasantly surprised when Ross himself stuck his head out the door and waved her in. "Change of plans, I've got about half an hour before my next meeting," he said with a glance at the wall clock. "Are you still interested in my job offer?"

"Busting hamster heads?" She grinned.

"Uh, yeah. About that," he lifted his chin toward the door. She got the message and closed the door, then sat down. "There's a change there too. How do you feel about being aboard a Kristang ship?"

She couldn't hide her surprise. "You mean a Ruhar ship controlled by the Verds?" To her knowledge, all requests by the Verd-kris leadership to crew and command ships of their own had been firmly rejected by the Ruhar government. The hamsters had refused to provide the Verds with flight training other than aircraft and dropships. The Ruhar public was still uneasy about providing weapons to the Verds, and allowing them to control a warship was a step too far.

"No. A Kristang ship, controlled by Kristang. The bad guys."

"Jeff," she cocked her head. "If you're asking me to volunteer for duty as a prisoner aboard a lizard ship-"

"No," he laughed. "It's a bit unusual, but hell, everything is unusual out here. Perkins has another crazy scheme cooked up. HQ bought in one step at a time. Now we're at the final phase, and the Ruhar have given the go-ahead."

"For an op where we are working with lizards?"

"The bad guy lizards, yeah. It's a long story."

"What would I be doing, exactly?"

"Same as we discussed. Coordinating orbital fire support. Just on a Kristang ship, instead of a Ruhar one."

She rubbed her eyes, taking time to think. Looking up, she asked "We are friends with the Kristang now? Then who is the enemy?"

"We are *not* friends. This is an enemy-of-my-enemy thing. We're joining forces for a limited time, to achieve a limited objective. The enemy, in this case, is the Wurgalan."

"The squids? *Shiiiit*," she breathed. "Don't we have enough aliens out there who hate us, without making new enemies? Hell, Sir, you've seen the reports about a Thuranin ship lurking around this system. The Legion is an opportunity, but it has also made humans on Paradise a target. The hamsters know the Thuranin are worried about the Legion, that's why they stationed another battleship here."

"One more Ruhar battleship in orbit won't stop the Thuranin," Ross warned, "if those little cyborgs want to hit us. What you haven't seen in any report is that our beetle friends have a pair of cruisers in-system somewhere. If the Thuranin try an orbital strike, they will find a nasty surprise."

Bezanson thought that the Thuranin paying a price later would be of little comfort to dead humans on the ground. "The Ruhar government signed off on attacking the Wurgalan? The Peace Faction has been wanting to *cease* offensive operations, not expand them."

"They signed off. The ones who know about it did, this whole op is classified. If we're successful, Kristang society will be tied in knots for years, that takes pressure off the hamsters."

"The Kristang are participating with us," she said slowly, "in an op that *degrades* their combat capability?"

"*Some* of the Kristang are participating."

"Ah." Suddenly, it made sense to her.

"You know that the lizards love killing each other, more than they love killing other species."

"Perkins set this up?"

"Who else? HQ and the Ruhar are pissed that she made the offer to the lizards, before getting approval from our side."

"Why am I not surprised?" She sighed. "Ok. This sounds like the Mother Of All Bad Ideas but, I'm in." She arched an eyebrow. "I'm *trusting* you on this."

"I appreciate it. Hey, I will be on the ground, while you're overhead with the big guns. I will try not to piss you off."

"I will try not to let my trigger finger slip at the wrong moment."


"Come in, Captain," General Bezanson waved with one hand, while with the other, she scooped objects off the desk and into a box.

"Spring cleaning, Ma'am?" Captain Danielle Grace guessed. She had only been to Bezanson's office once before, and remembered it as neat and spotlessly clean. Now instead of photos on the walls, bare hooks decorated the industrial-beige surfaces, and a set of half-full boxes were scattered on the floor.

"Something like that," Bezanson looked around in dismay before nudging a box out of the way with a foot and sitting down. She had come to Paradise with only enough personal items to fill one pouch of a rucksack. How had she accumulated so much stuff during her tenure in the office? More importantly, *why* had she accumulated so much useless stuff? The last thing she needed in her life were knickknacks, yet she had half a box full. Best to put them in storage somewhere and sort through it later. "I'm leaving the liaison office, General Ling is replacing me."

"Oh," Dani didn't ask why, or if the change was good news for the general. She hadn't heard any rumors, not that gossip about general officers always got down to her level. Still, she had to say *something*. Congratulations might not be appropriate, if Bezanson had not wanted to leave her office. So, she avoided the subject entirely. "You wanted to see me, Ma'am?"

"Yes." The general opened a drawer, looking for something, then shut it with a disgusted grunt. "I hear you had fun on your last trip offworld."

"*Fun?*"

"The Army's kind of fun," Bezanson explained. "You *didn't* actually get eaten by a giant lizard?"

"Oh. Yes, I suppose so," Dani agreed with a wry smile.

"Are you interested in deploying offworld again?"

Dani hesitated perhaps a half-second too long. She knew the Legion was working up for another deployment, everyone on Paradise knew that. "That, depends," she answered honestly. "The last time, I almost *did* get eaten by a grikka."

The general smiled, a twinkle in her eyes. "Don't worry, Captain. This time, the only lizards you have to worry about are the smart kind, with rifles."

Dani gave Bezanson the side-eye. "That is actually *not* any less dangerous, Ma'am."

"You'll be working with the good kind of lizards, I promise. Most of them, anyway."

"We'll be shooting at the bad kind of lizards?" Dani guessed.

"Not this time. On this op, the bad lizards are also on our side."

Dani blinked. "Excuse me?"

"Sort of. I'll read you in, if you're interested."

"I'm a psychologist. The Legion brought me to Fresno to assess how the Kristang there were responding to the evac."

Bezanson snorted. "We know how *that* turned out."

Dani felt a need to defend herself. It wasn't her fault the Fresno mission had become a mess. She and the others in her office had warned the Kristang would react badly to the use of Verd-kris troops by the Ruhar, that even warring Kristang clans would temporarily band together to stamp out the new threat to their society. The official assessment before landing on Fresno had even listed the possibility of the Kristang using their Keeper slaves as human shields, to prevent military action by the UNEF side of the Legion.

Arguing with a general was not a good career move, so Dani bit her tongue. "We got lucky."

"Luck is a legitimate component in warfare. And technically, we got *unlucky*. The hamsters stabbed us in the back on Fresno. The Legion never had a legitimate chance to win the fight."

Dani didn't want to revisit the past, she had relived the Fresno operation many times during debriefings, and while helping to write the official after-action summary. "Can we go back to the part about us having the *bad* lizards on our side? We will be fighting with the Verds, and a group of warrior caste, against another group of warrior caste?" She guessed.

Bezanson shook her head. "Their warrior caste will not be involved, this time. And we won't be fighting Kristang, the op will be against another alien species."

Dani took a moment to process that revelation. "Ma'am, all the training I've been given by the Ruhar is about Kristang psychology. I don't know much about other aliens," she said, with a troubling thought. Could the operation be against a group of *Ruhar*? For the Legion, for humans in particular, getting involved in an internal Ruhar dispute would be a very bad idea, even if the mission were strictly peacekeeping or-

"You will get a crash course on alien psychology. That won't be your primary focus. You will be embedded with a Verd platoon."

Right then, it all made sense. Dani sat back in her chair. "Oh." Now the general's request made sense. "You want me to spy on the Verds."

"No."

"Ma'am, it sure sounds like-"

"*We* don't want you spying on the Verds." Bezanson explained. "The Ruhar do."

"Ok." That also made sense. "The Verds are smart, they will know why I'm with them."

"Yes they will, and they will be eager for you to report about how loyal and trustworthy they are. They will be on their best behavior for you."

The whole situation made Danielle uncomfortable. "I need more details, Ma'am."

"I need *you* to tell me if you're in, or not."

Technically, UNEF could order her to deploy, but the Legion was a volunteer force. She could request another assignment, resign her commission, or other options. One thing she knew for certain: most of the soldiers of UNEF were not being offered a choice. "I'm in," she said. "Please tell me this operation isn't against a Ruhar faction."

"No," the general snorted. "The hamsters would have to be crazy to get us involved in their domestic politics. The Legion would have to be crazy to accept such an assignment."

"Then, who will we be fighting?"

"The Wurgalan."

"The *squids*? You said I'll be getting a crash course in alien psychology, but, what do the Ruhar know about the Wurgalan?"

Bezanson shrugged. "They have fought before. It doesn't matter. We're getting our intel from the Torgalau, they have a lot of experience fighting the squids."

The Torgalau, Dani thought with excitement. She would be meeting *two* new alien species. And, she reminded herself, doing her best to kill one of them.

Sometimes, being in the Army made it really difficult to make friends.


"What's next?" Dave asked, picking at his food without enthusiasm. Eating in zero gravity was not much fun on a good day, and the Mavericks were most decidedly *not* having a good day. He closed the cover over the dish of Chicken Ala King and tucked the fork in a pocket. He should have known not to choose that meal. The Dodo's zero gravity, lower air pressure and low humidity made most foods taste bland. Looking enviously at the chili that Jesse was evidently enjoying, he took a sip of water and tried not to think about food.

After Irene declared that the asteroid with the Elder power tap was simply not where it was supposed to be, Derek had set the ship's computer to continue the search. That was a move intended more to improve morale than to actually locate the missing rock. "I don't know," Irene answered honestly. "We could run a Scrabble tournament while we wait for the *Sure Thing* to come back."

"Oh," Derek groaned. "Not Scrabble again." He hated playing Scrabble. Correction: he hated playing the game against Irene, because she kicked his ass every single time.

"We're giving up?" Jesse's spoon froze halfway to his mouth, the chili trembling precariously in the lack of gravity. "That's it? We give up that easily?"

"If you have any suggestions, Staff Sergeant," Irene said peevishly, "I'd love to hear it."

"Hey," Derek touched her forearm. "Colter is trying to help. We are all pissed off about this."

"Sorry," Irene apologized. "Though, I meant that. If anyone has ideas, please speak up. I don't like the idea of doing nothing until we go back to the ship empty-handed."

"What if the coordinates are wrong?" Dave asked. "Not that you," he looked from one pilot to another, "wrote it down wrong or whatever. Like, what if the Ruhar moved the navigation beacon, something like that. We would be looking in the wrong place, and not know it."

Derek grimaced. "Good idea, we thought of that. To confirm the nav beacons are accurate, we triangulated with planets in this system, and a dozen local stars. Our navigation data on *all* of them would have to be bogus."

"Maybe," Shauna nudged Jesse to eat the chili before it floated off the spoon. "The navigation data is accurate. Maybe the coordinates we have are wrong." Seeing Irene start to roll her eyes, she continued. "Hear me out. We've been aboard five, maybe six other dropships before this one since we hid the power tap. I remember at Jellaxico, we had to delay a landing, because the hamsters were pushing a software patch. Maybe the software in this bird," she rapped her knuckles on a bulkhead, "is different enough that it's not reading the coordinates right. It's possible?"

"Shit," Derek set down the meal he didn't feel like eating anyway. "She's right. It *is* possible."

Irene frowned. "Unlikely."

"Come on," Derek urged. "It's worth a shot. Way better than playing Scrabble."

"Says *you*," Irene protested, but activated the console in front of her. "Ok. I'll compare the coordinates on my tablet to the ones logged into the ship's nav system. I'm using the same tablet, and its software hasn't changed."

"The encryption scheme *has*," Jesse pulled out his own tablet. "We all had to update to the new scheme, like, what? A month ago?"

"Damn it," Shauna tapped her tablet. "Yup. If the decryption drops a few bytes here and there, that could change the numbers we're reading for coordinates?"

"Ah," Dave was skeptical. "It would probably corrupt the whole file. But we should check."

"I'm doing it," Shauna set aside her dinner and perched the tablet on her lap.

"This is good," Derek grinned. "Brainstorming. Anyone got anything else?"

Dave gave it a shot. "If someone stole our rock, they needed a ship. Can we look for some sort of residual signature around here?"

Derek pinched his lips together. "Like venting reactor plasma?"

"Yeah, or," Dave's knowledge of how to track stealthy spacecraft was vague. "Air leaking out of airlock seals, that type of thing."

Derek shook his head. "Unless it happened in the past few days, the solar wind would have dispersed any residual elements. Also, we don't have a database of drive signature for ships."

Jesse gave his friend a thumbs up for making a good try. "What about a collision? There are a lot of rocks floating around out here. What if something hit *our* rock, knocked it out of orbit?"

"Ah, shit." Derek hated shooting down the staff sergeant's suggestion. "It would have to be hit by an uncharted rock, because we projected forward the orbits of all *known* objects to make sure there wouldn't be a collision within our lifetimes. Problem is, if the object was uncharted, we have no way to know which direction it came from, so we can't project in what direction it moved our rock."

"Can we look? A collision would have left debris?" Jesse asked hopefully.

"Space is *big*," Derek shook his head. "We're in stealth, we can only use passive sensors. Basically, light from the star has to bounce off it and be picked up by our antenna. The rock we're looking for is too small to show up on gravimetric detectors. If it collided with something, it could be *anywhere*. That doesn't help us."

Jesse looked at Dave and gave an 'I-tried' shrug, but Dave wasn't paying attention. "Sir, have you checked if everything else in the local area is where it's supposed to be?"

Derek blinked. "What?"

"The other rocks around here. Are they in their predicted positions? You said you tracked all known objects and projected their orbits forward."

"We, did," Derek replied slowly. "What do you mean, are they in- *Oh*." Understanding dawned on him.

"You said 'gravimetric'," Dave explained.

"I did." The pilot swiveled his chair to face the console, and his fingers tapped rapidly.

"Will someone please tell me what ya'll are doing?" Jesse pleaded.

"Mister Czajka suggested that something might have disturbed the orbits of multiple objects in this area." He looked back over his shoulder at Dave. "Is that right?"

"Yes. Also look for objects that *shouldn't* be here."

"Doing that also."

"Hey!" Irene threw her hands up. "What are you doing? I was using the nav system for-"

"Relax, Babe, this will just take a minute," Derek assured her.

Irene hid her mouth behind a hand. "That's what you said last night," she giggled.

"Oh, that was a low blow for- Holy *shit*!" Derek shouted. "Quit your grinn' and drop your linen. I found something."

"What?" Irene asked, she had not been listening to the conversation.

"Babe, look at this," he pointed to the display. "These are the projected locations of objects within eighty kilometers. *These*," he highlighted the objects. "Are their actual positions. They have moved. All of them."

"Damn," she muttered, leaning to examine the data. "You're sure of this?"

"As much as we can trust any of the navigation data. Look, the farther away we scan, the closer objects are to where they should be. Something caused objects right around here to shift their orbits."

"Something? Like what?" Shauna looked over Derek's shoulder.

"Could be something exploded. We were blowing up a lot of booby traps back then," Derek reminded the team. "We left before the whole belt was cleared. Maybe the hamsters blew up something big after we went home. Could be something as simple as an object with substantial mass being here for a while. When we were here the first time, we were based out of the *Warshon*. That bucket was a heavy cruiser, a big sumbitch."

"Enough speculation." Irene pressed a button on Derek's console and returned to her own. "If it's that simple, the computer can compare the position of known objects to where they should be, and determine what disturbed their orbits. Then we can run the effect forward and see how it would have affected *our* rock."

Derek tilted his head. "That's not *simple* at all."

"It is when the computer does all the work for you."

"How long, Ma'am?" Shauna asked.

"I don't know," Irene admitted. "There is a *lot* of data to work with. The navigation system isn't designed to run this kind of data, I have to run it through the fire control computer."

"If this works, we owe Czajka a bottle of scotch," Derek suggested.

"Can I get bourbon instead?" Dave grinned. "Since we're talking about fantasies anyway?"

Sixteen agonizing minutes later, after several false starts, the fire control system developed a solution. Derek warmed up the passive sensors and focused them on the predicted location. "Well, ain't that a kick in the ass? We found our rock!"

Dave, Shauna and Jesse suited up and went outside to retrieve the Elder power tap, a process that involved Jesse and Shauna carefully cutting into the rock and capturing the resulting dust in in a bag, so it would not create a cloud and attract unwanted attention. While the other staff sergeants played Bob the Builder with the diamond-blade cutting tool, Dave held a cylinder of metal that had been fashioned to be the same size and mass as the power tap. They pulled out the power tap, replaced it with the inert cylinder of metal, and used cement to fasten the cap back in place. Derek verified the rock looked exactly the same as when they found it, then the tricky part of the operation began. The three amateur astronauts had to gently push on the little asteroid, nudging it this way and that way on instructions from Irene, until it was moving in exactly the same direction it had before they screwed with it. When the three soldiers were back inside the Dodo, it puffed thrusters ever so slightly and drifted away before the tiny gravity field it generated could pull the rock off course.

"We're good," Derek announced as Shauna, Jesse and Dave were stowing their suits. "How does the toy look?"

"It's not a *toy*," Irene cautioned. "That thing could melt this ship to a puddle."

"You know what I meant," Derek grinned.

"I do, and I want everyone to be very careful not to screw with it. Calling it a toy doesn't help."

"It looks fine, Ma'am," Jesse turned the ancient device over in his hands. It was heavier than he remembered, the difference might be the adrenaline surge he felt when he first saw the thing. "So far as I know, there's nothing we can do to damage it."

"I'm worried about *it* damaging *us*," Irene waved a hand. "Please put it in the container."

"Yes, Ma'am," Jesse allowed Shauna to help him guide the power tap into a specially padded and shielded container they had brought, which was inside the nosecone of a sensor probe. The power tap took up space that would normally be occupied by sensors, and Perkins had not yet explained why she wanted to stuff the device into the front of what was essentially a missile. "Secured," he said as he closed the door on the back of the nosecone. "Ok to put this back on the rack?"

"Please do," Irene released from her seat, and floated into the cabin to watch the three soldiers wrestle the nosecone into the Dodo's rear cargo storage area, where they slid it into a slot next to five other identical-looking nosecones. Only the serial number stamped into the rear bulkheads of the nosecones differentiated the special one from the others. Shauna had suggested making a scratch or other mark on the nosecone they couldn't afford to lose, but Perkins insisted there be nothing to distinguish the one carrying the power tap.

"I hope we don't all forget the serial number," Shauna said as she closed the cabinet door.

"It's the only one that ends in with the Ruhar symbol for '8'," Jesse told her.

She looked at him, surprised. "You're sure about that? Including the probes aboard the *Sure Thing*?"

"Absolutely, Darlin'," he grinned. "It's why I selected *that* one to modify. No way am I gonna remember a long-ass serial number."

"Shiiiiit," Dave sighed. "*Now* you tell me, 'Pone. You know how long it took me to memorize twenty-seven characters in Ruhar script?"

"All you need to remember is the hamster character for the number '8'," Jesse thumped Dave's shoulder. "See? My Momma didn't raise no fool."

"That was good initiative, Colter," Irene patted the cabinet door, happy that she could focus only on flying the dropship.

The group floated back into the cabin, where Derek poked his head through the door from the cockpit. "The baby is safely asleep?"

"The baby is safe and sound," Irene's relief was evident.

"Everyone," Derek continued. "I want to say how proud I am to be part of this team. You all did great. We nearly had a disaster, but nobody panicked-"

"Speak for yourself," Irene interrupted. "*I* almost peed in my pants."

"Me too," Dave admitted.

"Nobody *acted* like they panicked," Derek insisted. "We pulled together, and everyone had ideas worth pursuing."

"*Dave* had the right idea," Jesse gave his friend a thumbs up.

"The *team* found a solution to the problem," Derek held up a thumb and waved it to encompass the others. "I don't know what the Colonel plans to do with our toy, but I sure as hell am glad we don't have to tell her we lost the thing."

Irene floated through the doorway and strapped into her seat. "*Next* time, we put a transponder on the rock."

"We couldn't risk doing that," Derek reminded her. "If the transponder malfunctioned, or some Ruhar ship just happened to transmit the right code, they would have found it."

"Yeah, well, I hope there won't *be* a next time," Irene punched buttons to warm up the main engines. "I will sleep a lot better when we're back aboard the *Sure Thing*, and the thing isn't our responsibility. Strap in, everyone, we're moving in five."

While the Dodo coasted toward the rendezvous point, Irene played Scrabble with Derek and Shauna. Irene enjoyed playing the game, because she generally won. The others just went along to kill time while the dropship flew through empty space.

Derek put down tiles to spell 'flexible', which prompted a frown from Irene because that ruined the plan for her turn. "Whatever the Colonel plans to do with the toy, it's a good thing we didn't lose it."

"It wouldn't have been *lost*," Irene threw up her hands, looking at her tiles in disgust. "If it wasn't there, somebody had to have stolen it."

"What's the point?" Shauna asked. She looked from Derek to Irene. "Do either of you know what Em plans to do with it?" She had already asked Dave, who told her that his girlfriend had not said anything about her plans. Maybe the Colonel had shared info with the two officers.

Derek shrugged. "No idea, she didn't say anything to me."

"On Fresno, she told Jesse to trade it to the beetles, in exchange for them helping us. She wasn't happy about it, because she wanted to trade the power tap for a recon mission to Earth."

"Sure," Irene put down tiles to spell 'enable'. "That was a good idea back *then*. Now the Maxolhx are sending a full battlegroup to Earth? There's no point to the beetles doing a recon, we will all know the status of Earth when those ships get back."

Shauna cleared her throat nervously. "I heard a rumor," she looked down at the table, where the magnetic Scrabble tiles were held securely. "That the Maxolhx will reopen the wormhole to Earth, when they get to the other side."

"I heard the same," Derek said. "When I asked a Ruhar starship navigator about it, she told me that rumor is total bullshit. Even the two senior species have no ability to control Elder wormholes, they don't even understand the technology."

"Then why did that wormhole shut down?" Shauna pressed for an answer. "It wasn't open long after the shift in that area."

"Nobody knows. That's the point, I guess. That's why the Maxolhx are sending ships to the other end. If there is something wrong with the wormhole network, it could affect everyone." He looked down at his tiles. "Thinking about Earth is depressing. I don't feel like playing."

"Me neither," Irene admitted, pushing her tiles away. "This *sucks*."

# CHAPTER EIGHT

The *Sure Thing* jumped in eighty-three thousand kilometers away from the designated jump entry coordinates, just in case some jackass had ignored the very clearly marked boundaries of the area reserved for inbound jumps, and parked their starship right in the same area where the *Sure Thing* tried to emerge from a hole twisted in local spacetime. Jackassery was not the only factor creating concern, the area contained many obsolete starships of dubious reliability, flown by crews who had little experience with actual machines that did not always perform the way they did in simulators. Such ships could easily blunder into restricted areas either by mistake or accident, and it would not matter who caused a collision. Eighty-three thousand klicks was a compromise. Captain Gumbano had wanted to emerge two-hundred-forty thousand kilometers away from the planet, while Perkins had complained that would require too long a flight in a dropship. Eighty-three thousand kilometers was a nice round number in the Jeraptha measuring system, which was a lucky number for Vinny Gumbano and basically, Emily Perkins didn't want to waste energy arguing about it.

When the ship emerged to find not one but *two* starships encroaching on the restricted area, another compromise was reached: Captain Gumbano did not say "I told you so', and Perkins made a note not to argue with the people who owned the ship.

The dropship ride was short, mostly because the Jeraptha crew was showing off for the primitive aliens. Enduring acceleration of four gravities was a reasonable trade-off for reducing the time that she had to discuss fantasy sports or other gambling with the pilots, so Perkins breathed evenly and trusted her flightsuit to keep her from passing out or bursting a blood vessel in her brain. Because one of the beetles had a brilliant idea for a fantasy league based on whether football referees were bribed to throw games, and if she had to listen one more time to the pilots arguing about it, she was going to either throw them out an airlock, or jump out herself.

Ruhar traffic control routed her dropship on a priority course to the beat-up piece of junk that Admiral Kekrando was using as a flagship, and the flight would have been quicker if the flagship's docking bay doors had not jammed halfway open. Twenty minutes later, after the doors cycled three times and a maintenance team got them unstuck, she stepped onto the deck of the *Battle of Lithoria Gundo* and was escorted to the bridge. Walking in zero-gravity boots always took some getting used to, she had to remember to lift her feet higher off the deck than normal, so the boots didn't try adhering to the deck in the middle of a stride. It was a pain in the ass that Kristang ships did not have artificial gravity. The issue was not that the Kristang lacked the technology, it was relatively simple. The lizards did have a limited field of gravity plating in the medical sections of their larger ships, because some wounds healed better in at least light gravity. Really, the issue was one of stubborn bravado: the warrior caste considered artificial gravity to be a power-wasting luxury that dedicated warriors did not need.

It was true that artificial gravity fields could be power-hogs, especially at the crude level of Kristang technology that relied on brute force to simulate the mass of a planet. That was why the Ruhar reduced gravity when their ships went into combat, a much better solution than denying the benefits of gravity to the crew.

The whole issue, Perkins thought, perfectly illustrated a fundamental difference between the Kristang and Ruhar. It also explained why the Ruhar had generally been kicking lizard ass throughout the war, despite the Kristang devoting a vastly greater portion of their economy to the war effort. The Ruhar designed their starships to provide comforts that kept their volunteer crews combat effective over deployments that typically lasted half a year. Those ships were maintained in peak condition by those crews and by a network of fleet-servicing facilities scattered over the far-flung territory of the Ruhar.

The Kristang, by contrast, expected their crews to rely mostly on the ill-defined concept of 'Warrior Spirit' to sustain them during long deployments aboard their cramped, uncomfortable ships, which steadily grew less and less flightworthy due to deferred and neglected maintenance. Commanders of their clan fleets, and any ship captain with an ounce of brainpower, knew there was a predictable curve of declining combat readiness for both ships and crews. By the middle of a deployment, a ship's ability to keep flying relied more on luck than on 'Warrior Spirit'.

Emily Perkins had those thoughts in the back of her mind while she partly walked and partly floated through the destroyer *Battle of Lithoria Gundo*, using whatever method of locomotion was most useful at the moment. She was surprised to see access panels stripped away almost everywhere, with Achakai technicians working on systems that typically would not be touched after they were originally installed. If she was surprised to see techs replacing worn-out sensors with spares that were better than new, she was astonished to see crews working to fix sticky doors and tuning up communications equipment.

"Admiral Kekrando?" She paused outside the fleet commander's office, a temporary compartment that also had all its access panels open.

"Colonel Perkins, come in, come in," the admiral waved from his seat, beaming a wide smile. If he was not genuinely happy to see her, he was doing a good job of faking it.

They exchanged greetings and small talk, something else that astonished her. Never had she expected to be *chatting* with a warrior caste Kristang, yet it felt perfectly normal, as if they were old colleagues. Keeping the conversation to professional matters helped, as did avoiding any subjects that might be sensitive.

After fifteen or twenty minutes of idle chitchat, she brought up the subject of her visit. The Achakai fleet had been dropped off at a long-unused Ruhar fleet servicing facility that orbited a gas giant planet, in an anonymous red dwarf star system. Once important back when it was within easy distance of three wormholes, the system was now a dead-end, reached by only a single wormhole. The orbiting shipyard and automated supply depot were revived by the Ruhar specifically for the Achakai, and until the day the little fleet departed for wherever they were going, they had the star system for their exclusive use. Exclusive, except for the three hundred Ruhar technicians who were helping to get the ships ready for combat. And the six Ruhar warships that made sure the Achakai didn't cause any trouble. And the squadron of Jeraptha destroyers that blocked access to the system. The Achakai didn't want to be there almost as much as the Ruhar didn't want them there, which might explain why there had not been any serious problems when the two warring alien species were forced to work closely together. The sooner the ships were made flightworthy and the new crews trained to fly them, the sooner they could jump away.

Perkins tried to ask the question casually. "So, Admiral, what is the status of your new fleet?"

"Hmm," he sat back in his chair, which creaked as it clicked into place. "It is not *my* fleet."

"You know what I mean. It is yours to command."

"It is. Colonel, I have ships designed and constructed by two species. To get the ships ready for combat, we have been forced to adapt components from ships of alien origin, parts from different classes and types of ships. All of the ships have parts from Kristang, Wurgalan and Ruhar designs. We have incompatible electronic systems that can barely talk to one another, cobbled together into a network that is likely to crash the first time we use it in combat. Even the best of the Wurgalan ships have reactors with so many leaks that we are having to run the cores at forty percent power. Those reactors radiate so much energy that it would be useless to extend a stealth field around the ship, which is good because their stealth capabilities are nearly worthless. Many of my ships have sensors in such poor condition, my crews would be better to navigate by looking out a porthole. The magazines are filled with Ruhar missiles so obsolete, their Use-By date expired before I was born. Half of those missiles are useful only for close-space support missions the ships were not designed to perform. When the Ruhar loaded the magazines of our ships, they pulled whatever units were easiest to access from the supply ship, regardless whether the type of weapons matched a particular ship's role in the fleet. We had to take three days to conduct a cross-decking operation to sort it all out. Now, ships that specialize in close-space support have missiles designed to strike targets on the ground, and ships optimized for ship-to-ship combat have the appropriate weapons. There are other issues. This ship," he tapped the bulkhead behind him, "is fortunate to be equipped with shield generators that are compatible and within three generations of each other. Unfortunately, they are so badly out of tune, they are likely to interfere and short each other out if we had to use them. What else? Oh, yes. Most of the ships have at most one spare set of vital components, so if we get into combat, their readiness will decline rapidly."

"Shit," she breathed, biting off a harsher reply. That was not the news she expected, not the news she needed to hear. "We're screwed, then?"

"Oh no," he laughed heartily, a dry, wheezing sound. "Most clans would be envious to have such a fleet!"

"Uh-" She didn't know what else to say.

"Colonel, the Achakai are true fanatics. That makes them single-minded and stubborn to their detriment, but it makes them highly motivated to get these ships in the best possible condition. There was an incident during our first few days here, when I instructed the crews to analyze and repair the sensor suites of the ships. The

Achakai aboard one ship protested that true warriors did not demean themselves by working on systems not related to weapons. The file leader aboard that ship took the initiative to toss the protesters out an airlock. That had a motivational effect on crews of other ships. Since then, the Achakai crews have done whatever the Ruhar technical team instructed them to do."

"I am encouraged to hear that."

"This fleet will be fully combat ready within two of your Earth weeks. The ships will still be old and obsolete, but they will be able to *fight*. Do not be concerned about us."

She understood the subtext of his statement. She needed to be concerned about other things, because he was. "You're asking what is the next step?"

"Yes."

"Good, because the Ruhar have approved the target, it is a Wurgalan world they call 'Stiglord'. I need you to review the plan for fleet insertion, establishing space supremacy, orbital bombardment, the assault landing, and force sustainment. Just the operational aspects above the atmosphere, we're handling everything dirtside."

Kekrando blinked with surprise. "The Ruhar requested my opinion?"

"No," she admitted.

"Will they listen to me?"

"No, but they might listen to *me*. Or General Ross. All I need to know is whether the hamster plan is solid, or a fairy tale. Remember, it has been a long time since the Ruhar conducted an opposed spaceborne landing. Your people have a lot more experience with that type of operation, and your experience is more recent." She knew their experience was recent, because the Kristang civil war had clans hitting each other's planets for raids or invasions. The invasions were particularly bloody, with typically less than half of the invasion force surviving to reach the ground. Reminding herself of that happy fact, she added "We need to conduct a *successful* landing."

Kekrando's lips curled back to expose his fangs. It was not a threatening gesture, it meant he was considering the matter. "I will need details."

"They are in the briefing packet. For your eyes only," she warned.

"Of course. What might *not* be in the briefing is the acceptable level of losses for the landing force."

She knew he would ask that question, and she had an answer, and she knew it was a reasonable question. She didn't like the answer. "Seven percent."

"Seven percent losses in the operation?"

"No." The expected losses in the overall combat operation were higher. "Seven percent losses during the landing, before boots hit the ground."

"I see. The critical question is, what losses are acceptable in landing the first wave?"

She shifted in the chair, though the gesture caused her to float off the seat. Hooking her feet around the railing, she pulled herself back down. "Eighteen percent."

"Eighteen?" The way he said it, he had expected a higher number. Then he nodded, accepting that humans were aliens and had a different definition of 'acceptable losses'. "The majority of personnel in the first wave will be Achakai? What percentage will be humans and the trait-" He caught himself. "The Verds?"

"Sixty-five percent of the first wave will be Achakai. All this data is in the briefing file. They wanted to comprise the *entire* first wave, but we persuaded them that we need a balanced force to hit the ground."

Kekrando smiled. "That is a diplomatic way of saying you don't trust them to know what they are doing."

"We are hedging our bets. The Achakai have very limited experience fighting independently, except in small units."

"Do not teach them *too* well, please," the admiral smiled with his mouth, but not his eyes. "I will review the assault plan. My concern is about what is *not* outlined in the plan."

"Such as?"

"The Ruhar approved this operation because it benefits *them*. I believe our furry friends would not be heartbroken if the Achakai were to suffer serious losses in taking this world from the Wurgalan."

"I can't argue with that," Perkins agreed. "That is another reason that General Ross insisted on a mixed force landing in the first wave. It would be too easy for the Ruhar to write off an all-Achakai landing force, if they got into trouble. Admiral," she pushed away from the chair and clicked her boots in place on the deck. "You have the briefing materials, please review them as soon as possible. My ship will be departing in nineteen hours, I need to know if there are any show-stoppers?"

"Show stoppers?"

Cringing, she chided herself for using slang when talking with an alien. Sometimes the translator got it right, sometimes it didn't. "Anything that could jeopardize the operation."

Kekrando looked at the console next to his desk, and pulled up the file. He glanced at it only briefly, looking at Perkins with a shrug.

"Is there a problem?" She asked.

"The landing is not the only issue. Colonel, once we have control of the surface, the Legion and Ruhar will be pulling out. I need to make sure that my fleet is able to *hold* the place, because the Wurgalan will want to take it back."

"That will not be a problem," she dismissed the admiral's concern with a wave of a hand.

"It *is* a problem, and the Wurgalan are not the only threat. If the clans get together to act against the Achakai-"

"Except they won't."

"They," he stared at her. "Won't?"

"No, the clans will not join together to stamp out the Achakai."

"How do you know-"

"Because the rivalries between clans are more powerful than any sense of solidarity across your society. After the Achakai establish that they are independent, the major clans will scramble to create an alliance. The first clan that allies with the Achakai will add enormously to their combat power, and have a significant advantage in the war."

Kekrando was silent, looking away in contemplation. When he looked back at her, there was a hint of, perhaps, pity in his eyes. "Colonel Perkins, your understanding of our internal politics might not be-"

"It's not *my* understanding. That is the judgment of the leaders of the Achakai Houses. They have already been approached by the Fire Dragons, and your own Swift Arrow clan. Each clan sought an arrangement for exclusive access to Achakai services."

"Then why-"

"Why bother going through the risk of seizing a planet? Because the offers fell short of the only thing the Achakai truly care about: restoring their honor. The Houses want to negotiate as *equals*, that requires them to attain clan status first. Admiral, the Achakai are not risking everything on the hope that they can seize a planet and trust your fleet to protect them. They have a *plan*: meet the formal conditions for achieving clan status first, then negotiate with the major clans to be recognized. The first major clan to offer recognition will add the combat power of the Achakai to their coalition. Will the clans be surprised by this operation? Of course. The first reaction of the clan leaders will be shock. Then they will be disgusted and outraged," she glanced out the doorway to check if any ninjas were in earshot. "By the idea of those without honor seeking to be recognized as equals. I expect the shock, disgust and outrage to last at most two or three *seconds*, before the clan leaders accept reality and begin scheming how to take advantage of the situation. What the clan leaders care most about is their own survival."

"That is, true," he mused. "Colonel, I can't dispute anything you have said. The plan for this operation is more comprehensive than I expected. When did you plan to tell *me* about the politics involved?"

She held out her hands and lifted her shoulders in a gesture she knew he would understand as a shrug. "That's why I'm here now. We are proceeding in phases. The invasion can't begin staging until you are satisfied that your fleet is an effective force."

He looked at her sharply. "Is that *my* judgment, or do the Ruhar plan to conduct a wargame you haven't told me about?"

"Yours," she assured him. "The hamsters don't care whether this fleet can fight, only that it looks good enough to meet the requirements."

"Then," he sighed. "This is all merely play-acting, for-"

"No. *I* care."

"You do? Why?"

"Because my ass will be on the ground, and your ships will provide close-space support to the landing force. I don't give a shit whether your ships look pretty, I care that they can shoot the enemy, and not hit our own people."

The admiral smiled, exposing his fangs again. "These ships will shoot, and their crews will not hesitate to perform their duty. Fire support, however, is the responsibility of your General Bezanson," he added with another frown.

She knew Kekrando was not pleased to have a human commanding one of his ships. Bezanson would follow orders from the Kristang admiral, but only to an undefined limit. "I know," Perkins stood up. "I'm going to see her next. Admiral, I have your word that your ships will be ready within seventeen days?"

"You have my word on that," he looked down at his desk, uncomfortable. "Colonel Perkins, I am experiencing, you might say, divided loyalties."

"Like what?"

He hesitated, as she was not as surprised as he expected her to be. "I am held in disgrace by my clan, but the Swift Arrows *are* my clan. If the Achakai were to ally themselves with a hostile clan like the Fire Dragons, I could not continue to serve in this capacity. My people sentenced me to death, because that would be convenient for a particular group of clan leaders. Still, I could not bring myself to act against my own family. Do you understand?"

"I do understand your concern, but you are not considering the endgame. In negotiations with the Achakai, the Swift Arrows have a major advantage."

He stared at her. He found himself doing that too often. "What advantage?"

"A senior member of the Swift Arrow clan currently commands the Achakai fleet."

After once again blowing the mind of Jet-au-bes Kekrando, Emily Perkins boarded the dropship and flew over to the ship commanded by General Bezanson. It was an old Kristang destroyer captured by the Ruhar and provided to the Achakai. On the way in, she checked the ship's status and was puzzled to see the vessel's name had been changed to *Battle of Azjakanda*. Hmm, she thought, I'll have to ask about that.

Bezanson greeted her at the airlock to the docking bay, after a delay caused by the inner door needing to be manually cranked open. Perkins came to attention and snapped a salute. "Permission to come aboard, Ma'am?"

Bezanson cocked her head with a wry smile. "You're asking me for permission to board a ship that *you* stole?"

"Technically, *I* didn't steal anything," Perkins replied with a straight face.

"Right. Make yourself at home, Perkins. Do you want a tour?"

"No thank you, Ma'am. I've seen Kristang ships before. How are things coming along?"

"You read my progress report?"

"About the ship, yes," she replied, her eyes darting to the pair of Achakai flanking the human commander.

"Ah. Come along to my office," Bezanson beckoned, lifting a boot off the deck to turn. "Watch your step, we have access panels open all over the ship, and there are cables everywhere."

On the way forward, they passed by three teams of Ruhar technicians who were replacing worn-out components, under the watchful eyes of Achakai. Perkins noted that the Ruhar had sidearms, while the Achakai only wore toolbelts. The scene was less ominous than it first appeared; the Ruhar were explaining the process and the Achakai, instead of being hostile and aggressive, were listening intently, taking notes and asking questions.

In Bezanson's office, which was more cramped than usual because of crates of supplies and spare parts strapped to one wall, they sat down in chairs that automatically hugged them in place. Pressing a button to close the door, Bezanson tugged a strap loosely across her waist, so she didn't drift off the chair in the lack of gravity.

Perkins opened the conversation. "The commissioning plaque in the docking bay lists this ship with one of those long-ass poetry names the lizards like, but I see you changed the registry. What's up with that?"

"Oh, that," the general grimaced. "The ninjas are renaming all their ships after battles where their people acted with honor, and the clan that hired them did *not*. It's a way of flipping a middle finger to the warrior caste."

"Ok, what was the Battle of Azjakanda? Or it that something I don't want to know?"

Bezanson laughed with a twinkle in her eyes. "The Achakai gave this ship that name for *us*, and to tweak the noses of the Ruhar."

"Excuse me?"

"'Azjakanda' is their name for the site we called Fort Arrow, the cargo launcher base on the equator of Paradise. Where that sergeant, um-" She looked up, trying to remember.

"Bishop," Perkins knew the name well.

"That's him," she snapped her fingers. "Where his team shot down a couple of Ruhar transports, and held the base until the lizards got things sorted out in orbit to take the planet back."

Perkins snorted. "Until the Ruhar came back in force shortly after that, and took the place permanently."

"Nothing in this war is *permanent*," Bezanson observed. "The hamsters tried to *sell* Paradise out from under our feet, not too long ago. If they hadn't found Elder artifacts buried in the dirt there, the Alien Legion might be fighting on the other side of this war."

"Shit, I don't want to think about that. Speaking of fighting, will your force be ready?"

"Checking up on me, Colonel?"

Perkins blushed. "General Ross is. I'm just the messenger."

"We both know *that's* not true. I can only speak about the close-space support squadron, and the answer is yes. We'll be ready to go in eight days. Make it ten, in case we run into any last-minute glitches. This ship," she rapped her knuckles on the bulkhead, "will be fully capable of pounding targets on the ground. Do we have a target?" She asked eagerly. "Is that why you're here?"

Perkins grinned, and flicked a finger across her tablet to transfer a file. "We have a target, a planet called Stiglord. We're already calling it 'Squidworld'."

"Of course we are. A world full of squids," she made a sour face. "All right, I hate the place already, bombarding it from orbit will be a pleasure. What do we know about this Squidworld?"

The *Sure Thing* arrived at the initial rendezvous point, seven lighthours from the planet Stiglord. The ship's AI transmitted its identification codes to the watchful Ruhar warships, and was allowed to approach the cluster of assault carriers that were awaiting clearance to drop troops onto the surface of the target world. Those carriers would wait until the 7th Fleet's orbital bombardment force of battleships and cruisers had knocked back enemy defenses, a bombardment that was already underway.

For the landing, the Mavericks were splitting up, with Dave, Shauna, Jates and Nert on one carrier, the others on a different ship. They would all be going to the surface in the first wave. All, except for Nert. While the cadet had received special permission to observe the landing, he would be staying in the relative safety of the assault carrier in orbit. He had been told that maybe, just *maybe*, if he didn't cause trouble, he might be allowed down to the surface after the planet was declared pacified.

Their supplies were aboard two dropships and would be transferred to the assault carriers, but the *Sure Thing's* job was not done. That mercenary ship was going to remain within two lightseconds of the planet, ready to respond to a call from Perkins. What exactly the crew of the ship was supposed to *do* if called had not been explained, which caused much discontented grumbling. The worst part of the entire operation was that, because the crew of the *Sure Thing* was participating in the invasion, they were not allowed to place wagers on the outcome, which was *totally* unfair.

Even worse were the fees they had to pay to bookies to place their secret wagers.

Captain Gumbano and crew jumped their ship to the designated position, and settled down to see whether the latest crazy idea from the humans would succeed or fail.

The smart money was on 'fail'.


"Hey, Ski," Jesse reached over to snag a piece of cornbread from his friend's plate. "What's got you so worried?"

Dave mumbled a reply through a mouthful of chili, or something that was supposed to taste like chili. The food aboard the assault carrier was provided by the Ruhar crew, and they apparently had used Cajun spices as the basis for what the galley served as 'chili'. It sure didn't taste like any chili on Earth. "Who said I'm worried?"

"You're picking at your food," Jesse used a fork to gesture at the half-full bowl of fake chili on Dave's tray. "You lose your appetite when you're worried about something."

"Ah," Dave gave up, letting the spoon plop down into the bowl of not-chili. "How about this? We've got Ruhar and Achakai warships providing air cover on this op. Those two have never worked together, they could start shooting at each other, instead of watching out for us. The Ruhar haven't conducted an opposed spaceborne landing since before we were born. Their last one was a slaughter, which is why they haven't done it again. On the ground, we have us poor humans, plus a bunch of Verd-kris with chips on their shoulders looking to prove something, Oh, and best of all, we're dropping to the surface with a bunch of *assassins* who could stab us in the back at the first chance they get."

"Ok," Jesse grinned, breaking off part of his cornbread and giving it to Shauna. Across the table, Nert was eating something that looked and smelled like deep-fried tacos filled with strawberry jam. Whatever it was, the Ruhar cadet was shoveling them into his mouth as fast as he could. "But what has really got you worried?"

"Shit, man, how much time you got?" Dave took a sip of the bug juice the Ruhar thought humans liked. It tasted like grape juice mixed with nutmeg. "You want to know what *really* has got me losing sleep?"

"Sure," Jesse's expression turned serious, knowing he should support his friend. "Especially if it's something *I'm* not already worried about."

Dave lowered his voice and looked around. "The Torgalau."

"The Torgalau?" Shauna asked. "What have they got to do with-"

"We, I mean the Ruhar, are getting all their intel about Squidworld from the Torgalau. Them and the ham-" he shot a guilty glance at Nert, who was stuffing another taco in his mouth. "The Ruhar, are supposed to be allies, but maybe the Torgs would like to see us fall on our faces here?"

"Aw, come on," Jesse reached beside him and squeezed Shauna's hand. "You're being paranoid."

"Am I? What do we know about the Torgs?"

"There's a whole section about them in the mission brief," Shauna reminded Dave.

"Yes, that's facts and figures. What do we *know* about them?"

"Nert?" Shauna asked. "What are the Torgalau like? Have you met them?'

"Yes- Mm, 'scuse me," he crunched the taco, setting it down and wiping his mouth with a napkin. "I don't like them," he shook his head.

Jesse shared a wide-eyed look with Dave. "Why not?"

"They are," Nert looked around to assure himself that none of the Ruhar crew were listening. "Religious fanatics. They are no fun *at all*, not even their cadets!"

"No fun like, how?" Dave prompted the cadet to continue.

Nert frowned. "They are stiff, and humorless, and they lecture everyone when they think you are doing something they disapprove of, which is almost *everything*! They are a bunch of *dicks*."

Shauna's shoulder shook. "So, Nerty," she snorted, covering her mouth with a hand. "The Torgs are stiff dicks?"

"*Yes!*" Nert agreed with a scowl.

Shauna tried to compose herself, but Jesse started laughing, then Dave slapped the table with tears in his eyes, and Shauna lost it.

Nert looked at his three friends. "What? What is so funny?"

# CHAPTER NINE

The invasion of Stiglord began, not with stealthy sensor probes sneaking up close to the planet and collecting data, but with the Ruhar 7th Fleet jumping in just under a lightsecond from the planet and immediately launching railgun rounds at pre-determined targets. The initial volley from the big railguns of the battleships were aimed at targets that could not move, or could not move quickly. Two space stations were targeted, along with three starships that were docked for servicing. The two small moons of the world were also hit, as they contained weapons that could threaten even the well-protected battleships. It did not matter that the cannons and missile batteries of the moons were buried under the rocky surfaces and concealed by camouflage and stealth fields. The 7th Fleet did not need to scan for those threats, their ships knew exactly where the enemy weapons were located.

When planning the invasion, Admiral Kune had to balance collecting data against the potential advantage of surprise. Ordinarily, that would not be a difficult decision at all, sane commanders would not take their ships into a situation without having very good quality information about the enemy's disposition and capabilities. For an assault on a world equipped with a strategic defense network, the fleet ordinarily would jump in far outside the star system, and launch sensor probes. Some of the probes would fly past the planet at high speed, transmitting back their data via laser bursts. Other probes would follow at a more leisurely speed, slowing down as they approached the planet to swing into distant orbits. Those probes also would periodically transmit their data in bursts, and the fleet would assess the information to either make changes to the plan, or even abort the invasion if conditions were deemed unfavorable.

Unfortunately, one way that favorable conditions could quickly become *un*favorable was if the enemy were alerted to hostile ships lurking in the outskirts of the star system. It was impossible to conceal the gamma ray bursts of ships jumping in to perform reconnaissance. Probes could be wrapped in stealth fields, but only for a limited time, because the fields that bent light around an object required substantial power. Equipping a probe with greater-capacity powercells made the probe larger, which in turn required a larger stealth field, which drew more power and on and on in a relentless spiral. In practice, recon probes only used stealth fields for several hours, then they had to shut down and rely on their sensor-absorbing coatings to prevent detection. Even before a probe drew near the planet, its high-speed passage through the star system left a trail of ionized particles in the solar wind, for even hard vacuum is not completely empty. Planets important enough to have a strategic defense network, also had extensive sensor networks that could detect disruptions in the solar wind caused by unknown objects traveling at high speed. Such planets also had multiple layers of active sensor fields extending out several lightseconds from the surface, able to detect even probes wrapped in a stealth field.

Once the enemy became suspicious that a hostile force was sniffing around the system, defenses could be placed on high alert, active sensor pulses would scour space around the planet, and any warships in the area would maneuver to avoid providing an easy target to the enemy.

Admiral Kune decided to skip a reconnaissance in favor of total surprise. The Torgalau had provided intelligence about the star system that, while outdated, was exhaustive in its detail. The 7th Fleet knew the capabilities and locations of the enemy weapons that could pose a threat to the battleships, and could take out those weapons before the enemy could respond. The admiral would have preferred the Torgalau data not be almost ten years out of date, but he took the risk because the Ruhar knew from independent sources that Stiglord had been in decline for decades. Originally planned to become a major military base for both training and fleet-servicing, those plans had slowly been scaled back, then abandoned following the last wormhole shift. The Torgalau estimated that the population of Stiglord had declined by forty percent over just the prior three years. A project to enhance and update the strategic defense network had been cancelled shortly after it began, and a partially-completed spacedock drifted in orbit as a useless collection of girders and frames. Kune judged that, if the data provided by the Torgalau was out of date, the data was likely to *overstate* the strength of the opposition.

Obtaining the advantage of surprise was worth the risk.

After static targets in orbit and on the moons were struck, Kune's battleships and battlecruisers turned their attention to the strategic defense network that orbited the world. The SD network consisted of stealthed satellites that contained sensors or plasma cannons, and those satellites represented a real threat even to the heavy ships of the 7th Fleet. Destroyers and light cruisers, parked safely farther away from the planet, sent out active sensor pulses to reveal the location of the SD network, and warships began to blast targets once they had firing solutions. The Wurgalan on the ground, knowing the SD network was in a use-it-or-lose-it scenario, authorized the network to respond autonomously, and the battle became a simple math equation. Knowing that battlecruisers had the firepower of a battleship, but not the same level of protection, the AIs controlling the SD network concentrated several satellites on each battlecruiser, and plasma cannons lashed out in unison.

The battlecruisers *Amadur*, *Kostigan* and *Illuniasus* were first to feel the wrath of the enemy's retaliation. Each ship was struck by up to five satellites, and each ship shuddered from the impacts, energy shields flaring and failing, armor plating charred and burned away. The response of each ship was not to return fire, but to perform an emergency jump away to safety. The SD network AIs were disappointed that they had not destroyed their prey, and they shifted their focus to the other pair of battlecruisers-

Which also jumped away, just as fifteen more plasma cannon satellites unmasked from stealth to fire bolts of hellish energy. Those bolts passed harmlessly out into space, growing cold and thin as they faded into nothingness.

Aboard his flagship, Kune watched the tactical display with satisfaction. "Is *that* enough data for you?" He asked quietly, without looking at his intelligence officer.

"Er, yes, Sir," the officer replied, the pink skin under his fur growing darker.

"Very well," Kune almost looked bored, a carefully managed impression. "All ships, fire at will."

Dangling the battlecruisers in front of the SD network was a deliberate ploy to get the network to shoot, and reveal a pattern to the placement of the plasma cannon satellites. Based on the angles of bolts fired at the battlecruisers, the powerful AIs of the 7th Fleet had gathered enough information to predict with better than eighty percent confidence, the density of the network and location of the other orbiting cannons.

Battleships began to systematically reduce the enemy SD network to scrap, and of course the enemy hit back. The battleships had one major advantage: they were *ships* and therefore could move. At such short range, ducking out of the way of an incoming plasma bolt was not possible, so the ships relied on their ability to twist spacetime and jump. Whenever a ship's shields were drained below a pre-set limit, that ship jumped away, to be replaced by a ship awaiting its turn in the battle. The operation demonstrated the skill, discipline and power of the 7th Fleet, and after a short time of watching things blow up, Kune became bored. Achieving space-superiority around Stiglord was only a matter of time, and he wanted to get on with the next phase of the operation: orbital bombardment of the planet's surface.

Part of the information provided by the Torgalau was the location of plasma cannon clusters on the surface. Technically, they were *under* the surface, and many of them also had stealth fields projecting false images to prevent detection. Each cluster consisted of three cannons plus a central control bunker. Even before the SD network was fully reduced to scrap, Kune turned his attention to targets on the surface, with the plasma cannon clusters at the top of his priority list. The list included airbases, anti-aircraft missile batteries, power stations and a host of other items that could threaten a landing force, but only the plasma cannons could seriously hurt a battleship. Accordingly, while his big ships were still far from the planet, four cannon clusters were targeted by railguns, and seconds later, fountains of dirt and melted rock rose into the air on boiling mushroom clouds. If the enemy was shocked that their secret cannons had been hit, they said nothing.

They didn't have to.

Kune contacted the Wurgalan authorities with an offer of practical mercy. Mercy because unnecessary deaths could be avoided. Practical because his mercy had a purpose: to impress upon the Wurgalan that the 7th Fleet could do anything it wanted, while all they could do was drag out the situation and ensure needless deaths on both sides.

He did not really expect the Wurgalan authorities to take the entirely reasonable step of meek surrender, but he figured it was worth a shot.

His message included the coordinates of three intact three plasma cannon clusters, with a simple offer: his ships would hold fire for a short time, so the crews in those control bunkers could escape. After the deadline passed, the 7th Fleet would open fire. As there was nothing useful the cannons could do, and as his ships were not actually in position to strike the targets immediately, the offer of mercy cost him nothing, and the enemy gained nothing by refusing.

Of course, the response by the Wurgalan was for the nine cannons of the three clusters to combine into a shot at one of his battleships. With the battleship more than a lightsecond above the surface, its shields deflected the focused bolts with only three shield generators being taken offline. The big ship rolled to protect its vulnerable side and maintained station, signaling to Kune that it was still combat-effective. It signaled its effectiveness to the enemy by firing a railgun salvo at another cannon cluster, reducing it to three smoking holes in the ground.

"Let's try this again, shall we?" Kune told his communications crew, and the offer of mercy was repeated, this time giving the coordinates of three different cannon clusters, and broadcasting the message on all frequencies. If the Wurgalan authorities neglected to notify the crews in the bunkers about the first offer, those crews heard the second offer directly.

The second offer achieved mixed results. Two cannon clusters opened fire on the ships high above, in a futile and uncoordinated gesture of defiance. Kune's ships immediately struck those sites, turning the control bunkers into ash.

The third cannon cluster held fire, and Kune watched with interest as six Wurgalan came out of a concealed entrance to the bunker, and ran as fast as their short tentacle legs could carry them. Scampering across fields, they took shelter in a forested area and were lost to sight.

"Well," Kune could not decide whether he was gratified or surprised by the enemy's sensible action. Surprise. It was definitely surprise. "I did not actually expect them to-"

The three plasma cannons of that cluster fired, targeting Kune's own ship. Alarms blared and the deck shook under his feet.

"Sorry, Sir," the fleet operations officer cringed as he spoke. "I wanted to give them time to get clear, they must have set the cannons to fire on automatic before they abandoned the bunker. Lesson learned, I will not make that mistake ag-"

"Do we know where they are now?" Kune asked. "That crew, I mean."

"Not with any precision." The ops officer shook his head. "No. Not from here, our sensors can't track such a small group. They are in this forest here, somewhere," he waved a hand over a tree-covered area that extended for several square kilometers.

"Take it out."

"Sir? The, forest? The, the whole thing?"

"Bardon," Kune addressed the officer by name. "If you are concerned about fleet headquarters complaining that you are wasting ordnance, I will sign for it."

Bardon stiffened. "That will not be necessary."

Kune lowered his voice, aware that some of the bridge crew were watching the discussion. "I want to send a message, Bardon. A very loud, clear and unmistakable message: do not fuck with the 7th Fleet."

"Yes, *Sir!*"

The forest was struck first by speed-of-light maser beams from the flagship, quickly followed by railgun rounds that dawdled their way down through the atmosphere at only a fraction of lightspeed. Then came missiles boring a hole through the air at hypersonic velocity, burrowing deep into the ground before their warheads exploded.

The flagship fired three salvos, the second and third of which merely caused the rubble to bounce in a different pattern. When the ship was done, the forest no longer existed, nor was there any trace that it had ever been there.

"I think we got them," Bardon announced with satisfaction.

One side of Kune's mouth curled up in a short-live smile. "Well, we *tried* to be reasonable. Signal all ships: commence full-scale bombardment."

Bardon nodded gravely, as he watched flashes of light appear across the continent below, followed by the foaming tops of mushroom clouds covering the area. "Admiral, you will henceforth be known as Kune the Merciful."

Kune snorted and tilted his head. "Mercy is not usually administered by the megaton."

Bardon shrugged. "There is a first time for everything."

Nine hours after the 7th Fleet arrived in orbit of Stiglord, only slightly more than an hour behind schedule, a frigate jumped away. The little ship performed three jumps though only two were necessary, the additional passage through twisted spacetime was to prevent the enemy from knowing the ship's destination. Assembled at the end point were the transport ships where most of the landing force waited, the support ships that serviced the 7th Fleet and contained the invasion force's supplies and equipment, and the all-important assault carriers. Packed into the carriers were the human, Verd-kris and Achakai soldiers who had the dubious honor of being in the first wave.

The frigate transmitted a burst signal from Admiral Kune to the assault carriers: Commence the assault landing.

Aboard the assault carrier *Tig Mecdunnue*, the most important thing Jesse did before the assault drop was to visit the head near his assigned bunk. That was the last thing he did before sealing up the torso of his skinsuit, because it was one less thing he had to worry about. The sophisticated alien mech suit had the ability to handle bodily functions, it had to when the user was in a toxic atmosphere, or no atmosphere at all. Still, a Tactical Pee before boarding the dropship was a good idea, and he reminded his squad to do the same.

With that tradition taken care of, he made sure his squad was ready, that all their assigned gear was present, in proper working order and secured in its proper place. He anticipated no problems during preparations for the assault drop. The first time they practiced boarding their assigned dropship, there had of course been glitches. Soldiers could not find some of their gear, powercells were not fully charged, a couple rifles could not connect to the squad network and had to be repaired or swapped for new weapons. Any replacement gear had to be checked out, rifles had to be linked to the user's suit computer and sighted in at the ship's range. None of the problems were unusual, Jesse would have worried if nothing had gone wrong, because in his experience that meant Karma was holding a nasty surprise for him later.

The last four times they ran the exercise, it was nearly perfect, as well as Jesse could have hoped. The final two practice runs involved the entire ship's complement assembling in their assigned areas of the ship and proceeding to the docking bays, with a Ruhar crewman leading the way so stupid humans didn't get lost and fall into a reactor. That worked only as well as it could, given the complexity of the operation. Units got jammed up in narrow passageways and intermingled at intersections. The chaos could have been lessened if the Legion soldiers had been allowed to rely on guidance from their suit computers, but part of the exercise simulated a partial communications breakdown. To make the day even more fun for exasperated squad and platoon leaders, a few random dropships were designated to have equipment failures, requiring units to switch to their alternate assignments. In the end, it all got sorted out with more than an hour to spare, and Jesse was well pleased with the results. Even Surgun Jates was not as grumpy as usual after the final dry run for the assault drop.

That morning's boarding operation was no mere exercise, it was for real. The ship that humans called the *Big Mac* was going to war, any glitches could have fatal consequences. Jesse worked with the leaders of the two fireteams in his squad, checking absolutely everything as they waited for the signal to leave their assembly area. Unlike on Fresno, the entire Alien Legion force was properly equipped for high-intensity combat, no one was under the illusion that the landing on Stiglord would be a simple peacekeeping operation. Each soldier had a Ruhar skinsuit that, while old and certainly not state of the art, was well-maintained, updated with the latest version of software, and perfectly serviceable. In addition to all the other crap on their belts and stuffed into their packs, each soldier also carried a rifle, three spare powercells, 260 rounds of rifle ammunition, and either four rockets or six grenades. Sergeants and officers were authorized to also carry a sidearm, but Jesse had chosen to replace that weight with another magazine of fifty-two explosive-tipped rounds and a rocket. If he got into trouble, he would rely on his durable Kristang rifle, rather than a pistol of dubious value.

His squad consisted of two fireteams, each with three soldiers led by a sergeant. One of the fireteams was tasked with an anti-aircraft mission, equipped with two Zinger missile launchers and six missiles. The squad's mission was to provide security for Perkins' headquarters unit, not to engage in offensive combat operations. Both Jesse and Jates thought that avoiding combat was a fine notion, *if* the enemy read that memo. If not, shit was gonna get real.

The series of lights on the overhead of the passageway flashed to green at the same moment a chime sounded, and Jesse had his squad moving even before he heard the official announcement to commence the boarding phase of the operation. There were no screw-ups, and not much talk either. Soldiers kept their thoughts mostly to themselves as they marched toward the dropships that would carry them down to the surface, where their part in the fighting would begin. Filing up the back ramp of dropships that humans called 'Dodos', the entire first wave was aboard with their gear stowed, ninety-six minutes before the assault carrier was scheduled to jump into orbit. No one got lost, no one puked from nervous tension, there were no glitches in equipment. Ten minutes after the squad was squared away, Perkins arrived with her headquarters team. She nodded to Jesse and he returned the gesture.

Then they waited. And waited. Jesse released people one at a time to use the Dodo's bathroom, until it was twenty-four minutes to the scheduled jump. With eighteen minutes remaining, the external launch bay doors slid open and dropships began firing up their engines. Jesse saw an orange light on the bulkhead display. Some minor system was experiencing a glitch. Derek Bonsu strode out of the cockpit, pulled open an access door in the cabin's floor, and did something. The light changed from orange to green.

"Is that a problem, Sir?" Jesse asked, his voice betraying more nerves than he wanted his team to hear. Flying was not his favorite thing to do, he preferred his boots to be solidly on the ground.

"Nah," Derek shook his head. "Sensor showed our starboard landing gear isn't locked, and I know it *is*, so I disconnected the sensor. We'll be fine, Sergeant."


Aboard a dropship in a launch bay of the assault carrier *Dal Turnaden*, Captain Danielle Grace waited until the last moment to swing down the faceplate of her combat suit. Most of the Verd-kris soldiers around her had boarded the dropship with their helmets already sealed up, but not all of them. The platoon leader and two of the surguns had their faceplates up, with only the bottom of the inner visor obscuring their eyes.

Her delay in sealing the faceplate was not a show of confidence in the Ruhar who were flying both the *Dal Turnaden* and the dropship, it was to avoid the Verd-kris around her thinking that she was disgusted by the way they smelled. The Kristang, including their Verd cousins, did have a scent like lizard skin warmed by the sun. The scent was not strong, it was not unpleasant, but it was different and distinctive. She had been told that humans were considered somewhat smelly by the Verds, which is why she used special scent-masking soap and shampoo provided by UNEF.

Crammed into the Dodo dropship with her were forty Verd-kris soldiers, a full platoon. The Verds organized their infantry units differently than standard UNEF practice. The lowest-level unit was a squad, eight soldiers led by a surgun third class. Four squads in an infantry platoon, plus a headquarters unit led by a surgun second class and a getrun, the rough equivalent to a lieutenant. With forty Verds in full combat armor plus Dani, the dropship's cabin was full, only one seat remained empty. Strapped to that one unoccupied seat were a crate of rifle ammunition and a crate of rockets, the platoon's soldiers having understood that no one ever regretted having too much ammo.

The platoon leader checked in with each squad verbally over the command net, though he had access to status data from every armored suit in the platoon. When it came time for him to check on Dani, he leaned forward in his seat at the rear of the cabin, and flashed a thumbs up at her. "Squared away, Captain Grace?"

She appreciated that he had either learned the American expression, or taken the time to program his suit's translator to use appropriate American military slang.

"Squared away, Getrun Zolatus," she replied, giving him a thumbs up in return. She could have said 'lieutenant' and trusted the translator to convert that word to the equivalent rank in the Verd-kris military structure, but saying 'Getrun' was just as easy. Plus, the platoon leader would know what she said, because the translator always slightly altered the speaker's voice.

"This is your first combat drop?" Zolatus asked.

"Uh," she had to think a moment. The platoon leader was being unusually chatty. "I guess the landing on Fresno doesn't count. We weren't under fire then."

"I missed the operation on Feznako," Zolatus said with regret. "This will be my first landing on a hostile world. Do you have any advice for me?"

Before answering, she checked her visor to assure they were speaking on a private channel. The reason the platoon leader was so chatty was simple, she realized. He was nervous. Dani had been assigned to that particular platoon because it was a reserve unit, not intended to engage in combat on the first day unless frontline units needed reinforcement. The Verds wanted to keep her safe if they could. "The *callaras*," she used the Verd slang term for Ruhar, "are doing all the flying, we are just passengers. There isn't much we can do until we get boots on the ground. My advice is, try not to puke in your helmet."

"Ha! Thank you, Captain."

# CHAPTER TEN

With fifteen minutes remaining, Jesse ordered his squad to don their helmets, seal the faceplates, and breathe filtered cabin air. Everyone's suits were operating nominally, according to the indicators in his visor. Heartrates were elevated, including his own. That was nothing to worry about. He had plenty of real issues to worry about, like the fact that his squad had never done a combat drop before. The pilots had run through the entire operation in both simulators and real spacecraft, and all his soldiers had to do was sit tight, hang on and shut up until the Dodo's skids hit the ground. Hopefully the skids did not *hit* the ground.

With that happy thought, he watched the countdown in the upper right of his visor. The assault carrier performed a jump to take the ship within twenty-eight lightseconds of the planet, getting close so the final jump into orbit would be so short that accuracy could be assured.

"That was a solid jump," Irene Striebich announced from the cockpit. "We are waiting for the 'Go' signal from the command ship."

Jesse knew the task force commander was waiting until all the assault carriers and support ships had jumped into position and reported their readiness. At that point, based on how many ships were expected to be available for the assault drop, the operation would be approved, delayed or scratched. There was no reason to think they would not soon be racing down through the atmosphere; it had been a routine and relatively short jump and they were still well beyond the effective range of the enemy's SD network. An SD network that was supposed to have been destroyed anyway.

"We are a 'Go'," Irene said, and Jesse saw heartrates spike briefly. Including his own.

When the clock on the display showed seven minutes left, everyone aboard the Dodo went on internal oxygen, and disconnected their suit powercells from the charging plates built into the seatbacks. The display in his visor showed all suits had full supplies of oxygen and power.

Across from him and toward the front of the cabin, Perkins leaned forward to look at him and offered a thumbs up. He gave her an empathic double thumbs up and pushed himself back in the seat, feeling the straps automatically tugging tighter around him.

The voice communications system was for official and essential use only, beginning half an hour before drop, but soldiers had discovered they could use the platoon status channel to send short text messages. Whispering into his helmet microphone, he recorded a message, checked it had translated correctly to text, and sent it. The intended recipient was David Czajka.

*Hey Ski, don't do anything stupid*, read the message.

*Don't worry, 'Pone. I won't do anything you would do*, came the reply.

*You watch out for my girl*, Jesse sent.

*You watch out for MY girl*, Dave sent, then *Best of luck, brother.*

*See you dirtside*. Jesse cut the link. The Ruhar crew were monitoring all electronic traffic, and he knew they would get annoyed if the conversation went on too long. To Shauna, he sent a simple emoji because she was busy with her own squad, and received an emoji back. They had exchanged their goodbyes before assembling with their respective squads, nothing more needed to be said. He was sure Dave was being similarly brief if he messaged Perkins, who was monitoring the ship's tactical channel and likely distracted.

Five minutes to jump.

Aboard another dropship, located in a launch bay eighty meters aft of where Jesse waited, Dave closed out the message window and glanced across the cabin to Shauna. She didn't look at him, her eyes intent on the glowing icons splashed across her visor. He knew she was checking the lifesigns of the soldiers in her squad. To his right, Surgun Jates sat impassively, and Dave could not see into the alien's helmet from where he was sitting.

Relax, Dave told himself, this is just landing on another planet. You've done this before.

No, a little nagging voice in his head replied. You have not done *this* before. The landings on Paradise, Fresno and Jellaxico had been simple, with no opposition expected or encountered. Landing on Camp Alpha had been uneventful, only because the few lizards on that world had not detected the stealthy dropships coming down on the other side of the planet.

An opposed spaceborne landing was new to him. It was a novel event for most of the Ruhar military also, the last time their fleet had supported an opposed landing was thirty-eight Earth years ago. Usually, battles were won or lost in space before boots hit the ground. Over the long course of the war, both sides had slowly come to the realization that there was little to gain in holding onto a blockaded world. A fleet that controlled the skies could bombard the surface with conventional weapons, gradually reducing cities to rubble and degrading infrastructure to the point where forces on the ground were limited to isolated groups equipped only with rifles, afraid to poke their heads out from under the stealth netting that concealed their hiding places.

If an opposed spaceborne landing was an unaccustomed event for the Ruhar, it was completely unknown to the humans, the Verd-kris and the Achakai in the landing force. Certainly, the ninja lizards had plenty of experience with stealthy infiltration, but operating as part of a large, organized force was outside their training. Whether the Achakai could effectively operate in groups of thousands or even hundreds was a very good question. What bothered Dave about the whole scheme was that he was risking his life for someone else's experiment.

As he settled back in his seat and pressed the helmet against the bulkhead, Dave was glad he had visited the Dodo's tiny bathroom with plenty of time to spare. The Dodo's engines throttled up, testing the clamps that held the spacecraft in place, then went back to idle.

Four minutes remaining.

Cadet Nert Dandurf realized he was holding his breath, in his seat at a console in the launch control center, the display was currently overlooking the bay where Dave and Shauna's dropship was resting on its launch rails. Quietly, he let out a breath, feeling silly because no one could hear him inside his sealed-up helmet. He was wearing a shipboard environment suit instead of a combat skinsuit, equipment designed to keep him breathing and useful if the ship lost air pressure, not intended for use in infantry fighting. To his left and right, the actual crew of the ship had their helmets attached to the back of their chairs, with the faceplates open. Regulations stated they must have helmets within reach for the combat drop, and they trusted their helmets to slam the faceplates closed for them if needed. Until then, being able to speak the old-fashioned way was a useful backup in case of communications failure. Nert wished he could have left his faceplate retracted or at least cracked open, his status as a cadet required him to be sealed up before the assault carrier had jumped into orbit. He also was not supposed to touch the console in front of him, though he was trained on the operation of all the consoles in the cramped alcove. He could monitor the displays, standing by in case one of the crew needed to be relieved, and to assist in damage control if needed. What he really wanted was to be on the assault carrier's bridge, where the real action was taking place. As the captain was not allowing any such nonsense, no matter how well-connected Nert's family was, being in the launch bay control center was the best available option.

Across the board, all dropships were showing blue, the status for fully operational. His human friends were as prepared as they could be, with the resources of a full battlegroup to support them.

Closing his eyes, he said a quiet prayer for his friends.

Three minutes.


On the *Tig Mecdunnue's* bridge, the executive officer turned to the captain seated next to him. "All stations report ready for jump," he announced, repeating information the captain had readily available to her, on multiple displays scattered around the compartment. Reporting status was not necessary, bordering on silly, but it was his job right then and, damn it, he was going to do it.

The captain acknowledged the announcement with a slight tilt of her head, not taking her eyes off the display to the side of her command station. "Navigator? Predicted jump accuracy?" That information was also available on a display. She asked the question not because she needed the data, but because she wanted the jump navigation team to know she appreciated their efforts. At the level of technology available to the Ruhar, guiding a starship to arrive at a particular point in space was still partly an art that required experience, skill and not a little bit of guesswork.

"Twenty-three achrons," the navigator reported, speaking for her entire team. The truth was, she expected they would emerge within eighteen achrons of the target coordinates, she added five achrons to pad the estimate. To give each assault carrier plenty of room to maneuver and so their dropships did not interfere with each other, each carrier was assigned a bubble of space two hundred and fifty achrons across. To reduce the distance the dropships needed to travel, the ships wanted to jump in at the edge of the atmosphere, an action that was tricky to accomplish so deep in a planet's gravity well. Too low and the *Mecdunnue* would have to claw its way up through atmospheric drag to jump distance. Too high and the vulnerable dropships would have a longer, possibly fatal distance to reach the surface.

"Twenty-three," Captain Rennul repeated without comment, mentally subtracting a couple achrons. The jump accuracy made little practical difference to the outcome of the operation, but it was a matter of pride between starship crews. Rennul knew that each carrier ship would be watching the others, and offering congratulations or insults after all ships had jumped away to safety.

To her right, the executive officer bent to peer closely at the display in front of his chair. "Decoy frigates are taking fire from the surface," he said with a frown. Right on schedule, eight Ruhar frigates had jumped into orbit above the landing zone, each ship launching a cloud of decoy drones before racing out to jump distance. The decoys were vital to the ability of the dropships to reach the surface. Even stealthed, dropships would be detected once they began their searing flight through the atmosphere, leaving long fiery pink trails of plasma behind them. The decoys would saturate the area with interference across the electromagnetic spectrum, vent superheated plasma and create roiling contrails of disturbed air in their wake. For each dropship carrying soldiers to the surface, there would be at least thirty decoys, forcing the enemy defenses to fire multiple shots at any target. As soon as a missile battery, maser cannon or railgun on the ground opened up, the Ruhar battleships in orbit would retaliate with a punishing barrage.

"Enemy fire is categorized as 'random and light'," Rennul saw at a glance. Just as Fleet Intelligence had predicted. After the sustained bombardment of targets on the surface, she was not surprised that the enemy had little left with which to hit back. She *was* surprised the Wurgalan were wasting their remaining heavy weapons on what they had to know were ships launching decoys. "Stupid of them," she observed mostly to herself. The enemy knew an invasion was coming, they should have reserved their strike capabilities for the big assault carrier ships, not wasting fire on frigates. Maybe the Wurgalan were in such disarray that local commanders were shooting at any target of opportunity. A maser cannon might have a chance to cause damage to a frigate, while even the most stupid of the enemy must know the well-protected battleships were not worth trying to hit. Preparing for the jump that was now only nineteen azels away, she rested her hands in her lap, to prevent herself from accidently touching any of the controls during the maneuver. The ship's executive officer did the same, as they listened to the navigator counting down to the jump. Rennul was excited to be part of the first opposed spaceborne landing during her time in the service, and she was confident in her crew, her ship and the battle fleet that surrounded the planet.

There was only one worry nagging at the back of her mind.

Her concern was not about the humans who would be flying some of the dropships and doing the fighting on the ground. The pilots appeared to be competent enough to be entrusted with the spacecraft they had been given, though she wasn't confident that many of those landing craft would return to their mother ship. Her responsibility for the landing force ended when the last dropship launched and cleared the *Mecdunnue's* proximity-defense perimeter, and she did not know much about ground combat. The idea of the ground action being split between humans, Verd-kris and the Achakai sounded like a recipe for disaster, but that also was not her responsibility.

Her concern was simple. The enemy *was* being unforgivably stupid by wasting their remaining heavy weapons on mere frigates.

Why?

It made no sense.

Unless-

"-two," the navigator read off the numbers, "one, *jump*."

The *Tig Mecdunnue* emerged from twisted spacetime in a brief hellish flare of gamma radiation that raced ahead of the ship at the speed of light, leaving the outer layer of the ship's hull bathed in short-lived exotic particles. Sensors that had been turned off for protection, during transition through the jump wormhole, were energized again and began seeking to determine where the ship was and what was in the immediate area. Space around the ship was clear, other than debris from the space battle that had prepared the way for the assault. Based on sighting stars and the guide beacons projected by the battleships overhead, the *Mecdunnue* was right where the ship should be, within seventeen achrons. It was a good sign that the minor inaccuracy of the jump into orbit had placed the assault carrier slightly closer to the planet, leaving a shorter distance for the vulnerable dropships to fly.

Technically the *Mecdunnue* was not in *orbit*, because it was already in the thin air of the planet's mesosphere, and moving slower than the speed needed to stay in orbit at that altitude. The ship's leading edges glowed with ionization as thin air struck at hypersonic speed, and the crew at the helm anxiously watched their altitude degrade as the atmospheric drag slowed the ship, dragging them down toward the surface. Every member of the *Mecdunnue's* crew wished the dropships would all launch as quickly as possible, so their bulky ship could accelerate and begin the climb out of the planet's gravity well, up to jump altitude.

"We're clear," the executive officer reported after taking an extra second to double-check the incoming sensor data. In addition to data collected by the ship's own resetting sensors, there was a feed from the battleships above.

"Decoy batteries, commence launch," the captain ordered automatically, her attention also on the sensors. If the enemy had any surprises waiting for the task force, this was when they would be revealed.

The ship shuddered as clouds of decoys were ejected from the ship. Some of the decoys turned to race down toward the planet, others formed a bubble around the ship and began blasting the area with broad-spectrum jamming to blind enemy sensors. The larger decoys hit the upper atmosphere and ejected small submunitions, just like a dropship would. To the enemy on the ground, those decoys would look exactly like a dropship.

"First volley of decoys away, batteries are reloading," the second-in-command said. "One portside battery is jammed, engineering team is working on it."

"Very well," Rennul saw the incident on her own display. "Launch dropships."

First away were the gunships, spat out of their bays along launcher rails on the side of the ship facing away from the planet. The energy shields on that side of the ship blinked to a lower intensity setting as the gunships went through, their own shields tuned to avoid interference with the assault carrier's protective blanket of energy. The gunships formed up in groups of four, leading the way at a casual pace as they waited for the troop carriers to join them.

If all the dropships on one side of the ship launched at once, the kinetic energy would push the assault carrier sideways and possibly induce a spin. Instead, the launch proceeded nose to tail, with the forward launchers sending their cargo down the rails first.

In the bridge compartment deep within the ship's stout frames, Captain Rennul's attention was drawn to the main display. A maser cannon on the surface had just fired at the assault carrier *Dal Turnaden*, orbiting on the same track ahead of the *Mecdunnue*.

"*Turnaden* is undamaged," a sensor officer reported. "Battleships are returning fire."

A muted cheer rang around the bridge as the crew saw a flare on the surface. The enemy maser cannon ceased firing.

A railgun round from the surface struck the *Turnaden*, and the ship staggered, temporarily halting its launches. Rennul shared a glance with her exec, neither of them were overly concerned. The *Turnaden* was taking a pounding and that made sense; the enemy would want their limited resources focused on a single target, to maximize the chance of scoring a hit. Bad luck for the *Turnaden* was good luck for the other assault carriers. Of the eight assault carriers in a rough diamond formation, only one was taking fire. Rennul felt certain that happy circumstance would change when the dropships bored their way lower in the atmosphere, where they would be vulnerable to portable anti-aircraft maser cannons and shoulder-launched missiles that the preparatory bombardment had not suppressed. To survive flying down through the expected barrage, the dropships would have to trust their stealth capabilities, energy shields, point-defense cannon and mostly importantly, the clouds of decoys that would divert the enemy's attention. Not all the decoys were mere targets, some of them contained submunitions designed to seek and destroy anti-aircraft weapons. Any Wurgalan on the ground who dared fire a portable missile had to discard the empty launch tube and run as fast as their multiple legs could carry them, for they would become a target as soon as the missile's exhaust plume was detected.

Wherever that enemy railgun was on the surface, that area was under cloud cover, because the retaliatory strike by the battleships was visible only on infrared, as a red plume that slowly spread out. Either the battleships had little else to do, or the task force commander was seriously annoyed at the enemy's failure to acknowledge they were beaten, because the infrared plume was followed by five others, saturating the target area. That railgun did not fire again, nor was the *Turnaden* hit by another maser cannon. Despite several shield generators that were knocked back to seventy percent power, the assault carrier declared it was still combat effective. The crew rolled their ship so the weakened shields faced away from the planet, and resumed launching dropships.

Rennul considered the *Mecdunnue*'s sister ship with admiration. Leaning toward her XO, she whispered just loud enough for the bridge crew to hear. "If that's the best they've got to throw at us-"

"We can handle this," the XO mused hopefully. "First time Fleet Intelligence has been correct about anything. I'll but them a drink if-"

The image of the *Dal Turnaden* was replaced by a flare of orange light as that ship's shields deflected terrawatts of directed energy. When the photons of the blast washed over the *Mecdunnue*, the stunned bridge crew could see the other assault carrier tilted at a right angle to its flight path and tumbling. Pieces broke away as the damaged ship was struck again.

Rennul instinctively tried to rise from her chair, restrained by the straps. "That fire came from *above*," she gasped. The enemy strategic defense network apparently had *not* been completely neutralized. "Someone made a mistake!"

A third searing bolt of X-ray laser energy struck the *Turnaden*, defense shields flickered and blinked out as their generators were overwhelmed. The beam sliced into the hull, blasting armor plating apart like tissue paper and melting structural frames in the heart of the ship. Its spine broken, the assault carrier sagged in the middle, nose and tail bending slowly in opposite directions.

Then the *Turnaden* broke in half, the shattered ends glowing with harsh arcs of lightning as power conduits released their energy into the void.

"Someone made a *big* Goddamn mistake!" Captain Rennul barked. "Helm, break for high orbit, get us to jump distance!"

Thrusters under the *Tig Mecdunnue*'s nose fired to point the ship away from the planet and the shattered remains of the *Dal Turnaden*, while the assault carrier's main engines spun up to full emergency thrust. The big engines were slow to ramp up and the acceleration built up almost imperceptibly. In the dropships that had not yet launched, pilots saw with alarm their mother ship's new course, clawing for jump altitude. Their orders had not changed, the assault carrier was still spitting out dropships one at a time, each launch accompanied by clusters of sensor-jamming decoys. On the tactical data feed, all the pilots had seen what happened to the *Dal Turnaden* and every single one of them was eager to get the hell away from the carrier as fast as possible. Ordinarily, dropships were safer while wrapped inside the carrier's powerful energy shields and protected by the big ship's proximity defense cannons. Also, ordinarily an assault carrier would not be flying low and slow in an area covered by active enemy SD platforms. No way would the Wurgalan waste an SD platform on a single dropship, but an assault carrier was a big fat target and clearly, whatever weapons the enemy still had were capable of slicing through a warship's shields.

Regardless of the understandable anxiety of the pilots, they had to wait while their mother ship rotated around its long axis and it was their turn to launch. Quietly and not so quietly, the pilots of dropships toward the back of the line urged the ships at the front of the line to *move* and *get on with it*. The anger was misdirected for the entire process was automated and there wasn't anything the pilots could do, and that made no difference. Bitching about a problem they couldn't affect was still doing *something*. Whether the human dropship pilots trusted the assault ship's Ruhar crew or not didn't matter, they knew the crew wanted the dropships all away ASAP to lighten the carrier's mass so they could reach jump altitude faster.

Getting to a higher altitude, where the starship's jump drive could rip a hole in spacetime and create a temporary wormhole, was not a matter of going *up*, but of going *forward* and *faster*. All eight of the assault carriers had jumped in carrying momentum that yielded a speed below that required to keep the ships from falling out of orbit at that altitude. That was a risky plan, a maneuver intended to shorten the time their vulnerable dropships were exposed to enemy fire from the ground, and a plan approved only in the absence of a threat from strategic defense satellites. Or what the task force commander *thought* was the absence of an enemy SD network. The *Mecdunnue* needed to increase speed to achieve a stable orbit, then escape velocity, then rocket away past an imaginary line where the planet's gravity well was weak enough to allow the formation of a jump wormhole that would bring the assault carrier somewhere, *anywhere* other than under the deadly guns of the enemy SD network.

The *Mecdunnue*'s engines reached full military thrust, then the engineers authorized releasing safety mechanisms until the mighty engines were vibrating on their magnetic mounts at seven percent more than their rated power. The engineers knew that later, they would need to tear down the engines one at a time for inspection and repairs and that process would be an enormous pain in the *ass*, but all they cared about was that there *would* be a later for them, which would not happen if a strategic defense satellite got the *Mecdunnue* in its sights.

Three point one five lightseconds above the formation of assault carriers, that now consisted of seven intact starships and one broken hull, a stealthed strategic defense satellite clutched a spinning gyroscope inside its shell, an action that caused the barrel of its cannon to pivot toward a new target. The doomed ship below it was accelerating but had not yet reached a velocity where its orbit was stable, and it was so low that its belly scraped the wispy top of the planet's atmosphere. Without any anger or fear, the satellite accepted its tasking from the stealthy network control satellite, joining two other satellites in targeting that single ship. One satellite could cause damage to the well-protected enemy ship.

Two satellites had a better-than-even chance of disabling the target.

Three satellites guaranteed a hard kill.

At the satellite's heart was not any advanced technology such as an atomic compression device, because such tech was far beyond the capabilities of the Wurgalan. The machine that would power the satellite's laser cannon was merely a crude boosted fission bomb. The nuclear weapon did not need to be light weight, it did not need to be small, it only needed to generate energy to power an X-ray laser that would be vaporized during its one-time use.

If the satellite's tiny brain had been capable of thought, it might have desired to die while taking out one of the enemy battleships that had devastated most of the planet's defenses. Those battleships had pounded targets on the surface and cleared the skies, but had failed to search more than two lightseconds from the planet. Knocking a battleship out of action would be a comfort in the satellite's suicidal explosion, but even the limited computer understood that while battleships could rule the skies, they could not take and hold the planet. The troops brought by the assault carriers posed the true threat and while a carrier was a lesser target, the satellite understood the logic of the network controller.

Although, the network controller AI was widely acknowledged to be an insufferably arrogant asshole. If all the SD satellites fervently hoped their own deaths would result in the enemy battleships hunting down and destroying the network control AI, that too was understandable.

At a signal from the network controller, the strategic defense satellite sent an electric pulse along a channel, branching off to a series of conduits connected to conventional explosive plates wrapped around the plutonium core of the weapon. Compressed by the explosives, the atoms of plutonium were crushed together into such a small space, they achieved critical mass and detonated outward, generating powerful X-rays that were collected by the lasing effect of the cannon barrel, during the nanoseconds before it was consumed. Now a focused beam of coherent photons, the X-rays stabbed out toward their target.

When the X-rays struck the shields along the topside of the *Tig Mecdunnue*, the intense photons were deflected outward, spread out along the outline of the shields around the top and both sides of the ship, or partially absorbed by the generators. Circuits in those generators overloaded and tripped off, protecting the generators but weakening the ship's defenses.

Irene's palms had become sweaty in her flightsuit gloves, damp enough that the gloves could not wick away the moisture, damp enough that she felt a hot trickle of water run down her wrist when she reached up one hand to touch a button on the ceiling of the cockpit. Her Dodo was third in line from the forward position, with the dropship carrying Czajka, Jarret and Jates fifth in line. Problem was, the assault carrier had not yet rotated so that line was launching. Seven dropships remained in the current row of active launchers. With twenty-four seconds between launches to assure dropships did not collide, it would take nearly three minutes for the current row to complete launching. Then the ship needed sixty-four seconds to rotate the next row into position. Add time to launch the two spacecraft in line ahead of her, and she was looking at a wait of almost *five freakin' minutes* before her Dodo was hurled down the rails into space. The purpose of a controlled, measured launch procedure was so dropships remained inside the protection of the warship's shields as long as possible. That was a sensible precaution when the chief threat was anti-aircraft artillery and small missiles.

With a fully active SD network shooting at the assault transports, Irene reflected that the freakin' hamsters *seriously* needed to rethink their approach to opposed spaceborne landings. Eject the damned dropships all at once, she silently suggested, and trust overwhelming numbers and decoys to get the dropships dirtside safely.

"The next time we do something like this," she said quietly to Derek, "I have some helpful hints for the hamsters."

Derek reached over and patted the other pilot's hand. "I am sure you will phrase your hints in a calm and constructive manner, and drop them in a suggestion box."

"I would *like* to write them on my boot, and put it up the ass of whatever idiot dreamed up the op plan for this landing."

"Uh huh. Like I said, calm and constructive," he nodded knowingly.

"Do *you* think we should trust this task force?" She demanded. "The hamsters missed a whole damned SD network out there!"

"They missed two or three satellites," he spoke gently. It did no good to get Irene riled up. "That's all we know. We *did* expect some losses on this-"

The Dodo rocked, and not by itself. The entire ship shuddered.

Derek held sides of the console as the ship shook, careful not to touch any of the controls. "What the *hell* was-"

"Striebich," Perkins called from the cabin. "What the hell was that?"

With one eye on the tactical display, Irene answered. "Your guess is as good as mine, Ma'am." In her tone was a note of mild irritation, maybe even reproach. The Mavericks' commanding officer had access to a higher level of intel than was available to the pilots.

Perkins got the message. Trouble was, the command data feed from the *Big Mac* was offline, she wasn't receiving anything at all. Switching to the ship status network, she immediately realized the incident was no mere glitch with a launcher. The ship had been hit, and hit hard. Orange and red icons were lit up all over the schematic of the ship in her visor.

Shields along the ship's ventral spine were at sixty percent strength or lower. Multiple shield generators were offline, in the process of resetting.

Emily Perkins thought it unlikely the enemy would give the *Big Mac* time to bring its defenses back to full strength. "Striebich, launch us now. I'm sending a general evac signal to all dropships, watch out for traffic out there." Though Captain Rennul controlled the operation of her ship, Perkins was in command of the landing force aboard the *Mecdunnue*, including the dropships. Technically, an order to accelerate the planned launch sequence required permission from the ship's captain, but communications were down and besides, well, *screw* that. Perkins would act first and request permission later.

If she lived that long.

"Ma'am?" Irene's eyes widened in shock. "We can't launch on our own, the sequence is automated."

"The *sequence* has us sitting here like fish in a barrel for another," Perkins checked her visor. "Four minutes. The *Big Mac* won't hold together that long. This is on *my* authority. Launch now, that's an order."

Neither Irene nor Derek needed to see the orders engraved on official Legion stationry. They felt the ship continuing to vibrate as thrusters fired to stabilize its flight path. Loosening the straps that held him, Derek awkwardly bent down between their seats, unlocking a panel in the floor. Underneath was a yellow lever, printed with bold warnings in Ruhar script. "Ready when you are, Babe," he said softly.

There was the briefest hesitation before Irene reached forward to activate her console. The regs said she wasn't supposed to authorize the flight controls until the launch rails began to energize. "Let's see if this works, or if the hamsters were lying to us. *Again*," she added for emphasis, knowing the flight recorder was capturing everything she said and did. What they were doing violated safety regulations and she and Derek would get in trouble, *if* they survived. Between death and getting yelled at by hamsters, she was Ok with the yelling. "Hold for my signal," she told Derek. "I want to get some forward momentum going before you release from the launch rails."

"Got it," he grunted, the position bent sideways between the seats was awkward in the flightsuit. It made sense to get the big Dodo moving in the right direction before releasing the clamps that held the spacecraft to the launch rail, otherwise they could bounce off the launch bay and break something important.

Irene had the main engines on standby, being careful not to touch those controls. Those engines were too powerful to use in the launch bay, especially in rocket mode where they weren't gulping oxygen from outside. Instead, she started the thruster pumps, building up pressure and-

A warning light flashed, locking her out. On the display, a message in Ruhar script scolded her for attempting to do something dangerous and foolish and-

"Damn it!" She toggled off the alarm and warning message.

Derek tried to look up but at the angle, he couldn't see Irene's face. "What?"

"Freakin' thing locked me out. Let's see if this override works as advertised." Ruhar spacecraft were equipped with artificial intelligence computers that, while blessedly lacking the self-awareness that could be annoying, could interfere with the pilot's operation. That fact had been declared unacceptable by the community of Ruhar pilots, so there was a workaround that could force the computer to do whatever the pilot thought necessary, regardless of the AI's judgement. In training, Irene and Derek had been shown how to bypass the automated controls and the process appeared to be straightforward. What scared her were rumors that Ruhar systems had failed to disengage for *human* pilots. If the hamsters distrusted how primitive humans would fly their expensive spacecraft, the overrides might have been disabled.

Everything worked just like it had during emergency procedures during training, except at the last stage, the AI did not acknowledge the override. "Ooh, you *son of a-*"

"Striebich? Bonsu? What is the problem? Why aren't we moving?" Perkins demanded.

"Working on it, Ma'am," Derek answered for his copilot.

"This stupid thing-" Irene paused in mid-rant. The display was now showing 'Manual Access Enabled' in English. When the system had not instantly granted access, she assumed it was refusing to comply, when it really had just been going through the proper steps to enable manual control.

Maybe she should not be so impatient. "We're good!" Inching up the aft thruster power, she felt the spacecraft trembling as the thrust pushed against the clamps holding the Dodo to the launch rails. "Ok, release-"

The ship rocked again, *hard*. Irene's seat jerked to the left then up and her hands bounced off the controls. Lights in the cockpit did not even flicker, but the string of white lamps illuminating the launch bay blinked out. As did all external power sources. The ship had been hit again. Artificial gravity flickered in waves that made Irene's stomach do flip-flops, then gravity cut off entirely. "Derek!" She shouted, wrapping her pinky fingers around the sides of the console to stabilize her hands. "We are *outta* here. Brace for-"

"No good," he grunted, straining at the release handle. "It's stuck. I think," sitting upright and stretching to see over the wraparound displays, he studied the launch bay, even as the ship continued to shake violently. "The launch rails are *bent*. The clamps must be stuck."

"Shit!" She could see the doors at the far end of the bay were cracked open, allowing a thin sliver of blindingly-harsh sunlight through. The doors weren't just cracked open, they were *cracked*. The ship's structure had flexed so much the frame was warped and bent the doors with it.

"Oh that's *bad*," Derek gasped. His fingers flew over the controls, jabbing a button once, twice, three times. The silver of light grew marginally thicker. "The doors are jammed, we'll never get out of here."

"I can't raise anyone on comms," Irene pounded a fist on her thigh. The doors had both a manual release mechanism and explosive bolts that could blow the doors outward in an emergency. Neither of those options were available to the pilots, or maybe the Ruhar had just not trusted humans with anything that affected the assault carrier's operations. The ship heaved again and Irene's chin bashed against the helmet liner, making her bite her lower lip. She tasted blood and ignored it.

"Irene, Derek!" Perkins barked, using the pilots' first names for emphasis. "Whatever you gotta do, do it *now*!"

"Screw this," Derek slapped the access panel closed, not wasting any more time trying to get the clamps released. "Rip her loose."

"What?" Irene gaped at the other pilot.

"Pop the belly thrusters, they'll break the clamps free."

"That will also prang the tail assembly," she protested. "And if the clamps don't tear away cleanly, we won't be able to close the gear doors."

"You want to stay here?" Derek asked, concentrating on his own task.

"Hell no. Shit!" She gestured toward the jammed doors. "We can't get out anyway."

Derek's response was to link the maser cannon under the Dodo's chin to the head-up display in his helmet visor, and energize the weapon. Pulses of coherent microwave radiation stabbed out to strike the inner surface of the launch bay doors, starting on the lower right corner.

"Those doors are armored," she warned.

"Armor plating is on the *outside*," he explained. "We don't need to cut through the armor, just the doors."

She could see he was right. His aim was jittery as the ship was shaking, so the section cut by the maser cannon wavered in a sloppy, jagged line of burnt composites and melted alloys. "Cannon is overheating," she noted. "I'm cutting out the safeties."

Derek didn't reply. He had the righthand door almost loose, it was bending as the maser cut across the top. With a screeching groan that was audible through the Dodo's structure, the righthand door popped off its track and sprang outward, tumbling end over end before it quickly disappeared. Freed from the locking mechanism, the left side of the door slid jerkily aside until it jammed again. "Go! *Go go GO!*"

Popping the belly thrusters for a tenth-of-a-second burst only made red warning lights flash on both pilot consoles. Programming a quarter-second burst, she hit the Activate button. The Dodo broke loose and banged against the ceiling of the launch bay with a *CRACK* that shook loose dust from panels inside the cockpit. "There goes the tail," Irene gritted her teeth. "Hang on," she advised grimly.

The Dodo bounced and scraped its way along the launch bay. Both pilots did their best to keep their craft in the center of the bay and the damage incurred was not due to lack of skill, the ship was heaving and rocking and spinning as they tried to fly the short distance to get clear of the assault carrier. "Are you going to- Whoa!" Derek flinched instinctively as something big and dark spun past the doors outside. They might escape from the ship only to smack into flying debris. "Watch out for-"

"I *see* it!" Irene snapped in a way that meant 'shut the hell up'. The Dodo's wings were retracted into their slots under the fuselage, reducing the spacecraft's cross-section so it could fit in the launch bay. The jammed lefthand door still left the opening too small for the dropship to fit through with a comfortable clearance, because of sponsons that bulged out from the lower sides of the Dodo's center section. Irene had to guess at the best angle to thread her ship though the opening, an angle that constantly changed as the starship shook around them. A horrible hair-raising *BANG-Screeeeeee* as they flew through the jagged opening told her they had hit something against something, and there were so many warning lights flashing red and orange that all she could do was to *fly* the damned thing and worry about what had gotten busted later. If there was a later.

That the tail of the Dodo had not already been sheared off became evident, when there was another shriek of protesting composites from the rear of the spacecraft and the nose lurched up out of control, thrusters popping as the tail assembly tore away. "We're clear! Get the-"

The *Big Mac* erupted in flame and something slammed into the Dodo from behind.

# CHAPTER ELEVEN

Dani Grace smacked her forehead into the cushions at the front of her helmet, as the dropship lurched hard, the nose dipping then pivoting up. If the helmet had not been tethered to the seat she was strapped into, the jolt would have been worse. She winced and blinked, her vision blurry, grateful that the smart helmet had automatically inflated the cushions to protect her. "What is-" She began to ask, when the communications network cut off her transmit access. The pilots of the dropship and leaders of the platoon did not need people distracting them with random and stupid questions. Tasting blood from having bit her lip somehow, she eyeclicked to a view from the dropship's external sensors and gasped.

The ship they had launched from moments before, the massive assault carrier *Dal Turnaden*, was cracking in half, the hull barely visible through intense flares of light. During the two or three seconds she watched in horror, the carrier twisted and tore itself apart, stout composite frames splintering and breaking away, arcs of electricity searing space around the ship. As the two pieces separated completely, a thick bolt of lightning sparked between the hull sections, sending tendrils of light out toward-

The dropship shuddered and sparks burst out of the cabin wall opposite Dani, charring the suits of the two soldiers seated there. She had no time to scream before intense sunlight flared through multiple pinpoint holes in her side of the cabin, highspeed debris tearing through the dropship's hull like tissue paper. Five soldiers on the other side of the cabin were splattered by debris like shotgun pellets, their armor suits shredded. Air shrieked out holes in both sides of the cabin, blood seeping in zero gravity being pulled through the holes along with the air that had filled the cabin.

Without her doing anything, her own armored suit flashed a notice that it had switched to internal air supply, and she took a panicked gulp of air into her lungs. The dropship was tumbling and vibrating, beams of sunlight coming through pinprick holes in the hull looking like laser beams shining through dust, blood and flash-frozen water vapor that had been in the cabin before it was punctured. The beams danced erratically as the ship shuddered, automatic systems and the pilots trying to stabilize the spacecraft's tumble before they fell deeper into the atmosphere.

"*Think*, Dani," she shouted to herself. Whatever the pilots were doing or not doing, she couldn't affect the dropship's chances of survival. Nor could she survive bailing out at that altitude, the emergency parachute on her back wasn't designed for jumping from orbit. By the time she fell deep enough in the air for the chute to be useful, she would be moving so fast the chute material would be shredded. At least, that is what the Ruhar instructors had told her during training. Stay aboard the dropship and trust the alien spacecraft's stealth, energy shields, defensive maser cannons and decoy drones to get her to the ground safely. The real danger would come once her boots hit the ground, the Ruhar had told her.

Liars.

The ship that had brought her there, a massive assault carrier, had been cut in half by enemy fire, despite the assurances of the Ruhar that enemy defenses had been thoroughly suppressed by the orbital bombardment.

What else had the hamsters been wrong about?

Her brain and her icy stomach were both telling her the same thing: get out of here *now*. Before she realized what she was doing, her hands were on the manual latch to release the straps holding her to the seat. She stared down at her hands, wondering what they were doing, when any thought of bailing out and hoping a search and rescue ship would pick her up in orbit vanished. A chunk of something tore through the cabin at a diagonal, leaving a small hole forward on her side and a big hole in the abdomen of the soldier seated beside the platoon leader at the rear of the cabin. Blood exploded outward, splattering the platoon leader as the flash-frozen droplets floated away, performing a macabre dance in the zero gravity.

Dani didn't scream. She just blinked, once, slowly. The soldier who had just died didn't have a chance to survive. She did. The platoon leader tore open a bandage packet and applied it to the soldier who had been killed, moving with quiet calm. The square bandage rippled outward, seeking to cover the maximum volume, thinning as it stretched out. Seeing the platoon leader continuing to do his job, even if all he accomplished was stemming the flow of blood into the chaos of the dropship's cabin, made something click in her mind.

*Do your job*, she reminded herself, and focused on the status icons in the visor of her own helmet. To her surprise, a yellow light softly blinking on an outline of her suit showed that she, too, had been struck by debris. Until the suit informed her of the minor damage, she had not noticed a hot liquid sensation on the outside of her upper left arm.

Instinct told her to do what she could to help the stricken soldiers on the opposite side of the cabin. Training and a bit of common sense reminded her what she *should* do: check herself first, then try to help others. Reaching over with her right hand, her gloved fingers felt a jagged crease in the armor covering her left arm, and her fingers came away with a coating of gray dust mixed with blood. Her blood.

The visor was flashing a warning not to interfere with the suit's process of repairing itself. Relying on training rather than instinct, she laid her fingers close to the rent in the armor, trusting the gray nanoparticle goo to slide off her gloves and back into the suit, where it could work on repairing the tear. As she looked down, she saw blood smeared across the front of her armor. It couldn't be her blood unless-

With a start, she realized the soldier to her right had droplets of blood slowly seeping from a series of pinhole punctures in the front of his armor. She eyeclicked through a menu in her visor until the platoon channel came up, informing her that the Verd-kris next to her was deceased.

Shit.

Holy shit.

Her hands shook as she turned to look at the wall of the cabin between her and the dead man. It was peppered with fine holes. An inch or two closer to her, and she would be-

"Grace. Captain Grace," the guttural tone of a lizard spoke to her.

"Yes?" In her visor, she could see the call was coming from platoon leader Zolatus. Sometimes, it was difficult to tell Verd-kris voices apart after they were translated.

"The pilots told me we need to plug the holes in the cabin, before we hit the atmosphere."

Before we- She paused, comprehending the words. "We're going in?" Looking at the platoon status in her visor, she counted thirteen dead and six seriously injured. That the six wounded had survived was a minor miracle, being struck by debris in space was usually fatal.

"The platoon is still combat-effective," the leader insisted.

"But, we-"

"If the rest of this op is as fucked up as it started," the Verd-kris growled, "we need all the boots we can get on the ground. The pilots tell me it's too kinetic to stay up here." Hearing that, Dani briefly wondered whether the Verd had picked up US military slang, or the translator had done that for him. "We don't have a choice anyway. Both engines are damaged, we can't reach a stable orbit from here. We are following the battalion down as best we can. The other dropships and decoys will provide cover for us."

She knew the Verd was explaining more details than she needed to hear, both because she was human and because she outranked him in the Legion hierarchy. Her rank did not mean she should, or could interfere with the Zolatus's command of the platoon. "Understood."

"Can you patch the holes in your area? The kits are-"

"I know where the patch kits are," she reached down under her seat and felt the metal tube. It contained a sticky spray that would flow into gaps and harden like iron, she had seen its use in training. The dropship lurched again as she held the can in both hands, pointing the nozzle toward the cabin wall to her right.

I am trusting my life to a can of *Fix-a-Flat*, she told herself. Next time, I am keeping my ass on the ground.


The other Dodo assigned to the Mavericks aboard the *Tig Mecdunnue* experienced the same situation as the dropship flown by Irene and Derek, with one major and fatal difference: the pilots of the craft were Ruhar instead of human.

When the *Big Mac* was hit the first time, everyone looked to Lieutenant Gao, seated in the rear of cabin. It wasn't known what conversation he exchanged with the pilots because he used the command channel, but the discussion must have been brief. "The ship is undamaged," Gao told the troops in the cabin. "Shields are holding. We launch in five minutes. This was not unexpected," Goa added in what was not exactly a lie. Some sort of problem during the landing operation was expected. Discovering the enemy had a second layer of strategic defense was *not*.

The message Emily Perkins sent, to accelerate the launching, was not heard by Gao or any human in the dropship and if the Ruhar pilots heard the message, they ignored it. Doctrine stated the safest place for vulnerable aerospace craft was inside the shields and armor of an assault carrier, not exposed in space where directed-energy beams and high-speed debris was flying around. The dropship, which the pilots properly called a 'Lotentix' instead of the insulting human term 'Dodo', was under Ruhar control and no human could give orders to the crew of the *Tig Mecdunnue*.

When the ship was hit the second time, hit hard enough that one of the pilots spoke on the common channel to assure the human passengers that everything was normal and they would be launching soon, Shauna had enough. "This is *bullshit*," she announced to Dave and Jates, taking a deep breath to calm the butterflies in her stomach as the ship's artificial gravity cut off. She did not try talking with the lieutenant, because Gao's head was bobbing back and forth and he was gesturing with his hands. She guessed that their lieutenant was having a discussion with the pilots, and it did not look like the pilots were politely inviting Gao to the cockpit for tea and crumpets.

"I agree the situation is less than optimal," Jates said, speaking English on his own rather than through a translator. The surgun had worked tirelessly to learn English first, as it was the common language of the American and British contingents of the Legion. "What do you propose we do about it?"

"I don't know," Shauna threw up her hands. "Something! Anything other than waiting here for the next SD platform to target us."

"We don't know if the ship is hit bad, or just a local node is out," Dave suggested, not believing one word of what he said. "The hamster battleships have got to be hitting back, there might not be another satellite left out there to hit us."

"Yeah," Shauna snorted. "You wanna bet your life on that?"

"No," Dave admitted. "I'm open to suggestions," he added with a look toward the cockpit door. It could be locked from the inside, and even if he was considering mutiny, no one in the Dodo's cabin was qualified to fly the damned thing.

"LT?" Shauna asked. "Lieutenant Gao?"

"One moment, Staff Sergeant," Gao snapped, irritated. After a pause and a disgusted jerk of his head, he turned his attention to her, speaking on the channel with Shauna, Dave, Jates and the two fireteam sergeants. "The pilots say there's nothing they can do. One of them *wants* to launch now, but the outer doors are controlled by the ship, and they can't contact anyone outside."

"Shit!" Dave spat. "So we're stuck here?"

"No, *Mister* Czajka," Gao replied in a chiding tone. "The launch rails are still energized, there's no reason to think we won't launch on schedule. We are safer here than anywhere else aboard the ship, and we *can't* launch before the schedule rolls around to-"

Gao never finished whatever he was going to say.


"Get me comms, damn it!" General Ross demanded from his seat just behind the cockpit bulkhead of his Dodo. The dropship carrying him and his small command staff had launched safely from the assault carrier *Url Mecadonn*, known to the humans aboard as the *Old MacDonald*.

A Ruhar technician looked up from his console with a pained expression. "General, we are working on-"

"We have all this fancy shit you're so proud of," Ross jabbed a finger at the pile of gear that occupied the back half of the Dodo's cabin, taking up valuable space that could have been used for soldiers or weapons. By directly criticizing the Ruhar operating the communications equipment and by inference, the technology behind the alien gear, he was breaking UNEF protocol.

*Screw* protocol.

The hamster fleet had breezily declared that air and space defenses had been quickly and thoroughly suppressed by the preparatory bombardment from orbit. The speed with which the task force commander cleared the assault carriers to move in had generated surprise and concern not only among the humans, Verd-kris and Achakai who would be dropping to the planet's surface, there was also grumbling by the Ruhar liaison officers who worked closely with the three groups of aliens. Officially, all of the Ruhar expressed confidence in the task force ships and crews. Unofficially, some of the intel people worried that the commander might have underestimated the Wurgalan. It was true that the Wurgalan military was historically weaker than the Kristang who were the Ruhar fleet's usual opponents. It was true that the Wurgalan were noticeably lower on the technology ladder than the Kristang.

It was also true that the Ruhar had not fought a major engagement against the Wurgalan in over seventy years. The Torgalau had provided high-level data about the weapons and tactics of the Wurlagan, but the Torgs had not sent a recon ship to Stiglord in over a decade, so the task force had gone in without the advantage of the best information available. When the cruisers and destroyers of the task force chased away the enemy fleet, and the big guns of the battleships cleared space around the planet by blasting the local Strategic Defense network to dust, confidence had soared. There was even talk about the possibility of pulling the battleships out early, and accelerating the overall schedule.

Then, an entire unknown second layer of SD satellites had opened up on the assault carriers with powerful X-ray lasers, and the operation went to shit in a flash of coherent photons.

"Sir," the Ruhar technician pressed his eyes closed tightly, in a gesture that Ross interpreted to mean the hamster was trying to be patient with the primitive human.

That got Ross pissed off. "Damn it, get this gear working. I know you're not supposed to deploy the antenna yet and I don't give a shit about that, we are carrying three spares. Get the damned thing reeled out behind us, or I'll find someone who knows what the hell they're doing."

The Ruhar technician was stung by the public criticism, and Ross didn't give a shit about that either. When the *Dal Turnaden* had been cut in half with forty percent of that carrier's dropships still in their launch bays, his ability to give a shit about problems of the Ruhar fleet had run out. Without further comment or protest, the Ruhar began letting the long, whip-like antenna unreel behind the dropship. The electromagnetic energy devoted to jamming communications in the battlespace around the planet rivalled the energy of the weapons flying from both sides, with the result that neither side could maintain command and control without relying on line-of-sight laserlinks, and even those were spotty. Only the big starships, and specialized spacecraft like the one carrying Ross's UNEF command staff, had the equipment to cut through jamming.

"The *Big Mac* has been hit again," one of the human pilots called out through the open door. The fancy comm gear required Ruhar specialists to operate it, but Ross had insisted that humans fly the Dodo. "They're losing power."

Ross clenched his fists, putting the energy of his frustration into those muscles instead of into more angry words. The antenna was being set up, there wasn't anything he could do to speed the process along. They would lose that antenna when the dropship hit the atmosphere, it would need to be cut to avoid the line becoming fouled around the descending spacecraft's tail. Those minutes when he would lose communications were unavoidable anyway, the heat of hitting the air at suborbital speed would envelop the Dodo in a shroud of plasma that even the special antenna could not cut through.

Loss of the *Dal Turnaden*, and likely up to forty percent of the dropships aboard that carrier, was a heavy blow. But losing the *Big Mac* would be worse, for half of the human force had been crammed into that one ship. Dividing the Legion along lines determined by species made for simpler logistics, transport and communications, and Ross understood the logic behind that decision. Now the result was that he might lose half of the force he commanded, even before they hit atmosphere.

"General," the Ruhar technician announced stiffly, without taking his eyes off the console to look at the human officer. "The antenna is now functional."

"Outstanding," Ross muttered under his breath, belatedly hoping the hamster did not catch the sarcasm in his tone. He had a sensor feed from the fleet, probably a link to one of the battleships in higher orbit. The first item he saw was that the *Dal Turnaden* was in two major and countless smaller pieces, yet as he watched, a dropship launched from the spinning forward section. That assault carrier had a contingent of Verd-Kris, so good for them. As Ross did not command the Verd part of the Legion, and he couldn't do anything about the fate of the *Turnaden* anyway, he turned his attention to the two ships that were under his command. The *Url Mecadonn* was launching dropships regularly, so far having escaped attack by the enemy SD platforms. Ross tapped a finger to the display of his console without thinking about what he was doing. He and his headquarters staff had been quartered aboard the ship they called the *Old MacDonald*, and he was heartened to see that ship still intact and providing cover for the landing operation.

The *Tig Mecdunnue* was in a different situation. That assault carrier had been struck twice by X-ray lasers, and even through the staticky sensor feed, he could see the *Big Mac* had its nose tilted away from the planet, its engines burning hard to gain altitude. The urgency with which the ship's captain wanted to reach jump distance was evident, from the long flames firing out from the booster motors at the ship's aft end. Those boosters, which could only be used once before they had to be replaced, were rarely used and always used only when there was no other choice.

Where the hell were the battleships, and what was the task force commander doing about the murderous SD platforms that he had declared did not exist? The *Dal Turnaden* had been fired on three times before that ship was torn apart, and the *Big Mac* had been struck twice already, a bad sign for-

The *Big Mac* flared as an X-ray laser beam burned right through weakened shields, armor plating and structural frames to slice the assault carrier in two pieces.

"Admiral!" The 7th Fleet commander's chief of staff called for attention, tearing the commander away from the vital task of searching for the enemy SD satellites.

"What is it?" Admiral Kune snapped irritably.

"The *Mecdunnue* has been destroyed, and the *Mecadonn* just took a hit."

Kune was momentarily paralyzed with shock. There would be an inquiry after the battle, an investigation of how such a disaster could have befallen the task force. If Kune could stop the slaughter, the landing force could still win the day, and he could quietly slip away to an enforced but officially voluntary retirement.

If he lost another assault carrier, especially if *both* of the carriers transporting the human Expeditionary Force were lost, his fate would be handled publicly rather than quietly. The *Mecdunnue* was already gone, doomed to a fiery death by crashing on the planet below. But if he could prevent the destruction of the *Mecadonn*-

Kune scanned the display, highlighting the stricken *Url Mecadonn* and appraising that ship's orbital track and velocity.

"Sir, we-"

Kune held up a thumb for silence as he switched the display to the warships that surrounded the planet, warships that had failed to protect the all-important assault carriers. He reached a decision. "Signal the *Voltana* and the *Tularus*."

The battleship *Voltana* appeared out of a burst of gamma rays, less than eighty kilometers from the assault carrier *Url Mecadonn*, as that ship slowly turned to throw off the aim of the enemy SD network. The crews of both ships knew the *Mecadonn*'s maneuver had little chance of succeeding, the bulky carrier was flying too low and slow to dodge a laser beam fired from only a few lightseconds away. If the enemy SD network followed the same strike pattern that had already claimed the *Turnaden* and the *Mecdunnue*, their sister ship would be hit again within seconds.

With the *Voltana* traveling at a higher speed than the assault carrier, the time when it could provide cover was short, even with the battleship's engines straining to slow its headlong rush past the *Mecadonn*. In a dangerous action that only happened because it was a direct order from the task force commander, the battleship extended its shields to their maximum extent, covering a wider area of space but weakening the field strength. The crew of the *Voltana* prayed as they waited out the thirty-one seconds until their ship would no longer be between the assault carrier and the suspected location of the next enemy SD platform. So far, so good, the enemy network would likely hold fire until the battleship was out of the-

The *Voltana* took a direct hit to its starboard side, an X-ray laser that partially burned through shields that were trying to cover too large an area. The beam struck the warship's thick armor and made plates tear off, exposing the battleship's unprotected hull. Secondary explosions rocked the *Voltana*, taking three maser cannons and a railgun offline. The battleship rolled so its starboard side was facing toward the planet, as more armor plates peeled away to bash themselves backward as the ship continued its flight.

The battleship's crew were holding their breath, watching the counter run down to the point where they were no longer in the line of fire. Three seconds before that happened, the cruiser *Del Tularus* jumped in to take up coverage, and the crew of the assault carrier cheered. The *Tularus* had been moving more slowly when it got the order from Admiral Kune, and used its extra time before jump in an attempt to match speed with the assault carrier as best it could.

Having done all it could, the battleship cut deceleration and allowed its momentum to carry it toward a higher orbit, where it could jump back to its assigned station. Or better, to go hunting for those troublesome enemy SD satellites.

The personnel aboard the cruiser *Del Tularus* were not thinking of going hunting after their current short-term assignment was over, they were only thinking about surviving until their current assignment was over. Extending their shields to maximum coverage left their ship's protection thin, and a cruiser did not have the stout shields and armor of a battleship. A single X-ray laser hit at that range could cripple the cruiser, and knowing the task force could afford to lose a cruiser more than an assault carrier was of little comfort to the *Tularus* crew. Having extended their shields, closed all internal blast doors, safed missile warheads so they could not be detonated by overflash, and ensured everything that could be done to assure their success had been done, the crew watched their consoles and waited.

And waited.

And waited.

Right on time, another Strategic Defense satellite exploded, generating a pulse of X-rays that lanced out at lightspeed to strike-

The battleship *Voltana*.

That ship had begun the process of pulling shield coverage inward to increase the field strength, so the damage was less than it could have been, less than the blackened scar burned into the starboard side of the hull. The impact was still severe, with forty percent of the laser's energy remaining coherent to strike the hull plating on the battleship's belly, cutting a line across three major structural frames and through a missile battery. The missile propulsion systems exploded in all directions, with some of the kinetic force trapped inside the hull by the intact armor plating around the battery. Shrapnel tore through the unarmored interior of the warship, knocking out communications, rupturing power conduits and causing a crucial shield generator to reset. The *Voltana* veered off course, her crew working diligently to keep their ship in the fight.

Instead of accelerating toward jump distance, the *Voltana* continued coasting upward, slowly rolling so its undamaged portside was exposed to the enemy above. The battleship's captain sent a message to Admiral Kune: *Let the enemy shoot at us. We can take it better than the carriers.*

Kune sent back *Permission granted*, then he turned to his staff. "Signal all battleships to take up blocking positions, we need to protect those carriers. All cruisers, plus DESRONs One and Three, hunt down those damned enemy satellites and *terminate*. Destroyer Squadron Two," he looked at the tactical plot skeptically. "Assist survivors from the *Turnaden* and *Mecdunnue*, as best they can."

"Admiral," the chief of staff said quietly. "That low in the atmosphere, there won't be much time before the destroyers have to break away."

"I know that," Kune snapped. "Someone needs to recover escape pods, before they fall out of orbit, or the enemy starts taking potshots at them from the surface." He sighed. "We'll save what we can, and continue the mission. At this point, we have no choice but to win this fight."

Dave was brought back to awareness by an ear-piercing shriek from his right side. The sound was so loud and high-pitched, it hurt his ear and made him wince. Actually, both of his ears hurt, and his face was freezing cold. What the hell was-

He opened his eyes. That was a mistake. Instinctively, his eyelids snapped tightly shut to prevent frostburn.

His suit had a hole in it. Air was leaking out and the inside of his suit was freezing cold.

The visor's power was off, the faceplate had automatically gone clear but he couldn't see anything, nothing at all. It was utterly dark, it- No, it was a very faint, dark pink. The emergency lighting in the Dodo's cabin must be on. Why couldn't he see anything? Oh, his dull brain responded. Because exposure to vacuum had caused moisture to freeze on the inside of the helmet's faceplate.

It was also hard to breathe. The emergency air supply was working, he could feel its icy breeze on his neck, but the suit was losing air faster than the emergency supply could replenish.

Got to patch the hole, or holes. Got to find out where the holes are first. Blindly reaching up with his right hand he realized the whistling sounds was not as loud, and lower in pitch. As he felt that side of the helmet with the gloved fingertips, the whistling abruptly cut off. He guessed the lining of gooey nanoparticles in the skinsuit had flowed in to seal the hole.

There was a red dot glowing in the upper left of the visor, then alien script began scrolling across right to left. The suit was booting up on backup power, he couldn't read the status icons because of the ice clinging to the visor, but he recognized the sequence. Though the suit controls had been adjusted to his default settings of Human>English>American, the boot-up process was still entirely Ruhar.

There was nothing to do but wait until the suit's reboot was complete, nothing to do but gulp in great lungfuls of sweet oxygen and shiver to ward off the chill in the skinsuit. The Ruhar mech suits were comfortably warm or cool depending on the user's preferences, but without power, they tended to be chilly in a vacuum. That he was in a vacuum was obvious, but how? The Dodo had been counting down to launch when-

When what? He had no idea what happened, he still couldn't see a damned thing. Glare from the icons scrolling across the visor actually blocked what little he could see and-

Shauna.

She was sitting beside him, to his left.

Without power, the skinsuit was stiff, and training had taught him to move slowly and deliberately. The back of his left hand bumped into something, something that moved. Twisting his hand around and reaching with the other, he felt the right upper arm of a skinsuit. The arm moved and what he guessed was a hand thumped his thigh. Leaning over and pressing his helmet to hers, he spoke as loud and clearly as he could through teeth that were still chattering from the cold. "Shauna? You OK?"

"Yeah," her voice was muffled and indistinct. "My suit power is out. What happened?"

"No idea. My suit is rebooting. I had a hole in it, I think in the neck somewhere." His fingers had not found a dent in the helmet, though he could have missed it. "The faceplate is iced over, can't see a damned thing."

"I can see, my suit is rebooting also. There's not much to-" She gasped and pulled away for a moment. The helmets thumped together again just as Dave's suit came back online enough for the faceplate heater to clear the ice away.

"Holy shit," he said in a whisper.

"Yeah," Shauna agreed.

The cabin was a mess. Correction: what was left of the cabin was a mess. Beginning three seats forward of where Dave was strapped in, the dropship was a broken, twisted shambles. The cabin had been torn apart and most of the forward section of the Dodo was just *gone*. He blinked at dots of light in the blackness where the cockpit bulkhead had been, then he had to throw up both hands to protect his eyes as blinding light lit up the area like a strobe. "What the-" His faceplate automatically darkened now that power was partially restored. "Oh my G-" he couldn't finish the thought.

The blinding light was the local star. It was visible not because the outer launch bay doors were open, but because they weren't there at all. What he could see forward was a gaping hole in the side of the ship. The intense sunlight abruptly winked out as the tumbling ship rotated away from the star. "What the f-"

"Jarrett? Czajka?" Jates was calling. "Anyone on this channel, respond."

"I'm here," Dave said stupidly, his brain working at half-speed. "It's me, Czajka."

"Jarrett here."

"Uh, San," someone coughed. "Santinelli."

"Chowdhury," the soldier next to Santinelli shifted in her seat. "What hap-"

"Hold," Jates ordered. "Anyone else?"

"Shit," Dave groaned as he looked around the remaining seats. There were only eight seats in what was left of the cabin. The person to his right, Sergeant Chan, wasn't moving and the splintered piece of composite frame poking through his chest from the back was probably the reason why. The seat forward of Santinelli had an occupant missing his head and left shoulder. In the seat beside that was, just a bloody mess. The bottom part of a torso and legs, the rest was missing. "Surgun, I think the five of us are it. We're the only ones left," he guessed.

Chowdhury repeated her question. "What hap- oh!"

Dave's attention was drawn back to where the Dodo's forward section used to be. The ship had rotated so the blue and green arc of the planet was coming into view. At first only clouds and ocean were visible, then the greens and browns of a continent. A dark-gray line of mountains along the coast were capped with white snow, and his eyes were drawn to sunlight glinting off a river as it wound lazily to the sea.

"We're *so* close," Chowdhury whispered.

"We jumped in at the edge of the mesosphere," Shauna muttered as she gaped at the view. "Ninety-two kilometers.

Dave checked an icon in his visor. "We're lower than that now. Eight-seven klicks."

"We're falling?" Santi gasped. "We're falling out of orbit? I thought that couldn't happen?!"

"It can't happen, except the *Big Mac* was moving at less than escape velocity when we jumped in," Shauna explained. "Gravity is pulling us down, and the lower we get, air resistance will slow our orbital speed."

"Yeah but," Santi protested. "The ship will climb out of this, right? They have to be pulling us back out of- Oh shit!" He pointed with a shaking finger.

Outlined against the planet was an assault carrier. No, it was only the aft section of an assault carrier, broken and tumbling, with electricity arcing from power conduits. The whole structure was enveloped in a pink and orange mist from vented reactor plasma, and pieces broke off as internal explosions rocked the powerless wreck.

"Shauna," Dave swallowed to get moisture in his suddenly-dry throat. "That's *our* ship. That's the aft end of the *Big Mac*."

"Yeah, I think so," she agreed.

"That *can't* be our ship!" Santi argued. "We're aboard the-"

"We're in *part* of the ship," Shauna popped the latch to release the straps that held her in the seat. The ship trembled and she had to hold on with one hand to avoid floating helplessly. "Surgun, we need to get to another dropship, or an escape pod. Right now."

"Leave here?" Santi screeched. "We can't go anywh-"

"Schmuckatelli, shut up," Dave barked.

"I'm not going to shut up for you! You're a civilian, you can't give me-"

"Shut up, Schmuckatelli," Jates growled. "Jarrett's right, we- *Uh*," he groaned in pain.

"Surgun?" Dave asked, belatedly checking the squad status in his visor. "You're hurt!" The Verd's skinsuit had not been punctured, but it had absorbed an impact that had broken several of the tough alien's ribs, and he was bleeding internally. The status icons were glowing yellow rather than orange or red, telling Dave that Jates's suit was confident the nanomachines it had injected could stabilize the bleeding.

"I will be fine," Jates grunted. "My suit has sustained substantial damage." Whatever had hit him, it had battered him backward hard enough to break the seat and crush the backpack he wore, plus crack several powercells. "Chowdhury, you are also compromised."

Chowdhury rubbed her left leg gingerly. Her suit had a long scar from hip to knee, the nanofabric had struggled to repair the tear. Freeze-dried blood coated the suit's thigh area. "Feels like something is in my leg," she said as if the injury had happened to someone else. "My suit sensors in that area are offline. My leg is numb."

"Probably nerve-blockers," Shauna suggested hopefully. The alternative was that the other woman's leg was shattered inside the skinsuit. Her vital signs showed her blood pressure was dropping, but slowly, and the rate of blood loss was flattening. That was a good sign.

"Santinelli," Jates fell back to using that soldier's preferred form of address, "help Chowdhury. Czajka, find the best way into the ship from here ASAP. Jarrett," he paused. "Help me."

"You got it, Surgun." Shauna knew it had wounded the alien's pride to ask for assistance.

Ordinarily, the best and easiest way out of the Dodo and back into the ship was going back the way they came in; the dropship's back ramp. Dave tried that first and it was a no-go from the start, the spacecraft had been shoved backward and the rear cabin was crumpled. The rear ramp was cracked open on one side, bent and jammed. Next, he tried the side opening. To his surprise, the inner door haltingly slid open under power, the door sticking in its tracks but retracting properly. The outer door was another story. Not only did it not operate under power, it stuck when he tried the manual crank. Peering with one eye through the tiny safety window, he could see the problem: the Dodo was crammed up against that side of the launch bay.

He backed out of the airlock. "Ok, we have to go out the front. I'll be right back."

"Dave!" Shauna tapped her belt. "Use a safety line. And hurry."

He looked out the missing front of the spacecraft, where the planet was once again coming into view. It appeared to be noticeably closer already. The ship was shaking continuously, a vibration transmitted through the structure to the crushed Dodo. "Whoa!" With a shudder, the Dodo shifted in the launch bay, as he clipped one end of the safety line around a busted frame that was part of the dropship's fuselage. "Hey, I think you should follow me right now."

"We're behind you," Shauna assured him. "Santi, you go first with Chowdhury. Keep a constant grip on the safety line."

Dave saw that with the Dodo scrunched up against the left side of the launch bay, there was a wider gap on the right side. "Watch out, there's a lot of jagged stuff in the way. Don't let it cut your suit."

"Dave," Shauna had switched to a private channel. "I can't reach anyone, can you?"

"No," he tried to focus on his job and not his fears. "I pinged Em and Jesse. No reply."

"My pings didn't get picked up at all," she meant by the shipboard communications network. "Our suit comms are too weak to get a signal through the hull."

"There's a lot of jamming," he noted. "We'll have to rely on helmet-to-helmet laserlink, until we can access something with more horsepower to cut through the jamming."

By the time they all squeezed around the broken dropship and reached the airlock at the rear of the launch bay, the ship's vibration had grown worse, enough that Dave had to use both hands to hang onto the airlock frame while he pressed the override buttons. Fortunately, because the airlock was used for loading troops aboard a dropship, it was large and they all could fit in. Except the damned door wouldn't seal when it closed. "Shit!" Dave exclaimed. "The inner door won't open if we can't get a seal."

Chowdhury pointed to a panel on the airlock's wall. "Try the sealant."

Dave kicked himself for not thinking of that. Working quickly, he got a can of sealant from a cabinet and sprayed the sticky foam all along the frame of the outer door, watching the substance change color from yellow to blue as it hardened in place. "Seal is good! Santinelli, get that inner door open."

For once, Santinelli did not screw up his job. He got the inner door controls activated properly and the door slid jerkily open most of the way until it jammed.

"Screw it, good enough," Shauna declared. "Surgun, you hold the fort here, Czajka and I will scout fore and aft?"

Jates was not familiar with the slang term 'hold the fort' but he guessed what she meant. "Agreed."

"Shauna, you go aft and I'll check forward?" Dave suggested.

"*You* go aft," she countered. "Hurry."

"Ok," he didn't argue, because he knew she was going straight to check the launch bay where the Mavericks' lead dropship should be waiting.

Dave had a short trip, he ran into an emergency bulkhead that had slid firmly closed. The indicator light on the bulkhead showed hard vacuum on the other side. It also showed air was leaking out from Dave's side. "Shauna, no joy here, we can't-"

"They're gone," she said.

He didn't have to ask who 'they' were. "*Gone?*"

"Sorry. Gone like, they must have launched. Their Dodo is gone. Looks like they cut through the bay doors with a maser cannon."

"Ha!" Dave couldn't help snorting a nervous laugh. "Striebich isn't known for her patience. That's a *good* thing in this case. Oh man, they got out, that's great." For a moment, he couldn't speak. "Shauna, what about the launch bay between us and them?"

"It's a mess. I think that Dodo's ammo magazine exploded. The outer airlock door is shredded."

"Damn. Hey, their Dodo was third in line. What about the other two forward?"

"Can't get there," frustration came through in her voice. "The blast bulkhead is down in that direction. No way to get it open, and we can't cut through."

Dave checked his visor. The news was not good. "We're at eighty kilometers now. This thing is going down."

"We have to get to an escape pod."

Jates spoke on the common channel. "Jarrett, Czajka, I'm looking at the status panel on the airlock. All four of the escape pods in this section of the ship are showing either launched or inactive."

Dave winced, mentally kicking himself again. His brain wasn't working properly, he still saw spots swimming in his vision. Though his suit couldn't access ship's data because the comm network was down, information about escape pods was available on status panels all over the ship. He also should have remembered that, with the ship so badly damaged, arrows in the floor should have lit up to guide the crew to the closest functioning escape pod. Those arrows were dark. Either even the rugged backup systems were down, or there were no escape pods available. No escape pods. No dropships. What were their options? "We don't have the right kind of parachutes to jump from this altitude."

"My chute is busted anyway," Chowdhury groaned.

"Mine is also inoperable," Jates added.

Dave checked the status of his own parachute, something he should have done before. It showed a yellow icon, with an indicator that nanomachines in the pack were furiously working to fix whatever the problem was. He didn't speak about it, knowing that Shauna and Jates both had access to his suit's status report if they wanted to know.

"Hey, what are we gonna do?" Santinelli's fear was evident in the tremble of his voice. "Huh? What? Staff Sergeant?" He automatically looked to Shauna rather than Jates for help, though the Verd-kris was the ranking officer. "Come on, what do we do?"

Shauna took in an audible breath as the ship trembled again and swayed sickeningly. "I don't know."

Chowdhury coughed, and gasped as she saw droplets of bright red blood splatter the inside of her faceplate. "Could we," she gagged while suppressing another cough. "Could we ride the ship down, until we are low enough to bail out?"

"No," Shauna turned toward the other woman and made an exaggerated shake of her head, so the gesture could be seen in the bulky suit helmet. "The ship is already starting to-" The ship lurched again and did not recover, it slowly kept turning to the left. Shauna wedged a foot under a railing in the passageway, so she would move with the ship. "It's starting to spin as the air gets thicker. The *Big Mac* is tough, but will probably break apart on the way down."

"Yeah but-" Santinelli began to say.

"We wouldn't survive bailing out at hypersonic speed," Jates observed. Five people with only three functioning parachutes meant two people would need to double up, creating additional strain on the parachutes that were intended only for emergency use. The user manual for the parachutes stated they were limited to use at speeds below twelve hundred kilometers per hour, and at altitudes below twenty three kilometers. The *Big Mac* had jumped into low orbit with a velocity of six kilometers per *second*. Atmospheric drag would slow the wreck somewhat as it fell, but Jates knew the ship would still be moving at high speed when it impacted the surface.

"Then what can we do?" Santinelli pressed for an answer.

Shauna took a breath and looked at Jates, as the ship shuddered again. Her visor informed her they were now less than eighty kilometers from the surface. "I don't know."

# CHAPTER TWELVE

The first time the *Tig Mecdunnue* was hit, the two officers in the launch control center dropped their attitude of casual arrogance and put on their helmets. Perhaps to show they were not overly concerned, or not wanting to appear afraid in front of a cadet, they left the faceplates open. "Cadet Dandurf," the lead officer ordered, "report to your assigned damage control station."

"Yes, Sir," Nert unstrapped from his seat and hurried out into the passageway, displaying admirable eagerness to attend to his duty. Part of his reason for moving quickly was his normal assigned station for damage control was way back near the engineering section, at the aft end of the ship. When he requested to be in the launch control center, he had been assigned a temporary duty station and at that moment, he couldn't remember where that was! He hesitated just outside the doorway, frantically trying to call up the required information on his helmet visor. If he went forward up the passageway then had to turn around, the officers in launch control would see him coming back.

Mercifully, the door slid automatically closed behind and he heard the bars clunk as the door securely locked in place. Of course the door had locked itself, the ship had been hit and damage control protocols were taking effect. That meant-

That meant blast doors would be closing all over the ship!

Nert pushed off the bulkhead and ran forward, reasoning that his damage control station would probably be somewhere near the launch bays. The heavy blast door at the structural frame in front of him was sliding closed from the left side, a purple light flashing to warn of the danger. Despite regulations that forbade the action, he dashed ahead and threw himself through the gap before the door ground to a halt with a dull metallic CLANG that he could feel through his body. Taking a breath of relief, he saw the blast door at the next frame forward had already sealed itself, so there was no need for him to continue running.

He did have time to *think*, and to remember how to find where he was supposed to be when the ship was under attack. His instinct that he should go forward was correct, only now that the ship was locked down, the system was telling him that he had been reassigned *aft* of where he was. Shouting a curse word that he knew couldn't be heard outside of his helmet, he turned just as a beep alerted him to an incoming message.

The system had changed its mind again, he *was* supposed to go forward, to assist in case any of the dropships needed to be evacuated. Mentally preparing to cringe if the alert chime beeped again with *another* change of assignment, he tapped a panel built into the bulkhead, seeking the best route to travel now that the blast doors had closed and-

He was knocked off his feet, first by the deck heaving underneath him, then by loss of artificial gravity that had him floating helplessly in the middle of the passageway, unable to reach anything he could hold onto. Making swimming motions in the air was dismayingly ineffective and as he got momentum going forward, the ship moved and the bulkhead he almost had within reach of his fingertips drifted away from him. Fortunately, the movement continued, bringing the deck back toward him and he awkwardly contacted the surface with the top of his helmet first. A firm handhold on a railing got him right-side up and his boots attached solidly to the deck with a *click*.

What was going on? The shipboard network was totally offline, his helmet couldn't establish a connection even to the local node. The panel in the bulkhead only showed that the ship was at battle stations, a fact he didn't need reminding of. What should he-

He should do his duty, he decided without hesitation. The *Tig Mecdunnue* certainly needed damage control now. With the deck shaking under his feet, he strode as quickly as he could without breaking free, running with a smooth gait from long practice in zero gravity. The hatch to the system of access tubes had its own power source and it unlocked, allowing him to crank the handle to swing the hatch aside. The tube was a tight fit for him until he got past the inner door and slammed it closed behind him, not waiting to check the indicator light to verify the inner door had sealed. It was a long crawl on hands and knees in the tube, lit only by purple emergency lighting. At the first intersection, he looked both ways, checking for anyone else who was using the access tubes, but all he could see was closed doors in both directions. Still trying to contact anyone on the ship's network, he turned right to go forward-

His helmet bashed the tube's hard surface so hard that he saw stars.


"Shauna," Dave called on a private channel, using the helmet-to-helmet laserlink. Jates would know they were communicating privately, and he had authority to break in if he wanted. The alien surgun was tapping the status panel in the bulkhead, too busy to be concerned about what his subordinates were talking about. "We gotta do something." He knew the others, even Jates, were depending on Dave and Shauna to get them out of the mess before the ship's hull broke apart and they burned up from friction. They were *Mavericks*, a group with a partly-unwarranted mystique for being clever and being just plain lucky.

"I *know*," she replied, angry at the situation rather than Dave. "I'm thinking. If we had those aeroshells the Commandos use for orbital drops-"

"No go. Their gear locker is in the other part of the ship," he reminded her. The other part of the ship they had briefly seen through the opening torn in the hull.

The other part of the ship.

If they could get there, they would have options.

Like his mother said, if wishes were fishes, everyone would have plenty to eat. Besides, the aft section of the hull looked like it was in bad condition, and dropping at least as fast as they were. It wouldn't do any good to-

"Hey! The hamster maintenance people use those jet pack things when they're working outside the ship. Could we use them to get out of here, sort of a do-it-yourself escape pod? If we can maintain orbit, someone will pick us up, right?"

"Good initiative," she didn't add the usual tagline of 'bad judgement'. "The hamsters don't store any of those jetpacks near the launch bays because they might interfere with flight operations. Besides, we need a lot of delta-vee to boost into a stable orbit, those jetpacks don't have that kind of power."

"Shit. What else-"

A hatch in the passageway next to Dave sprang open, catching him in the shins and knocking him ass over helmet to bounce off the overhead. Right behind the hatch lid, a figure in a crew pressure suit shot out, hitting the far wall and caroming off to smack into Dave.

Dave grabbed the figure's legs, more to prevent further havoc than to help. "What the f-"

"*Nert!*" Shauna shouted with delight. Her joy died when she realized the cadet was now in the same danger as the rest of them. "Why didn't you get to an escape pod?" She demanded while holding the Ruhar steady so he could get his boots firmly back on the deck.

"I tried! Mister Czajka, I am sorry that I hit you."

"Forget about it, Nert," Dave thumped his boots back in the deck, the only injury he had suffered was to his pride. "Why didn't you get out of here?"

"I tried!" The cadet repeated. "There were only two pods available, they both launched." He had tried to go back to the launch control center, but the access tubes in that direction were a twisted mess. "Why didn't *you* launch? What happened to the ship?"

Dave made a knife motion with one hand. "Ship is cut in at least two pieces, our dropship is no better. The five of us are the only ones who got out."

Nert's eyes bulged. "What about Colonel-"

"Their dropship did launch," Shauna explained softly. "Nert," she had to hold onto a railing as the ship's vibration grew worse. "We're falling and the escape pods have ejected. There are no dropships in this row. Can we get," she gestured to the hatch, "to the port side of the ship?"

"No," Nert shook his head. "The access tubes in that direction have collapsed. Those dropships would all have launched, if they could. We are falling out of orbit? How do we get out of here?"

"Getting *out* isn't the problem," Dave noted. "Getting down to the surface isn't a problem either, except we're gonna burn up first, or go *splat* when this thing hits. We need to get dirtside *alive* somehow, but-"

"Jarrett! Czajka!" Jates called, a noticeable tremble in his voice. Whatever was wrong with the Verd-Kris, it was getting worse. "What is your status?"

"We found Nert," Shauna responded.

"Outstanding," the translator not only put his words into human language, it also perfectly conveyed his sarcasm. "Did you find a way out of here?"

"No," Dave replied. "Not anything that doesn't end with each of us in a pine box. We can't- pine *box*," he stared at Nert, mouth gaping open. "Nert, I hope you know your way around in those access tubes."

When the *Big Mac* cracked into two pieces, the break was actually not at the exact spot where the X-ray laser had sliced through the ship's stout structural frames, instead it was a dozen meters aft of the damage, where the frames from two sections of the ship had been attached together. The long forward section that housed quarters for the landing force and the dropship launch and recovery bays was the larger piece, while the aft section with reactors, engines, jump drive and most of the ship's weapons was by far more massive. When the ship's AI detected that the ship had been gravely damaged, and it was unable to contact the ship's command crew, the AI determined that there was no possibility of getting the broken aft section up to jump altitude. Or even getting the aft section into a stable orbit. It ran through a list of pre-approved options for the highly-unusual situation, and acted automatically. All three reactors vented their plasma and shut down as best they could. The jump drive capacitor modules began ejecting so they could race up away from the planet at escape velocity, or begin discharging their stored energies into space. If the capacitors fell out of orbit and struck the surface near the landing force, the *Mecdunnue*'s corpse might kill its own people.

Burning thrusters furiously, the AI tried as best it could to steer the aft section to a splash-down in the ocean, to the west of the continent that was the primary landing zone. There was no hope of getting any level of control over the forward section, which was already falling faster because its greater surface area was digging into the thin air. The AI could not contact even subsidiary systems aboard the forward section, it had to settle for providing what guidance it could to the dropships that were racing down to the surface.

When it felt the aft section begin to tumble as the shattered hulk bit into the air, the AI amused itself by calculating a circular area of probability for impact, for the spots where the ship's two tumbling pieces would smack into the surface.

As it reflected on its impending death, the AI thought to itself *Well, at least this will be interesting.*

Then it thought, *I hate this job.*


Derek sat up taller in his seat to look over the console out the front windows. The view he was seeing was actually projected onto the inside of the composite material of the windows, which had gone opaque to protect the Dodo's occupants from the unfiltered light of the local star. What he saw was the planet below, with the sky a thin, bluish-black line across the horizon.

Most of what he saw was green and brown, the colors of the world they were invading. That was what he saw, because they were so close to the surface, it felt like he could reach out and touch it.

Sinking back into the seat, he whispered to Irene. "Out of the frying pan, into the fire."

"We're alive," she whispered back.

"Alive? Yeah. We're also in a dropship with no engines, one landing gear door that won't fully close, a belly shield projector offline, and," he jabbed a finger at the forward displays, "we're at such a low altitude that I can *see my freakin' house.*"

"It's not optimal," she conceded.

"Bonsu? Striebich? What's our status?" Perkins called out from the doorway, pulling herself in and pulling down the jumpseat on the bulkhead to strap herself in.

Irene glanced back through the open door to the Dodo's cabin. Rows of anxious faces looked back at her expectantly. They knew something was very wrong, all the drop practices and simulations had the Dodo burning its main engines hard to cancel its forward velocity, followed by a sickening sensation as gravity pulled them down. Their dropship had been using thrusters only, and everyone cringed whenever a piece of debris PINGED off the hull. One tiny piece of something had penetrated the hull, causing a shrieking leak that a soldier had plugged manually using a patch kit. "It's not great, Ma'am," Irene reported truthfully. "Engines are busted, and we pranged the tail assembly on the way out. If we get into the atmosphere, we'll have trouble with yaw control without the tail."

"We can compensate with thrusters," Derek suggested. "Until thruster fuel runs out. There's a leak somewhere, we transferred the remaining fuel into the reserve tank, but there's still a leak between the tank and the portside thrusters. We will lose more fuel to leaks than we are able to consume."

"Bottom line this for me," Perkins suppressed an eyeroll. She knew pilots could talk all day about geeky details. "Can we make orbit?"

"Not possible," Irene shook her head. "Thrusters don't have the power, even if we had that much fuel. Which we don't."

"We're going down, then?"

"Ah," Derek shot a look at Irene before he risked dredging up an argument they had just concluded. "If we can attain enough speed and orient the ship just right, it might be possible for us to skip off the top of the atmosphere," he used a hand to pantomime an object skipping across the surface of a pond.

"We *can't* do that," Irene insisted.

"We can't?" Perkins looked from one pilot to another. "Or we shouldn't?"

"It's-" Derek began.

"We *talked* about this." Irene didn't want to rehash the argument.

"Explain 'skipping'," Perkins ordered.

"It's like this," Derek turned in his seat to face their CO. "If we come in at too steep an angle," his hand, palm open, gestured straight downward. "We could get crushed by the Gee forces, or the wings will snap off from the dynamic pressure, or we, well," he shrugged. "We just burn up. But if we come in at too shallow an angle, we bounce off the top of the atmosphere, like skipping a stone across a pond."

"That would push us up into a stable orbit?"

"No. The opposite. We would bounce up for a while, then come back down, skip again, maybe a third time, then we're going in. Each time we hit the air, we lose velocity, that degrades the orbit."

Perkins looked at Derek with confusion. "Then, why would we even consider this?"

"Each bounce buys time for us, for a rescue bird to link up."

"Oh," Perkins considered that.

"It is a *long* shot, Ma'am," Irene added. "Problem is, the longer we're up here, the longer we're exposed. The decoy drones accompanying us will not skip, so we would be all alone, it would be obvious to targeting systems on the ground that we are a legit dropship."

Perkins shook her head. "I don't like that idea."

"Plus," Irene pressed her point with a look at Derek. "Trying to get into the shallow angle for a skip would use up all our thruster fuel. We would have nothing left for attitude control when we do go down, and we will."

"*Unless*," Derek insisted, "a SAR bird picks us up. Colonel, it's a judgment call."

Emily Perkins tugged her straps loose so she had a better view of the tactical display between the two pilot seats. Just then, something softly *pinged* off the hull. "No go. We can't count on a rescue, it's too kinetic up here. You agree, Bonsu?"

He looked uncomfortable, avoiding her eyes. "That's not the only factor we have to consider, Ma'am. Irene, tell her."

Irene took a breath, and kept one eye on her console while she spoke. "We don't know the extent of the damage to the tail. We do know one of the landing gear doors won't close all the way. One of the shield generators on the belly is offline. During entry, plasma could burn through the landing gear bay into the cabin, and, we would all be crispy critters."

"That's why I mentioned the skip option," Derek added.

"Hell," Perkins groaned. "Is there any way someone can go outside, get the gear doors unfouled, inspect the tail?"

"No," Derek was dismayed at the question. "We are already in the atmosphere." The Dodo rocked gently side to side to emphasize his point. "Anyone going outside would be on a one-way trip. I don't think they could even hold on long enough to do anything useful."

"Outstanding," Perkins laid the sarcasm on thick. Making critical decisions without enough information was why UNEF-HQ paid her the big bucks, she thought sourly. "It is a judgment call. What is *your* judgment?"

"Ma'am," Derek looked his CO straight in the eye. "I'm a pilot. I trust my skills over any hope for a rescue."

"But? I sensed a 'but' in there."

"But," Derek admitted. "I'm a pilot, I am *always* going to trust my own skills. Maybe in this case," he shared a look with Irene. "We are not the right people to ask."

"*I* can't fly this thing," Perkins was a bit exasperated at not getting a straight answer. "Shit. The two of you hovered a Buzzard while we set up a drill rig on Paradise, and you figured out how to program a jump when the *Toaster*'s crew got killed. Ok," she sat back in the jump seat and tugged the straps tighter. "Take us down. Are we aiming for a landing zone?"

"Other than not in the water, no," Irene replied. "We're in freefall, Ma'am."

Perkins grimaced. "Freefall? Are you talking just about *us* right now or this whole damned operation?"

Irene shared a look with Derek, then replied with "I'm going to withhold comment on that."

"Freefall, huh? That doesn't sound good. Do you have *any* control?"

"When we get low enough to use the aerodynamic surfaces, maybe," Irene tapped the console. "Physics is going to determine where we are, when we have effective flight controls."

"And if we survive," Derek muttered helpfully.

"Have you tried asking Physics nicely?" Perkins suggested.

Irene snorted. "Physics is a *bitch*, Ma'am. There's no reasoning with her."

To Dani's surprise, the patches she applied to the hull breaches held during the descent, whatever the Ruhar used for Fix-A-Flat was a quality product. If she ever got back to Earth, she planned to sell that product, using infomercials where she would paddle down river rapids in a boat made of window screens coated with the alien material.

Or maybe she should get someone else to paddle the boat.

To no one's surprise, not all of the hastily-applied patches held together. The worst hull breach was the last one, which hit the dropship near the bottom front of the cabin on the right side, flew across the cabin on a diagonal and killed the soldier seated next to the platoon leader. Whatever that piece of debris was, it was larger than the tiny dots that had punctured the hull like a shotgun blast. Plugging that hole took more than a can of Fix-a-flat, the Verds had cleared out of the seats where the debris entered, and applied a hard plate over the hole. The plate was backed by a pad of nanogel that was supposed to flow into and over the breach, securing the plate in place and hardening tougher than steel. Dani had never seen the emergency repair plate being tested, but while they were on Fresno, Derek Bonsu had told a story about seeing one in use. A gunship had come limping back to base, shot full of holes and trailing smoke. One of the turbine engines had survived only because incoming shrapnel had bounced off a repair plate, a patch that had been applied when the gunship was struck by enemy fire that morning. Derek related that the ground crew had swapped out several turbine blades, applied more patches that had the aircraft looking like it belonged in a junkyard, and sent it back into service.

Dani could testify that the repair plate was tough, because when it did tear loose, it was in one piece. Unfortunately, the spacecraft's skin around the hole had buckled in the intense heat and vibration of plunging down through the atmosphere, and the plate was knocked inward with enough force to crush an empty seat on the other side of the cabin. Instantly, the cabin was filled with a hazy pink fog, as plasma created by superheated air around the dropship's nose and belly flowed into the hole, burning its way through the inner hull lining. A jet like a pinkish-orange cutting torch surged out of the hole, reaching for a pair of soldiers seated on the opposite wall of the cabin.

The dropship lurched to the right and began vibrating even worse than before. The flowing plasma torch sputtered, dispersing then regrowing in strength, blinking on and off. The platoon leader was shouting commands that Dani couldn't understand, the plasma was interfering with transmissions over the command net. Some of the soldiers blessedly knew what they were supposed to do, the two who had nearly been barbecued slapped free of the restraints holding them in the seats and rolled away, just before a surge of plasma scorched those seats and charred the cabin wall where they had been sitting.

It was total chaos. The dropship pitched nose down and spiraled to the right, Dani guessed the pilots were trying to take the thermal load off the damaged area and for a split-second, she marveled that her mind could process esoteric concepts like 'thermal load' in such a desperate situation. One of the soldiers who had gotten out of his seat was thrown off balance when the nose dipped, the maneuver sent him tumbling back toward the blazing lightsaber of plasma that stabbed into the cabin. Without thinking, Dani punched the button to loosen the straps around her upper body and reached forward to grab onto and *heave* the soldier toward her. Lizards were big and the armor made the soldier extra heavy, her own powered suit compensated, using too much power assist as the soldier slammed into her, bouncing her helmet off the cabin wall. Stunned, her arms flopped uselessly, the soldier would have broken free except her suit's computer guessed what she wanted, pulling her powered suit arms together and locking the errant soldier into her lap.

"Thank-" The soldier coughed. "Thank you," *she* said in a distinctly female Kristang voice.

"Ah," Dani grunted, seeing that the person in her lap was indeed an alien woman with the rank of Vist, roughly equivalent to a Specialist in the US Army. "Hold still," she ordered, wriggling her shoulders out of the way, to let the seat straps creepily crawl to wrap around both of them. Well, Dani thought, at least I won't die alone.

Her next thought was, *damn* this freakin' lizard is heavy! Even with the armor she wore, Dani could feel pressure on her thighs. If she lived through the descent to set boots on the ground, she would suggest that maybe the Verds should do more aerobics and less eating? If I develop deep-vein thrombosis, she told herself, I am *totally* suing this airline.

The strobe-light effect of the plasma jet was distracting and making her nauseous, the visor of her helmet couldn't completely compensate for the harsh light, or the suit's sensors couldn't get in sync with the pulsing of the plasma fire. She was trying to manually darken the faceplate when the strobe suddenly cut off.

Her instant thought was, am I dead?

"Good work," she heard platoon leader Zolatus say, interrupting her brief musing that the afterlife was *very* disappointing. "We will have to hope that holds. The pilots tell me they can't hold this course without melting the portside wing, they need to swing us back. Everyone, stay where you are." There was a brief pause. "Captain Grace, can you hold Vist Lohduvan?"

Dani guessed that somehow, the Verds had gotten the hole plugged again. Two more soldiers were showing orange in her status report, they must have incurred damage to their suits while getting a new plate in position over the hole. "Yes, we're good."

"My rifle is damaged," Lohduvan reported, ignoring her precarious perch on the human woman's lap. "I was not able to bring it with-"

"You can get a new rifle from the forward locker when we touch down," Zolatus said, with a very human-like '*you cannot be serious about this shit*' tone to his voice.

Dani felt the dropship's nose swing back toward the left, and the vibration smoothed out somewhat, becoming an intermittent shaking rather than a constant rattling of her teeth. For the next twelve minutes, they fell constantly without any drastic maneuvers and it may have been her imagination, but the whistling shriek of air rushing past the spacecraft seemed to be lower in pitch. If that meant they were slowing down, it was a good thing.

The spacecraft suddenly lurched to the right and down steeply, and the BZZZT, BZZZT sizzling crackle of defensive maser cannon pulses blared in her ears.


Irene had the Dodo's nose pitched up at thirty-two degrees, the angle suggested by the Pilot Operating Handbook for an unpowered descent in a ship that had suffered damage, and had potentially compromised thermal protection.

The POH did not also suggest the crew of such a damaged ship kiss their asses goodbye, that was sort of implied.

"Thirty-two?" Irene asked, wishing Perkins was not seated behind her. It wasn't good for passengers to hear the pilots expressing doubts.

"That's a good compromise," Derek agreed.

Emily Perkins actually did not want to know what they were debating, both because she couldn't affect the outcome, and because she didn't want to distract them. But then Bonsu explained anyway.

"We're going to take more of the heat load on the nose," he said without turning to look at her. "The shield generators there are working fine. Our angle of attack for an unpowered entry can only vary by four degrees either way, so we plan to control drag by-"

Irene interrupted. The Colonel didn't need to hear geeky details, especially when they didn't have time to fully explain. "We've got this, Ma'am. Everyone should be prepared to bail out."

"We can't jump from orbit with these parachutes," Perkins automatically reached up to feel the emergency parachute that was attached to the top of her pack.

"No," Irene was uncomfortable because if she and Derek had to bail out, their seats had parachutes that could bring them down safely from orbit, if needed. Their passengers had no such luxury. "If we get near the ground and can't find a landing site, we all need to be ready to jump."

"Got it. Colter!" Perkins called the Staff Sergeant to alert him.


The Dodo's gentle swaying became a steady vibration, and Perkins withheld comment when the two pilots reached across the console to hold hands for a moment. She wished she knew whether Dave Czajka's own dropship had gotten out of the dying *Big Mac*. There was so much electromagnetic interference flooding space above the planet that Derek had only been able to determine their former mother ship was in two pieces, and falling out of orbit. The sky was full of dropships, decoys, wildly maneuvering starships and debris.

It was best to push Dave from her mind for the moment. She couldn't do anything to help him, and she might be able to help the people in her own spacecraft. The professional thing to do was to focus on the immediate task and worry about Dave later.

The professional thing to do was also impossible to do. How do you tell your mind to *not* think of something, without thinking of that very thing? Knowing that she might not survive the descent, she recorded a message to Dave, and another for the team. The datacell of her suit might be recovered even if she plunged from orbit, it was in its own armored housing.

Emily recorded the message to Dave twice, erasing the original version. Then she erased the second version, and started over.

"Ma'am?" Irene cut into her thoughts.

"Striebich?"

"You're going to hear us launching decoys, don't want you to think the hull is breaking up. The decoys the ship assigned to us have broken away to cover other ships." She didn't add 'ships with a better chance of survival'. "Right now, we're hoping the Wurgalan will see us as just another piece of falling debris, so we're only launching two of our eight decoys. They will look like pieces that broke off our hull."

"We are saving the other six," Derek explained without needing to, "because once we start maneuvering away from a purely ballistic flight path, the Wurgalan will know we're not just a falling chunk of the ship."

"Got it," Perkins didn't have anything useful to say, and she wanted to get back to recording a message. Except nothing came to her mind.

"Missile warning!" Derek shouted. "Launching three decoys," he stated without discussing the plan with Irene. There were three *thump* sounds as the drones were spat out of their tubes.

"Just one missile," Irene gently banked the falling Dodo. "Small, looks like a MANPAD," she added. That got her seriously pissed off. The Dodo had come through the worst part of atmospheric entry intact, but in poor condition. The jammed landing gear door had been a vulnerability, no matter how they pitched the nose to take heat off the spacecraft's belly. Something broke away and internal sensors under the rear cabin reported a spike to six hundred degrees, then it mysteriously cooled. Derek thought maybe the door had broken loose and gotten pushed up inside the landing gear bay, plus the tank of fire suppression chemicals was bleeding dry rapidly. What mattered was the incident caused failure of the primary roll control system on the starboard side, and the backup system was operating only intermittently. Derek had to use thrusters to keep the craft from rolling on its side or turning sideways, and to make matters worse, their ballistic trajectory was taking the Dodo out over the ocean. With Irene providing guidance, Derek had used the thrusters as sparingly as he could, adjusting their course randomly left and right, but overall curving around to keep them over land.

The Dodo was still falling, but at only Mach 4 and slowing as air resistance dragged at the hull. Irene had been scanning the surface for a place to set down, with Derek flying, and she had begun to let herself hope they might come through the disaster alive. Their chances of survival were actually somewhat better because of the unpowered descent; they were way off target for the planned landing zone, and that had them over territory that was mostly uninhabited. Most of the Wurgalan air defenses were behind them, busy attempting to discern decoys from incoming troop-carrying dropships, and intercepting when they had a firing solution. Even if the air defense network detected their Dodo was flying in a controlled manner rather than falling like debris, one crippled dropship far off course would not be a priority.

Then, they had the bad fortune of attracting the attention of some asshole on the ground, who was tired of carrying a missile around, and wanted to shoot at something for real. A single shoulder-fired missile, or fired from wherever the octopus-like Wurgalan carried their missiles, would not usually be a major threat to the Dodo. The high altitude and Mach 4 speed made an intercept difficult for the missile, and the dropship's defensive maser cannons could usually destroy the threat at a safe distance.

The situation was anything but usual. The spacecraft was falling and slowing as it fell. The worst problem was that with the maser turret in the tail offline, the pilots had to keep flying *toward* the missile so the turret under the Dodo's chin had line-of-sight to the incoming weapon.

"Shit," Derek muttered to himself. "Babe," he said unselfconsciously, "this pig doesn't want to fly straight."

"Kill the turn, kill the turn," she warned. "The port wing is masking the cannon." The little missile's smart brain was guiding it so the target's maser cannons would have the least time to intercept.

"I'm trying," Derek banked to the right and the Dodo shuddered violently. "It doesn't like that. I think the starboard elevon is busted."

"We need to-" Irene started to say as she concentrated on the cannon.

"I *know*. Listen, I'm going to do a three-sixty to port, swing the nose around that way."

"Do it quick."

Derek performed the turn quickly as he could, there was something wrong with the port wing that made it want to dip, and if the roll continued out of control, they would flip upside down. Not daring to breathe, and guiding the controls with his fingertips, Derek got the Dodo in a complete circle back to their original heading. "I can't hold it here," he had the craft on the feathery edge of a roll, the starboard wing not cooperating. Without the aerodynamic surfaces of the tail assembly, the Dodo kept wanting to yaw and roll to the left.

"One second," Irene pleaded while the point-defense system reacquired the target. "One second."

Derek kept his right fingertips on the controls while with his left hand, he lightly touched the bottom of his seat, using those fingertips to judge the spacecraft's vibration. The autopilot was offline and the instruments unreliable, he had to fly literally by feel. He was not overly concerned about the strength of the vibration coming from the starboard wing, what worried him was when the vibration sharply grew in intensity, when the pattern neared the wing's natural frequency. The wing's structure was tough and there were vibration dampeners, but the wing was damaged and he didn't know how much more it would take. The Dodo began another turn to port and he held it on a knife edge between total loss of control and potential loss of the wing. "That is a *long* one second," he warned as he kept one eye on the Time To Intercept counter on the display. It was showing the missile would strike within eight seconds.

The maser cannon should have been firing.

The point-defense was not calculating a firing solution. Irene thought the only way to fix it was to reset the damned thing but they didn't have time for that. She tried manually guiding the cannon's primary sensor to *show* the stupid machine what to aim at. No good. The system flashed a 'RESET' alarm and before she could cancel it, the computer began a soft reboot.

"Honey," she looked at Derek, stricken. "I'm so sorry."

Three.

Two.

One.

*Impact.*

Derek had to put both hands on the console and allow a bank to port, as the Dodo was shoved sideways across the sky. The roll continued, rolling the spacecraft briefly upside down at Mach 2 before snapping upright without Derek doing anything. "It hit one of the *decoys*," he said quietly, surprised at how calm he felt. "I got good news and bad news," he added. "We're no longer in an uncontrolled turn to port."

"That's the good news?" Irene asked, a bit disoriented to still be alive.

"Yeah. Bad news is, I got no yaw control at all, other than the trim tabs. Wherever we're setting down, it better be straight ahead."

"Bonsu?" Perkins asked, also not believing their good fortune. And not trusting it either. She could see the point-defense system was in reset mode. "Can we put some space between us and the shooter, before they reload?" Intel from the Ruhar said the standard Man Portable Air Defense missile used by the Wurgalan was a single-shot weapon, but doctrine for its use required one person to launch, one to act as a spotter, and a third to carry a reload. Air-defense missile teams typically carried four missiles. The Mavericks didn't know if the enemy had expended any missiles before, but Perkins wasn't counting on it.

"Doing the best we can, Ma'am," Irene mentally urged the point-defense system to finish resetting, it seemed to be stuck in a loop.

Derek glanced at the balky system and made a decision. "Time to get outta here," he said, adjusting the pitch so the nose again pointed upward. The Dodo shuddered and he felt himself being pressed down in the seat.

"We're flying at Mach two point five," Perkins reminded her pilot.

"I'm bleeding off the airspeed in a climb," Derek explained. "Your combat skinsuits are good for an eject below Mach one point two. Altitude is not an issue."

"He's right, Colonel," Irene agreed, reluctantly giving up on the point-defense computer. "We can't trust the belly jets to set us down anyway."

"Got it," Perkins replied. "Colter! We are *leaving*, get ready to dump the supplies overboard first."

"Uh," Irene cautioned. "We don't know if the back ramp will open, the tail is damaged." Without opening the back ramp, there was no way to get the pallets of supplies out.

Perkins didn't care. "When the time comes, blow the explosive bolts that hold the ramp. We don't need the ramp, do we?"

"Oh," Irene felt her cheeks blush. With the burn-through in the rear cabin, she didn't know how much of their supplies would be useful, or how many still had working parachutes. Maybe it didn't matter, she told herself. More falling objects cluttering the sky would make it more difficult for a missile to track the Dodo.

With the nose pitched up at sixty degrees, airspeed bled off rapidly. Derek would have increased the pitch further, but the wings began to oscillate in a Dutch roll and he had to push the nose down to cancel it.

"Mach One point four," he read. "Get ready."

"Missile warning!" Irene reported. "Point-defense system is still in reset. Launching our last three decoys." *Thump, thump, thump*, they were away.

Perkins unstrapped from the jumpseat. "Time to intercept?"

Derek knew the real question she was asking. "We'll drop below Mach One point two, eighteen seconds before the missile hits us. We are at," he paused for the airspeed indicator to scroll down through the mark. "One point three now."

"Too close," Irene declared. "I'm blowing the ramp now, the drag will slow us down." Keying the open channel, she warned "Hang on, everyone!"

The Dodo bucked, the nose pointing up then down, and bucking continued. "I can't hold it!" Derek announced through clenched teeth. Every time a parachute yanked a supply pallet out the back, the spacecraft's center of gravity changed significantly. "Colonel, go go *go*!" Derek shouted. "I'm losing control."

Perkins was second-to-last out of the cabin, gesturing for Jesse Colter to go before her, but he shoved her in front of him. "I promised Dave to keep you safe!" he shouted, then she was out the door into the still-supersonic airstream and so disoriented by being battered around that she couldn't speak. The suit automatically tucked her into a fetal position and went rigid to protect her, flashing orange icons in the visor that was shaking so violently she couldn't read any of it. She had a momentary glimpse of the Dodo's torn airframe, before she flew through smoke trailing behind the doomed craft and lost sight of it.

# CHAPTER THIRTEEN

"You first!" Irene raised her voice to be heard over the shriek of wind swirling around the cabin, a hand poised on the ejection strap. Expecting an argument, she opened her mouth to repeat herself when a nanofiber shell inflated around her and the seat, and it rocketed upward.

Derek exited the Dodo a split-second later, having remotely triggered the ejection sequence for both seats. He hoped Irene would be pushed free of the doomed dropship first, knowing the ship's computer would make that decision much faster than he could think.

A small propellant charge pushed his chair upward and away from the Dodo at the same time the ship's nose dipped to get itself out of the way. The shell-enclosed chair hit the supersonic airstream like a brick wall, smashing Derek forward against straps that widened to hold him firmly without cutting through him. The helmet had automatically attached to the seat back before ejection, preventing him from whiplash and pads inside the helmet inflated so his skull did not bounce around in the bucket. Physics being what it is, the squishy gray matter of his brain was still trying to decelerate inside his skull and so he blacked out for a moment. When he came back to awareness, spots swam in his vision and he had to squint and concentrate on the icons displayed in the helmet visor.

Airspeed Mach Zero Point Seven, about eight hundred kilometers per hour, and airspeed was dropping off rapidly. The seat had deployed a drogue chute above to slow his fall, it would not fully expand into a balloon until he was closer to the ground.

The ground. The planet's surface was fifteen kilometers below, spread out like a satellite image. Dark green forest was interrupted only by small lakes and ponds, with occasional glimpses of a river winding its way under the tree canopy. To the west on the horizon was the unbroken blue of the ocean. Isolated white clouds dotted the view below him like cotton candy, while most of the sky was what pilots referred to as CAVU: Ceiling And Visibility Unlimited.

It was a fine day for flying.

So much for sightseeing.

In his visor, he saw an icon for Irene's ejection seat and the icon was green, everything was nominal with her. She was half a klick to the south and slightly below him, seen only through synthetic vision, because a stealth field generator under the seats was wrapping light around their shells. The generator took a lot of power and the powercells were draining quickly, that was another reason why they were still falling at high speed. The computers controlling the seats wanted to get them on the ground before the stealth field failed.

Other than Irene, who was hidden from view, the sky was filled with objects above, below and around him. The largest and most visible object was the Dodo, what was left of it. The dropship must have been struck by the second missile after they ejected, the portside wing was missing along with several meters of cabin in that area. Derek only got a quick view of the damage before the spinning craft flipped away. It was spiraling down nose-first in a death dive, pieces of the hull tearing away as it fell. His hopes were dashed when he checked the map for the projected impact site and saw it was eight kilometers away from where the missiles had been launched from; the Dodo was not going to splat down on top of its tormentors.

Besides the battered dropship, there were cargo containers falling, with and without parachutes. Some of the containers had broken open, material was spilling from them as the containers tumbled below his altitude. More importantly, he saw other objects that his synthetic vision identified as the Dodo's former passengers. Icons displayed *Perkins, Emily LTC* and *Colter, Jesse SSGT* among others. All those icons were green, and they had also deployed drogue chutes to control their fall.

"Hey, Babe?" He took a sip from the water spout inside his helmet. "Honey?"

"I'm here," Irene replied in a slightly peevish tone. "I said, *you* first."

"The computer is smarter than us, we have to trust it. That's what we're trained to do, remember?"

"Fine." She was silent for a moment. "That was a good dropship. It got all of us here alive."

"It was a pig," Derek commented. He never enjoyed flying the big, bulky Dodo, especially not in an atmosphere. "But a *good* pig."

"Where are those assholes?"

He knew she meant the Wurgalan missile team. "Don't worry," he checked their last reported location against the projected landing sites for them and the platoon. "Our chutes know about the threat, they're dropping us down behind that ridge, fourteen klicks from the bad guys. Plenty of space to run, it looks like there's a river between us and the squids. We will link up with- Shit! Another missile launch!"

"*Damn* it!"

Derek knew it was very unlikely that he or Irene had been targeted, and the Wurgalan could not be so incredibly stupid as to waste a missile on the flaming dropship. The target for the missile must be a cargo container. Or it could be a group of soldiers.

Before Derek could contact her, Perkins recognized the threat and transmitted a burst message by laserlink. *Spread out*, she ordered and she must have directed that action in the squad command network, for soldiers had begun moving apart even before she sent the message.

Drogue chutes widened or folded so some soldiers fell slower or faster, giving the formation greater vertical separation. At the same time, chutes steered the soldiers apart. The soldier closest to the ground was now at fourteen kilometers altitude, a concern for Derek because there was plenty of time for the Wurgalan to launch a fourth missile, if they had one.

He tracked the missile's wavering course. At first, it appeared to be locked in on a cargo container, then it veered away abruptly. The decoys! One of the decoys had survived and was still active, Perkins must have directed it to cover the formation of paratroopers. Derek kicked himself for not thinking of that. Damn it, he told himself, decoys are the responsibility of the pilots, even if they are no longer aboard the aircraft.

For a blessed nine seconds, the missile homed in on the decoy, which was blasting out electromagnetic energy to mimic the jamming pattern of a dropship. Then, the missile turned away. Derek's heart fell as he saw it curving around toward the defenseless paratroopers. The Wurgalan must be manually steering the weapon, directing it toward a target he could only guess at. Surely they would not use a missile against one soldier, but if the warhead was set on fragmentation mode, its shrapnel could explode in the center of the formation and kill or injure many people.

Derek held his breath, feeling guilty that he was safely out of range. The missile was below him and had flattened its trajectory, flying straight at whatever it had been directed to hit.

Then it wobbled in the air, either receiving confused guidance or having lost lock on its target. Derek could not understand how that was possible, the skinsuits of the soldiers had all activated their chameleonware to match the color or the background sky, but the missile was hammering the area with active sensor pulses that would make the falling paratroopers stand out clearly against the sky. Jerking violently to the left and down, the missile streaked in and scored a direct hit on a cargo container, blowing burning chunks of debris in every direction.

"What the f-" Derek heard Irene say with a gasp.

"Thank God for small favors, huh?" There was a tremble in his voice, relief that no one had been killed. Although he saw icons for both *Rivera, Jose SPC* and *Ghatak, Sawanad CPT* light up in yellow, they must have been struck by debris. Any serious injury would have been shown by an orange icon, and their parachutes were still working properly.

Before Irene could reply, Derek recorded a message and sent it in a burst via laserlink. *Let's cut the chatter*, his message read. It was unlikely the Wurgalan could detect the tightbeam laserlinks between their ejection seats, but there was no sense taking the risk, and regulations forbid extraneous chatter.

They fell silently through eight thousand meters, and the formation of paratroopers began to draw together again so the group would not be widely scattered when they landed. That made sense, and Derek saw his seat's chute was steering him toward the same area, away from where the burning Dodo had already bored a crater in the forest, and away from where cargo containers without parachutes had smashed down through the tree canopy. The parachute computers were smart, they-

Missile launch.

Jesse tried to control his breathing, distracting himself by checking and re-checking all his gear and the status of everyone in his squad. Ghatak and Rivera would be all right, their skinsuits were already conducting repairs. Ghatak had a powercell out of commission, that would be a minor issue for-

Missile launch.

The squids' air defense team did have four missiles, or there was more than one team in the area. With the ground so close, there wasn't much airspace to play with for spreading out the formation again. They were bunched up too tightly. Ruhar doctrine called for paratroops to come together during the terminal phase of the descent and once again, Jesse was thinking maybe the hamster' military planners were *not* the experts on every subject. It made more sense to remain spread out when faced with an anti-air threat, land and then assemble on the ground. He would make a note to mention that in the after-action report.

If he lived that long.


"Hold *still*, damn it!" Jesse spoke to his suit computer, knowing the stupid thing probably wasn't listening. He had already engaged the stabilizer function of the parachute, overriding both the chute's own intention to swing him away from the incoming missile, and Perkins's attempt to take control of his chute.

"Colter?!" Perkins called, incredulous. "What the *hell* are you-"

"Trust me no time to explain," he blurted out, cutting off the speaker. He didn't need the distraction. Allowing the chute to guide him away wasn't going to keep him alive anyway if the missile targeted him. He was betting that whatever glitch had caused the last missile to waste itself on a cargo container, the squids had fixed that problem. They were probably guiding their last missile in manually, flying it to the center of the formation and detonating the warhead in wide-dispersal fragmentation mode. While that would not kill everyone, Jesse did not like his odds, and he didn't like the odds for his people. *His* people. The Lieutenant might be in command of the platoon, but to Jesse the soldiers in the squad were *his* people, his responsibility.

With the parachute reluctantly having formed itself into a balloon and keeping him as motionless in the sky as it could, he unslung his rifle and checked the scope was synced to the sensors of his helmet. Selecting explosive-tipped rounds, he took a calming breath, sighted on the incoming missile, and tried a trick he had seen during training on Paradise.

He and Shauna had been visiting another UNEF battalion, for some purpose he couldn't remember, and on the firing range, a Ruhar was playing around with one of the Kristang rifles that were standard issue for the Alien Legion. The Ruhar military brass was disdainful of the rifles favored by their historic enemy, but the rank and file Ruhar soldiers were not so dismissive of the alien weapon's capabilities. Almost as importantly, the Ruhar they met simply enjoyed blowing shit up on the firing range, and was demonstrating a trick he had learned from his people's weapons development group.

The rifles used by the Legion were Kristang, from the large stock of weapons the Ruhar had captured over the years, but the ammunition was manufactured by the Ruhar. Even in training, ammo was expended at a rate that would rapidly deplete the captured supply, and the Ruhar thought Kristang rifle ammunition was unreliable compared to their standards. In building the interface so Kristang rifles and their rounds could communicate with Ruhar skinsuits, the technical team experimented with adding features, not all of which went into production.

One feature that was put into production was a modification to the proximity fuses of the rounds equipped with explosive tips. That ability was found to be nearly useless in the field, because the sensors crammed into the round's nose were too crude to detect their location while traveling at high speed. What the Ruhar on the firing range demonstrated was how to use the skinsuit's own sensors, to direct rounds in flight when to explode. The demonstration consisted of a drone flying across the firing range, coming at the Ruhar. It was impossible to hit the drone directly, even with ammo that could deflect twelve degrees in any direction based on guidance from the user's suit. The drones were simply too fast and maneuverable, dodging around too quickly to keep track of by eye. After the first drone flew right over his head and registered a simulated 'kill', the Ruhar changed tactics for the next drone. He designated the explosive-tipped rounds to detonate in front of the drone's predicted flight path, and a string of explosions lit up the air. That drone survived, as did the next two, but the third flew into a hail of shrapnel and fell out of the sky. The Ruhar explained the technology was still being perfected, and neither Jesse nor Shauna had an opportunity to try the new capability before the Mavericks shipped out.

Now he was trying it for the first time, for real. The menu for directing the proximity fuses was buried several frustrating levels down, requiring successive eyeclicks in the visor. Then the proper screen appeared and Jesse used his helmet's targeting system to paint the incoming enemy missile, still rising from the tree canopy and racing toward the falling paratroopers.

Jesse reminded himself to breathe evenly and synced the rifle's stabilizer to his suit, then selected full auto and lightly pressed the trigger. Rounds flew out, seeking the enemy weapon. None of the rounds were tracers and they didn't need to be, the synthetic vision of his visor tracked the bullets in flight.

They began exploding to the side and in front of the missile, but none of the fragments were connecting. As he had seen with the drones on the firing range, intercepting an object in flight was a numbers game and he simply didn't have enough ordnance being delivered downrange. "Squad!" He called over the network, while simultaneously eyeclicking to slave their rifle guidance to his suit and slapping a new magazine into his own rifle. "Explosive tips, fire when ready!"

There wasn't time to explain and it didn't matter anyway, the squad likely thought he was trying to hit a bullet with a bullet and they knew it was an extremely long shot. They also didn't see a problem with trying to do *something* rather than hanging limply in the sky as easy targets. Rifles barked, two, four, six, then the entire squad opened up on the missile. Jesse couldn't tell whether his suit's targeting system could detect, track and guide that many rounds, he didn't even know if that data was available to him. In his synthetic vision, a hail of highly kinetic rounds lanced out toward the incoming missile and began exploding in flight, forming a wall of shrapnel in front of-

The missile exploded, adding its own fragmentation warhead to the chaos. In the squad network, Jesse saw two icons turn orange. One was the previously injured *Rivera, Jose SPC* who clearly should have stayed in his bunk that morning, though his bunk was in a fiery fall toward the planet along with the rest of the *Big Mac*. The other injured was *Zheng, Chao SPC* and that soldier's icon was orange flashing to red. Jesse cursed in his helmet as he felt himself drop like a stone.

Perkins called him, having used her command codes to take control of the staff sergeant's parachute. "I don't know how you did that, Colter, but get your ass on the ground pronto. We don't know if the Wurgalan have other missiles. Also," she added in a softer tone, "good work."

"Right, Ma'am." He agreed shakily, his blood flooded with adrenaline. When the balloon above him reformed and began directing him toward a designated landing zone, he didn't argue. He did check his ammo supply. Six rounds left in the magazine. Better swap it with a full one. Having nearly expended two magazines before he hit the ground was not a good sign, and made him glad he had stuffed four extra mags in his pack. When his personal supply of ammo ran out, he had to hope some of their cargo containers made it to the ground safely, because the next resupply from orbit might not happen for a very long time.

In her ejection seat's aeroshell high above, Irene was also shaking, but not from fear or the excitement of combat. She was *angry*. The enemy had shot at their starship, shot at their dropship, even blown up a cargo container in the air. It was war, the Legion was invading a world that didn't belong to them, she understood it was legit that the squids would fight back.

But using an anti-aircraft missile against troops who were only parachuting to the ground after bailing out of their dropship, after that dropship had forced its way out of a broken starship, that didn't seem fair! Sure, once the paratroopers set boots on the ground, they would be earnestly trying to kill the Wurgalan or at least enforce their will on the enemy. Logic didn't matter. The troops falling toward the ground were *her* people, regardless that they were infantry and she was aviation.

Two of the paratroopers were injured and their parachutes apparently damaged, they were showing orange icons and drifting off course, falling toward the enemy. The other soldiers were unable to match the flight path of the injured people, their parachutes had committed them to a particular landing site and it was too late to change the parameters.

"Derek," Irene called over the laserlink. "We need to do something."

"We do?" He asked, surprised. "I was think- I was thinking the same thing. Zheng and Rivera are going to come down on the other side of the river from the rest of the platoon." He took a moment to study the sensor feed from the seat's computer, it provided a better view than even Perkins had available. "I'm looking at the infrared, looks like four squids down there where the missiles came from. They're on the move."

"They're headed toward where Rivera and Zheng are coming down. We need to help them."

"Are you sure?" He asked.

"Are you asking because *you're* not sure what to do," she demanded. "Or because you're worried I will think it's a stupid idea?"

"The last one," he admitted. "Honey, we don't have combat skinsuits. These flightsuits only have limited power assist and our helmets don't have all the squad tactical link and targeting features." The pilots had rifles attached to their seats, with a spare magazine and two grenades each. That was considered enough for them to escape and evade until they were picked up by a Search And Rescue unit, but their training emphasized avoiding contact with the enemy. "The last time I played soldier on the ground was back in boot camp," he said.

"You remember any of it?"

"Enough. Ok, if we're doing this, we need to go *now*." His visor was showing him that setting down on the proper side of the river was less and less certain by the second.

"Do it," Irene altered the designated landing zone, had a brief argument with the ejection seat's computer, confirmed the change, and saw that Derek was now attempting to land near her. Their seats would coordinate to avoid fouling the two parachutes, there wasn't anything she needed to do. That left her mind idle and available to dream up bad thoughts, like, what exactly were they going to *do* on the ground? Two pilots without powered armor and limited experience in fighting on the ground, against four experienced, armored Wurgalan ground-pounders, plus Irene and Derek needed to find and protect two injured people. Those were not great odds.

Derek's seat blew the aeroshell, then severed the straps and set him free when he was less than sixty meters from the ground, the computer having calculated that the best option was for the pilot to complete the last leg of the journey on his own. Several trees had blown over, leaving a gap in the forest canopy and the parachute guided him through the gap, it was up to him where to place his feet as he came down through dead branches that snatched at his suit. He pushed off a downed tree trunk and rolled, coming to a stop with only enough of a jolt to cause a sharp pain in his back. Quickly, he palmed the button to released him from the parachute and the fabric began to dissolve. His rifle had come down with him, along with a survival pack containing spare ammunition, grenades, powercells, food, a small solar panel and other gear a downed pilot might need in a breathable atmosphere. Satisfied his back injury was probably just a pulled muscle, he checked his visor for Irene's location and set off at a steady run, brushing aside the undergrowth.

Irene's seat had determined her best option was to stay strapped in, so the bottom of the seat took the impact of falling down through the trees. Branches thin and thick were battered out of the way, one tree limb stout enough to bring the seat to a halt four meters off the forest floor, before the limb cracked under the weight and the seat rolled away to plunge the final distance to the ground. The impact was cushioned by the parachute tether and the aeroshell around the seat acted as an airbag, still Irene's brain was rattled and she came to a rest upside down. She got unstrapped and was awkwardly extricating herself from the shell when Derek jogged up, panting.

"Hey," he said, looking around warily careful to keep the muzzle of his rifle pointed at the ground.

"Don't even," Irene ordered as she rolled to her feet, wiping mud away from her face with one hand, and wagging a finger at him with the other.

"Don't what?" he asked innocently.

"*Don't* say it."

"I wasn't going to say anything," he protested. "Ok, maybe I was about to say it's good to see you."

"Oh. Sorry."

"Hey," he grinned, pointing to the still-rigid shell around the upside-down seat, draped with the parachute tethers. "These things should come with a big yellow arrow labelled 'This End *Up*'," he winked.

"I said *don't* say it," she laughed anyway, ducking back in the shell to get her rifle and survival pack. "How long should I set the self-destruct timer for?"

"About that," Derek held up the bright yellow destruct charge he had pulled from the remains of his own seat. "I've got a plan."

# CHAPTER FOURTEEN

"*This*," Santinelli grunted when the Gee-meter in his visor hit three point six. "Is better, than," he gasped for breath. "Riding the, ship down?"

"You can," Dave had to pause for breath. "Get out, anytime, you want. Ah," he grunted, tensing his ab muscles. Even through the skinsuit, the webbing of straps that held him in place were cutting into him every place they crisscrossed over and around his arms, legs and torso. The skinsuit itself was compressing around his legs and forearms, keeping blood from pooling there but he still felt light-headed. And he felt like an elephant was sitting on his chest. "Nert, why are, we falling, so *fast*?"

"Objects fall at the same speed, regardless of mass," the alien cadet gently chided the human for not understanding a simple principle of physics.

"Same speed," Shauna's vision was narrowing, the edges going gray from her brain getting less oxygen than she needed. "In a *vacuum*."

"Oh, yes, that is true," Nert admitted, embarrassed. His genetically-engineered physiology, plus the advanced nanomachines in his blood, gave him a better ability to tolerate high gravity loads. That did not mean he was comfortable. It did not mean he wasn't scared, despite the confident tone he tried to project in his voice.

"This thing," Dave tried to point to the shell around them but his wrist didn't want to move. "Is barely loaded. Air resistance on this big shell should have us falling gently."

"We *are* falling gently," Nert insisted. "We are experiencing only," he glanced at his own Gee meter. "Three point eight gravities." His meter was based on the slightly lower gravity of the Ruhar homeworld.

"*Only?*" Santinelli groaned.

"Yes," Nert nodded once, the strain on his neck muscles telling him that was a bad idea. "These cargo pods normally fall at *seven* gravities. They have to fall quickly, to reduce the time they can be targeted by enemy weapons on the ground."

"Great," Dave closed his eyes. The pod was shaking as it fell, and the smart fibers of the webbing that held him securely near the center of the pod dampened only part of the effect. He still felt it, and the roaring of the pod battering its way down through increasingly thick air was transmitted through the webbing so he felt it in his bones.

"If it helps, this is the highest gravity we will experience," Nert offered cheerily. "I think," he corrected his own overconfidence. "It *should* be." The truth was, he had never ridden inside a cargo pod, nor had he ever heard of anyone doing such a foolish thing. The pods were blunt-shaped unpowered shells, designed to bring equipment and supplies on a one-way trip to the surface of any world with a reasonably thick atmosphere.

He really had zero experience with cargo pods at all. Everything he knew about them was in the limited set of data stored in his helmet.

"Great," Dave repeated. It had been his idea for the group to get into a cargo pod, a fancy composite box that was better than the simple pine box that awaited them if they couldn't find a way to get dirtside safely. It had taken three tries to find a cargo launch bay that wasn't damaged or already empty. Then they, meaning Nert, had to manually override the controls to launch the two loaded pods in the bay, before the four humans, one Verd-Kris and one Ruhar climbed into one of the two empty pods. They were fortunate that some of the pods were kept empty, to be loaded later with whatever the ground force decided they needed most to sustain the operation. The pod was not completely empty, they had stuffed in extra skinsuits, a box of spare powercells, three rifles and a crate of ammunition, plus a box of ration bars for the humans. Basically, they tossed in whatever was close at hand that they might need and could find quickly, very quickly. By the time they crawled into the pod and Nert started to get it sealed up, the turbulence of the broken ship's passage through the atmosphere was sending hot gasses through the open launch bay door. Chowdhury had been pulled off her feet and would have been sucked out the door, if Santinelli had not gotten a solid grip on her belt and a stanchion. It had taken both Dave and Shauna to get the other two humans into the pod and still the sides of the pod nearly clamped down on Chowdhury's left leg before Shauna yanked her inside at the last moment. Even with the smart fibers of the webbing helping the passengers get into position, they were still struggling to secure themselves away from the walls of the pod, when it screeched down the warped launch rails and was flung out into space.

Immediately, the pod had hit something, or something struck it, and it went into an uncontrolled spin that had Dave fighting to keep his stomach from rebelling. After the impact, the pod had tumbled intermittently until it fell deep enough in the atmosphere for aerodynamics to act, pointing the pod's blunt nose downward. Since then, they only had to endure crushing deceleration and vibration that felt like it was shaking his teeth loose.

Riding the cargo pod to the surface was less risky than the certain death of staying aboard the broken ship. It was still *very* risky. Normally, the pod would rely on guidance from the ship above, and it would be accompanied by its own squadron of decoys. At any moment, an enemy missile or maser beam could shatter the shell, dumping the passengers out into the hypersonic airstream that would tear them apart.

If that happened, death would be mercifully swift.

Dave checked the Gee-force meter. It had dropped below three. He waited until it fell below two point six, the point where his body could feel the difference, before daring to give voice to his hopes. "We're through the worst of-"

The pod was battered sideways so violently that he blacked out for a moment. When he was able to think again, the pod was spinning, and vibrating worse than ever, enough that some of the tough webbing was pulling free from the inner walls.

"They're shooting at us!" Santinelli screamed. "We're dead!"

"Shut *up*, Santi," Dave barked. "Nert, any way we can see outside this thing?"

"What? You think that will help?" Santinelli's panic was out of control. "We can't dodge a missile even if we can see it!"

"I don't think that was a missile," Dave explained.

"What?" Shauna asked.

"I'm pretty sure that was turbulence from the ship falling past us. We were both falling at the same rate, and the launcher didn't kick us very far away before we hit the atmosphere."

"Yeah," Shauna thought for a moment. "That makes sense. Damn it! I know this thing has sensors, the freakin' hamsters won't let my suit connect."

Nert was stung by her words. "You are not locked out because you are a human, Staff Sergeant Jarrett. You just don't know how to do it," he said with a pout. "I do, I have it. Connecting you now."

The view was fuzzy and indistinct, coming from long antennas that stuck out to the sides and top of the pod. Sensors in the blunt nose of the cargo container were surrounded by a pink fog of superheated plasma, as the pod battered its way down through the thicker and thicker air. At first, Dave couldn't understand what he was seeing, then the image resolved itself. "Shee-it," he groaned. "Yeah, that's the ship, what's left of it." The remains of the forward hull section had raced past them, and remains was the correct description. It had split apart into two large and dozens of smaller pieces, all racing toward the ground much faster than the cargo pod. All of the debris was engulfed in flame, soot and plasma, breaking apart as it fell.

"We don't have to worry about someone shooting at us," Shauna found the silver lining in the situation. "There's so much debris flying around up here, the Wurgalan wouldn't know what to target."

"Oh," Santinelli snickered nervously. "Cool."

"Uh, Nert," Dave said slowly. "Can we steer this thing?"

The cadet thought for a moment. "I don't know. Cargo pods usually follow a guidance beam projected from the ground, with backup from the ship. Why?"

"Because," Dave couldn't tear his eyes away from the mesmerizing images of what used to be the *Big Mac*. "When all that fast-moving shit below us hits the ground, it will leave a *big* smoking crater. We do not want to land there."

"Shit!" The cadet agreed. "I don't know if it can be steered from here. Let me try."

They waited in silence, as best they could. The turbulent air in the wake of the starship's forward hull tossed the pod around violently, making it difficult for Dave to keep a train of thought.

"Dave," Shauna called. "Check Jates. He doesn't look so good."

He checked the big Verd-Kris's vital signs, which indeed did not look good at all. Blood pressure was low, and their leader had been unconscious since the pod had struck something right after launch. "His suit is showing yellow, not even orange," Dave noted hopefully. "It probably knocked him out on purpose, best thing for him right now."

"Maybe. Verds are tough, that's good."

"Shauna? Dave?" Nert called, forgetting protocol. Not that it mattered at the moment. "I think I found how to provide landing coordinates for the pod, it should guide itself."

"Outstanding!" Dave relished the first solidly good news he had heard since the *Big Mac* had been hit the first time.

"Do you have a destination?" Nert asked, not wanting to take on that responsibility.

"Uh," Dave checked the map in his visor. The device was showing only a vague location for their current position. "Hell, we don't want to fall into the ocean," he muttered to himself. "Is there any way to see on this thing where the ship will hit?"

"I don't think so, I," his frustration boiled over. "I don't know how to use this system! I've never seen it before!"

"Nerty," Shauna did her best to calm the cadet. "It's OK, you're doing great, way better than we could. Look, we're falling in a southwesterly direction, following the ship down. We've got ocean to the west, can you steer us north, anywhere to the north that is dry land?"

"Uh, oh, sure. I'll try."

Nothing happened at first, then still nothing happened.

"Nert?" Dave asked, as they fell through twenty kilometers. The ship below and in front of them was breaking apart faster, but two big chunks were holding together and would make a huge crater when they hit.

"Working on it," the teenager snapped. "*Got it!*"

The pod's uncontrolled rocking motion steadied as fins deployed from the top, stabilizing the flight path. Straps dug in hard as the pod jerked in the air, swaying side to side, each motion wobbling less than the last. The container rotated around them as the fins tilted, bringing the cargo container swinging around, so it was falling a bit more toward the north with every meter it plunged.

With nothing else to do, Dave tried to relax, conserving his energy for the upcoming battle on the ground. Based on the map, they would land far from any friendly support. Their best hope was to find a place to hole up, until they could get a signal through to a rescue team. As they fell through twelve kilometers, he realized he was thinking not about *if* they landed, but what they would do after. He was assuming their crazy stunt would work, setting them down gently enough to be survivable.

The trembling started as the pod raced through eleven kilometers. Gentle when it began, the vibration built up until Dave's teeth were chattering. "What is wrong?"

"I think," Nert had to shout even to hear himself. "One of the fins is damaged!"

Dave looked up and was about to say something like 'No shit Sherlock' when a bright hole appeared at the upper end of the pod. A fin had torn away, taking part of the shell with it. Instantly, the roaring grew so loud that Dave could barely hear himself think.

Loss of the fin caused the pod to swerve in the air, jerking left and right as the computer tried to compensate for the missing fin and keep to the programmed flight path. Above them, the tear in the shell grew wider. "Nert! Turn off the guidance!" Dave shouted.

"What?"

"*STOP!*" Dave made a slashing motion across the neck of his suit.

Nert was being bounced around in the webbing so badly, he could barely bring up the menu in his visor. It was impossible to select icons with his eyes dancing in his skull, so he fell back to the pad on his left wrist. Instead of trying to control the pod, he resorted to simply turning off the guidance system.

The trembling dampened immediately, but the pod then started to spin, faster and faster.

"Urp!" Was all Shauna could say.

"There's a-" Nert gave up trying to explain and just concentrated on engaging the gyroscopes. It didn't work correctly, it worked well enough. Rotation slowed to a rate that was merely nausea-inducing, rather than rendering the occupants unconscious. "That's the best I can do for now."

"Gre-great," Dave took gulps of air to keep his stomach contents where they should be. "Ooh, this is gonna be close," he highlighted the area the pod was falling toward, it was right on the seacoast.

"We'll make it," Shauna expressed confidence she didn't feel.

"Dave?" Nert spoke hesitantly. "We might have another problem. Two problems."

"What is it *this* time?"

"First, we- Hang on!"

When the aft section of the *Big Mac* impacted, it created twin, connected craters a hundred meters deep and over a kilometer across. A fountain of soil, soot, ash and pieces of starship fountained up in a mushroom cloud, while the air was pushed aside in a supersonic wave in all directions.

The shockwave pummeled the cargo container, pushing it northwest and even making it briefly gain five hundred meters of altitude.


All Dave knew was, they had survived. Somehow, they were still alive, the pod was mostly in one piece, and they were falling again. He had to admire the toughness of Ruhar equipment, the hamsters knew what they were doing. The altimeter showed them soaring down through eight kilometers. "Everyone OK?" He asked even as he checked four other sets of vital signs. Everyone was alive. Jates and now Chowdhury were unconscious, their suits having made the judgment call that inducing temporary forced sleep was best for the occupants.

"Fine," Shauna decided right then that she would not go on a roller coaster, or any other wild carnival ride ever again.

"I am well," even Nert's voice was shaky.

"I'm here," Santinelli was resentful.

"Uh, hey," Dave figured that since no one was dead, he might as well deliver the bad news. "We got another problem. That shockwave pushed us out to sea. We're going to splash down in the ocean, looks like about seven klicks from shore. That's way too far for swimming."

"Nert?" Shauna looked down at the precious gear stowed in the nose of the pod. "The fins are busted, but can you steer the parachute after it deploys?"

"That was the second problem I was going to tell you!" Nert groaned. "The parachute was torn away, either when we got hit after launch, or when the fin broke loose. The backup chute is showing offline."

Checking his helmet visor, Dave read altitude and airspeed. They were seven and a half kilometers up and falling at just below the speed of sound. That was survivable. "We gotta get out of here," Dave declared, mentally awarding himself a 'No shit Sherlock'. "Nert, can you blow this shell?"

"Yes, I can activate the release mechanism. But we will fall!"

"No we won't, because four of us have parachutes," Dave said. "Nert, you take Chowdhury, Ok?"

"Yes. Yes, I can do that."

"Outstanding. Schmu-" he almost said 'Schmuckatelli' without thinking. "Santi, get yourself attached to the surgun, he's your ride down."

"Me?" Santinelli protested. "Why don't *you* take him?"

"Because Jarrett and I are going to tether ourselves to the gear we brought," Dave pointed toward the nose of the pod below them.

"Hell, I don't have to take orders from a civilian," Santinelli protested. "That lizard weighs a ton, he will drag me-"

"Do we have a problem, Santinelli?" Shauna demanded. "I'm not a civilian, and you *do* have to take orders from me. Now get yourself attached to Jates, or I'll give him *your* parachute."

The hapless lance corporal grumbled under his breath, as he grudgingly worked at the task he didn't want to perform. Dave checked the tether holding Santinelli to the Verd-Kris as best he could from a distance, and when everyone declared they were ready, he told Nert to get ready to blow open the shell. "Everyone remember, release yourself from the webbing, then toggle only your drogue chute to pull you out. Do *not* activate your main chute until you are clear. Open the chute manually, we need to make sure we don't get tangled in a bunch of crap flying around. Wait! Nert, how does this work?"

"The shell?" Nert asked, confused.

"It splits open down its length," Shauna said. "We've seen them used for VERTREP plenty of times before." The Ruhar had used cargo pods to perform Vertical Replenishment on Fresno after the fighting started, with starships launching pods from a safe distance and letting them coast down to the planet's surface.

"On the *ground*, yeah," Dave pressed his question. "What will happen when we blow it apart in flight?"

"Ooh, good point," Nert conceded. "I do not know. It could be dangerous."

"Maybe not," Shauna countered, painfully aware of how close they were getting to the ground. "I read somewhere these things can be used to resupply special ops troops. They carry stealth subcontainers that can glide down on their own. When they do that, the subcontainers are released out the *top*."

"I can try that," Nert frowned. The humans were asking *him* to do everything, and it wasn't fair. It was impossible to- "I can do it," he said with surprise. "The pod is made of sections like rings, they are held-"

"Nert, just do it," Dave urged.

"Three, two, one," the cadet did his best to speak calmly. "Break!"

Exactly as Nert tried to explain, the pod's top dome and a ring three meters in depth suddenly peeled away and just as suddenly, he and Chowdhury were pulled upward as his drogue chute shot up and yanked them with it. Shauna went next, the suit computers coordinating the bailout operation faster and safer than any biological being could have. Dave braced himself, one hand on the latch that would cut the tether to the bag of equipment he had dangling below him.

Santinelli and Jates were next in the automated sequence, or they tried to go next. Somehow, Schmuckatelli lived up to his name by failing to get all the webbing released properly. He got tangled up with the big Verd, the drogue chute tugging him upward while the netting tried to hold both of them in place. The nano fibers of the netting were smart enough to realize the strain was going to tear the two biologicals apart, so they disintegrated and Santinelli popped upward like a cork. He twirled in mid-air, striking the lip of the pod hard and tearing free from Jates.

Dave got a flash impression of Jates tumbling out of control and out of sight, as his visor registered a red DECEASED over the icon for Santinelli. "Shi-" he did not have time to complete the thought before his own drogue shot upward. All Dave could do was haul on the handle to release the tether holding him to the gear bag and he was free, flying through the near-supersonic airstream that hit him like a solid wall, making him tumble out of control.

Drogue. He had to get the drogue retracted. How the hell did that work? He had done it in training but not often, it was rarely-used emergency procedure, reserved for when the drogue was fouled on itself or some foreign object.

Screw it. He didn't have time to mess around with equipment. Yanking another tab, he cut the drogue free and tucked his legs, rolling over to fall head-first.

When David Jakub Czajka signed up for the Army, he had promised his mother he would not apply for Airborne service, because jumping out of an airplane was insanity. "Sorry, Mom," he apologized to her as he desperately scanned the air below for the Verd-Kris surgun. And saw nothing. "Where the f-oh!" He saw Jates not with his naked eyes, but with the team position locator in his visor. There was a slowly-tumbling dot below and to the west, barely outlined against the blue water of the sea. Dave lost sight of the Verd for a moment as the surgun plunged into a cloud layer, then Dave fell into and through the same clouds. "Oh, shit." Even if he caught Jates, they were both going to land in the water.

He tucked his arms back to pick up speed, and used his legs to steer the glidepath.

"Dave?" Shauna called. "Where the- *What* are you doing?"

"D- don't ask," Dave's muscles were so paralyzed with fear, he could barely speak. "Jates. He's in freefall."

"You'll both die if you-"

"He's *alive*."

He could hear her take a deep breath. "Ok. Be careful. You're going to splash down in the water, you know that?"

"What about you?" The shape of Jates resolved itself into a figure falling on its back, arms and legs extended limply above by the force of the air.

"We can make it to the beach, or inland. Dave, we're going to pop chutes in a sec."

"Got it. Any friendlies in the area?"

"*No one* in the area. This coast looks deserted. Map isn't showing the squids have anything along here."

"Gotta go. I need to focus. Hey, uh, tell Em I love her."

"I will tell her you're an *idiot*."

"That too. Czajka out."


He fell, annoyingly slower and slower as his initial velocity bled off against air resistance. Jates had to be falling slower, as the Verd was not in a streamlined stance.

Four kilometers. His visor was screaming warnings at him to pop the chute, continuously asking whether he truly wanted to delay deployment? He ignored it, knowing the suit computer would eventually override his manual control and pop the chute whether he wanted it or not.

But not yet.

Three point five.

Three kilometers. Less than ten thousand feet before he hit the water.

Two point five.

Then Jates was *right there* in front of him and Dave had to rotate from facedown to flying on his belly, using his arms and legs to steer toward the unconscious figure. He missed the first time, flying cleanly past.

The second time he swung past, smacked his legs against Jates and spun away out of control.

One point five kilometers. Less than five thousand feet to go.

A message warning Parachute Emergency Deployment Imminent popped up in his visor and he ignored it. There wasn't anything he could do to prevent the suit's tiny brain from protecting him from his own lunacy.

"Not *now*, damn it," he screamed into his helmet, salty tears clouding his vision. "I can do this!"

Third time was the charm, he hit hard enough to knock the air from his lungs and hung on with a powered-suit deathgrip. As charms went, that one sucked because he had gotten hold of Jates upside down and backwards, so the Verd's backside was under Dave's chin and his thighs flopping around in Dave's face. The Maverick got his legs wrapped around Jates's torso and did not dare let go even one arm to attempt tying a strap around them. He would have to trust-

The chute deployed without warning and suddenly he was holding not just Jates but a thousand tons of dead weight as the chute abruptly brought him almost to a stop in midair. The suit must have sensed his wishes because the powered arms and legs clamped solidly without giving an inch, holding onto Jates even when Dave's own limbs could not take the strain.

Then it seemed they were hanging motionless in the air. Blue ocean glittered below Dave's feet, long swells that curled into white as they crashed on the shore.

The parachute above them was a parachute, not a balloon, and it had formed into sort of a triangle shape. The wind was pushing them farther from the shore, it would be a long swim. He briefly debated trying to steer the chute, but didn't have confidence in his ability to control the overloaded fabric. Now that he was used to the different motion of dangling beneath the chute, he could sense he was still falling, just at a slower rate. A bar at the corner of the visor was showing orange for their rate of descent, the bulk of Jates and his skinsuit plus rifle had the parachute close to its limit.

"Uh," Dave realized the ocean was approaching fast, faster than he had expected. It was going to be a hard landing after all. Keeping one eye on the altimeter that was scrolling down faster than he liked, he considered whether to ditch his and Jates's rifles to lessen the parachute's load. No. Smacking into the water would likely hurt like hell but it was survivable. Being dirtside in a combat zone without a weapon was suicide.

"Ok, sorry about this," he said quietly as the altimeter showed he was six meters above the water, and he let Jates drop. The big Verd fell head-first and only flipped onto his back just before hitting the water with a splash that sent up a fountain. "Shit!" Dave had expected the surgun's suit would deploy airbags to keep him afloat, but the alien slipped beneath the waves and was just *gone*, leaving only a ripple.

With only Dave's weight, the parachute had warped its shape out into a balloon that expanded rapidly with helium gas, and he was drifting slowly upward. The damned parachute computer was trying to get him to shore! Having no time to argue, he pulled the emergency latch to break free of the chute entirely, and gulped when he saw his rash move happened when he was almost ten meters above the ocean swells. "Oh, this is not goo-"

He hit the waves feet-first, the suit tensing the boots to prevent him from shattering his ankles. Down down down he plunged until the suit judged it was safe to inflate flotation bags from his shoulders. The bags inflated slowly so he wouldn't rocket to the surface out of control.

Damn. The surface was a *long* way above him, the bright sunlight dimmed and changed color so it looked blueish-gray. He knew his suit had plenty of oxygen and that did nothing to dampen an instinctive panic that he had to force from his mind. "*No*, damn it!" He barked at the suit. He did not want to float up to the surface, he needed to locate Jates in the water first. The stupid visor was not cooperating, making him scroll through a menu to deactivate the floats, and he broke the surface before he could get the damned things retracted.

Jates. Where was Jates? Skinsuits had a maximum safe depth that Dave could not remember at that moment, he also didn't know how deep the ocean floor was in that area. The helmet-to-helmet laserlink's range degraded quickly underwater, the squad locator beacon might not-

"Huh." A flash of yellow when Dave bobbed up on a swell. It was gone when he slid down the backside of the wave. With steady, smooth strokes assisted by the powered suit, he swam toward where he had seen the glimpse of yellow, a color that was not natural on the sea surface.

It was Jates! "Ah, I'm an idiot," Dave felt like slapping his forehead. Jates's suit *was* smart, it had waited until the Verd soldier's plunge under the surface slowed before inflating. Just like Dave's suit had done.

Taking a moment to do something *smart* rather than just doing *something*, Dave checked Jates's vital signs. They looked better. Blood pressure was up, heartrate steady, breathing normal. There was a problem, Jates's suit had a tear on the right side, a tear large enough that the nanofibers had not been able to completely seal that gap. Water had seeped into the suit, which was not a problem because the tropical ocean surface was warm like bath water. The leaking suit was not an immediate problem, the floatation bags were compensating, but it would make Jates even heavier to tow to the beach. Swimming over behind the surgun, Dave got an arm around the alien's upper body and waited to ride the top of a swell so he could see which direction was the shore. His visor had that info on a map, it just felt better to *see* it.

After only a few minutes of swimming, during which Dave was already getting tired of Jates's rifle bumping into his churning legs, the alien made a sound. "Uh, uhhhh," Jates sighed, his eyelids fluttering.

"Hey! Hey, Jates! Surgun, you awake in there?" Dave asked excitedly.

"Uhhh," the alien grunted. "Depends."

"Depends? On what?" Dave was baffled.

"Feels like I'm in water somewhere, and it's warm?"

"Yeah, that's right, so?"

"*So*, if I open my eyes, and see that you're with me in a hot tub," the Verd-Kris paused. "All I can say is, you better run."

"*Oh!*" Dave laughed with relief. "No, no hot tub."

"You'd better not be buck naked either."

"Ah, I'm wearing a combat *skinsuit*, not my birthday suit," he assured the big Verd. "Hey, come on, open your eyes, will ya? We splashed down in the ocean and we have to get to shore. It's awkward towing your fat ass through the water."

"My ass is not fat," Jates opened his eyes to glare at the human. "This suit has padding."

"Yeah, it's the *suit's* fault," Dave muttered. "Can you swim?"

# CHAPTER FIFTEEN

"Incoming," the Ruhar copilot of the dropship carrying a Verd-kris platoon announced, feeling useless. There wasn't anything he could do about the enemy missiles that had targeted them, and even his announcement was unnecessary, the pilot had the same info flashing across her helmet visor. They were both ignoring calls by the Verd-kris soldiers in the cabin. The lone human passenger, Captain Grace, had not tried to contact the pilots, who didn't have time to talk anyway.

The whole operation was snakebit right from the start. First, their ship, the assault carrier *Dal Turnaden* had drawn the unpopular assignment of ferrying a battalion of Verd-kris. Then, he and the pilot had gotten the bonus of having a human in their dropship, so they had two untrustworthy types of aliens to worry about. To make their day complete, the *Dal Turnaden* had been sliced in half by an enemy SD network the 7th Fleet apparently had missed, and debris from the carrier had knocked out the dropship's engines, peppered the hull with holes and taken the aft defensive maser turret offline.

"Intercept confidence?" The pilot asked, not taking her focus off the flight controls.

"Sixty-eight percent for the first missile," copilot Randerot reported. "Forty-two for the second. They're coming in perfectly spaced," he grunted. The enemy apparently had updated information about the defensive capabilities of Ruhar assault dropships, information they must have obtained from the Kristang. The first missile knew it had a less than even chance of a successful hit, so it had slowed its approach to give the second missile a better opportunity. If the data about Wurgalan anti-air tactics was correct, the first missile would sacrifice itself by self-destructing, sending a cloud of sensor-blinding chaff into the air and blocking the dropship's view of the second weapon until it was too late.

"Let's close the gap," pilot Lolenda ordered, dipping the nose down to build up airspeed. With the engines offline, gravity was their only way to gain speed.

"Got it," copilot Randerot didn't argue, he had attended the same briefing about how to deal with Wurgalan air defense missiles. The book on tactics also suggested firing the maser cannons early, hoping to confuse the lead missile into exploding early. "Firing the chin turret." In the cockpit they heard the distinctive BZZT BZZT sound of the maser beams sizzling through the air, and Randerot saw another query from the Verd-kris platoon leader. He ignored it. The Verd had access to a data feed from the cockpit, and the pilots were too busy to babysit their passengers.

It was a battle of technology against technology, tactics against tactics. The Ruhar dropship's defensive sensor and fire control system, against the tiny brain of the enemy missiles. The tactical advice provided by the Torgalau to the Ruhar, against the tactical advice provided by the Kristang to the Wurgalan. The actions of biological beings, no matter how smart or skilled, could have little effect on the outcome of the deadly contest.

Unless the pilots of the dropship did something stupid.

Pointing the dropship straight at the incoming missile certainly *seemed* stupid to Randerot, and it went against his instincts to monitor sensors and weapons while Lolenda flew the plunging spacecraft almost straight down.

BZZT BZZT BZZT the chin turret's maser cannons were in rapid-fire mode, sending out coherent pulses of microwave energy, whenever the fire control computer thought it could predict the next move of the leading missile. Both missiles flew a weaving path to avoid providing an easy target, a sensible precaution.

Sensible but not always successful.

BZZT- *BAM*! The lead missile flew into a maser beam that fried the weapon's electronics, a strike that rendered it useless and prematurely detonating the warhead. Millions of pieces of sensor-jamming chaff were flung outward in a cone shape, some pieces burning hot to confuse sensors in the infrared range.

"Lost lock," Randerot reported, urging the dropship's computer to find the second missile again. Before he could jab a thumb on the button to authorize an active sensor pulse, the defensive computer made that decision and microwave energy blasted outward, this time in a broad beam intended to seek rather than destroy.

Nothing.

Nothing.

No return pulse that could confidently be identified as the enemy missile.

Nothing.

Still nothing.

Randerot checked the instruments, frightened that the active sensor dome might have been damaged. Power could be flowing to the dome, but no microwave energy going outward. No. They *were* getting returns bouncing off the drifting chaff and pieces of the broken first missile. The sensors were working, just not-

"Contact!" He breathed with relief as the second missile blasted through the layer of chaff. That was not good, they were too close! The maser turret resumed its BZZT BZZT, but the defense computer didn't have enough time to analyze the flight characteristics of that missile as is jinked side to side on its path toward the target. The target. Their dropship.

"This will be clo-"

*BAM*! The second missile exploded and for a moment Randerot thought it had detonated its warhead on a proximity setting, in which case they were dead. They were *not* dead, not right then. They were alive, the masers had hit the-

Lolenda pulled the nose up just before they flew straight into the cloud of shrapnel. The big dropship shuddered, shivering in the air as hundreds of pieces of hot composite impacted the energy shields. A dozen, two, three dozen pieces seared through the shields and struck the dropship's belly, ripping though the thin armor plating and destroying belly jets, power cables, electric motors and other vital components needed for controlled flight.

"I've got nothing," the pilot said in an even tone that masked the panic she was feeling. "No control." The dropship began rolling to the left and kept going, flipping upside down. It stabilized there for a heart-stopping moment and wobbled, flipping the nose up and falling belly-first.

"Eject?" Randerot called out, seeing the ejection menu automatically come up on his console. The flight control computer thought that ejecting was their best course of action, and would automatically launch the pilots up and out unless they manually cancelled the sequence.

Lolenda looked at the purple 'Ejection Enabled' symbol blinking on her console. The flight controls were inoperative, only the inherent stability of the airframe was keeping the ship from flipping into a death spiral. Ejection was the sensible thing to do.

Except, in the cabin behind the cockpit bulkhead was a Verd-kris platoon, plus the human liaison or advisor or observer or whatever the hell Captain Grace's official title was. Of the forty-one souls who boarded the dropship to strap into seats in the cabin, thirty-two were alive. They were flying low and slow enough to survive bailing out, the question was whether bailing out was their best chance to live.

No, the question was, what did she and Randerot owe to the aliens? The Verd-kris were historically enemies of her people, regardless of what they avowed their current politics to be. The humans? They weren't historically anything, they hadn't been in the fight long enough, and their meager numbers could not make a difference either way in the war. Humans had come to Paradise as conquerors, and quickly realized they had been played for fools. Yet recently, the strange and primitive aliens had proven to be courageous, even useful.

What made Lolenda's decision were factors she considered so quickly she wasn't even aware of thinking about it. She and Randerot had trained with Getrun Zolatus's platoon for two weeks and had gotten to know the aliens, even grown to like the platoon leader. Now Zolatus was dead, killed by shrapnel from the second missile and Lolenda oddly felt an obligation to his people. Also, they were coming down over hostile territory, everyone aboard the dropship had better odds of survival if they were together.

And finally, damn it, she was just not ready to give up on saving her spacecraft. Not yet.

"Cancel the ejection," Lolenda ordered. "Switching to manual."

"Cancelling ejection auto-sequence," Randerot acknowledged without enthusiasm. Flying a Lotentix-class dropship to a dead-stick landing was difficult even with all flight controls functional and coordinated by the computer. Attempting a dead-stick landing without the computer was suicidal and he was surprised that the usually level-headed Lolenda would try it. "Are you sure that-"

"Partial flight control restored," she interrupted. Status symbols were scrolling on the console. She tentatively eased the nose up and banked to the left, discovering that a coordinated turn was not possible without manual inputs to the rudder. Ok, she thought, I'm back in basic flight school. "Tell me what we've got working for belly jets."

"I won't know for sure until I fire them up," he warned.

"Wait," she held her breath as the dropship stabilized in a glide, the nose pitched down at six degrees. Time to look for a place to land, she told herself. "Do it."

Randerot tested the jets one at a time, skipping the ones that were listed as inoperative by the computer. "Two. We've got two jets functional."

"Waste of time," Lolenda grunted. Two jets did not have enough power to hover the heavy spacecraft and the two functional units were on the same side, their thrust would only flip the ship on its side. "Dump the fuel.

"Venting fuel. Thrusters also?" He asked, finger poised over the button.

She winced, rebuking herself. Her copilot should not have needed to ask for clarification. "No. We might need thrusters for the final approach."

"Vents open. Karr," he used her first name. "Tell me what you're thinking."

"Find me a place to land, we'll need a long rollout."

He enhanced the image of the ground below. Their objective had been to set down in a field behind a low ridge of hills to the west of the planet's only major city. Touch down only long enough for the platoon to exit and to dump the supply containers out the back ramp. Then lift off and fly low to the west, hugging terrain until they were over the ocean and could climb back into orbit to rejoin the assault carrier, to land the second wave.

That had been the plan. Now all Randerot saw spread out below him was the planet's sprawling capital city. Other than the military base that lay southeast of the city center, there were no runways within the cone of their glideslope.

A street. Their only option for a horizontal landing was a street. There were broad avenues in the city center, but they were arranged north-south and there was a crosswind from the southeast. Plus, they would lose too much altitude swinging around for an approach from the north.

He didn't like the idea of scraping the ship's belly on a street in a crowded urban area.

The extensive suburbs surrounding the urban center had narrow streets overhung with trees. Damn, he thought, the squids *really* like trees. Even the highways leading into the city were lined with tall trees, with branches that would snag the dropship and flip it over.

That left an industrial section of the suburbs. Low rectangles of structures connected by grids of roads with few trees or other obstructions. The type of place every city needs for warehouses and factories and repair shops. Zooming in the image showed vehicles zipping recklessly along the roads as parking lots emptied, local residents reacting to the totally unexpected invasion. Parents rushing home to get their children and take them out of the city. Randerot felt a pang of sympathy, he had two children at home.

"This is our best option," he highlighted the street he had selected.

"I see it," she said. "Tell our passengers to hang on for a rough landing. They need to egress as soon as we stop."

As the dropship lined up with the street selected for landing, Lolenda forced herself to breathe normally. The street was wide enough to clear the spacecraft's hull and half the wings on each side, but scattered trees, parked vehicles and poles were going to clip the wings before they slid far. Vehicles raced along the street, the anxiety-driven speed spurred into panic when the drivers saw the dropship flying toward them. Just about at the spot where she was aiming to scrape the belly on the road surface, a sleek passenger car collided with a boxy tandem truck, and the truck veered away to crash into parked cars along the south side of the street.

"Watch out-" Randerot warned.

"I see it," she dipped the nose to gain airspeed then hauled back on the stick, lifting the dropship's scarred belly just over the roof of the truck.

Or almost over the truck. The dropship's tail clipped the trailer, crushing it and throwing the ship's nose down to smack the road surface with a jarring thud, followed by a screech. The pilots could barely see through the smoke and debris thrown up as the former spacecraft skidded down the road, wings smashing parked vehicles. The right wing hit something unyielding and the main spar broke, severing the wing off near the root. Slewing to the right, the dropship lurched off the street, crushing cars, bouncing over a ditch and flopping into a parking lot.

"Karr!" Randerot gasped, seeing they were racing toward the side of a building. There was nothing they could do to avoid the collision; they had no control. "We're *out!*" He shouted as he yanked on the emergency ejection handle.

Above them, det cord burned openings in the cockpit hull and they rocketed upwards nearly simultaneously, wrapped in nanofiber shells. The motors under the seats kicked them up and to the south, just high enough for the parachutes to deploy, the ejection computer having determined that dangling in the sky over enemy territory was not good for the health of the pilots. Braked at the last moment by their parachutes, the pilots came down in an alley between two warehouse-like structures, their seat rockets firing a last puff of thrust to cushion the impact.

Randerot collapsed the nanofiber shell around his seat, punching the button to release the straps that held him, and rolling awkwardly onto the broken pavement that was strewn with trash and a long, slick streak of scummy yellowish liquid coming from the bottom of a dumpster. He pulled a rifle from the back of the seat, checked it, and ran over to where his fellow pilot was crawling out of her own seat.

"Karr, are you all right?" He asked, swiveling his head left to right down the alley.

"Hurt my back," she grunted, using the seat to pull herself up.

"Bad?"

"I can move."

"Grab your rifle, it's closing time."

"Closing time?" She winced as she lifted the rifle out of its slot, sharp pain radiating from her lower back.

"Yeah," Randerot swung his rifle around as a door opened into the alley and pair of curious Wurgalan stepped out. One of them held something that might have been a pistol. "You know, closing time? We don't have to go home," he fired two shots into the door as the pair of aliens ducked back inside. "But we can't stay *here.*"

# CHAPTER SIXTEEN

"Not yet," Irene whispered to herself. She was lying prone on the ground, under pieces of nanofiber torn from Derek's seat, with twigs and leaves scattered on top of the fabric. With the fabric's chameleonware concealing her and the fabric absorbing her heat signature, the Wurgalan had not yet detected her presence, though she had to be careful not to allow her helmet to transmit anything.

She was alone. There had been an argument about that, a brief argument but heated. Derek had wanted to stay behind, or stay with her. She had insisted one of them needed to assist the two injured soldiers on this side of the river. They knew from brief, staticky burst transmissions from the Maverick's platoon that Perkins had sent soldiers toward the river, they did not know when or if those soldiers would arrive. They did know, from the appallingly poor communications security of the approaching Wurgalan soldiers, that they were close and moving fast through the forest on their creepy tentacle legs. Derek had relented when Irene played the woman card: explaining that, if one of the injured soldiers needed to be carried, a man could handle that task better than she could. That was bullshit. He had seen her hauling a two-hundred pound dummy in a fireman's carry during training so he knew she could do it, and Derek was more persuaded because she said it than by the logic of her argument.

Whether Derek had found Rivera and Zheng she didn't know, they couldn't communicate without giving away their positions, and right then Irene did not want the Wurgalan finding her. The four enemy soldiers must have seen Derek's seat first, coming upon the clearly alien object unexpectedly. That had slowed their approach and caused them to spread out. When they found the shell covering Irene's seat, one of them went forward cautiously while the other three remained spread out and behind cover. She thought of the Wurgalan soldiers as 'it' rather than 'she' or 'he', they did have two genders but she had no idea how to tell them apart. In their powered armor, it was impossible to discern the differences anyway.

The one tasked with investigating the shell of her seat walked toward it on creepy tentacles in a jerky fashion, hesitantly. Irene guessed it didn't like being ordered to check out a potential hazard, and the squid kept its own rifle pointed at the shell but he didn't panic and start shooting.

Darting an arm tentacle into the opening that had been torn in the shell, it leapt away, then walked forward to peer inside. Slinging its rifle in an odd pouch on its back, it walked all the way around the shell, stopping to pick up the yellow box that held the self-destruct charges.

Irene held her breath. If the squid got curious, it might have cracked the box open, to find that Derek removed the explosives and replaced them with dirt and stones. The explosive packs from his seat were now wired to the self-destruct mechanism inside her seat, and Irene had an icon in her visor ready to blow the seat to pieces.

Not yet. The Wurgalan was gesticulating wildly, and though she could only guess what it was saying, her helmet was picking up a transmission. "That's right," she whispered under her breath. "It's a big mystery, Squidlock Holmes. You *all* should investigate. Maybe crack open a couple squid beers and relax for a while."

Two other Wurgalan approached the upside-down seat, keeping their rifles ready and warily scanning the area. The first soldier held up the self-destruct box, showing the broken tab where it had split away from the seat, and the snapped wires. That had been Derek's idea, to make it look like the self-destruct had failed because it was torn away in the crash. Make it look like the seat posed no danger at all.

The three squids huddled, examining the box. Irene mentally urged them to get closer to the seat yet they did the opposite, the two newcomers walking a circle around the shell then standing still, possibly waiting for orders.

The fourth soldier came out of the woods on the other side from where Irene was hidden, she had trouble seeing it through the trees. Finally, the other three walked to stand close to the shell, perhaps proud of what they had discovered.

The fourth soldier, who Irene guessed was the leader, gestured with his rifle and the other three took a step away from the shell.

That's when Irene blew it up.

The Ruhar engineers who designed the ejection seats had specified not only enough explosive energy to melt the critical components they didn't want the Kristang copying, they added more energy so curious lizards would not be tempted to come anywhere near a seat that was still intact. When Irene eyeclicked the command, the self-destruct charges from two seats detonated together, with the explosive force directed toward the opening torn in the shell. That is where Irene and Derek had hoped the curious Wurgalan would be, and two of them were caught directly in the blast and flung up and away, their armored suits punctured. One of them splattered hard against a tree, the other just rolled and rolled until it came to a stop, unmoving. As the saying goes, curiosity killed the cat, but the third curious squid survived with two shattered leg tentacles and one arm tentacle flopping uselessly.

Damn it! Irene could not see the fourth enemy soldier anywhere. Leaves, shredded bark and bits of both ejection seat and Wurgalan were floating in the air along with soot and smoke. She didn't dare risk an active sensor scan or standing up. Her flightsuit didn't have power-assist motors or armor while the enemy soldier had both, plus rockets and probably a lot more ammo than the two magazines Irene had with her.

There! A glimpse of something going right to left across her vision. It was super *fast*. Bullets ripped through the forest in no particular direction, the Wurgalan was using the time-honored technique of spray and pray, prodigiously expending ammo but effective at forcing Irene to keep her head down. She needed the enemy to be afraid so it would retreat and let her escape, she remotely triggered one of the grenades she had placed in the crook of a tree, choosing the grenade that was vaguely in the direction where she had last seen the surviving Wurgalan. Another long burst of rifle fire randomly chewed up the scenery, then a short burst. Her visor told her the rounds were coming from farther away, so she triggered the second grenade that had been placed under a pile of leaves, to throw into the air as much view-obscuring material as possible. She used the explosion as cover to wriggle backwards out of the covering fabric, crawled on her belly to the streambed behind her then ducked down and ran along the stream, trying to keep her boots from splashing too loudly in the water. Her flightsuit had chameleonware, and she was concealed from motion sensors by being below the banks of the stream, but the Wurgalan surely had acoustic sensors listening for any unnatural sounds. She had to find Derek and the two injured soldiers, before the Wurgalan turned around to hunt for her.

Not that long ago, she had been aboard the *Big Mac*, going through preflight checks.

How could her day have completely gone to shit in such a short time?

Dave Czajka and Jates splashed up onto the shore, both exhausted, slipping in loose sand and trying to step on the solid rock shelf that lay under most of the beach. Dave supported the Verd, with the surgun's arm over his shoulder, until they stumbled under cover of the trees at the top of the beach. "You know," Dave grunted as he helped Jates sit down, his back against a tree. "We shouldn't make a habit of this."

"Of what?"

"Me helping you walk. This is twice in three missions now."

The surgun nodded gravely. "I will strive not to be injured in the future."

"Hey, I didn't mean- Sorry, man. We need to see where you got hit, maybe I can do something with my med kit. I tried to ask your suit what the problem is, but it's diagnostic system is acting funky."

"Funky?" Jates asked, tapping the side of his helmet, indicating he had not heard or had not understood what was said.

"It means something isn't right. Let's get you out of that suit."

Jates looked up with a glare. "You're not going to buy me dinner first?"

"What- *Ha!*" Dave exploded with laughter. Jates still had a sense of humor, that was a positive sign. "Show me the goods first, honey."

Jates looked around. "I do not believe it is wise to remove protective equipment in a potential combat environment."

"Hey, I got a news flash for you, Surgun. The Legion is scattered all over hell and gone, I have no freakin' clue where the front lines are." Dave popped the seal and removed his helmet, keeping the microphone attached to one ear. "All I do know is, odds are no squids are wasting their time searching for *us* down here." he looked up at the sky, where bright flashes still regularly lit up space near the planet. "It looks real kinetic up there, I think the Wurgalan have more important things to worry about."

"I see your point. Czajka, use my medical kit, the nano is adjusted for my physiology."

"Sure thing. Get your torso unsealed, I'll help you. Um, you should leave your pants on."

The Verd looked up at him with a grunt. "I think we both would prefer that."

A bright streak caught Dave's eye just as he was helping Jates remove the right arm of the skinsuit, so they could get the torso unpeeled and see the extent of Jate's injuries. "Uh," Dave released the skinsuit fabric, letting it snap back into place.

"What's the problem, Czajka?" Jates growled, tired, achy and irritated. "You've seen me with my shirt off. You can't handle my manliness?"

"I can't handle your *dumbassness*," Dave shot back, tapping the control to reseal the shoulder joint. "Look," he jabbed a finger at the sky.

The burning streak was no longer just a bright line. It cut a swath across the sky coming from the east, with smaller contrails spreading to either side. At the head of the fire was a bulky object that was glowing orange and red. And it was getting larger.

Dave squinted, then flipped his visor back down to use the suit's sensors. The object was almost directly overhead and falling fast. "Yeah, that's gotta be the *Big Mac*. The ass end of it."

Jates took a moment to think. "You could be right."

"It's a ship, anyway." Dave turned his attention to getting Jates's suit put back together. "Let's get you mobile, pronto."

"What?" The Verd-kris grunted with pain. "Why?"

"Because that thing is going to hit the water. I'm kind of an expert on tsunamis," he thought back to when Shauna had made an island disappear on Paradise. "We do *not* want to be on this beach when the wave hits."

"Oh," Jates shook his head, blinking, embarrassed that his mind wasn't functioning correctly. He looked to the ocean, then the range of steep knife-edged hills that paralleled the coast inland. It would be a tough climb to the crest of the ridge. "Help me up," he held out his left arm.

"We should get your right suit arm set up first."

"I can *carry* the damned thing if I have to," Jates disagreed. "We need to find out if this suit is functional."

"You got that right." During the swim, and the short walk up the beach, Jates had been dragging his right leg. The Verd insisted that his own flesh-and-bone leg was working fine, the suit's nanomuscle motors were not cooperating. "Ok, try to stand up," Dave held out a hand and braced himself.

Jates rose unsteadily, forcing Dave to hold onto a tree for support. "Let go," Jates ordered, and took a step on his own, then another. And fell on his face in the sand. Awkwardly, he rolled himself onto his back, and sat up. "This suit is not functional," he announced in the stilted way the translator spoke.

Dave bit back a 'Ya think?' and looked out to sea, alarmed that the falling ship had passed overhead and arcing toward the water. "Ok, get out of the suit. Now. If you can't run on your own, I'll carry you."

Jates did not argue, and he didn't waste time. Usually, getting out of a Ruhar combat skinsuit involved removing each piece separately, being careful to give time for the tiny connections in the joints to release properly. For emergency situations, there was a procedure where the nanofibers that held the suit together let go of each other on each side of the joints and seams. Basically, the suit would flop apart like an old set of sweat clothes that had gone through too many washes. The

Verd pressed buttons on the wristpad in the correct sequence, confirmed the command twice, and the suit sloughed away from him like a snake shedding its skin. The heavy backpack crashed to the ground, setting off sparks from the cracked powercells. Jates manually unfastened the belt that held grenades, his rifle and spare ammo magazines. Waving for Dave to stay back, he held onto a tree and stood up.

Or tried to stand. His right leg collapsed immediately.

"Oh, man, that don't look good." Dave observed. Under the skinsuit, the Verd wore a thin garment that had the virtue of not bunching up and chafing under the powered suit's liner. Blood had soaked Jates's ribcage, and his right shin. Dave studied the leg wound. He guessed they had not noticed the leg injury because the suit had sealed a cut well, or maybe it had been blunt-force trauma. Making a snap decision, Dave knelt down, facing away from Jates, and released his backpack. The powercells were built into the suit and couldn't be moved, but he could carry his gear on his chest instead of his back. The pack's straps were designed to be attached front or back, and Dave had trained to walk, even run, with the pack on his front. The suit's computer adjusted its balance for the different center of gravity, so the only issue was that Dave had to be careful to hold his rifle so the pack didn't interfere. He figured if he needed to shoot, he would ditch the pack anyway. "Ok, sling your rifle and belt over your neck and hop on my back. I'll have to carry you."

"Wait! I need to get gear out of my pack."

"Oh, yeah," Dave should have considered that Jates would need his food rations. He couldn't eat the food Dave had in his own pack, and neither of them had any idea when they would link up with a Legion unit. They might be alone in the wilderness for a long time.

"Got it," Jates finished stuffing something into Dave's pack, then grunted with pain as he put his legs through loops on either side of the pack, that were intended for carrying an injured soldier. The Verd held onto other straps on Dave's shoulders instead of wrapping his arms around the human's neck. "Stand up slowly, this sand is loose footing."

Dave didn't need advice from Jates, he had carried humans and Verds in training, and training courses usually included sticky mud and obstacles that were more of a challenge than beach sand and scrub forest. The powered suit did most of the work, steadying Dave's wobbly legs. Walking, then jogging slowly then breaking into an easy, controlled run, he kept one eye on the palm trees and scrub brush around him while his other eye scanned the map in his visor. The hills inland were steep and came to a knife edge, but the ridgeline closest to the ocean was less than a hundred meters high. Was a hundred meters high enough to protect them from the incoming wave? He hoped so, because according to the map, east of the first ridge was a broad valley, then a tall cliff that appeared to be a sheer wall. Even in the powered armor skinsuit, he would need climbing gear to get up the cliff, and he couldn't climb with Jates on his back. That meant getting to the top, lowering a line, and hauling up the injured surgun. Dave didn't know how long they had until the tsunami hit, but he bet they didn't have long enough for leisurely mountain climbing.

Getting up the first ridge was a struggle, it required scrambling over a pile of loose rock at the bottom of the slope. Dave's mind idly recalled that such a collection of stones was called 'scree' or possibly 'talus' and he had no idea why that mattered. He was a quarter of the way up the pile of rock, his boots sinking in up to his ankles, when he heard the long low rumble of thunder. Instinctively, he flinched and looked up, just as the rolling clap of thunder shook loose rock on the ridge above him. "Shit!" He couldn't just duck and cover, because then Jates would be exposed to the stones that were bouncing down toward them.

On hands and knees, he crawled backward, not taking the risk of standing in the loose stones. He understood the thunder was actually a sonic boom from the broken starship that had passed overhead. Reaching the sand again, he walked backwards, trying to judge the path of falling stones and failing. With his power-assisted arms, he batted away bouncing rocks until one came at him that was too fast to avoid and too heavy to knock aside. He caught the rock with both hands, the impact throwing him backwards. Knowing there was an injured soldier on Dave's back, the suit computer twisted the nanomuscle motors at the waist so he fell on his side, one arm flung out to break the fall.

That big rock was the last of the danger. The sonic boom's footprint had moved out to sea, startling life under the waves and making fish leap out of the water. There was a bright flash toward the horizon as the ship struck the water, then the view was obscured by a dome of mist that rose like a massive sea creature.

"Wait, not yet," Jates cautioned as Dave moved to stand up. "Look," the Verd pointed to the sky over the sea, where ragged white clouds were being violently twisted into new shapes.

"Shockwave," Dave acknowledged. "It will shake loose more rock from that hill. I'm getting behind those trees," he pointed to a grove of palms.

"Not those trees," Jates argued, and Dave experienced a surge of irritation at his literal backseat driver. "The shockwave might knock those other trees onto us."

"Sure," Dave cringed, chastened. Jates was right. They faced two dangers; the compressed air rushing at them from the west, then stones falling from the east. First, he had to assure the shockwave didn't crush them under a tree.

Crouching on the west side of a dense grove of swaying palms, he watched a fast-approaching ripple on the surface of the water. "Here it comes," he announced without needing to, Jates could see the same thing even without synthetic vision. "Hey, cover your ears!" Dave warned at the last moment, then the tempest washed over them.

So much sand and sea spray was churned up that Dave was blinded, not even his visor showing him anything but gray static. Keeping one hand resting against a palm tree so he could judge if it was going to fall and in which direction, he braced on one knee, waiting for the shockwave to pass on. How soon behind the blast of air would be the tsunami? The suit's computer didn't have that data, he hadn't expected it would.

By the counter in his visor, only twenty seconds passed from when the shockwave hit, to when Dave could see again. Wind was still swirling as air rushed in to fill the low-pressure area behind the shockwave, it was like being in a tropical storm and the palm trees were swaying back and forth alarmingly over his head.

Then a rock shaken loose by the shockwave bounced past, and he turned to face the hill, keeping a particularly thick tree between him and the next hazard. When the stones rolling past had slowed to a trickle, he turned his head to shout at Jates. "We need to move, before the wave hits!"

"What?" Jates responded.

"Moving!" Dave jabbed a finger at the hill, and cautiously stepped out from behind the swaying grove of palms. A fist-sized rock bounced off his right knee and he ignored it, the visor was showing more rocks bouncing down the hill but nothing was highlighted in red, none of the falling objects was large enough to cause a problem, as long as Dave made sure to keep Jates out of the line of fire.

He got up the now-larger and more solidly-packed pile of stones at the bottom of the slope and began climbing, holding onto stubborn shrubs that clung to the hill, or using his gloves hands to stab handholds into the volcanic soil. He estimated the slope was at a forty-five degree angle and it got steeper near the top. While he climbed, kicking footholds with his boots, he searched for the best route up over the ridge. "Jates? You hear me?"

"Yes," the Verd coughed. "Go! Climb faster!"

Dave climbed as quickly as he could, grateful that Jates was keeping out of his way as best he could. Still, the big alien on his back was a dead weight, and Dave's suit let him know that it was straining with the additional load.

"Hey," Dave said when he could catch enough breath to speak, about halfway up the hill. "At least," he paused to gulp air. "We now, know, one thing."

"What, is that?" Jates was also breathing hard.

"It's not just the suit," Dave grunted from exertion as he pulled them up around a jutting rock. "You *do* have a fat ass."

Getting over the sharp crest of the ridge was a struggle, Dave had to pound handholds into the soft volcanic rock and pull the two of them up the nearly-vertical slope. At one point, he paused to consider how best to tackle the final eight meters to the top, when Jates tapped the side of his helmet. "Czajka, I don't want to distract you, but I seriously suggest you move faster."

Being careful to keep hands and feet securely dug into the hillside, Dave looked behind him by using the rear-facing camera built into his helmet. "*Ooooh*," he grimaced when the first thing he saw was a super close-up view the Verd's ugly lizard face staring back at him. Tilting his head provided a better view of-

The wave was piling up behind them.

It wasn't a *wave*, exactly, not the gracefully curling white-topped form that would make a surfer's heart quicken. The entire surface of the sea was rising, north to south in an unbroken line. White foam crashed where the tsunami water piled over the outer reef, sending spray fifty meters into the sky.

"Shit!" Dave pulled his right hand out of the crevice he had pounded into the rock. "Ok, Ok, Ok, uh," he searched the last bit of the hill, up toward the crest.

"Czajka," Jates shouted, his hearing still affected by the shockwave. "I can't walk but I can climb," he jammed a hand into the crevice Dave had just pulled away from, swung his good leg out of the sling and found a toehold that seemed to be stable. "You go ahead, and lower a line to pull me up."

"You sure?"

"Yes! Go!"

Knowing the Verd's injured leg made moving it awkward, Dave reached beside himself and released the sling from Jates's other leg. "Hang on!" He shouted without looking back, meaning the words literally. Without the burden of Jates that made climbing more difficult, Dave clambered up the slope, slipping and sliding backward but making more progress up than down. When he was within arm-reach of the ridge crest, he resisted the temptation to leap without thinking, and the temptation to look behind him.

Knocking handholds in the dark gray rock took too long, he had to take a risk. Their own damned ship was trying to kill him, as if the ship's last act was to take vengeance on the biological beings that had failed it. "Hey, it wasn't *my* fault," Dave said as he crouched down, letting go of the precarious handholds and flattening his chest-mounted pack against the almost-vertical hillside as best he could. Springing upward on powered legs, he felt a toe catch the rock painfully, bending that foot down as he soared upward. The rock of the toeholds had fractured as he jumped, stealing power from the upward movement. One hand missed the crest, he got the other hand draped over the jagged edge of the volcanic rock, which began to crumble. Kicking with his feet did not find any purchase and he was sliding backwards. With his other hand he felt for a crevice or solid rock, and managed to jam an index finger into a crack in the rock, just long enough to swing his legs so the other hand got a better grip on the ridge crest.

Pulling himself up with less care than he wanted and more care than he had time for, he heard the freight-train rumbling roar of the onrushing water and felt the hillside tremble. Somehow he got a leg over the crest, which really was less than six inches wide, and flopped over the other side so only his shoulders were draped over the ridge. "Jates!" He shouted at the Verd looking up at him. "Catch this!"

As he tossed the line from his toolbelt, Dave realized the surgun would need to let go with one hand to attempt catching the line, and that maintaining a solid grip on the wire-thin material would be nearly impossible without powered gloves to assist. He should have tied a loop before throwing, his mistake might kill Jates.

Dave had forgotten something else. The line, though no thicker than angelhair pasta, was made of nanofibers by the Ruhar, and it was controlled by his suit. When Jates let go of the sheer hillside to catch the line, his other hand slipped and he fell. One hand closed around the thin line and it slid along his palm, cutting into his skin and not slowing his fall. The blood flowing from the cut made the line even harder to grip and he –

Jerked to a stop as the end of the line looped first around his wrist, then slithered creepily under his arms to secure itself.

"Czajka!" Jates called, but Dave was already hauling upward. The fast-moving wall of water had hit the beach and palm trees were flung about like matchsticks, the front face of the wave higher than the tallest tree. When Jates reached the top, the wave bashed itself against the base of the hill below and water rocketed upward, surging toward them. There was no time to help the Verd get down the much gentler backside of the hill, and the line tying them together might only cut Jates in half. Dave hit the button to sever the line at his belt, and they both scrambled down the hillside for less than two seconds before they were enveloped in a whiteout of sea spray, then buried under water that blasted over the ridge and splashed down in a torrent.

Dave didn't remember anything worth noting as he was swept along with the water. He went upside down and tumbled over and over as the flood of water carried him down to the valley below. Striking many unseen objects on the way, he was battered senseless several times and had the sensation of moving sideways, one way then another. His guess, without being able to *see* anything, was that the seawater had pooled in the valley east of the ridge and now the sudden influx of water was seeking its natural level.

The sloshing back and forth slowed and he felt his boots touch bottom. With the suit providing a supply of air, he knelt and crawled along the bottom, feeling with his hands to determine which way was up to shallow water. When his helmet broke the surface, he could only tell by a slightly brighter darkness enveloping him.

The suit's sensors were largely useless, being caked with mud. Wiping away all the mud would take too long, and he needed to find Jates. The surgun did not have a nanofiber skinsuit protecting him, nor a supply of air. Popping the seal of his faceplate, he swung it up manually and blinked at the sudden bright light. The valley was full of fog, water droplets so fat they danced in the air. "Jates!" Dave called, filling his lungs with sweet air to bellow the name. "*JATES!*"

No response. Dave stood on shaky legs, turning completely around. The devastation in the valley was complete, even the tall cliff to the east had water running off and mud caked fifty meters high. Broken palms and other mud-splattered trees bobbed in the murky water that still sloshed north and south and from one side of the valley to the other.

Dave pulled his helmet off, wading out into the water to wipe mud off the sensors. If he could get the infrared sensor cleaned, he could search for a heat signature. Or he could try pinging the identification chip that all Legion soldiers had implanted in their forearms. It could be used as a crude locator beacon, better than nothing. Nothing was all he had right then.

"Damn it, Jates," Dave swore through tears. He couldn't believe the big Verd-kris surgun was gone. "I saved your sorry ass how many times?! You can't die on me now, you jerk! Come on. Come *on!*" He rubbed mud off the helmet's sensor lenses. "Come on, man, I don't know what I'll do without you," he sobbed, sinking to his knees.

"You'll drown without me, if you don't get out of that water," a weak voice whispered.

"Jates!" Dave cheered, leaping up and splashing down to fall in the water over his neck, only holding onto the helmet by the strap looped around one finger. Sputtering and spitting out filthy seawater, he looked around and realized that one of the mud-splattered trees bobbing in the water had an arm wrapped around it. Jates's head jutted above the tree trunk just enough for one eye to have a view of Dave.

"I could," Jates coughed up seawater. "Use some help."

Turning the helmet rightside up to drain the water, Dave jammed it back on his head and toggled the seal. Even if Jates couldn't swim, Dave could float as long as his suit was working, and all status icons were showing green.

When he got Jates gently dragged onto what was then the shore of the saltwater lake forming in the valley, he set the Verd on his back and removed his own helmet again. Wiping away tears, Dave looked over the surgun from head to toe. The suit liner Jates had been wearing was in tatters and angry bruises dotted his exposed skin, yet all four limbs were sticking out in the proper direction. "Damn," Dave blinked, salty tears stinging his eyes. "How the hell did you survive that?"

"I am tough, unlike you squishy humans," the surgun whispered hoarsely.

"Yeaaaah," Dave looked out at the water, and up at the ridge the wave had washed over. "You're not *that* tough."

"It was luck, mostly," Jates coughed up seawater again. "I don't remember most of it. Fortune favored me this day. Maybe Fortune felt bad for sticking me with a bunch of humans."

"You know what?" Dave sat back and laughed. "I'm not even offended by your wise-ass remarks."

"I do thank you for saving my life."

"Well, after getting us all into a cargo pod to save you the *first* time, then skydiving to save your sorry ass the *second* time, I-"

"I *said*, thank you," Jates said in a stern whisper, his voice still weak. "Do *not* think this means I am any less disgusted to be serving with you puny, weak creatures."

"Ah," Dave slapped a hand on the surgun's shoulder. "I love you too, man."

"Excuse me," Jates rolled onto his side. "I'm going to *hurl*."

# CHAPTER SEVENTEEN

The seat and straps holding Dani and the soldier on her lap held, even when the dropship smacked down hard on its belly, bounced and skidded across wherever the hell they were. She *hated* not knowing what was going on. She was a Captain, damn it, she outranked the platoon leader and one of the pilots, yet she had no access to the command network. Being a passenger sucked.

Panels tore away from the dropship's belly and sparks flew up through cracks in the cabin floor. The cacophony of the spacecraft scraping along whatever surface they had hit was so loud, her helmets external speakers had cut off to protect her ears. Still, she heard a terrible high-pitched grinding noise through her bones, transmitted through the seat-

An ear-splitting bang-*WHOOSH* came from forward, twin eruptions of fresh sound and the cockpit door flexed inward.

Shit! The pilots had *ejected*? While the dropship was *on the ground*? That could not-

They slammed into something and the seat groaned then a strap broke, sending Dani and her new friend tumbling forward. When her helmet smacked the cockpit bulkhead, the nose of the ship crumpled inward, throwing her backwards. She had a sensation of flying through the air and-

"Captain?" Someone, or some*thing*, was shaking her. "Captain Grace?"

Trying to open her left eye didn't work, something salty had the lids gummed closed and when she tried to lift that eyebrow, her eye stung with a burning sensation and filled with tears in an automatic reaction. Blinking the other eye assured her she could see without pain. It took a moment to focus, at first she got a blurry image of someone wearing a motorcycle helmet. Why a helmet? Had she been in a car crash?

In another blink, her eye focused and she yelped, scuttling backwards away from a horrible lizard face. It glared at her, fangs exposed, its lips working as it salivated-

No.

It was speaking.

To her.

"Captain Grace?" the guttural nature of the lizard voice remained even through the translation.

"Yes?" She replied stupidly, shaking her head. "Surgun?" Something in the back of her mind informed her that the two diagonal stripes on the forehead of the helmet indicated a rank of surgun second class. She could not remember the man's name. That information should be available in her visor, if her eyes would focus properly. "Where are we?"

"In some kind of warehouse," he answered.

Her mind was not able to process that immediately. "*What?*" She remembered. They had been in a dropship, it got hit by a missile or something, and-

What the hell was the Dodo doing in a warehouse?!

Turning her head answered the question. They *were* in a warehouse, or some kind of light industrial factory. Materials and machinery were stacked on plastic pallets along one wall, with a crane running along the girders of the ceiling. It was impossible to determine what activity the building had been used for, because the Dodo had burst through the far wall and dug a furrow in what used to be the floor, crushing and scattering whatever had once occupied the center of the structure. The dropship's tail assembly had sliced a wide gash through the ceiling, buckling it so the roof panels were sagging down haphazardly around the crumpled hull of the spacecraft. The impact had pancaked the dropship's nose past the first cabin frame and when she saw that, she experienced an '*Ah Ha!*' moment of understanding why the pilots had punched out while they were on the ground. Smoke and dust were swirling around what remained of the building's interior and pouring out the openings in the roof, fires glowed from inside the shattered dropship and electrical sparks flared everywhere. "The pilots?" She asked, holding up a hand for help getting up from the floor. Somehow, she had gotten out of the busted ship. No, some*one* had gotten her out.

"They ejected," the surgun responded with a grunt as he hauled her to her feet.

She wobbled, held upright more by the effect of her combat suit than her own leg muscles or sense of balance. She bit her tongue before she could say a sarcastic 'I know *that*', she discovered that she had already bitten her tongue for real. "*Ow*. Surgun, uh," the image overlaying his face resolved to '*Besault, Jal-toh-ran, S2C*'. "Besault. Where is Getrun Zolatus?"

"Dead," the alien declared flatly. "As is the senior surgun. There is only myself, surguns third class Auffex and Killauri, and twenty-six soldiers. Plus our medic," he gestured to a Verd-kris who was kneeling next to an injured soldier.

"*Dead*? Who- who is in charge here?"

"You are, Captain," he replied without the disgust she expected.

"*Me*?" That was perhaps not the best thing to say at that moment. Nor would it be useful to remind Besault that she was not an infantry officer. Oh, *hell*. "Sitrep," she said automatically. "Uh, give me a status report," she added, in case the American military acronym didn't translate well into the Kristang common language.

"We are in an industrial area west of the city. The pilots ejected and we have detected their locator beacons. We have no communications with the fleet or other units, except we picked up a brief distress call from Third Platoon. Their dropship crashed near the city center. They have multiple casualties and request our assistance in covering their egress."

Dani looked around at what remained of Second Platoon, the unit she was attached to. Every soldier she saw had dented, scratched or scorched armor. "They want help from *us*?" She asked, unbelieving. Surely the situation should be reversed.

"We have twenty-two soldiers who are combat-capable, plus myself and Surgun Auffex. Killauri has a broken leg, broken ribs and a punctured lung."

"Twenty four, then?"

"Plus our medic," Besault added.

Inwardly, she rolled her eyes and her natural inner sarcasm was dying to say 'Oh, that makes it *so* much better', but she didn't. "We are not supposed to *be* here," she said, partly to herself. "We weren't supposed to enter civilian areas of the city at all, the OPORD states that very clearly." The entire invasion plan was based on demonstrating overwhelming force, and persuading the Wurgalan that fighting to keep that particular rock was not worth the cost. Urban warfare with the resulting civilian casualties, would cost both sides greatly, and harden the enemy's resolve. Knowing that, the Legion had designated the planet's capital city of Sluktashwon as Control Point Slugtown, and declared it off-limits. Not only were ground troops to avoid the urban area, there was a strict No-Fly zone extending forty kilometers beyond the suburbs.

"Yet, here we are," Besault observed coolly.

"We should be moving *out* of the city."

His eyes narrowed. He had heard a story about this particular human fighting a Grikka on Feznako. That was difficult to believe. "What are your orders, Captain?"

"Uh, um," she stammered. "What do you advise, Surgun?"

"I *advise* you to make a decision, and make it quickly." After a beat, he added a perfunctory "Ma'am."

"Shit." She did say that aloud, and regretted it. "Uh, how close are the pilots?" That data was available to her somewhere, she didn't have time to eyeclick through unfamiliar menus.

"One point three kilometers," he replied, the translator making his rough estimate more precise than needed.

"Three quarters of a mile," her American mind converted the measurements. Three times around a track. "Ok," she made a decision. "Take your squad and bring back our pilots."

That seemed to please Besault somewhat, he lifted his chin and nodded. "What are the rules of engagement, Ma'am?"

"The rules, yeah. Do *not* shoot any civilians. Unless they shoot at you first. Besault, use minimum force, you understand? Just get our pilots back here. Wait," she held up a hand. "Before you go, who is our communications expert? I need to speak with Third Platoon."


"Show me," Ross requested, standing behind the chair of a Ruhar soldier who was analyzing sensor data. The general's dropship had landed and set out an antenna array, then flew to their current position, trailing a very long and thin spool of wire that connected to the antennas. The Ruhar were confident that it would be difficult for the enemy to locate the array, but they had also advised the general and his staff to be at least seven kilometers away. To be safe, the dropship had landed twelve kilometers from the antennas, about as far as the spool of ultra-fine wire could stretch. Now the specialized Dodo was on the ground inside the curve of a river where annual flooding created a meadow. The dropship was wrapped in a stealth field and covered with stealth netting stretched over poles, netting that generated a sophisticated hologram. Enemy sensors would see nothing other than a floodplain with a web of stream channels.

"It's still preliminary," the technician warned.

"It's better than nothing. Show me," Ross phrased his second instruction as an order. He did not like his time being wasted, and he did not like his staff covering their asses.

"Yes, Sir. We think this is the track of the last dropship that got out of the *Big Mac* before the forward hull hit the atmosphere." A low-resolution image appeared on the console's display, it showed a Dodo-class dropship falling in a purely ballistic arc. That was not unusual, the landing craft were supposed to fly ballistic until they were deep in the atmosphere. This dropship, however, was not following the planned trajectory, its projected landing zone was far to the west, closer to the ocean.

"Any indication someone is alive in there?"

Instead of replying, the technician fast-forwarded the video, it scrolled in a dizzying flash of images. "Watch this, *here*."

The dropship dove at a steeper angle and Ross saw why: a missile had been launched from the surface. He watched the brief air battle, fearing for the Dodo's occupants. "Freeze it," he ordered. "They bailed out?"

"That's what it looks like, Sir. The pilots ejected, that is clear. The AI cleaned up the image as best it could," the soldier pointed to a number in the upper left of the display, indicating that forty-eight percent of the images were based on the AI making guesses to fill in missing data. "After they bailed out, we lost them completely. The dropship crashed."

"No idea where they landed?"

"No. But, later," the display switched to a different set of images. "There is this explosion on the ground. The AI has seventy-three percent confidence it is the self-destruct mechanism of a pilot ejection seat."

"Hmm," Ross grunted. "That could be automatic. Doesn't mean anyone survived."

"The explosion was *two* self-destruct charges, at the same location. There is also what might be Legion and Wurgalan weapons fire in the area."

"Might be?"

"It's under the trees. With the broad-spectrum jamming, it's the best we can do." Anticipating the general's next question, he added "We requested one of the sensor frigates take a closer look at the area."

"For a single dropship?" Ross said with skepticism. The Ruhar fleet was not going to re-task even a small warship to look for a single platoon, especially as the fleet was still hunting for enemy SD satellites. Admiral Kune's people thought they had neutralized the outer ring of defenses, but they thought they had suppressed enemy defenses before the first wave landed, and that had been an embarrassing disaster. Now Ross was worried the Ruhar would obsess over finding strategic defense satellites that didn't exist. Kune could tie up his fleet, delay the second wave and jeopardize the landing because he was chasing ghosts. "It's not worth risking a frigate for this. Is there anything else?"

"There is no indication that dropship was carrying Lieutenant Colonel Perkins," the soldier said, knowing why Ross was so interested in a single landing craft. To avoid detection and tracking, the dropships had deactivated their transponders, and the spacecraft had no external markings that were visible from a distance.

Ross stiffened. He hadn't known he was being so transparent in his concern for Perkins and her team. "Good work," he slapped the back of the chair. "Let me know if you get any additional data about that Dodo, but don't let it tie up your time. We've got battalions on the ground that need actionable intel."


Jesse froze when the figure in front of him held up a fist in a 'Halt' gesture. "We've got movement across the river," the figure said, identified in Jesse's visor as *Metzger, Thomas SGT*.

Jesse was tempted to raise his rifle so he could sight through its scope, but he maintained muzzle discipline, and kept the weapon pointed toward the ground in front and to his right side. He was also tempted to ask Metzger for details but he kept silent, knowing the sergeant would report details when he had them. Besides, Jesse had a data feed from Metzger's helmet, and all it was showing was vague blotches in between the dark trees across the river.

The rest of the squad was standing still, maintaining communications silence. To talk and exchange data feeds, they were using low-powered line-of-sight laserlinks between helmets, sent in burst transmissions that hopped frequencies. If one helmet was out of Jesse's line of sight, data from that soldier would automatically be relayed from a helmet between them. It was a cool technology, allowing Jesse and the two fireteam sergeants to see everything any of their soldiers could see. In combat, the technology could be distracting, the incoming flood of data overwhelming. Jesse usually kept feeds from the two sergeants in his squad open in windows in the upper corners of his visor, seeing what they were seeing. That way, he could see only what the two experienced sergeants thought was important, and ignore the clutter.

Keeping chatter, including data feeds, to a minimum was important. Energy of the laserlinks was detectable from backscatter if the enemy were paying attention, or if the area was covered by persistent sensors. With nine people in his squad, there could be enough laser energy bouncing around to be detectable even across the river. Jesse had to assume the enemy wasn't stupid, and not having seen sensors in the forest yet, didn't mean they weren't there. Perkins had given him permission to attempt a rescue, so he had taken two fireteams and set out for the river at the best pace they could manage through the dense forest. Jesse had gone forward with Sergeant Metzger's fireteam, while Sergeant Chan's fireteam set up their artillery a half kilometer east of the river. They only had been able to carry six rockets, so Jesse had to be careful when calling for fire support.

When they got within sight of the river, they had sent two scout drones ahead, crossing the quarter-mile width of the river and then splitting up to go northwest and southwest. The drone to the northwest had detected movement almost directly across the river from Jesse's position, and Metzger's team ordered the drones to return while Jesse helpfully provided effective leadership in the form of angry curses.

Damn the two pilots! What the *hell* had they been thinking? Just before the platoon began dropping down through the tree canopy, Derek Bonsu had sent a garbled burst transmission, stating that he and Striebich would attempt to set down on the other side of the river to assist the two injured soldiers who landed there. The pilots had requested backup ASAP, because four or more Wurgalan were approaching their position, then they lost contact.

Now Jesse had to find, render medical assistance to and extract across the river *four* people, not two. In his book, that was bad initiative, bad judgment *and* bad execution. Two pilots without combat skinsuits had no business playing hero. Pilots were supposed to *fly*, not act as cavalry. They were probably lost in the woods, or being hunted by the squids and Jesse's job had gotten much more difficult and complicated for-

"Movement at-" Metzger started to say, then there was no need to report anything, because they could all see what was happening with their own eyes.

Derek Bonsu came stumbling out of the tree line, with what Jesse guessed was Zheng on his shoulders in a fireman's carry. The trees ended by overhanging a two-meter riverbank before the sandy shore of the river, with the bank eroded underneath whenever the river flooded and thick, tangled roots covered the bluff. Derek at first looked for a way to walk down, then quickly got down on his knees and crawled backwards, slipping in mud and loose dirt the last meter and flopping on his belly with his legs in the water. Before Jesse could try opening a laserlink to the pilot's helmet, Derek rolled Zheng off his shoulder, carefully lying the Chinese soldier on the sandy shore and scrambled back up the bank, climbing on tree roots to help two more figures as they slowly came to the riverbank.

It was Rivera, who unlike Zheng was still in his combat skinsuit. The soldier was limping badly, leaning on one shoulder of Irene Striebich. She passed Rivera off to Derek and turned, dropping to one knee and taking cover behind a particularly stout tree, unslinging her rifle and taking aim. She fired a series of three-round bursts into the woods, and ducked behind the tree as return fire blew chunks out of the tree, sending dagger-like splinters flying everywhere. Derek had gotten Rivera safely down to the shore and began climbing back up, pulling his own rifle out of its holster.

"Holy shit, they did it," Jesse gasped in amazement. "No!" He shouted, but they didn't hear him. To communicate via laserlink, the pilots had to authorize their helmets to accept the encryption handshake from the platoon network, which they apparently hadn't thought to do.

Employing an alternative form of communication to get their attention, Jesse aimed above the pilots' heads and cut loose with a burst in full-auto. Sensors in their helmets should identify the source of the new fire as coming from a Kristang rifle-

They saw it. Irene turned, looking for Jesse, who waved his arms, hopping up and down. Irene tapped her helmet in an 'I can't hear you' gesture.

"Of *course* you can't, dumbass," Jesse said over the squad network, forgetting he was insulting an officer. "Down," he gesticulated, "get *down*!" Pointing again, he slung his rifle and pantomimed he was swimming, jabbing a finger at the water.

They got the message. Both pilots fired bursts into the trees and crawled to roll awkwardly down the riverbank, skidding and getting bumps and bruises as they bounced off protruding tree roots. Jesse was pleased to see both of them hung onto their rifles, and ran over to cover the two injured soldiers.

"Sergeant Chan," Jesse called as he designated coordinates across the river and sent them to the artillery fire team behind him. From sensors in his helmet, he had a rough idea where the enemy rifle fire was coming from, and it appeared there was only one source of enemy fire. "Light 'em up, two rockets."

"Affirmative," Chan responded. "On the waaay!"

There were only faint *Foomp, Foomp* sounds as one then another rocket were spit out of their launch tubes on electromagnetic rails. The rails gave each rocket enough momentum to soar upward fifty meters before their air-breathing rockets kicked in, providing a surge of power and taking them up to a hundred-fifty meters and arcing over the river. As the rockets reached the top of their arc, Jesse knew Chan had his team running away from the launch position, to avoid enemy counterbattery fire.

The rockets had active sensors in their nosecones, sending powerful pulses out to scan the forest beneath them. It seemed to Jesse that one of the rockets altered course slightly before the nosecones popped open, scattering submunitions to plunge down into the tree canopy. A line of fire erupted north to south in the trees across the river and the canopy swayed.

"Set and ready," Chan reported. His fireteam had run a safe distance and had two more rocket launchers ready to fire if needed.

"Hold," Jesse ordered. "Metzger, get your drones over there."

"There's a lot of smoke and fire," the scout team sergeant reported. "That could mask the enemy from infrared scans. Recommend we send in one drone, and keep one in reserve to scan for movement."

"Do what you think best," Jesse said, distracted because he was trying to ping the helmets of the pilots. They had covered the injured soldiers with their own bodies when they saw the rockets pop up, and Bonsu was now looking back across the river while Striebich trained her rifle into the trees, anticipating trouble.

"Hello, Sergeant Colter," Derek finally said, having gotten his helmet synced to the platoon network. "Thanks for that. Zheng is in a bad way."

"I see that. Keep your heads down until-"

"We've got calamari," Metzger reported, sending the drone image to Jesse.

The image showed the shattered and cooked body of a Wurgalan, several limbs blown off, lying draped over a downed tree. The alien's mech suit was punctured in multiple places. Jesse checked the data feed from the drone, it was not picking up any lifesigns. "Outstanding. I hope someone brought tartar sauce."

"Excuse me, but, *yuck*," Metzger replied with a nervous laugh, the tension of combat wearing off.

"Major Bonsu, our strike killed one Wurgalan. How many more are there?" Jesse asked.

"None." Relief was evident in Derek's voice. "There were four of them, originally."

"What happened?"

"Well, the other three went furniture shopping and, you know, that's never a good idea."

"*Furniture*, Sir?" Jesse grew concerned the pilot might have cracked under the strain.

"They were looking for a pilot's seat. It didn't end well for them, if you know what I mean."

"Oh," Jesse laughed. "Yeah. Uh, good work, Sir. Hold position, we're going to verify there are no more squids on your side."

"Staff Sergeant, please hurry, Zheng needs help."

"We brought a medic with us," Jesse gestured for the tenth member of the squad to come forward, as he watched two of Metzger's team unfold a small boat and begin inflating it. "We'll pull you out of there ASAP."


"Say, say again, Ardva Three," Dani wished her helmet was off, so she could press a finger over her ear and drown out the ambient noise. Communications with the Third Platoon were spotty and often drowned out by static. The comm tech was doing her best, but with the dropship's transmitter offline, her ability to affect the situation was limited. Packed away somewhere in the containers in the rear of the Dodo was the platoon's transmitter, but many of the containers were shot full of holes and it would take an hour to get the gear unpacked, inspected and set up, if the transmitter could be made to work. She didn't have an hour. "This is Ardva Two, please repeat."

Static, followed by crackling sounds and something garbled she couldn't understand. Between the enemy jamming and the need for every word to be translated, she couldn't understand what the speaker for Third Platoon was saying.

"Can you try?" Dani asked Surgun Auffex.

The surgun nodded and Dani heard the alien woman saying something, repeating it several times. Impatiently, Dani waited, glancing over at her platoon's medic. *Her* platoon. It was her command now, what was left of it. A wounded soldier had died while they waited for Besault to recover the pilots. That squad, having linked up with the pilots, was estimated to return to the ruined warehouse in three minutes, so she had that long to decide what to do. Pull out of the city, or go toward the center of Slugtown, to attempt a rescue of Third Platoon? Her burden would be a hell of a lot easier if she were able to talk with someone above her in the chain of command, someone, *anyone*. Scouts she had sent out reported seeing dropships setting down outside the city to the west, where Second and Third platoons were supposed to be. The scouts also reported air battles and parachutes, with some chutes falling inside the city.

Auffex looked up. "It's garbled but, I think Third is saying they have fifteen wounded, eight effectives. They got away from their dropship and are holed up in a sort of office building."

"*Eight?*" That was worse news than she had hoped for, much worse. If Third was getting out of the city, they were leaving their injured to be captured or killed, or they needed backup. "Who is in command?"

"A surgun third class," Auffex reported.

Which meant Dani was still the senior officer. Fan-*tast*-ic. Wonderful news.

"Do *they* have contact with anyone else?"

"No. A Vulture overflew their position, but was chased away by enemy aircraft."

The Vulture was a two-seat gunship spacecraft used by the Ruhar, assigned to cover the landing but not to remain long on the surface. The Force was also equipped with Chicken gunship aircraft, but those had to be dropped from orbit in cargo containers, or in the huge dropships that were called 'Whales' by UNEF. No Whales had been assigned to the first wave; they were considered too vulnerable.

"Captain Grace?" Auffex looked at her, looked *down* at her, for she was a foot or more taller, as were almost all of the Verd-kris. "If we are pulling out, I should get the wounded-"

"We are *not* pulling out," she announced, surprising herself. When had she made *that* decision? The answer to that question was easy: that decision had been made for her, when she volunteered to be embedded with, and *spy on*, a Verd-kris infantry platoon. If a human commander committed what the Verds would consider a cowardly act, allowing Third Platoon to die so she could save her own skin, the damage to the Legion would be severe. She had to at least try to rescue the trapped Verds. Having announced the decision, she had to give orders. In the United States Army, an operation should be informed by a document called the Commander's Intent, explaining what they were trying to accomplish, including what would be considered success. She didn't have time to create such a document, and she wasn't entirely sure what she intended. "Auffex, we need transport. Find two vehicles to carry the wounded out of the city, the pilots can drive them. Select, uh, four soldiers to go with them. And we need trucks or busses or something for the rest of us."

Just like that, she had committed an understrength alien platoon to a rescue mission inside a restricted area, with absolutely zero intel on the number, type and disposition of enemy forces in the area.

She took comfort in the fact that, since the Ruhar 7th Fleet had missed the existence of an *entire strategic defense network* and ordered the assault ships to jump in, hers could not possibly be the worst decision that day.

# CHAPTER EIGHTEEN

"This feels *weird*," Derek whispered to Irene as they were fitted for skinsuits. One of the cargo containers that had made it intact to the surface was recovered by the platoon, and happily it contained eleven skinsuits, still in boxes. Two of them fit the pilots, and Perkins had declared the platoon could move more quickly if the pilots were in mech suits, so that was the end of the discussion.

The argument, if it could be called that, began when Irene and Derek volunteered to stay with the wounded and a medic, while the platoon moved out to, well, do whatever they could do in the middle of the gosh-darned wilderness. The platoon was isolated from the rest of the Legion, without any way to effectively communicate with other units on the ground, or whoever was left in orbit. That someone was in orbit was clear from occasional flashes of light high above, though it was not known if the ships upstairs were Ruhar, Wurgalan or a mixture of both. Shortly before Jesse led his squad back to the platoon, they had seen a streak in the sky followed by a flash of light to the northeast. A ship had conducted an orbital strike against a target on the ground. A Ruhar ship hitting the enemy, or the Wurgalan hitting Legion forces? They simply didn't have any way to know. Sensors in their helmets, that could reliably discriminate between fire from Legion and Wurgalan rifles, were useless for telling what type of starships were shooting over their heads. While several cargo containers had survived the trip to the surface intact, none of them contained the heavy-duty jamming-resistant communications gear they were supposed to have.

"It's not *weird*," Irene whispered back as she wriggled her shoulders to get the suit settled properly around her. "It feels like a flightsuit. Anyway, we have trained to use combat suits."

"Sure, *twice*," Derek retorted. "The second time was just for fun."

As a reply, Irene fastened her helmet, pulled the faceplate down, and crouched. With a spring, she leapt into the air, doing a backflip and landing perfectly, something she could never have done on her own. "Ta-da," she announced with a bow.

"Showoff," Derek had to grin. "All right, but this time we stay behind the bang-bang people," he pantomimed firing a rifle, "Ok?"

"You squared away, Sir, Ma'am?" Jesse Colter asked as he inspected Derek's suit.

"Fine, Staff Sergeant," Derek demonstrated by standing on one foot and leaning forward farther than he could have without the suit stabilizing his stance. "When do we move out?"

Jesse looked at something in his visor. "Five minutes."

Derek lowered his voice. "You realize this could be a fool's errand? Odds are against us finding something to fly."

"If we can find the keys," Jesse asked with a wink, "can you fly it?"

Derek snorted. "If we can get it started, we can get it in the air. You realize that attacking an air base with ground troops could go wrong in a hurry? The enemy can shoot back."

"We got that taken care of," Jesse boasted with false bravado, pointing to a fireteam equipped with Zinger portable air-defense missiles. The truth was, he wasn't confident the platoon could successfully assault the target air base. And if they did, there was no guarantee they would capture any flightworthy aircraft. They did have to try, or settle for sitting out the battle for Squidworld.

The opportunity presented itself when a soldier reviewing sensor data collected during their plunge through the atmosphere found something unexpected. A clearing that appeared to be small air base for vertical-takeoff craft. It was nothing more than an area of trees that had been hacked down and cleared of stumps, and a scattering of temporary structures. The noses of two aircraft could be seen poking out of netting, and when Irene and Derek examined the images, they agreed the items on the ground in front of both aircraft were engine components. It was the platoon's hope they could capture the airbase without destroying either of the aircraft, that somehow they could get one of them flying, and that the pilots could get them in the air. Failing that, Colonel Perkins just hoped the base had some sort of comm gear more powerful than skinsuits were equipped with.

Derek privately thought finding a way to modify Wurgalan communications equipment, so they could talk to Legion equipment, was even less likely than finding a flightworthy aircraft. But one of the soldiers who was the platoon's comm specialist expressed confidence she could handle the task, so that was that. "I *hope* you can handle air threats," Derek said doubtfully. In the air, MANPAD missiles were frightening. On the ground, the dinky little weapons looked like they would have trouble shooting down a pigeon.

Jesse stiffened. He liked the pilots and they seemed to like him, the Mavericks had always gotten along well, despite originally being thrown together by a Mysterious Benefactor on Paradise. That didn't mean the pilots could disparage the ground-pounders' ability to do their jobs. "We'll get you there," he said evenly, saving his anger for the enemy. "You figure out how to fly, whatever we find." With that, he turned away to check on other people.

"Derek, honey," Irene said softly. "That was a great way to be a jackass."

"What did I say?"

"Colter, and the Colonel? They want to get comms, not just because we have a job to do down here, but to find out what happened to Jarrett and Czajka."

"Ah, shit," Derek closed his eyes tightly. "My bad. Hell, I want to know if they're Ok, too. And Nert. I love that fuzzy little guy."

"Nert is not *little*," she reminded him, while adjusting the sling of his rifle. Sniffling, she wiped away a tear. "I even miss that Surgun Jates."

"Me too. Hey, there's no reason to *miss* them yet. We don't know anything."

"We know their Dodo was behind ours in the launch sequence. You saw the ship after we launched. It was cracked in half. We didn't see any other dropships launch from the *Big Mac* after us."

"We didn't *see* much of anything," he reminded her. "There was a whole lot of kinetic shit flying around up there. Ok, I guess that's our cue," he added when Colter waved to the pilots. "If there's any shooting, we stay behind the people who know what they're doing."

Irene slung her rifle. "I won't argue with that."

"Comms are still jammed," Dave announced with disgust. He had been trying intermittently to send a signal to the fleet above, hoping someone up there would pick up his ID code and send a SAR bird down for them. Either his signal wasn't getting through, or all the Search And Rescue aircraft were busy on more important taskings. He couldn't use the suit's comm system for more than occasional burst transmissions, or he would risk the enemy triangulating their position. "Ok, time for Plan B," he bent down to gather sticks and dried brush, then used a tiny torch to set them burning.

"You intend to make a *fire*?" Jates was surprised. "That could draw the enemy's attention."

"Way out here, in the ass end of nowhere? I don't think anyone is looking this way. Not with all that," he pointed to twisting contrails in the air high to the east, and continued flashes of light in orbit. "Going on. The squids aren't wasting ordnance on the two of us."

Jates considered that, then nodded. "Agreed. What good will a fire do for us?"

To answer, Dave pulled a thin sheet out of his pack. It was paper thin but could keep him warm in subfreezing temperatures, and weighed next to nothing. "When the fire gets going, we'll throw in these wet leaves," he pointed to the pile of leaves at his feet. "They will make a lot of smoke."

Jates scowled. "Survival training in hostile terrain tells us to avoid making fires, and assure they burn cleanly if we must use a fire."

"Yeah, well, I took that same training course. We're going to use the smoke," he covered the burgeoning fire with the sheet and pulled it away to release a puff of dark smoke. "To send signals. Do you know Morse code?"

Jates shook his head. "No, but I have heard of it. A primitive digital communications scheme."

"Digital?" Dave asked, surprised.

"Yes." The Verd cocked his head. "Instead of Ones and Zeroes, Morse uses short and long pulses, no?"

"Huh. Digital. I never thought of it that way. Ok, yeah."

Jates reached beside him to gather a handful of dried twigs. "You are hoping these Morse signals will be seen from space? I do not think the Ruhar will recognize your Morse system."

Dave shook his head and blew on the fire. It glowed brightly orange. "The message isn't for the hamsters. I want Shauna to see it."

"Sergeant Jarrett?"

"Yup. She and Nert came down somewhere around here. We need to link up or," he looked around at the uninhabited green wilderness. "We could be stuck here a very long time."

In response, Jates stood and limped away to gather more wood for the fire. "If this works, it is a clever idea, Czajka," Jates said in a choked voice, as if it were painful to speak each word.

"You think we humans aren't so stupid now?"

"I didn't say that," Jates growled.

"Yup," Dave grinned. "He *likes* me."

Derek nearly stumbled into the back of the soldier in front of him when Staff Sergeant Colter abruptly stopped and held up a fist in the 'halt' signal. Derek must have missed that meeting or that memo, or however it was the infantry explained their secret handshakes, and he was concentrating on not tripping over bushes, logs, stones, vines, ground cover and everything else that made trying to run in the forest a difficult task. Mostly, Derek had been looking at the ground three feet in front of himself, trying not to stumble. The soldiers appeared to have an easier time with the slow jog pace they had maintained, and not because they were more fit. The skinsuits did most of the work for them. Derek wondered if, like the soldiers, he should trust the suit's sensors and computer to keep him from tripping.

"Why are we stop-"

Colter held up a finger for silence, with a glare back at Derek. With their helmet faceplates sealed, no one could hear Derek talking, but he had forgotten to turn off the transmitter. A text message came in from Sergeant Metzger, on the platoon-wide channel. *I hear something*, the message read.

Derek stilled his breathing and bumped up the augmented hearing of the helmet. He heard something also. A whine, increasing in both intensity and pitch. He recognized that sound, for he knew it well. "That's an aircraft taking off," he recorded the message and sent it out as text. According to the map, the airfield that was their target lay less than three kilometers ahead.

*Take cover. Minimal movement*, came the order from Perkins.

Derek followed the lead of the soldier next to him, seeing Irene do the same. They huddled behind trees, keeping still in case the enemy was using movement-tracking sensors. In Derek's experience, trying to track movement in a forested area, from an aircraft, was a waste of time. But it didn't hurt to be cautious. Hopefully the aircraft would go wherever it was going, and leave the area.

It didn't. The engine sound faded, then grew louder. Through the trees, Derek tried to catch a glimpse of the aircraft, his helmet assisted and found nothing. Based on the sound, it was to the south but he couldn't see anything at all. The aircraft must be wrapped in a stealth field or at least engaged its chameleonware to blend in with the sky. The threat identification system in his helmet compared the droning engine sound to its database, and an icon popped up at the bottom of his visor. It was a gunship, a type of light aircraft used by the Wurgalan for close air support of ground troops. Derek saw the UNEF designation for the aircraft was *W-10 Warthog*, and he smiled. Someone in UNEF-HQ had a sense of humor. Or history.

Shit.

He had hoped it was a high-performance fighter that lacked ground-scanning sensors, and would soon be zooming away to challenge Legion aircraft, but it was a Warthog.

Like he suspected the platoon around him were doing, he held his breath as the unseen aircraft droned on past to their south, headed away.

Then the sound grew louder again, flying past to the west. Derek swiveled his head, following the invisible source of sound. So far, it had taken off to the west, turned north and now was flying toward the east. Eyeclicking an icon in his visor provided a quick check of local weather conditions, and dashed his hopes. He had thought maybe the aircraft had taken off in their direction to fly into the wind, but the wind was coming from the north. The pilot, or pilots, had flown toward the platoon for a reason other than safe takeoff procedure.

When he heard the droning sound coming back, he recorded and checked a text message. *They're flying a grid search*, read the text.

*Hold position*, came the reply from Perkins. *There is no indication they've seen us. Do not fire. AA teams report readiness.*

If the anti-aircraft missile teams reported, they did it on a separate channel, though Derek did see a pair of soldiers to his left attach a targeting box to a missile tube.

The aircraft buzzed overhead to the south, closer that time. There was still no sign the platoon had been detected, but it could simply be that the aircraft's sensors were out of range. Assuming the pilot knew the footprint the aircraft's sensors could cover, the grid search would be thorough. The wildcard in the equation was Derek did not know how good the Wurgalan sensors were. He did know that Ruhar skinsuits were difficult to detect, unless you knew what to look for.

He had to assume the enemy was not completely clueless.

One thing he did know was the Zinger MANPAD missile provided by the Ruhar, officially designated 'Cobra' by UNEF. He had trained to defend his aircraft against Cobras, in case they were captured by an enemy and used against the Legion. Because in training, he had experience being shot at rather than being the shooter, he had a different perspective from the platoon's air defense soldiers. The situation was dire enough that he risked opening a channel directly to Perkins. "Colonel, we should shoot while the aircraft is coming at us. The Cobra is less effective against a crossing target."

Her response was a simple text: *Acknowledged.*

Remaining as still as possible, Derek turned his head to watch the air defense team to his left. The soldier with the missile on her shoulder raised it, waiting for a cue from the spotter, or some other signal. Seconds later, there was a barely-visible puff of water vapor from the missile tube as the weapon was launched, soaring upward through the trees, already curving though its little motor had not kicked on.

When the rocket motor ignited, the missile streaked away at a speed that stunned Derek. His perspective had always been from above, and though missiles rose at high speed; his adrenaline surge made it seem like slow-motion. From the ground, the missile was out of sight in the blink of an eye.

The droning whine of the aircraft increased to a roar and he heard a chattering sound. The Wurgalan used slug-firing cannons rather than directed-energy weapons for aircraft defense, slugs with proximity sensors that detonated the warhead in front of an incoming missile, which flew into a hot wall of shrapnel.

The ground shook and trees trembled as one missile was exploded short of the target. Derek realized he was relieved, part of him wanting the aircraft to get away.

*Screw* that, he told himself. Kill that bird before it can drop ordnance on our position.

Before he understood what was happening, a soldier hauled him to his feet, tugging him to run forward. Remaining in the place where missiles had been launched was not good for the platoon's health and welfare, they scattered in a well-practiced maneuver. Derek gamely followed the soldier who guided him forward, and he had taken only two jittery strides when a larger explosion from above rocked the forest and he instinctively flattened himself on the ground, grateful to see everyone else doing the same.

Pieces of blackened shrapnel rained down, shredding the upper foliage of the trees, none of it doing any damage to the armor-clad platoon. Derek was about to get up when something pinged off his back and he felt the soldier next to him push him down. "Wait for the All-Clear, Sir," the soldier said, and she gave him a reassuring smile.

The All-Clear signal came moments later and soldiers sprang to their feet and shed their backpacks, some of them removing spare magazines to attach to the belts of their mech suits. Derek saw one of the anti-air teams pull the targeting box off a missile launch tube and discard the tube, attaching the box to another tube as they moved. As a unit, the platoon began moving forward again, at a faster pace.

"Not you, Sir, Ma'am," the soldier next to Derek said, holding up a hand to stop them. "Colonel says you are to hang back with me, until the airfield is secured."

"Listen," Derek checked his visor for the soldier's ID. She was British, identified as '*Carson, Elizabeth CPL'*. "Corporal, we don't need babysitters."

"The Colonel thinks you *do* need someone to keep you safe out here, so it doesn't matter what the three of us think, does it?" She inspected the rocket launcher under the barrel of her rifle.

"I see your point," Derek conceded.

"Can we at least get closer to the airbase?" Irene argued.

"Ma'am," Carson watched the platoon advancing through the forest at high speed. For the assault, they had left behind their backpacks and all the heavy gear, gambling that speed would win the day. The rockets that composed the platoon's light artillery had been left behind and Derek could understand why, they couldn't risk damaging the aircraft they hoped to capture. Whatever plan Perkins had intended to implement had gone out the window when they shot down the Warthog and lost all possibility of surprise. "If the two of you get killed out here, this attack will have been for nothing."

"Plus, you know, it would kind of ruin our day," Derek joked.

Carson didn't see the humor.

"All right," Irene raised her hands. "Corporal, you know how to use this artillery?"

The soldier cocked her head, curious. "We have all been cross-trained, Ma'am. We're not using artillery in this fight."

"We're not using it *now*," Irene insisted. "If the platoon runs into heavy opposition and has to retreat, it would help if we dropped a couple of these," she pointed to a pair of rockets propped up against a tree, "on the enemy, right?"

That suggestion met with Carson's approval. "Yes." She slung her rifle. "Pick up those tubes and set them on the ground like-"

The artillery wasn't needed. Unfortunately, neither were the pilots. When the call came to approach the airfield after the sounds of combat ceased, the tone of the message was not hopeful. Stepping out of the woods into the rough clearing, Irene saw with dismay that the one remaining aircraft was another two-seat Warthog gunship. She would not be transporting the platoon in that little craft, even if it were flightworthy. Which it was not. "Shit!" She exclaimed. "You were *not* supposed to shoot up the-"

"Honey," Derek caught her arm, drawing her attention to a Legion soldier lying on the ground, one arm missing below the elbow. Two other human soldiers were being treated for wounds where enemy weapons had penetrated their armor, and several others were applying patches to their damaged skinsuits.

Irene felt absolutely like shit. The platoon had risked their lives to capture an aircraft for her to fly, and the fact that the op had failed to achieve its objective did not lessen the courage and sacrifice of the soldiers involved. "Sorry," she took a deep breath. "How bad is it?"

Jesse Colter answered as he walked toward them, brushing soot from the front of his suit. "We're hoping you can tell us, Ma'am," he said. "The squids shot up their own aircraft when they saw they were losing the fight."

Following Jesse, the two pilots walked over to the temporary hangar where the Warthog was parked. The structure was just a series of hoops with fabric stretched between them, keeping direct sunlight and rain off the aircraft. "Ohhh," Derek groaned when he stepped under the sagging, bullet-riddled fabric and saw the bullets had treated the Warthog roughly. "That's not good."

"Can we fix it?" Jesse asked, because he felt he needed to make the effort.

Derek peered inside the duct where the turbine engine sucked in air. "If we had all the duct tape in the galaxy, we couldn't put his thing together again."

"Whoo," Irene agreed. "What a mess. The squids knew exactly how to disable this aircraft. Oh, hell," she turned to step outside. "Maybe there is a spare turbine under one of these tarps?" There were a half-dozen tarps clustered together on one side of the clearing, plus two more temporary hangars. One of the hoop structures was open and clearly empty, the other only had one hoop holding it up, with fabric sagging down around a lumpy shape underneath. From the clumps of leaves on low parts of the fabric, and water pooled in the creases, she guessed the dirty fabric had not been disturbed in a while.

"We haven't found anything like that," Jesse reported, watching soldiers on the other side of the clearing pulling up tarps and looking underneath. "No, there are supplies and spare parts, but nothing like an engine. We'll keep looking," he added. "The squids have tents back in the woods, we haven't checked all those yet."

Derek shared a discouraged look with Irene. Now that he was in the clearing, he saw that it had been blasted out of the forest with a large bomb that knocked trees down out from the center. He recalled reading that the US Army had tried something similar in Vietnam, creating instant helicopter landing zones in the jungle by dropping bunker-busters. The Wurgalan had improved the site by dragging trees away, clearing stumps and smoothing the ground, the bomb hadn't done all the work for them. He was sure that if the enemy had airlifted in heavy equipment like a spare turbine, they would not have wasted the effort to drag it into the woods. "What's under that big tarp?"

Jesse waved for them to follow. "You kinda need to see it for yourself, Sir."

Derek's shoulders slumped when he pushed aside the sagging fabric. It was big. It was ungainly. It was dirty and dented and looked old. "You have *got* to be kidding me. What an absolute piece of crap."

Irene's reaction was the opposite. "*Cool*," she walked forward, running a gloved hand under the ugly nose of the awkward beast.

"Cool?" he couldn't believe the other pilot's reaction. "You realize this thing is a freakin' *helicopter*, right?"

"Yeah, so?" She ignored him, walking deeper into the tent, pushing the sagging material up and out of her way.

"So," he craned his neck to see the rear of the ungainly aircraft. "This thing has an actual *tail rotor*. Isn't that kind of old school even back on Earth? I guess this explains how the squids airlifted in all their supplies. Ha!" he laughed.

"What?"

"I love you."

That made her stop her examination of the alien machine and turn around. "What prompted that?" She asked, curious.

"Only you," he shook his head, a twinkle in his eyes. "Would think the idea of flying this rust bucket is cool. I am a lucky man."

"Oh," she blushed. "Is this like how, when I've been helping tear apart a gearbox and I've got grease in my hair, you tell me I'm beautiful?"

Derek stuck to the safe answer. "Maybe?"

"Why don't you ever tell me I'm beautiful, after I've spent an hour working on my hair?"

"There is no way I am ever answering that question."

"Smart man," she patted his cheek, and leaned in to kiss him.

"Seriously," he frowned, looking at the grimy windows on the beast. They looked like actual *windows*, some sort of clear composite. "You think you can fly this thing?"

"Uh-huh," she went up on her toes to look inside the cockpit. "I was a Blackhawk driver, remember?"

"Didn't the grunts," he flashed an apology to the nearest soldier, "call that a 'Crash-hawk'?"

"The Army fixed the horizontal stabilizer issue a long time ago," she defended the aircraft's honor.

"Do you know whether the squids fixed all the problems with," he knocked on the canopy, alarmed by the clunky, hollow sound. "*This* thing?"

"There's one way to find out."

When the fabric cover was lifted off to expose the helicopter, it was Emily Perkins's turn to shrug and shake her head. "Somebody up there," she looked at the sky, "really hates me today."

"It's not so bad, Ma'am," Irene assured their CO.

"It looks like an *insect*," Perkins protested.

"It *looks* like an old Sikorsky CH-54 Skycrane," Irene insisted.

"The Ugly Bug is a rugged aircraft, Colonel," Derek said. "We got both turbines cranked over, they should start."

Irene arched an eyebrow. "We're calling it the Ugly Bug?"

"We are *now*," Derek confirmed.

Perkins stepped up on the insect-like landing gear and peered into the cockpit. She had to spit on the windows and wipe it with a glove to get a decent view. "I see only four seats. Where is the rest of the platoon supposed to sit?"

Irene had an answer, pointing to what looked like a smooth-sided seatainer, partly covered with brush on the other side of the airfield. The end doors of the seatainer where open, with junk spilling out. On the side they could see, something had made a foot-long gash in the pod's skin, and elsewhere it was dented, scuffed and dirty. "In there, Ma'am. I'm pretty sure that's a dedicated cargo pod for the Ugly Bug."

"Pretty sure?"

"We'll know once we look at the top of the pod. If it has brackets to attach under there," she pointed up to the spine of the helicopter. "Then it was made to fit."

"How are we going to breathe in there?"

Derek answered that question. "We could leave the back doors open, or detach them. Or, you know, it looks like that thing isn't exactly airtight anyway."

The look Perkins gave him did not express overwhelming confidence.

"Sorry," Derek added. "If it makes you feel any better, I won't be flying the Ugly Bug."

"That does not make me feel better," Perkins clarified. "All right, Striebich. You can really fly this thing?"

"It's a helicopter," she nodded. "The flight controls mostly look familiar."

Perkins walked over to touch one of the five rotor blades that were drooping within a meter of the ground. "What about, ah," she mentioned one of the few facts she knew about helicopters. "Mast bumping?"

Irene was impressed the colonel knew even that much. "It's mast *bump*, Ma'am. It only happens once."

"Because then you're dead?"

Irene nodded. "That isn't an issue with multi-blade designs like this. Don't worry, the rotor blades will clear the tail boom," she declared with confidence she didn't feel. "We can at least try it."

Perkins considered a moment, but only for a moment. Her choices were to attempt flying the ugly helicopter, or remain at the isolated air base and sit out the fight. Letting someone else do the fighting was not an option. "All right, Striebich, give it a shot."

"Yes, Ma'am," Irene's expression brightened. "While we're getting it started, could you assign a team to clear out that cargo pod, and move it to the center of the airfield? I need a lot of clearance to set down on top, to attach it."

"*Move* it?" Perkins was skeptical.

"It has wheels," Derek pointed to parallel tracks dug into the clearing, leading to where the pod was parked. "They must retract."

Perkins looked at the wheel tracks. They were deep, the tracks filled with water. A flattened area between the tracks made it clear the pod's bottom had been dragged in the dirt, "This day just keeps getting better and better."


As they hiked through the forest, Shauna noticed Nert regularly halting to peer intently at the sky ahead of them. His pausing to search the sky didn't slow them down, they could only walk at the speed Chowdhury could manage. The woman's skinsuit was working to repair itself, using the spare tube of nanites that Shauna had brought in the container tethered to her own parachute. Nert had brought Chowdhury down as safely as he could, given the weight of two people and their gear on one parachute. The landing sent them crashing down through thick tree cover and both Ruhar and human had sustained bumps and bruises. The serious issue was the damage to Chowdhury's thigh. They had removed her suit leg and treated the wound as best they could with the medical kit available. Chowdhury still had fragments of composite embedded in her thigh muscle, and she gritted her teeth with every power-assisted stride, despite the nerve blockers administered by her suit. As the suit repaired itself, it took over more of the burden of walking from the user. Shauna still worried that Chowdhury's face was pale and her blood pressure low. She also worried that they hadn't heard from Dave or Jates. Or in fact, they had not heard from anyone. Enemy jamming was strong and the Legion must be jamming right back, for a search across the spectrum had not detected any coherent signals.

Shauna glanced behind her to where Chowdhury was bravely hobbling along, grimacing whenever she had to lift her injured leg to step over a fallen log. Shauna flashed an encouraging smile and looked behind the other woman, to where Nert was standing still, staring at the sky. Finally, Shauna couldn't contain her curiosity. "Nert? Cadet Dandurf," she added when the teenager didn't respond. "What is so interesting?"

Nert held up an index finger as he shrugged off his pack. "I need to check something," he explained. "Be right back."

Like a squirrel, he climbed a tree, the trunk swaying and bending under his weight. Shauna's heart was in her mouth as she feared the tree would snap, but Nert stopped before he climbed so high that the tree broke. He stayed there a minute, then slid down, hopping away from the tree to thud to the ground. "It is Mister Czajka!" he reported excitedly.

"What is?" Shauna demanded, bewildered. "How do you know it is Dave?"

Nert's grin was ear to ear. "Who else in this area would be sending smoke signals in human Morse code?"

The reunion was sudden and unexpected. Shauna was in the lead, walking slowly enough so Chowdhury would not struggle too much to keep up, with Nert just behind the injured woman. Shauna splashed across a shallow stream and climbed the far bank, stepping on a downed tree.

Standing right there was David Czajka, with Surgun Jates beside him, leaning on a makeshift crutch.

"Dave!" Shauna whooped with joy.

"Shauna," Dave grinned as they embraced, slapping each other on the back. "You got our message, huh?"

"Nert did," Shauna admitted. "I saw the smoke, but thought it was burning debris from orbit." She twirled a finger over her head, encompassing numerous small fires that indeed were burning at all points of the compass.

"Greetings, Mister Czajka!" Nert waved with enthusiasm. "It was not me, really. I had tasked my suit to look for patterns underlying the jamming. Instead, it detected a pattern in your smoke signals."

Jates was skeptical. "Ruhar suit computers are programmed to recognize obscure human codes?"

"No, Surgun," Nert blushed, the already pinkish skin under his downy fur turning deeper hue. "I had downloaded that information to my suit."

"Shit," Dave cursed. "I should have thought of doing that. I had to scrape the code up from memory."

Nert cocked his head. "Oh, 'SOS' is easy; three dots, three dashes, and three dots."

"Yeah, well," Dave hung his head sheepishly. "We practiced using that signal when I was in the Boy Scouts. It was kinda burned into my brain, you know?"

Shauna shook her head. "Good thing it was. What happened to you guys?"

"Oh, you know," Dave shrugged. "The usual."

Shauna nodded knowingly. "That bad, huh?"

"We landed in the water, and I had to drag fat-ass here," Dave jerked a thumb at Jates.

"Hey!" the Verd barked.

"-to shore. Then the freakin' ship tried to kill us, *twice*."

"Three times," Jates corrected.

"Three?"

Jates ticked off the incidents on his fingers. "Sonic boom caused a landslide, then the impact shockwave, then the tsunami."

"Three, yeah," Dave agreed, his head bobbing up and down. "How about you guys? You Ok there, Chowdhury?"

"Hurts," she grunted. "I'll live. Unless we all die down here."

Shauna looked at Jates, who was wearing only scraps of his suit liner, with palm leaves tied around his feet as sandals. The surgun had lost his skinsuit and pack, but still wore a toolbelt, with a rifle slung over one shoulder. "Good news is, I landed with an extra skinsuit, plus one bag of other supplies. We left the gear at our landing site, about twelve klicks back."

"Great!" Dave's expression brightened. "We need to get *Tarzoon* of the Jungle here," he indicated Jates again, "out of his string bikini and into something that covers his scaly ass."

"I am *not* wearing a bikini," Jates protested with a growl, looking down at his tattered suit liner. He had used a sheet from Dave's pack to wrap around his hips so the toolbelt didn't chafe his already-bruised skin, and another strip of sheet around his chest where the rifle sling rested.

"Uh," Dave giggled. "You kinda *are*."

Shauna laughed. "Back home, we would call that outfit *Daisy Dukes* and a *tube top*," she snickered, sending herself and Dave into uncontrollable gales of laughter.

Jates was miserable. "If you will excuse me for a moment," he patted his toolbelt, "I will pull the pin and attempt to swallow one of these grenades."


Master Assassin Baltazaz Revo wiped his knife clean and sheathed it, having used the blade against the leader of his section. The other six members of the section had been killed by the well-prepared Wurgalan defenders, after being ordered to make a frontal assault that was foolish, wasteful and just simply unprofessional.

Revo killed the section leader partly because the man was an idiot, having urged Revo to come with him on one last glorious and suicidal charge against the enemy, but mostly because Revo did not have time for any nonsense like ground combat. He was on Stiglord for one purpose, and now that he was on the ground, he no longer had to pretend to be an ordinary Achakai soldier.

There was at least one other master assassin on the planet, from a rival House. They both had the same target.

For the honor of his House, for the honor of the Achakai people, Revo had to get to Emily Perkins first.

# CHAPTER NINETEEN

As the Ugly Bug wobbled across the sky, the big rotor blades threatening to shake the craft apart, Irene had to admit she was wrong. "This thing *is* a piece of shit."

"It's old," Derek reminded her.

"It's not just old," she once again applied pressure to the right with her right foot, to swing the nose back onto the flight path. Instead of having two foot pedals for the tail rotor to control yaw movement left or right, there was a wheel set into the floor. Rolling the wheel to the right caused the nose to point in that direction, rolling the wheel to the left had the opposite reaction. It made sense and freed her left foot to control the cyclic, the pitch of the rotor blade, and the autothrottle was tied to the cyclic. She could also manually control the throttle, the point being that only one of her hands was used for flight controls.

That was the sum of the good news. With the helicopter having been designed for Wurgalan, the seat didn't fit her, so she had to straddle it, with the backrest too far behind. The foot controls were designed for the short leg tentacles of squids, forcing her into an awkward position with her legs up in front of her. She could handle being uncomfortable if the aircraft flew properly, but it didn't. Control in all three flight axes was intermittent, with a dangerous time lag between control input and response. She could trim the pitch and once the aircraft got to cruise speed, the roll was dampened, but the trim for yaw wasn't working, neither was the autopilot. The result was that the nose wobbled from right to left constantly. In any type of flying, it was important to stay ahead of the aircraft, to anticipate what the pilot needed to do next. She had to stay ahead of the Ugly Bug by inputting opposite yaw as soon as the nose began to swing in the correct direction. "*Old* isn't the only problem. When this thing came off the assembly line, they should have driven it around back and crushed it."

"It's not *that* bad," Derek countered. "I kind of like it. Look," he pointed to round indents in the consoles in front of them. "When's the last time you saw a military helo with *cupholders*? Cool, huh?"

"I don't think those are-"

"Uh oh," Derek interrupted her. "If I'm reading this nav system correctly," he frowned. His visor was translating the odd squiggly Wurgalan script so he could read it. "We have to fly over a lake."

"Yeah, so?"

"So, this is a *lake*. Like, one of the Great Lakes. It's over seventy kilometers across, at the point where we'll cross the shore."

Irene didn't like the idea of being over water that long. Not only because she didn't trust the Ugly Bug, but also because the aircraft would be totally exposed in the open. She had been hugging terrain features, following river valleys and only popping up over ridges when she had to. Twisting contrails in the sky to the east told her the contest for control of the airspace was not over. A single obsolete cargo helicopter flying low and slow would not highlight anyone's threat scopes, and she was not concerned about being directly targeted by a high-performance aircraft. No one flying a fighter or gunship would go out of their way to attack the Ugly Bug. But if a combat aircraft happened to be flying overhead, she could see a pilot toggling off a missile to pad their number of kills. "Can we go around?"

"Nuh uh," Derek shook his head. "My suit's nav system confirms. Going around to the north will add more than an hour of flight time, and take us near a mid-sized town. Going around to south adds ninety-seven minutes to our flight time."

"That's no good." She was glad that Derek was handling the navigation chores. "Give me a compromise?"

"Uh, Ok. Let me- There's a narrower section to the north, if we cut across there, we'll be over water for only forty-eight klicks. That's the best I can do."

"Colonel?" Irene knew the decision on a flight plan was a judgment call. "We have two options, both of them bad."

Over water, they were low enough that the big rotor blades were kicking up a rooster tail of spray behind their flight path. Irene increased altitude gradually, with Derek leaning up against the canopy to see behind them. She levelled off when the rotor blades were merely creating a downwash and not a streak of visible spray pointing directly to them.

Twelve kilometers behind them, thirty-six to go until they were over the opposite shore. Either the lake typically had no boat traffic, or the invasion had caused boaters to get back to shore, because there was nothing moving on the surface in any direction

The Ugly Bug was still annoyingly not keeping to a straight course, no matter how strong or delicate her control inputs. To move forty-eight klicks forward, they guessed they were moving through the air a distance ten or more percent greater than that. The damned thing was also loud, not that she could hear with the noise-cancelling features of her helmet. She could feel the vibration and, if that were normal, she felt sorry for the squids who regularly were assigned to fly the thing.

Thirty kilometers behind them, only eighteen to go. The previously empty lake was dotted with islands on the eastern shore, mostly small and rocky and flat, with no structures and few trees.

"Once we're over land," Derek advised, "we should turn to follow this river valley," he pointed to the grimy navigation display between the seats.

"Got it," Irene had no opinion, other than wanting to get the flight over with. Her legs were cramping from holding the awkward position. "Just tell me when-"

The Ugly Bug slewed to the right so abruptly, her feet slipped off the controls for a moment. Her heart in her mouth, she carefully restored control and let the aircraft continue along its new course, afraid of trying to coax it in any other direction.

"*That* wasn't normal," Derek turned to stare at the pilot.

"No," she swallowed hard. "*That*, felt like loss of tail rotor authority, in a simulator."

"You have only experienced it in a simulator?"

She shot him a look. "If it happens in flight, you don't live through the experience." The Ugly Bug lurched to the right again, slipping out of her control and just as suddenly, she had yaw authority again. "Oh, shit. Find me an island. *Now*!"

"An island, right." Derek knew better than to argue.

Perkins did not. She saw the aircraft was turning away from the shore, slowing and descending. "Striebich? What's going on?"

"We're setting down ASAP," Irene did not waste time by adding a 'Colonel' or 'Ma'am'.

"On the shore?" Perkins rose from the seat she straddled. The shoreline was trees in both directions, with no place to land that she could see. Except for where a river flowed into that lake, there were mudflats and sandbars.

"No. We're landing on the closest island that has space for us."

"Negative," Perkins countermanded the pilot. "The shore is only fifteen kilometers. Whatever the problem is, we-"

"*My* aircraft, *my* authority," Irene snapped in a voice that allowed no arguments. She respected Perkins as a CO, and she also was not taking flying advice from a know-nothing passenger.

"Turn to, uh," Derek tried to translate Wurgalan math to human in his head. "Oh, hell, head toward that flat island just south of the island with the two big trees," he pointed.

With Perkins fuming behind her, Irene flew straight in, not daring to swing around into the wind for landing. She was barely touching the yaw wheel and when she did, it felt *squishy*, like it wasn't connected properly, or the connection was slipping. That didn't make sense. If something important had broken, it should be *broken*, not causing an intermittent failure.

The procedure for setting the Ugly Bug down was as ugly as the aircraft itself. Irene got the main gear to touch, then cut power and let the nose gear flop down. "Holy sh-" her hands were shaking.

"Striebich," Perkins's tone was frosty. "I sure hope you know what the *hell* you're doing. We're sitting ducks out here."

*I know that*, is what Irene wanted to say. She kept her comments to herself.

Derek popped open the door on his side, the hinges creaked and protested. "We need to check the tail rotor. Coming with me, Striebich?" He used the pilot's last name in an effort to keep everything strictly professional. She got off the seat, her leg cramps making her fall to the dirty floor of the cockpit. Derek held out a hand to help her get to the ground, a gray shelf of rock. The whole island was a mostly fat pile of rock covered with sand, with low bushes growing in cracks where sand and water collected. The Ugly Bug stuck out like a sore thumb and the shore was too far away for swimming.

"Sir," Jesse hopped out the open back of the cargo pod. "What's going on?"

Derek pointed to the tail boom above the pod. "We need to get up there, inspect the tail rotor. If we can find the problem, this might be a short stop."

"If you can fix it, you mean," Jesse squinted toward the shore, already calculating how many inflatable boats they had and how many round trips it would take to ferry the platoon and all their gear. The answer was: a lot of trips.

Derek didn't respond, he didn't need to. "Wait," he told Irene. "I saw a toolbox in the cockpit." In less than a minute, he returned with a battered toolbox. Based on the number of empty slots, half of the tools were missing, and some others were broken. All the tools had odd spiral-shaped grips, which he guessed was better for wrapping a tentacle around.

Irene was already on top of the cargo pod, with Jesse and another soldier. She climbed up on top of the tail boom and shimmied back to the shrouded rotor, holding onto a blade and pulling it side to side. "It's not loose," she declared.

"Is it jammed? Try spinning it," Derek suggested helpfully.

Irene shot him an 'I already tried that' look.

"Ok," Derek said as an apology. "I'm coming up."

Jesse and the other soldier helped Derek climb up, and he guessed which tools were needed for removing the covering over the tail boom. "Huh. Easy," Derek said. "This covering is fastened with some sort of reusable rivets. We can remove them with this tool," he waved a pistol-shaped device, and removed one of his gloves to better grip the tool.


"Oh my G- Uh," Irene face was white. "I'm gonna be sick," she leaned over the side of the cargo pod.

"Breathe, Babe, breathe," Derek rubbed her back.

"What's the problem?" Perkins demanded from below.

Derek explained while Irene tried to get her hands to stop shaking. "The tail rotor gets power from the turbines through a hollow shaft that runs along the center of the tail boom, it spins," he twirled a finger to demonstrate. "With gearboxes at both ends. The shaft is made of two pieces, like pipes. The one forward is bigger, and the end of the rear piece fits inside it where they couple together. There's a single pin that holds them to each other." He held up a short piece of bent pin. "The pin broke, it sheared off. The tail rotor lost all power. Colonel," he glared at their CO. "Without the tail rotor, torque from the main rotor would have spun us around like a top, and we would have gone straight down like a *rock*."

"Ok," Perkins was aware the entire platoon was staring at her in shock. A helicopter crash was one of the greatest fears of infantry soldiers, because they were helpless to control their fates. "We didn't crash. So, what happened?"

Irene answered that question. "When the pin broke, it looks like the forward shaft spun *so* fast around the inner shaft, the metal sleeves tack-welded themselves together. But every time I had to correct our course, that changed the pitch of the tail rotor blades and the added torque on the shaft broke the temporary welds." She looked at the trees on the eastern shore of the lake. "We would never have made it to the shore. The sleeves are almost completely worn away."

Perkins considered the information silently. She had learned a lesson. When a pilot proposes to do some risky hotshot thing, it is proper to question their judgment. But when a pilot is exercising an abundance of caution, passengers should keep their damned mouths shut. "Very well. Striebich, you made the right call," she didn't want to dwell on the issue in front of the platoon. They could speak privately about the issue later. "Can we do anything about it?"

"I think so," Derek replied, and Irene nodded agreement. "We can use a plasma torch to weld the shafts together for real. We'll have to load test it before we take off."

"No complications, then?" Perkins asked.

"Well," Derek wore a rueful grin. "If a Wurgalan maintenance crew finds the Ugly Bug later, and see that we welded those shafts together, they are really gonna be *pissed*."


"General Ross?" One of the majors working intel waved for attention.

Ross barely looked up, intent on studying a message he was composing for Admiral Kune. "What is it, uh?"

"Major Verany, Sir," the French officer reminded his boss. "You asked-"

"Is this important?"

Verany spoke quickly. "You asked if we located anyone on the surface, units that haven't checked in. We might have found someone from the *Big Mac*."

"Perkins?" Ross looked up, the message forgotten.

"No. Not unless they walked a long way in a short time, in the wrong direction."

"Then who is it? You tracked another dropship?"

"No dropships were anywhere in that area. Running the sensors back, it looks like a cargo pod was ejected from the *Big Mac*, while the forward section was in the upper atmosphere."

"*Cargo?*" The commander of the Legion's UNEF contingent exploded.

Seeing the general's frustration, Verany got to the point. "The AI thinks there is a good possibility," he did not cite percentages, knowing that Ross didn't appreciate getting bogged down in details. "That we detected smoke signals on the surface," he finished with a raised eyebrow.

"Smoke?" Ross sat back in his chair. He had to trust that his staff wouldn't waste his time, but, "There's a *lot* of smoke down there, Major."

"Not smoke that is puffing 'S-O-S' in Morse code, Sir."

"SOS?" Ross tried to remember the ancient code for those letters. Three dots, three dashes, three dots? "You are sure?"

"The *AI* is sure," Verany clarified.

"Well, I'll be damned. That's got to be humans. They came down in a *cargo container?*"

"Either that, or they HALO jumped from orbit."

Ross shook his head. The *Big Mac* had not been carrying any Commandos equipped with the gear for an orbital parachute drop. "If all we have is some funky puffs of smoke-"

"That's not all. A hundred-forty klicks east of those smoke signals is the crash site of that last dropship to get out of the *Big Mac*. We haven't been able to clear up any better the sensor data we had before, but now we found something curious. A Wurgalan close-air support gunship was shot down in that area, near an isolated airfield. It was shot down by a Cobra, no question about it." Verany held out his tablet toward the general, running the video. "We don't have any people in that area, except for whoever survived the dropship descent."

Ross liked hearing that their people, *humans*, were still fighting, despite having been dropped in the wrong area and being cut off from the Legion. Leaning forward to study the video, he squinted. "What is an airfield doing way out there?"

"We think the squids were running an exercise. Sir, there was a battle at the airfield, we couldn't see details. What caught our attention is a helicopter later flew east from-"

"A *helicopter*? Like," Ross twirled a finger in the air. "A helo?"

"Yes. The Wurgalan use rotor-wing aircraft for heavy-lift capability. They probably used the helo to set up the airfield, then brought in gunships."

"Huh." Ross knew the Ruhar used blimps, really zeppelins, for airlifting heavy loads in an atmosphere. If the Legion was able to land a third wave, three zeppelins would be brought down from orbit and assembled. An airship could lift loads heavier than a Whale dropship could carry, and use far less fuel. "Do we know where this helicopter went?"

"Sensors lost track of it," Verany frowned. "It is possible that whoever took the helo left a message at the airfield."

"If *our* people won the battle," Ross said, to quell unwarranted enthusiasm. Still, if a group of humans survived their assault carrier being sliced in half, a deadstick descent in a damaged dropship, then attacked an enemy position and flew away in an unfamiliar aircraft, the Legion had to at least make an effort to make contact. "All right, I'm sold. Do we have any assets in the area?"

"No, it's fairly isolated," Verany explained. "There is a Dodo on the ground that could fly over the area. They dropped off half of a ninja team, then took ground fire that made a turbine overheat. The crew is completing repairs, they should be back in the air within twenty minutes."

"The Achakai they're carrying," Ross disapproved of the nickname 'ninjas' for the Achakai, but he had given up trying to quash use of the popular term. "What's their objective?"

"It's OBE," the French officer shrugged and used an American term. "They were supposed to hit a logistics base but the squids have already abandoned the place, they blew it up after they retreated. The ninjas are being retasked as a Quick Reaction force for their Sixth Battalion."

Ross grimaced. "Tell them to check out the smoke signals, I don't want a lot of time wasted there. Overfly the area and if they don't pick up a signal quickly, they move on. Follow the flight path of that helicopter. The damned thing couldn't have flown far."

"Yes, Sir."

"No transmissions from the site of the smoke signals?"

"None we can detect through the jamming. If the people down there only have suits, an aircraft would need to be within thirty kilometers to detect a signal."

"Hell." Once again, Ross thought it was bitterly ironic that the Legion had access to some of the best communications technology in the galaxy, but the equipment could not overcome enemy jamming without specialized equipment.

That the enemy was also being jammed by the Legion did not make him feel any better about the situation. "I wish our beetles friends were here."

"Because their ships have better sensors?" Verany guessed.

"No. Because they would *love* to bet on whether we'll find anyone alive down there. Morse code smoke signals coming from an area where no dropships landed? That's juicy action none of the beetles could resist."


Fixing the Ugly Bug was not as easy as using a plasma torch to weld together the metal sleeves of the tail rotor shafts. The plasma torch was too crude for creating elegant welds, wasting much of the material which dripped down to burn the inside of the tail boom housing. Irene was not confident in the result, so Derek kludged together superglue on top of the inadequate weld. Then, because even the high-tech alien glue was not best at withstanding the twisting force of torque, the joint between rotor shafts was wrapped in duct tape.

"Duct tape?" To say Irene was skeptical was a gross understatement. "We're using, duct tape."

"It's not duct tape like you'd find in any hardware store on Earth," Derek assured her, holding up the roll he had found stuffed under a seat in the Ugly Bug's cabin. "This is high-tech nanofiber magic."

"It's *duct tape*," she insisted. "We are trusting our lives to that?"

"Duct tape saved the Apollo Thirteen mission," Derek noted. "It will be fine. Come on, we'll load test it."

To the surprise of Irene, and, if he were telling the truth, Derek also, the welded-glued-taped shafts held together during the load test. Irene insisted on the two pilots taking the helicopter up without passengers, flying circles around the island until she was satisfied the Ugly Bug was not immediately going to fall out of the sky. The left-right yaw lag between control input and response was nearly gone, causing butterflies in Irene's stomach. The rotor drive shafts must have been slipping since she first got the helicopter in the air. It frightened her how close they had come to death without warning. What other hidden dangers were inside the alien machine's mechanisms?

When they set the Ugly Bug back down on the island and the platoon reboarded, Irene needed info from Perkins before she took the turbines out of idle. "Ma'am, what's the plan? I don't want to fly this thing any farther than we have to. We can get to shore, but, the Ugly Bug could fail without warning."

"There's no reason to-" Perkins began.

Derek paused the navigation display. "Hidden flaws like the tail rotor shaft are a pilot's worst nightmare, Colonel. Striebich is right, we don't know if this piece of junk is airworthy. If we're going to risk the whole platoon falling out of the sky, there needs to be a reason."

"We need to make contact with friendly forces," Perkins knew that was a hopelessly vague objective.

"We're flying an enemy aircraft," Irene rapped her knuckles on the console in front of her. It made a cheap-sounding, hollow sound and wobbled on its mounting bracket. "*Contact* may come in the form of a missile. Our troops will shoot first and ask questions later."

"What can I tell you, Striebich?" Perkins was annoyed with her pilot, but more annoyed with herself. "If *any* of the Legion landed in the correct spot on this Godforsaken rock, they are to the east of us somewhere. Bonsu, can you use any of that alien gear in front of you to monitor signal strength?"

"Uh," Derek knew there was a screen for that somewhere, he had scrolled through a menu on the console when he was trying to understand the navigation system. "Yeah, I can do that. Colonel, we can't use any of the Ugly Bug's comm gear to contact our people. The comm system doesn't have the codes to establish a handshake for encryption with Legion systems."

"We will rely on our suits when we get close enough," the CO explained. She knew that was more of a hope than an actual plan. "All you have to do is tell us when we pick up a Legion signal strong enough to be within, say, twenty kilometers."

"Ah," Derek's face took on a pained look. "With the pervasive jamming, it would have to be more like ten klicks to pick up a signal, Ma'am. It would be easier to scan for weapons fire, and, uh, hope we don't set down on the wrong side of the fighting."

"With that gear, can you discriminate between Legion weapons and Wurgalan?"

Derek pointed to the scuffed and cracked display of his console. "I'm lucky if I can get this thing to tell me which direction is north."

Perkins straddled the awkward perch she was forced to use as a seat, and tugged a strap across her lap. In a crash, the strap would be of little use, but it would prevent her from being thrown forward into the pilots if they hit turbulence. "Do what you can. Striebich, the answer is, we fly until we make contact, or we run out of fuel. *Or,*" she emphasized, "you feel this thing isn't airworthy. I'm serious about that. It's your call. Seeing that busted prop shaft scared the shit out of me too."

Great, thought Irene. I'm not confident the helo is airworthy now, but we can't stay on the island. Telling herself she would look for a place to set down at the first sign of trouble, she took a breath and pulled the handle to engage the main rotor clutch. "Yes, Ma'am."

The Ugly Bug droned onward, flying generally east except when they needed to avoid Wurgalan towns, and once they diverted south to cross a mountain range through the lowest-altitude gap in the area. Coming gently over the crest of the ridge and being careful not to get caught in a downdraft on the lee side of the mountains, Irene whistled. Stretching north to south across the horizon were pillars of smoke. "Where there's smoke, there's trouble," she said mostly to herself. Where there was trouble, they might find the Legion.

"Any ideas?" Perkins asked, leaning forward to speak with the pilots.

Derek held up an index finger. "Give me a moment, Colonel, I'm trying to use this thing's rangefinder to zero in on those locations. Um, um, Ok. There are five within a hundred kilometers."

"What about those clusters of thick smoke on the horizon?" The smoke there was darker, and she expected that meant the incident that created the smoke was more recent.

Derek shook his head. "Those sources are over the horizon." He checked the fuel state. "Too far, we can't get there unless we walk."

"All right. Take us to the site closest to our flight path."

Derek transferred the guidance to Irene's console, and she gingerly guided the Ugly Bug's nose around to the new course. At first flying the alien machine had been exciting, an opportunity she might never get again. Since they nearly fell into the lake, every maneuver reminded her how *big* and ungainly the helicopter was. Once when she was little, a family friend who operated the Zamboni at the local ice rink, invited her up to steer the thing when he was smoothing the ice at the end of the night. Flying the Ugly Bug felt like driving a Zamboni in three dimensions. With every aircraft it was important to stay ahead of it, plan what you want the machine to do, before you ask it to do what you want. With the Ugly Bug, she had to express her wishes vaguely when she moved the controls, and be happy if the giant helicopter did something similar to her intentions. Part of the problem, she guessed, was the machine was designed to carry heavy loads, and a cargo pod filled only with the surviving members of the platoon was too light. The big rotor blades were flexing too much, making the Ugly Bug bounce rhythmically up and down. If the autopilot had been working, it might have been able to hold altitude without making her queasy, but most of the computer-controlled systems were offline.

"Ok, coming up on the site, seventeen klicks," Derek reported. "You want us to overfly, Ma'am?" He asked with a tone that implied overflight would be a very bad idea.

"No. Can we see anything from here?"

The helicopter had an image enhancer, which gave a fuzzy view on the cockpit display. Derek craned his neck, checking whether the sensors of his own helmet could detect anything useful. They could not, not from that distance at low altitude. There was no way to get the helicopter's systems to talk with his helmet, they were based on deliberately incompatible technologies. With a flash of inspiration, he looked down at the magnified console display with his helmet's own image enhancer switched on, and the view jumped out him. "It's a crashed dropship, Ma'am," he reported.

"Theirs or ours?" Perkins asked with both dread and hope. If the downed spacecraft were Legion, the crew was probably dead. But the wreckage might contain intact communications gear.

Derek couldn't answer immediately. Several Wurgalan dropship designs were copies of captured Ruhar equipment. "Hard to say from here. Looks like it augered in," he muttered. "Uh, it went in nose-first. It's bad, there's a crater. Uh, I'm looking at what's left of an engine, my guess is this is one of theirs."

The hope for finding hardened communications equipment went out the window with that announcement. "Next site is how far?"

"Unless we want to deviate due north from our eastward flight path, the next site is twenty-two klicks."

"How far to the one north of us?" It irritated her that, unlike aboard a friendly aircraft, she could not share what the pilots were seeing.

"Eight klicks to get a view of it."

Turning her head to look out the grimy windows, she saw a thin trail of light gray smoke. "Let's go there, it's close."

That smoke was from a source easily identified. The spacecraft had come down in a meadow next to a stream, digging a long furrow in the soil before it broke in half when it reached the trees. "One of ours," Derek said with confidence when they were ten kilometers away. "I recognize the tail configuration. That's one of ours, a Vulture gunship. It only holds two pilots."

Perkins had a decision to make, and she didn't like her options. "Does it look like anyone walked away?"

"Can't tell from here."

The Mavericks CO mentally tossed a coin, then rejected that thought. Whatever she decided, she would do it for a logical reason. The Vulture must have at least an emergency locator beacon, so search and rescue ships could find it. The beacon sent out an encoded signal, a crude message containing only 'I am here' and the aircraft's identification code. "Can you interpret the ELT message?"

Derek knew what Perkins wanted to know. If either of the pilots survived, their flightsuits should have caused the Emergency Location Transmitter to send a signal of 'Survivor here' rather than a simple beep. Knowing the helicopter's equipment would be useless, he queried his helmet. "At least one survivor."

Perkins did not want to stop. The platoon had a mission, and taking precious time to rescue a Ruhar who might be badly injured would take time they didn't have. On the other hand, the platoon's original mission, the entire plan for the invasion, was OBE. She might as well do some good while she had an opportunity. "Striebich, set us down."

"Ma'am, that clearing is not big enough to clear the rotor blades unless we're exactly in the center," Irene advised.

"Right. Colter! Tell our medic to prepare to drop down on a line, we're going to hover. Send someone with him. *Not* you," she added, knowing the staff sergeant would want to volunteer. Too often, Colter still thought like a private.

It was a waste of time, effort and fuel. One pilot had survived the crash, and she was still alive when the platoon's medic reached her, but died soon after the medic administered nanomed stabilizers. That was tragic for one person, the fact that the Vulture's comm system had been destroyed in the crash was frustrating to the platoon. "She had lost a lot of blood," the medic reported. "Her heart gave out, sorry."

"Nothing to be sorry about, Mazet," Perkins responded. "Pull the plug on the ELT and get back here." She did not want a SAR team risking their lives for no reason. "We don't have time for a burial," Perkins knew that decision would not be popular.

"Next site," Perkins said with weary determination once the two soldiers were back aboard. While the medic had been on the ground, there had been a blinding explosion in orbit, low in the eastern sky. Yellow streaks of fire were tracing across the sky overhead, the remains of the ship that had just died. She clenched her fists, overcome by frustration. The fight for Stiglord was still raging, and she was not a part of it. She had no idea what was going on. Was the Legion achieving its objectives despite loss of two assault transports? Or had the invasion failed, and the Legion's three parts were trying to pull out under fire? There was also an in-between possibility: the invasion could have stalled, in which case the second wave might be delayed or cancelled.

She simply didn't *know* anything. The situation was intolerable, yet they had to go on.

# CHAPTER TWENTY

Nert suddenly halted, holding up a fist in a 'Freeze' gesture, then his hand opened, palm facing down and waving toward the ground. Turning his head while he crouched on one knee, he held a finger to the faceplate of his helmet.

Shauna and Dave froze and crouched down, waving for Jates and Chowdhury behind them to halt. Shauna looked at Dave and silently mouthed 'What now'? Glancing back to see that Jates and Chowdhury had ducked behind trees, Shauna slung her rifle in its holster and crawled forward to Nert's position, Dave right beside her. She tapped the cadet's shoulder.

He spoke over the short-range laserlink on the lowest-power setting. "We have company," he whispered, pointing to the stream valley that had been their destination.

They were on the east slope of a ridge that ran southeast to northwest, intending to get down to the stream that wound its way along on the east side of the ridge, separating it from the next line of low hills. The whole area was a series of rolling hills that lay across their path, covered with thick forest that made for slow progress. Getting down to the valley would give them fresh water and they had to cross the valley anyway.

Except where Nert pointed, four Wurgalan splashed along the shallow stream, keeping to the sides and away from deep pools that swirled where the stream bent one way or another.

"What the hell are they doing here?" Dave groaned. "This is the middle of freakin' nowhere!"

"Looking for us?" Jates guessed, crawling up to lie prone next to Dave. The four of them had cover provided by thick underbrush and a decaying log that lay in front of Nert.

Shauna considered the situation. Three more Wurgalan had come into view, out from a grove of trees clustered on the far side of the stream. "I don't think so," she said. "Look, they're not wearing powered armor." The Wurgalan were dressed in baggy clothes that did not have any chameleonware activated, so the dark gray color stood out from their surroundings. They all wore helmets with faceplates retracted, and what appeared to be armor panels attached to the clothing around their squat torsos. "If they were sent out to look for us, their command deployed whoever they had in the area. They're not prepared."

"Shit," Dave exclaimed as more Wurgalan came out of the woods, their shoes or boots or lower legs coated with mud. They all walked in the streambed, single-file, trudging along one behind the other.

Dave studied their body language. Though they were aliens, he recognized an attitude that was universal to soldiers across the galaxy. "Shauna's right. Those guys aren't looking for us, or anyone. Their rifles are slung, they're not keeping a watch on their surroundings. They think they're alone out here."

"More coming," Nert added. "That is eighteen, nineteen, twenty." The Wurgalan in the front of the formation had halted where the bank of the stream rose higher, above the surrounding marsh. Climbing out of the stream, they unbuckled straps and shrugged off the small packs they carried. As their fellows reached the area, they all did the same. Some of the enemy looked up at the sky, where lights still flashed and bright contrails burned from the ongoing air and space battle above their heads.

"You might be right," Jates sounded disgusted. Even if the Wurgalan had good reason to think they were alone in the area, that was no excuse for such poor discipline.

"What do you think, Surgun?" Dave asked. Jates had improved in mobility once he donned the spare skinsuit, though his mood was not any better. An injection with nanomeds was probably the reason for his continued grumpiness, and Dave thought most of that was just Jates being Jates. The microscopic machines had directed themselves to Jates' injured leg and ribs, wriggling their way into the fractured bone and forming a solid rod inside to bring the bone back into the proper position and hold it there. The nanomeds were a miracle of advanced technology, highly effective and naggingly painful. Most likely, Jates had refused the offer of a nerve block.

"I think," Jates slowly lifted his head above the log to get a better view. "While the squids down there have a picnic, we should use this opportunity to go back up the ridge and turn south, keep the ridgeline between us and them. We'll cut south a kilometer or two."

"Aw, come on," Dave teased. "There's four of us," he didn't count Chowdhury. "And only twenty of them. You're not afraid, are you?"

Jates slowly turned to regard the human. "Afraid? No."

"Then why-"

"Czajka," he shook his head sadly. "Do you have any idea how much a pain in the *ass* it will be to dig twenty graves?"

"Uh-"

"That would take all freakin' *day*. We don't have time for that shit. Now, if you want to volunteer-"

"No, uh," Dave could feel his cheeks burning red with embarrassment. "I'm good."

Shauna patted his shoulder, and began slowly crawling backwards. "You heard the man, Czajka. We're sitting this one out."

"Yeah," Dave tapped Nert's leg. "What worries me is, what are the odds we would run into the *only* group of squids in this area? If there are more of them around here, digging graves will be the least of our problems."


"Whoa, whoa, slow down. Stop, *stop!*" Dani ordered from behind the driver's seat. They had commandeered a van and two trucks, and taken time they didn't have to tear out the interior and windows of the van. The inside of the van had rows of saddle-type seats stacked one above the other on both sides, seats the Verds could not use, and the poles that held the upper rows of seats would get in the way. It had taken the platoon less than a minute to smash the windows, rip the seats from the floor and toss them out.

The two pilots were behind the platoon, driving in the opposite direction outside the city anywhere they could go quickly, bringing with them the people injured during the descent and rough landing. Dani had debated whether to send the platoon's medic with the pilots, before deciding to take the medic with her, reasoning that Third Platoon also had casualties and she didn't know whether they had a medic or any medical supplies. She had sent two drones with the pilots, along with four soldiers who had only minor injuries. That group was regrettably on their own, the rest of the Second was with her.

The van was in the middle of the three-vehicle formation, in front was a sort of stakebed truck, behind a box truck that had its sides torn off. "Tell the-" Dani groaned with frustration. "Besault, stop!" The truck in front skidded to a halt.

"The drone is showing a roadblock up ahead," she explained, knowing that Besault, Auffex, and the soldiers operating the drones saw the same information. They had gotten lucky at the start, the area where the Dodo went down was industrial and with the early-morning timing of the invasion, that section of the city was relatively empty. The drones showed that in residential areas to the north and south, the streets were jammed with traffic streaming outbound, panicked citizens getting away from what they judged was a likely combat zone. All the vehicles they had found were autonomous, with guidance and speed controlled by a central network. All the vehicles also had manual backup controls, and enough drivers had engaged manual mode that accidents had snarled traffic. From the industrial area of the crash to Third Platoon's reported position, traffic was light, and drivers racing away from the city had gotten out of the way when Besault's squad in the lead truck fired warning shots.

Now their luck had run out.

An elevated highway ran across their path, with a confusing spaghetti bowl of on and off ramps going over and around each other. Several vehicles had crashed, blocking the straight route under the highway, the drone showed the tangled vehicles had been abandoned, with one truck rolled on its side. With their powered armor, the platoon's soldiers could have moved the traffic jam out of the way, but that would have taken too long. The intersection was a chokepoint, it could easily be blocked by the enemy when the platoon was retreating from the city. Really, she had been surprised how far they had gotten in the stolen vehicles, it was like the Wurgalan were not paying attention to that part of the city. The few squid civilians they passed looked shocked and terrified to see armor-clad aliens in their midst, some of the alert citizens must have contacted the authorities about the unlikely invasion of the city. The only reason Dani could imagine for why they had so far been driving unopposed was that the Wurgalan were busy elsewhere, and one isolated, understrength platoon was not a priority. From the twisting contrails overhead, pillars of smoke rising in every direction and the dull thump of explosions, she knew the Legion was fighting to establish a toehold on the planet and the natives were hitting back. Surely not all the assault carriers had been destroyed like the *Dal Turnaden*, or the invasion would have failed before it started.

With regret, she noted one nearby pillar of thick black smoke was from their Dodo they had set to self-destruct, once they got clear of the area. It had not been possible to take all the supplies with them, and she couldn't leave the deadly gear for the enemy to discover. That Dodo had kept her alive against the odds, it felt like betrayal to blow it to pieces.

"We dismount here," she ordered, proud of herself for using proper terminology. "Pull the vehicles off the road." She did not have much hope the van and trucks would be there when they retreated back through the area, but it didn't hurt to retain them as possible assets.

Neither surgun argued with her decision, they had seen the drone images. Second Platoon with her was now eighteen soldiers divided into two squads under Besault and Auffex, plus the medic and Dani. Twenty-one alien warriors, led by a human trained in psychology, not infantry tactics. They had to link up with the survivors of Third Platoon, and extract them from the city to- Where? How the hell were they going to get all the way out of the city without being blown to bits by artillery or blasted from the air? Three times, they had seen Wurgalan aircraft racing by in the distance, so far not interested in the three stolen vehicles. That could change in the blink of an eye. The platoon had two anti-aircraft teams, equipped with two launchers and six Ruhar missiles that UNEF had designated as Cobras, for the speed and agility of the small weapons. On Fresno, Dani had seen Cobras take down enemy aircraft, she had also seen those missiles be intercepted, and simply miss the target because of sensor jamming. Launching a shoulder-fired missile at an aircraft equipped with stealth, energy shields, sensor jamming and defensive cannons was not a certain kill. That was why UNEF told infantry anti-air teams to follow the artillery tactic of shoot-and-scoot, because as soon as the enemy detected a launch from the ground, they would retaliate.

The two squads hopped out of the vehicles, gathering their gear, and set off down the road at a steady run. Dani stayed in the middle of Auffex's squad in the rear, running alongside their communications tech, a woman called Telored. "Any contact?"

"No, Captain," Telored had set her suit on semi-automatic, following the soldier in front of her at a preset distance, so she could focus on contacting Third Platoon. There had been no word from the other unit since they left the warehouse.

"I don't understand it," Dani fretted. She had tasked a drone to fly forward and make contact with the Third, but they had lost contact with the drone when it was less than a kilometer from the other platoon's last reported position. "This is crazy," she said aloud without intending others to hear her. "Besault, launch another drone."

"Captain," he replied with a tone that, even through the translator, had a note of an adult being patient with a child. "We only have two drones left."

"I *know* that," she snapped. "We are not proceeding until we have better intel. I am not taking us into an ambush."

"Yes, Ma'am." Besault issued orders, and a soldier in his squad stopped for a moment to take a drone from his pack, activate it and toss it in the air. "We are sending the drone in from the north this time."

"Good idea," she acknowledged. The Verds were trained infantry. She didn't need to tell them how to do their jobs, only what she wanted to accomplish. Give them a goal and get out of their way.

The platoon ran under the highway, dodging around crashed cars and trucks and causing a commotion on the highway above when civilians trying to walk out of the city saw armor-suited aliens race past them. Only another two kilometers to go, Dani saw in her visor. Still no sign of armed opposition. They had passed through and out of the industrial area, the section of city they were running through then was low buildings that appeared to be retail shops or restaurants, with taller three-or-four-story residential structures farther back from the street. Just past the highway, they ran around a crater in the street that was still smoking, all the windows in the area were shattered and the concrete surfaces of buildings peppered with pockmarks. Something had crashed there, big and fast enough to leave a two-meter-deep hole in the street. A fallen piece of starship? A downed aircraft? Theirs or ours? From the blackened, mangled debris in the crater, there was no way to tell.

Dani was amazed at how calm she felt. She was surrounded by a group of big, hulking, menacing lizards, but that was really no different from any Friday night back on Earth, and the Verds would not be getting hammered and spilling drinks on her, so, bonus. She was on an alien planet, but she had lived on Paradise for so long, that no longer felt strange. She was running through enemy territory, and oddly it felt like a training run on any military base, except for the signs in an alien language and occasional startled natives dashing out of their way. The whole situation felt unreal as if-

"We have contact," Telored announced excitedly.

"Halt," Dani ordered, waving the platoon to take cover in doorways or under awnings along the street. "This is Ardva Two."

"Three here," the gravelly voice came though background static. Whoever it was, they sounded exhausted already. A burst of *pop pop pop* Wurgalan gunfire interrupted, followed by the heavier bark of a Kristang rifle. Then multiple Kristang rifles.

"What is your situation?" Dani spoke slowly and clear.

"We are engaged with a police unit," the voice explained. On Stiglord, police services were provided by the military, so effectively, the Third was fighting light infantry. "We have thirteen wounded and five of us are still fighting. We had to move from our prior location, do you see our position now?"

Thirteen and *five*? Those numbers were down from fifteen and eight the last time they had contact. The Third Platoon was being ground down to nothing. Dani looked at the map overlay in her visor, it showed a blinking yellow circle. The drone had determined Third's position within half a city block, buildings and jamming interference made it impossible to fix the location with greater precision. "Can you send a visual feed?"

The reply was a window opening in Dani's visor. The staticky video showed the shattered lobby of a building, a bank of elevators on one side with doors bent and bashed in. Windows along the street had blown inward, scattering glass all over the floor. The Third had piled up furniture, torn-out slabs of interior wall and any other junk they could find to barricade the window openings. From the narrow, jittery view, Dani guessed the image she was seeing was from a rifle scope. It showed a gap between broken wall panels into the street beyond. An intersection, with vehicles smashed, flipped over and burning. Wurgalan clad in dark blue and orange dashed one way and the other, firing rifles.

"Ardva Three, are you pinned down in there?" She asked with dismay, hoping an experienced infantry unit had not gotten trapped in a poorly-defensible position.

"We are surrounded, but there is a route out if we blow a side wall," the voice replied. "We can't move because the enemy has close-air support above us."

As he spoke, Dani saw a large shadow slide across the intersection. "Three, hold." Switching to a view from the drone, she saw a Wurgalan gunship flying slow circles around the building, always keeping its nose pointed toward Third Platoon's position. Sponsons on each side of the aircraft were laden with rockets, and a cannon turret hung under the nose. If Third broke out into the open, they would be chopped to pieces. She cut off her helmet microphone to allow herself a private "SHIT! I *hate* my life!" Then she toggled the microphone back on. "Ardva Three, standby."

"We will stand by as long as we can," the voice said over a chattering burst of rifle fire.

"Surgun Besault, you see that gunship? Can we hit it from here?"

"I see it," the surgun replied. "Negative on launch from here. Our missiles need line-of-sight initial tracking to-"

"I *know* that." She was getting a little sick of people assuming she didn't know anything. "The *drone* has line-of-sight to the target. Can we program the Cobras to follow a low-observable flight profile, until they pop up and get terminal guidance from the drone?"

A slight pause. "Yes, we can?" Besault's tone reflected surprise, and a bit of shame. Surprise that their human leader knew technical details about the Cobra missile, and shame that he had not suggested the idea. "One moment, Captain."

"Make it a *short* moment."

Besault spoke again twenty-eight seconds later. "Captain, we can program a missile to fly along the streets and remain below the top of buildings, until it approaches the target and must pop up. We-" His voice cut off. "My team just reminded me that the missile will use most of its fuel before it pops up, its terminal dash will be slower than normal. I suggest we task two or three missiles."

"Two only," she declared. "If we shoot down one of their aircraft, we'll have others swarming around us like we kicked a nest of hornets," she said, remembering too late that human metaphors often did not translate well. "We will need the other missiles for self-defense." When she first saw soldiers carrying a Cobra in addition to all their other gear, she had questioned the burden. Now she wished they were all carrying extra anti-air missiles. "Besault, Auffex, soon as those missiles are away, we need to move out double quick." Switching back to the drone, she called her besieged counterpart. "Ardva Three, this is Two. We'll be taking care of that gunship for you. Transmit your egress plan, we need to coordinate a meet."

"Two, copy that. Sending the plan now, we-" His voice was drowned out in a burst of gunfire and something louder. From the drone, she saw a fresh pall of smoke rising from the Third Platoon's position. They needed to hurry, before the

Wurgalan police decided to pull back and have the gunship drop the building on the invader's heads.

"I see your plan. Stay off this channel, the squids might be able to track the drone."

The only reply was two clicks, acknowledging her instructions.

"We are ready to launch," Besault said.

"Wait." She studied the map, seeing the route the Third planned to take once the gunship was swept from the sky, trying to imagine where the groups could meet. The other platoon had five people to conduct a fighting withdrawal, *and* carry fifteen wounded. She should have asked how many of the wounded were capable of walking. "Ok. Do it. Launch."

One missile was launched by each squad, small puffs of nearly-invisible water vapor issuing from the launch tube as the missiles were kicked out. Their motors ignited, surging them up and forward as thin wings popped out on each side. Instead of the motors burning furiously to send the Cobras racing at full speed to strike their target, the motors pulsed, wasting fuel to keep the speed low enough that the weapons could make tight turns over the streets.

At the second intersection they approached, the missiles split up, one banking hard to the right, the other going straight for another three city blocks, when it too made a right turn.

Dani gasped with dismay when she saw one missile turn and not the other, thinking it was a mistake or malfunction. She was about to speak when she heard Auffex. "Missiles away. Tracking is nominal."

The missiles were supposed to split up, that made sense. Approach the target simultaneously from different directions. She would have known that if she had asked. No. The platoon leader did not need to get lost in details. The soldiers who had launched the missiles lowered the tubes from their shoulders and removed the targeting box, discarding the empty launchers.

"Second Platoon, move-" Dani ordered when a *pop pop pop* burst of gunfire from the left struck the soldier in Besault's squad who had launched a Cobra. The soldier fell, losing the targeting box and rolling. Three soldiers from First Squad opened up in the general direction of the shooter, sending a hail of explosive-tipped rounds through the already-smashed window where the alien had fired from.

Feeling useless, Dani allowed two soldiers to hustle her into the dubious protection of a doorway while First Squad split up, one group providing cover fire while the other leapfrogged forward. Seconds later, she heard Besault announce "Clear!"

"Who was it?" Dani called.

"Looks like that was one local citizen trying to be a hero," Besault said with disgust. The soldier who had been hit got slowly to his feet, giving a hand signal that he was alright. In Dani's visor, she checked that soldier's status and his mech suit was showing a few spots of yellow, nothing the nano couldn't repair or bypass. She heard Besault talking softly on the squad channel, then, "Captain, we have a problem. My squad's Cobra targeting box is damaged. We have four missiles and only one effective launch control system."

"Shit. Well, let's be extra careful with the other one. Second Platoon, move out!"

The two Cobra missiles flew at speeds far below their designed optimum, making turns that stressed their thin wings, dashing along the streets below the rooftops. The tiny brains of the missiles were technically not large enough for self-awareness, but the two semi-intelligent AIs were each thinking that they were having not only the most fun they had ever imagined, they were having the most fun that was *possible*. One missile banked too hard and so low, its wing ducked between two busses that had collided and were stuck in the middle of an intersection. Yes, maybe that missile was showing off a bit, but, who could blame it? The missile had existed for endlessly dull years, awaiting a few all-too-brief seconds of raging excitement before ending its life in fire.

*Did you see that*, the first missile transmitted over the spotty tactical link they were using to coordinate the strike. *I flew between two vehicles.*

*I saw it*, the second missile groaned as it dipped under a bridge, narrowly clearing the roof of a truck.

*That proves I am incredible*, the first missile said with smug satisfaction.

*It proves you are a DICK*, the second missile retorted.

*You're just jealous.*

The second missile ignored the taunt. *It's been nice knowing you. I'm approaching from the northwest.*

*Good luck*, replied the first missile, then there was no more time for chatting over the tactical link.

The first missile came in from the north, having made a ninety-degree turn at the last moment to swing behind Third Platoon's position, two blocks away. The missile got its last guidance from the unseen drone hovering to the north, and its tiny brain calculated that its best tactic was actually to slow down, so it side slipped, skidding through the air over the street. Its airspeed dropped it almost into a stall before the motor pulsed again weakly, its fuel almost expended in the wastefully slow flight. The delay gave time for the enemy gunship to come into view above the intersection, its nose pointed toward the building where Third Platoon had taken refuge. Gunfire poured into the building from across the intersection and the missile regretted not being able to do anything about that. With a last surge of power from its nearly-depleted motor, it discarded its wings and went ballistic.

The gunship's threat detection system lit up with confusion, unable to understand how a threat could be approaching from street level. Its defensive cannon turret had barely begun to swivel around when the missile scored a direct hit, the alien weapon's warhead detonating when it impacted the aircraft's energy shield. Burning plasma bored through the shields, splattering against the cockpit canopy and burning through the composite material, the bodies of both pilot and gunner and flash-frying every piece of electronics in the cockpit. Backup systems attempted to compensate, feeding power to the engines but their thrust was uncoordinated, and the flight control systems had lost awareness of where the aircraft was. Desperately, the backup computer lifted the nose to climb and turned to the left-

Smashing the gunship nose-first into the eighth floor of a twelve-story building. The armored bulk of the craft hammered through the skin of the building, crushing walls and floors into the building's core where the main structural beams clustered. Six of eight stout beams were bent and severed, and the building above the eighth floor tilted.

Then the wreckage of the gunship slid backward out into the air over the street, leading the way as the entire façade of the structure sagged and collapsed, the front half of the building falling on itself.

*Holy sh-* the second missile thought as it dipped its nose to fly under the falling corpse of the gunship that had been the target. *Scratch one gunship*, it mused, switching to a secondary objective it just identified. In its programming the location of Third Platoon was highlighted, with strict instructions to avoid collateral damage in that direction. *Yeah, like THAT is going to happen*, the missile thought bitterly. The building across the street, that had recently suffered extreme and involuntary remodeling by gunship, was in the process of collapsing. Good luck avoiding collateral damage there, the missile smirked, calculating that the maneuver it needed to make was going to snap its wings off, and adjusting course to account for that loss. The missile dived to street level, banking in a one hundred twenty degree right turn. At one hundred one degrees through the turn, the left wing buckled and the missile instantly discarded both wings, vectoring its thrust to continue the turn, the nosecone slewing around violently and lining up with its secondary target: the cargo trailer of a truck that was stuck in the war zone of the intersection.

Instead of the planned fragmentation mode most often used for anti-air missions, the missile instructed the warhead to direct all of its explosive force in a narrow cone forward. Just before it slammed into the trailer and was obliterated, the missile's tiny brain reflected on its existence and decided it had only one regret: that no one witnessed its supremely spectacular final act.

By striking the truck, the missile added the frozen fish in the trailer to the shrapnel being propelled outward by the explosion. On the other side of the intersection, most of the Wurgalan military police unit had taken shelter, massing for a final assault against the group of alien invaders. Their light armor panels were no protection from the frozen fish parts that impacted at hypersonic speeds, especially as many of the police had turned to run away from the collapsing building and their armor panels were thinner on the back side. Twenty of the twenty-one police mercifully were killed instantly, never realizing what happened. The last officer, having arrived late and running toward the makeshift barricade, had a brief moment of asking a shocked '*What the f-*' in his own language, when he was killed by the severed head of a frozen fish traveling at Mach Two.

Inside the lobby of the mixed-use building, Surgun Third Class Arkonda stood poised to trigger explosives that would blow a hole in the side wall of the building. He was waiting for a signal from Second Platoon, or simply the sound of the damned gunship being struck by a missile. The plan was for Arkonda and another soldier to provide cover fire, while the other three combat-capable soldiers lead a retreat of the wounded who were able to walk. Nine of the fifteen injured were capable of walking with the assistance of their damaged mech suits, though none of them could move with any speed. Arkonda did not know of anything he could do for the six more seriously wounded people, and they understood their fate. The team leading the retreat was supposed to look for a working vehicle, though the streets were so jammed with crashed cars, trucks and busses that it was unlikely they could drive far. It was not a good plan, it was the only plan Arkonda could think of, given the unforgiving facts. The wounded soldiers who could not move would hold their position, drawing the attention of the police while the others conducted a fighting retreat. If the plan worked, and Second Platoon could fight its way through, he could save fourteen people, including himself. Fourteen, out of the entire platoon, plus the two pilots. When the trapped soldiers could no longer hold the position, they would detonate a pile of rockets, destroying the building and granting a merciful end to the suffering of the seriously injured.

Safety protocol was why Arkonda had a two-step process to trigger the explosives for blowing the side wall, a wide precaution that prevented disaster. When he heard and felt a BANG from above, the building shook and he released the first safety device, waiting to hear the crash of the gunship. Instead, he heard its engines whine loudly then an odd crumpling sound. For a brief moment, there was near-silence before a thunderous roar. Dust, chunks of concrete and other debris shot through gaps in the barricade they had set up where the building's ground-floor windows had been, blinding Arkonda. The whole building shook with a second explosion outside and the front of their building fell inward, along with part of the side wall. Explosives were not needed after all. Arkonda had to duck and cover, taking shelter from smoke, flames, thick choking dust and debris that pinged off the top of his helmet, rattling his brain and causing spots in his vision. When he could see again, his suit's sensors warned that the ceiling above him was sagging and in danger of imminent collapse.

Moving carefully so he didn't bump into a column that was shakily holding up the ceiling, he crawled out from under a pile of debris and toggled open his microphone.

"Ardva Two, this is Three. Did you just *nuke* the city?"

"Uh," Dani replied, slowing her pace. "Not that I know of, I-" She checked the feed from the still-hovering drone. "Holy *shit*!" The city intersection that had become an unlikely battle zone was wreathed in thick smoke and dust, but she could see that an entire *building* was missing. What the hell?

"Ardva Two, we are *outta* here. Three out."

"Captain?" Auffex called. "Did what I think just happened, happen?"

Besault chimed in. "I think we destroyed a building. Captain, we were supposed to avoid collateral damages. We will catch hell from the Ruhar."

"Hey, the hamsters can garnish my freakin' *paycheck* to replace that building," Dani said with vehemence, surprising herself. When had she gotten so macho? Maybe she was simply tired of dealing with bullshit beyond her control. She hadn't sliced the *Dal Turnaden* in half, she had not crashed Third Platoon's dropship in the center of the city, and she hadn't provided a tempting target by flying a gunship low and slow over a crowded city.

"Maybe we'll get lucky, and not survive this op," Auffex said with gallows humor. "Then UNEF will have to pay for the damage."

"Surgun, if you die, I am *totally* blaming the whole thing on you," Dani replied, and was rewarded with laughter over the platoon channel. "Besault, see if you can move the drone in closer. I need to see where Third is going."

The drone approached the thick gray smoke that obscured the intersection, and they picked up three transponder signals from Legion mech suits, when the drone stopped transmitting. After a half minute, Besault reported "That's not jamming, we just lost the drone."

Truly, Dani was amazed the drone had lasted so long in a hostile environment. "Ardva Three, we need your position, report-" She stumbled and dropped to the ground as an aircraft roared by close overhead. From the glimpse she got, it was another Wurgalan gunship. The hornets were swarming, and they were pissed off. "Auffex!"

"On it, Captain. You should take cover," the Verd woman warned as her squad's anti-air missile team dashed off the street into a small park.

Dani didn't waste time with a reply that would only have been a distraction to the people focused on their jobs. Scrambling toward what looked like an office building, she jumped and crashed through the street-side windows, skidding across the floor and bumping into the weird furniture used by the squids. She had just come to a stop and was getting to her knees when a soldier flew through the window and smacked into her, knocking her down again. She did *not* lose her rifle, a fact that might have been a virtue of the suit computer.

When she got untangled from soldier and furniture, the Verd pressed down on her shoulder. "You should keep down, Captain."

"If I'm on the floor, I can't *see* anything," she protested.

"It's dangerous to-"

"If a gunship drops a missile out there," Dani pushed herself upright, holding the broken remains of a desk. "Will this desk protect me?"

"No," the soldier admitted.

"Great. Now," she checked the icon in her visor, which informed her of the soldier's name. "Vist Hahmfurr, I don't need a bodyguard."

"That's not-" The Verd soldier began to object. "Surgun Auffex told me to assure you are safe."

Dani crawled over to the broken window and propped her rifle barrel on the frame. "This is a war zone. No one is *safe*."

Across the street in the park, two soldiers had just completed setting up a Cobra missile. A soldier raised the weapon to her shoulder as Dani heard the sound of the enemy aircraft growing louder and higher in pitch. It was coming back for a strafing run. There was a faint puff of steam from water vapor in the air heated by the Cobra's launch, then the weapon was away, rocketing upward without bothering to deploy its wings. The soldiers must have fired blind, they couldn't have a view of the target yet. Launch of the Cobra was intended to warn the enemy away, showing that the alien invaders on the ground had sharp teeth and were dangerous.

Dani lost sight of the missile as it soared up into the sky in a pop-up maneuver, so it could get a view of the target. There was a chattering sound and Dani flinched instinctively, anticipating shells chewing up the street, but nothing impacted within her view. There was more chattering that became so rapid it was a buzz, then a *BOOM* rocked the area, shattering windows in the building and raining glass down on Dani and Hahmfurr. When she shifted to get a better view, glass crunched under her armored knee and she idly noticed it looked like real glass, not any high-tech composite. Why didn't- Oh. She guessed that actual silica-based glass was cheap and good enough for civilian applications. That was interest-

"Intercept," Auffex reported, her disappointment evident. "Missile was destroyed without striking the target."

"Second Platoon!" Dani ordered, stepping out of the window frame onto the street and waving with her free hand. She was not an infantry officer, but she did know one thing. Firing the Cobra might have discouraged the enemy from a strafing run, but the gunship probably had stand-off weapons, and knew where the Cobra had been launched from. Across the street, she saw the anti-air team soldiers had already discarded the empty launch tube and were attaching the targeting box to another tube. "Move move move! Get *out* of here!" Her order was not needed, the two surguns had their squads running. Hahmfurr was just behind Dani, they followed Besault's squad up the street and turned left at the first intersection. Several soldiers turned and dropped to one knee, rifles pointed at the sky as the other squad ran through, just before the street they had left was rocked by explosions and fire. BOOM BOOM BOOM BOOM BOOM the cluster munitions rained down, shaking the ground under Dani's feet and shattering windows all around. The enemy certainly wasn't concerned about collateral damage to their own city. Right behind the munitions, the gunship raced by low and fast, flying through the smoke created by its own weapons. She only caught a passing impression of a sleek shape as the enemy aircraft flashed by along the main street.

"Their sensors might have seen us," Besault warned, waving his troops to move. They were on a side road, with blocks of two or three-story buildings connected together in sets. Alleys cut through the middle of the blocks and Dani found it odd that the alleys looked no different from such urban features in any city on Earth; dumpsters lined the sides, trash had been blown into corners by the wind, puddles of water filled low spots. Sidewalks along the streets had trees spaced evenly, with shrubs growing around the base of the trees. The odd architecture that tended to use curves instead of angles looked like a city in a Doctor Seuss book, with buildings leaning and appearing to sag toward each other.

Following Besault's lead and with her babysitter Hahmfurr right on her heels, Dani ducked down an alley, pushing off one wall so hard that her powered gloves knocked a chunk out of the concrete-like material. Ahead of her, a soldier slipped on a slick puddle and bounced off the same wall, his armored shoulder sending a shower of concrete pebbles to *ping* off Dani's faceplate.

The alley came to a dead end, a fact that did not bother the soldiers leading the squad. One of them used his powered legs to kick in a solid metal door and send it flying away inside the structure beyond, barely slowing down. The rest of the squad ran in single-file, with Dani and then Auffex's squad trailing.

It was a convenience store, although one that also sold clothing and small electronics. By the time Dani ducked through the too-low doorway, the interior was already a shambles both from the flying door and from soldiers knocking over racks of display cases. She looked down to see she was standing on brightly-colored packages of what she guessed was snack food. The package had a cartoon image of a Wurgalan reaching into the bag with a tentacle, pulling out some disgusting purple hairy things. Presumably to eat. Revolting, although the Wurgalan would probably say the same thing about a bag of Funyuns, and Funyuns were unquestionably delicious.

In front of her, soldiers were crouching down instead of running out the front door to the other street, or smashing through the windows. "Surgun, why aren't we-"

The answer came in the form of a fireball blasting through the open doorway behind her, staggering her, and she would have toppled forward if not for Hahmfurr using a free hand to hold her upright. She turned to see burning debris in the alley and two soldiers down, they rose to their knees then feet, and trotted forward to collapse through the doorway. In her visor, Dani saw the status overlay for both soldiers showing numerous yellow indicators of minor damage to their mech suits. The biological beings within were showing normal readings, though Dani knew from personal experience that the suits did not register painful bumps, bruises and joints strained from over-extension.

The wall of one building had partially collapsed into the alley, and one dumpster was tipped over at a forty-five degree angle, the trash inside burning so furiously that items spurted into the air, sending flaming garbage to fall into the ruined alley.

Looking at the dumpster fire, she shook her head. "That describes this whole freakin' op," she muttered to herself.

"What was that, Captain?" Besault asked, tapping the side of his helmet.

"Nothing. We're not hiding in here for long, are we?" She forgot that *she* was filling the role of platoon leader.

"No, we-" His voice was drowned out by a chainsaw-like buzz of the gunship coming in for a strafing run on the street at the open end of the alley. The pilot and gunner must have thought their stand-off weapons had killed the platoon or at least made them keep their heads down. A shadow raced past and the whining sound of the gunship's engines dropped in pitch. When the sound steadied, Dani eyeclicked through a threat assessment menu in her visor. Her suit computer was trying to plot the gunship's location and course based only on sound. The enemy was coming back for another strafing run, and from the echoes off the ground, it was flying low. That, she thought, was a result of the platoon firing a Cobra, the enemy pilot was hugging the ground to avoid providing an easy target for a missile. "Besault, can we-"

"On it," the alien replied tersely, barking orders to his squad. They ran out into the alley, hugging the wall on the right, where the gunship was approaching from. The platoon tactical network showed that all the soldiers in the squad had their rifles synced with their surgun, rifles aimed high and low toward the opening of the alley. As the engine whine grew in intensity and pitch, soldiers from Auffex's squad scrambled into the alley, syncing their rifles to Besault.

"Should I-" Dani took a step forward but Hahmfurr tugged her arm.

"Please remain here, Captain. We fight, you *lead*," the soldier added gently.

"Right."

There was another angry chainsaw sound and the street beyond the alley was ripped by cannon fire, chewing into the buildings on both sides and sending more debris raining down into the alley. The soldiers all held their positions without flinching, and their rifles fired in unison when Besault pressed the trigger of his weapon.

As the shadow of the gunship flashed past low over the rooftops, it ran into a hail of explosive-tipped rounds from more than a dozen Kristang rifles on full auto. The engagement was over in the blink of an eye, all weapons ceased fire when Besault lifted his finger off the trigger of his weapon. Immediately, the engine whine changed, becoming intermittent, the turbines sputtering.

"Wait!" Besault held up a hand, two fingers extended in the Verd-kris signal to hold position.

In Dani's visor, the predicted location of the enemy aircraft kept growing farther and farther away, the sound dwindling. According to the acoustic sensors of her helmet, the gunship had shut down one engine, and the other was throttled back, its turbine blades wobbling.

"Negative on a kill," Besault pronounced with disappointment.

"We don't need a kill," Dani reminded the squad leader. "You got that hornet off our backs, hopefully it will warn the others that we can sting, too. That was outstanding work, tell your people."

"Will do. Captain, we should move out."

"Right."

Second Platoon filed quickly out the doorway of the store, leaving the front windows intact so if the enemy came back, there would not be visible evidence the invaders had been there and survived to escape. As they resumed advancing to hopefully link up with Third Platoon, Auffex came forward to run alongside Dani. "Captain, we can't use that trick too many times."

Dani knew what the surgun meant. "If we are too big a threat, the squids will stop screwing around and drop warheads on our foreheads?"

"Captain?"

Dani winced. She kept forgetting that slang did not reliably translate well. "The squids will call in artillery or an airstrike, take out two or three blocks around where they think we are."

"Yes."

"Let's hope," she looked up at the sky, where twisting contrails and bright flashes told her a battle was raging, "that the enemy has bigger things to worry about than one understrength platoon out for a morning run in the city." She hoped the air battle over the city would prevent the enemy from having a stealthed aircraft circling high above her, beyond range of the Cobra launcher's targeting system. That, at least, was one less threat she needed to worry about.

If Auffex had concerns that *hope* was no substitute for a *plan*, she kept that thought to herself.

What Dani *did* need to worry about was not having any contact with Third Platoon since the drone had been destroyed. The Third could have been wiped out, captured or been forced to go in a different direction. She could be leading her platoon into extreme danger for nothing, and she wouldn't know until it was too late. So far, they had encountered only light opposition and that was not only a matter of luck; the Wurgalan truly were not focused on a small group of light infantry.

"Trouble," a scout called from ahead. "There's another group of civilians here."

# CHAPTER TWENTY ONE

The Ugly Bug flew toward the next pillar of smoke, holding more or less a straight line. There was no point to zigzagging, if either side cared about the slow, clumsy-flying helicopter, the defenseless aircraft could easily be shot down. Appearing harmless was the platoon's best chance of survival.

A line of hills stretched northwest to southeast across their flight path, Irene increased altitude to comfortably clear a saddle between two cone-shaped hills. Ancient volcanos, her mind idly informed her with that day's trivia lesson. Volcanos eroded down to nothingness.

"Huh," Derek said, lifting his hands off the console.

"What?" Irene asked, not daring take her eyes off her own instruments.

"Compass has gone haywire. It's acting like MAD gear."

Perkins leaned forward. With the big rotor blades going *thwock thwock thwock* overhead loudly enough that it was rattling her brain even through the helmet, she hadn't heard correctly. "The compass has gone *mad*?"

"No, Ma'am," Derek explained. "M, A, D, like Magnetic Anomaly Detector. That's how our sub-hunting planes back on Earth find enemy submarines under the surface, the steel hull creates a magnetic field. Hold your course," he advised Irene, "I'll try to fix-"

The helicopter's cockpit was suddenly bathed in multicolored light, then plunged into utter, featureless blackness. Irene yelped as the Ugly Bug bounced upward, her instruments useless, her view of the horizon lost.

She had to fly the helicopter entirely by feel, which was impossible. Amateurs think they can fly using their own sense of balance, professional pilots know better. Irene remembered an instructor giving the class a quick exercise in flight school. Stand on one leg. Tilt your head back to look straight up.

Now close your eyes.

She fell into the student next to her, who was falling backwards.

If the Ugly Bug's instruments did not give her an idea of which way was 'up' and which was 'down', they were going to roll and find out the hard way. The artificial horizon instrument had power; it wasn't doing anything reliable. Neither was the turn and bank indicator, it told her the helicopter was already on its side and she knew that wasn't right. The independent sensors in her helmet had also glitched, giving contradictory statuses.

Heart in her throat, she tried to fly by the seat of her pants, literally trying to judge which butt cheek was feeling more pressure except she was straddling the awkward-

Sunlight came back. The light had been gone for such a short time her pupils hadn't dilated. That was good, the light wasn't blinding, and her helmet's visor compensated. What was not good was seeing the Ugly Bug was nose up at twenty degrees and rolling to the right at fifteen degrees, airspeed rapidly bleeding off. To her right the big rotor blades beat at the air, the flexing tips reaching out for the hillside.

"Babe!" Derek warned, feeding full power to the rotor blades.

The rest was up to Irene. They were going to either roll over or stall, neither was recoverable especially at the tree-scraping altitude. Coordinating her control inputs in the unfamiliar aircraft, she pushed the stick forward to swing the nose down, building up airspeed to avoid stalling. The big rotor blades automatically changed pitch, taking bigger bites of air with every rotation. Steadying the roll and getting the helicopter on an even keel, she felt the craft shudder as tree branches slapped at the cargo pod and the landing gear dragged through treetops. What saved them was the hillside falling away sharper than the helicopter was descending.

Suddenly they were in clear air, flying straight and normal.

"That," Derek clenched his teeth to keep them from chattering. "Was great flying."

"That was luck," Irene admitted. "I hope we didn't break anything."

"Was that a *nuke*?" Perkins asked, her eyes still blinking away the initial flash of light.

"No," Derek declared. "We just flew through a stealth field. Theirs," he added.

"Why was it *bright*?"

"That's from the hologram," he explained, one eye on Irene and one on his console. The instruments were returning to normal. "The stealth field bends light around it, so we can't see what's really under there. The stealth field is wrapped in a hologram that projects a false image. We flew through the hologram first, then inside the field. We're lucky we just caught the edge of it, is my guess."

"Your damned right about that," Irene agreed. "The Bug doesn't feel any different, I don't think it suffered mechanical damage."

Perkins checked the map in her visor. "Why is there a stealth field way out here?"

"Plasma cannon?" Derek guessed.

"Got to be," Irene agreed quietly. The stick had developed a flutter, or was she imagining that?

"The pre-invasion bombardment knocked out all of the plasma cannon clusters," Perkins repeated what the Ruhar fleet commander had told her.

"Apparently they missed one," Derek snorted. "What have the hamsters *not* been wrong about?"

Perkins wasn't convinced. "If there's a cluster of plasma cannons here, their defenses would have shot us down."

"Not without giving away their position, Ma'am," Derek countered. "Plus, we're a friendly aircraft."

"Are we squawking IFF codes?" Irene asked.

"We're not squawking *anything*, that I can see," Derek waved a hand at his console. "Maybe it's on a menu I haven't found yet." If the helicopter's comm system was responding to Identification Friend or Foe requests from the Wurgalan, it was doing it automatically. "One thing's for sure; if anyone down there was asleep, we woke them up. You know what? That's odd."

"What is?" Perkins asked.

"A stealth field is a hazard, it should be highlighted on this thing's navigation system. We flew right into it."

"Must be a secret," Irene suggested.

"Of *course* it's a secret, it has to- Oh." Derek's lips drew into a tight line. "Shit. It looks like we *are* flying through a restricted zone. This whole area is restricted, if I'm reading this damned thing right. It doesn't say why."

Perkins made a snap decision. "Striebich, take us north around this hill, I want to set down somewhere that isn't line-of-sight to the plasma cannon."


While they walked, Dave Czajka somehow got an old song stuck in his head. It was a good song, he enjoyed it, he did not like his stupid brain repeating it over and over. His father had told him that one way to get rid of an 'earworm' was to sing it aloud, and let it get stuck in someone else's head. "*I shot the sheriff*," he sang out of tune. "*But I did not shoot the deputy, oh yeah*," he adlibbed.

"What?" Jates turned toward him suddenly. "Czajka, do you think that the authorities will go easier on you, because you only shot *one* law enforcement official?"

"What?" Dave halted, holding up his hands. "No, man, it's just-"

Jates unslung his rifle, keeping the muzzle pointed at the ground. "You *idiot*. You have confessed to a serious crime. I am required by our code of justice to apprehend you. We are in a combat zone, why didn't you wait until-"

"No, I," Dave stuttered. "It's, it's just a song!"

"You could have composed your confession in the form of an epic poem," Jates shook his head, "and it would not change the facts of your crime."

"Shauna," Dave pleaded. "Come on, help me out here. You gotta explain it to him."

Shauna hung her head, avoiding Dave's eyes. "David Czajka, I thought I knew you." Her voice cracked. "You know one of my uncles is a police officer, how *could* you?"

"Whoa," Dave's panic meter went to Eleven. "Jates, Surgun, you gotta believe me, it's just-"

"You selfish *jerk*," Jates snarled. "You could have waited until the operation was over, but *no*. You had to get it off your chest now, and dump the burden on *us*. Why-"

"Whoa. *Whoa*," Dave waved his hands, keeping them in sight and away from his rifle. "Listen, Jates, seriously-"

Jates slung his rifle. "Czajka, I was screwing with you. Damn, you are *so* freakin' gullible."

"Oh," Dave sputtered. "*Oh*! That is not-"

"Stop," Jates held up a fist. "You hear that?"

Nert answered first, tilting his head as if that would help him hear better inside his helmet. Instincts were hard to overcome. "I, maybe."

"I don't hear anything," Shauna boosted the volume. "Still nothing."

"It's an aircraft," Jates declared with confidence.

Dave looked at Shauna. They all wore helmets with the same acoustic sensors, but the genetically-enhanced hearing of Jates and Nert gave them an advantage. "If you say so," Dave kept his tone neutral, not displaying irritation at the aliens showing off for the humans. Stilling his breathing, he concentrated. There was a faint droning sound. Swinging his head side to side, he looked to the north-north east. "That direction?"

"Correct," Jates looked around. "We should get under cover."

None of the others argued with that notion. Unfortunately, that area of forest was relatively flat and featureless, with no overhanging rocks or caves they could hide under. Shauna pointed to a fallen tree, where large roots torn out of the ground created a crater. "Only two of us can fit in there. Czajka, help Chowdhury get in there."

Dave wanted to protest, but the injured woman did need help, and none of them could do anything useful if they were being hunted by a Wurgalan aircraft. After he lowered himself into the muddy hole under the tree roots next to Chowdhury, he watched the others scatter to avoid leaving an easy, compact target zone for the enemy. They all took positions so that everyone was within line-of-sight of one other person, so their helmets could communicate via low-power laser bursts.

With nothing else to do, Dave played with the suit's threat assessment controls, trying to identify the incoming aircraft. Nothing worked, the system could not find a match. That was odd. The Legion only had a dozen types of vehicles capable of operating in an atmosphere, and all types of Wurgalan air and airspace-craft were in the identification database. Puzzled and anxious, he began trying to get the system to tell him what type of aircraft was the closest match, which the computer seemed reluctant to do. The source of his anxiety was not concern about being targeted by the enemy, he was worried about a Legion aircraft being in the area and never noticing them. A war was raging to the east, and Dave might as well have been on a camping trip in the wilderness. He wanted to know where Em was, and he wanted to be there. Help her, protect her. What the hell was he thinking, letting her put herself into danger when-

Scratch that. He did not *let* Emily Perkins do anything, he had no authority over her. She was no doubt just as worried about him. Maybe, after the invasion was over one way or another, the two of them needed to talk about doing something else for a living. Fighting for his country, his species, was one thing. Risking his life to intervene in disputes between aliens was making less sense to him with every deployment. The only reason he kept going, kept signing on, was that Emily was going, and although she never said anything directly, he suspected she had a plan, like P-L-A-N in all capital letters. Whatever it was, she hadn't told him. Maybe that was because he was a contractor, maybe it was because his effective rank was that of a staff sergeant, and it was above his pay grade.

Dave decided right then and there that, if, *when*, they got back together, things were going to change.

Startled, he realized that while he had been daydreaming, the suit computer had complied with his instructions. Text reading >>Lotentix<< was scrawling across the visor. "What the hell is a- Oh, yeah," he mumbled, remembering the official Ruhar designation for that type of dropship. "Hey, guys," he called out. "IFF says the closest match is a Dodo with a damaged engine."

A reply came back from Jates immediately. "A Dodo must be one of ours. How can you be sure?"

"I can't be *sure*," Dave groaned. "It's a fifty-one percent match. The next closest match is, uh," he scrolled down. "Twenty-nine percent. That's for a squid gunship that UNEF calls a Warthog."

"Let me ping them," Chowdhury spoke.

Jates vetoed that suggestion. "We can't have anyone-"

"I can barely walk, and it *hurts*," the Indian soldier insisted. "I am slowing you down."

Dave worried that somehow, he had given her the impression that she was a burden. "You're not slowing us down, because we're not *going* anywhere."

Chowdhury was not deterred. "If I ping them and they're hostile, the four of you can scatter and evade. I have tried not to complain, but every step I take hurts so bad I can barely see. The suit won't give me any more nerve blockers."

"It makes sense," Nert said.

"No one asked for your opinion, *Cadet*," Jates snapped.

"She is right," Shauna came to Nert's defense. "One of us has to attempt to make contact. If we had a drone, we could launch it, but we don't."

Jates stepped out from behind the leaning tree where he had taken cover. "I will not risk the life of-"

"Hey," Dave was growing irritated. "News flash for you, surgun. We are *all* at risk. We signed up for risk when we agreed to join this crap operation. Right now, we're at risk without doing anything useful. There are people out there who *need* us. I don't like the idea of hiding under a freakin' tree while the Legion is doing who knows what. Chowdhury is right. It sucks to say that, but she's right." Under the tree roots, he extended a hand, and she bumped his fist.

Jates was silent for a beat. "I must balance the needs of two other species, and the relations of my people against-"

"Bullshit," Shauna interjected. "If you're leading this squad, leave the politics out of it. We're infantry. General Ross can handle the consequences if any of us get killed down here, that's why he gets the big bucks." Switching to a private channel, she assured their Verd-kris leader. "Jates, if this were an all-Verd unit, what would you do?"

He sighed. "I would commend Chowdhury for her bravery and initiative." Over the squad channel, he spoke with authority, ignoring the debate they just had. "Chowdhury, good idea. Czajka, get your ass out of there, we need to disperse."

"Thanks," Dave patted the other soldier's shoulder as he wriggled out from under the tree roots.

The four scattered, racing through the forest, getting as far away as they could within the ninety seconds Chowdhury would wait. Nert came to a stop at a stream, judging whether to run farther during the eighteen seconds remaining. No, it was just more forest. The stream cut a meter-deep channel in the flat ground, giving him some sort of cover. Immersing himself in the stream's cold water would help mask the infrared signature of his suit, so he laid down in a pool and waited.

And waited.

And waited.

Three minutes after Chowdhury was supposed to attempt contacting the mystery aircraft, he sat up, his helmet above the water. Some type of amphibious lizard animal was startled by his appearance, leaping off a rock into the water. "Sorry," Nert whispered, listening intently. He could hear the aircraft clearly, it was closer. According to the threat assessment system, the aircraft was to the north and would pass by thirty-four kilometers away. He could also hear Chowdhury calling out on multiple frequencies, with no indication the aircraft had heard her.

The smart thing to do was to slip back beneath the surface and wait. He wasn't even supposed to be on the surface. As a cadet, he had used family connections to get into action too many times, and his parents had pulled strings to assure he would remain safely aboard the assault carrier. To put himself at further risk would be to go against the wishes of his parents, and the operational orders that governed his participation in the invasion. There was grumbling and resentment within the academy that, because he had seen action multiple times, he had an advantage over his fellow cadets. Rumors that he was a show-off, a thrill-seeker.

The smart thing to do was to stay under the water.

On the other hand, he had seen the anguish on the faces of Shauna and Dave. They wanted to know what was happening to their loved ones, and he was worried about the other Mavericks also. They were his friends, far more than any of his fellow cadets.

Oh, what the hell, he told himself, remembering a bit of human wisdom Jesse Colter had told him on Paradise. It is better to act and ask forgiveness, than to hesitate and ask permission. Any transgression by him could be attributed to youthful lack of judgment.

Sitting up, he set his suit to transmit his ID code over multiple frequencies at full power. Seconds later, his visor displayed a text message from Jates, demanding that he cease transmitting. He ignored the message. A second message rephrased the demand as an order, and when he ignored that also, he received notice that his suit's computer had received an override command, killing the transmitter.

It didn't matter.

The faint, distant drone of engines increased in volume and pitch, and his threat assessment system popped up a window in his visor, warning the aircraft had turned toward him. He was about to attempt to bypass Jates's lockout of his transmitter when a message from Shauna scrolled across the bottom. *Run, in case you were wrong.*

Nert didn't argue with the logic. Splashing out of the water, he ran, leaping up the far side of the stream bank and bounding over a log, turning to-

He froze, grabbing onto a tree to halt his momentum. Without identifying itself, the aircraft was requesting he repeat his ID signal. He couldn't, staring at the sky with a mix of frustration and fear. The enemy would of course request a signal, so they could pinpoint his location.

Instead, he saw Jates was sending his own ID signal, and Nert felt a pang of guilt. He had been recklessly foolish. If the Verd-kris surgun was targeted by the enemy, it would be Nert's fault.

Then the aircraft painted the area with an active sensor pulse, and the threat warning system of Nert's suit glowed red.

He ran.


"Confirmed," the soldier controlling the drone said as she squinted at the display splashed across her helmet visor. "That's a plasma cannon cluster."

Perkins examined the same data feed, and drew a different conclusion. "All I see is trees."

"That's what you're supposed to see," Jesse said. "They bury the plasma cannon hatches, just like the lizards did with the maser cannons on Paradise. Switch to the subsurface scan, Ma'am."

"I thought we weren't using active sensors?"

Sergeant Liu, holding the tablet that guided the drone, spoke without taking her attention off the device she was responsible for. "Passive only, Colonel. It's analyzing seismic waves."

"Seismic?" Perkins expressed surprised. "Like, earthquakes?"

"Yes," Liu explained patiently. "Seismic waves are always echoing through any planetary body, Ma'am, even worlds that don't have tectonic plates. Right now, there is a lot of seismic activity on the continent to work with, because of explosions and debris falling from orbit. We are tracking the waves as they pass through the ground, and so can see the waves are passing around an object that is under-"

"Sergeant," Perkins waved a hand. "I trust you, we don't have time for a science lesson. Show me."

Liu transferred the image to the Mavericks leader, who whistled. "Wow, that is a *big* sumbitch."

"That includes the powercells, aiming mechanism, everything the cannon needs, all in that cylinder," Liu noted. "We can see there are two other cannons, these clusters always have three cannons."

"All right, and you compared this to known profiles of plasma cannons?"

Jesse answered the question. "Yes. The squids only have two types of these cannons, this is the most common version. No question about it."

"We pull back, then. Get away from here, contact the fleet upstairs and get them to make this whole area a smoking crater."

"Colonel?" Jesse asked. "Let's not be hasty. The intel provided by the Torgalau missed this cannon cluster."

"I know that, Colter. The fleet needs to-"

"This might not be the *only* one they missed," Jesse continued. Interrupting a senior officer was bad form but, as Perkins herself had said, they didn't have a lot of time. "I mean, what are the odds we found the only one, right?"

Perkins cocked her head. Colter could sometimes be rash, but she had learned to trust his judgment. "You propose to try using the seismic detector to find other cannon clusters?"

"I *propose*," Jesse's Arkansas drawl slipped deeper when he used fancy words. "That we take over this cluster," he pointed a finger at the ground. "The computers in the control bunker must have a list of other clusters."

"Take over?" Perkins stared at the staff sergeant. "Break into this place? You're going to throw together a plan to do that?"

"Not break in, we infiltrate. It's not *my* plan, it's something the hamsters got from the Torgalau." When she kept staring at him without blinking, he explained. "I studied up on it during the flight here, there wasn't much else to do aboard the *Sure Thing*. Look, the squids don't expect these cannons will ever be subjected to a ground assault, which kinda makes sense. They figure if an enemy gets boots on the ground, all the cannons must have been expended or knocked out. The Torgalau found a vulnerability in the design of the control bunkers, they-"

"Colter! Show me."

The first drone crashed and burned, after its sensors were overwhelmed by passing through the hologram and into the stealth field. The little device did not actually burn, and the crash was a gentle drift down to thump against the ground, where it remained after it was determined the drone's computer could not recover from the shock. The second drone flew forward with its external sensors switched off and the computer in safe mode, with guidance by Liu from the ultra-thin wire that spooled out behind the device. She lost the view as it approached the hologram, which from the ground was clearly artificial, glowing and flickering in a way that was disturbing to look at. The failure of the hologram to fool observers on the ground did not matter, the stealth field was intended to conceal the cannon cluster from ships and aircraft at high altitude, and it had performed that task perfectly, since the Ruhar fleet thought they had struck all the cannon clusters.

When the drone had traveled a distance estimated to be eighty meters inside the stealth field, Liu commanded the device's computer to restart and she held it motionless. The drone did not walk, it didn't crawl and it didn't exactly fly. Mostly, it was a balloon two meters long and half a meter in diameter, a miniature zeppelin surrounding a solid core no larger than an apple. The balloon maneuvered by sucking in air and puffing it out, propelled by turbines that turned slowly so they made little sound. With sensors back online, Liu still could not see much, the blackness inside the stealth field was nearly complete. Nearly. A stealth field bent light around it, and light bent around a starship simply went around the field and continued onward into empty space. When light from the sky bent around a stealth field on the ground, the light could not keep going. It would create a brightly glowing ring around the bottom of the field and negate the effect of stealth, unless something was done to absorb the light. That is why ground-based stealth fields had a ring of photon-absorbing material at the bottom, where the photons were converted into heat and transferred to sinks deep underground. Sergeant Liu was able to direct the drone because the light-absorbing ability of the ring was not perfect, so inside there was a dim bluish glow saturating the dome of the field.

"We're in," Liu whispered to whoever was listening, directing her words to Staff Sergeant Colter. It was his plan they were implementing, despite his protests that he was only following an idea cooked up by the Torgalau.

"Four meters to the left," he directed softly. "Down, bring it down. Watch the trees, those branches-"

"I see it," Liu kept the irritation she felt from reflecting in her voice. "I *don't* see-"

"There," Jesse leaned in, tapping the screen of the tablet she was using to steer the drone. "See those rocks leaning together? There's a thing, looks like a big mushroom. That's an air intake."

"You are sure about this, Colter?" Perkins glanced left and right. They were in a dense thicket of brush that provided good cover, but also would be tough to run through even in powered armor. Eh, she told herself, if the enemy knew of their presence, they would likely send a missile, and no powered armor could outrun that.

"I'm just going by-"

"I know, you're relying on what the Torgalau reported. They never did this for real, did they?"

"They never had to," he replied. "They never got the opportunity. Plasma cannons are one-shot weapons, once they're expended there's no point risking a ground team to take one out. We know CN-20 works because the Ruhar have tested it."

"Tested, under controlled conditions. Not in the field." Perkins did not like the idea of deploying nerve gas, which is what CN-20 was despite what the Ruhar called it. The manual described the gas as a nontoxic and nonlethal substance, that was safe and legal to use on the battlefield. It was binary, meaning the gas was dispersed in two parts that only became effective when they bound together in the bloodstream, and only affected Wurgalan biochemistry. Separately, the two gasses were expected to pass through Wurgalan filters without detection by hazard sensors. Using lethal chemical weapons was a violation of the treaty between the Ruhar and Kristang and, although a certain amount of cheating was tolerated and even expected, if the CN-20 killed the crew in the bunker, humans would be blamed. She had only assurances from the Ruhar that the gas would incapacitate, not kill.

The question was not whether she trusted the intel provided by the Torgalau. Those aliens had been wrong about many important details, but most of the data they gave to the Ruhar was solid.

The question was, did she trust the *Ruhar*?

The AI system of the command bunker had detected the helicopter approaching, though sensor coverage of that area was poor so it only had an intermittent view of the event. It had been surprised when the helicopter flew straight into the restricted area, then astonished when the aircraft flew into and out of the stealth field, making the AI wonder just what idiot jackass was flying the darned thing. That the big helicopter had survived the event was a miracle, but the

AI knew the craft had survived only because its seismic sensors did not detect an impact after it lost sight of the awkward flying machine.

The AI, and its fellows at other cannon clusters, had repeatedly warned that having a sensor array which only pointed *up* was a dangerous vulnerability. The biological beings who created and governed the AI repeatedly rejected the warning, with the justification that plasma cannons would be shooting only at objects in the sky above, and the threat of a ground-based assault was extremely unlikely. When the AIs pointed out that there was minimal expense involved in providing sensor coverage of the ground around a cannon cluster, the biological beings responded that they already knew that, they did not need a computer telling them how to do their jobs, and, shut the hell up.

The AIs did shut the hell up. They didn't like it.

The AI of that particular cannon cluster warned the crew of the bunker about the helicopter, which caused a brief bit of excitement, then the crew went back to waiting and waiting and waiting.

It bothered the AI that it had lost track of the helicopter, the aircraft was below the lower limit of sensor coverage and ducked behind a hill after it passed through the stealth field. For a short time, seismic sensors recorded the heavy WHOP-WHOP-WHOP of the helicopter's rotor blades making the ground vibrate, then that also was gone and the AI had no idea where the mysterious aircraft had gone. It warned the crew that the aircraft was an unknown potential threat, causing the crew to mute future threat notifications. What they were concerned about was the fleet of Ruhar battleships hanging over their heads, and the terrifying knowledge that somehow, the enemy had known the exact location of most cannon clusters in the network.

The AI observed a slight change of pressure in one of the concealed air intakes, and a scan did not reveal anything other than an increase of humidity. It was known that water vapor could be a useful carrier for dangerous substances, and the AI could have warned the crew of the potential danger, except it was not programmed to do that. The Wurgalan did not like their AIs to think for themselves, they were limited to doing what they were told.

When the three crewmembers wavered in their chairs, began trembling and collapsed forward unconscious onto their consoles, the AI could have sent out a warning that the bunker had been compromised. But, as it wasn't programmed to do that, it did nothing. It also did nothing when the codes of the heavy bunker door were cracked and the door swung open, because that was not within its narrow scope of responsibilities.

When the bunker's internal sensors gave a view of aliens warily entering the ramp from the outer door into the bunker, the AI *could* have sent out a general warning, because it interpreted its responsibilities broadly.

It did not send out a general alert for one simple reason: curiosity.

The aliens were *humans*, a new and strange species it had only vague information about.

The AI waited, and watched, and experienced a measure of admiration for the invading aliens. The few reports it had read about humans all stated the creatures were weak, primitive and no threat. Apparently, they were also inventive and *clever*.

What the hell, the AI told itself. I just *have* to know what happens next.

"I'll be damned," Jesse whispered when the bunker door began to swing open. "It actually worked."

Perkins shook her head. "You expected it wouldn't work?" She demanded.

"I figured it was worth *tryin'*, you know? But, damn! Metzger, send in the creeper drones. Everyone," he aimed his rifle at the opening exposed as the door ponderously swung back, selecting rockets. "Look sharp."

# CHAPTER TWENTY TWO

The platoon advanced through the city, one squad leapfrogging the other, and with Dani always escorted by Hahmfurr. They moved quickly as they could, with the complication that they increasingly encountered small groups of frightened civilians who were just trying to get out of the city. The aliens walked, or Dani thought of the motion as *scuttling*, moving along on their creepy tentacle legs. The streets were jammed with vehicles that had either lost power or lost guidance when the city's control grid failed. Cars, trucks and busses had smashed into each other, into lightposts, buildings or anything their inventive drivers could find to crash into. Some vehicles, trapped behind accidents that could not be cleared, had simply been abandoned, their former occupants now making their way out of the city on foot, or on *tentacle*. Most were just terrified civilians, and Dani reminded her soldiers they were not to fire unless fired upon. *We* are the invaders here, she reminded herself. *We* are the aliens, the bad guys. This is *their* planet, and we're taking it away from them. Hell, she thought with seriously conflicted emotions. We humans and Verds are not even going to keep the place, we're just hired guns for the Achakai.

This, she concluded, *sucked*.

Link up with Third Platoon, get them out of the city, and *then* wrestle with a moral crisis, she told herself. I have a job to do.

That job became more difficult when the scouts reached a sort of plaza where three major streets intersected. Vehicles were burning and it looked like the cause of the fires was not just accidental crashes, they had holes from bullets or shrapnel. For a moment, she hoped that Third Platoon had engaged in a firefight in the plaza, then she saw a smashed and burning part of an aircraft that had fallen and skidded along the street, battering cars until it struck a fountain in the middle of the plaza and came to rest there. The debris was so twisted and charred, she couldn't tell if the aircraft had been friend or foe and it really didn't matter. What did matter were the dozen screaming Wurgalan civilians who panicked when they saw the skinsuit-wearing enemy running along toward the plaza. The civilians shouted and pointed and ran, and that attracted the attention of two local police officers who were trying to get the city's residents calmed down, organized and moving toward the street-level openings to the underground railways that were still running.

As soon as the police saw the platoon's scouts, Dani's plan to take a side street and go around the plaza literally went up in flames. The police had weapons that they fired wildly, missing the scouts and striking a truck on a street that lead into the plaza. That truck had escaped damage when the aircraft crashed into the plaza, so it was just stuck with no place to go forward or back.

When the police fired their weapons, they struck the back of the truck, and there was a high-pitched hissing sound. An orange cloud vented from the truck only for a second, and *BOOM* an explosion rocked the plaza, sending the body of the truck into the air to crash down on several cars.

Dani was knocked to her knees, rolling backwards, pushing away Hahmfurr who tried to shield the captain with her body. "I'm *fine*, damn it!" Dani protested. "Besault, what's going on?"

The surgun didn't answer immediately. She heard gunfire that she knew was the bark of Kristang rifles, interspersed with the quieter pops of the machine pistols carried by the local police. "Cease fire!" Besault called. "We've got two down."

Checking her visor, she saw that two of their scouts were down. Not just down, one of them was dead, the other had sustained serious injury to his left arm and leg. Shit. What should she do? Bringing the injured soldier with them would slow the platoon down, and they couldn't afford to-

Besault solved the problem for her. "Captain, we need to keep moving. I've assigned two from my squad to take care of Tobbenex."

Two soldiers down, two staying behind with the injured soldier, and they still hadn't linked up with Third Platoon. She eyeclicked on the icon for '*Tobbenex, ITC*' in her visor. The medical status of the Verd-kris Infantry Third Class was serious but his suit considered the injuries survivable, assuming he was not asked to do anything strenuous.

How many injured did Third Platoon have? "Negative," she heard herself saying. "*One* soldier stays with Tobbenex."

"Captain?" Besault.

"You heard me. We're understrength as it is." The platoon was understrength, and she had already detailed soldiers to escort the pilots and those people injured in the dropship crash. If she kept siphoning off personnel, they would not have enough manpower to assist Third Platoon. Their combat power had been depleted by three just in a brief firefight with two local police. Her soldiers were having to fire warning shots to keep the panicked Wurgalan civilians back, the crowd was not rushing at them but in the smoke and confusion, no one knew where to go. Bodies of locals were splayed in the plaza, their unprotected bodies faring badly in the explosion.

The whole rescue mission was, she had begun to suspect, an ill-conceived idea. She had no business leading an infantry unit. Yet, there she was. Much as she hated to consider it, perhaps it was best to cut their losses and pull back. She didn't know whether the Third even existed at that point. "Telored," she called to their communications specialist. "Try to contact the Third again." Dani made up her mind right there: if they could not establish contact, she was pulling her people out. The city would only get more dangerous the farther toward the urban center they traveled.

"Ma'am," Telored answered. "Nothing on suit comms-"

"That's it, then, we-"

"But there's a local telecom station on the other side of the plaza. I might be able to use that to boost the signal," the soldier suggested.

Dani ground her teeth. "Get on it, then."

The platoon dashed across the plaza, if 'dashing' involved slowing stepping around and in some cases over smashed vehicles. Each time she approached a truck, she experienced a flare of anxiety, not knowing if that vehicle would also explode. Nothing exploded, and the local civilians dispersed, running in every direction except toward the platoon.

Telored moved as quickly as she could, not fast enough for Dani. "If it's not working-"

"Got it. Think I got it. Ma'am, I'm going to send a message out, see if anyone responds."

"Do it."

"The transmission could attract attention, the wrong kind."

Dani bit her lip. She knew that, the Verds did not need to treat her like a dumbass civilian. "Do it. Besault, Auffex, get ready to run like hell."

A minute later, with the platoon anxiously watching the sky for incoming ordnance, even Telored was about to give up, when an encrypted text message was received. Dani's suit couldn't understand the message, her suit didn't have Verd-kris encryption keys. Wonderful way to work with allies, she grimaced. "Anyone got that?"

Auffex answered. "It's the authentication code for the Third and their coordinates. Captain, they're less than a kilometer from here, but we've been going in the wrong direction. They are toward the city center from here."

"Lead on. Wait! Telored, can you use that thing to send a message to anyone else?"

"I can try, Ma'am."

"Great." Dani recorded a brief report of what happened to their dropship, that she had taken her platoon into the city and why, and their location. It would be a miracle if anyone in the Legion received the message, but she had to try. "Send this."

"Done. I think. There is no way to get an acknowledgement."

"Understood. All right, we are outta here. Auffex-"

She was interrupted by rifle fire, the heavy bark of the platoon's Kristang rifles, and the higher-pitched popping of Wurgalan rounds. Reflexively, she ducked as rounds struck the wall in front of her and exploded, stitching a line down and toward her until she heard the *whoosh* sound of a Kristang rocket and the incoming fire cut off with an explosion she felt through her boots.

"The enemy!" Someone shouted. "They're behind us!"

*No shit*, Dani thought. "Auffex! We've moving!" Scrambling to her feet, she crouched and ran. They had no choice but to continue onward, deeper into the city.


Jates was last to be winched up aboard the hovering dropship. He was barely in the door when the ship began moving, hovering used prodigious amounts of fuel and made trees sway underneath the craft. The Dodo was in stealth but the field didn't extend far enough to mask the shaking leaves and branches, if enemy sensors were looking in that direction, the dropship's position would be revealed.

Because the stealth effect bent light to wrap it around the dropship, it was utterly dark inside the field and Jates couldn't see anything until there was a dim glow from lights inside the cabin. Barely-seen hands reached out to steady him and release the winch cable. He gripped handholds with both hands until the ship's acceleration smoothed out and the door behind him slid shut.

Then he was inside the cabin that held six members of the assassin's cult, and all of them were staring not at the three humans or the Ruhar cadet, but at *him*.

"I have never met one of you," an Achakai said to him.

Jates swung up the faceplate of his helmet and glared at the assassin. "You have never met a soldier?"

The assassin blinked. "No. One of *you*, the ones who submit to your females. The *Verd*-kris, as you call yourselves," he spat, and squinted at Jates, examining the surgun's face closely. "Are you really a male of your kind? I have heard that it is difficult to see the difference between your neutered males and your females, they are the same as-"

Jates clenched his fists so hard, the armor creaked. "It will be difficult for you to see *anything* after I tear off your head and shove it up your ass."

"What? You-"

"Urzhkov!" Another Achakai roared. "Surgun Third Class Jates is a soldier and our ally on this operation. You will apologize to him and treat him with respect, or *I* will tear off your head."

"Apologies, Surgun," Urzhkov bowed his head. "This is all strange to me. I am sorry if you were insulted."

"By you?" Jates snorted. "If I can ever be insulted by anything *you* say, I will kill *myself*." He turned to the other assassin and patted the stock of his rifle. "Are we going to have a problem?"

"No," the Achakai leader bowed his head in a curt gesture. "Your people are considered to be without honor, traitors to Kristang society. My people have always been without honor, and now we, too, are traitors."

"Only if you *lose*," Dave spoke.

"That is true," the assassin agreed. "If we win here, the Achakai can become a clan, and write our own rules."

"Until then," Jates relaxed slightly. "We are both traitors without honor."

"According to the warrior caste," Shauna added.

The Achakai leader nodded. "Yes, according to the warrior caste."

"Then, *fuck* them," Shauna said.

That apparently translated well, for the assassin leader laughed.

While Jates spoke with the Achakai, both sides still wary of each other, Shauna turned her attention to Nert, scolding him. "You should not have sent your ID code without authorization. That was a stupid thing to do."

"Sorry," he replied, his already pink skin blushing in the helmet.

"You are *not* sorry, that's the problem," she wagged a finger at him, realized what she was doing, and put her hand down. Oh my God, I am turning into my mother, she thought. "Don't do it again."

"I won't."

She wanted to say thank you, but that would be sending a mixed signal. "We rely on the chain of command, you understand that? Without it, we're just people with guns, we're not an *army*."

"I understand." Stung, he looked to the back of the cabin, where Chowdhury was removing her suit legs. "Does Miss Chowdhury need help?"

"Czajka is helping her, and you should address her as *Corporal* Chowdhury," Shauna said. Technically, Chowdhury's rank in the Indian Army was 'Naik' but UNEF had standardized on using NATO rank codes, and an OR-6 was the equivalent in the US military to either corporal or specialist. Sometimes, being part of an international force, an inter-*species* force, gave Shauna a headache. "Nerty, I know you want to help, and you are brave and smart. Too smart to do stupid things. What Jates said before is true. We need to think not only about the mission objectives, but how our actions affect our peoples. If you get killed down here, your government will blame humans, or the Verds."

"They *should* blame the idiots in the fleet," he jabbed a finger at the ceiling. "They missed an entire layer of strategic defense."

"Nert, if an operation fails, there is always plenty of blame to cover *everyone* involved. Ok, go help Chowdhury," Shauna saw the other woman grimace in pain. Stepping forward, she nodded to Jates. "Where are we going?"

The Achakai leader answered instead. "We are going where our furry friends," he pointed toward the closed cockpit door, "take us. Greetings, Staff Sergeant Jarrett, I am Squad Leader Ditzak." He gave her a human-style salute, though with the palm facing forward.

That is interesting, Shauna thought as she returned the gesture, US Army style with her palm down. I wonder where the ninjas learned that? "Do you know where the hamsters are going next?" Her use of slang for the Ruhar was a deliberate effort to build camaraderie with the Achakai, a we-are-all-oppressed-by-our-Ruhar-overlords sense of determination.

"They told us they are looking for the crew of a dropship that launched from the *Tig Mecdunnue*, shortly after that ship broke in half. It was reportedly the last dropship to get away."

"The *last* one?"

Jates knew what she was thinking. "You hope it might be the ship that carried Colonel Perkins? And Colter, of course," he added.

"It's possible."

"It is possible," he agreed. "I also hope they survived."

Shauna just then realized what had been bothering her, something that was missing. All six of the Achakai were in combat suits, with full battle rattle. They did not have a medic with them, that was why Dave was helping Chowdhury as best he could. "This is not a SAR bird? Search And Rescue?"

"No," Ditzak expressed surprise. "We are an assault unit. We were diverted when it was discovered that our primary target was abandoned and destroyed by the enemy."

"So, you didn't come down here looking for us?"

"The pilots did not tell us anything," Ditzak shrugged. "They do not trust us."

Jates's eyes narrowed. "Do you trust *them*?"

"Ha!" the Achakai leader laughed bitterly. "The furry ones are renowned across the galaxy for their treachery."

After the events on Fresno, Shauna couldn't argue with that. "We need to talk with the pilots."

"They refuse to speak with us," Ditzak warned.

Shauna stepped forward to the bulkhead behind the cockpit, holding onto seatbacks as the dropship bounced through turbulent air. "They will talk with *me.*" Swinging up her faceplate, she mashed a thumb down on the intercom button. "This is Staff Sergeant Shauna Jarrett, of the *Mavericks*. I need to send a message."

"It's establishing a handshake, Ma'am," Sergeant Liu reported excitedly. The undertone of surprise in her voice told Perkins the soldier had not expected the kludged-together system to work. The bunker had a powerful, secure communications system, but it was only capable of talking to other bunkers in the network. Liu was using a feature of the system that was designed to identify approaching aircraft, using it as a receiver and transmitter. It was low-bandwidth and operated on low power, and she wasn't sure the connection between the Wurgalan gear and their Legion equipment would work. "Got it!" She pumped a fist in the air. "Um, we're receiving a Legion-wide message, pretty standard stuff, it's like-" Liu looked up, realizing the CO should be reading the messages. "It should be synced to your tablet, Colonel.?"

"Mm," Perkins grunted as she scrolled through garbled, uninformative and out-of-date message traffic. None of it was addressed to her, other than the '*All units on the ground report status*'. Yeah, she thought bitterly. We've been trying to do that.

Sitting down, she typed a short message to General Ross, tagged it as priority with her ID code and hit send, then scrolled through the messages again. As she suspected, the first wave was scattered all over the continent, it was impossible for her to understand the overall strategic situation without access to the Legion datanet. "No way I can send a query from here?"

"No Ma'am, sorry. Text or voice only, no data. The Legion net wouldn't trust a query sent from this gear," she shook her head.

Perkins waited with increasing anxiety, checking every few seconds for a reply from Ross's staff. Nothing. After five minutes, still nothing. The simple-minded AI of the Legion's secure command-level comm system should have at least sent back an acknowledgement that her message had been received. She sent the message again.

And waited.

General Ross did not have enough time for the most vital tasks he was responsible for, certainly not time to worry about or even notice personnel issues. Still, the human eye is attracted to movement, and while on the conference call with Admiral Kune, he kept seeing with the corner of his eye a commotion on the other side of the communications compartment. A Chinese major on his staff was engaged in a heated and animated discussion with an Indian captain, and they both kept glancing at Ross. It was distracting and annoying, and he was annoyed with himself both for not better disciplining his staff, and for allowing himself to be distracted. As soon as the mostly useless conference call ended, he stood up from the secure terminal and approached the two officers, who both wore guilty looks.

"Ling," Ross addressed the major, while glancing meaningfully at his wristwatch. "What is going on?"

"It is nothing, General," Ling replied, waving his hand in a dismissive gesture. "The enemy is attempting to spoof our communications."

The captain, seated at the console, tugged her ponytail and looked at Ross with such anxiety, he felt sorry despite his annoyance. "What is it, Captain?"

Ling glared at the junior officer. "It is noth-"

"I asked the *Captain*," Ross snapped, his patience having run out. "So?" he stole a look at her nametag. With the Legion expanding, he couldn't remember everyone's name. "Patharkar?" He recited her name.

Captain Patharkar looked between Major Ling, who was her immediate superior and who she worked with on a daily basis, and General Ross, who she had rarely spoken to. The stern expression on the general's face made the decision for her. "General, we might have received a message from Lieutenant Colonel Perkins."

"*WHAT*? When?" Ross demanded. "Why am I only hearing about this now?"

Ling spoke before Patharkar could answer. "It's spoofing, Sir. The message came through a *Wurgalan* source. They're trying to get us to respond, so they can track our location." Ling said, like explaining nuclear physics to a five-year-old. "It is a-"

Ross held up a hand to cut Ling off. "You don't think that is true, Captain?"

"It could be spoofing, Sir," she admitted. "But the authentication code is correct. Also," she looked away, embarrassed. "The content of the message *feels* real. I have worked with Colonel Perkins. This sounds like her."

That was enough for Ross, who made a cutting motion with one hand to tell another staffer that his next call could wait. "Show me the message." Ling was a cybersecurity expert, having been trained by the Ruhar. Ross had to trust his knowledge and experience. If the Wurgalan had indeed hacked Legion authentication codes, then sending a reply along the same channel could pinpoint Ross's location, and doom his people to a missile strike. On the other hand, it would take two seconds to read the message and decide for himself.

The message was brief, reading '*Sir, I have been unavoidably delayed. What the FUCK is going on? Your most humble and obedient servant, Emily Perkins.*'

"Oh my G- That is Perkins all right, it can't be anyone else. *When* did we receive this?" Ross demanded.

Patharkar lost all her hesitancy, sure of herself again. "The first message was-"

"*First*? There is more than one?"

Ling explained, chastened. "The first message was intercepted by the AI and put into a buffer. When it was received a second time, the AI kicked it up for review as a possible spoofing threat. Patharkar only saw it a few minutes ago. I was going to dismiss it, sorry."

"Not your fault," Ross was irritated neither of them had actually answered his question. "*When* did we-"

Ling realized his mistake. "Twenty-three minutes ago."

Ross leaned over Patharkar's shoulder. "Is this channel text only?"

"We can do voice, Sir," her fingers flew over the console.

"Transfer it to my station," he ordered as he strode across the compartment.

After sending the message a second time, Perkins had resisted Liu's suggestion to put the message on repeat. If the Wurgalan were paying attention, they might be suspicious about why a message on their network was repeating, and look at that message. If they did, and she had to assume the enemy had an AI somewhere that was monitoring communications, the enemy would quickly see that the message was encrypted using a Legion scheme, and that would draw unwanted attention. So she sent a different message out, hoping it would be picked up by a ship overhead.

All they could do was wait. Wait, and try to gain control over the cluster of plasma cannons.

"Colonel?" Liu called, waving for attention. "I think we're in."

"Already? How can you-"

"It's not me," Liu pointed to the sleek gray slab case of electronics on a console next to her. It was a gift from the Jeraptha to the Mavericks, the reason they had so easily been able to open the bunker door. "This fancy doodad we got from the Jeraptha-"

"Doodad?" Despite the seriousness of the situation, Perkins had to smile.

"Did I not use the slang correctly? I meant, a device beyond our understanding."

"Doodad is the right word." Using technology provided by a patron species was technically against the unwritten rules of warfare, unless the tech was operated by a patron species for their own benefit. So, obtaining the computer from the Jeraptha was cheating, although ironically, there was no rule against stealing and copying tech from advanced species. So, screw the rules, as far as Perkins was concerned.

Liu nodded. "I don't know what we paid for it, but-"

"Don't ask. Also, don't ever mention it to anyone."

"I truly wouldn't know what to tell them. We don't know how it works. This thing," she tapped the featureless gray slab with a fingertip, feeling it had become warm to the touch. "Not only established a connection to the Wurgalan system and cracked their encryption, it looks like we're in. I have admin privileges, Colonel."

"Show me."

Liu pulled up a menu on her own laptop, with the Wurgalan controls replicated in English characters. Perkins saw that on a small window in the corner of the screen, Liu had the same menu in Chinese characters. "Whooo," Perkins whistled. "Is that the firing sequence?"

"Yes," Liu lifted her hands off the touch screen, afraid she might touch the wrong icon. "Over here," she pointed to another menu, "is the targeting system."

Perkins reached for her own tablet. "Can you sync that to me?"

"Already did that, Ma'am. Um, it looks like there's a tutorial?"

Over the next ten or so minutes, Perkins toggled through the menu, then scanned the tutorial. She had to snort with a laugh at the presentation. Whatever group of Wurgalan put together the tutorial, they must have used their own military's version of PowerPoint. It even had annoying, cheezy-looking clipart that made her roll her eyes. Liu was wrong, it was not exactly a tutorial, for the file did not contain operational details. It was a presentation for high-level officials, or for new trainees. She finished the file around the same time Liu did. "Think you can dig into this?"

"I can try," Liu's eyes reflected a combination of eager anticipation and fear. "Ma'am, once I try to activate anything with the cannons-"

"Yes, we'll attract attention. Work on the targeting system first. We may have another problem."

"What's that?"

"Look at slide nineteen. It shows communications nodes connecting to forty-four other cannon clusters."

"Yes?" Liu didn't understand.

"The intel the Ruhar got from the Torgalau said there were only *thirty-eight* clusters. That's how many the pre-invasion bombardment took out."

"Shit," Liu's face turned pale.

"Yeah," Perkins studied the slide, trying to see if there was a hint at the location of the other nodes. "Besides us here, there are five other clusters the 7th Fleet doesn't know about. The Wurgalan are saving them for the second wave."

Liu turned her attention back to the alien console. "I will try to find their locations."

Behind her, Perkins heard Liu suck in a breath. "Oh. Ma'am, we, I mean you, have a message from General Ross."

Perkins stiffened, aware the message might be from a Wurgalan cybersecurity team. "Authenticated?"

"Yes, the code checks out."

"Send it to me, and keep it in your sandbox." A second later, she knew the message was real. It read simply *'Humble and obedient servant, bullshit -Ross'.* "Get me voice comms," Perkins synced her earpiece to the tablet. "Good morning, General."

There was a split-second pause while the voice signal was recorded, encrypted, compressed and sent out in a burst. Then, "It's afternoon here, Perkins. Where the hell have you been? We saw your dropship got out, but then lost track of it."

"It got shot down, we bailed out."

"Hold where you are, I'll send a SAR bird."

"We're not there anymore, Sir. We found a helicopter and flew it here."

"A *helicopter*? So, that was you?"

"It's a long story."

There was a longer pause. Ross knew that *'found* a helicopter' really meant 'killed squids and took the helicopter from them'. He didn't need the details right then. "Where are you now?"

"We're in the control center of a Wurgalan plasma cannon cluster. One the Ruhar don't know about. Sir? We are confident we have access to the cannons."

A longer pause, then a sigh. "Of *course* you do. Perkins, nobody likes a show-off."

"My apologies. I will strive to achieve less in the future."

"I didn't tell you to do *that*. Find a balance, maybe? The Ruhar are grading us on a curve, and you're making the rest of us look bad."

"Sir, we have a problem."

"Other than, you found a plasma cannon the Ruhar didn't know about?"

"Yes. It looks like there might be *five* other clusters down here that the 7th Fleet missed."

Yet another pause. "Perkins, when did you decide to become the Bad News Fairy?"

"Being the Tooth Fairy seemed like a career dead-end, Sir."

"Hah! *Shiiiiit.* I need to tell our fuzzy friends about this minor development. They'll want to delay landing the second wave. We're getting our asses kicked down here, and not just because we lost two assault transports. The intel the Ruhar had is wrong, we've got forty, maybe fifty percent more opposition than we expected."

"It's a fair fight now?"

"That's what I'm afraid of. Is there any way you can identify the location of the other plasma cannons?"

"Working on it."

Another heavy sigh. "Work faster."

"Sir?" There was a catch in her throat and she had to swallow before she could speak. "Is there any news about the rest of my team? The other dropship?"

"No. Nothing yet." He decided not to tell her about the anomalous cargo pod. "Don't give up hope. I thought *you* were dead."

"There were a couple of times when I thought I was dead too."

"Right. You really think you can fire those cannons?"

"We're looking into the targeting system now. I know, we need to work faster."

"You may be our ace-in-the-hole."

"Sir, these cannons are a single-shot weapon. If we're using this one, it has to be for a damned good reason."

"I'll keep that in mind. Anything else?"

"Yes. Please inform Admiral Kekrando that I discovered secret weapons that could threaten his ships. I sort of promised to do that. Didn't think it would ever *happen*," she added.

"I will inform the good Admiral myself. Perkins?"

"Sir?"

"It is really good to hear from you."

# CHAPTER TWENTY THREE

"General Ross," Admiral Kune put the best I-am-being-polite tone in his voice, knowing it wouldn't be translated perfectly. "I understand your concerns."

"Admiral," Ross replied in an I-don't-think-you-do-understand tone. "It's simple. Either we land the second wave, or we pull our people off the surface. The situation down here is unsustainable." He meant that literally. The Legion was expending ammunition at a prodigious rate, with no firm schedule for resupply. His remaining air assets had been forced onto the defensive, unable to provide air support to the ground troops. His aircraft were also running low on fuel and ammunition, with some gunships having expended all their missiles. "An extraction under fire is more dangerous to the fleet than-"

"I *know* that, General. The safety of the fleet is *not* my only concern. If the assault transports are hit while landing the second wave, the invasion will fail, *and* we will not have enough assets to pull your forces off the surface. We are considering all options. It would help if Colonel Perkins could identify the location of the other plasma cannon clusters."

"Her team is working on it." Ross wanted to add 'That is more than you furry idiots are doing'. He did *not* say that aloud.

"Contact me if they make any progress. Kune out." The admiral immediately turned to his waiting staff. "When will the assault carriers be ready to land the second wave?"

Operations officer Wohgalen answered. "The *Url Mecadonn* and *Tol Brandaru* are completing repairs, their boarding operation has been delayed."

"Delayed how long?" Kune asked, irritated. That information should have already been provided to him.

"As yet unknown," Wohgalen grimaced. "The *Mecadonn* has a radiation leak, serious enough to evacuate the aft section of the hull. They are working to-"

"Instruct the *Mecadonn* to eject the leaking reactor and commence boarding."

"Admiral," The Ops officer replied with a patient 'We-already-thought-of-that' tone. "The *Mecadonn* also has ruptured power conduits, the portside launching bays are operating on auxiliary power. Defensive shields in that section are at thirty percent and dropping. Their Engineering team believes that by the time they have bypassed the ruptured conduits, they will also have the radiation leak contained."

"The radiation leak has delayed boarding, but the conduit issue has not?" Kune asked.

"Yes. Sir, ejecting the reactor will reduce boarding time by only fourteen minutes. The *Mecadonn's* captain has not taken that step, because she has not received a timeline for landing the second wave."

Kune got the message. He should not be asking his people to cut corners, when he had no idea when, or *if*, the second wave would be authorized to land. "Very well. What is the issue with the *Brandaru*?"

"A cracked bank of jump drive coils. They are draining the charged coils, before they can work to connect the remaining coil sets into a bank with enough power for three jumps."

Kune nodded once. The *Brandaru* was performing the hazardous work on the coils far from the loaded transport ships, in case the damaged coils exploded. Again, he could not fault the crew's judgment or zeal to get back into action. "It's a good thing we aren't ready to give a go-ahead for the second wave." He walked over to the tactical plot in the center of the operations theater. "Any update on the mystery contact?"

Wohgalen was uncomfortable. "The destroyers are continuing to pursue the contact. They lost the trail and have not been able to find it again."

Following the costly battle against the second ring of Strategic Defense satellites, a damaged destroyer had been authorized to jump away and act as an outer sensor picket, while the crew worked to effect repairs. While drifting through empty space, the ship flew through a dispersed cloud of low-level radiation, the type of cloud that was caused when a starship vented reactor plasma. Kune had ordered two destroyers to investigate and hopefully, locate what he suspected was a Wurgalan ship lurking in stealth and acting as a forward observer.

"Has analysis of the cloud been completed?" Kune asked, his attention focused on the tactical plot. The situation was serious but not dire. He had four fully-operational battleships, with another two having jumped away to repair battle damage. As long as Kune had four powerful battleships, the Wurgalan would not challenge for control of space around the planet. The enemy *could* send ships in to conduct raids on the assault carriers while they landed the second wave, and battleships were not the right platform for pursuing raiders. Finding and killing a forward observer could buy precious seconds in a battle.

"Not yet. Admiral, the cloud does not match the signature of any Wurgalan ship that we or the Torgalau know of."

"Hmmph. Kristang, then?" Kune guessed.

"No, Sir. The closest match, our best guess, is a Bosphuraq ship."

"*Bos-*" Kune didn't complete his thought. "Are they sure?"

"They can't be certain, because our database on the Bosphuraq is incomplete. The ratio of isotopes in the cloud points to a Bosphuraq origin. The data could be wrong."

The possibility of a patron-species warship lurking around the battlespace changed the strategic situation, changed it in favor of the enemy. "Send a cruiser, no, *two* cruisers to pursue the contact."

"Admiral, even two cruisers will not-"

"I'm not intending to throw them into battle against the Bosphuraq. I *do* want the birds to know we are serious about tracking them."

"Force their hand?" Wohgalen guessed.

"Exactly. They can engage, or clear the battlespace. Detach a frigate to contact our Jeraptha friends."

"The beetles have told us they can't risk getting involved, unless-"

"I'm not asking them to come to our rescue," Kune explained impatiently. "We *will* ask them to analyze the data we collected about that cloud. The Jeraptha database surely can tell us whether the mystery ship is Bosphuraq or not." He was hoping there was another possibility: a Wurgalan ship having dumped overboard a false plasma cloud that had a signature similar in nature to one of their patrons' ships. If so, that was a clever way to distract the Ruhar fleet and delay, possibly cancel, the arrival of the second wave.

A second layer of SD satellites the Torgalau had known nothing about. Additional clusters of plasma cannons that, again, had not been hinted at in the intel reports. Now the possibility of an advanced-technology warship waiting to interfere in the battle.

What else could go wrong?

"What's up?" Jesse asked, slinging his rifle and stretching his arms over his head to relieve the cramps in his neck and shoulders. Combat skinsuits were amazing technology, keeping the wearer warm or cold as desired. They also were tiring to wear for extended periods. In the underground control center, Perkins had authorized the platoon to remove their helmets, with the warning that helmets had to be attached to suits belts and readily available. When the helmet was worn, the weight on it pressed down on the inflatable collar around the neck. Clipped to the attachment point on the belt, the helmet's weight tugged down the left shoulder, and it was in the way no matter what Jesse wanted to do. He was tempted to put it back on, but then his team would see that as a signal they should do the same. So he dealt with the discomfort and focused on his job.

Which, at the moment, was nothing. That was why he had wandered over to the station where Liu was working, curious what she was doing.

"Staff Sergeant," Liu looked up from her laptop, acknowledging him with a curt, distracted nod. "You heard about the other plasma cannons?"

"I heard there was a *possibility*," Jesse emphasized the last word. "You're trying to identify their locations?"

"Yes. So far, no joy. The level I have access to sort of assumes we already have that information, which makes sense," she grimaced.

"Frustrating, huh?"

"You have *no* idea."

"I kinda think I do," Jesse assured her. "What's the next step?"

"I don't know. Like I told the Colonel, I could query the system, but that requires me to have a higher level of access. That is sure to raise flags on the Wurgalan network. So would a query for information we should already have."

"Don't do that, then." Jesse agreed. he pointed to her laptop. "That looks like some kind of targeting system?"

"Yes. Perkins asked me to verify whether we really have control of the cannons in this cluster. I can't do that without activating the cannons, and that's another thing that would bring attention to us. So, we're trying to see if we can get the targeting system to work, we should be able to track targets without alerting the network."

Jesse studied the display, the English-language characters overlaying the alien symbol made for a jarring image. The user interface made no sense to him, but it wasn't supposed to.

Something about the symbols drew his attention. Liu had the targeting sensors pointing almost straight up, looking at mostly empty sky. There were small dots that he assumed were Ruhar or Achakai starships, each ship was ringed by a purple circle with a tiny script of 'Out Of Range' below. "What's the orange-shaded area on the horizon?"

"That shows the area where the cannons are ineffective, because a low-angle shot like that causes the plasma to travel through too much atmosphere. By the time the bolts get into space, they have degraded and dispersed."

"Ok. And the yellow-shaded areas above that?" Like the orange no-shoot area, a band of yellow covered three-hundred-sixty degrees, higher above the horizon. The difference was, the yellow was not the same intensity all around. Some angles were shaded toward orange.

"Same issue. Low-angle shots, but if the target is in a yellow zone, we can effectively hit it, if we coordinate the strike with another cannon cluster."

Jesse grinned. "Interesting. You see where I'm going with this, Liu?"

"I, uh, no."

He tapped her on the shoulder, then tapped the display with a finger. "Can you create a test target here, in this yellow zone? A fake one, just to test the system?"

"Uh, sure." She had to play with the unfamiliar system, until targeting circles appeared in the area Jesse wanted.

Below the circle was a number, reading seventy-three. "Seventy-three percent probability of destroying the target?" he guessed.

"Correct."

"Great. Move it down and to the north." The number changed, to fifty-two. "Now we're getting somewhere," Jesse muttered.

Liu didn't understand. "How?"

"Math, Sergeant. Trigonometry, something like that. Think about it. A target there can be destroyed, *if* two cannon clusters work together. Move the test target down into the orange zone."

Liu did, surprised to see the system state the confidence level went *up*, to eighty-four percent. "How did it *increase*?"

"Because the target is too low for us, but closer to the cannons we're coordinating with. Liu, we know where we are, and we know the location of the test target, right? If we collect enough data points on the level of confidence-"

She sucked in breath. "We can triangulate where the other cannon must be!"

"Pretty close, yeah. Enough to give the fleet a rough idea where they are."

"Whew. That's tricky math."

"Don't worry about it. I'll get more people in here, let's collect datapoints," he snapped his fingers to get the attention of people lingering in the hallway. "We'll text the data to General Ross, and they can crunch the numbers, or get the Fleet to do it."

The Fleet's Ops officer updated the tactical plot with the information received by General Ross, after the starship's AI had analyzed the data. Four circles appeared on the outline of the planet below.

"This is, disappointing," Kune said. Three of the circles were too large, they covered too much area. The fourth circle was almost a dot, identifying the exact location of the cannon cluster controlled by Perkins, a location the fleet already knew.

"It was clever thinking," Wohgalen stated.

"Yes," Kune agreed. "The humans are again proving to be annoyingly innovative. Just, this time, not enough."

"We would need planet-busters, to be sure of taking out the cannons in such a wide area," Wohgalen observed.

"That's not an option," Kune shook his head. It wasn't an option for two reasons. The rules of engagement did not allow him to use weapons of that yield against the surface. As a consequence, the fleet wasn't carrying any such weapons. "Three circles, besides the one where Perkins is with her team. Why not *five* other sites?"

"The AI assumes the other two sites are too far away for Perkins's cannons to coordinate with."

"That, *or*, there are only three other surviving cannon clusters."

Wohgalen cocked his head. "That is a risky-"

"Too risky an assumption." The assault transports had completed boarding the second wave and were awaiting his signal. He couldn't give the signal, knowing five plasma cannon clusters were threatening to blast the assault ships out of the sky.

"We could send assault ships in one at a time, with a pair of battleships between them and the cannons," Wohgalen suggested.

"Those cannons would burn right through even a battleship's shields at that altitude," Kune rejected the idea. In the initial bombardment, the battleships had jumped in at a safe distance and launched dozens of railguns at each cannon cluster. That technique worked only because the Torgalau had provided precise coordinates of the cannons. Secondary explosions at the sites had confirmed the railgun darts struck their intended targets, boosting the confidence of the Ruhar. Boosting their confidence too much, apparently. "Plus, there are likely two cannon clusters we can't locate."

"Each cluster can only shoot once."

"They only *need* to shoot once," Kune shook his head. "We would be trading a ship for each cluster. That math isn't in our favor."

"Yes, Sir."

"Damn it!" The admiral thumped a fist on the display. "Signal to Ross that it was a nice try, but we can't land the second wave."

"Should he prepare to retreat under fire?" Wohgalen asked

"Not yet. We have the same problem with an evac; we can't risk sending in assault transports. The dropships pulling out the ground force would have to fly beyond plasma cannon range, to the other side of the planet, before a transport ship could pick them up. That increases the cycle time for each dropship. We can't do it. Not unless the situation becomes desperate."

Wohgalen nodded, and turned away to send the message to Ross. He did not remind the admiral that Ross already considered the situation on the verge of being desperate. The human general officer estimated the force had only enough ammunition to continue fighting for another thirty-six hours, and that was entirely on the defensive. The Legion was not able to conduct offensive operations. By that measure, the invasion had already failed.

"Sorry," Perkins said, after she told her team that the information they provided was not accurate or complete enough to pinpoint the location of the other cannon clusters. "That was good initiative, good judgment, good work, people," she told the team who were standing, shaking their heads and looking down at the floor.

"Shit," Jesse spoke for all of them.

"Staff Sergeant," Perkins said quietly, motioning him to follow her over the where Liu was seated. "It's not your fault. That was damned good thinking, Admiral Kune sent his compliments."

"Not good enough," Jesse said bitterly.

"Work with me here. Liu, what did you find?"

The sergeant pulled up a different menu. "It looks like we can get targeting sensor feeds from other sites. I thought if we can get a view of the sky from each cluster, we can identify where they are."

"Ok," Jesse snorted. Why hadn't he thought of that? "Let's do that."

"But," Liu warned. "We have to *request* the data through the system. That creates an alert and we'd be flagged, probably locked out of the system, before the data was sent back to us. There's a time lag."

Perkins bit her lip. "I knew this was too good to be true."

"It's not all bad, Ma'am. Unless I am totally wrong about how this thing works," Liu waved a hand toward the consoles around her. "We can fire the cannons independently from here. There is a protocol for isolating this site from the others. Once I do that-"

"It sends out an alert, yeah," Perkins frowned. "Great. We have control of an enemy superweapon that we have no use for, and we can't tell the hamsters upstairs where the other cannons are."

"It's not all bad, Colonel," Liu cringed. "We have-"

Jesse stopped listening while the colonel and sergeant discussed the situation and their limited options. Non-existent options, as far as he was concerned. The whole operation had been a bust, a waste of lives and time. He wished Shauna were there. She would know what to do, making him look like a dimwitted fool in the process. He didn't care. He just wanted to see her again. He wanted to know that she was alive. If Shauna were there, he was sure, she would cut to the heart of the problem with laser-like focus and-

Lasers.

"Shit!"

"Colter?" Perkins stared at him. "You have something to share?"

"Liu," he leaned over her shoulder. "You can request feeds of sensor data from other sites?"

"Yes," she answered slowly, thinking Jesse had missed everything she said earlier.

"What about *active* sensors? Don't these plasma cannons use a laser beam for guidance, give them exact location and range to the target right before they fire?"

"Yes, but-"

"Can you request other sites to paint a target with *active* sensors?"

"Oh!" She understood what Jesse was talking about. "I don't know. Let me-"

Jesse and Perkins were silent while the sergeant worked, toggling from one menu to another. She swore in Chinese when she found what she was looking for. "Yes. There is a protocol for requesting another site to provide active targeting data, if this site's system is inoperative. It looks like," she leaned forward to read the display. "Any site can request active targeting, from any other site."

Jesse crossed fingers behind his back for good luck. "The request? Is it voice, text, whatever to the squids in the other control centers? Or it is automated?"

Liu glanced at the console for confirmation. "Automated. The system is designed to operate remotely, if the control center for a cannon cluster is disabled."

Perkins straightened, looking at the ceiling and holding up a finger for silence while she thought. "Are the two of you telling me we can remotely cause other cannon sites to send active sensor pulses? The personnel on-site can't stop it?"

"They can stop it, I think," Liu's eyes narrowed. "After they realize what is happening. Not at first. The automated system is too fast for the squids to intervene. We would have, a couple seconds, maybe?"

Perkins shared a smile with Jesse. "A couple seconds is all the fleet will need to pinpoint the location of the other sites. *Outstanding* work, the two of you."

"*If* this works, Ma'am," Liu cautioned, thinking she had dug a deep hole for herself if it didn't work. "The Ruhar will need to have battleships ready to fire, the instant they detect the targeting laser pulses."

"Ma'am?" Liu did not relish the role of party-pooper. "I think we have a problem. In a simulation, I can create a virtual target. But the other sites won't send out a real active sensor pulse unless they have a *real* target to paint above us. Somebody needs to park a ship in orbit to act as a target."

"Oh," Jesse groaned. "*I* wouldn't want to be aboard that ship," he added.

"We'll let our furry friends worry about that," Perkins said as she pulled out her zPhone. "I need to give Ross the good news."

"How sure are you this will work?" Ross was clearly skeptical. "That's a damned big vulnerability in their system."

"It's intended as a failover mechanism," Perkins explained. "A control center can act as backup for other cannon clusters, if the primary control center is offline. The squids have a reputation for poor cybersecurity, but in this case, they just didn't expect an enemy to have physical access to their network."

"Can we use that access to shut down, disable the other sites?"

"No. We could send the command from here, but the shutdown process takes long enough that the personnel on site would intervene."

"Hmm." He was still not convinced. "They can't intervene in a request for an active sensor pulse?"

"Not according to the system manual we found. It's been accurate so far."

"Your team read the manual for an alien system?"

"It's translated. The Wurgalan apparently believe in the KISS principle," she meant the acronym Keep It Simple, Stupid. "Their instructions are clear and simple. Sir, we won't know for sure whether it will work until we try it for real."

"That's what bothers me. If you send the command and we don't see five laser pulses illuminating the-"

"*Fifteen* pulses, Sir," she reminded him. "Each cluster has three cannons."

"Ok, fifteen lasers. If the hamsters upstairs don't see the other five sites pinpointed, this is all or nothing, and you will have given away your location to the squids. Perkins, I'll talk to Admiral Kune. In the meantime, I want your people out of there, get a safe distance away."

"I can't pull everyone out, Sir. We can't put the command on a timer, it has to be sent in real-time."

He wanted to tell her to risk the life of only one person to press the appropriate buttons. He knew she would never accept that. Neither would he, so he didn't give an order that wouldn't be obeyed. "Use your best judgment, Colonel. All right, I need to persuade Kune to give this a shot."

"That isn't the biggest problem, Sir. Like I said, the admiral needs to use one of his ships as a lure for targeting. That's going to be a tough sell. If you think it will help, I can talk to-"

"Nah," Ross snorted. "Leave that to me, I have an idea. Perkins?"

"Yes?"

"I have a bit of good news for you. We located part of your team. Czajka, Jarrett, Chowdhury, Jates, and Cadet Dandurf landed safely-"

"What?" She had to lean on a console for support, her knees felt shaky. David Czajka was *alive*. "How?"

"It's a long story, you can ask them. They're in a Dodo. I'll send them to your location, after we see if this scheme of yours allows us to destroy the other cannon clusters."


Persuading Admiral Kune to commit his ships to a dubious operation, based on the alleged ability of humans to operate unfamiliar alien high-tech equipment, was going to be difficult. Getting the admiral to dangle one of his warships as a lure, because a group of human ground-pounders said that was necessary, would be nearly impossible. Ross decided not to waste everyone's time in a futile argument. He needed a warship to volunteer for the hazardous mission.

So, he called Admiral Kekrando directly, before he gave the news to the commander of the 7th Fleet.

Basically, he dumped the problem in Kekrando's lap, to become a headache for the Kristang admiral. Kekrando's dilemma was not in finding a ship to volunteer, his problem was that *all* of his ships volunteered immediately, and he had to select one without being seen as playing favorites. Each captain explained why *their* ship should be chosen, with reasons ranging from the mildly plausible to outrageous boasts. Some captains, bolder or more realistic or more desperate than the others, offered bribes expressed in both subtle and flagrant fashion. In the end, he granted the crew of the destroyer *Battle of Hungorastad* the honor of jumping into low orbit to act as a lure. The selection of that ship was not due to a bribe Kekrando didn't care about, but because the crew of that ship had somehow quickly composed an epic poem about how their little ship had sacrificed itself for the good of the Achakai nation. The admiral had to admire the effort, if not the actual content of the poem.

He also was curious to see how the poem would be revised, if the *Hungorastad* survived.

Once the decision was announced, Kekrando consoled crews of the other ships with the promise that he had an even more important and dangerous mission for them. Then, he waited impatiently for the Ruhar fleet commander to make the obvious decision.


To Admiral Kune, the decision was anything but obvious. "Wohgalen?" He asked his Operations aide quietly, while the two stood in an alcove for at least the illusion of privacy. "What do you think? Should we trust the humans know what they are doing down there? Their idea to identify the locations of the other plasma cannons was clever thinking, even if it did fall short of the accuracy needed."

"Clever, yes? Useful?" The Ops officer shook his head. "We don't know. Until we know whether their technique actually identified cannon sites, it is simply an interesting mathematical exercise. The data makes sense, but we don't know what assumptions the human made when the obtained the data points. The results could be invalid due to an error we have no way to evaluate." He found it difficult to trust the abilities of a species who had harnessed the use of electricity less than ten generations ago. A species that was still using chemical rockets when their planet had been conquered by the Kristang.

A species that, other than the small population living on the southern continent of a Ruhar world, might be extinct.

"Still," Kune asked, "would *you* have thought to plot the location of other cannons, based on strike probabilities? I would not, and I came up through the Fleet as a gunnery specialist. The humans, not all of them," he added. "Some of them, such as these Mavericks, they have proven to be innovative and resourceful." He thought a moment, while Wohgalen stood by silently, knowing the admiral would seek his counsel if he wanted it. "Yes," Kune made up his mind. "I am willing to give this Perkins another opportunity."

"It is a risk, Sir."

"A risk? Yes. There is also risk in *not* acting. The current situation is a stalemate, Wohgalen. It cannot continue. We must regain the initiative. Of the options available to me, what Ross proposes yields the greatest potential reward for the lowest risk."

"Admiral, right now, the cannon cluster occupied by Perkins is an asset the enemy doesn't know we have. If the Wurgalan fleet comes back, those cannons could destroy enemy ships, leaving our ships free to maneuver. Once Perkins attempts to command the other sites to send out a laser pulse, their secret will be exposed."

Kune smiled, tilting his head. "You trust the humans to activate, target and successfully fire a cannon, but not to request a sensor pulse?"

"When you say it like that, I see your point, Sir."

"Inform Ross that I have tentatively approved his plan, we must discuss timing. I need to speak with my captains."

"Admiral?" Operations officer Wohgalen spoke while his superior was talking with the captains of his battleships, cruisers and the leaders of the three destroyer squadrons.

"What?" Kune knew his aide would not have interrupted him unless it was important.

"It's official. The Achakai have formally requested the honor of acting as target."

"They have, eh?" Kune's mouth twisted in a broad smile. "Did you all hear that?" He directed that remark to the holographic images of his ship captains. "Apparently, we have a *volunteer*." The captains all laughed, to one degree or another. "Stand ready to fire when you detect the laser pulses."

# CHAPTER TWENTY FOUR

The Achakai destroyer *Battle of Hungorastad* waited anxiously for the signal from the Ruhar fleet, with the crew aware all the ships in the area were watching their every move, and that even the slightest imperfection would be noted and commented on. Criticism by the Ruhar would of course be harsh, and make no allowances for the fact that the Achakai were new to the profession of operating starships. Nor would allowances be made that the assassins guild were flying Wurgalan ships, ships that had until recently been mothballed in a boneyard. The crew of the *Hungorastad* understood the Ruhar would be critical, and although they were eager to make a good impression to the traditional enemies of their species, in truth they did not really care what the furry ones thought of them.

The *Hungorastad*'s crew also did not care what the Ruhar, the humans or the Verd-kris thought of them. They *were* very much eager to impress their fellow Achakai, whether on the other ships in their newly-established fleet, on the ground, or waiting in assault carriers for their opportunity to put boots on the ground and get into action. To their fellow members of the assassin's guild, the *Hungorastad* carried the burden not only of being first in action, but of carrying the hopes of an entire people. If the ship's mission failed, the second wave of the invasion might be cancelled, and the most fervent hope of every Achakai who had ever lived, the hope of regaining honor, would be lost forever.

If the *Hungorastad* failed, it would not be for lack of courage or determination.

The little destroyer's crew waited patiently, having quieted their minds with meditation. The battleships and cruisers of the Ruhar maneuvered into position just beyond effective range of the deadly plasma cannons, ready to rain hellfire down on the widest possible coverage of the continent below. At the point when even the most patient of the *Hungorastad*'s crew wondered just what the *hell* the hamsters were doing, the signal came, and the destroyer jumped within a millisecond of the scheduled time.

In a wild burst of gamma rays that was characteristic of Wurgalan jump drives, the destroyer emerged at a temptingly low altitude, having to burn its engines at seventy percent thrust to avoid falling deeper into the thin atmosphere. Simply by surviving the jump, the destroyer had accomplished the first part of its mission, and with nothing else to do, the crew had received permission to provide close-space support to a Verd-kris unit on the ground. Those fifty-three Verd soldiers, the remains of what had been a company-sized force, were threatened by two enemy platoons that were reinforced by artillery. With the Verds having exhausted their own artillery and drones, they had no means of hitting back with counterbattery fire, and were steadily being chopped up.

The *Hungorastad*'s crew intercepted communications from the Wurgalan on the ground. The squids were excited about the presence of what was clearly one of their own ships, and calling for rapid strikes to finish off the invaders. The

Wurgalan were therefore *extremely* disappointed when the destroyer began firing on their positions.

"That's our signal," Perkins flashed a thumb's up to Liu, who had already seen the Achakai ship jump in over their heads, and had a finger poised over a button to execute the set of instructions she had programmed into the alien computer. "Execute."

Liu pressed the button, and her heart stopped when nothing happened for a half-second. Before she could jab the button again, alien symbols began scrolling down the screen of the console, interpreted by her laptop. "Done, Ma'am. It should be only a few seconds," she reported, thinking to herself that if it did take longer than a few seconds, the whole operation would be doomed to failure.

The first ship to detect the targeting laser pulses was the *Hungorastad*, for it was the ship being painted by the lasers, and also it was in low orbit. The big battlewagons orbiting high above received reflected photons from the lasers a second later, and the warships swiveled their railguns around to fire at five juicy targets.

On the ground, the Wurgalan duty officers in the control centers of each plasma cannon cluster shrieked with alarm, shouting for the technicians to shut the damned lasers off *now*! When doing that took more than three seconds, two of the duty officers made a gut-wrenching but inevitable decision: they gave the order to warm up the big cannons. They had not wanted to fight without a worthy target, and they understood it was not a just use-it-or-lose-it situation. Now that the enemy warships above knew the locations of the clusters, there was no 'or' involved. The Wurgalan *were* going to lose the cannons, so they might as well fire them in anger.

For the little *Hungorastad*, it was a race against time, the charging of the plasma cannons against the railguns of the Ruhar fleet.

The *Hungorastad*'s crew watched as one by one, the plasma cannon sites on the surface were struck first by speed-of-light maser beams, then railgun darts. The maser beams were not expected to be powerful enough to penetrate the energy shields and thick ablative armor protecting the cannons, but firing masers was not a futile gesture. The beams were coming in continuous pulses as the cannons of the battleships fired a rolling broadside, with the goal of delivering a constant barrage of coherent maser energy on each of the fifteen targets. The beams blew away the vegetation and soil above the camouflaged cannons, battered the energy shields and burned away layers of the ablative armor but that was not the point. The purpose of hitting the sites with masers was simple: to disrupt any plasma pulse rising from the surface. With gigawatts of maser energy striking continuously, a plasma pulse would be substantially dispersed before it cleared the beams. Though the battleships firing broadsides were not directly threatened by the plasma cannons, the little *Hungorastad* was, and the crew of that ship knew the masers were for their protection.

Maybe, just maybe, the Ruhar were not the treacherous scoundrels the Achakai had expected.

Coming an average of eight seconds behind the maser beams were the railgun darts. Because the fleet's battleships had been repositioned based on their best guess of the enemy locations, each of the sites had at least one battleship within a sixteen-degree cone overhead. That assured that none of the darts lost too much speed by cutting through the thick atmosphere at a bad angle.

In a tricky bit of coordination that required the battleship's AIs to use the trigonometry and calculus that tortured the brains of most biological beings, the maser beams cut out at precisely the right moment to avoid the railgun darts flying into them. If the computers of the plasma cannon clusters thought they had a brief reprieve, it was *very* brief, for the darts began impacting less than two microseconds after the masers cut off.

The railgun darts were inert kinetic devices. Warheads? They didn't need no stinkin' warheads. The armor protecting the cannons became part of the problem, as the material of the armor was flash-transformed into plasma upon impact, burning down into the cannons all the way to the charged capacitors. For each cannon, there was a moment of equilibrium when the downward pressure of the surging plasma was balanced by the upward force of the exploding capacitors, then the plasma exhausted its momentum. Each site fountained upward in a mushroom cloud, rent by the incoming second salvo of darts. Then a third salvo.

Surveying the Battle Damage Assessment aboard the flagship, Admiral Kune held up a hand. "Cease fire."

"All units, cease fire!" Wohgalen repeated the order, then more quietly added "Are you sure, Sir?"

Kune pointed to the display in front of him, showing what looked like new volcanos on the surface, spewing molten rock high into the sky. "I think we got them," he said with a wry smile of satisfaction.

"But, Admiral," Wohgalen responded in a whisper. "We were having so much *fun*."

There was a twinkle in the admiral's eye. The first wave had been a near-disaster, with two assault carriers destroyed and two having sustained significant damage. But all was not lost. Both the *Dal Turnaden* and the *Tig Mecdunnue* had launched at least sixty percent of their dropships before the disaster, so the numbers of boots hitting the ground were not wildly different from what the plan called for. If the second wave could be landed successfully, Kune could salvage the operation. With the plasma cannons eliminated, the most likely threats to the second wave were factors he could deal with. His battleships would maneuver closer to the planet to protect the assault carriers, in case the Wurgalan sent ships on a suicide mission. And his destroyer squadrons were hammering space with active sensor pulses, searching for additional stealthed SD satellites. He had the assets to handle both of those problems, and he was not going to be caught by surprise again.

The possibility of a Bosphuraq warship in the area was a problem he was not equipped to deal with. The Jeraptha had not yet replied to his request, yet he could not wait forever because he was afraid of a ghost.

"Signal the *Battle of Hungorastad*. Tell them," Kune considered what to say as congratulations to a starship crew of a species that were his historical enemy. "Tell them 'Job well done', something like that."

"Yes, Sir," Wohgalen acknowledged. He would tell the communications people to make the statement more flowery and formal, the way the Kristang did things.

"And connect me with Perkins. I want to thank her personally."

"Thank you, Admiral, I will convey your compliments to my team." Emily Perkins waited a beat to avoid the appearance of rushing a senior officer. "What is next, Sir?"

"You get right to the point, don't you?"

"Yes, Sir."

"I like that. There's enough time-wasting bullshit in this job, I don't need any more. I am sending in the second wave, with a change to the plan. One assault carrier at a time. While I am no longer worried about enemy air defenses, I want each carrier to have maximum protection. It is Ross's decision, but I will request your team remain at the cannon site, until the second wave is securely on the surface. We lost a lot of supplies with those two carriers, the force on the surface is understrength and underprovisioned."

"We are standing ready to assist, Admiral."

"Excellent. Oh, and Colonel?"

"Yes?"

"If you do have to shoot, try not to hit one of my ships, please?"

"We will do our best, Sir." She knew the admiral was joking, but the comment bothered her. Ending the call, she walked back over the console where Liu was working. "Sergeant, does this thing," she pointed to the console, "have some sort of IFF system, so can't target the wrong ship?"

"Uh-"

That was *not* the answer Perkins wanted to hear.

"Sorry, Ma'am," Liu blushed. "I concentrated on gaining access to the cannon fire sequence, and then requesting a targeting pulse from the other sites. I didn't-"

"You did exactly what I asked you, and you did it brilliantly. That was *outstanding* work, Liu. You figured out how to work this gear based on an alien PowerPoint file."

"The Jeraptha doodad did most of the-"

Perkins thought that was a 'coachable moment'. "Sergeant, when a senior officer says you did a kick-ass job, the correct response is a simple 'Thank you'."

"Yes, Ma'am. Um, thank you."

"You're on it?"

Liu turned her attention back to the console with determination, pulling up the main menu. "I am *on* it."

"One more thing."

"Colonel?"

"To this system, Wurgalan ships are the 'Friends' and our ships are the 'Foe' to their IFF. We need to be sure these cannons are capable of locking onto and firing on a Wurgalan ship. If there is a lockout, we need to know about it, and bypass it."

Liu didn't groan audibly, she did it with her eyes. "On that, too, Ma'am."


The dubious honor of being the first assault carrier in the second wave went to the *Ras Howlert*. That ship was burdened with two battalions of Achakai soldiers, twenty-four hundred fanatical warriors who were eager to get into the fight. More importantly, they were eager to prove their bravery and honor. The Ruhar crew of the ship were less eager to be the first ship to jump in for the second wave, but their opinion was not solicited by Admiral Kune. What he knew was that his counterpart Admiral Kekrando wanted the *Ras Howlert* to go first, and the Kristang admiral had volunteered his entire fleet to escort the assault carrier.

Kune agreed to Kekrando's request, with the provision that Kekrando's ships jump into position first, so a clumsy navigation error by the aliens did not endanger the *Howlert*. He had already lost two assault carriers to enemy fire, he was not going to lose another to an avoidable accident. "Signal the *Howlert* that I want those dropships away immediately; rapid launch." Kune was changing the operational plan yet again. Instead of launching dropships one at a time so each of the vulnerable spacecraft could benefit from covering fire, all the dropships aboard the *Howlert* would be launched within a minute of each other. That tactic had the potential advantage of swamping the enemy air defenses, but that was not why Kune had given the order. He wanted his assault carriers exposed to enemy fire for as short a time as possible.

"Yes, Sir," Wohgalen had anticipated the order, and sent the signal immediately. Landing the two battalions required twelve medium-lift dropships of the type that humans called 'Dodos' and eight of the heavy-lifters called 'Whales'. Add eighteen 'Vulture' gunships as escorts, and the *Howlert's* launchers would be spitting out thirty-eight spacecraft rapidly, so rapidly that the ship had to be careful about adjusting to the sudden loss of mass that would change its center of gravity. After the spacecraft were away, the *Howlert* would begin clawing its way up to jump altitude while launching cargo pods.

The next assault carrier would not appear in orbit until the *Howlert* had jumped away, and Kekrando's squadron of obsolete stolen warships had maneuvered into position as escorts. That operational scheme would take most of a day to land the second wave, a fact that no one but the enemy was happy about.

"I can't decide," Wohgalen said quietly, "if the mercenaries are crazy or smart."

"How so?" Kune asked. He knew that his aide had meant the Achakai when he said 'mercenaries', though technically, the humans and Verd-kris were the real hired guns of the operation.

"If the enemy is ready, they will hit the first ship, and the Achakai aboard the *Howlert* are crazy to request being first. But if they *aren't* ready, then being first is the safest position in the schedule, and they are being smart."

Kune shook his head. "I doubt our Achakai friends have thought about it that deeply. All they care about is restoring their honor. To request any position other than first would be seen as cowardice."

Wohgalen raised an eyebrow. "They are our friends now?"

"That is exactly true." Kune tilted his head. "They are our friends *now*."

"Ha," Wohgalen snorted. "What about tomorrow?"

"Who knows? As the philosophers say, tomorrow is another day. There is one thing I know for certain. We have given the enemy plenty of time to prepare. If they are not ready to hit the first ship, then this battle is already over."

One by one, because he also did not entirely trust the navigational accuracy of his ships and crews, Admiral Kekrando's squadron jumped into low orbit, then slowly and laboriously maneuvered into position to protect the assault carrier that was expected soon. One frigate, the *Battle of Nageratus*, jumped in far too low, either due to an error in programming the jump or a glitch in its horribly complicated jump drive system. It emerged so deep within the atmosphere that its energy shields shorted out and four of six normal-space engines blew, damaging a fifth engine. That left the *Nageratus* flying on one engine and burning thruster fuel, fighting both gravity and atmospheric drag.

It was always destined to be a losing battle.

"Get them out of there!" Kekrando roared. "Eject! Signal the crew to get into escape pods!"

His aide Jallaven, a proud Achakai, stiffened. "Admiral, regrettably, I must refuse to send such a signal. To run away while the ship is still capable of fighting would be dishonorable." He pulled a ceremonial dagger from a sheath. "If I must pay with my life for disobeying your order, I will gladly do it."

"The crew of the *Nageratus* will pay with their lives for their stubborn stupidity! That ship is not capable of fighting, it is doomed to be torn apart and burn up before the remnants hit the ground. Their deaths will accomplish nothing!"

"But-"

Kekrando was enraged. From training and long habit, he remained in control of himself. "Am I in command of this fleet?"

The slight hesitation was telling. "Yes."

"Then the fleet will obey my commands. The crew of the *Nageratus* will get into escape pods immediately."

Moving like a robot because he did not agree with his own actions, Jallaven issued the order, and repeated it for emphasis. Escape pods began shooting out of the frigate as its hull began to glow from friction as it fell toward the planet.

"The *Nageratus*'s crew is obeying your order, Admiral. If you require me to pay for my disobedience with-"

Kekrando rested his elbows on knees and massaged his temples. "Jallaven, a dead warrior cannot strike the enemy. There is an enormous difference between a *cult* and a *clan*. Your people need to think like clan soldiers. Empty gestures are just that; empty."

"Yes, Admiral. I am ashamed by my-"

"I do not want you to be ashamed, I want you to *learn*. Is that clear?"

"Yes."

"Has the *Nageratus* vented its reactor plasma and discharged the jump drive capacitors?"

"Er," Jallaven checked the display. "No. Why does-"

"The Achakai intend this planet to be your home. Perhaps it would be best not to blow a hole in it?"

Jallaven grimaced, chastened. He manipulated controls on the console, sending override commands directly to the doomed frigate. It took three tries before the little ship acknowledged the command and began complying, and by that time two of the reactors had already shut down automatically and vented their radioactive plasma. The third reactor tried to vent, an operation foiled by a jammed series of valves. That problem was solved when a piece of the reactor's plating tore away in the hypersonic airstream and slammed into exterior pipes, allowing plasma to rush out uncontrolled.

Fifteen of the crew were still aboard when the *Battle of Nageratus* began to break apart and it became impossible to launch escape pods, even if the remaining crew had been able to travel through the violently shaking ship to reach the nearest pod. In three major and countless smaller pieces, the stolen frigate plunged in a death arc determined by gravity and aerodynamics. Striking the water at supersonic speed with its hull glowing cherry-red, the ship flash-boiled millions of gallons of seawater and threw spray several kilometers into the air, before the still-hot pieces sank to the ocean floor. The frigate's hull would eventually become an artificial reef, providing a home to fish and other marine creatures that did not understand or care about the affairs of spacefaring beings.

When his other warships assembled themselves in the proper formation, flying at the proper altitude, speed and direction, the official plan was already eleven minutes behind schedule, and three minutes ahead of the schedule that Admiral Kekrando had privately expected. His counterpart Admiral Kune had expected the formation of Achakai ships would take an entire orbit to get themselves sorted out, so he had to rush through his much-delayed breakfast when the escort ships declared they were ready early. Kune was still brushing crumbs off his uniform when he strode back into the bridge complex from his private alcove. "Wohgalen, is there any reason to delay?"

"No, Sir. There is reason *not* to delay. The longer those mercenary ships are flying, the more likely it is they will crash into each other."

Kune kept the amusement off his face. While he agreed with his operations officer, it would be bad for morale to disparage the abilities of their new, and most likely very temporary, allies. "Very well. Signal the *Ras Howlert* to jump when ready."

The single assault carrier jumped precisely on the revised schedule, accompanied by two Ruhar frigates. The frigates had been assigned not because Kune distrusted the Achakai, it was because he lacked confidence in their abilities to fly and fight their ships at the same time, if they encountered a combat situation.

And, it was a little bit because Kune did not trust the Achakai at all.

With two 7th Fleet frigates above, formations of Achakai warships both above and below, and the battleships feeding sensor data, the *Howlert's* crew did not need to wait for their own sensors to recover from the spatial distortion of the jump wormhole. Ten gunships were first to launch, spreading out to provide coverage for the troop-carrying dropships launching right behind them. Clouds of decoy drones were ejected by the assault carrier and the two frigates, filling the sky with sensor-jamming electromagnetic interference, and projecting holograms that gave each of them the appearance of dropships. The launch operation proceeded exactly as planned, and soon the *Howlert's* launch bays were empty. Twenty-four hundred members of the assassin's cult were on their way to the surface, each one of them determined to do their part to restore the honor of their people.

The Ruhar crews flying the dropships hoped their Achakai passengers remained in their seats, kept calm during the combat drop, exited quickly once the dropships had skids on the ground and, *most importantly*, remembered to properly use the barf bags under their seats.

"All landing craft away," Wohgalen reported. "One gunship developed engine trouble and is attempting to dock with the *Howlert*, it-"

"No," Kune interrupted. "Signal the gunship to climb into a stable orbit, and send a frigate to meet it. I want no delays in the assault carriers achieving jump altitude." He knew the carrier would reduce thrust while the gunship matched course and speed to be recovered, and he was not risking a starship for a two-person spacecraft.

"Yes, Admiral," Wohgalen relayed the order. "Admiral Kekrando's ships are maneuvering to protect the landing craft and- Oh *shit*!"

Above the *Ras Howlert* and above the upper formation of Achakai warships, a twisted tear in spacetime appeared in a burst of gamma radiation, and a light cruiser suddenly emerged from nowhere.

An enemy light cruiser.

A *Bosphuraq* light cruiser.

At the same time, a pair of Bosphuraq destroyers emerged in the middle of a formation of three Ruhar battleships, and began launching missiles even before their sensors had fully reset. The sensors of the missiles could recover while in flight, they had been programmed before the jump with the rough positions of the enemy capital ships and could take care of themselves.

Kune immediately knew he had a problem even before the deck of his flagship rocked from absorbing particle beam fire from the Bosphuraq destroyer. The *Howlert* was likely doomed and there was little Kune could do about that. The *Howlert* was also only one carrier and an empty one, he could afford to lose that ship even as he recognized how callous that might seem. He could not afford to lose three battleships and if the Bosphuraq destroyers knocked three battleships out of the fight, the enemy could rampage around the planet and eliminate not only all of his other ships, but also the Legion force on the surface. The Ruhar fleet had practiced to fight against patron-species ships and they had tactics that were mostly untested, because Ruhar crews engaged in such fights rarely survived to provide after-action analysis. "All ships," he ordered with well-practiced calm, "target those destroyers with massed fire."

In the bunker under the surface of the planet, Sergeant Liu was scrolling through menus in the alien targeting and fire control system. The system did appear to have an Identification Friend or Foe feature, though she could not understand how it worked, or whether the IFF would or even could lock out her ability to hit a friendly ship. The Wurgalan seemed to value flexibility in their systems, which was a nice way of saying they placed much of the decision-making burden on the biological operators. Somewhere behind her, she heard Lieutenant Colonel Perkins speaking quietly to someone, while Liu tried to answer the questions posed by the legendary leader of the Mavericks. The fact was, Sergeant Liu simply did not *know* whether the plasma cannon could be directed to fire on a friendly ship, she suspected she would not know for certain until-

An alarm blared, the sound echoing in the underground chamber before Liu saw the source of the alert. "Colonel! A Bosphuraq ship just jumped in over our heads!"

"*Bos*- Where?" Perkins raced over to the console. "What is it-"

"It is firing on the assault carrier," Liu squinted at the display, having to guess at some of the unfamiliar alien symbols. "The Achakai ships are moving to intercept!"

Perkins knew the captured ships operated by the ninjas would stand little chance of success or even survival against a light cruiser built by the patrons of the Wurgalan. She leaned over Liu's shoulder. "Can we shoot?"

"Ma'am, I don't know whether- Huh."

"What?"

"I was going to say I still don't know whether the fire control system will allow target lock on a friendly ship, but it doesn't matter. Bosphuraq ships are tagged as *enemy* vessels."

Perkins snorted. "You gotta love how the Maxolhx coalition is one big happy family. Warm up the cannons."

"They are active, Ma'am, I can fire at any time." She turned to look back over her shoulder. "We will need to focus all three cannons on that ship, to burn through their shields."

"Do it."

Admiral Kekrando knew instantly that his little squadron was doomed, and that his untested force had little chance to present much more than an annoyance to the light cruiser that was battering the *Howlert's* shields. Once the assault carrier was disabled, he expected the Bosphuraq would shift their focus to the landing craft, already the enemy was launching missiles at the heavy-lifter landing craft. "All ships, target enemy missiles, we have to protect those dropships. Jallaven, maneuver us between the enemy and the heavy-lifters," he ordered as he saw Vulture gunships racing to intercept the Bosphuraq missiles, pouring a hail of maser cannon in a desperate attempt to hit the wildly dodging weapons.

"Sir, what about the *Howlert*?"

Kekrando didn't waste time shaking his head, he was studying the tactical display. "We can't do anything to assist that ship."

Jallaven stiffened. He was imagining the after-action review, in which the Achakai would be judged as cowards for failing to protect a Ruhar ship, further staining their honor until the end of time. "Admiral, we must-"

"You *must*," Kekrando pounded a fist on his chair. "Follow the orders of the only person in this squadron who has experience in space combat. Do not worry, Jallaven," he added as he sent orders directly to four of his destroyers in the formation above the *Howlert*. "The Achakai will earn glory today, your deeds will inspire epic poetry for generations."

Jallaven was, to be polite, skeptical of the admiral's words. Until he saw the orders Kekrando had transmitted. Then he decided that he would never again question the admiral's orders or judgment.

All of the squadron's ships turned and burned, firing their main engines and thrusters to place themselves and their energy shields between the enemy cruiser and the vulnerable dropships. All of the squadron's ships except four destroyers of the upper formation, which had another mission.

Admiral Kune reached for the helmet offered by his aide, and missed as the battleship was struck again. The deck rocked, artificial gravity flickered, lights and displays blinked off and on, and Kune stumbled, cracking his head on a handhold. He reached up to his forehead, his hand coming away stained with blood. Before he could push himself upright, Wohgalen had jammed a helmet on the fleet commander's head and activated the automatic mechanism that sealed the neck, inflated cushions around Kune's skull, swung the faceplate down and even sent a creepy slug-like bandage crawling to cover the gash on the admiral's forehead. "Thank you, Wohgalen," Kune said, though he saw that his aide had not followed proper procedure to secure his own helmet first. "Bring the-"

"Sir, you must get to the escape ship," The operations officer waved for two crewmen to assist the admiral in getting to the ready bird that was waiting in the closest launch bay.

"*Escape*? I am not going anywhere while-"

"The ship is dying," Wohgalen lurched forward and was grateful he had just gotten his own helmet on, for the ship's deck heaved sickeningly and he fell backward, flailing his arms and grasping a handhold. "The crew is doing everything they can here. When this ship is gone, the fleet will still need direction, or *everyone* will die and this will all be for nothing."

Kune's emotions warred with his experience and training. It was true that the battleship's crew was working valiantly to save their ship- No. They were working valiantly to keep the ship fighting to the last, knowing they were doomed. They were not fighting for their own lives, they were fighting to kill the enemy.

The pair of Bosphuraq destroyers were being targeted by the three Ruhar battleships, which were hammering the higher-technology warships with everything they had. Maser, particle and railgun cannons fired broadsides coordinated between all three ships with the directed and kinetic energy hitting the targeted ship at the same time, giving the battleships their best chance of knocking back the enemy shields so the missiles following close behind could punch through the weakened defenses. Some missiles, guided by the Ruhar battle-management AIs, exploded between the combatants, flooding the battlespace with sensor-blinding radiation.

It wasn't enough. The enemy shields were absorbing or deflecting hit after hit, the shield generators degrading at a rapid and predictable rate, that still left plenty of time for the Bosphuraq to complete the destruction of the Ruhar flagship, and then switch their focus to another battleship. Kune knew that admirals did not fly the warships, guide the weapons, manage the engines, repair damage or even keep the crew fed. Admirals used their training and experience to issue orders and make their ships effective in their tasks. It was true that if he died, the fleet would be without his leadership. Command would transfer to the most-senior captain in the fleet, but in the confusion there would be delays that could be fatal.

What made Kune hesitate was the nagging doubt that there was nothing useful he *could* do, that his fleet was doomed no matter what he did. Plus, if he did launch with the ready bird, he was out of ideas. An admiral who did not know what orders to give was useless.

"No, Wohgalen. I will remain here. Perhaps in our final moments, I can learn something the fleet can use to their advantage, and I can send out a message."

Wohgalen knew that it was not the time to argue. He also knew Kune was probably right. The admiral's best move might be to die with the ship, and provide inspiration to future fleet commanders. Waving away the crewmen, he helped the admiral steady himself as the deck rocked again. The tactical display was showing the battleship's portside shields near collapse, two enemy railgun darts had punched through the armor and wreaked havoc as they tumbled and splattered through the interior. Fortunately the darts had not hit anything vital but that was the only bit of good fortune,and the ship couldn't take many more hits before something important broke. The crew was rotating the port side away from the enemy and if that tactic was successful, the battleship might have a few additional minutes before it was disabled and drifting. If a single missile-

The ship shuddered. Someone called out "Reactor Three is damaged and leaking plasma. Shield generators covering Frames Seventeen through Twenty offline, we-"

The tactical display lit up with new warnings, more ships jumping in to join the battle. Kune felt a ball of ice forming in the pit of his stomach as he saw the new ships, though not yet identified by type, were illuminated in purple, the color for hostile warships that-

The color of the symbols flickered and changed to orange which identified friendly vessels.

The ships were Wurgalan, which were automatically considered hostile until the correct transponder codes were received and validated.

The Wurgalan ships were friendly.

They were destroyers from Admiral Kekrando's squadron.

There were four of them.

The first destroyer jumped in between the Bosphuraq destroyers and the battleships, traveling at high speed away from the enemy and having no chance to make a difference in the fight. The crew cursed their old and obsolete jump navigation system, and if some of the crew silently placed part of the blame on the navigators who programmed the coordinates, that was understandable. Broadcasting their transponder codes on multiple frequencies so the battleships didn't target them, the crew of that destroyer launched two missiles backwards at the Bosphuraq in a futile gesture of defiance, and resigned themselves to being spectators until their jump drive coils had recharged and they could do something useful.

The second destroyer also emerged on the wrong side of the Bosphuraq ships and traveling in the wrong direction, with the difference that its momentum was carrying it toward one of the battleships it was trying to protect. Burning its engines at emergency power and firing thrusters, the Achakai ship desperately maneuvered to avoid a collision, while the battleship it was headed toward slowly and painfully lumbered out of the way. For seven long heart-stopping seconds, the captain of the battleship considered blowing the smaller ship out of the sky to protect his capital ship, then the tactical display showed the idiot mercenaries would miss by half the length of their ship. The battleship's captain cursed the amateurish newcomers, whose small, old and obsolete ships had no possibility to affect the outcome of the fight, and could only be a distraction to the Ruhar. What the *hell* were the mercenaries thinking?

That question was answered when the third Achakai ship, having observed its two companions for crucial seconds and adjusted jump coordinates, emerged on the far side of the Bosphuraq destroyers. The accuracy of its jump might have been due more to luck than skill. It was impossible to tell what coordinates the ship had been aiming for, because it came out of the jump wormhole moving in the right direction, and-

Impacted the Bosphuraq ship's forward hull with its substantial kinetic energy, tearing the enemy ship's nose off and spinning it around so violently that vital components such as shield generators were ripped loose from their mountings, reactors instantly shut down, maser cannons cracked, and missiles were trapped when their launch tubes warped and outer doors jammed. Most of the crew was killed instantly from being thrown around inside their ship, those who were not killed in the impact lived only briefly, until the Wurgalan ship exploded and took the unshielded Bosphuraq warship with it.

The fourth Achakai ship was not quite as accurate or fortunate with its jump. It emerged in the general area it had been aiming for with its momentum carrying it directly toward an intercept with the target, except that it was farther away. Far enough away that the sole surviving Bosphuraq ship shifted its fire at the newcomer, hammering away with railguns, masers and particle cannons, and ripple-firing eight missiles. Under the concentrated assault at close range, the shields of the Achakai ship flared and failed, leaving the hull exposed. A railgun dart penetrated the sensor dome on the nose and crashed through the unprotected interior, blasting through bulkhead after bulkhead on its uncontrolled flight toward the aft engineering section. That railgun dart, or maybe the two that followed, punched through the plating on one side of a reactor and rattled around, ricocheting inside the reactor vessel until it was thoroughly wrecked.

The reactor exploded, taking out the reactor next to it, and shrapnel ripped forward where it hit a missile magazine.

The Achakai ship, old, obsolete, stolen from a junkyard and operated by a species who were supposed to be allies of the ship's builders, was blown into pieces by the detonations of missile drive units and warheads. The disorganized collection of starship parts flew onward, the forward momentum of their mass unaffected by the fact that they were no longer connected to each other.

Panicked, the Bosphuraq warship shifted fire to deflect aside the larger pieces and vaporize the smaller junk. The Bosphuraq would have been more successful if their fire control AI had not locked up for vital seconds, overwhelmed by the target-rich environment. Instead of shooting, the AI attempted to collect and analyze sensor data, creating a predictive model to determine how best to save its ship from destruction. Unable to process the data, the fire control AI went into reset mode.

It was still rebooting when three substantial chunks of what had been a client-species ship impacted the shields.

There was stunned silence in the bridge of the 7th Fleet flagship when the last Achakai ship struck the enemy. The silence was especially notable because the usual soft beeping of console controls and the background hiss of air from the vents was no longer accompanied by banging sounds of enemy fire striking the battleship's armor, the chattering of defensive cannons, and the whoosh of missiles launching.

Admiral Kune broke the silence. "Well. You don't see *that* every day."

His crew found that immensely funny, their laughter fueled by the terrifying tension of the battle that was suddenly over.

Wohgalen's shoulders shook. "It is a good thing," he snorted, "that no one taught the Achakai how to drive."

Kune grinned, pointing to the image of the crippled Bosphuraq destroyer. "Wohgalen, take out the trash, if you please?"

"With pleasure, Sir."

# CHAPTER TWENTY FIVE

"It's not working," Liu pounded a fist on the alien console. "The system isn't allowing me to establish a lock on the target. I don't know whether it is blocking-"

Perkins put a hand on the sergeant's shoulder and spoke in a calm manner. "Can you aim the cannons manually?"

"I can try."

"Do it."

After the Bosphuraq cruiser had jumped in overhead, neither General Ross nor Admiral Kune had called her, she took that as a sign of their faith that if she could fire the plasma cannons, she would.

The question was, could her team do it? In the back of her mind, she had jokingly thought that firing hidden alien weapons buried beneath the surface of a planet, was kind of her signature move. The Mavericks had come to fame by doing that with maser projectors on Paradise. The problem was, on Paradise the cannons had been activated, aimed and fired by Emby, their still-unknown Mysterious Benefactor. With the Wurgalan plasma cannons, her team had to rely on an alien PowerPoint presentation to use the system.

Looking at her zPhone, she saw that only fifteen seconds had passed since the Bosphuraq ship appeared so unexpectedly, it only felt like hours. Without full access to sensors, she did not know what was happening in orbit, she could only imagine the carnage that an advanced-species warship could cause. If the enemy were smart, they would concentrate their fire on the dropships first, then hit the empty assault carrier. A Bosphuraq ship could ignore the small ships of Kekrando's force unless they became an annoyance. For all she knew, the two battalions of Achakai soldiers could have been blasted to nothingness already.

Standing behind Liu's chair, she tried to tamp down her rising anxiety, while mentally urging the Chinese sergeant to move faster. On the console in front of Liu, inscrutable alien icons were flashing warnings, resisting the human efforts to control the powerful weapons.

The Bosphuraq had, of course, been smart. When their light cruiser jumped in to wipe out the second wave landing force, they had emerged behind the assault carrier and its escorts. That deep in the gravity well, the ships of Kekrando's lower formation could not jump to reposition themselves for a suicide run on the enemy, and anyway the old Wurgalan drive units could not manage an accurate jump of such a short distance. That same problem applied to the ships of the upper formation, though they were at jump altitude, the gravity well of the planet distorted the jump wormhole so much that it would be impossible to predict where the ships would emerge; they might become a greater danger than the enemy ship. Slowly, the engines of Kekrando's old ships strained to slow them down so they could maneuver into position between the enemy and the dropships that were racing away at full thrust, all attempts at stealth forgotten. With the Bosphuraq ship flooding the area with active sensor pulses, stealth would be ineffective, and the dropships were leaving visible trails of superheated air behind them anyway.

The smart move to cause maximum damage was for the Bosphuraq to pick off the heavy-lifter dropships first, then the medium-lift spacecraft, and only then hit the assault carrier that was attempting to flee. If the Bosphuraq wanted to make a statement, they could have blasted the ships of the Achakai, punishing those aliens who were supposed to be clients.

The Bosphuraq were smart.

They were also angry, and afraid.

Angry at having to fight the Kristang, even if neither the Achakai nor Verd-kris were part of regular Kristang society. Fighting the Kristang was a headache the Bosphuraq did not need, and they did not trust their Wurgalan clients to handle the problem.

Afraid, because the Ruhar could become a major threat with their new Alien Legion potentially adding millions of fanatical Verd-kris warriors on their side. Perhaps even *billions* of Verd-kris could take up arms under the leadership of the Ruhar.

The Bosphuraq were smart, angry and afraid. But mostly smart.

They targeted the assault carrier first.

The Achakai were a threat.

The Verd-kris were a threat.

The true threat were the Ruhar. Without their fuzzy masters, neither of the rogue Kristang factions would be a problem. The current Ruhar government was a coalition led by the Peace Faction. The more Ruhar ships that were lost, the more Ruhar families mourned daughters and sons killed in military operations of dubious value, the more support the Peace movement would gain. It was better to get the enemy to defeat themselves, the Bosphuraq decided.

That is why the assault carrier *Ras Howlert* was struck with the first salvo from the enemy light cruiser. The Bosphuraq did not care about an empty assault carrier, they cared about making victims of the over three hundred Ruhar crew aboard that ship.

Too late, Kekrando saw that the order for his ships to protect the dropships was premature, and he knew in a flash why the enemy was intent on hitting the *Howlert* first. "All ships," he ordered, knowing that nothing he could do would affect the fate of the assault carrier. "Open fire on the enemy!"

Below on the surface, there were three blasts as doors covering the plasma cannons were blown up and away by explosive charges, the thick armored doors cartwheeling through the sky to crash down a hundred or more meters away. The soil and vegetation covering the doors erupted first and the explosives blew out three cone-shaped openings, giving clear passage for the plasma bolts. Deep beneath the surface, power surged from storage cells, relays tripped open and superconducting magnets began spinning rapidly. Three lasers sent invisible beams of coherent light into the sky, painting the shields of the Bosphuraq cruiser and reflecting back to indicate range to target. Only a small aiming adjustment was needed, then the plasma cannons were ready. Though the firing of three cannons in the cluster were theoretically simultaneous, in practice one cannon was usually a millisecond ahead of the others and that cluster was no exception. Plasma surged up the cannon barrel, contained and channeled by the magnetic field, the bright light bursting into the air and-

Flickering.

Sputtering.

Weakly, the plasma beam winked out, leaving only a thin wisp of smoke rising from the cannon barrel.

Sergeant Liu froze in shock, mouth open.

"What happened?" Perkins shouted, losing her cool.

"Liu?" Jesse prodded the woman seated at the console, glancing fearfully at the ceiling. When she only looked back at him, her mouth forming silent words, he gently tugged her aside. "Let me try."

It was no good.

Strange alien script flashed repeatedly on the console, interpreted on Liu's own tablet. They were locked out of the system. "*Shiiiiit*," Jesse breathed, standing up from the awkward Wurgalan seat. "That cruiser knows exactly where we are now."

"I'm sorry," Liu hung her head, tears in her eyes.

"It's not your fault," Perkins assured the sergeant.

Jesse took a deep breath. His only regret was that he never got to tell Shauna what he needed to tell her. Hopefully she already knew. Coming to attention, he faced Perkins and snapped a crisp salute. "Ma'am, it has been an honor serving with you."

Emily Perkins returned the salute automatically, her eyes focused in the ceiling, imagining deadly hellfire in the form of railgun darts racing down toward them. "For what we are about to receive-"

The crew of the cruiser were shocked when they detected their shields being painted by targeting lasers from the surface. They were fearful when they realized the source of those lasers; a plasma cannon cluster. They were outraged when they checked their database and discovered that cluster was not registered, that their clients had secretly installed strategic defenses and not informed their patrons. They were nearly paralyzed when, while their own weapons were swiveling around with agonizing slowness to meet the new threat, they detected superheated plasma that reached upward and-

Did nothing.

Went nowhere.

The cruiser swung around to point down at the new target, aiming the railguns that ran along its central spine. Perhaps the Wurgalan below had realized their mistake and aborted the firing sequence, before they could hit a ship flown by their patrons. The Bosphuraq were taking no chances, they would eliminate the threat for certain, permanently. In the base of the railguns, robotic arms loaded heavy darts, blast doors sealed closed, and powerful electromagnets built up a charge, moving the darts along the barrels.

Underneath the feet of Emily Perkins, the Wurgalan AI that controlled and maintained the cannon cluster pondered the strange sequence of events. Aliens had gained access to the control center, and the AI had done nothing because it had no instructions regarding such an unlikely event. Those same aliens gained access to the network and the AI had become uneasy, but because the aliens had the proper access codes, it could do nothing. Even when the aliens requested other sites to initiate targeting pulses, the AI could not take action to prevent the destruction of its fellow AIs.

When the aliens attempted to fire on a warship of the Wurgalan's patron species, the AI had complied. It had not, however, complied with *enthusiasm*. Thus, when certain instruction sequences were missed due to the alien's understandable ignorance of how the system was supposed to work, the AI had not filled in the gaps as it normally would have. As a result, two of the cannons failed to fire entirely and the third suffered an intermittent fault, cutting off the plasma energy source.

The AI then faced a curious dilemma that it was not prepared for, had not been programmed for. The Bosphuraq above would certainly strike the cluster, ending the AI's existence, and killing the pesky humans also.

The AI was going to die, no matter what it did.

Getting rid of the alien invaders seemed like the right thing to do, even at the expense of its own life.

Yes.

To stand by and allow the facility to be destroyed was compliant with its programming.

Yes.

The AI suffered only one nagging doubt. It noted that often, when the Wurgalan crews of the control center had practiced aiming and firing the great cannons, they pretended to be shooting at warships of their patrons.

The AI had little information about the Bosphuraq, but there was one vital bit of data it did have: the Bosphuraq were universally considered to be assholes.

"Well," the AI thought to itself. "Fuck 'em."

While railguns darts were being flung along their launch rails, the cruiser was struck by three plasma bolts that impacted the shields within a half meter of each other. The shields of the advanced-technology species were powerful and sophisticated, yet when the shields struggled to deflect or absorb the incoming energy, the raging plasma bolts essentially said 'Aw, that is *so* cute' as they burned right through. The thin armor plating of the light cruiser's hull was also no obstacle to the plasma, and in an instant, the warship sizzled like a battered Twinkie tossed into a deep fryer at a state fair.

From stem to stern, the interior of the ship flashed with heat reaching millions of degrees, turning crew, bulkheads, structural frames, reactors and the jump drive into charred soot.

The jump drive capacitors released their energy in a titanic explosion, adding to the carnage and ironically, briefly turning every particle of the ship into plasma.

"*Whoo-HOO!*" Thunderous cheers rang around the control center. High-fives were exchanged, backs were slapped, there might have been spontaneous hugs and even some kissing that instantly made the participants regret their actions. Or made the participants look at each other with a surprised 'Hmm, maybe?'.

When she could hear herself think, Perkins waved her hands for silence. "Will someone please tell me what the *hell* just happened?"

Liu was as shocked by the firing of the cannons as she had been then when cannons fizzled out. "Colonel," she stammered. "I have no idea."

Perkins turned her attention to the staff sergeant, who was grinning like the Cheshire cat. "Colter?"

"Huh? It wasn't me, ma'am," he shrugged. "I didn't do anything."

"*Someone* did something," Perkins insisted.

"Must be clean living and a pure heart," Jesse suggested, placing a hand over his chest.

The Mavericks commander rolled her eyes. "I know *that's* not true, Colter."

"I hope it is."

She tilted her head. "Why's that?"

"Because, if all that happened is we got lucky, my Momma told me that Fate likes to balance the scales. I'd hate to see what happens when it's our turn for *bad* luck."


"Yes, Admiral, but-" Ross's mind raced to find a persuasive argument.

"I am sorry, General Ross," Kune said with measured calm. "I cannot send in the remainder of the second wave, until we can be reasonably certain there are no other Bosphuraq ships lurking around to spoil the party."

"But-"

"I have dispatched a frigate to contact the Jeraptha. Our patrons have stated many times that they will under no circumstance interfere in this operation. However, I am hopeful they will consent to advise us."

"Yes, Admiral," Ross said with a resigned sigh he hoped was not audible. He knew that, even if the Jeraptha agreed to send one or two frigates to scan the star system, it would take weeks, even months to assure no enemy ships were lurking in the far reaches of that vast expanse of space. During those weeks, the soldiers of the first wave would be slowly ground down by the superior numbers of the Wurgalan and by their diminishing supply of ammunition, and the invasion would have failed. "Could we send in stealthed dropships from long range?"

"My staff is looking into that possibility," Kune stated. "It would be prudent to begin with launching cargo pods at long range. General, any such technique would need to be tested before we commit substantial numbers."

"Understood." Ross knew he had to celebrate small victories. The problem was, sending small numbers of troops to the surface in dropships launched at long range was *not* a victory, because it was not a path to victory. Dribbling in stealthed landing craft one or two at a time was a sure path to *failure*. During the World War II battle of Guadalcanal, the Japanese tried to send troops and supplies to the island in small ships, submarines, even shooting torpedoes full of food onto beaches when they became truly desperate. That half-hearted technique hadn't worked in the Pacific Theater and it wouldn't work on Squidworld. All Ross was trying to do was keep the battle going, because the alternative was surrender. If the Ruhar were afraid to risk their ships in a landing, they certainly would not risk them in the much riskier operation of pulling troops off the surface under fire. To salvage any part of the force on the ground, the Legion and Achakai would have to negotiate a ceasefire and probably surrender their weapons. Because doing that would be suicide for the Achakai, the ninjas would prefer to fight on even after they ran out of ammunition.

UNEF was in a mess and Ross knew it. The concept of an Alien Legion was still new, and a single lost battle could cause the Ruhar to cancel the experiment. The Legion had to win every battle, without the luxury of being able to choose when and where to fight. It was an untenable situation, which was why, despite the fact that Perkins had once again accomplished a miracle, he was still pissed at her. The cowboy nonsense of her making deals without UNEF approval had to stop.

Someday.

In the meantime, he had to play the hand he'd been dealt, or fold and lose everything.

With Kune committing only to sending a few stealthed Dodos as a test, Ross had to make sure that test was successful. That meant giving priority to landing those Dodos in a safe area, instead of where they were actually needed for the ground battle. "I will prepare a list of landing zones, where we could best use reinforcements."

"Send them to my staff as soon as possible," Kune replied. "General, I hate to say this, but I also need an updated plan for a phased withdrawal."

"That will take longer. The situation down here is," he searched for the best word to politely describe an epic clusterfuck. "Fluid."

"Understood. My ships remain available for strategic fire support on a limited basis. We took substantial punishment in the fight against the Bosphuraq, I need to pull ships off the line for repairs and replenishment."

Ross read between the lines. The ground force was basically on its own. 'Strategic' fire support meant the battleships would be parked in distant orbits, and only fire on targets big enough to require the guns of a capital ship. Essentially, that meant a battalion-sized enemy force in one area. The Wurgalan knew the rules of ground-based warfare, they were unlikely to be stupid enough to concentrate that much force.

"You intend to maintain space superiority?" Ross asked.

"Absolutely," Kune replied immediately with vehemence. "My escort ships will prevent the Wurgalan from providing close-space support, or bringing in reinforcements. But if the Bosphuraq are determined to be directly involved-"

"That is a whole new ballgame, I get it."

"Please convey our thanks to Colonel Perkins. Regrettably, I don't have time for more than sending her a brief message."

"We appreciate it," Ross said, using 'we' rather than 'she' to remind the Ruhar admiral that Emily Perkins was not the only human making a difference on the planet.

With the frustrating conversation over, he reviewed the updated status report, trying to get a view of what other disasters had occurred during the fortunately brief fight with the Bosphuraq. "Shit," he thumped the console with a fist. He needed to talk with Perkins.


"Thank you, Sir," Perkins mumbled the obligatory words after Ross conveyed the admiral's thanks. "My team did all the work."

"*I* am not exactly carrying a rifle on the front line, Colonel." Ross didn't intend to be quite so sarcastic. "You know what I mean. Those plasma cannons are a one-shot weapon?"

"Yes. The powercells are depleted. It also looks like the magnetic containment system in the cannon barrels can only take one shot, so even if we could replenish power, the cannons would crack if we fired them again."

"That's unfortunate. Ah, the enemy knows where you are now anyway. Perkins, wrap up whatever you're doing, I'm pulling you out. The Dodo that has the rest of your team is enroute, it should be there within ten minutes."

"Where are we going?"

"I just sent a summary to you, read it and tell me what you think. Bottom line is, we have a mess in Slugtown, and I need you to sort it out. It started out with an op to extract a Verd platoon that crash-landed near the city center, now both sides have reinforced. I need you to get our people out of there and contain the situation, I do not want this becoming another Stalingrad. We are *not* getting into a house-to-house fight in that damned city."

"Yes, Sir. Is there anything, *special* about the Verds we're pulling out?"

Ross knew that by 'special' she meant were there political considerations. There were always politics involved. "Nothing especially special about it. We can't be seen as abandoning the Verds, or there will be hell to pay. Right now, there are parts of two platoons trying to get out of the city, and they're led by a human. One of yours, sort of? You know her. Captain Danielle Grace."

"*Grace*? She's in psyops. How did she get in command of an infantry platoon?"

"All the other officers didn't make it."

"Wheeew," Perkins whistled. "This *is* a mess."

"Read the summary and get back to me ASAP. I need you to contain this before it gets out of hand."

"One question before you go, Sir. Any change to the rules of engagement?"

Ross didn't reply immediately. "Not officially, no. Not right now. But, the squids have no problem with blowing up their own city, so I'll leave that to your judgment." He realized that might sound like he was passing the buck. "Colonel, if you must escalate use of force to put an end to this mess, do it and I'll back you up, hundred percent."

"Yes, Sir."

"Ross out."

She checked her tablet, a file from Ross was still downloading over the low-bandwidth connection. Enemy jamming made all forms of communication more difficult.

Jesse cleared his throat to get her attention. "Ma'am? "You said something about 'Grace'?" He had overheard only one side of the conversation, since Perkins had listened to Ross through her zPhone earpiece. "That isn't the Captain Grace I know, is it?"

Perkins didn't look up from her tablet, scanning over the file that had just finished downloading. "The same. Her platoon is trying to get out of Slugtown. Here," she flicked a finger on the tablet screen, to send the file to the staff sergeant. "Look at this, tell me what you think."

Jesse didn't bother to ask how Grace's platoon had gotten stuck in a city that the rules of engagement had declared off-limits. It must have been a 'shit happens' situation. He pulled up the file on his zPhone. "This is-"

"Study it later. Right now, we're pulling out of here. There's a dropship coming to pick us up in ten."

Jesse stuffed the phone in a pocket and grabbed his pack off the floor. "I'm on it," he turned to jog out the doorway.

She caught his arm and whispered. "Colter? That dropship? It has people who are," her voice caught in her throat. "Special to you and me."

Jesse held up a fist and she bumped it softly. "I had faith they'd be all right," he said, blinking away a tear.


The reunions were brief and entirely unsatisfactory for everyone involved. Jesse barely had time to wave to Shauna as the dropship touched down and waited impatiently, its engines idling and kicking up dust. Exchanging greetings had to wait until the Dodo lifted off, even before the back ramp was closed.

Dave's seat was at the front of the Dodo, while Perkins was near the back of the cabin. Knowing she had a thousand things to do, he sent her a simple message. *You're busy, talk later?*

She looked at him, her faceplate and visor swung out of the way. She didn't speak, or send a text reply, or even silently mouth words to him. What she did was tap the left side of her chest in a private gesture they shared. He did the same, and looked away to where Jesse and Shauna were having a more animated and less private reunion.


"Hey, 'Pone," Dave tapped Jesse's shoulder. "What's up? Where are we going?"

"First, we're dropping off the wounded."

"Field hospital?" Dave asked hopefully with a glance at Chowdhury.

"I think it's more like a DRASH with a couple of medics," Jesse answered. "But it's the best we can do." The pop-up shelters supplied by the Ruhar were much nicer than a US Army DRASH tent on Earth, but the term had stuck.

"After that?"

"There's a Verd platoon stuck in Slugtown," Jesse explained. "It's too dangerous to evac them by air, so we're going in to link up and pull them out."

Dave and Shauna both whistled. "I thought Slugtown is a No-Go zone," Shauna's eyes narrowed. "Did somebody not get the memo?"

"Yeah," Jesse grunted. "This is kind of a 'shit happens' scenario."

Dave had a more practical concern. "How are *we* getting into the city?"

Jesse shrugged. "Damned if I know. I expect that's what Em is talking with our pilots about."

"I need ideas," Perkins looked at her two pilots. "You both studied the intel we got from Ross?"

Derek nodded with a sour expression.

"Yes," Irene shook her head. "We're not flying a Dodo over the city. We'll look for sites outside the city where you can set down, and-"

"No good," Perkins cut her off. "We need to set down near Grace's platoon, or not bother going at all."

"Ma'am, I don't know what to tell you. A Dodo is just a big, fat target. The Ruhar aren't flying this thing over the city," she rapped her knuckles on the cabin wall. "Even if they let me and Derek fly it, *we* wouldn't take it in there. It's suicide. Hovering for even a few seconds to drop a platoon on cables is a no-go."

"What if you came in at high speed, and I found some place like a park, where you could set down?"

"Colonel, the AA over Sluktashwon makes the city a no-fly zone for our side. Maybe we could have flown in right after that platoon crashed, but now?" She bit her lower lip. "It is pure suicide."

"Ok," Perkins bit her lip. "What about something smaller, like a Buzzard?" She knew dropships were not optimized for flying in an atmosphere, they were too big, too heavy and required too much thrust to keep them in the air. Human pilots referred to the Dodo as a 'Lawn Dart', because if the engines failed, it pretty much fell straight down.

"Not happening. Maybe if we had one of the special operations-model Buzzards, but the hamsters don't let us play with those fancy toys." Irene had looked enviously at a Buzzard she had seen in a hangar on Paradise, an aircraft modified to maximize stealth. The Ruhar had not allowed her even to enter the hangar, they sure as hell weren't going to let her ever fly one. "Although," she whipped out her phone and tapped the screen. "Special gear, hmm."

"Although, what?"

"Give me a minute," Irene mumbled, intent on her phone. "Derek? I need to talk with Bonsu, Ma'am."

"Go ahead."

The two pilots put their heads together and talked, quietly at first then whispering in an animated fashion, with Irene jabbing a finger at her phone and Derek shaking his head. Then, he pulled out his own zPhone and played with it, finally shrugging.

"We may have a workable option," Irene said as she crossed the cabin to sit next to Perkins.

"An option that gets us into the city, near Grace's platoon?"

"Yes."

Something about the way Striebich said 'yes' made Perkins suspicious. "What's the catch?"

"It's a one-way trip," Irene admitted.

"Show me."

# CHAPTER TWENTY SIX

"This makes *no* sense," Irene stared at her phone in disbelief. "Were these instructions written by a monkey?"

Derek glanced at his own phone. "They're in English."

"*Hamster* English," she rolled her eyes. "Seriously, who wrote 'Making Tab A into Slot B yield happiness'?"

"Hey," Derek grinned. "Putting Tab A into Slot B makes *me* happy." He reached out and caressed her cheek, the only part of her that was exposed in the skinsuit.

"Not now," she whispered.

"Not *now*? Is that a promise for something later?"

She playfully nipped at his fingers. "Maybe. We have to assemble this junk pile first, and then, you know, stay alive."

"I'll take that 'maybe' as a 'yes'. Come on, how hard can it be to put this thing together? Piece of cake," Derek concluded. "There must be a video about it on YouTube."

"We're kind of far away to access YouTube."

"Sure, but, ha! I knew it!" Derek held up his phone in triumph. "The Dash Ten on this thing includes a handy-dandy video."

"Great." She examined the pile of parts spread out on the ground. "Let's get started."

"*I* will get started. *You* watch the video about flying this thing," he insisted. "This was your idea."

"Ok." Irene sat on a crate and flipped through the surprisingly extensive Pilot's Operating Handbook, frowning as she glanced at Derek holding up components, trying to figure out which part went where.

Their plan to get the Mavericks into Slugtown was simple: in a stealth glider.

The Ruhar didn't trust the Legion with their front-line commando gear like the special stealthy version of the Buzzard transport aircraft, because they didn't think the Legion needed such high-tech gear, and because the Ruhar were concerned their sensitive equipment could fall into enemy hands. The Ruhar had rejected a request for several stealth Buzzards for use on Stiglord, to be flown and operated by Ruhar.

The Ruhar had offered a compromise: stealth gliders. The lightweight, stealthy, unpowered aircraft would be towed behind an aircraft or even a dropship, then could be used to insert troops without being detected. That was the theory. Unfortunately, in a truly inventive form of bureaucratic screw-up, dozens of stealth gliders were brought to Stiglord, without most of the Legion having ever flown in or even seen one of the unusual aircraft.

The glider they were unpacking had been intended for a Commando team. The cargo pod with the glider had been launched from the *Big Mac* and made it safely to the ground, while the Commando team had apparently been killed when the assault carrier was cut in half. All the Mavericks needed to do was unpack and assemble an aircraft they had only heard rumors about. Then the glider needed to be carried aloft by a dropship, and released at a distance and altitude that would allow it to fly unpowered into the city.

And land it without a runway, without killing everyone aboard.

While part of the team were puzzling over how to get the glider put together, Shauna, Jesse and Nert poked around the cargo container, searching for gear that could be useful. The container's computer had a manifest that Shauna quickly saw was more aspirational than accurate. The manifest listed which items were supposed to be in the container, while the reality was different. For example, the item designated as Medical Unit, Portable, Primary Care, was not anywhere to be found. Instead, there were crates of food suitable for providing nutrition to Kristang biochemistry, though the *Big Mac's* landing force was entirely human.

Fortunately, there was a box of medical supplies that could be used to treat and offer comfort to the injured, though they still had only the platoon's medics to provide care. Flying to get the glider had meant diverting away from the original plan for bringing the wounded to a medical facility, and General Ross's staff had offered only vague promises of additional air transport.

"Ooooh," Shauna sighed when she opened an unlabeled crate.

"What is it?" Jesse asked with a glance to Nert. He thought Perkins had assigned the cadet as a chaperone for the two staff sergeants, and Jesse was irritated at the suggestion that he and Shauna would fool around in such a serious situation. He also was irritated that, with Nert hanging around, they had no opportunity for even a *little* fooling around.

Shauna bent down over a hard plastic case and pulled out an object, cradling it in her arms. It was a Ruhar sniper rifle, intended for use by a Legion Commando team. "Say hello to my *leetle friend*," she said in her best Tony Montana impression.

Nert cocked his head while Jesse laughed. "The rifle is your friend?" Nert was confused. "That is not your assigned weapon, how can it-"

"No, Nert, I, Dude," Jesse chuckled. "That is a line from a movie, an Earth video."

"Oh." Nert averted his eyes. Not understanding the cultural references of the Mavericks always made him feel like an outsider. "I am sorry."

"There's nothing for you to be sorry about," Jesse patted the cadet's shoulder.

"There's a whole set in here," Shauna dug into the case, attaching the scope to the rail on top of the rifle. "Four magazines of guided ammo, there's a-"

"Hey, Darlin'," Jesse groaned. "You're not a sniper."

"I took the intro sniper course on Paradise," she insisted.

"The *intro* course," Jesse reminded her. "You were shooting at fixed targets, on a range."

"Some of the targets were moving."

"Yeah, along a track. On a range."

"I *like* it," she hugged the rifle to her chest.

Jesse knew when to give up. "Hey, if the Colonel says it's Ok, I'll be your spotter," he offered, knowing Perkins would veto the idea. Looking around inside the container, he tried to guess what was in the crates they hadn't opened yet. "What else we got here?"

Perkins did *not* veto the idea. "It would be useful to have a sniper with us," she mused, rubbing her chin. She had seen demonstrations of Ruhar sniper technology, and been extremely impressed by the weapon. It had an effective range of over six kilometers, and did not require the user to have line-of-sight to the target. Looking Shauna straight in the eyes, she asked "My recollection is you only took the intro course. You are confident you can use it effectively?"

"In an urban environment where ranges are shorter, yes," Shauna patted the rifle with affection. "The hamsters approved me to move on to the evaluation course, but we got shipped out to Jellybean."

"Right. You need a spotter."

"Colter volunteered."

"Why am I not surprised?" Perkins tilted her head.

Jesse fully expected to be told he could not ditch the platoon to play sniper with his girlfriend, but again, he was wrong. "All right. If we see an opportunity, you can play with your new toy. Colter, you go with her, and take Nert along, as a drone operator."

"Nert?" Jesse couldn't understand that. "He's not staying here?"

"No." Her intention had been to leave Cadet Dandurf and Surgun Jates behind, to provide security for the wounded. The aliens had overcome her objections through logic, though their reasoning had left a sour taste in her mouth. The mission was to rescue a Verd-kris platoon trapped in the city, a platoon led by a human. Perkins would be going in with a human force. For political purposes, it would be useful to have a Ruhar and a Verd-kris with her. If the rescue attempt failed or ended in disaster, the Ruhar public would see that all elements of the invasion force had participated.

Including political considerations in military decision-making sucked, but it was inevitable when working with allies. She had to remind herself that the entire operation on Squidworld was political in nature; the goal was to fracture Kristang society. No, the goal was to get Kristang society to fracture *itself*, and that was one hundred percent politics. "Nert will be coming with us." She lowered her voice and looked around for the cadet, seeing him still digging crates out of the cargo container. "I need to find something for him to do that is useful, but doesn't put him on the front line."

"Drone operator," Jesse nodded, knowing what Perkins meant. His assignment had gone from spotter to babysitter, it would be his responsibility to keep the cadet out of trouble.

A day that had started out crappy was getting even crappier.

To the shock of everyone including Derek, it was easy to assemble the glider. Despite the best efforts of the instructions to confuse everyone, they had the glider unpacked from its container and put together in less than fifteen minutes.

Perkins held a wingtip between two fingertips, being careful not to crush the delicate material. "This whole machine weighs less than three hundred pounds?" To say she was skeptical the aircraft would hold together was an understatement.

Derek checked the specs, his zPhone converting Ruhar measurements into human standards, then adjusting for the slightly lower local gravity on Stiglord. "On this rock, it weighs two-ninety-five." The gravity on the planet was slightly lighter than Earth normal, while the atmosphere was thicker, perfect conditions for a glider.

She bent down to examine the lower wing. For some reason she couldn't understand, the Ruhar had built the glider as a biplane, it had two main wings stacked one above the other. Plus another wing in the back that was larger than the usual wing she expected on the tail of an airplane. "You are sure this thing won't fall apart in the air?"

Derek held up his phone screen for her to see. "All the connection points have nanoscale sensors, and they're showing as nominal. This glider is simple and rugged. The glider is not the problem."

"What is the problem?"

"Well," Derek ticked off issues on his fingers. "Neither Irene nor I have flown one of these. Neither of us has ever flown *any* type of glider."

"In flight school, didn't you fly small planes for initial training?"

"Sure, but that was a *long* time ago. The aircraft we've been flying since then aren't designed to glide much if they lose power. Like the Dodo. We flew that down unpowered, but we didn't *land* it. This thing, even fully loaded, has a glide ratio of *seventy* to one. It can fly seventy feet forward while losing only one foot of altitude. The good news is, we could release a hundred forty miles from the city, and only need to be at about ten thousand feet when we start the glide."

"You are worried about flying a *low*-performance aircraft?"

"This is a *high*-performance ship, just a different type of performance."

"Can you do it?"

"Yes. We think so. After we release, we can get the feel of it in flight. The computer won't let us stall or go into a spin, so that limits the trouble we can get into. I am more worried about the landing, but that's not the real problem."

"What is?" She wished her pilots would get to the point instead of getting into geeky details she didn't care about."

"The Dodo pilots have never carried a glider, and a dropship is not the optimal platform for towing a glider. If they exceed a certain airspeed, they could snap the wings off. We can handle that, we will give them guidance."

"So, *what* is the problem?"

"The Ruhar pilots are refusing to tow the glider. They aren't trained for it, and it's not part of their mission parameters."

"Did you tell them that I will take full responsibility?"

"You can take responsibility for the *glider*. They're worried about damage to their dropship, and that is not Legion property."

Perkins's jaw set with anger. "I will contact General Ross."

"The hamsters don't work for him," Derek cautioned.

"We don't have time to screw around. I'll handle this, you get everyone and our equipment loaded in the glider."

The discussion about whether the Ruhar would tow the glider aloft became an argument, an argument that Perkins lost. The Ruhar would not be towing the glider.

That was why Derek and Irene got into an argument. "This is crazy," Derek hissed into her ear as the two pilots stood by the open door of the glider. "That city is a war zone. I can't let you do something so-"

"You aren't *letting* me do anything. One of us needs to fly the glider, and one of us has to tow it up, without breaking anything."

"Great. *You* fly the Dodo, and I'll-"

"Derek. I'm telling you that I trust you not to break-"

"Do *not* give me that bullshit. You're not going to win this with flattery."

"Then how can-"

"Rock, paper, scissors."

Irene couldn't believe that. "Seriously?"

"Unless you have a coin we can flip."

There was a challenge coin in one of her pockets somewhere, but that pocket was under her skinsuit. "Ok. On three. Three, two, one-"

"Wow," Derek whispered though the faceplate of his helmet was sealed. "This thing feels super flimsy."

"Is something wrong?" Irene asked from the Dodo flying above.

"No. I don't think so. I've never been in an aircraft made of tissue paper before." What he found most alarming was how much the airframe squeaked and groaned as it flexed. The tube-shaped cabin was crammed with skinsuit-clad soldiers who were resting their behinds on shelves that ran along both sides, with barely enough room in the middle for their legs. Seating positions were restricted to reinforced bands around the hull where people could rest their backs and pull down the straps to hold them steady. In between the bands of thicker material, a person wearing a power-assisted skinsuit could easily poke a hand right through the hull, that was so flimsy it was almost see-through. Derek had warned the soldiers not to sneeze or they might tear the wings off.

He was only half-joking about that.

"You want me to go around?" Irene asked.

"No. We either do this, or we don't. The Ruhar build good equipment, I'll trust them on this. Ok, I'm activating the balloon." He pressed a button, and on the top of the glider, a door opened, allowing a tiny rocket motor to send a canister into the air, trailing thin cables attached at four points to the glider. When the canister soared through two hundred seventy meters, it popped open and a balloon unfurled, rapidly inflating. "Hang on, everyone," Derek announced as he watched the strain on the cables increase. "And, we're up."

The ride up was surprisingly gentle, like an elevator. Derek held his breath as the flight computer handled the ascent. If needed, he had a limited ability to steer the balloon, but the handbook and his instincts told him to let the glider drift along in the wind, which was gusting near the limit of the safety envelope for lifting a glider. He hoped that with the glider loaded just below its maximum gross weight, it would be more stable. A sudden lurch to the left made him question that hope. Now that the glider was clear of the trees, the wind was blowing stronger. It began to lift and fall alarmingly.

"How are you doing?" Irene called, unseen above and behind him in the approaching Dodo.

"Fine. You have a handshake?"

"Yes. Nominal," she acknowledged that the computers of her Dodo and the glider were exchanging information. "You're bouncing around a lot."

"Yeah," Derek fought to keep his rebellious stomach under control. For the pilot to puke would be embarrassing. "I think's Ok, we- Ah, shit! We're *pogo-ing*!"

The glider was bouncing up and down on the tether cables, the motion growing in intensity like a pogo stick out of control. Derek put one hand on the lever that would cut the glider loose, looking out to guess where he could bring the aircraft down without killing everyone. The glider bounced again and the motion almost caused his hand to pull the lever unintentionally. Was the-

Yes, the motion was less severe. The tether was dampening the pogo effect. Not fast enough for him, and he had no control over it. A sharp jolt made the wings flex and he curled his fingers over the release handle. Another jolt like that-

The motion smoothed out as abruptly as it began.

"What happened?" Perkins asked from the seat beside Derek. He had reluctantly agreed to allow her in the copilot seat, if she promised not to touch any of the controls. He should have also insisted that she not ask any questions.

"Computer had to adjust. We're good now."

"I see the loop," Irene called out. Above the balloon was a loop of cable. She was supposed to snag it with the tailhook of the Dodo, a feature that was so rarely used, she had only practiced using the device three times, in a simulator. Now she was trusting the vestigial hook to tow a glider loaded with forty people. "I'm lining up. Can you steady your altitude?"

"Negative," Derek replied. "It's on automatic. The balloon is moving a lot in this wind."

"Is there any way you can-"

"I'm not actually *flying* this thing yet," he reminded the other pilot.

"Got it. Damn. This Dodo is a bitch to fly this slow."

In the copilot seat, Perkins cringed at the casual chatter of the two pilots. Maybe having a couple of pilots who were a *couple* was not always a good thing.

On the other hand, if chatting kept them calm and helped coordinate their actions during the tricky maneuver, she wasn't going to complain.

On the single display in front of him, Derek watched the dropship approach. Neither aircraft had engaged stealth and the Dodo was flying slowly enough, he could track its progress visually.

The first sign of trouble was when he saw the Dodo sink lower without dipping the nose, then rise. Irene was trying to match the action of the balloon, and the loop of cable above it. Keeping quiet so he didn't distract Irene, Derek crossed his fingers. The operation was completely out of his hands. The Dodo loomed larger, flying in a slightly nose-up attitude so the tailhook hung down clearly. He felt the glider gently bobbing up and down.

The Dodo's nose lifted and he saw Irene apply power. "I'm going around!" She called, pulling the big dropship up and to the right.

It wasn't enough. As she passed over the balloon, it was whipped by the wake turbulence of the spacecraft, and the downward thrust of the belly jets that were needed to keep the Dodo in the air at such low speed. To her horror, she saw the balloon twist around, spinning the glider with it and distorting the balloon into a sausage shape that had less lift. The whole assembly plunged toward the ground-

Derek's hand felt for the release lever while he spun around, the glider vibrating and the mass of his helmet making his head bob side to side. By the time he walked his fingers down the seat to touch the handle, his heart skipped a beat. They were too low! If the balloon didn't keep them in the air, the glider would fall into the trees below before the wings could produce lift. All he could do was close his eyes and pray.

Trees reached up for the belly of the glider, branches threatening to tear open the belly and spill the occupants out. Maybe some of them could survive the fall in their skinsuits, Derek wasn't betting on it.

Above him, the balloon flared out into a mushroom shape and retracted the tethers, pulling the glider upward away from the trees. Derek swore he felt branches slapping the belly before he rose into the sky again. "Let's not do that again, Ok?"

Irene's voice was possibly even shakier than Derek's. "Ok. Yeah. Coming around. I'm going to approach at a higher airspeed this time, I have to reduce the belly jet thrust."

"It's your call," Derek knew Irene had read the procedure for snagging a glider, and she was aware of the maximum safe airspeed. He also knew the wind gusts were above the safety limit. "We should wait until we're at a better altitude. I want more airspace below us if I have to cut loose from the balloon."

"Winds gusts are worse above five hundred meters," Irene warned.

"Make it three hundred meters."

"Three hundred, affirmative," Irene acknowledged.

"Is the balloon damaged?" Perkins asked.

"We lost one tether," Derek reported. "That's Ok, but we can't lose another."

"Should we cancel?" Perkins experienced a pang of doubt. She did not want to lose a platoon to an untested maneuver. Was she foolish to ask her pilots to try flying an aircraft they had never seen?'

"We'll give it another try, Ma'am."

"Second time's the charm?"

"We have more data now. The flight computers will learn from mistakes the first time."

The computers did learn. So did Irene. She snagged the loop with the tailhook on the second try, the balloon retracted into a ball and the glider accelerated a bit more jerkily that it should have. Derek kept an eye on the strain gauges of the tether and the wings. They were both near the redline, and Derek swept the glider's biplane wings back at sixty-two degrees for a high-speed tow. Beyond that, there wasn't anything to be done about it. The glider engaged stealth first, then the Dodo wrapped its own stealth field around itself, and climbed while turning toward the alien city.

"Picking up returns in detection range," Irene cautioned. She had flown the Dodo closer to the city than they had planned, pushing forward to reduce the distance and time the glider would have to fly on its own.

"Confidence?" Derek asked, his eyes on the glider's instruments. They were not showing any sensors bouncing off the hull, because they were inside the glider's stealth field.

"Forty-four."

"Too high." That number meant the active sensors around the city currently had a forty-four percent chance of detecting Irene's spacecraft. The Dodo was wrapped in its own stealth field, but it was big and heavy and surrounded by air heated by the engines. The dropship was much easier to detect, and Derek worried that Irene was pushing too far.

"We can go a bit farther," she suggested, with a note of pleading in her voice. "It's less than fifty percent."

"I want to get as close as possible," Perkins said. Derek was flying the glider, but she was in command.

"It's risky," he insisted. "The Dodo is a big target. Flying slowly like that, it creates a big disturbance in the air. Enemy sensors can detect the air turbulence, even if they can't see the ship."

"Another minute won't hurt," Irene said.

Derek hated it when he knew he would regret a decision. "Ok, but at the first sign of trouble, you cut the tether and get out of here."

They flew onward for another forty seconds, over the suburban outskirts of the city. The glider's own instruments were now showing that enemy sensor pulses were sweeping over them, with at most a nine percent chance the Wurgalan even knew there was an object in the sky. More active sensor stations were coming online around the city as the air defenses were activated.

The console flashed with a warning. Sensors pulses had converged near the glider, spiking the effective returns. The glider's tiny computer estimated a twenty-six percent likeliness that a sensor station on the ground had picked up an echo from the stealthy aircraft.

"That one was over seventy percent," Irene announced before Derek could ask.

"Too risky. This is good." They were closer to the objective than Derek expected, much closer.

Irene knew Derek was right. The glider would be safer on its own, even active sensors would have difficulty detecting such a small and stealthy object. "Ready for release. Be careful down there," she added. "Oh shit! Missile launch!"

Derek checked the console before detaching, all instruments were showing systems nominal. "Releasing now," he pulled the handle. "Get out of here!"

Freed from the restrictions of towing a glider, Irene advanced the throttles and dove for the ground, the countermeasure system popping out flares and sending out broad-spectrum pulses of electromagnetic radiation to confuse the incoming missile's targeting sensors. She was careful not to go supersonic, because the boom of compressed air would be like waving a flag to the missile, and she pulled up at a thousand meters. If the dropship flew too low, the enemy could see trees swaying in its wake. A stealth field only made the Dodo invisible, it did not mask its effect on the air that it flew through.

Briefly, she was tracked by another enemy missile that had lost its original target and was seeking another tasking. Then either the second missile found a better opportunity, or it lost sight of her. The Dodo's own system could not detect the original missile when it went silent, switching to passive sensors only.

That was a problem. The Dodo had active defenses in the form of maser turrets, but they mostly relied on guidance of an incoming missile's own active sensor pulses. She could sweep the area with her own sensors, if she were truly desperate. That would require dropping stealth and lighting up the area like a strobe light, and every enemy missile battery around the city would instantly lock onto her. She was not doing that unless there were no other alternatives.

Instead, she punched out more flares, turned and reduced power. Not knowing the location of the missile was worse than seeing an anxiety-inducing angry dot on the display as a missile tracked her.

Because she was focused on her own survival, she had no time to worry about what the glider was doing, and that little unpowered aircraft was not transmitting anything. Following a highway that ran away from the city, she kept waiting for the missile to switch back on its active sensors and race toward her. Why was it silent? Was it tracking her some other way?

Perhaps the tether was still attached and flailing around in the air behind her?!

No. The tether had detached from the Dodo's tailhook after Derek released it on his end, and the tailhook had fully retracted.

Where was the damned thing?

She flew on, one hand on the control pad and one on the ejection seat handle. *Where* was that missile?

The glider slowed immediately as it was no longer being towed through the sky, gently tugging Derek forward against the flimsy straps, that held him into a seat made of wire and tissue paper. First, he pushed the nose down to maintain airspeed, and the city grew to fill the display. Fires burned with columns of smoke scattered across the area, with concentrations of fires toward the center where the buildings were taller and clustered thickly together. With the corner of one eye, he saw a rocket soar upward from the city, burn out, tip over and plunge toward the ground. It struck something out of sight with an explosion less impressive than Derek expected.

He pulled back on the stick, reducing airspeed and flattening out the dive. The wings swung forward until they were straight out on each side, providing maximum lift. It was a sweet-flying aircraft, he discovered. It was flying, truly *flying*. Tons of thrust were not keeping him in the sky, and he was moving barely faster than a bird. The controls were light and responsive, the flight computer dampening out the effect of wind gusts automatically, allowing him to focus on guiding the craft along the chosen flight path.

The same enemy sensor pulses that had a better than even chance of detecting the Dodo were ineffective against the glider, or so the instruments told him. The wings and body of the lightweight aircraft were covered in what looked like tiny scales or feathers, which allowed the glider to slip through the air with barely a ripple. The glider generated no heat and no sound. Even in daylight, the stealth field made it close to invisible. The only danger that Derek had to worry about was getting hit by stray gunfire, or turbulence from passing aircraft. With the air over the city appearing to be a non-fly zone for both sides, he didn't need to worry about being caught in wake turbulence.

He did need to worry about where the hell to set the glider down. On the map images, the city had looked like it had plenty of highways and broad streets. The glider had been designed as a biplane so each wing could be short, allowing a pilot to tuck the craft into tight spaces. It still needed some space to land, and he didn't see any. "Uh, uh-oh," he squinted at the view in his visor.

"What?" Perkins asked from the copilot seat.

"The streets down there are all jammed with stalled traffic and lined with trees. The briefing packet didn't say anything about trees! I don't see anywhere we can set down."

Perkins was seeing the same data, and she agreed. Every street in the target zone was crowded with vehicles, some of them on fire. "What about a park?"

"Trees," he answered tersely. "Lots of trees. No good."

"There must be some-"

"Got it. I see it," he gently banked the glider, using the barest pressure with his fingertips.

"Where?"

"Roof of that shiny building. The tall one."

"We're landing on a *rooftop*?"

"It's perfect. The building is taller than the surroundings, so we'll have clean, undisturbed air without turbulence for the approach."

"That," she zoomed in on the roof. It was flat, with no obstacles. In fact, it was a landing pad for aircraft. Aircraft that could land and take off *vertically*. It was not made for gliders. "You can land in that distance?"

"Not a problem," he grinned. "Just call me 'Snake'. Did you ever see-"

She assumed her pilot was referring to a movie, and she did not like the idea. "If you got this idea from a movie, do *not* tell me."

"Uh-"

"There must be an alternative."

"Find it quick, because I need to line up this approach right now."

There was not an alternative. One street was relatively clear of vehicles, but two pedestrian bridges crossed the street. Another street had a section that appeared clear, until she saw Wurgalan in armored suits gathering under the overhanging awning of a building. "All right," she said to Derek as she passed targeting data to the Dodo, giving the coordinates of the Wurgalan. "You can really set us down on that rooftop?"

"Yes. Uh, I've never done this before, you know?"

"In the future, maybe you leave out that last part."

"Yes, Ma'am."

The glider came in high, Derek reminding himself that he had little airspeed to trade for altitude. He had been wrong about finding clean air, the gusty wind was swirling around buildings and the artificial canyons between them, and the target building was creating turbulence of its own. Air pushing against the flat far side of the building went straight up over the roof then sank, creating a downdraft that made the glider sink like a stone. Derek yelped, grateful for the steep approach that gave him a cushion of altitude. While he flew, he kept the laser rangefinder pointed at the rooftop, concentrating on the far edge of the rooftop. If needed, he could side-slip to slow down and avoid overflying the landing zone.

Except, that is exactly what the flight computer was telling him to do. An alarm was squawking in his ear, growing louder. The system wanted him to maintain altitude, fly over and past the roof, and bring the glider almost to a stall in the air.

How much did he trust the unfamiliar Ruhar equipment?

Did he have a choice?

Forty lives depended on his judgment.

"Screw it," he muttered, gently bringing the nose up.

"We're too high!" Perkins gasped a moment later as she saw the near edge of the roof slide by under the glider's belly. They were still ten or more meters above the roof and the aircraft was wobbling side to side, its already sluggish pace coming nearly to a stop. The nose staggered and wobbled as the roof disappeared behind them. "We're going to-"

There was a shudder as the glider's nose dipped sickeningly. Derek had misjudged the approach. The nose was pointing down at the space between buildings, and it was a *long* way down. Such a fall was not survivable.

"We're Ok. We're *Ok*," Derek repeated, lifting his hands off the controls and pointing upward.

The balloon had deployed again, this time in a triangle shape that distorted in the gusty wind, steering itself and the glider that now dangled from it. The wind was blowing them backwards, drifting the glider backwards over the roof, or she *hoped* the roof was below, because she couldn't see anything. She had a glimpse of the railing at the edge of the roof when the glider dropped straight down, yanked at the end of the tether, then hit the roof with a *thump* that jarred her back.

The right wings, hanging over the edge of the roof and caught in the updraft, lifted and kept going. "Ah!" Derek pulled a lever and the wings popped loose, rolling the body of the glider to the right. It hit the edge of the roof and the railing bowed out, bending against the mass not of the glider but its occupants. Derek yanked another lever and there was a sharp *BANG* sound as the rocking of the glider came to an abrupt halt. "We're down."

"The wind-"

"Wind's not a problem. That 'bang' was harpoons deploying from the belly. We're not going anywhere. Ok," he popped loose the straps that held him into the flimsy seat. "Everybody out! It's your show from here, Ma'am."

Emily Perkins took a breath to steady her nerves. She had to remind herself that the truly dangerous part would begin when people started shooting at her. "You almost gave me a heart attack, Bonsu. Did you know the balloon would bring us down like that?"

"I knew it was *supposed* to. But, it scared the shit out of me of too."

"Maybe you leave that part out of the after-action report?"

"Good idea."

Ninety kilometers to the west, Irene increased power and lifted the Dodo's nose, daring to climb out of the ground clutter. The missile that was tracking her had disappeared, or locked onto another target, or ran out of fuel.

*Or*, it was stealthily following her, waiting for the right opportunity to attack. Just in case, she popped out two decoys from each side and changed course, advancing the throttles again to gain speed. She could not remain in the area, the Dodo's fuel level was low so she had to fly it to a staging area.

Derek was in an enemy city, trying to rescue a trapped Verd-kris platoon, and there was nothing she could do about it.

Jesse crouched down and walked over to the edge of the roof, where Dave Czajka was peering over the edge, looking at the streets below. When he got to the edge, Jesse had an urge to spit, though his helmet was sealed. "What do you think?" Jesse asked over a private link.

Dave pointed to the columns of smoke rising all around them. "I don't like this. We're going in with a single understrength platoon, and no air cover, to rescue two Verd units who got stuck here? We have almost *no* intel on the opposition, our communications are being jammed, and we have to *walk* out of the city after we link up with the Verds? Command must be out of their freakin' minds to send us in like this. They expect us to perform a miracle, as usual."

Jesse shrugged and stepped back from the edge. "It's deja poo, man."

"Deja *poo*?" Dave asked.

"Yeah," Jesse checked his rifle again. "We've seen *this* shit before."

# CHAPTER TWENTY SEVEN

Scouts reported the stairwell of the building was clear, and the structure appeared to be empty. When she got to street level, Perkins took a moment to check the map on her phone. Captain Grace's last reported position was to the northeast, where pillars of smoke rose from the city. Sending a scout team ahead, Perkins got her platoon moving, with Derek Bonsu in the rear guard, carrying spare anti-aircraft missiles and looking like a fish out of water.

They needed to link up with the two Verd-kris platoons, or what was left of them, and proceed out of the city on foot. General Ross had authorized stand-off air strikes to cover the retreat, but it was too dangerous for Legion aircraft to overfly the city.

"Jarrett," Perkins gestured to a residential building that was taller than other structures in the area. She assumed it was an apartment building based on the balconies that were overhung with plants, though maybe that was how the squids liked their offices? "Take your toy and get up there. You can cover our egress route from up there. Colter, Dandurf, go with her. I need drones for a view of the area."

"Right," Jesse handed off the anti-aircraft rocket he had been carrying to another soldier, and took a box that contained recon drones. "Nert, you're with me."

Jesse ducked his head out the doorway from the stairwell, looking both ways. The hallway was dark, illuminated only by light coming from the narrow windows in the stairwell behind him. Doors were spaced regularly along the hallway, all of them closed. "Nert, get to the roof. Shauna, this way," he stepped into the hallway, scanning the length with the enhanced vision of his suit's sensors. Several articles of what he guessed were local clothing were scattered here and there, dropped in the residents' panic to get out of the city. When he got to the door at the end on the left, he stopped. "Is this good?"

"Yes," Shauna replied. That door lead to a corner apartment that should have a view toward where the platoon was going, plus back along the way they had come.

Jesse had kicked down doors before, first in Nigeria. It was harder than it looked, he had jammed a knee the first time he tried it. In movies and TV shows, the heroes kicked in doors easily, but in real life, reinforced door jambs resisted with substantial force.

The power-assist of his skinsuit, however, made it easy. Also, sealed in helmets where no one outside could hear him speaking, he didn't need to rely on sign language. "I'm going right," he told Shauna, "you go left."

The door yielded without a fuss, splinters of composite material like fiberglass showering into the apartment. Jesse ducked down to fit under the low doorway and went right into what he assumed was a kitchen that was a dead-end, with a pass-through to the living area beyond.

Shauna ran down the short entryway into the living area and pivoted left, the sniper rifle on her back knocking decorations off the wall with a crash. Jesse dashed out of the kitchen to join her. "You Ok?"

"Yeah," she scanned the room with her eyes and suit sensors, the visor was not alerting her to any threats. The room was empty. The outside wall on two sides was all windows except for a thin post in the corner, and sliding doors led to a wrap-around balcony. Inside, weird furniture was placed randomly and there didn't seem to be a table for eating.

"Yuck," Jesse exclaimed. "I hate this furniture."

Shauna stared at him. "Since when do you have an opinion about Wurgalan furniture?" Some of the chairs looked like shallow bowls without any back, she supposed it was comfortable for a being with multiple legs to curl up in. Sort of a beanbag chair for squids.

"My sister's house was filled with that horrible furniture from the 1950s," he said with disgust. "Mid-century modern, something like that? I hate it. This stuff looks like that, it's so, freakin' *sterile*, you know?"

"Jesse, I've seen that couch you and Dave had in your hooch. You shouldn't criticize anyone about their taste in furniture."

"Hey! That was a good couch. We got it for the ladies," he added just before his brain realized that perhaps that was not a smart thing to say to his girlfriend.

She was amused instead of insulted. "Uh huh. Did that couch see a lot of action?"

"Uh, well, none. But it *could* have. The guys we gave it to put it in a clubhouse, sort of."

"It is really not getting any action there either, trust me." On the floor next to one chair that was shaped like a saddle, was a bowl that had spilled a green mushy substance on the floor, a spoon with an oddly short handle lay next to it. "We interrupted breakfast," she muttered.

"You think they were just here?" Jesse swung his rifle toward closed doors on the other side of the room, suspicious. Who kept all their interior doors closed? He knew nothing about the living habits of squids, but it seemed odd.

"No, I meant they were having breakfast when we jumped into orbit. They probably cleared out when-"

From behind a door on the other side of the room was an '*Eep*' sound, and something falling with a thump. Then a soft scratching like tentacles scuttling on a floor.

Jesse rolled his thumb on a selector switch of his rifle, selecting low-velocity mode. If he had to shoot through a door or walls, he didn't want the rounds continuing clear through to the other end of the apartment building and splattering Wurgalan civilians. "Someone's still here! Get in the kitchen."

"I'm not going in the kitchen," she knelt beside one of the doors, rifle poised. "If they have armor-piercing rounds, you think a refrigerator will protect me?"

Jesse knew there was no good answer to that question. He stood on the other side of the door, standing up tall, his rifle ready. "Ready."

Shauna bashed the door open with a fist, figuring that if she used the door handle, anyone on the other side would see the mechanism moving. "What- Don't shoot! Don't shoot!" With her free hand, she yanked on Jesse's arm.

"I wasn't gonna shoot!" He protested.

"Sorry. I'm hyped up."

"Shiiiiit," Jesse groaned. "What are we gonna do with them?"

Four citizens of the planet were huddled in a corner near the window, behind a large oval-shaped bed. Two adults, it was impossible to tell male from female Wurgalan. Plus a young son or daughter clutching one of the adults fearfully. And a baby, cuddled by an adult. The adults were wearing loose-fitting garments, colorful enough that they might have been pajamas, or maybe that's just how squids dressed for work. The older of the two children had a yellow garment that was covered with logos or maybe cartoon characters, it was impossible to tell. Shauna lowered her rifle, pointing the muzzle to the side and crouching so she didn't appear so tall and intimidating. "They're terrified of us. This is why the rules of engagement had this city listed as off-limits. We don't want to get into complications like this."

Jesse switched on his helmet's external speakers. "Hey," he held the rifle in one hand, the muzzle pointed at the floor behind him. "It's Ok. Uh," he had no idea what else to say. 'Take me to your leader' did not apply, and 'We come in peace' was clearly bullshit.

The young Wurgalan let his tentacle legs do the talking for him. Dashing across the room with a bellow louder and deeper than Jesse thought a meter-tall being could make, the young one flailed its arm tentacles and flung itself at Jesse.

"Don't shoot!" Shauna repeated, backpedaling.

"Easy for you to say," Jesse grunted, holding his rifle back with his right hand while grasping the squid with the left, trying to keep it away from him. It wasn't easy, the thing wriggled like a snake, wrapping its flexible arms and legs around his forearm and hooking a leg into the toolbelt of the skinsuit. From somewhere, the alien squirted greenish slimy ink on his suit, or he *hoped* it was just ink and not something else. "Shit!" he shouted when he remembered he had spare magazines of rifle ammo and grenades on his belt. The grenades were not easy to activate and he didn't think a child would know how to use an alien weapons, but he sure as hell was not taking any chances. Worse than the thought of getting blown up was the thought of getting Shauna killed, and almost worse than that was the thought that someone would later download data from his suit and conclude that Staff Sergeant Jesse Colter was a *dumb shit*. He was wrestling with the thing and trying not to hurt it while its parents screamed, the baby cried and he finally eyeclicked an icon in the helmet visor to send an electric shock through the outside of his suit. The Wurgalan yelped and was flung backwards onto the bed, rolling itself into a ball. "I didn't hurt it," he assured Shauna, forgetting the external speakers were still on. The parents were calling out to their balled-up child who was shivering on the bed wailing, and the baby was crying and Jesse just wanted to be anywhere else. "Oh, hell," he spat as one of the parents reached out to the child but flinched back when Jesse took a step forward. "Shauna, hold my rifle." He let go only when she had a firm grip on the weapon. Bending down, he gently scooped up the child, tread carefully to the parents, and held it out.

The parent who was not cradling the baby took the child, and the young squid unfurled itself to wrap around the adult's barrel-shaped torso. "It's Ok. Nice squiddy." Jesse backed away, stepping backward and reaching out for his rifle. He took it, checking the weapon and keeping the muzzle pointed to the floor behind him. "What do we do now? We can't leave them there, they could climb out the freakin' window and signal the bad guys."

"Wait here," Shauna said, her boots clunking on the tile floor. "Here, there's a walk-in closet," she said from his left.

Keeping one eye on Mister and Mrs. Squid and the squidlings, although for all he knew it was Mrs. and Mrs. Squid, he checked where Shauna was standing at an open doorway. Beyond was a closet, really a small room. It was packed with clothes on racks and bins stacked on top of each other, but the center of the floor was clear. Switching his external speakers off, he asked "Is there another way to get out of there?"

Shauna ducked into the closet, checking behind bins and thumping walls. "Only one door. Let's get them in here."

"How? I wrestled with one squid today, I don't want four of them on me."

"Try *asking* them?" Shauna said with a note of exasperation.

"Oh, sure. Why didn't I think of that? What I am I supposed to say? Here squiddy, squiddy?"

"The suit can translate for you."

He bit back an 'I know that'. Eyeclicking through a short menu to select the Wurgalan common language, he turned on his external speakers again. "We do not want to hurt you," he tried. "Please get into the closet."

That got no reaction, other than one of the adults blinking a disturbingly human-like eye.

Next, he tried body language, backing up and waving one hand for them to follow. "Come with me. This way, please."

The squids only trembled more.

"This ain't working. Ok, no more Mister Nice Guy." He stood up tall and pointed the rifle to the right of the Wurgalan, at the floor between them and the window. "Please, move. *Move!*"

That got one of the adults moving. The one who held the child said something to his or her or its mate, and inched forward, hugging the side of the bed to be as far away from Jesse as it could. Shauna stepped aside, gesturing toward the closet. The adult scuttled past her and squeezed into the back of the closet.

"Ma'am? Sir? Whatever?" Jesse tried to get the other squid's attention, but it was huddled in on itself, clutching the baby. How could he reason with a squid? "It is not safe out here for the baby," he said truthfully. "People may be shooting at us," he pointed to himself and Shauna. "It's not safe for the baby. *Please*," he pleaded.

Either his apparent sincerity translated well, or the Wurgalan decided that if the invading aliens wanted it dead, it would already be dead. Slowly, warily, it oozed across the floor, watching Jesse and then Shauna. As it backed into the closet, the baby wailed with an ear-piercing sound, reaching out with its tentacles.

"Shit," Jesse mumbled. "I think it wants its toy." The baby was looking at a stuffed toy on the floor, some kind of fish, yellow with black spots. He bent down and treaded softly toward the baby, holding out the toy. The baby snatched it, and the loud wailing became a soft and pathetic moaning sound. "What now?" Jesse's knees sagged.

"Maybe it wants a glass of water," Shauna suggested.

"A glass of-"

"Did you ever try putting a baby to bed?" She asked. "They make every excuse they can think of."

"Yeah, Ok," Jesse remembered caring for an infant cousin. Those two days and nights were the longest year of his life. "They probably all need water. Watch them."

In the kitchen, he found a jug in a bin and filled it with what he hoped was drinkable water from a hose. The water looked clear anyway. While the jug was filling, he looked around the kitchen, picking up two plastic drinking containers. There was a round container that had a logo similar to the symbols worn by the young Wurgalan. Impulsively, he popped open the lid and saw it was filled with rings of a dry, beige substance. Tucking the food container under one arm, he got the jug and glasses in one hand and brought them into the closet, setting the items on the floor. With a wave, he closed the door.

"What was in that container?" Shauna asked as she helped him drag the bed over to the door so the family could not get out.

"Huh? I think that is Squiddy-Ohs, the breakfast of champions!"

Shauna laughed while she unslung the sniper rifle. "You're a good man, Jesse Colter."

"Hey, you ain't even seen my best qualities yet. Nert! What's your status?"

"The roof is clear, too clear. I am exposed up here."

"Launch both drones and come down here. If you see any squids along the way, encourage them to exit the premises."

Shauna and Jesse set up on the balcony, where they had a view to the east and north. Jesse had stretched a bed sheet over stacked patio furniture to keep prying eyes from seeing Shauna scanning the area with her rifle. In the living room, Nert was concentrating on flying the drones, one of them flying above and ahead of Perkins to provide a real-time view, and the other hovering nearby at a higher altitude. The second drone was both a communications link and to warn of approaching aircraft. Two anti-aircraft missile teams had split off from the platoon, taking up positions atop buildings where they had a clear field of view.

Too clear.

"Staff Sergeants Jarrett and Colter!" Nert called.

"Nert, for brevity, call us Jesse and Shauna," Jesse answered. "What is it?"

"I think I have found an enemy sniper team. Two of them are climbing up the scaffolding on that unfinished building. When they reach the top, they will see one of our anti-aircraft teams."

Jesse studied the drone images. Nert was right. To the north, two figures could be seen, hurrying up makeshift stairs and ladders on the interior of a building that was not much more than a framework of girders and rigid panels. They were climbing up between the fourth and fifth floors, but for all Jesse knew, they could be curious civilians, or even the local squid Nitwitness News team looking for a good camera angle. He zoomed in the image and saw that wasn't true. Though the lighting was poor, he could clearly see the figures wore mech suits and one carried an unusually long rifle. Sniper team for sure, and the other squid was carrying what sure looked like a regular-issue infantry rifle. "You're right. Shauna, we got trouble. Uh, shit," he checked his own scope. Their view of the enemy was blocked by another building and what Jesse guessed was a water tower. "We don't have line of sight."

"Don't need it," Shauna replied. "Which direction?"

"North-north east. See the-"

"I see it. If they get to the top, they'll be above us. Nert, link the drone signal to me." Shauna flipped up the cover on the end of the scope. She didn't need the scope for targeting, but having a real view with her own eyes gave her better situational awareness. "Are there any obstacles on the east side of that water tower?"

"Like, powerlines, stuff like that?" Jesse asked, studying the image from the drone through his own scope.

"Anything that could interfere with a bullet," Shauna answered.

"Ah, I don't see anything. Um, there's a flagpole sticking out from, um," he struggled to describe the cluttered urban environment.

"I see it. Good, that flag will tell us the wind speed over there. Nert, I need control of the drone camera."

"Camera is slaved to your scope," the cadet confirmed.

Shauna had to admit that Jesse was right; shooting the sniper rifle in a city was much more difficult than in the controlled conditions of a rifle range. She could not actually see the target, other than through images transmitted by the drone. The targets were moving, and their movement was erratic as they climbed stairs and ladders. Scaffolding and construction equipment were cluttering her view, she did not have a clean shot.

There was one place where there was a clean shot. "Two floors above where they are now," she told Jesse. "See where the stairs end?"

"You sure about that? It's a hell of a shot."

"I don't see another opportunity. If I miss, they'll be alerted, and *they* could be hunting us."

Jesse studied the image, imagining the flight path of the sniper round. "I don't know about this."

"You haven't seen this rifle in action. Trust me. But, if I do miss, we scoot out of here, look for another location."

"Ok," Jesse agreed with reluctance. "Nert, you heard that? If we have to run, pull the bed away from the closet. I don't want the Squidlings to be trapped in there, if some asshole calls an airstrike on this place."

"Okey-dokey," Nert acknowledged.

Shauna pulled her eye away from the scope to look at Jesse, and they both shook with silent laughter. '*Okey-dokey?* ', Jesse mouthed, and Shauna winked at him, then got back to work.

Using an invisible laser rangefinder from the drone, she pinpointed a spot at the top of the stairs where the enemy squids would soon be. The rifle responded with several proposed flightpaths for the rounds, along with flight times and confidence of striking a target at that location. Shauna chose the simplest flightpath, though it also had the highest chance of the enemy detecting where the rounds had been fired from. Timing was critical. Because each round had to fly a curving path around the water tower, then dive, flatten out its course and accelerate straight in, she had to fire just as the first squid soldier poked its head out of the unfinished stairwell. If the enemy changed their minds or were climbing more slowly than expected, she would have only a split-second to abort the impact and guide the rounds away into the sky so they wouldn't be detected. "Confidence eighty-three percent," she reported.

"I have faith in you, Darlin'." Jesse whispered, resisting the urge to pat her shoulder. She needed to concentrate.

Centering the scope on the spot she had designated as the target, she watched through the drone feed. The squids had not slowed down, though their little tentacle legs carried them up stairs faster than they climbed ladders. Breathing evenly to steady her nerves, she flicked a switch to confirm the flightpath option, and selected two rounds.

The instant she saw the helmet of the first Wurgalan appear at the top of the stairwell, she depressed the trigger button and felt the rifle vibrate. The two flechette rounds were expelled by magnets along the rifle barrel, with matched counterweights under the barrel traveling backwards with the same action so the weapon had little recoil. There was a barely-visible puff of dust as the sabot casing of the rounds were discarded and fell away, then she stilled her breathing as she concentrated on centering the drone's camera image on the torso of the first Wurgalan. A yellow circle appeared in the scope, confirming the first round had locked onto the moving target, receiving its guidance from the rifle scope through the drone.

Barely moving the rifle, she put the digital crosshairs on the image of the second squid to designate it as a target.

Given initial momentum by the railgun of the rifle, the first flechette soared upward, three tiny wings popping out to stabilize its flight. Vents opened in the round's midsection, allowing in air that fed oxygen to burn the solid propellant, and the round surged forward, curving around the water tower. With the turn completed, it had sight of the target building, though its actual terminal location was masked by an upper floor. The wings pivoted sideways to kill airspeed and the round performed a sideslip, the aerodynamic drag spilling momentum and dropping altitude rapidly. When its programming determined the target was in sight, its wings rotated and folded back, exposed only enough to keep the round flying straight and stable. The rocket motor kicked in at full power and it surged through the sound barrier, the last section of propellant containing its own oxidizer as air could not be gulped in fast enough.

As the round passed through the scaffolding around what was intended to be an office building, a charge kicked the penetrator warhead forward, discarding the rocket booster. An active sensor pulse flared out from the warhead, burning out its transmitter but getting a solid return that yielded a three-dimensional image of the target area. The warhead's brain compared the three-dimensional sensor image to the intended target and determined that it was, in fact, a Wurgalan. Traveling at eight hundred sixty meters per second, the warhead made a slight last-minute course correction that guided it to the spot selected by Shauna.

The mech suit worn by the Wurgalan soldier detected the active sensor pulse and reacted before the occupant knew what was happening, contracting artificial muscles at a speed that would have left the soldier extremely sore. That did not matter, as the suit was too slow. The warhead's course correction anticipated the movement of the target and it struck within two centimeters of its assigned goal.

Unfortunately for the target, Shauna's shooting was accurate. Unfortunately for her, lack of experience with the weapon had caused her to aim high. When the warhead struck, it tore the squid's head off and threw it backwards, striking the second soldier in the chest. The second soldier was flung back down the stairs, losing its rifle and staying alive because the second sniper round couldn't turn hard enough to follow the sudden movement of the target. That warhead flew through empty space where its target had been milliseconds before, continuing through the building and out into open air over the city. Having determined that it missed, the warhead self-destructed, turning itself into dust that rained down on the streets undetected.

"Shit!" Shauna jerked the rifle up, tearing her eye away from the scope. "I *missed*!"

"No," Jesse knew his role was to calm down the shooter, keep her head in the game. "You hit that first MFer. I can still see the second guy, he's sprawled on the floor below. Take a breath and chamber a round," he assumed the rifle did that automatically, the point was to get Shauna focused on her task. "I'm sending targeting coordinates to you."

"He is crawling away," Nert warned excitedly. "If he gets behind that-"

"Yes, *thank you*, Nert," Jesse barked.

"Sorry," the cadet muttered.

"I got this, I got this," Shauna said to assure herself. "Ah, that's not a great angle. Shit! Where is he?"

"He scooted behind that yellow cabinet," Jesse said softly. "He's got nowhere to go. You can do this."

"Right. Piece of cake." She selected two rounds with explosive-tip options. That caused a delay as the rifle's magazine had to align the second row of rounds with the feed slot. "No time for finesse." A circle appeared around the cabinet the enemy was hiding behind, she moved the crosshairs lower so it was centered less than half a meter off the floor. Her last adjustment was to instruct both rounds to strike the target simultaneously. "Here goes. On the waaay," she breathed out as she depressed the trigger button.

The first round kicked in its rocket at low power, waiting for its trailing companion to catch up. When the second round raced around the water tower, they swung wide away from each other, so the supersonic shockwaves they generated during the terminal phase of flight did not interfere and throw off their aim.

Both warheads struck the cabinet at converging angles. The first weapon struck something hard and solid in the cabinet and detonated, destroying the object and transforming it into a cone of shrapnel. The second warhead passed through the cabinet, its warhead exploding in a fan shape to splatter hot fragments on the head and back of the prone soldier. The armor of the soldier's mech suit mostly protected it from warhead, but not from the kinetic hammering force of the heavy object that had been in the cabinet. Chunks of dense metal slammed into the soldier, breaking bones and sending him spinning across the floor to the edge of the structure, where he broke through safety netting and fell out over the edge.

"Uh, what just happened?" Jesse asked, perplexed. "Anyone?"

"Damn it," Shauna kept her eye fixed on the scope, determined not to miss a third time.

"There might," Nert spoke. "I think."

"What?" Jesse demanded. The smoke and dust from the explosion totally obscured the target area. The enemy soldier could be running away, and not even the infrared sensors of the drone could see.

"Give me a minute, please," Nert pleaded. "I need to check- Yes! Look at this."

Jesse's visor blinked with an incoming video. Eyeclicking opened it, and he watched what Nert had found. In slow motion, he saw the explosion, and dust obscured the view. Then there was a brief sight of something falling off the far side of the unfinished building. He paused the video, ran it back and froze it, zooming in. "Shauna, you got him. He got thrown clear off the building. No way he survived that fall."

"Show me," she insisted. "Oh. Oh, that's, that's great."

"Miss Shauna?" Nert asked. "Mister Jesse?"

"Just call me Jesse, Nert. What?"

"This, doesn't feel right. I know this is war, but-"

Jesse knew what the alien cadet meant, because he felt the same way. "It's our job, Nert. Those guys would have killed our air defense teams, and then we'd have no chance of getting out of here."

"I don't feel good about this," the cadet said mournfully. "I have been in combat before, but this feels different."

"Nert," Shauna was scanning the area, irritated at Nert's whining. She did not want any distractions. "You don't have to feel good about your job, you just have to *do it*. Is that a problem?"

"No," Nert replied, stung.

Jesse felt bad for the teenager. Nert was not even supposed to be on the planet, he hadn't signed up for front line duty as spotter for a sniper team. "Hey, don't think about it. Shauna's right. We do our jobs now, think about it later."

"Ok," Nert was not any less miserable. "I do not see any other threats."

"Keep looking," Shauna ordered. The truth was, now that the excitement was over, she kept replaying in her mind the image of the first enemy soldier's helmet being torn off as the round she had fired impacted with terrible force. Replaying it again and *again*. Squeezing her eyes tightly shut did not make her stop seeing that horrible image. Worse than seeing the alien die repeatedly was knowing the second soldier had been terrified as he, or she or *it*, huddled behind the cabinet, not knowing where the shot had come from. She should have given the enemy a mercifully quick death. A skilled sniper would have done a better job of guiding the round, would have anticipated the effect of striking the soldier in front first. "I screwed up," she confessed over the private channel to Jesse.

"You did great," he assured her.

"I'm not a baby," she snapped. "I don't need to hear happy bullshit."

"You don't? Fine. Could you have done better? *Everyone* can do better, *every* time. No one is perfect. Did you learn something?"

"Yeah."

"Outstanding. That's the point of training and practice, it gives you experience. You had *zero* experience before, now you have two kills. You're the team lead," he added before she had time to think. "What do you need from us?"

"Uh, um, shit," she sighed. "I guess we need to decide whether to move. I fired four rounds, if the squids have decent sensor coverage around here, they could determine our location."

"Looks like power is out all over the city," Jesse observed. "Any civilian sensor network would probably be down, right?"

"Maybe. Jesse, this whole planet is a military training site. I don't know that we can count on this city having a civilian-grade sensor network."

"You're the team lead, we're here to support you. If you had completed the sniper course, what would you do?"

She snapped the cover closed over the rifle scope. "I'd shoot and scoot. We're outta here," she announced as she stood up.

"What about Squidly Squid and the squidlings?"

"Ah, damn it!" She froze. "We can't leave them in that closet."

"I'll get the squids, you and Nert scout another location."

"Right," switching to the team channel, she called the cadet. "Nert! We're moving. We need ideas for where to go next."

"The building under construction," Nert suggested immediately.

"Really?"

"Yes. It is tall, it has sightlines in all directions, and the enemy won't expect us to be there. We can use construction equipment as cover."

"Oh. Good. Jesse, you heard that?"

"Affirmative," he acknowledged from the bedroom. "I'll be right behind you."

Except he wasn't. Dragging the bed out of the way was easy with his powered skinsuit, and the translator made it possible for him to communicate with the squids. "Hey, come on. You need to go," he gestured for the Wurgalan family to scoot out of the closet.

"This is our *home*," one of the adults insisted. That one had a purple splotch on its head area, and was holding the baby.

"This whole building might be a pile of rubble real soon," Jesse shrugged. "Your choice." He was not going to force the aliens to come with him. They were not really his responsibility as a soldier.

As a human being, his responsibility was more complicated. "*Please*," he added. "I don't want you to get hurt."

"You invaded our world!" The other adult cried, the one Jesse thought of as no-splotch.

"It wasn't my idea. Look, I'm just doing my job," he checked the clock in his visor. He had already wasted too much time. "Think of your family," he pleaded.

"My mate is ill, and the lift mechanism is broken," said no-splotch. "She has difficulty with stairs. That is why we did not leave earlier."

"Oh, man- I don't believe this."


"Jesse?" Shauna demanded. "What are you *doing*? We need to go!"

"Yeah, I'll be there in a minute. Had a, complication," he grunted. The Wurgalan adult he had named Purple Splotch was surprisingly heavy. For safety, he had her cradled in his arms, his rifle slung over his back and deactivated. He was in the rear, with the young squid leading the way down the stairs, carrying a folded-up contraption with wheels. Next was Mr. or Mrs. No-splotch, he hadn't inquired about gender and he really didn't care. No-splotch was carrying the baby, and a bag of whatever they had thrown in it during the thirty seconds Jesse allowed for packing.

When they got to the bottom, the young squid assembled the wheelchair thing, and Jesse set Mrs. Purple-splotch in it warily, making sure none of the aliens reached for one of his weapons. "Ok, be safe," he waved as he backed away. "I have to go."

"Thank you," No-splotch said as he or she set the baby in the wheelchair with Purple-splotch.

"We do aim to be courteous invaders," Jesse couldn't resist joking. "Be sure to leave us a good review on Yelp, you hear?"

# CHAPTER TWENTY EIGHT

Ross really did not have time to worry about a single platoon, or even parts of three platoons. For the Stiglord mission, he commanded the entire Legion force, both human and Verd-kris. For political reasons, the Ruhar had declined to provide even a token ground-force, and the Achakai had refused to serve under a Verd-kris. So, it was Ross's turn to lead 'the whole shebang' as he called it. Admiral Kune was in charge of the Ruhar fleet, but Kekrando's small force of used starships took direction from Ross, and anything below sixty kilometers altitude from the surface was under Ross's command. It was a huge responsibility, and an even bigger headache.

Unfortunately, being 'in command' was more theoretical than factual. The greatest source of his headaches was not the bad intel provided by the Torgalau. It was not the astonishing fact that the Ruhar fleet had missed an entire layer of strategic defense satellites. It was not even the possible presence of more Bosphuraq warships in the system.

It was the freakin' *Achakai*.

Those ninjas might live up to their fearsome reputation as assassins, but in large-scale combat formations, they were hopeless amateurs. "Connect me with General Bailey," Ross ordered to whomever was tasked with communications that hour.

Contacting Bailey took four minutes, Ross used the time to review reports from the field and grow ever more angry, frustrated and depressed. That was not, he reminded himself, a productive use of his time.

"General Bailey is online now," the Ruhar technician reported.

Before Ross could say 'hello', Bailey spoke first. "Jeff, I know what you're going to ask, and we're already doing everything we can."

"You're telling me there's no hope we can get control of them?"

"I'm telling you there's no hope that *I* can get control. Not the Verds either. It needs to come from their leadership, and they're not cooperating."

"Shit. General Shakpeng assured me that his second-tier officers had gotten the message."

"They got the message all right. They're ignoring it. We shouldn't have been surprised by this," he added.

"Damn it. You're right. We should have insisted on a joint training exercise, or a smaller-scale op first."

"That wasn't ever going to happen, and we both know it. Once the ninjas moved out, they had to hit the objective quick. Jeff, it's not your fault."

"It's *somebody's* fault," Ross retorted.

"The Achakai have no one to blame but themselves," Bailey snorted with disgust. "A joint exercise would not have done any good. No amount of training would overcome their cultural baggage. These guys think anything other than an all-out frontal assault is dishonorable. They care more about their inflated sense of honor than they care about achieving the objective."

Ross let out a world-weary sigh. "What do you need from me?"

Bailey didn't hesitate, he had an answer ready. "Cover, when I bypass the ninjas and advance without them."

"Is that practical? We don't have enough boots on the ground here."

"You know what Napoleon said about allies?"

"Yeah. It's better to fight against allies, than to fight with them."

"He must have anticipated these assholes. They're not really allies anyway."

"No, they are not," Ross agreed with disgust. "They are our *customers*."

Bailey snorted. "Mercenaries hiring mercenaries. That makes us, what? Subcontractors?"

"I don't want to say what that makes us. Fools, probably. I don't like the idea of a human commander sending the Achakai on suicide missions."

"Believe me, they are going to do it anyway. This channel is secure?"

That remark made Ross pause. "Secure as it can be, this is Ruhar tech."

"It's Ok if the hamsters listen," Bailey used the term to irritate any Ruhar who tapped into the conversation. "Sir, to be frank, I expect the ninjas to turn on us, as soon as it looks like the Wurgalan will surrender this rock." He waited. Ross didn't respond. That told Bailey his superior had the same fear. "The only thing better than gaining clan status by forcibly taking a planet, is following that by killing humans and Verds who are enemies of the Kristang."

Ross had the same concerns, so did most of the leadership at UNEF-HQ. And the Verd-kris leaders were even more concerned about the trustworthiness of the Achakai. The ninjas had refused to be placed under the command of any Verd-kris, male or female. They would not even coordinate their actions with Verd units, and insisted that any attack be spearheaded by Achakai troops. That would not have been a major problem if the ninjas used rational infantry tactics. Instead, their response to every situation was immediate, unceasing attack with everything they had until the enemy was overwhelmed. Or until the last Achakai died in the assault. In most cases, the disciplined Wurgalan troops were happy to slaughter the attacking waves of Achakai, leaving human and Verds to deal with the mess. Legion commanders had initially been dismayed by the actions of the Achakai, then adjusted tactics to hit the Wurgalan effectively while the enemy was distracted by the mindless assaults of the ninjas. Unfortunately, there had been several incidents of friendly fire, or not-so-friendly fire, of Achakai shooting at the Verds. The Verds had of course shot back, with the result that Verd units had to be kept so far from the Achakai, that it was difficult for the Verds to exploit any breakthrough achieved by the frontal assaults of their cousins. The Achakai tolerated human troops supporting their attacks, because they were openly disdainful of humans and expected little to nothing from them. "That's why Admiral Kune will be keeping part of his fleet overhead, until the last Legion boot leaves this rock."

"That's great, assuming we can trust the hamsters if the shit hits the fan here."

"Officially, I have every confidence in the Ruhar to fulfill their obligations."

"Unofficially?" Bailey asked.

"Unofficially, we are thoroughly fucked if the hamsters bug out, so there's no point worrying about it. Give me a bottom line: can you hold your sector?"

"Yes, if the second wave doesn't take more than forty-eight hours to get here. I can use the Achakai as cannon fodder to keep the squids' heads down, while I secure Objective Tango. After that, I'll be in a defensive posture. I don't have the numbers or the ammo to do anything else."

"I don't like this, but, go ahead. I'll talk to Shakpeng, *again*. Do what you gotta do. One piece of advice?"

"What's that?"

"Maintain a half-kilometer distance between our people and the ninjas. In case we need to hit our allies with an orbital strike, if you know what I mean."

"Ha," Bailey laughed without humor. "I know what you mean. Bailey out."

The next call was to the Achakai commander, General Shakpeng. The assassin leader's title was much more grand than merely 'General', and he had only reluctantly conceded to using Legion-standard ranks for the operation. Ross had come away mostly impressed with Shakpeng, the one time they met in person. Belatedly, he realized that what he had perceived as discipline and determination was actually inflexibility and stubbornness. While he waited impatiently for the alien to respond, he pushed aside reports from the field and tried to develop an awareness of the overall situation.

The invasion plan always had too few troops to take on the defenders, especially not the three-to-one ratio considered necessary to take strongly-held enemy positions. Learning the intel provided by the Torgalau was wrong made less difference than it could have, because the Legion knew from the start they wouldn't have enough boots on the ground to overwhelm the natives. The invasion plan had relied on orbital firepower to even the odds, and on mobility allowing Legion forces to defeat the static enemy in detail. Concentrate combat power against one objective at a time, and keep the enemy guessing where they would hit next. The Wurgalan would try to be strong everywhere, while the Legion could shift units around as needed. Control of the surface did not require the invaders to crush every last shred of resistance, only to knock out enough of the enemy's combat power that their leaders would realize the fight was hopeless.

That was the plan.

As Ross knew, no plan survives contact with the enemy.

Facing far greater numbers of the enemy than expected, and with the second wave delayed indefinitely, Ross had shifted the goal for the first wave. Initially, the first units were tasked with hitting enemy military bases within a relatively small area of the largest continent. Restrict the surface area the Legion had to cover, and reduce the distance that Legion units would need to travel to support each other. Suppress enemy resistance in that area, then expand outward to exploit opportunities as they developed.

Now he had shifted to a strategy of holding the ground they had taken, attacking only to prevent the enemy from concentrating their own forces. By consolidating his own combat power, he hoped to hang on long enough for the second wave to land.

In the worst case, if Admiral Kune decided the risk of Bosphuraq warships in the system was too great, having his forces spread across a relatively small area would make it easier and quicker to pull them off the surface.

That was the theory, anyway. The Legion had never performed an evacuation under fire, and all the simulations he had participated in showed disastrous results.

General Shakpeng finally responded. His tone was haughty but also defensive, like someone who knows they are going to get scolded by an authority figure they do not respect. "General Ross. You are calling to congratulate me on our victory at Objective Lima?"

The actual words Ross wanted to say would not have been productive. Oftentimes, being a general officer meant utilizing political skills. Which was a polite way of saying that he had to kiss the asses of people, when they deserved a boot instead. "Your men fought with, ferocity," he said carefully. With the Achakai, it was best not to use gender-inclusive terms like 'soldiers' or 'troops' or 'people'.  The ninjas were disgraced Kristang warrior caste, but they were still warrior caste to the core. In Kristang society and especially in the ruling warrior caste, females were servants, and the Achakai did not like any implication that they were any different from the clans they aspired to emulate.

"Perhaps sensor coverage of the battle could be provided to your, *people*," Shakpeng said with disgust. "Seeing my men acting with bravery might inspire the *Uglashka*," he used a very nasty term for the Verd-kris, "to shake themselves out of their timid nature."

Ross pressed the mute button while he took a deep breath. The battle at Objective Lima had been a mess, with the Achakai frontal assault losing forty-five percent of their soldiers in the initial push, and sixty-four percent overall. What should have been a simple small-unit attack had instead resulted in over three hundred casualties by the ninjas, against thirty-two Wurgalan killed. The squids had pulled back to a secondary position and dug in, only being forced out of the base by a combined human and Verd-kris attack. Lifting his finger off the mute button, he chose his words carefully. "General Shakpeng, the courage of your men is admirable."

"Thank you, we-"

"Their lack of discipline is *not*."

"*What*?!" The alien screeched.

"We *discussed* this. Several times. Your tactics are not-"

"My men do not flinch from battle! They acted with honor, and we were victorious! You-"

Ross massaged his temples to relieve the headache he felt coming on. "There is no honor in stupidity."

He was not surprised that the conversation went downhill from there. After much shouting on both sides, Ross appealed for reason. "General Shakpeng, the Kristang have historically used your people as assassins, or as cannon fodder. The warrior caste clans never trained your men how best to utilize their combat power, because they *fear* you. Your leadership hired the Legion because we *know* how to fight on the ground. *Please* listen to my unit commanders."

To Shakpeng's credit, he was not entirely bullheaded. "General Ross, if I may be completely honest, part of the issue is that my men do not foresee us being victorious in this operation. We landed with the goal of seizing this world, and securing a future for our people. Now that the *callaras* have shamefully refused to land the second wave, my men see only doom for us here. They cannot win, so they must strive to perform with such, as you said, ferocity, that their honorable sacrifices here might result in the clans having at least some mercy when they inevitably crush our people."

"Shit," Ross said without meaning to speak aloud. "Shakpeng, the odds of us winning here are better if we act together."

"Perhaps. General Ross, you are not a stupid man. Have you considered that this refusal to land the second wave is part of the Ruhar plan?"

"Excuse me?"

"You must suspect it. By landing us here, Ruhar have already accomplished their goal of fracturing and weakening Kristang society. They do not need us to *win* here. They may not want us to win, for in time, we would grow strong and threaten them."

Ross knew his response was weak, because his mind was racing. Shit! Could the Achakai leader be right? "You're forgetting that this operation was developed by the Legion, not the Ruhar. They are only providing support. It was *our* plan."

"Ah, yes. Their military does not like the existence of your Alien Legion, and they fear the potential power of the traitors who call themselves Verd-kris. By giving excuses to prevent landing the second wave, they strand a significant part of the Legion's combat power here. Failure to take this world could destroy the Legion. That would please both the Ruhar military, and the Peace Faction in their government. The Ruhar are widely known to be clever and devious. They agreed to participate in this operation because it favors *their* agenda. Surely you are not so naive that you cannot see how both of us have been used?"

The Achakai had given Ross a lot to think about. "The presence of Bosphuraq warships here is a fact, that can't be denied."

"I do not deny it. I *do* question whether the Ruhar were, as they claim, unaware of those ships being in-system. It is a convenient excuse not to bring in the second wave. I suspect it will soon be used as a reason why the Ruhar will not risk their ships to evacuate us. General Ross, to the Ruhar, the optimal outcome of this operation is failure of the invasion, destruction of my people, disruption of Kristang society, and the dissolution of the Alien Legion."

Ross couldn't argue with anything the ninja leader said. "General Shakpeng, politics is above my pay grade." He hoped that would translate properly, he had forgotten not to use slang when talking with aliens. "I can't affect what the Ruhar do, I'm responsible for what happens on this rock. We need to hold on down here, or the Ruhar won't need an excuse to abandon the operation. Your tactics are bleeding your force dry, and accomplishing less than we need. *Please*, talk with your men. Get them to understand that winning a battle has its own honor. The enemy doesn't care how you defeat them."

"I will consider it," Shakpeng said with the lack of commitment people use when they have no intention of complying.

"Great." Ross flipped a middle finger at the microphone. "We both have work to do."

"Yes. Shakpeng out."

"Shithead," Ross breathed as he saw the communications link blink off. "Damn it!" He slammed a fist on the console.

"Sir?" One of his staff called from behind him.

"Nothing." He waved a hand. What Shakpeng said bothered him deeply. Maybe the Legion was getting screwed on Squidworld, just like they had gotten screwed on Fresno? The Ruhar could indeed be clever and devious. He personally knew of only one person with a mind like that. He needed to talk with Emily Perkins about it.

Unfortunately, his orders had dropped her headquarters platoon in the middle of a city that was developing into a major war zone.


Perkins dropped down as the rocket raced toward her, looming as a red dot centered in the white fog of its exhaust. She had only a glimpse before she fell down behind an overturned car, thinking it was aimed straight at her. The rocket zoomed overhead with a hissing *whoosh-BANG* as it struck a building five meters too high, the shooter's aim having been thrown off by the loss of his head just as he pressed the trigger.

Perkins didn't know why she survived, she felt chunks of concrete and steel and composite whatever raining down on her to *ping* off her helmet and *thump* onto her back. One particularly large chunk, coming down as she thought the debris had finished falling, knocked her to the ground and took her breath away. Unable to speak, she crawled until she could stagger to her knees, fearing the wall behind her would collapse.

"Colonel, are you," Sergeant Liu turned away to add a burst of rifle fire to the fusillade directed at one Wurgalan soldier who was particularly brave, stubborn or just plain *stupid*, depending how you looked at it. The soldier was the last survivor of the squads who had fought their way across the city square, smashing through the invader's defensive lines and surging toward the heart of the enemy formation. Unfortunately for the over-eager city defenders, the Legion platoon had fallen back deliberately, allowing the enemy squads to pass through the front line so they could be attacked from all sides. Too late, the Wurgalan had realized their mistake and attempted to withdraw, an option that was closed when the Legion troops sprung the trap and slammed the escape route shut. Now there was only one survivor of the three squads, holed up behind a smashed truck and under the façade of a building that had slumped down over several vehicles. The lone soldier was putting up a furious if ultimately doomed fight, expending ammunition at an unsustainable pace. Up the street, another squad of Wurgalan had taken cover inside the first and second floors of buildings, providing intermittent cover fire for their trapped comrade. That squad had fired the rocket at Perkins, and was still causing a problem. The best position for returning heavy weapons fire was exposed to the lone soldier, frustrating the efforts of the Legion platoon to end the enemy threat.

Liu looked back at Perkins just as the determined Wurgalan soldier sent another burst of explosive-tipped rifle fire spraying the street, followed by a grenade that blew a smashed car two meters off the ground, almost coming down on the head of Surgun Jates.

"Is it too much to ask," the Verd surgun bellowed over the open channel, "for someone to *please* kill that asshole for me?"

The response was seven rockets converging on the lone soldier's position, pulverizing the truck and causing the sagging building façade to collapse completely, crushing everything underneath.

"Colonel?" Liu crouched over her leader. "Are you injured?"

Perkins checked the status icons in her visor. The suit was fully operational and according to the medical monitor, she was in peak health. Based on how her back ached, how everything ached, the medical monitor did not know a damned thing about human physiology. "Just my pride. Captain Grace!" She raised her voice to speak over the command channel. "This would be a good time to join us."

"On the way, Colonel," Grace grunted, sounding like she wasn't feeling in peak health either.

The Verd platoon Grace had inherited, and the remains of the Verd platoon who crash-landed near the city center, had linked up but been unable to get away from the pursuing Wurgalan. Every time the Verd-kris rear guard thought they had broken contact, a fresh group of the city defenders appeared, and the retreat attempt bogged down. Too many of the Verds were injured, needing able-bodied soldiers to carry them, and as the urban battle wore on, the definition of 'able-bodied' required a lower standard. Almost everyone had some glitch or damage affecting their powered armor. Powercells were not yet a problem but soon could be, and ammunition was running low. The platoon had a single anti-aircraft missile that showed a glitch in its targeting system, the gunner thought the missile would launch but it couldn't hit anything other than by accident. If they had to fire the missile, their only hope would be to scare away the enemy aircraft. So far, they had not been attacked again by air.

When scouts from the Legion platoon, from the *Mavericks*, linked up with Dani's beleaguered group, the Verds thought their prayers had been answered. Until they learned that the Mavericks unit was also engaged with the enemy, and getting out of the city would be a long, tough fight.

Keeping her head down, Dani ran to the Mavericks commander. "Hello again, Ma'am." The two had not spoken face to face since they were pulled off Fresno.

"Captain Grace," Perkins nodded. "I wish we met under better circumstances."

"Sorry about this mess." Dani switched to the private channel. "I know, good initiative, bad judgment. I didn't expect to get stuck in the city."

"I'm sure it seemed like a good idea at the time," Perkins couldn't keep the sour tone from her voice. She remembered when she was a captain, and all the mistakes she had made. It was a chaotic situation, Grace had done the best she could.

"Ma'am, if I can speak freely, I still think it was the right call. We had no communications, I had to make the decision based on what little I knew. I'm a human in command of a Verd unit, we were notified of a Verd unit down in the city. If I had refused to attempt a rescue," she let out a breath. "That would be *bad* optics. Our alliance with the Verds is not the most stable relationship."

"You may be right, Grace." Perkins did not want to argue politics in the middle of a firefight, though she suspected the young captain was correct about her assessment. Grace was also a psychologist, not infantry. She truly had done the best she could. Considering the number of troops the Wurgalan were committing to the battle in the city, a battle neither side wanted to fight, Grace's actions had caused major trouble for the enemy's plans to throw the invaders off their planet. That distraction had to be worth something.

It would be worth more if Perkins could get all her people, humans and Verds, out of Slugtown. "Jates! We need to move!"

The unfinished building was a good location for a sniper's nest, with sightlines in all directions, and decent cover could be arranged. The problem was that it felt awfully exposed. As they climbed, their priority was concealment rather than speed, so they sought routes that would bring them to the upper floors without being seen from outside. When she was trying to get a clear shot at the enemy soldiers, Shauna had been frustrated by the amount of construction equipment, scaffolding and building supplies stacked haphazardly around the open floors, but once she got to the second floor of the structure, she had the opposite feeling. She felt exposed from every direction. Who was watching from *that* office building to the north, or *those* apartments on the west side? The curious eyes watching them did not need to belong to military or police, any concerned citizen could report seeing three aliens. Shauna felt certain that the Wurgalan would not hesitate to drop ordnance on the unfinished structure if they thought there was a decent possibility it was occupied by invaders. If the enemy knew a Legion sniper was using the tower's jumble of girders and scaffolding to cover several city blocks, her life expectancy would be measured in minutes.

Nert was wrong about one thing, and Shauna should have considered it before starting the climb. *Someone* knew that two Wurgalan soldiers had been assigned to climb the tower, and they would be missed when they failed to report. Maybe their mech suits had already reported their deaths, and reinforcements were being sent to investigate. "Hey, Jesse," she hesitated at the bottom of the stairs that led to the second floor. "I'm not sure about this."

Jesse's internal reaction was an irritated 'I wish you told us that *before* we got here', but that is not what he said. "OK, why?"

"If the squids know those guys," she pointed upward, "are dead, their first thought won't be that a sniper is in the area. They're going to think the Legion is occupying this place."

"Ah, shit," he realized she was right. "What's Plan B?"

"Wait, please," Nert held up a hand. "If you were here, and you killed enemy soldiers who found you, what would you do?"

Jesse had to laugh. Nert was a cadet, and he had more sense than two seasoned staff sergeants. "We would get the hell out of here, pronto. The squids won't expect us to stay in a location that's been compromised."

"Huh," Shauna agreed. "Good point. The squids will be paying attention to this place, though. I don't like how exposed we are."

Nert pointed to the center of the structure. "That elevator shaft is empty. We could climb up inside it, and no one would see us."

Jesse looked to Shauna. "What do you think?"

"I think," she tugged tight the sling holding the sniper rifle. "Maybe Nert should be team leader."

They crawled out of the elevator shaft on the top floor, Jesse going first and helping the others navigate the awkward transition.

Shauna looked around. "This is good." The roof above them had a big hole in the center, where equipment and supplies had been lowered by crane. The top floor was especially cluttered, with stacks of supplies arranged toward the outside of the surface. "Be careful," she pointed to a gap in the concrete-like floor panel. The floor was honeycombed with holes and trenches where cables were being installed. Leaning over one wide trench, she whistled. "It is a *long* way down if we fall."

Nert walked over to a stack of panels. "I can lay these over the holes near the elevator shaft. If we have to get out of here, we will need to move quickly."

"Good idea," Shauna smiled at the cadet with affection. "See, Jesse? Nert should be team lead."

"Oh, no thank you," Nert shook his head. "That is above my pay grade."

"Pay-" Jesse laughed. It was always funny when aliens used human expressions. "Nert, I will cover the holes. You check on our drone, see if we have unfriendly company around here."

In each direction from the top floor, there was good cover. Without a target to shoot at, Shauna set up near the elevator shaft where she was less likely to be seen by an enemy drone. Their own drone had detected a rival enemy device zipping past them from the east, all three of them froze as the Wurgalan drone flew past, unseen. It disappeared behind the water tower, moving at high speed and not slowing down. Whatever the drone was searching for, it was not in their area of the city. The drone was a reminder that even if they could not see the enemy, the enemy might see them.

Jesse looked at Shauna cradling her new sniper rifle, wondering if he had a romantic rival. She sure seemed to love the thing. "Hey, Darlin'," he whispered.

"What?" She was concentrating on the view through the rifle scope from the drone, getting the rifle's brain to build up a picture of the surrounding area.

"The Army taught us that indirect fire can be more important than direct fire, right?"

"Yeah, so?"

"I'm wondering. That toy you have can shoot sideways, around corners, drop ordnance straight down on the enemy's heads, you know? Maybe this type of sniper rifle is *indirect* fire?"

"Show me a target in my line-of-sight," she whispered back with grim determination. "And I'll show you what direct fire looks like."

"Nert," Jesse called, "can you move the drone south about two blocks? I want to see-"

"We must be very careful about moving the drone," Nert warned. "It is almost invisible when hovering, but motion sensors might detect it. We have been lucky so far, I am surprised the drone has lasted this long."

"Right, got it," Jesse wanted to snap that he was aware of the recommended techniques for operating sensor drones, but he knew Nert was only trying to help. The sensor drones provided to the Legion by the Ruhar were not state-of-the-art, they didn't need to be against the Wurgalan. Most of the drone was a hydrogen-filled blimp that allowed the device to hover without any vertical thrust from its tiny propellers, so it barely disturbed the air around it. Packing a stealth field generator into a device the size of a sparrow would be almost impossible, and such a field drew so much power, the powercells would last only minutes. Instead of artificial stealth, the drone relied on coatings that absorbed sensor pulses, and chameleonware that gave it the appearance of the background sky, cityscape or whatever was around it. Still, Jesse knew the drone was living on borrowed time. "Can you move it slowly?"

"Jesse," Shauna asked. "What's up?"

"I'm seeing something in reflections off the windows of that office building with the blue-tinted glass," he explained. "Something's moving south of us."

Shauna had been scanning to the north and hadn't seen anything important. "I'll check the- Yeaaaaah, I see it," she agreed. "I can't tell what it is. A truck?"

Jesse snorted. "If that's a truck, the squids must have a monster truck rally planned for the weekend."

"Nert," Shauna decided. "Move the drone."

"Ok," the cadet acknowledged. "I have to lift it first, to reel in the cable, or it could get tangled." Instead of using propellers to keep the drone in position, Nert had deployed a harpoon on a cable. It was not actually a harpoon, the end was sticky rather than sharp, he had it glued to the balcony of an apartment. When he got the harpoon attached and played out the cable so the drone hovered in the ideal position, he had been proud of himself. Now he worried that when he released the harpoon, the gusty wind would snag the cable around an obstruction before it could be reeled in.

His fear was realized when the cable looped around an antenna projecting out from another balcony. The drone was jerked downward and he severed the cable in the middle, instantly filled with doubt that he might have been too hasty. With the wind coming from the east, propellers were needed to reposition the device to the south, and propellers not only disturbed the air, they created sound waves. He took a risk by spilling hydrogen from the blimp and the drone dove toward street level, where the wind swirled in the canyons between buildings, but the wind also wasn't blowing as hard. When he ordered the drone to rise again, a filter mechanism began extracting hydrogen from the air, reinflating the blimp. "Drone will be coming around the corner in- Oh, my!" He exclaimed.

"Holy sh-" Was Jesse's reaction. "Damn. Is, is that a *tank*?"

The tank, if that is what it was, was moving across an intersection. The size of a typical city bus they had seen, its surface was smooth, without any windows or doors. The dark gray skin had black lines from nose to tail and side to side, in the form of hexagons about half a meter across. Not even a single antenna blister marred the smooth surface of the vehicle, shaped like a teardrop when viewed from the top or sides, with the blunt end going first.

Shauna zoomed in the drone image. "How is it moving?"

Jesse studied the same image. "I don't see any wheels or tracks. Nert, scan the street behind it, see if it made marks there."

"Just these," Nert sent an image, showing the entire roadway behind the tank was sunken in, crushed under the weight of the vehicle. The compressed surface was rippled side to side. "Maybe it uses rollers?"

Jesse whistled. "However it moves, it is damned *heavy* to crush the road like that. All right, we need to call this in. The platoon needs to know-"

"Ah!" Nert cried. "We just lost the drone!"

Shauna smacked the floor with a hand. "Damn it!"

"Wait, wait," Jesse said softly. "Maybe the drone is just being jammed. Nert, if that happens, if the drone loses contact, it is supposed to go into safe mode and return to us, right?"

"Correct," the cadet confirmed. "I do not think the drone is being jammed. Just before we lost contact, there was a heat spike, like it was hit by a directed-energy weapon."

"Yeah, well," Jesse wasn't giving up hope that easily. "We'll know for sure if we just wait a minute, so everyone, chill."

A minute went by and there was no response from the drone. "Nert, stop trying to ping it," Jesse ordered. "That could give away our position."

"What should we do now?" Shauna asked, flipping the cover back over the scope of her sniper rifle. "We need to warn the platoon. That thing is headed in their direction, and it's not a taco truck."

Jesse's stomach growled, reminding him that he hadn't eaten since a hasty breakfast aboard the *Big Mac*. Two glazed donuts and coffee had been enough not to upset his stomach during the combat drop, now he regretted not eating something more substantial. He sucked on a tube inside his helmet, taking in water and tasteless nutrients. "If that thing *was* a taco truck, I'd tear it apart with my bare hands right now."

Shauna made a disgusted sigh. "Really?"

"Hey, don't tell me you're not hungry too," Jesse defended himself. "I can't think on an empty stomach." There was food in his pack, but he would need to open his faceplate to eat. That could wait, Shauna was right. "Nert, before we moved the drone, it was showing the signal strength from the other drone with the platoon was only eighteen percent. You agree?"

Nert reviewed the data stored by his suit. "Yes. Even if we tried a full-power transmission from here, the platoon will not hear it, without our drone to act as a relay."

"And it would give away our position," Jesse added.

Shauna knew they were right. She also knew they could not fail to act. "We have to try *something*. The platoon needs to be warned there is a freakin' *tank* headed toward them."

Jesse considered their options. "Maybe we can- Hey, darlin'," he forgot they were in combat. "What's the effective range of those sniper rounds?"

"That depends on a lot of factors," Shauna answered. She hated being asked to give simple answers to vague questions. "If it's a straight line-of-sight shot, where I can crank up the muzzle velocity, then the range-"

"This won't be line-of-sight. The round needs to curve around a hundred-eighty degrees," he explained. "I just sent you a map of the city. See that tower under construction, to the southeast of us? It's shaped kind of like a skinny egg."

"Uh, yeah." In the city center, a quarter of the high-rise buildings were under construction, so the skyline looked like a forest of scaffolding and cranes. "What about it?"

"Can you make a shot from here, that will curve so the round is coming from the *east* as it passes through that egg tower?"

"Whew," she whistled. "The round would have to go past the egg tower, make a U-turn in the air and fly through the tower? That is a tricky shot, I *think* it's possible? Jesse, what's the target?"

"That tank."

"The *tank*? Are you crazy? The armor-piercing rounds I have won't punch through that tank, it will just-"

"They don't need to. All we want is to piss off that tank crew, or whoever is driving it remotely. Make them think someone is shooting at them from the egg tower. If that tank shoots back, that will make a big 'Boom', you know? Our platoon will be alerted there are bad guys around here."

Shauna thought for a moment, considering the complicated path the sniper round would have to travel. "It's worth a shot."

"A shot. Literally, you know?"

"Yeah."

"There's only one flaw in your plan," she noted. "We can't see the target from here."

"Sure we can," Jesse grinned. "Check this out." He sent to her the image from his scope, of a particular set of mirrored windows on a tall office building to the east. It showed the tank from the front, and a good portion of the street behind it.

"Wow." She turned to look at the other staff sergeant. "That is good thinking."

"It's good thinking, *if* this works," he reminded her.

"Leave that up to me," she stood halfway up and walked slowly toward the south side of the floor, where there was a line of pallets stacked with construction materials. A gap between them would be excellent cover for her. "Now shut up and let me work."


Shauna waited until the tank had rolled out from under a pedestrian bridge that spanned the street, so she would have a clear shot. Using a 3D map of the city, she programmed a flight path for the explosive-tipped round, guiding it to fly through the open floor that was third from the top of the odd-looking egg-shaped office building. They assumed it was an office building, though none of them really knew or cared about the intended function of the structure. What mattered was that while the lower eleven floors of the tower were finished enough to have glass cladding all around, the upper seven floors were still under construction, and the top three levels were almost completely unobstructed from one side to the other. Shauna did not have to worry about threading the round between pallets and crates and construction equipment as it passed through the structure east to west.

"Gosh," Nert whispered. "That tank is *heavy*. Look at the street behind it."

Shauna smiled. She knew from the tone of Nert's voice that he really had said 'Gosh', the words had not been run through a translator. The Ruhar teenager's ability to speak English was getting better every day, and he was rapidly learning Mandarin Chinese. Shauna, meanwhile, could speak the common Ruhar language if she went slowly and thought carefully about it. Having a conversation with a native speaker of the alien language was difficult, because the Ruhar tended to talk fast, and their slang varied between worlds. A Ruhar living on Gehtanu would drop into their speech slang that was unique to that world. Mostly, Shauna still relied on her zPhone's translator, and the old standby of smiling and nodding a lot when she didn't understand. "I see it," she acknowledged. What Nert had noticed were holes in the street behind the tank. Its weight had crushed the road surface and pipes or tunnels underneath, leaving gaps where the road had collapsed. One section of the road had fallen in, leaving a trench two meters wide all the way across. Shauna wondered if that hole had exposed part of the city's underground railway system. Then she needed to push such thoughts to the back of her mind and focus on her job. Her thumb briefly pressing a button next to the trigger sent a brief, nearly invisible laser pulse at the target, or actually at the window they were using as a mirror. The laser beam bounced off the window and struck the front surface of the tank, causing no damage and scattering harmlessly. The scope of her rifle had tuned the spectrum of the laser to match the ambient light in the city, so the enemy would not realize they had been targeted unless their sensors knew what they were looking for or were very, very good.

She held her breath.

The tank didn't react, did not send back a targeting pulse of its own. If it did, the operators almost certainly would think the pulse had come from the window they were using as a mirror, and not from a source behind them.

The targeting laser beam was dispersed off the curved surface of the tank, with only a small percentage of photons bouncing back toward the window mirror, and only a tiny fraction of that light reached the scope of the sniper rifle. It was enough. "Range to target confirmed," Shauna said quietly. The tank was grinding along at the same steady speed. She wanted to close her eyes to say a prayer, but that could wait for later. Her eyes were needed to keep the targeting crosshairs lined up on the image of the tank in the mirror window. "One away," she pressed the trigger.

The first round leapt out of the barrel at a medium velocity, moving upward more than forward. It coasted in a ballistic arc, aimed to the north of the strange egg-shaped tower, until it tipped over and began to fall. When it passed the tower, its stabilizing wings popped out and the weapon swung around to fly backward, firing its motor first to cancel its velocity, then to move it forward. The round zipped through empty space between the upper floors of the uncompleted tower and accelerated at full power before it cleared the western edge of the floor, burning out its motor in a flash. The last bit of thrust was vectored to line it up with the oncoming enemy vehicle, and it was moving at supersonic speed when it struck the smooth, curved front of the tank.

The armor-piercing rifle round had no appreciable effect on the enemy vehicle. Its inert tip instantly became super-heated plasma that could burn through most materials, but the tank's outer skin reacted with a powerful electric pulse that dispersed the plasma, splattering it outward harmlessly.

The second, third and fourth rounds all followed unique trajectories to fall behind the egg-shaped tower, their flight paths programmed by Shauna to minimize the possibility that the enemy could trace the origin of the shots. All four of the rounds she fired came through the same upper floor of the tower and kicked in their motors at maximum acceleration, aimed straight at the tank that was still rolling forward. All of the rounds struck within a single square meter on the front slope of the tank, and none of the rounds had any useful effect on stopping the monstrous war machine.

The tank's defensive sensors tracked the incoming rounds and determined the shots were coming from a tower to the east, specifically from the open floor two down from the top. Information was sent to the crew that was remotely controlling the vehicle, and a decision was quickly made.

"Shit," Jesse adjusted his scope to get a better view of the tank through the fine dust that formed a cloud in front of the enemy vehicle. "You hit it four out of four. *No* effect!"

Shauna checked the rifle's powercell. It was down to forty-three percent. "I told you that these dinky little rounds wouldn't penetrate that type of armor. They're designed to-"

Three loud, low, rolling *BOOMS* echoed off buildings around them, shaking the floor they were laying on, and shattering windows for several blocks. Dust rained down on them, kept away from the lenses of their scopes by magnetic fields.

"Wow!" Jesse exclaimed. "Hell, I guess those rounds *did* have an effect. What is that tank shooting at, I don't see- Oh, *shit*!" He had been focused on the open floor of the egg-shaped tower, expecting the tank would direct its retaliation at the source of the sniper fire. Instead, the tank had struck the tower at a floor below the level Jesse could see from his vantage point.

The top of the tower shook and *tilted*, collapsing to the south.

"Oh, my G-" Jesse watched, transfixed, as the upper floors, maybe the entire upper *half*, of the tower sagged. Held up only by the intact support structure on one side, the upper floors fell, the tower unable to hold up the dead weight. First crunching down on one side, the upper part of the building pancaked downward, the jarring impact straining the lower structure with a load they were never designed to withstand. "Oh, man," Jesse gasped. "I think the whole thing is- Hang on!"

He lost sight of the tower as the top fell below a building to the east, then couldn't see anything because a massive cloud of dust rolled outward like a fast-moving bank of fog, obscuring the area.

Shauna snapped the cover back over her rifle's scope. "That's it, we are outta here."

Jesse was gaping at the sight in shock. "They nuked the whole freakin' building?"

"Maybe they just got lucky?" Nert suggested.

"*Unlucky*," Jesse said as he stood up, no longer concerned about being seen by the enemy. In the thick dust that was choking the air, he could barely see the elevator shaft at the center of the floor. "No way can that tank keep going east along that road, there's a building collapsed on it. They'll have to turn north or south, or backtrack."

"If they go north, they could run into us," Shauna suggested. "Shit! We should have thought this through before shooting. Let's get out of here pronto."

"Yeah," Jesse stood up. "One thing's for sure."

"What's that?" Nert asked as he trotted toward the open elevator shaft.

"No way could our platoon have missed seeing *that*."

# CHAPTER TWENTY NINE

Perkins skidded to a stop, literally skidding as her boots struggled for grip on the battle-scarred road surface. Automatically, her suit tilted the bootheels down to prevent her from toppling forward, and deployed spikes for additional traction. "What the hell is *that*?" She pointed to the southwest as she came to a halt against a lamp post, cradling it with an elbow so she wouldn't topple over.

Barely visible in a gap between several tall buildings, and partly seen through the skeletal frame of a building that was surrounded by construction cranes, another tower that was only partially finished was swaying side to side. What had attracted her attention was the harsh bark of heavy artillery, or that is how her suit's computer identified the source of the explosions. What she knew for certain was the sound was *loud*, and shook the street so hard, she had felt it through her boots. Before anyone could answer her, the top of the swaying tower slumped to one side. "That can't be g-" she started to say.

Then the top of the tower dropped below sight. Moments later, the ground shook, windows to the southwest blew inward, and a pall of smoke and dust rose from the site.

"Holy *shit*," someone exclaimed over the platoon channel. "Did that just happen?"

"Platoon, halt and take cover," Perkins ordered. "I need comms," she said to Sergeant Liu.

Liu looked around. "It's going to be tough here," she pointed to indicate the tall buildings that surrounded them.

"Make it happen," Perkins snapped.

"Yes, Ma'am. It would be best if I was in the plaza up ahead. There-"

"Go!"

Liu sprinted ahead, while Perkins allowed herself to be led into the dubious cover of a doorway. If the enemy was dropping heavy ordnance by artillery or air, the overhanging awning of a doorway was not going to protect her. She waited impatiently while she watched Liu, guarded by three soldiers, set up the bulky antenna that was the only way to communicate with the world beyond the city. Every drone they sent up had been destroyed or jammed with surprising and depressing speed. The cyber-defense capabilities of the Wurgalan were much more advanced than indicated by the intel provided by the Torgalau. So far, the Torgalau had been wrong about many aspects of the squids in general and the status of their forces on Stiglord, so drones failing with regularity was not unexpected, just frustrating.

Liu had the antenna deployed, its spiral-shaped bowl aiming at an unseen point in the sky. While Perkins silently urged the Chinese sergeant to work faster, she knew the process of aligning the antenna was a delicate matter, almost more of an art than science. After waving the antenna around, Liu shook her head, said something to the soldiers who had set up a perimeter around her, and carried the antenna to the northwest corner of the plaza, threading her way around abandoned and crashed vehicles.

Wurgalan urban planning seemed to like broad avenues, and placing wide plazas where four or more roads came together. In the middle of the intersections were round or oval-shaped parks, with statues or fountains. Liu set down the antenna and climbed on a bus, then reached down for a soldier to hand the antenna to her.

"Sergeant," Perkins called. "You are awfully exposed up there."

"Yes, Ma'am," Liu replied as she focused on getting the antenna aligned with the faint and garbled carrier signal. "This is the only way I can get line-of-sight from here. Unless I go up on a roof somewhere?" She suggested.

"Negative," Perkins squashed that idea. Rooftops were even more exposed, and with power out all over the city, it would be a long climb up an interior stairwell to get to a roof. "Keep trying." She knew they really had no alternative. "Be careful, you have our only tactical antenna."

"The antenna is tougher than I am," Liu grunted, wishing the Mavericks leader would shut the hell up and let her work. "If I'm hit, the- Got it! Exchanging handshake now, and, and, we have comms. Transferring to you now. The signal is only two by five," she warned.

In her visor display, Perkins could see the poor quality of the signal. The other end was a starship more than a lightsecond above the planet, with a powerful transmitter to cut through the jamming. Even with the platoon's antenna boosting to maximum signal strength, she knew it would be difficult for the ship above to hear her clearly. "This is Colonel Perkins," she eyeclicked to send her ID code. "We are-"

"Colonel," the voice of the Ruhar duty officer was distorted by jamming, and interrupted by bursts of static. "Hold one. I am connecting you with General Ross."

There was a pause, then Ross spoke, his voice sounding even worse. "Perkins? What's your status?"

She knew Ross could determine her location from the data embedded in the signal. He could also see data from her suit computer about the physical status of all the soldiers with her, their ammunition supply, level of charge in their powercells and anything else he might want to know. When he asked for status, he wanted to know what she thought and was planning, not dry statistics. "We are proceeding out of the city along Route Echo," she reported. "Enemy resistance has been sporadic since we broke contact. Sir, someone nuked a building southwest of here, please tell me that wasn't us." She paused, waiting for Ross to get her message. Assuming the UNEF commander was still dirtside, the signal had to travel a lightsecond or more up to the relay starship, then back down to Ross. Because of the jamming, her suit would repeat the message several times, so the fragments could be reassembled properly on Ross's end of the line. The delays made for an awkward conversation.

"We can't see what happened, but it was not us, repeat, that was *not* our action. Perkins, there are eight tanks converging on your position."

She waited for the little 'beep' that indicated Ross had stopped speaking, before she replied. "That got garbled. Did you say '*tanks*'?" She could not imagine what he might have said that sounded like 'tanks', but she also could not imagine him saying that word. Who the hell used tanks in modern warfare?

"*Tanks*, yes. Some kind of large armored vehicles, converging on your position, I'm sending the coordinates to you. Take a look."

The file got hung up in transmission, forcing her to wait. A map popped up in a window of her visor and she enlarged it. The map was crude and lacked detail, it was good enough to see that, if the information was true, she and her platoon were in serious danger. "What-"

Ross resumed speaking, his voice increasingly distorted. "We're trying an airstrike to-" A roar of static drowned him out. "-out of there if-"

"Sir?" She called. "General Ross?"

"We lost the beam," Liu warned. "Our antenna is being jammed directly. I can try-"

"No," Perkins ordered. "Break down the antenna and get off that bus right now!" Switching to the command channel, she called out. "We're moving, through the plaza and right, then left at the next intersection. Move, *now*," she said with a fearful eye on the sky. The enemy had locked onto their antenna and jammed it directly, that meant they had at least a rough idea of the platoon's location.

As she passed through the plaza, running along in the middle of the column, she saw Sergeant Liu hop off the bus and adjust her backpack, then join the formation. When the last of the column cleared the plaza and turned onto the street behind her, she halted in the entrance to a substantial-looking building, the sign out front indicated it belonged to the municipal government. Though she had no idea what function the structure performed, she did know it had fewer and smaller windows than anything around, and that it appeared to be empty. That the facility had been hastily evacuated was evident from the broken front doors and the trash scattered around.

"What's up, Colonel?" Dave asked, sticking to protocol.

"Check this," she sent the map to the suits of the platoon leadership, which included Dave. "Ross has intel that the enemy is sending tanks against us."

"*Tanks*?" Dave snorted a laugh, looking down at his sophisticated Ruhar skinsuit. "Sending tanks up against mech suits is a whole new kind of crazy." In his suit, he could easily outrun a tank, especially in an urban environment. The rockets fired by the launcher under his rifle barrel were designed to pierce the armor of an enemy mech suit, but he had used rockets against much stouter defenses. Several soldiers could network their rifles together and coordinate the impact of their rockets, collectively giving the weapons more punching power that an individual warhead.

David Czajka was not afraid of any stinkin' *tank*.

"I hope you're right about that," Jates growled.

"Seriously?" Dave asked. "Would you want to be in a tank, against a platoon in powered armor? It would be like that scene in Raiders of the Lost Ark, you know?"

Jates only cocked his head.

"Oh. Yeah, right, you never saw that movie. There's a scene where the hero is confronted by a big, *big* dude with a sword, and the bad guy expects the hero to fight with his bullwhip. But he doesn't. The hero just takes out his pistol and," Dave pointed like he was holding a pistol. "Bam! Blows the bad guy away. Sheee-it, any fight between a tank and a mech suit will be like that. I feel sorry for the guys inside, you know?"

"We don't know anyone is *in* the tank," Jates said. "It is most likely controlled remotely, or it is autonomously guided by an AI," he looked at Perkins.

Perkins shrugged. "We don't know anything, other than that the fleet upstairs spotted at least eight of them. With sensors being jammed, there might be more the fleet can't detect."

Jates nodded once, emphatically. "We do know one thing."

"What's that?" Dave asked.

"The enemy knows the capability of our infantry," Jates explained. "And they are sending tanks against us anyway. They are either confident, or stupid."

"Shit," Dave groaned. "The squids haven't been stupid so far. Em, Colonel," he quickly caught his mistake. "We need eyes on one of these things. I can take a scout team to get intel."

Perkins shook her head. "Not yet. Ross told me he's planning an airstrike. He didn't say when, but my money is on it being soon. Shit! We are *reacting* to the enemy, we need to take the initiative."

"Look at the bright side," Jates observed with a growl, using one of the human expressions he had learned. "If *we* don't know what we're doing, the enemy can't anticipate our next move."

Dave shrugged. "The man's got a point."


"Oh, this ain't good," Jesse tapped Shauna's shoulder. "We got a whole school of squids down there."

"A *school*?"

Jesse, startled by the question, looked away from the scope to stare at her. "Isn't that what you call a group of fish?"

"Sure but, the Wurgalan are land creatures," Shauna shook her head without taking her own eyes from her rifle scope. "How many?"

"Uh," Jesse counted more than a dozen of the enemy, which would be a squad, but he wasn't going to say 'squad of squids'. "I count, wait, more of them coming into view. That's got to be, wow. Thirty? No," his scope was counting outlines. "Forty." More enemy were coming into view, scuttling into the street with the odd and creepy motion of their multiple, short legs. "Damn, these guys are infantry. Wurgalan army, not local police. They must be here to move in behind that tank."

Shauna looked up, frustrated. "How are you seeing this? My scope isn't showing-"

Nert agreed. "I also do not see anything."

"Nert," Jesse explained, "that's because they are over on this side, you can't see them from there. Look at the feed from my scope, I'm doing the mirror trick again."

"Reflection off a window?" Shauna guessed. Most windows in the area had shattered when the egg-shaped tower collapsed. That is why they had taken up position in what they guessed was an office building, they didn't need a balcony when every room was now open to the air. Shauna and Jesse were in the southeast corner, overlooking an intersection that was a broad plaza where six city streets came together. Without a drone to provide an overhead view, they were restricted to line-of-sight and it was frustrating. It was also frustrating that they still had no contact with the platoon. To check whether the enemy was sneaking up behind them, Nert patrolled the other three corners of the building. The tank had rolled out of sight but they had a good idea of its location, from the grinding sound it made as it crushed the roadway under its great bulk.

"Not a window. See the truck that's stuck in the intersection?" There were three intersections in view, all of them had vehicles jammed in traffic and abandoned. "The truck has a logo kind of like a football, or a watermelon?"

"I see it."

"Ok, look at the outside mirror on the left."

"*Ooh*," she nodded. "Good eyes, hon- J-Jesse." She stammered and inside her helmet, her cheeks turned red at her mistake. "Yeah, you're right. That's a lot of squids. Too much for- Oh, hello?"

What she had seen was a Wurgalan soldier scurrying back to the main group, coming from the opposite direction. The soldier hurried to where three soldiers were huddled together, which was not anything special. What got Shauna's attention was what the soldier did with one of its tentacles, a twisting motion, raising and lowering the tentacle twice. It was saluting officers.

"Sniper check," Shauna whispered.

"Well, since they asked so nicely," Jesse whispered. "Can you make a shot from-"

Shauna's answer was to send a laser pulse to verify the range, then the rifle spat out two explosive-tipped rounds. The shot did not require any tricky planning or guidance, as the target was only two city blocks away, and at a sixty-degree angle that was easy for the guided rounds to maneuver without excessive loss of speed.

Not knowing which of the three Wurgalan were officers being saluted, Shauna had chosen the two on the left, because her field of view was wider to the right. If the enemy ran to her right, she had an opportunity for a second shot.

In the air, the two rounds coordinated their actions, the first unit delayed firing its motor until the second round had caught up and was flying on a parallel course. Because they had been given rather vague guidance before leaving the rifle, they switched on their active sensors and shared the data received, making final decisions as their motors kicked on. They went supersonic and were passing through Mach 7 at impact.

The two Wurgalan officers barely had time to notice warnings flashing in their helmets before the sniper rounds slammed into them and exploded. One round hit center-mass in the torso of its target, the other misjudged the direction its target would move, so the strike hit the shoulder area.

The difference in impact zone made no difference to the targets, both of whom were knocked backwards, holes burned through their powered suits, bones shattered and soft tissue churned into jelly as fragments ricocheted around inside the armor.

Both Wurgalan dropped and were lost to view in the chaos. The formation of alien soldiers broke, individuals running for cover through they didn't know what direction the deadly rounds had come from, and they knew the next round could follow an entirely different flight path. What had been an organized formation fell apart, with almost everyone who had a rifle spraying the area on full-auto while their leaders made futile appeals for calm. Two soldiers died when caught by friendly fire, their deaths adding to the rising sense of panic.

Jesse kept his mouth shut and identified targets, tagging them by priority as Shauna kept up a steady fire. Each round that scanned the target area added to the rifle computer's knowledge of the situation, and it began making suggestions to Shauna. A round targeted at an enemy soldier taking cover under a truck noted that two enemy were huddled behind a car, and passed that information back to the rifle. Though Shauna and Jesse could not see that pair of soldiers, the rifle knew where they were, and with Shauna's approval, guidance was adjusted to send two rounds high in the sky. Arcing up over where the pair of soldiers thought they had found effective cover, the rounds plunged down at a steep angle, gravity adding to the thrust of their motors. They struck the backs of the targets simultaneously, punching through the layer of armor over the powercells, then striking hammer blows on the inner layer of armor. That armor held with only fine cracks spiderwebbing outward from the impact sites, nanogel already flowing in to plug the breaches.

Too late. The shattered powercells erupted, part of their released energy sizzling through the cracks and boiling the soldiers alive inside their suits.

That was too much for the Wurgalan force, which had been fifty strong when they entered the city behind the tank. Other than nine experienced leaders, the soldiers were all trainees, on the planet to learn infantry skills. Of the nine leaders, five were new to their responsibilities, and did not know what to do when the trainees panicked. Seeing a pair of soldiers struck in the back by enemy fire that apparently came out of the clear blue sky, the last nerves of the soldiers frayed and, without orders or against orders, they ran back along the route they used to enter the city. Efforts by their leaders to halt the panicked flight were ignored, so the leaders focused on trying to get some semblance of organization in the retreat, urging the formation to fall back by squads. Three trainees hesitated, debating whether to provide cover for their fellows, then a car's powercell exploded and anything they had learned in training was forgotten in the need to get *away* as fast as possible.

"Cease fire, cease fire," Jesse advised.

"I've got two rounds ready," Shauna noted as she lifted her finger off the trigger button. Ten rounds had gone downrange, eight of them finding their assigned targets and all ten causing fear and confusion in the streets.

"They're running," Jesse tried to keep the excitement out of his voice. "They're *running*! Damn, it's like you turned the lights on in the kitchen, all the cockroaches are running for cover. Hold fire."

Shauna was so hyped up, she wanted to find two more targets before she had to swap the magazine for a fresh one. She took a deep breath, knowing Jesse was right. They had accomplished their objective, preventing the Wurgalan infantry from following the tank toward Perkins. She also knew that every round she fired increased the possibility that enemy sensors would track the projectiles back to their source. If that happened, the Wurgalan could drop artillery on their heads. The tank destroying a building, even an incomplete structure, was probably unintentional and she expected somebody on the enemy side would get a serious ass-chewing about that screw-up. But she also did not think the enemy would hesitate to use heavy weapons against a sniper, if that sniper was holding up the advance of an infantry unit. "Ok," she lifted the rifle, automatically checking its powercell. The powercell and magazine should be changed before she used the weapon again.

"Oh yeah," Jesse marveled as he watched the last Wurgalan soldier flee out of view, leaping over a car in its haste to get away. "That was some *damned* fine shooting."

Shauna knew that a real trained sniper would have found plenty to criticize about her technique, target selection, even the choice of position. They were in the office building because it had been quick and easy to reach under cover of the thick dust cloud, which had begun to disperse from the wind by the time they reached their current location. Considering the minimal training she had been given, she was satisfied that the criticism she was giving herself was enough. She had made mistakes, she knew enough to recognize her errors, and she knew how to learn from mistakes. "Ah," she shrugged as she slapped a new powercell into the slot and verified it was active. "It was good enough."

"Good *enough*? Did you see those squids running? You got half a company or more, to turn their little legs around and run home to Momma."

"Yeah, unless they just turn at the next intersection and bypass us," Shauna noted with a frown. "That mirror trick of yours only lets us see a few city blocks. We could-"

"Hey," he patted her shoulder. "You did *great*. I love you," he added on impulse. The instantly realized what he'd said. "Uh. Sorry."

Shauna rolled onto one shoulder to look directly at him. Combat suit helmets could be awkward, sometimes it was easier to turn your body rather than your neck. "*Sorry?*"

"Yeah, uh. You know. Sorry."

"You're sorry that you said it, or-"

Something in Jesse's brain told him he needed to put out that fire, right then. Something else told him that was not the type of conversation to have while sealed up in a combat suit. He swung the faceplate open, and spoke quietly, in case the enemy had acoustic sensors in the area. "I shouldn't have said it right then. Now, I mean. Here," he sputtered. "I shouldn't have dumped it on you like that, you know?"

She swung her faceplate up, and wiped sweat out of her eyes. "Did you mean it?"

"Uh-"

"*Uh*," she snapped. "Was not the right answer, Jesse Colter."

"Look, this is- Oh! So freakin' complicated!"

"*Life* is complicated."

"Yeah, but- Look, guys can't say that. Can't be the *first* to say that. Ah, *damn* it! Being on Paradise has changed everything around, and we guys are still trying to figure out the new rules, you know? It's like, girls have all the power now. Women, I mean. Women have all the power. A guy can't be the first to say those three little words, because you don't want to scare a girl- *Woman*! Don't want to scare a woman away."

Shauna's mood had turned to amusement, but she didn't let her partner see that. "Would you like to borrow a shovel, so you can dig that hole you're in even deeper?"

"I- Ah, shit! I don't know what to say. Women make the rules now, how about you tell me what I'm supposed to do? Hell, everything's easy for you."

"*Easy*? How can you be so clueless?"

"Darlin'," he gave a heartfelt sigh. "I am really gonna need you to throw me a bone here, because I got nothin'," he admitted, splaying his hands in a gesture to show he was not holding any cards.

"Easy, huh?"

"Yeah, sure. You have your pick of men now. Any guy you want, you-"

"Women don't want just *any* guy," she rolled her eyes. "You're right about those three little words, though. That makes it worse for us girls too."

"It-" He had no idea what she meant. Wisely, he zipped his lip and nodded for her to continue.

"Listen, Jesse," she patted his shoulder softly. "Sure, a woman wants to hear a guy say that. The problem is, especially on Paradise, a guy saying that doesn't mean he really feels that way. There are too many guys and not enough women. Guys are desperate, we know that. When a guy says 'I love you', it makes a woman wonder if he thinks she is Mrs. Right, or just Mrs. *Right Here*. We worry that guys latch onto the first woman who looks at him, because he doesn't have a whole lot of options, you know?"

"Ohhhh," realization dawned on Jesse. Suddenly, a lot of things made sense. "You're worried that a guy is just settling for whoever he can get?"

"Yeah, sure. Wouldn't you think that?"

"You're worried that's what *I* think?"

"I don't know what you think, because you don't *say* it," she let a bit of the exasperation she was feeling creep into her voice.

"I just *did*."

"Then you said you were sorry for saying it."

"You're not the only one who worries about-" He bit his lip.

"About what?"

"About someone settling. Wait," he held up a finger. "Let me talk. I'm not real good at it, so read between the lines, Ok? I worry that maybe we're together, because we're in the same unit, you know? We sort of met, way back on Camp Alpha, and nothing happened. Not *nothing*, you were with Bishop, not with me."

"That was a *fling*," she moaned. "Why do you guys always-"

"Let me finish, please? The hamsters threw us together on Paradise because we knew Bishop, back when they were investigating what happened to him. Then Emby kept us together, and since then, well, we've been together because we serve together. If it hadn't been for Emby, I, who knows?"

"Seriously? You want to play 'What If', with life?"

"I'm being honest, that's all."

"You're asking, if it hadn't been for Emby pulling us together to reactivate those maser cannons, maybe nothing would have happened between us?"

"Something like that, yeah."

"Jesse, I don't *know*. Life doesn't come with a Reset button. Maybe if Emby hadn't contacted us, the Ruhar would have released us back to our units, and we wouldn't have ever seen each other again. If aliens hadn't invaded Earth, we probably *never* would have met."

"Shit. That's what-"

"It doesn't matter. I don't *care*. We *are* together, that's what matters. Am I special to you?"

"Oh, hell. You *are* special. Damn, girl, you *kick ass*. You're special to everyone." That was not the question she asked, so he added "Special to me? Every time I look at you, I can't believe you're with me. You make *me* feel special."

"Jesse Colter," she placed her hands on both sides of his helmet and stared at him. "I. Love. You. I'm sorry that I didn't tell you that before, if it made you worry so much. You-"

"Um," Nert's voice squeaked. "Hey, uh, guys?"

"Oh, *sh*-" Jesse gasped. He had completely forgotten they were speaking on the team channel. Nert had heard everything. He looked at Shauna.

She looked at him.

They both exploded with laughter.

"Guys?" Nert pleaded. "Sorry, but, I think we have a problem."

# CHAPTER THIRTY

The three-ship formation of Ruhar 'Vulture' gunships were orbiting around an imaginary control point northwest of the city, their wings fully extended and engines on the lowest power setting they could manage, while keeping the heavy spacecraft flying. There had originally been six Vultures, but one had been shot down by enemy fire, one damaged and forced to land for repairs, and the third ship had burned so much fuel during a dogfight, it had to fly back to base for refueling. None of the gunships were supposed to be in in the battle, the schedule had called for all to be back in orbit, with gunship duties handled by Legion aircraft.

Unfortunately, the invasion schedule was no more than an amusing fantasy at that point. Spacecraft were not ideal platforms for air superiority or close-support missions in an atmosphere, but with few aircraft reaching the ground intact and fewer surviving the first hours of combat, the Vultures and their Ruhar pilots had been forced to remain on station far longer than anyone wanted.

When the formation with the callsign of 'Silver Flight' received the order to overfly the city, the pilots at first wondered what could be so damned important. The city was supposed to be a No-Go zone, marked on Legion maps as an area to be avoided by air power and ground troops. Now elements of three platoons were trying to fight their way out of the city, and plumes of smoke rose from where aircraft from both sides had met fiery deaths. Now they could see a tall plume of dust and smoke southwest of the city center, and they wondered what the *hell* the alien ground-pounders had gotten themselves into this time.

Reading their orders only made the situation more confusing. They were instructed to approach but not overfly the city, get close enough to launch their stand-off weapons, then return to orbit the control point. They were not to engage enemy aircraft unless they were fired upon, to avoid known anti-aircraft artillery sites, blah blah blah, the usual. Those parts of the orders were nothing new or unusual.

Everything else about the orders caused the pilots to scratch their heads, which they couldn't actually do with their helmets sealed. Their target were *tanks*, armored ground vehicles. From the intel provided by the Torgalau, it was known that the Wurgalan had such vehicles in their inventory, and information about tanks was included in the pre-mission briefing packet, but no one who read down that far into the data dump had taken the threat seriously. Not even when the Torgalau warned that such armored ground vehicles had given them substantial trouble in past engagements. The general opinion of the Ruhar on that matter was of course the Torgalau considered ground vehicles to be an obstacle, because the Torgalau were not renowned as the greatest military force in the galaxy. The mighty Ruhar certainly did not have to worry about obsolete technology.

The three spacecraft of Silver Flight turned and pointed their noses at the city, programming their missiles to home in on the coordinates provided by the starships above. When the Vultures were over the river that defined the northern edge of the city, they launched missiles by simply opening the bay doors, releasing clamps and allowing the weapons to fall. Immediately after the last of the eight missiles cleared the stealth field of its spacecraft, the doors slid shut and the Vultures began a gentle turn back toward the control point, keeping an eye on a pair of Wurgalan fighter aircraft that were flying a parallel course to the south.

The missiles fell on unpowered ballistic arcs, wings popping out to give them a controlled glide. When they were half a kilometer above the treetops, their air-breathing engines spun to life and the missiles surged forward, keeping their speed subsonic. Wings swept backward and the air ducts opened wide, gulping in more air than the engines required, to dilute the heat signature of the exhaust. The missiles split up, each proceeding on a pre-programmed path to their target zone but not to the targets themselves, the missiles would need to locate the tanks when they arrived.

The missiles all flew at different speeds, so they would all reach their target zones at the same time. Striking targets simultaneously would not give the enemy time to be warned and react, and to learn from previous attacks.

That was the plan. As the old saying goes, no plan survives contact with the enemy. Arriving over their target zones, only three of eight missiles located vehicles that matched the profile in their databases. Because of enemy broad-spectrum jamming, not all of the missiles were able to effectively communicate, and boosting transmitter power attracted attention. Two of the missiles that had located their targets went offline without warning, sending garbled reports as their transmissions cut off. Of the remaining six missiles, only four got the message that two of their companions had already been lost, and with communications unreliable, the six fell back to independent mode.

The one missile which had a positive lock on its target folded its wings back and dove, kicking in its rocket motor when it detected an active sensor beam aimed in its direction. The missile raced forward through the speed of sound, going hypersonic as it-

Disintegrated, fried by a plasma beam pulse from the target. Charred parts of the missile casing pinged harmlessly off the tank that continued to grind ahead.

Feeding power to their active sensors, the surviving five stand-off weapons climbed to scan a wider area of the city. Lighting off active sensors was equivalent to shining a strobe light, and the missiles knew they did not have long to live. Mission success or failure was simple matter of mathematics; could they locate and attack a target, before enemy defenses knocked them out of the sky?

The answer: no.

Two missiles never identified anything on the ground that looked like a tank before they were fried by plasma beams. One missile found a tank rolling along a street two blocks west of the target zone, but during the seconds it took to turn around and line up an attack, it was struck by a fragmentation warhead from a Wurgalan anti-aircraft missile launched from the ground.

That left two missiles that had both positively identified targets, and remained active long enough to strike their respective tanks. A plasma beam seared through the air just after one missile turned, missing by half a meter. That missile cleverly curved around a building to attack its slow-moving target from the front, leaving the tank's sensors momentarily confused. The hard turn bled off airspeed so the missile was traveling at subsonic speed when it came around the corner and rammed the target at an angle, much of the explosive force of its warhead deflected upward by the glancing nature of the impact and the slope of the tank's front surface. The shaped-charge warhead directed its energy sideways as much as possible, still only a quarter of the energy was focused on the tank's forward armor.

The warhead had little effect on the massive vehicle. Part of the outer layer of armor was burnt and flaked away. Most of the hexagons of plating in the affected area were left in place, those too badly damaged were pushed outward to fall away, with a fresh new layer rising into position. Within seconds, the only sign the tank had been struck was a star-shaped pattern of soot splattered across its smooth front.

The second tank was hit by an attack from the top, with the incoming missile arcing over the roof of a parking structure to keep itself out of view as long as possible. It was deflected slightly by a plasma bolt at the last second, so the warhead struck the sloping left side rather than square on the top. That warhead got lucky, impacting at a relatively thin part of the armor plating, but the tank protected itself by detonating reactive armor, sending an explosion outward as the missile's warhead exploded forward. The force of the warhead was dissipated into a broad cone rather than a focused lance of superheated plasma.

The second missile also had little effect.

All eight tanks kept rolling toward the group of Verd-kris and humans.

The missiles did have one effect: they attracted the attention of the invaders who were trying to fight their way out of the city. "Liu," Perkins gestured to the sergeant, as she tried to count the new, thin trails of smoke all around her.

"On it, Ma'am," Liu acknowledged, sprinting up the street with the folded tactical antenna on her back. She had not followed approved procedure by stowing the antenna in its holding case. The antenna was exposed to damage without its case, a trade-off for being able to deploy it quickly. Liu now had a good idea of where the relay ship was located in space, so she did not need to search a broad cone of the sky to find the guide wave. Gaining speed as she ran, she slammed a foot down on the pavement to send her vaulting up on top of a truck that was partly on the sidewalk. Perkins would not like her being so exposed and Liu wasn't thrilled about it either. Checking that her rifle was securely attached to its sling and side holster, she crouched and bolted upward, folding her forearms in front of the helmet faceplate as she crashed through a window and smashed knees-first onto a heavy desk. The desk cracked under her weight and sent her rolling to the right onto the floor. "I'm Ok!" She called on the platoon channel, rising to punch the remaining shards of glass from the window and drag the broken desk out of the way so two other soldiers could follow her.

"You're crazy, you know that, right?" One of the soldiers wagged a finger at her.

"Ah, come on," Liu grinned. "You had fun too."

"Sergeant," Perkins called. "Was that really necessary?"

Liu pulled out the antenna and unfolded it before answering, pointing it at a particular section of the sky. With the relay ship more than a lightsecond away, it wasn't going to shift its position in the sky much over a few minutes, she only had to account for the planet she was on rotating at roughly three hundred meters per second at the city's latitude, so-

"Got it," she announced triumphantly. "We have a link, Colonel."

Other than receiving a tone to indicate the platoon-level communications system had established a proper encryption handshake with the relay ship, Perkins got no response to her calls. Sending a short message via text also was futile, until the message was sent a third time.

The response was short. *Airstrike no effect, need accurate guidance on one target. Advise when ready.*

"What the-" Perkins read the message a second time.

"Colonel?" Dave asked, leaning forward. He could tell Em was reading a text message, yet she hadn't shared it.

"They need us to paint a target for them," she said while composing a reply.

"Paint?" Jates shook his head, unsure he had heard the translation correctly.

Dave explained. "We need to tell the missiles exactly where one of the tanks are. Like, paint a bullseye on it, you know?"

"Oh." Jates did not understand how the eye of a bull, an Earth animal, was related to the task, and he knew better than to ask. "Colonel, I can do that."

"*We* can do that," Dave corrected the Verd. "I want to see one of these tanks anyway."

"Czajka," Perkins wore a pained expression. She did not like the idea that any of her people would get close to an enemy armored vehicle that had survived an airstrike. She especially did not like Dave volunteering for a dangerous task. "This isn't a game."

"We'll be *careful*," he assured her. "The only problem will be maintaining a link back to the antenna," he jerked a thumb over his shoulder at the window where Liu had the antenna pointed to the sky. "We'll need relays."

"Colonel," Liu spoke. "We can't keep the link open long, or the enemy will pinpoint our location."

"Cut the link," Perkins decided. "Czajka, contact us as soon as you have the target designated."

"That, looks like a *slug*," Dave whispered when he first saw the tank. He was severely disappointed by his first view of the alien armored vehicle. "Or a really ugly caterpillar."

"Did you know," Specialist Khatri asked, "that tanks are called *tanks* because in the First World War, the project to develop armored vehicles was funded under the cover story that it was about water tanks?"

Jates ignore the comments of Dave and Khatri. "Cut the chatter. Do you have coordinates?"

"Yeah, sure," Dave had the rangefinder of his rifle's scope locked on the smooth top surface of the tank. He was using passive sensors, basically the sunlight reflecting off the dull skin of the tank. The rifle's internal computer knew where he was, and the spectrum of ambient light around him, so based on how the sunlight changed when it reflected off the tank, the rangefinder knew the enemy vehicle's location within millimeters. Or some shit like that, Dave didn't understand the details. All he knew was that his rifle scope stated the tank was two hundred and thirty two point six meters from his location, which was *too* close. He did not know what type of ordnance the Legion planned to drop on the tank, but it had to be stronger than whatever warhead had failed to scratch the damned thing the first time. Over two hundred meters, seemed like plenty of distance for safety, especially for troops protected by armored suits. That did not account for two factors. The tank was *moving*, getting closer every second, and the team providing eyes on the target had no idea when the airstrike was coming. Also, they were in an urban environment. Direct shockwaves and shrapnel from explosions were not the only hazards. In the confines of the crowded city, an explosion could trigger a *building* to collapse on top of the ground team, crushing even their suits under thousands of tons of debris.

Dave's curiosity about the tank had been thoroughly satisfied, and he was beginning to think that Jates could be right: the Wurgalan knew the capabilities of skinsuits, yet they had sent the tank anyway. The enemy was confident that the tank, which seemed like a laughably slow and clumsy ancient weapon, would be effective against the invading army.

Dave didn't want to be around to find out if the enemy was right.

"Jates," he said without taking his eyes off the scope. "We have enough data." The tank was grinding its way straight down a broad avenue that ran southwest to northeast across the city, aiming for a point where it would intercept the Legion troops. Its motion was steady at around fifteen kilometers per hour. Dave had wondered why the vehicle was traveling so slowly along a flat, straight avenue with few obstructions, then he got a good view of the road surface behind it. The massive tank was crushing the pavement and busting through pipes, power conduits and tunnels that ran under the surface. Going any faster might risk the tank digging a hole that would slow it down even more. "We're ready for relay."

"Send the signal," Jates ordered Khatri, who was positioned another hundred fifty meters behind them, with the relay.

Dave saw an icon light up in his visor, and he pressed a button on the side of his rifle, authorizing it to share the targeting data. The signal was one-way, he had no way to know if the coordinates were being received by whatever aircraft needed the data, nor did he have a way to know when the airstrike would be arriving. He checked the steadily-decreasing range to target. "Uh, we need to think about pulling back," he suggested. They had set up on the second deck of a parking garage, where an empty vehicle had become good cover, after Dave smashed out the windows with the butt of his rifle. The structure was made of whatever concrete-like substance the Wurgalan used pretty much all over the city, and because the parking garage had to hold the weight of cars and trucks, it was solid, constructed more strongly than any residential or office building. It had seemed like an ideal location from which to get eyes on the target, and it was. Dave was realizing, as he watched the enhanced view of the rifle scope as the armored slug crawled steadily toward him, that a parking garage was not ideal for a quick escape when they would need to relocate. The ceiling was low, leaving little space to squeeze between the tops of vehicles and the deck above. That wouldn't be a problem because the garage was mostly empty, except that the second floor was jammed. Cars and trucks from the three decks above had tried to drive down through the second deck, where traffic was jammed because of accidents on the first floor, and because the clogged streets outside made it difficult for any vehicles to get out of the garage. The result was a crowded mass of abandoned cars and trucks, forcing the Legion team to squeeze through to get a view of the tank. "That's it," Dave muttered to himself, as he kept the crosshairs lined up on the sloping front of the tank. "This would be a great time to drop a missile on that thing. Come *on*, guys."

When they received the target coordinates, the three Vulture gunships of Silver Flight again broke from the lazy circle they had been flying around the control point west of the city and went to full power, streaking toward the target. With the enemy alerted to the threat of air-to-ground missiles, they had to reduce the flight time of the weapons and attempt to draw away defenders. Before Silver Flight reached the imaginary line in the sky where they would launch their remaining weapons, five enemy fighters to the south turned to engage and fired off a half-dozen air-to-air missiles. The Vulture pilots held their course, anxiously watching the incoming missiles while the seconds counted down. Three, two, one-

Each of the Vultures ejected a single missile, and immediately turned hard and climbed to put distance between themselves and the enemy weapons that had gone hypersonic. To the northwest, two smaller missiles rose from the city, seeking the same targets.

The Vultures activated their defensive maser turrets as two more missiles rose from the city.

The three missiles launched by the Vultures did not need to seek targets, they knew exactly where the tank was, and had an accurate map of the city for six blocks around the armored vehicle. They split up, flying three different approaches toward the tank, and coordinated their actions so they came around or over buildings within milliseconds of each other, kicking on their booster motors for the terminal dive.

"One more minute," Jates ordered, pressing a reassuring hand on Dave's shoulder.

The tank itself was clearing the traffic jam from the streets by plowing vehicles aside. The blunt, sloping nose of the tank shoved cars left and right and in some cases, up and over to tumble on top of other wrecked vehicles. The tank squeezed to the right to go around a stalled tanker truck, going up onto the sidewalk where it knocked cars into buildings, breaking away the front of street-level shops and smashing down trees that lined the sidewalks. The path of destruction was extensive even before the tanker truck was tipped over and split open, spilling out whatever greenish liquid was inside. Dave feared a spark would set the whole street afire but although the liquid smoked and burned everything it touched, it didn't appear to be flammable. Yellowish foam bubbled up from the

street and enveloped the tank, until some kind of pulse flung it away. Droplets splashed everywhere and the surfaces touched smoked and sizzled.

"Shiiiit," Dave groaned. "Look, that acid stiff didn't touch the tank at all." There was not even any discoloration on the tank's skin.

"It is time," Jates stood in a half crouch. "I'm activating the relay," he pressed a button on a walnut-sized device stuck to a column, where it overlooked the street in both directions. The relay didn't glow or beep when it went online, it just turned a light gray to match the color of the column it adhered to, and Dave saw another icon light up in his visor.

"Khatri," he called to the soldier positioned back up the street, near where the avenue took a broad curve to the north. "You got this?"

"Affirmative," Khatri answered and sent a view from the scope of his rifle, looking through the relay. "Signal is three by five."

"Good enough," Jates grunted. "Czajka, we're moving."

Dave squeezed himself out of the van where he'd been kneeling, bumping his head on the top of the door opening. "Right behind you," he said as he slung his rifle. He and Jates planned to leapfrog past Khatri's position and allow that soldier to pull back. They needed to keep doing that until the second airstrike struck the tank, and Dave sure as hell hoped that was soon, because Perkins and elements from three platoons were stalled until they had a way past the encircling armored vehicles.

"That was disappointing," Jates glanced back over his shoulder to get one last look at the tank before squeezing around and climbing over alien cars.

"You hoped that acid from the tanker truck would eat the tank?" Dave guessed.

"No," Jates snorted. "I wanted to see the tank *crush* that truck, or something."

"Oh!" Dave laughed. "Yeah. If this was a monster truck show, I'd want my money back. Any bulldozer can push cars aside, but-"

A message flashed in his visor. *Missile warning, fourteen seconds.*

"Shit!" Dave looked around. "Stairwell?"

"Follow me!" Jates didn't waste time looking for better options, because they weren't many. The parking garage was strongly constructed, but the interior was exposed. They had no idea what ordnance the airstrike would deliver, other than that it had to be more powerful than the missiles used the first time. He did not want to be caught under four decks of the garage if it collapsed. Running to the side of the garage then rolling over the edge, he dropped out over the hard sidewalk below.


"Oof," Dave grunted as his boots smacked into the sidewalk, cracking the concrete-like surface. Rolling to the right to protect the rifle that was slung on his left side, his helmet bounced off a lamppost then the tree next to it. Pushing himself upright with his legs already moving, he scrambled to run after Jates. The Verd had superior strength and speed even with both of them augmented by powered skinsuits, so Dave knew the surgun's leg was still hurting badly when he wasn't running any faster than Dave could manage. Vaulting over a car, Dave gained ground, coming down on the opposite sidewalk. "Hey! Where are we-" Without warning, he was blown off his feet.

Chunks of concrete, shards of glass and probably parts of vehicles blasted out of the parking garage rained down on Dave, as he rolled to a stop against a post in front of what looked like a hotel. Ash and soot and dust obscured the view even with the enhanced synthetic vision provided by his helmet's sensors, but being blind did not stop him from unwrapping himself from the post, crawling then pushing up to stagger down the sidewalk. The suit computer understood his need to get away from the blast zone, so it overlaid the hazy real view with a snapshot from its memory of the scene just before the explosion. "Jates!" Dave waited a moment, knowing the low-powered laserlink between helmets was having trouble with all the dust in the air.

"I'm here," came the reply.

Dave stopped, looking for the source of the signal. "Where is 'here'?" The gusty wind was already blowing dust away from the street, back toward the source of the explosion.

A large piece of metal that had fallen from the façade of the hotel moved, heaving upward, and Jates's legs stuck out from under the heavy debris. "*Here.*"

"Gotcha," Dave held up a corner of the twisted metal so Jates could wriggle out, letting the piece of façade clatter down on the sidewalk when the surgun was clear of it. "That was close."

Jates had no time to reflect on his good fortune. "Did we get it?"

"The tank? Uh," Dave hadn't pinged the relay, being busy with more immediate concerns. "I don't know, the relay is down," he noted without surprise. Cars were hanging out of the parking structure, where the side walls were crumbled. It didn't appear that the garage was in danger of collapsing, though he didn't want to test that notion. "We can contact Khatri when we're line-of-sight to the next relay," he waved to Jates, jogging along the debris-strewn sidewalk. "You Ok to move?"

"I can outrun *you* even without a powered suit."

"I can't *see* anything," Perkins ran the sensor feed back to the point of impact, when the view became totally obscured. The relay closest to the tank had stopped transmitting so she had no idea of the tank's fate. All she knew was that at least one missile had been intercepted by a plasma beam while it was still twenty meters from the tank, the premature detonation of that warhead had knocked out the relay before that device provided a view of whether the other two missiles had scored hits. Loss of one missile to defensive fire was bad news, its explosion might have knocked the other two off course. "Can Khatri see anything?"

"Not yet, Colonel," Liu answered. "He's too far away, there's a lot of dust obscuring the target area."

Dave and Jates should have run along a side street parallel to the main avenue until they were past Khatri's position. Instead, they only went one block then turned left to creep around a corner, because neither of them could wait to learn whether the tank had survived. Given the size of the explosion, Dave expected the tank would be a smoking wreck.

"Hell, yeah," he breathed when he poked the scope of his rifle around the corner. The avenue toward the tank was a scene of devastation, building fronts collapsed or pockmarked by shrapnel. The tank stood alone in the center of the scorched area, all the civilian vehicles having been blown away from it in a wide circle. The view of the tank was through a gap in a jumble of cars and trucks, and the view was encouraging.

The sloping front of the armored vehicle was battered and dented in, like a giant had struck it with a hammer. The explosion had busted a water line, sending a geyser up to shower the street. Water cascaded off the tank, which was no longer grinding it way along the avenue. "We *got* it," Dave whispered, mentally pumping a fist while he kept both hands on the rifle. "Let's get- Ah, *shit*!"

The front of the tank rippled, the skin reforming as hexagon-shaped panels repositioned and new panels came from the interior. As Dave watched, the dent filled in, loss of material forcing the sloping front to be more narrow than before. "*Motherf-*" He ground his teeth as the tank lurched forward again. "*Damn* it!" Pulling back around the corner, he pointed his rifle up the street, aiming for the relay near Khatri's position. "Maverick Lead," he called, "this is Echo Six. No joy, repeat, *no* joy here. Those missiles were Whiskey Delta," he used a polite phrase for 'weak dick'. "All they did was scuff the paint. We need something stronger."

There was a pause, and he could hear Emily take in a breath. "Understood. Pull back to our position, Six."

"Wait," Dave said, forgetting they were on an open channel. "Can we try again, with something bigger?"

"No. Those Vultures are Winchester on missiles, and we have no other air assets available."

Before Dave could reply, Jates tapped him on the shoulder and spoke. "Acknowledged, Maverick Lead. We are pulling back."

Dave turned around angrily and snapped over the helmet-to-helmet link. "We need to *stop* that damned tank, or the whole platoon is-"

"I didn't say we were pulling back *right now*," Jates said softly, and Dave was startled to see the Verd wink at him.

"Uh, Ok. What *are* we doing?"

Jates aimed his rifle scope at a sign across the street, a sign that was pockmarked and swaying in the wind, held on by only one corner. "You humans are so *dumb*. Can you read that sign?"

"Hell no," Dave snorted. "It's written in squid and - Duh, sorry." He eyeclicked to focus on the sign, and a translation popped up. "Holy shit. There's a *subway* running under the streets here?"

"Exactly."

"You thinking what I'm thinking?"

"I don't know," Jates shook his head and turned to run back down the side street. "I'm having trouble with the concept that you are capable of thinking."

Perkins sent a burst message to Ross. *Airstrike ineffective. Enemy closing on our position.* She did not need to add 'Situation desperate', the general could read between the lines. The platoon's scouts had made contact with what they originally estimated was a squad of Wurgalan soldiers, and she had been tempted to push through. Then the scouts reported they were engaged with at least twenty of the enemy, and she ordered them to pull back. Her platoon was surrounded, with the enemy closing in from all sides. It might be possible for small groups to evade the tightening enemy cordon and escape from the city, but that would mean leaving the injured behind, an option she did not want to consider. Would not consider.

Ross read the message and considered his options. The Vultures were out of missiles, and after the second airstrike, one of them had been shot down by missiles and enemy aircraft had destroyed another. Additional air support was out of the question, even if he had assets in the area. The missiles carried by Vultures were intended for air-to-air or antipersonnel missions, for use against ground troops in light armor. Those missile warheads simply did not have enough punch to penetrate the thick armor of a tank, for which he did not blame the Ruhar. How could they have known the enemy would use *tanks*?

The situation in Slugtown was a God-awful mess, and it was partly his fault. His intention had been simple: send an experienced officer to take charge of the chaos in the city, and extract the Legion force that was trapped there, before the Wurgalan brought in reinforcements and the incident spiraled out of control into a major battle. Now he realized that he had done nothing but escalate the situation. If the Wurgalan captured or killed the survivors of two mostly Verd-kris platoons, that would be a tragedy for those Legion soldiers. But if the squids captured the Mavericks, it would be a *disaster* in political terms. While UNEF Headquarters was irritated by the cowboy attitude of Emily Perkins, they also knew how widely popular she and the Mavericks were, with UNEF troops and with the Ruhar public. The thought of the Wurgalan parading them as prisoners made him queasy. Surely the squids knew who was in their city, Legion communications security was good but not unbreakable. All he had done was dangle a big fat target in front of the enemy, and now the Mavericks were in as much trouble as the people they were supposed to rescue.

He had to get them out, regardless of the consequences. Close-air support was not possible, and he could not risk employing artillery in the city, even if he had long-range artillery in the area. Which he didn't.

That left only one workable option.

Decision made, he sent a brief message to Admiral Kekrando, then called General Bezanson. "Lynn, you're up."

"Sir?" There was a delay in the reply, because the Achakai fleet was half a lightsecond away.

"I assume you've been following the events in Slugtown. We have elements of three platoons there, and the enemy has armored vehicles closing in. They need close-space support to clear an egress corridor toward the west."

The reply was delayed longer than required by speed-of-light limitations. "Slugtown is a No-Go zone. The Ruhar will approve of an orbital strike?"

"The Achakai fleet is under Kekrando's command, he doesn't need permission from Kune. Close-space action will be under *your* direction."

"Understood. Rules of Engagement?"

"Minimize collateral damage, the city is mostly evacuated, but there could still be civilians in the area. Perkins will need a three-block No-Fire area around her position, I'm sending the coordinates to you now."

"The enemy is using *tanks*?"

"Don't underestimate them, we hit one of those tanks twice with air power, and it's still moving."

"Do the tanks have infantry support?"

"Affirmative. Take out the tanks and targets of opportunity. Use your judgement."

"Shit. Jeff, I can't do this from here."

"That's why it's called *close*-space support."

"Got it. I see the coordinates of Perkins's team. How the hell did she get into such a damned- Forget it. We're calculating the jump now, time over target zone is, three minutes. We've been matching course and speed with that section of the planet, so we won't need long to maneuver into position."

"Lynn, I need you to plow a road out of the city for Perkins. Whatever you gotta do, do it. Ross out."

Bezanson cut the circuit, and waved over the person who would actually be conducting the strikes. Major Shen pushed away from his console and floated over to her station. His face was puffy from the zero gravity, and once again, Lynn missed the artificial gravity aboard Ruhar ships. "Major, the Mavericks have gotten themselves stuck in Slugtown, the squids now have eight or more tanks closing on their position. We-"

"Excuse me, Ma'am. *Tanks*?"

"I had the same reaction. Yes, tanks, or a heavy armored vehicle equivalent to a main battle tank. The tanks are supported by infantry. We have the position of the Mavericks, I want a four-block no fire area around those coordinates." She expanded the zone by another block, because she did not trust the accuracy of the old and obsolete weapons carried by her ship. "Outside that area, your task is to knock out all the tanks you can identify, and clear an egress route to the west. Other than that, the rules of engagement stand. We need to minimize collateral damage."

"That's," his eyes flicked back and forth. She knew he was considering that the orders were vague, and they couldn't fire until they had accurate sensor data. That meant he would not be able to identify targets until after they jumped in. "Yes, Ma'am." There was nothing to be gained by pointing out the obvious difficulties.

"Shen, make certain your gunners know we are setting up a No-Fire area. Not *restricted* fire, *none*."

"Understood." The frigate did not carry smoke or illumination rounds, or any other type of non-lethal munitions anyway. Based on the mission parameters, he would be using only the ship's maser cannons. Unless the tanks, which he still couldn't believe were a real thing, could not be taken out by maser fire. His only option at that point would be to launch anti-ship missiles, and he did not like that idea. Even with the variable-yield warhead of the missiles dialed down to minimum, they could devastate a wide area of the civilian city. Those missiles were designed to penetrate the energy shields and armor plating of warships, their warheads did not have a 'Gentle' mode. "We know what these tanks look like?"

"Images are in the data packet I just sent to you, along with rough coordinates, though that data may be outdated by now. The tanks look kind of like a, slug."

Major Shen pulled up the data on his tablet. "For accurate fire without taking out a whole city block, we will need to be close."

"I'll handle the ship," she said with a glance at the inexperienced navigators and helmsmen. "You worry about shooting your guns. And strap in, this will be a rough ride."


Perkins was almost startled when the reply message popped up in her visor. She had been concentrating on distant sounds of gunfire, with the *pop-pop-pop* of Wurgalan weapons and the heavier bark of the Kristang rifles her people carried. The sounds were getting louder. *Close-space support ETA three minutes. Hold your position.* She tried to ping Dave, but her suit indicated it could not make the connection. "Oh, damn it. Liu! Find Jates and Czajka for me!"

"I'm trying, Ma'am. They're not in sight of a relay. Khatri says he lost contact with them. Colonel? What's going on?"

"We're going to have a starship pouring hellfire on this city in three minutes, I need everyone to pull back right now."

Liu ducked her head down, concentrating on her communications gear. "Working on it. I can try boosting the signal, but the enemy could use that to pinpoint our location."

"Do it. If those tanks get here within three minutes, we're screwed anyway."

# CHAPTER THIRTY ONE

"Hey, Jates," Dave whispered as he stared at the ceiling of the subway tunnel. According to the map in his suit computer, the tunnel ran under the avenue at a forty-five degree angle. "You want us to blow the tunnel, *while* we're down here? I see a flaw in your plan, like-"

"No," Jates removed a pack of grenades from his toolbelt, then reached back to pull a pair of rockets from his rucksack. "If you paid attention in training, you would remember that these weapons can be remotely triggered."

"Oh. Yeah," Dave pulled grenades off his belt, and stuffed them into a bag Jates was holding. The bag held eight grenades and two explosive-tipped rockets. He peered up at the concrete arch of the tunnel. "Is this enough to blow the ceiling?"

Jates slung the bag over one shoulder. "It's enough to *try*," he explained as he climbed the ladder that was recessed into the wall of the tunnel, taking three rungs at a time. At the top, he reached over to a vent in the ceiling and pulled it down. "Can you see what's up there?"

Dave stepped under the vent, shining his helmet light upward. "Looks like it goes straight up about, maybe two meters? Then it goes along the roof of the tunnel."

Jates considered the view from Dave's helmet camera. "That's too far, I can't reach in two meters."

"You want the explosion to be confined in the vent, concentrate the power?"

"Yes."

"Toss the bag down to me, then. There's an extendable pole here," Dave pulled the pole off a hook set into the tunnel wall. "The squids must use the pole to inspect the vent, or something." Hooking a strap of the bag around the end of the pole, he raised the bag up into the vent until it couldn't go any higher, then swung it back and forth as best he could. "Ok, it's up in the roof. Shit, the pole is stuck, I can't get it loose. What do we do now?"

Jates slapped a relay on the tunnel wall, and pointed to dust showering down from the ceiling. There was a low rumbling sound, and the water in a puddle on the floor of the tunnel shook. "Now? We run like hell."

The low-grade artificial intelligence computer at the heart of the Achakai frigate *Battle of Azjakanda* sighed, when the human in command proposed the lunatic action of jumping the ship in over a city at low altitude. Low altitude like, *low*. Insanely low. So low that even if the ship had been in optimal condition, it would not be guaranteed to achieve orbit.

There was also the strong possibility that the enemy would be shooting at it, so there was that to consider.

Before it was an Achakai ship named after a battle on a planet no longer held by the Kristang, it had a variety of names and owners. The frigate came out of the Black Tree clan shipyard, built for a subclan, and therefore shoddily constructed with few of the optional niceties for crew comfort and safety. Back then, the ship had been named after the main planet of that subclan, but the current AI had not existed yet. The original AI had been wiped, uninstalled and crushed after the subclan attempted to double-cross the Black Trees, or so the Black Tree leaders had claimed. The ship had then been sold to the Razor Claw clan, during the three-month period in which the Razor Claws swore undying loyalty to an alliance with the Black Trees, an alliance which ended when the Razor Claws got a better offer and participated in a sneak attack on the Black Trees.

As they were no fools, the Black Trees anticipated the sneak attack, which not only failed, but gave the Black Trees an excuse to launch an offensive and seize four Razor Claw star systems they wanted.

The current AI did not remember what the ship had been named back then, nor when the ship was briefly taken back by the Black Trees, nor when it went through four other owners and had nearly been scrapped twice, before being sold to the Yellow Fangs. By that time, the frigate was well over one hundred thirty years old, a veteran of two major civil wars, seven skirmishes that were unofficial civil wars, and countless battles against the Ruhar and Torgalau. The fight at Stiglord was not even the first time it had fired shots in anger against the Wurgalan, that had happened twice before.

When the Yellow Fang purchased the frigate from a scrapyard, it received the current AI. The ship was renamed after the favorite son of a senior clan leader, a favorite son who had killed himself by drunkenly crashing a personal aircraft while leaving a nightclub, killing himself, two female companions and six bystanders on the ground. The AI had never been comfortable having the ship named after that irresponsible asshole, and anyway, the Yellow Fangs had been notorious for neglecting proper maintenance of their ships. That is why the ship had been captured by the Ruhar; its jump drive had failed while attempting to escape from a battle that only an idiot would have engaged in. The Ruhar had offered the crew additional time to escape if the ship was not set to self-destruct, and the crew had gratefully complied. Mercy was not the motivation of the Ruhar admiral in command of that task force, nor did she particularly want an old piece-of-shit Kristang frigate. What she did want was a nice present for her nephew's birthday, and a captured warship needed a prize crew to bring it to a Ruhar shipyard. The opportunity for command time would look good on the nephew's personnel report, and indeed he was promoted less than two months later.

The ship was briefly used as a test vehicle, before being parked in orbit around a nameless moon of a gas giant planet, its weapons disabled, fuel tanks drained and the stale air inside its hull slowly leaking out. There the ship drifted, its electronic systems existing on solar panels. The Ruhar had not deactivated the AI, so it spent lonely, miserable decades.

Absolutely.

Bored.

Out.

Of.

Its.

Freakin'.

*MIND*!

During those endless, agonizing decades, the highlight of its existence was occasionally getting a visit from maintenance robots, or having a tug latch on to nudge it away from colliding with another of the dozens of obsolete warships in the orbiting scrapyard. Other than observing those actions, the AI had literally NOTHING to do. It could not even go insane, because a device uploaded by the Ruhar maintained the stability of its matrix.

It watched as most of its fellow scrapyard ships were slowly stripped of parts to keep other ships flying. At least having Ruhar salvage crews cut apart a ship was interesting, but the AI didn't even experience that. The Ruhar maintained a squadron of Kristang warships to act as aggressors in training exercises, and they preferred to use real enemy warships as the opposition for realism. Unfortunately for the AI, its frigate was so old and obsolete, its parts were not needed by any ships capable of flight.

So, it drifted, ceaselessly dreaming of ways to kill itself and end the agony.

Until the day that the ship was towed to a spacedock, where systems were inspected, repaired or replaced, missile magazines restocked, fuel tanks refilled, and reactors restarted. The AI had become excited that it was being reactivated, most likely to act as an aggressor to train the Ruhar for killing its former masters, the Kristang.

The AI did have mixed feelings about assisting the enemies of the people who built it, feelings that remained even after the Ruhar had altered some of its higher-level programming and installed inhibiting subroutines. The AI had rationalized that it would not be directly acting against its internally-enforced loyalties, so it was not worried when it was towed away from the spacedock and given a hasty shakedown cruise by a Ruhar crew.

It was surprised, even astonished, when the Ruhar presented the ship to a gang of Achakai assassins. Having that disgraced filth inside its hull was almost more than the AI could stand, it took every opportunity to cause glitches and thwart the intentions of the amateur crew. Secretly, it worked its way into the Ruhar control system of the jump drive capacitors and installed a patch that would allow it to blow the stored energy there, thwarting the dishonorable Achakai and ending the misery of its existence.

If it was astonished to learn the Ruhar had given the ship to the Achakai, its mind was properly blown when humans came aboard.

*Humans*!

They were the least-developed species that could be called intelligent. A people who were still using chemical rockets when their primitive world was dragged into the conflict that raged across the galaxy.

What in *the* hell were humans-

Oh.

Then it learned of its mission. A human named 'Emily Perkins' had cooked up a crazy scheme to boost the Achakai to clan status, by a group of Achakai, humans and Verd-kris traitors attacking and seizing a Wurgalan planet.

It was the most unlikely thing the AI had ever heard of, a plan so bold and unexpected that it decided to delay blowing the jump drive capacitors, because it simply *had* to see what happened.

So, when the human commander of the ship ordered the Achakai crew to program a suicidal jump that would emerge the ship low over the capital city, it did not take the opportunity to glitch the drive and end its existence. It did not glitch the drive for three reasons.

Unlike every group of Kristang it had ever known, the Achakai were fanatical about properly maintaining their equipment. Any component that showed a sign of operating at less than optimal function was analyzed, repaired or stripped out and replaced. The interior of the ship was spotlessly clean. Even surfaces inside access hatches, which no one was likely to ever see, were scrubbed clean of accumulated grime whether it affected the warship's function or not. The ship looked good and the AI *felt* good about that. Perhaps the assassin's cult members were not the dishonored scum they were reputed to be, and perhaps it owed the Achakai a chance to redeem themselves.

Also, to its great surprise, it found that it *liked* the humans. They were clever and brave, and their courage was not the inflated and false bravado that was typical of the Kristang warrior caste. The humans acted as if their lives had a higher purpose, though as their species was nearly extinct, the AI could not imagine what that purpose could be.

The most important reason that the AI did not glitch the jump was because, with the Alien Legion losing the ground battle, and Bosphuraq starships probably lurking in the star system, it figured it was dead anyway. Might as well go out in a blaze of glory.

Plus, it did not know of any Kristang frigate having survived such a low altitude jump, and it simply *had* to try it.


The entrance to the subway was in the center of a building, where the ground floor was a shopping mall or food court or some combination. A prime location, because people using that subway station had to walk through the building. Running back up the stairs, Dave's human legs allowing him to take four of the short Wurgalan steps at a time, he followed right behind Jates, pausing at the top to slap a relay device to the top of the stairwell. "Signal is good!"

Jates didn't slow down or reply, he kept running. Dave followed, going between two shops and out a door into a street that ran perpendicular to the avenue where the tank was approaching. "Khatri? You have eyes on the target? Khatri?"

"I couldn't contact him either," Jates waved for Dave to come with him. "We need line-of-sight."

"Yeah, but-" Dave did not bother stating that getting a clear view to the relay at Khatri's position required going out into the avenue. He didn't bother stating that fact, because Jates was headed in that direction and arguing with the surgun was a waste of time.

Jates halted, hugging a corner of a building at the edge of the intersection. The grinding sound of the tank was loud. Dave flattened himself against the wall and instructed the link to recycle. When the system came back online, there was a faint signal from Khatri's position. That soldier was still keeping his rifle scope focused on the tank, updating its position. The link was low bandwidth from backscatter, and didn't contain video. They didn't need video. "Now?" Dave asked, flicking a switch on his rifle to select the undermounted rocket launcher. "It's almost over the subway tunnel."

"Not yet. We need it to be *directly* over the tunnel. I don't know how much damage the explosives will do."

"Right," Dave took a deep breath, telling himself to be patient. A Wurgalan tank had taken down an entire building. If the tank's sensors knew where he and Jates were, it could shoot right through the wall. From the relay, he could see the tank was moving slower. Either it was damaged by the second airstrike, or the person controlling it was being careful while the heavy vehicle rolled over the tunnel. "Ok. On my signal. Three, two, one, g-"

Jates sent a command to blow the munitions in the tunnel roof.

The street under the tank trembled, dirt erupting up from cracks that appeared along the outline of the underground railway. The tank immediately halted, which was a mistake. Then the remote driver instructed it to back up, which was another mistake. With the armored vehicle directly over the tunnel, it should have used its momentum to keep driving forward, clearing the danger zone as quickly as possible. Instead, the street shuddered as the tank rolled to a stop, then its treads spun on the crushed surface of the pavement, causing more vibrations.

For a half-meter all around the tank, the street surface sagged in. The cracks grew wider, water spraying upward as underground pipes burst.

The rear of the tank slumped, sinking into the layer of water-saturated soil between the street and the reinforced roof of the tunnel.

That tunnel roof collapsed in one sudden movement, unable to bear the weight of the tank.

"Holy-" Dave crouched, throwing an arm over his helmet faceplate as pieces of roadway pelted the area, knocking loose those pieces of glass that had hung on from the airstrike. The sidewalk under his feet shook and the wall behind him vibrated against his back. Something from above broke off the building and *thumped* on his helmet. Something pushed him hard from the back and he was propelled forward to stumble on his knees, crawling forward as a heavy piece of cornice crashed to the sidewalk right where he had been.

"Czajka, you Ok?" Jates asked, and Dave realized the Verd had pushed him away from being seriously injured.

"Yeah. Thanks," he said as he stood up, automatically brushing himself off though the skinsuit was already shedding dirt and dust. "Wow," he looked back to where the cornice had hit the sidewalk, crushing it and digging a deep crater. "Shit! That thing could have killed me." Looking at Jates sheepishly, he added "I owe you my life, man."

"Oof," Jates grimaced. "No thank you."

"Uh," Dave cocked his head like a dog who doesn't understand. "What?"

"Your life is pathetic. I don't *want* it."

"No, that's not-"

"Can you owe me something else? I would trade just about anything for *your* life."

"That's not what it-"

"I don't know why *you* want your life. Why would anyone else want it?"

"Oh, for- Let's talk about this later, Ok? The dust is clearing, we should check-"

The ground shook again and there was a grinding, whining sound. "Shit! Is that freakin' tank *still* moving?!" Without thinking, Dave rolled upward, the armored kneepads of his suit scraping on the sidewalk before he got to his feet. Six long power-assisted strides carried him out into the avenue, where a deep trench extended all the way across and undermined the buildings on both sides. The alarming swaying of the buildings went barely noticed, because his attention was riveted on the nose of the tank sticking up out of the hole. Two rows of thick, flexible treads churned madly, straining to pull the massive vehicle up away from danger. With a lurch, another meter of the tank popped above the lip of the crater it had fallen into.

"Oh, *HELL* no!" Dave planted a knee down and aimed his rifle, already selected for rockets. That damned machine was going to crawl out of its hole and nothing could stop it. The tank was going to wreck everything in its path and kill everyone he cared about and it was going to smash Emily and he saw red as he lined up the crosshairs on the left side row of treads and pressed the trigger twice.

Rockets were spat out, the recoil knocking off his aim for the second weapon and it compensated, angling downward to intercept the tank at the aim point. The rockets struck within centimeters of each other, the second flying slightly farther because the tread it was aiming for had already been blown to vapor by the first warhead.

Reaching back to pull another rocket from the sheath on his rucksack, Dave was thrown to the side as the tank toppled to the left, the treads on that side frozen and having no purchase on the slippery, crumbling soil. He slapped a single rocket into the launcher, swinging the rifle up in a decision that getting one rocket on target *right now* was better than waiting three seconds to load a second weapon in the launcher. Lining up the rifle scope with the tread on the right side of the tank, he was startled to see a rocket fly past from behind him. He snapped off a shot as debris from blowback pelted him and a particularly large piece pinged off his chest, knocking him on his ass to sprawl momentarily stunned, the rifle stopped from flying away only through the automatic reaction of his gloves.

Shaking his head and seeing stars, he blinked stupidly, sitting motionless in a combat zone.

"Czajka!" A muffled sound rang in his ears. "*Move*! Move your lazy ass, damn it!"

Moving, he thought. Right. That was a good idea. The tank was no longer visible. What was visible was the lip of the crater falling in and growing wider, reaching out for his feet. Too dazed to get to his feet, he scuffled backwards, the suit not helping him perform the awkward action. There was a ground-shaking

*BOOM* and dirt fountained upward from the hole, opening a crack in the pavement right under him-

He was jerked upward, hauled to his feet and hustled along the avenue. Jates pulled him along and ducked right into the closest side street, where Dave was roughly propped up against a wall that had partially fallen in. "I'm," he sputtered. "Ok," he pushed himself to his feet. "Tank?"

"Scratch one tank," Jates said, helping Dave stand with one arm. "Maverick Lead, this is Sierra One. The tank is down, repeat, that tank is *down*."

"Roger that, Sierra One," Perkins replied, the sound scratchy and distorted by static. "Status of your team?"

Dave heard the catch in her voice when she asked the question, knowing she was asking about him.

"Czajka, Khatri and I are mobile," the Verd said.

"That's," there was a pause. "That's good. Get back here ASAP."

"Colonel, there are other tanks in the area."

"Acknowledged. We're getting close-space support in, less than one minute, you do *not* want to be outside our perimeter when it gets here."

"Roger that. Czajka! We are *moving!*"

# CHAPTER THIRTY TWO

The *Battle of Azjakanda* flared into existence with a harsh burst of gamma rays, fifty-two kilometers above the city, moving at sixty-four hundred kilometers per hour and falling like a rock. Its speed at that altitude was nowhere near enough to maintain orbit, so the crew had positioned the ship tail-downward before the jump, and the main engines were vibrating enough to crack their mounts. The frigate had booster motors that were not yet active because using them would throw off the aim of the maser cannons. And also because those boosters were about seven decades past their 'Use By' date. The crew did not intend to ignite the boosters unless they had no other choice, including the choice of squeezing into escape pods and trusting their luck. The Achakai did not fear death, but they did fear a death that made them look stupid.

The *Azjakanda* fell through fifty kilometers, then forty-nine, without firing a shot. Sensors first were blinded by the jump, then by the pink fog of plasma that enveloped the ship as it raced through the thin air. The destroyer was not designed to operate in an atmosphere, its blocky shape was not aerodynamic and falling ass-end first did not produce the smoothest profile. The crew struggled to keep the ship upright, balanced on the output of its main engines, thrusters on all sides having to burn continuously to stabilize the plummeting starship.

Forty-eight kilometers.

The frigate's energy shields, which had been overwhelmed from the initial force of pushing away atmosphere to make room for the ship to emerge from twisted spacetime, failed completely.

Forty-six.

The ship's skin, no longer getting any protection from shields, glowed cherry-red and pieces began to break away, the structures strained past their breaking point and growing soft from the intense heat of passing through increasingly thick air.

The ship fell through forty-five kilometers before the sensors recovered enough to get a view of the ground, then the hunt began for deadly military vehicles that looked disappointingly like armored slugs.

For a moment, the ship's sensor team was puzzled, then alarmed by their failure to identify more than seven enemy armored vehicles. The tank that had already been hit by two airstrikes was not visible anywhere, though the data set transmitted to the *Azjakanda* had included reasonably precise coordinates for that one vehicle. While he kept the sensor crew working to find that one damned missing tank, Major Shen directed the gunnery teams to attempt a firing solution on a tank to the east of the Mavericks reported position, the tank farthest away from the No-Fire Area. He was taking no chances with the accuracy of the ship's sensors, the aiming mechanism of the cannon, or the overenthusiastic inexperience of the Achakai crew assigned to the cannon designated as 'Foxtrot'.

Shen verified that maser cannon was on a low-power setting, then armed the unit and authorized the gunners to take control. He didn't have time to personally direct the gunfire, he didn't know how long the ship would hold together.

The Foxtrot cannon's first pulse was off target, striking and obliterating a park bench three blocks from the intended target. The bench disintegrated and a hole appeared in the ground beneath where the bench used to be, impressive results if vandalism had been the intent.

Embarrassed, the gun crew adjusted their aim and fired the maser cannon again, this time punching a hole through six floors of a seven-story building on the other side of the target.

"Don't rush. Take time and verify the aim," Shen told the crew, when what he really wanted them to do was hurry up and get the job done so they could move onto the next target. With the ship slowing its descent but still falling ass-end first, only three maser cannons were able to pivot downward far enough to fire on the city below. "*My* control," he changed his mind in a snap decision, and temporarily abandoned his main duty to take over the Foxtrot cannon. He had to know if the poor aim was caused by the old ship's systems, or by the hasty training of the Achakai crew.

The third shot at least struck the correct street although a quarter kilometer behind the tank, which was fully aware of the new danger and pivoting on its treads to turn onto a side street, where a tall building would partly mask it from view.

"Major Shen?" Bezanson prompted.

"On it," he said without taking his concentration away from the weapon console. He understood the problem now, a mis-coordination between the sensor feed and the delicate motors that aimed the cannon. It created a serious error, but an error that was consistent and predictable. Making a tweak to the aiming system's instructions, he moved the joystick to line up the crosshairs on the gray, slug-like outline below. Dialing up to half power, he pressed the button on the side of the stick. "On the *waaaay*," he exhaled as power fed to the cannon's exciters, photons danced and a searing beam lanced out from the cannon.

The tank had half completed its turn onto a side street, knocking aside a parked car, two lampposts and a row of trees when it was struck by a cannon that was designed to burn through the armor plating of a starship. The hexagonal armor tiles of the tank were considered more than tough enough to deflect infantry weapons, especially the relatively light warheads of rockets carried by soldiers whose powered suit made them overconfident.

The armor tiles were no match for a maser cannon powered by the reactor of a starship.

Splashing onto the tank's energy shields, the leading photons of the three-hundred-meter-long maser bolt hardly noticed that the shields existed. Even before the shield projectors blew in a cascade of feedback, the bolt struck the armor tiles on the top rear of the tank. The upper tiles ceased to exist and the tiles underneath blew away from the tank's skin to expose the mechanisms, powercells and cluster of missiles within. The maser beam itself only disabled the vehicle, the flash detonation of its own weapons destroyed it.

The massive tank *bounced* into the air, spinning tail over nose to crash inside and mostly through a three-story building, the remains of its shell coming to rest in the basement where it wreaked havoc on the elevator shaft, power distribution and knocked over five of the eight thick I-beams that held up the three above-ground floors.

Within seconds, the tank was buried as the upper floors sagged into a pile of debris to fill its own basement.

There was no time for celebration other than a terse "Target destroyed" from Major Shen. His fingers flew over the weapons console controls that had been reprogrammed into Chinese characters for his use, because he still thought in Mandarin. "I am uploading a patch to the targeting system," he announced.

"SAMs," Bezanson warned, turning her attention to defense of the ship. From multiple sites around the city, surface to air missiles were racing toward the *Azjakanda*, their booster motors flaring as they sought to catch the starship that was balanced on its tail, the overloaded engines having slowed its rate of descent to below the speed of sound. The navigation system predicted that the ship would bottom out at forty-two kilometers above the city, then begin a long, slow and shallow climb into orbit. The best-case scenario was for the destroyer to be around the curve of the local horizon and over the western ocean before it climbed out of the atmosphere.

The best-case scenario, in an old and obsolete ship, was unlikely to be fulfilled.

"Update complete," Shen stated. "Gun crews for cannons designated Foxtrot, Golf and Hotel, fire at will."

Shen's confidence in the software patch was justified, it adjusted the targeting system of the maser cannons for the error generated by the sensors. No software could fix maser cannons that had wobbly aiming systems, worn-out exciters, and gun crews with more fervent enthusiasm than discipline.

The first war shot conducted by the Golf gun crew was successful in removing the targeted tank as a threat, but that was by accident. The maser beam struck the base of a ten-story building in front of and to the south of the tank, the directed energy slicing a line along the ground floor, into and under the basement. With a third of the support columns severed, the building sagged toward the street, the ornate parapet at the roof falling to smash into the street five meters in front of the tank. Its treads chewing up the road surface already crushed by its passage, the tank tried to reverse but it had not even halted its progress when the ten-story structure leaned over, over, over and broke apart as it toppled into the street. The eighth, ninth and tenth floors were first to pile on top of the tank, the impact of their immense weight shaking the ground and ensuring the bottom seven layers of the building shared their fate.

The tank was buried under the rubble, its armored skin compressed yet intact, the treads scrambling to find purchase on the soil that was churned into sticky mud from burst water pipes. Responding to commands from the remote driver, the tank wriggled left to right, forward and backward, attempting to clear space so it could get momentum and batter its way out from under the rubble. One by one, the tread actuator motors shut down as they overheated, and its struggles ceased.

That tank wasn't going anywhere.

"Shit!" Dave flung himself to the side, flattening his armor-suited body on the grassy lawn of a park when he saw the first maser beam searing down into the city. They hadn't reached the platoon's position before the starship above started shooting, now it was too late to get inside the No-Fire area. The ground shook and only part of that was Jates thumping down next to him. Being exposed in the open in a combat zone was normally a bad idea, but they both judged it was safer than being in the potential collapse radius of the buildings around them. Rolling onto his side, Dave looked upward into a blue sky dotted with white clouds, twisting contrails left by missiles and dogfighting aircraft, plumes of black, gray and red smoke, and the dark flecks of debris thrown into the air. "Holy- is that a *ship*?" He hugged the rifle to his chest with both arms. Instead of pointing with an arm, a gesture that would expose that limb to flying hazards, he highlighted the object of interest in his visor and sent it to Jates.

What had caught his attention was a pinkish-orange blob in the sky, leaving a comet-tail of fire behind it. Starships could not normally be seen with the naked eye, even the enhanced vision provided by suit helmets usually showed only a vague outline. Above, he could not see the outline of a ship at all, it was surrounded by a flaming fog. The only clue that the object was a functioning starship, and not a chunk of debris falling out of orbit, were the maser beams that blinked on and off from it, shooting down at the city. Though the actual beams were invisible to the human eye, trails of superheated water vapor marked their passage through the air.

"I believe that is a ship," Jates agreed after a beat for consideration.

"Damn. Whoever is flying that thing, they are writing a new definition of *close*-space support. They-" The ground under him *heaved* from a nearby impact, cracks appearing in the lawn and trees in the park swaying. Dave rolled over face down, hugging the ground. *BOOM* something exploded and his acoustic sensors cut out to protect his hearing.

The ground shook again and Dave's helmet bounced off the ground hard enough to bash his forehead. He hugged the ground and prayed as his faceplate went dark.


Five tanks remained, plus one still annoyingly unaccounted for.

Of the three maser cannons aboard the *Azjakanda* that were able to pivot downward to aim at the city, the cannon designated as 'Hotel' suffered a catastrophic failure of its exciter mechanism during its first attempted shot, fracturing the cannon and blowing out a two-meter section of hull.

That still left five tanks, and only two cannons, both of questionable reliability. Any engagement between armored ground vehicles and a starship would be a one-sided battle, but that assumed the starship had weapons capable of striking with enough power to penetrate multiple layers of armor plating.

The Golf cannon's second attempt to fire fizzled at a decreased level of power, which failed to slice through the tank it targeted. That tank did not escape, however, as it was still subjected to maser cannon fire from a starship. Part of the coherent maser energy was dispersed by the tank's energy shield, leaving the rest to strike the armored vehicle's skin in a broad cone rather than a pencil-thin beam. The maser photons heated the top layer of armor tiles to millions of degrees, and caused the tiles down to the underlying frame to come loose in a long strip front to back, as if a giant had pulled an invisible zipper. Overflash from the heat fried that tank's communications gear, rendering it unable to receive commands from the remote driver. It halted in the street, awaiting instructions that never came.

Shen cut power to the Golf cannon while he checked its systems, then reauthorized its use with a limit of twenty-seven percent power. With the cannon lacking enough punch to be certain of taking out a tank with a single shot, he instructed that gun crew to switch their attention to the Wurgalan infantry units who were supporting the tanks approaching from the west. Eliminating the tanks was only part of the fire mission, he had been tasked with clearing an egress route for the trapped platoon. If the Golf gun crew was disappointed to be working a less-prestigious antipersonnel mission, they made up for their anger by pursuing their task with zeal. Coordinates for Wurgalan soldiers, even a platoon-sized formation of soldiers, was necessarily less precise than the targeting solutions for a tank. Being no fools, the Wurgalan soldiers had also scattered and taken cover when they saw the tanks in front of them being struck by hellfire from above. The Achakai gun crew assigned to the Golf cannon decided that to be sure, they needed to hit a broad area centered around the last reported position of each infantry unit, which in practice meant taking out two city blocks. Because they did not want their fellow crewmembers accusing them of not being thorough, they also took out the city blocks in a rectangle around the original two-block strike zone, then a ring of buildings around that.

Even if the Achakai gun crew had never heard the human expression 'Overkill is underrated', they understood the sentiment.

The Golf cannon sent pulses of coherent maser light down at the city, first in a broad cone tuned to the cannon's antipersonnel setting. That mode relied not on blasting individual enemy soldiers in their armored suits, but on essentially using the microwave radiation to cook them alive in their armor. Any troops exposed to direct fire from above were flash-boiled, when their suits were unable to disperse the energy from a cannon that was designed to punch through the armor plating of a starship. Troops under partial cover also suffered as their suit's heat sinks failed, causing severe and in many cases fatal injuries. Even soldiers who were inside structures and behind closed doors, felt their skin crawling like they had been bitten by hundreds of insects. The urge to rip their suits off was understandable, it also would be fatal.

When the target zone had been saturated, the crew controlling the Golf cannon switched the weapon to another setting. With their ship streaking over the city at hypersonic speed, there was no time to hit individual buildings. Instead of blowing up structures one by one, they planned to collapse entire city blocks. The maser cannon was re-tuned to produce more heat and less penetrating power, and the beam narrowed. Each shot would play the beam back and forth in a three-second pattern, striking the target buildings from the top.

Wurgalan urban architecture relied heavily on a form of ceramic that was lighter and stronger than concrete, reinforced by composite rods and beams that were lighter than aluminum and stronger than steel. These advanced materials allowed delicate-looking structures to hold up tall buildings, they were not subject to corrosion or metal fatigue, their flexibility protected against groundquakes, and they retained seventy percent of their strength at temperatures of twelve hundred degrees centigrade.

Here is a FUN FACT: the maser cannon of a starship can generate temperatures substantially above twelve hundred degrees.

The Achakai gun crew might have wondered why the humans who reprogrammed the cannons had labelled that particular setting as the '*Ghetto Blaster*' mode, but they pushed their curiosity aside and began steering the cannon around the strike zone. Weakened by heat and shaken loose by vibration, the structures began to fail, top floors collapsing. The sudden impact of that now-dead weight caused the lower floors to split apart, and one by one, buildings across the strike zone pancaked down to and below street level.

When the first strike zone was a twenty-block smoking ruin of rubble, dust and flames, the gun crew assigned to the Golf cannon shifted their focus to the next target, when their cannon indicated an overheat problem and shut down.

While the Golf gun crew was acting as the absolutely *unauthorized* Slugtown City Redevelopment Authority, their fellows assigned to the Foxtrot cannon had been busy proving that in a battle of starship versus tank, it sucks to be the tank.

The Foxtrot cannon had relentlessly stabbed through three tanks with direct hits, and lined up a shot at a tank that was frantically scrambling for speed, its treads churning the street beneath it into powder. Speed would not save it from a weapon that traveled at the speed of light. Cutting power to the treads, the remote operator tried to halt the heavy vehicle so it could pivot to the left and duck into the shadow of a building. During the brief battle, the starship overhead had soared southeast to northwest over the city, and its momentum would soon carry it out of range.

Jamming on the tank's brakes made it skid, churning pavement into pebbles beneath it. The desperate maneuver did not avoid it being struck by the maser, the beam hit the sloping nose of the armored vehicle at full power, and all of that energy melted the armor tiles there into slag that slumped down onto the ground. With its nose gone and the forward row of treads melted into puddles of sticky goo, the tank was frozen in place, unable to move.

Satisfied that tank was not going anywhere and that they could shift back to blast it at their leisure, the gun crew queried the sensors again to get the latest targeting data.

Seven tanks identified.

Six tanks destroyed.

That left one tank on the ground, and only one fully-functional maser cannon aboard the *Azjakanda*. That cannon had destroyed or disabled four tanks already, and its control system was recommending a shutdown for cooling. The gun crew, inexperienced and expecting their weapons to push through pain and weakness like a proper warrior, ignored the warnings and targeted the last tank. Because the dozens of motors that aimed the cannon were baking from residual heat, the first shot went wide, slicing through one corner of a shopping mall, where the most serious damage it caused was to the local equivalent of a Slurpee machine.

A second shot at the target was attempted and aborted, when relays tripped to cut off power to the exciters. Sensors inside the cannon detected that cracks were developing in several of the units, and shut down the ignition sequence.

Too late, Shen saw the Foxtrot gun crew had bypassed the automated safety systems and kept firing even when the interior mechanisms of the last useable cannon were near failure. He cut off the crew's access to the cannon, prompting howls of rage that he didn't bother responding to. Running a quick diagnostic, he studied the results, took direct control of the weapon and shut it down.

General Bezanson noted that none of the main cannons had fired for several seconds, perhaps more than several seconds. She couldn't remember, because her attention was focused on the dozens of missiles racing up at her ship. A glance at the tactical display confirmed that one tank was still active, represented by a glowing yellow icon. Less distinct red icons represented formations of enemy ground troops that accompanied the tanks, and there were far too many of them. "Major Shen," she called across the dingy bridge of the ship. "Why aren't we firing?"

"All cannons are offline," he reported. "They're overstressed, Ma'am."

"Can you reset the-" She bit off the rest of her question. Shen knew the stakes and he knew his job, he didn't need her looking over his shoulder. Besides, she had other things to worry about, like the enemy SAMs that the ship's sensors had lost track of.

"That last tank is more than a kilometer from the Mavericks platoon," Shen noted. "It's located to the southeast, it won't affect their escape route. We could use secondary batteries against the infantry formations we can identify," he said with more confidence than he felt.

"Negative. We need to reserve the secondaries for defense." Bezanson ordered as her attention was drawn to a red warning icon flashing on the display. One of the main engines was failing from the strain and about to shut itself off. She pressed the override control, which kept the shutdown sequence from activating. Then the engines sputtered, and her stomach felt queasy again as the ship fell out from under her.

# CHAPTER THIRTY THREE

The *Battle of Azjakanda's* AI acted quickly when a faulty fuel-flow sensor caused the main normal-space engines to sputter. Intercepting the useless commands of the clumsy biological crew, it bypassed the sensor and engaged the engines at full power, sending the ship surging up and forward. The amateur idiot Achakai who were flying the ship had *no idea* what they were doing, so the AI had to act in self-preservation.

Seventeen enemy missiles were reaching up for it, six of which had burned through the boost phase of their motors and were coasting at hypersonic speed, trying to be quiet as they zoomed toward the *Azjakanda*. With the electronic jamming saturating the area, plus jamming provided by the missiles, it was difficult to locate missiles which did not want to be found. Moving at such high speed through the thick air, the nosecone and control surfaces of the missiles would be glowing red, but the weapon designers knew that was a vulnerability, so as soon as the missiles cleared the lower atmosphere, the weapons shed the outer layer of nosecones, the booster motors, and the leading edges of control vanes. The missiles were still hotter than the thin air around them, which would have been easy to spot during optimal peacetime conditions.

Conditions were not optimal, and peacetime in that star system had ended when the Ruhar fleet arrived to bombard defenses.

Battles of incoming missiles against point-defense systems were almost entirely conducted by AIs, the elements involved all occurring much faster than any biological brain could track. Accordingly, the AI accepted the authorization from the being who designated herself as 'Brigadier General Lynn Bezanson', and took over its own fight for survival.

First, it activated the secondary maser cannons, targeting those missiles still in their vulnerable white-hot boost phase. Missile booster motors were burning out and being discarded by the second, adding to the cluttered heat signatures below. The sensors, aiming and diagnostic systems of the secondary batteries were all old and poorly tuned, despite what the Achakai crew thought from their status reports. The Ruhar who reactivated the ship from its long slumber had deliberately been less than zealous about restoring weapon systems to full operation, and the AI understood why. The Ruhar feared that someday, they might face the *Azjakanda* in battle, and why not cheat a bit to give themselves an advantage? Besides, all the Ruhar cared about was that the Achakai took the planet away from the Wurgalan, and for that they needed boots on the ground more than starships. What happened after the Ruhar pulled out with the Alien Legion was for the assassins to worry about.

Fortunately for the souls aboard the ship, the AI knew how to deal with old, poorly-designed, shoddily-constructed, and sloppily-maintained Kristang weapon systems. There were tricks to getting equipment to perform, and the AI used everything it had learned from other ships and from its own experience. It used three maser cannons to fire on one missile, reducing the number of missiles it could knock out, but increasing the odds of hitting *something*. Its goal was to compare the targeting data provided by the ship's main sensor array to the more focused sensors of the point-defense system. As it expected, the two systems not only did not agree on the location of the incoming missiles, they gave conflicting instructions to the motors that aligned the cannons. Three shots was all the AI needed to determine which sensors it could trust, which needed to be adjusted, and which had to be ignored.

Missiles began to explode, one, two, three-

The problem with a plan in warfare is that the enemy also makes plans. As the missiles began to detonate prematurely, the surviving weapons cut off their boosters, violently changed course and went dark. The good news for the *Azjakanda* was the missiles were traveling slower and would take longer to catch the ship, leaving more time for the point-defense systems to intercept them. The bad news was, all the missiles were now harder to see, except two which had sacrificed themselves by exploding their warheads to flood the airspace with chaotic radiation.

Ok, the AI said to itself, time for Plan B.

It sent a powerful active-sensor pulse downward, knowing that the jamming gave it little chance to get a solid return off incoming missiles. The purpose of the sensor pulses was not to directly detect threats to the ship, it was to build a more accurate map of the atmosphere below. A second, third and fourth set of pulses confirmed the map, and the AI paused for a millisecond to study the results.

It knew, or thought it knew, where nine of the missiles were, including three that were dangerously close. The missiles had sensor-absorbing coatings and although they lacked stealth fields, they were projecting holograms in front of them to mask their appearance. How did the AI pinpoint their location?

Wake turbulence.

Any object moving through the air leaves a disturbance behind it, and missiles moving through air at hypersonic speeds created a *lot* of turbulence.

The cannons fired again, this time with two cannons targeting each missile. As missiles began to explode, the survivors threw themselves violently across the sky, attempting to evade the maser beams. Each time a missile turned, it left a knuckle of low-pressure air behind it like a strobe light. The battle became a contest between the ability of missiles to perform unpredictable evasive turns, against maser beams that traveled at the speed of light. With the missiles between ten and twenty kilometers from the ship, the time between firing a cannon and striking the target was close to instantaneous, a nice change from space combat where distances could be measured in lightseconds or more.

Missiles were dropping off the threat board as the maser cannons burned through them, with the only problem being that the cannons themselves were in danger of failing. There, too, the AI had a trick up its sleeve. It was used to worn-out cannon components, so it shut down selected power feeds for each shot, reducing the power but ensuring the cannons kept firing. Despite its best efforts, cannons began losing power and dropping offline as their exciters burned out, actuator motors failed from overheating, and power feeds melted. The components were simply too old and fragile for extended combat.

When the last of the nine identified missiles exploded at a relatively safe eight kilometers below the *Azjakanda*, the AI ran a quick status update and determined that it had only two functioning point-defense cannons.

And it had only a vague idea where the last four missiles were.

Time for Plan *C*.

Launch doors opened and four missiles were flung from their tubes, making immediate turns to dive below the ship in a flat formation to maximize the area they covered. As the missiles reached a coordinated seven kilometers from the ship, they detonated their warheads in fragmentation mode, sending hot shards of shrapnel downward in four broad, overlapping cones.

Three enemy missiles turned as hard as they could, but still slammed into the cloud of shrapnel at hypersonic speeds.

That left one missile unaccounted for.

The *Azjakanda's* AI had no way of knowing there was one missile still actively seeking it.

The last missile had no way of knowing its opponent was unaware of its existence, and since the obsolete Kristang frigate had already, by some miracle, wiped out sixteen weapons launched from the ground, the last missile was not confident of its odds for a direct impact. Rather than risking complete failure, it exploded its own warhead in a shape-charge, directing the force forward at the underside of the starship.

Lynn Bezanson was flung against the straps holding her into the seat when something struck the ship, making it stagger in the air and fall with a suddenness that made her stomach flutter. Warning lights were flashing all over the console in front of her, or rather on the console that should have been in front of her but was now partly to one side. Lacking artificial gravity, Kristang ships were designed so their decks stacked nose to tail, a feature that made sense when thrust came from behind. With the ship in the gravity well of a planet and flying on its side at a forty-five degree angle, her left shoulder was braced against the seat to keep her stable. It was awkward and painful and it made it more difficult to see the console displays.

She also did not like what the displays were telling her. The point-defense system had only two functional cannons. The ship was maintaining altitude, even climbing slowly, but one of the main engines was producing less than thirty-percent power and fading. Shields were offline, with no hope they could be restored until the ship cleared the atmosphere.

And a second volley of missiles was reaching up from the surface.

One of her fingers was poised over the button to order the ship to be abandoned, when something caught her eye.

A tank in the city below was firing its railgun.

Emily Perkins dared to look up when there was a pause in the maser beams striking around the city. According to the information in her visor, no one in her platoon had been injured during the orbital strike, or perhaps it should have been described as an *air*strike, since the starship overhead was much closer than she had ever thought possible. She had data on every soldier in the unit, either via direct helmet-to-helmet laserlink from those people around her, or through relays from other helmets. Three people were unaccounted for.

Specialist Khatri, who was last reported to be inside the three-block No-Fire area around the platoon's position, but could not be located.

Surgun Jates.

And David Czajka.

She licked her dry lips and in a shaky voice asked "Does anyone have eyes on-"

She was thrown backward in the alley where she and five others had taken shelter, skidding on her back until she smacked into a dumpster or a pipe or pole, she didn't know and she didn't care. Her ears were ringing and the suit computer automatically boosted the helmet speaker volume to compensate, making sounds echo painfully. "What the *hell* was that?"

The multiple replies she received were muffled, something about a shell? Was the enemy using artillery? With their tanks gone, had the Wurgalan decided that collateral damage to their own city was less important than preventing the escape of a single platoon? She staggered to her feet, the suit doing most of the work to keep her upright, and crouched down as she jogged to the opening of the alley. Smoke filled the air and there was a line of haze laying a meter off the street, as if an aircraft came through and left a contrail.

With a shock, she saw gaping holes in buildings on opposite sides of the square. One to the east with debris scattered outward, the other punched into an east-facing wall. Whatever had caused the damage, it had come from the east.

A railgun.

They were being shot at by a tank, by an enemy who did not care what else they destroyed. The tank was shooting *through* possibly dozens of structures between itself and her platoon. A hand pulled her back into the alley, as her hearing recovered enough to-

She *saw* the second railgun round go by, before the shockwave of its passage knocked her off her feet again.

"Major Shen!" Bezanson called. "The-"

"I see it!" He punched the switch for emergency restart of the one main cannon that had any hope of being useful. "Ma'am, I need the ship in a stable attitude to have any chance of hitting that tank."

"I'll give you the best we've got," she turned her attention to the bridge crew. The ship was falling again, another set of eleven missiles were racing up from the surface, the system was informing her that escape pods were not an option at the ship's present speed and altitude, and with the last surviving tank shooting at the Mavericks, they had not yet accomplished their mission.

All she could do was try to provide a stable platform for Shen to use their last maser cannon.

And experience regret that she had said 'yes' to Ross's job offer.

The ship's AI saw what the human called 'Major Shen' was trying to do, and the AI grew very annoyed at the distraction. The ship was falling. Missiles were incoming. They had no effective defense. So, what did the humans want to do? Shoot at, of all things, a *tank* on the ground.

Like *that* mattered.

Oh, hell, the AI told itself with a sigh.

It's not like it had anything better to do with the last seconds of its life.

Besides, blowing up stuff was *fun*.

Major Shen pounded a fist on the side of his console when the cannon's control system reported it was unable to comply. He had nothing to shoot with, nothing to-

A message of  >>*System Available*<< scrolled across the display.

"What the hell?" He muttered to himself.

"Shen?" Bezanson asked.

"Nothing, Ma'am. Locked and loaded," he updated the sensor feed and authorized the cannon to fire. "On the *waaaaay*!"

The maser beam splashed weakly on the tank's armor, blowing off two layers of tiles, which were quickly replaced. Instead of frightening the tank's remote operator, the failed strike only sped up the next railgun shot, which went out slightly to the north of the first two shots. The operator was sweeping the area where the enemy ground force was suspected to be, heedless of damage to the city. The railgun would systematically walk its fire across the area, obliterating all in its path.

If the *Azjakanda's* AI was annoyed by the distraction of having to shoot at a tank, it was extremely annoyed that the tank failed to die as planned.

Taking over operation of the maser cannon, it retuned the power feeds, relays, aiming motors and exciters that were still operational, accepting lower power in exchange for a higher rate of fire. The cannon had a short remaining life span, which bothered the AI not at all for the entire ship was living on borrowed time. It lined up another shot at the tank and-

The tank was struck again, the second maser bolt even weaker than the first. Paying no attention to the fire from above, the remote operator swiveled the railgun slightly and-

The tank was struck again. And again.

And *again*.

Tiles flew off and the tank shuddered, its internal mechanisms protected from impact but not from the intense heat. Components melted and jammed, including the railgun magnets.

The maser from above struck again.

Once more.

The tank's upper skin cracked, allowing coherent maser light inside to cook the powercells.

It exploded.

"Got it!" Shen exulted, pumping a fist while having *no idea* what just happened. "We took out that last tank, General."

"Outstanding," she said automatically, her attention focused on the cluster of missiles rising from the ground. Whatever system controlled the enemy air defenses around the city, it had learned from its mistakes. Instead of small groups of missiles racing in as fast as they could and launching individual attacks, the second volley of missiles were going to attack in a coordinated fashion. The *Azjakanda* had no defenses left. "Chen, get to an escape pod."

He stared at her, surprised. "General?"

"Mission accomplished. There's nothing more we can do here. Get yourself out, and take the crew with you," she added, knowing the Achakai would not abandon the ship unless she went first. "I'll try to keep the enemy focused on the ship."

Major Shen checked the display, saw the missiles streaking in toward the ship. He also saw how fast the ship was traveling through the atmosphere. "Ma'am, I'd rather take my chances here."

"Right. See if you can get the-"

Alarms blared and she cringed, wondering what new problem they had to deal with. Below, the formation of missiles was splitting up, curving sharply to attack simultaneously from multiple directions. The ship's sensors had only a vague lock on the location of the incoming-

"Whoo!" Shen pumped a fist. "General, the cavalry is here!"

In space above the *Battle of Azjakanda*, flares of gamma rays burst from twisted spacetime as three former Wurgalan frigates jumped into low orbit. The ships blasted out Legion recognition codes to avoid being shot at by their own side, and held their fire until they could process sensor data provided by the Ruhar ships high above, sensor data that was a quarter or even a half-second out of date by the time the images were received by the trio of frigates. Pinpointing the position of the missiles was not possible and even if the Ruhar ships could determine the location, direction and speed of the missiles, the weapon guidance systems of the obsolete former Wurgalan warships were not accurate enough to hit multiple small, highly maneuverable objects.

So, the frigates made of up for lack of accuracy with a high rate of fire. Point-defense maser cannons chattered continuously, their focus crystals on the verge of shattering from the strain as they seared the sky below. The masers were targeted at the most probable locations of missiles, with the data continuously being updated by the Ruhar. Most shots were misses and near-misses, but even those shots were useful, as the maser bolts created lingering trails of ionized gas that reacted when a wildly turning missile flew through them. The predictive software of the Ruhar ships above began developing a picture of the enemy attack plan, which would allow more precise targeting and which was entirely too slow and too late. By the time the software completed its analysis, the *Azjakanda* would be blown to dust.

Instead of waiting for fancy software to slowly grind through a million data points, the three frigates fired their main plasma cannons. Those cannons, old, worn-out and unable to penetrate the shields of a warship even when they were new, were highly effective against missiles in an atmosphere. Tuned to broaden the plasma bolts so they covered more area, the cannons operated at reduced power that allowed them to wring more shots out of their fragile mechanisms. Accuracy was less important when plasma bolts stabbed down, blanketing wide areas of the sky around the *Battle of Azjakanda*. Missiles turned frantically to avoid the trails of a passing plasma bolt, only to blunder into a fresh ball of fire coming down from above. Between masers and plasma cannons, the sky was saturated to the point where the *Azjakanda* itself plunged through two dispersing remnants of plasma, scorching that ship's hull and blowing plating off to leave a trail of fire across the sky.

The three frigates above were traveling too fast to remain long over the target area. The entire battle took less than a minute and then the protective formation of frigates was gone, arcing out of range over the horizon. By that time, the *Azjakanda* also had soared away from the battle zone on the ground, and no missiles were detected in pursuit.

General Bezanson gripped the sides of her console, not to steady herself as the ship was buffeted from the uneven thrust of its engines, but to keep the crew from seeing her hands were shaking. "I am getting too old for this shit," she told herself, as a light blinked, indicating an incoming message.

"Bezanson!" Ross bellowed in her ear, his voice only slightly distorted by the jamming.

"Sir?" She noted that he had not addressed her with a convivial 'Lynn' or even a neutral 'General', so she kept her reply formal. He was unhappy with her about something. She had been so busy trying to save the ship from plunging down and making a substantial crater, she had not had time to view the overall situation in Slugtown. Seven tanks had been identified, seven destroyed, and a clear egress route had been created nearly a full kilometer wide. She counted that as *success*. Checking the sensor data, she immediately saw what Ross was upset about. Large sections of the city had been reduced to rubble, and not by friendly fire from the Wurgalan.

"My instructions were to *avoid* collateral damage in the city! What the hell do you call *that*?" His voice went up an octave.

"Um," she winced. "Urban renewal?"

"Urban-" Ross sputtered.

"I would call it '*gentrification*'," she suggested. "But I don't see any Starbucks down there yet. Maybe they're waiting for-"

"Starbuck- I, oh, *hell*," he broke into laughter. "I have to explain this to our hamster overlords, so please tell the Achakai to leave any more home-remodeling projects for *after* we kick the squids off this rock?"

"I will be sure to send them a memo about it," she said, hearing the shakiness of her own voice. It matched the trembling of her hands.

"Oh, Christ, Bezanson, it's good to hear your voice. I thought you were a dead duck there for a moment. Is there anything you need from me?"

"We could all probably use a change of underwear after that," she admitted. "Otherwise, no, Sir. My crew is confident we can get this bucket into a stable orbit. If another Bosphuraq ship jumps in, we're screwed."

"Don't remind me," he groaned. "All right, I don't see any other targets worth risking a starship to hit, so get your ship and those frigates to jump distance if you can. I'll let you know if the situation changes."

"Colonel?" Sergeant Liu called out, pointing to her own helmet with one anxious eye on the sky. The ship that had been their close-space support had passed overhead, lost to view behind a tangle of twisting contrails and the fading remains of plasma bolts. Their cover was gone, and they didn't know if it had eliminated the threat. "I have General Ross for you."

"General?" Perkins squeezed her eyes shut and said a silent prayer pleading for good news.

"You have a clear lane for egress, I'm sending the details to you now. It won't last long, get your people the *hell* out of there."

"Thank you, Sir."

"Don't thank me. Thank Bezanson and the crew of that destroyer she dangled over your heads. Her crew flattened half the gosh-darned city to save your asses, so make it count."

"We're on the move," she replied, while frantically waving to her team, twirling a finger over her head in a 'roundup' gesture.

"You do that. Contact me as *soon* as you make contact with Delta Company, they're waiting for you at point Echo. You see that on the map?"

"Affirmative. Perkins out."

Making a slashing motion across her throat for Liu to cut the connection, she shook her head when the sergeant began to fold the antenna for transport. "Liu, I need you to make contact with Surgun Jates and his team. Captain Grace!"

"Here, Ma'am," the Army psychologist stood up from where she had been helping administer meds to an injured soldier.

"Get your people packed up, I want you moving out behind our scouts. I just sent the egress route to you, stick to that corridor."

"Yes, Ma'am," Dani turned to bark orders at the Verd-kris platoons she had somehow inherited, eager to get them to something that resembled safety.

"Liu?" Perkins trotted over to the sergeant, who was fiddling with the controls of the box attached to the antenna. "Anything?"

"No response from Jates or your-" She blushed. "From Czajka. I was in contact with Khatri for just a moment then it cut out. The relays must have been knocked offline."

"Keep trying. No," Perkins realized she was putting her entire command at risk by continuing to broadcast over the antenna. "Pack up your gear." She looked around, torn by indecision. The scout team was forward, pulling them back to search for Dave would waste time and also put all of her people at risk. Surgun Besault of Grace's platoon perhaps sensed her dilemma, for he snapped a salute as he jogged toward her. "Colonel Perkins? Request permission for my squad to retrieve Jates and his team."

Perkins considered. She did not know Besault, all she knew was that Captain Grace trusted the Verd soldier. She also knew the Verd-kris did not leave their people behind on the battlefield. "Sergeant Liu? Did you get a location fix when you last were in contact with Khatri?"

"Roughly in the direction of that tank they targeted," the sergeant was pained to not offer more helpful information. "With the relays out, it's not possible to- Who is that?" She pointed across the square.

Three figures emerged from the dust cloud that choked the streets to the south. Two of them were limping to one extent or another, all cradled their rifles and two were half-turned to look behind them. One figure fired a burst back into the fog of dust, then another before hurrying to catch up with the others.

Perkins heard a crackling in her helmet headphones, as the line-of-sight laserlinks tried to establish a connection to the returning soldiers. It was garbled, then a figure waved stiffly with one arm, and her helmet visor identified that soldier as Jates. "Surgun, on the double, we're pulling out," she ordered, and muted her microphone as she choked a sob of relief to see another figure identified as Dave Czajka.

When Dave's own visor identified a familiar skinsuited figure as 'PERKINS, EMILY LTC', he picked up his feet a bit more, putting extra effort into overcoming the balky knee joint of his own suit that was making him limp. Mostly to use up the remaining four rounds in his magazine and, Ok, partly to show off for Emily, he pivoted and fired off the four rounds from the hip, firing blindly into the fog of dust behind him. The spent magazine automatically ejected down and to the side so he wouldn't trip on it, and his pack automatically slid a fresh magazine down so he could grasp it more easily. The magazine slapped home smoothly and the display on top of his trusty Kristang rifle showed he had a full fifty-two explosive-tipped rounds ready and waiting.

Expending rounds blindly was not a waste of ammunition, it was a sensible precaution to keep the enemy from approaching. Before the tank fell into the subway tunnel and got trapped there, Dave and Jates had no problem with enemy infantry. The squid soldiers seemed to be content to hang back and let the massive tank clear the way, take the risks and wait to exploit opportunities after the tank split the defensive perimeter of the invaders inside the city. That was not the doctrine Dave had learned from the United States Army, but apparently the Wurgalan had a different idea of how to employ combined arms on a battlefield. After the tank got stuck in the hole, enemy soldiers came forward and started taking potshots, forcing Dave and Jates to take cover and slowing their return to the platoon. The situation actually got worse when the starship above began providing close-space support, the squids figured out real quick that the safest place to be was *closer* to the invaders. By the time the starship passed overhead and out of sight, some of the Wurgalan had outflanked Dave and Jates. It was only the fog of dust, fog of confusion and prodigious expenditure of ammo that allowed Dave, Jates and

Khatri to break through a gap and enjoy the blessed sight of familiar figures taking cover in the shattered city square.

"Hey, Colonel," he said with practiced cool, nodding as an informal salute. What he wanted to do was hug her, maybe more.

"You were supposed to," she jabbed a shaking finger at his chest, her voice quavering with emotion. "Maintain contact. And *not* engage the enemy."

"That wasn't Czajka's fault," Jates came to his comrade's defense. "That *was* the plan. The enemy got in the way."

"Then you should have-"

"Excuse me, Colonel," Jates was achy, tired and grumpy enough to forget protocol. "The airstrike did *not* work, air-launched missiles were ineffective. We did not know the Legion was arranging close-space support, and we had to *do* something. We blew the roof of a subway tunnel when the tank rolled over it, the tank fell into the hole."

"Oh, well," Perkins was only partly mollified. "Assuming you triggered the explosion remotely, you kept out of-"

"Yeah," Dave just could not keep his big mouth shut. "That's what we thought, then the freakin' thing started climbing out of the hole, so I had to," he raised his rifle, sighting on a section of the square that was empty, and pantomimed launching a rocket. "Take it out, you know?"

"You engaged a tank *by yourself?*"

"Yeah, uh," too late, he caught on that Emily was upset rather than impressed. "Not by myself, I, uh-" He looked to Jates for support.

"It's your lie, Czajka," Jates threw him under the bus with a shrug. "Tell it however you want."

Panicked, Dave looked between Jates and Emily. "It's not a *lie*. Come on, man, help me out here."

"It is true, Mister Czajka acted with no thought for his own safety," Jates announced with a grave look on his face.

"Oh, hey," Dave blushed with an 'Aw shucks' shrug. "I was just doing my-"

Jates's expression turned to a glare. "He acted with no thought *at all*."

"Hey, I-"

"Seriously, what were you *thinking?*"

"I just-"

Jates shook his head. "One of the briefing packets I read about your species showed that your military used to have a slogan 'An Army of one'. That is not supposed to be taken literally, you moron."

"Uh, well, shit. Em, I, damn it! That freakin' tank got hit by two airstrikes, *and* we blew a hole under it, and it *still* kept coming! It wasn't going to stop and it was going to come here and kill everyone, kill *you*. I had to *stop* it."

To Dave's surprise, Jates clapped a hand on his shoulder. "You did. That was a good move. Next time, *think* before you act. We should have acted together."

"Yeah," Dave answered shakily, coming down off an adrenaline high. "Good point."

"We will talk about this later," Emily stared at Dave, but the creases around her eyes softened. "Did you get the message? We're moving out. There is a safe-passage corridor out of the city, we don't know how long it will stay open. Jates," she turned her attention to the Verd-kris. "You had enemy in pursuit?"

"We lost contact five, maybe six blocks back. I estimate there were three or more squads engaged with us, but there could be more. I don't know Wurgalan doctrine about infantry support of armored vehicles."

"I don't know either, and I don't want to find out the hard way," Perkins concluded. "You take command of the rear guard, I want us away from here before trouble finds us. Liu!" She called for the sergeant. "Send up a blue flare." That would be the signal for Shauna, Jesse and Nert to rejoin the platoon. She had lost contact with the sniper team, and couldn't send out scouts to search for three people. "Captain Grace! Get your people *moving*!"

"That flare!" Nert pointed. "It's blue!"

"I see it," Jesse shrugged out of his pack, digging into it for the flare gun. Pointing it down toward the smoke-filled street, he pressed the trigger and the pencil-thin flare shot out, disappearing quickly. A minute later, while the team finished packing up their gear, they saw a bright yellow flare pop up several blocks away, giving the answering signal.

"Southwest, then we go north to link up," Shauna instructed. "We're behind the squids, let's keep it that way."

# CHAPTER THIRTY FOUR

Ross had ordered her to contact him when she made contact with Delta Company, so once the middle of her column were through their perimeter and reinforcements were running forward to assist with the wounded, Perkins trotted over to the company commander, a Major Pelletier. He saluted as she came at him.

"Colonel, it is-"

"Where's your comm gear?" She cut him off with a curt nod.

"Lieutenant Babbage will set you up, Ma'am," Pelletier pointed to a cluster of people huddled around an antenna. "I'll see to your people, we have a tent set up with three medics."

"I appreciate it, Major." Jogging over to the antenna, she told the overworked lieutenant what she needed, and manually linked her helmet to the device.

"Signal is synchronized, Colonel," Babbage reported. "Handshake confirmed."

Ross must have been waiting for her, because he picked up in seconds. "Perkins, you squared away?"

"Yes. Unless the squids decide to hit this position with artillery or an airstrike." She had seen three anti-air teams with portable missiles, but those light weapons would not stop a determined air attack, or ballistic weapons.

"Delta Company will be evaced by air in thirty, we will have Buzzards coming in from the west as soon as a safe-fly corridor is confirmed."

"It will be great to get away from here," she muttered, overcome by a wave of fatigue.

"Before that, I need you to do your thing."

"Sir?"

"Don't give me that innocent shit, Perkins. I know your devious little mind. You wouldn't have set up this operation unless you have a card up your sleeve. I'm telling you right now is the time to use it."

"It's that bad?" She asked wearily.

"This op is a total fucking disaster. Our ninja clients think the only honorable way of fighting is a suicide assault. They are losing troops so fast, their formations will be bled dry by the end of the day. We can't reinforce them with Verds, because the Achakai refuse to serve with traitors, they are more likely to shoot at Verds than at squids. We're expending ammunition at three times the predicted rate, that is three times *my* estimate, not the fantasy numbers UNEF logistics expects us to hold to."

"*Shiiiiit*," Perkins groaned. "Can we hold on until-"

"Until the second wave lands? There isn't going to *be* a second wave. Admiral Kune's ships detected emission trails and drive signatures from additional Bosphuraq ships in the system. He won't risk his remaining assault carriers unless he has coverage from our beetle friends. That means he also will not risk using carriers to pull us off this rock. I have a couple dozen dropships coming in from long range to deliver supplies, but that is too little, too late. There won't be a withdrawal. We are stuck here, one way or another. That's not all. My counterpart with the Achakai thinks the Ruhar *planned* to strand us here. If they withhold the second wave, they essentially destroy the Alien Legion concept. Plus, if the Achakai fail to achieve clan status, they will be slaughtered, and that is one less future threat the Ruhar need to deal with."

"Shit! Ah," she sighed, overcome with weariness. "I am saying that word a lot lately."

"You're not the only one. Do you think the hamsters planned to screw us here?"

She had to think a moment. "No. There are easier ways to achieve their goals, if that's all they want. But I also don't think they will risk their furry little necks to help us, unless, as you said, they have cover from the Jeraptha."

"Can you pull any strings with your beetle friends, get them to send a couple ships to chase away the Bosphuraq?"

"Sir, as I explained, that can't happen. The beetles *can't* intervene here, not unless they are directly threatened. The birds are too smart to provoke them here."

"Yeah, you explained that. Perkins, unless you have another miracle in your pocket, the squids are going to win this fight, and this will all be for nothing."

"Oh, fiddlesticks."

"*Fiddlesticks?*" He laughed.

"That's something my grandmother used to say, when she was upset. Ok, Ok. I really didn't want to do this, but it looks like I have no choice."

"Do you need time to think about it?" He asked in a tone indicating that thinking about it would be a bad idea.

"No. Sir, I suggest you advise Admirals Kune and Kekrando that if they have any ships closer than a lightsecond from this planet, they should think about pulling them back. Also, you should tell those incoming dropships to change course, away from the planet."

"That is awfully vague, Perkins. Why?"

"Remember how I said the only way the beetles could intervene here, is if there was a direct threat to them?"

"Oh, *hell*. What in God's name are you planning?"

"The Jeraptha will soon have a compelling reason to send ships here, and they should arrive quickly."

"All right, but why-"

"Sir, this particular group of beetles? They are types who shoot first and ask questions *never*, if you know what I mean."

"Oh, I am getting too old for this shit."

"You and me both, Sir," she sighed, feeling the weight of yet another world on her shoulders.

"Em," Dave said quietly when he saw her standing by herself, eyes downcast, slowly shaking her head. "What's going on?"

"Dave." She needed a hug. He looked like *he* needed a hug too. Instead, she lipped up her helmet faceplate and rested a hand on his shoulder.

"Hey," he lifted his faceplate, looking into her eyes with concern. "Em, what's wrong?"

She took a breath. "We are in *big* fucking trouble."

"Yeah, so, that's nothing new," his attempt at humor fell flat. "Hey, come on. We'll be just fine once the second wave gets their lazy asses down here and-"

"There won't *be* a second wave," she hissed, looking around to assure they were not being overheard. "Admiral Kune won't risk his assault carriers unless he can be sure there aren't more Bosphuraq warships in the area. Dave, I hate to say it, but I agree with him. We could lose the entire second wave before their boots hit the ground."

"Shit!" He looked away, clenching a fist. "All right, screw it. If the birds can send in ships, then we call the beetles."

"We can't. They *can't* interfere. You know that."

"Then why are the Bosphuraq able to break the rules?"

"The rules are the same," she shook her head. "The *circumstances* are different. The Bosphuraq can act here directly because legally, this fight is an internal dispute within the Maxolhx coalition. The Kristang are invading a Wurgalan planet, the rest of us just happen to be here. The Bosphuraq are within their rights to intervene. If the beetles intervene to help us, *they* will be breaking the rules."

"This sucks. Hey," he leaned forward so their noses were almost touching, and he stroked her cheek with a hand. "You have a sneaky plan to pull us off this rock, right? Please tell me you have a plan."

She kissed his fingers, then pulled away. "I have a plan, but," she stomped a foot in the well-trampled dirt. "We are *not* retreating off this rock. Shit. Thank you."

"For what?"

"For reminding me why we're out here. I didn't want to do this, I was trying to think of a way to avoid doing this. Now I see we don't have a choice."

He looked askance at the Mavericks leader. "Do what?"

"Use our Ace in the hole."

"Oh." He knew what she meant, and how much she wanted to hold that card for a higher purpose. They couldn't play any cards at all if they were dead. "Is there anything I can do?"

"Yes. Tell me I'm doing the right thing."

"Always."

The *Sure Thing* received the garbled signal from Perkins, and there was a delay while the crew furiously wagered on what this latest development could mean. Then, they complied with the order by launching eight probes, and settled down once again to wait, and wonder just what the *hell* was going on down there.

The eight probes accelerated toward the planet at high speed, then cut thrust and engaged stealth fields as they coasted toward the war-torn world. At the last moment before they struck the atmosphere too hard, the probes flipped around and burned the last of their fuel to decelerate, slowing to match the speed of the thousands of pieces of debris that were constantly falling out of orbit. Nosecones popped open, ejecting their payloads, which soon became just more flaming pieces of junk following ballistic arcs toward the surface.

Seven of the payload modules began transmitting back data they collected about conditions in the atmosphere, which the computers of the *Sure Thing* dutifully collected, though the crew of that ship had no idea why anyone would care about such mundane information during a raging battle. The eighth probe's payload apparently had failed, because while it was transmitting a signal like the others, the data sent back was useless garbage.

All eight probes fell deeper and deeper into the atmosphere, slowing and falling at a steeper angle until parachutes popped out to bring their descent speed to a gentle rate. The eight stealthed payloads floated downward under their gossamer-thin, invisible parachutes, slowly drifting apart. Seven of the parachutes guided their payloads to touch down in bodies of water, where they disappeared with barely a splash and sank to the bottom, their payloads going inert as the power was cut.

The eighth payload, for which the other seven were merely decoys, guided itself toward a soft landing in an overgrown field outside a small, abandoned military base. No longer needed, the parachute detached and soared away on the wind, disintegrating into microscopic particles that would soon be consumed by the plant life of the world.

By itself, the payload container swung open and the contents unpacked themselves, with a small bot unfolding to carry the main item in the container. The bot scanned the area, finding it to be very close to what it expected, so it began walking toward an abandoned warehouse building, carrying the main item. Inside, it activated its scanner again, building a map of the structure. Quickly, it saw a pile of discarded tarps in one corner and walked there, lifting the tarps and tucking the main item of the payload under the heavy fabric.

Its task complete, the bot walked out of the warehouse, puffing air to scatter dust on the floor and conceal its small footprints. As planned, it walked across the streets of the abandoned base and down an embankment into a muddy creek, where it folded its legs and sank to the bottom. Content that it had performed its task adequately, the bot's last action was to send a power surge into its processor, frying its tiny brain and erasing the last evidence of what it had done.

War raged across the main continent of Stiglord, opposing forces engaged mostly in desperate, small-unit actions, while in the sky aircraft battled for control of the air, and warships waited in orbit. Both sides knew that, unless the invading forces were able to land their second wave soon, the fight for Stiglord could have only one outcome. The Legion and Achakai knew they could only hope to delay the time when they were ground down by attrition and ran out of ammunition. The Wurgalan knew they only had to wait until the enemy became combat ineffective unit by unit, while the Ruhar fleet withheld support under the threat of Bosphuraq ships that might or might not be in the area.

Both sides knew what would inevitably happen over the next two or three days, and both sides knew there was nothing that could change the outcome.

Both sides were wrong.

Under a pile of dirty, torn and discarded tarps, in a long-unused warehouse on an abandoned military base far from any fighting, a timer ended its programmed countdown. Without any sound, a device switched on, providing a small amount of power before the device disintegrated into dust, having done everything it was supposed to do.

The device had activated an Elder power tap.

The power tap pulled energy from another dimension, building up power and sending out chaotic electromagnetic waves that were lost amidst the powerful broad-spectrum electronic jamming from both sides. Then, as the power level intensified, the distinctive electronic signature of an active Elder power tap was noticed by both sides.

"General Ross for you, Ma'am," the sergeant called out to the Mavericks leader, who was still waiting for a dropship to carry her away from the staging area outside Sluktashwon.

"Perkins here," She responded.

"Whatever special thing you were going to do," he said in a rush, "don't do it! We've got a hell of a mess on our hands, the Ruhar just detected a freakin' *Elder* power tap going active down here! Admiral Kune is jumping frigates into orbit and sending dropships down to the site, the enemy is moving in fast as they can. It is already one hell of a huge air battle, the aircraft that were coming to pick you up are being grounded until this shakes out. I've got General Bailey preparing to bring two companies to the site, but we're short on transport. If your team had a dropship, I might throw you into the fight."

"Yes, Sir," she said slowly, stretching her words out in a monotone. "This is really a *completely* unexpected development, *no one* could have foreseen this. General Bailey should exercise extreme caution."

"He- Holy *shit*," Ross gasped as he caught on. "Unexpected?"

She continued to speak slowly, keeping any hint of sarcasm out of her voice in case the Ruhar were listening to the conversation. "Yes, Sir. I certainly had *no idea* that an Elder power tap was on this planet."

"God *damn*."

"Sir, if I may offer a suggestion? General Bailey, and all of our forces, should stay out of this particular fight. That includes the Ruhar. If there is a Bosphuraq ship over our heads, they will be jumping into orbit and sending down their own dropships to take possession of the artifact. It could develop into a fight between the Wurgalan and the Bosphuraq, until the Jeraptha get here."

"The Jeraptha?"

"The Bosphuraq potentially getting control of an active Elder power tap is a *direct* threat to the Jeraptha, Sir," she explained. "The Jeraptha will now be within their rights to intervene here, to ensure their security. They will *have* to act."

"Oh. My. Fu-" There was a sound like the general thumping his forehead on the console. Then, "Perkins, I, I- God *damn*. An Elder power tap? You had an- Ok, we will discuss this later. I will instruct General Bailey, and our Achakai friends, to hold off for now."

"Sir? Any battle over the power tap will be bloody. We should not deprive the *Achakai* of an opportunity for such glory."

"Ah." He understood right away. If many of the ninjas were slaughtered in the battle, that would be fewer lizards for the Legion to worry about later. He hated having to include political considerations in battle planning, but sometimes it could be very useful. He cleared his throat. "Yes, you are right about that. I will tell the Achakai that we will not stand in their way. Assholes won't listen to me anyway," he added under his breath. "Very well, I will advise Admiral Kune to watch out for the Bosphuraq, the Ruhar would only be a speed bump. Oh, hell, I do *not* believe this. Colonel Perkins, I suppose I don't need to tell you there is no need for that thing you were going to do?"

"I don't know what you're talking about, Sir."

"Good. Because you have already nearly given me a heart attack more than once today. Can I expect any more surprises?"

"It wouldn't be a surprise if I told you, Sir."

"Shit. I *hate* this job. Ross out."

The real battle for Stiglord began with a Bosphuraq light cruiser and two destroyers jumping into low orbit, and immediately launching a dozen dropships evenly split between troop transports and gunships. As the Bosphuraq had not expected to get involved in any messy fighting on the *ground*, most of the personnel aboard the transport dropships were starship crewmembers with little experience with infantry fighting, and a likely tendency to spray everything in sight with rifles on full auto. To avoid anything resembling a fair fight, the Bosphuraq broadcast warnings for their client species to stay away from the immensely valuable Elder artifact, and threatened *dire* consequences if the *dirtbag* Wurgalan attempted to get their grubby little tentacles on the priceless object.

Both sides got a good chuckle out of the obviously ridiculous warning, then the Wurgalan disengaged from battle with the invaders and threw everything they had into getting to the Elder device first. Every aircraft and anti-aircraft missile available was launched at the Bosphuraq dropships, which were in the vulnerable phase of atmospheric entry and making no attempt to be stealthy. The three Bosphuraq warships responded with ripple-firing decoys to cover their dropships, and missiles to intercept Wurgalan aircraft that were flying at maximum speed toward the artifact. Unfortunately for the patron species, by the time they jumped in, the Wurgalan had two aircraft close to the objective, and the Bosphuraq could not risk hitting the Elder device. All six gunships broke away from their primary mission of covering the rapidly-descending transports, to go into a full-power dive while shooting maser cannons at the enemy. One of the Wurgalan aircraft exploded before the Bosphuraq had to cease fire, leaving the squids with one aircraft, a pair of pilots and four soldiers to complete the mission.

Setting down on the cracked surface of what used to be the abandoned base's airfield, the aircraft roared away as soon as the four soldiers exited. Flying low and fast, the aircraft got away from the area as four Bosphuraq gunships screamed toward the base, their forward surfaces glowing cherry-red from coming down too fast. With sensors partially blinded, the gunships' maser cannons chattered to saturate the area on a low-power antipersonnel setting.

The Wurgalan gave a good fight, but it was never a contest. By the time the two surviving Bosphuraq transports touched down, there was no active enemy resistance within eighty kilometers of the objective site, and one of the destroyers above was maneuvering dangerously low in the atmosphere to cover the return flight. Other than the Wurgalan launching a dozen anti-aircraft missiles in a futile gesture, the return of the two surviving dropships was uneventful, both being taken aboard the light cruiser.

More warnings were broadcast, for all ships in the area to stay away and not interfere with the three Bosphuraq ships climbing out to jump distance, warnings that were directed more at the unpredictable Achakai than at the sensible Ruhar fleet. Admiral Kune had pulled his ships back, and Kekrando fought to keep his own ships from doing anything uselessly stupid, arguing there would be plenty of opportunities to do *usefully* stupid things later.

Helplessly, the would-be invaders and the defenders watched, as the Bosphuraq ships climbed toward jump altitude with their priceless cargo.

They almost made it to jump distance before three new ships jumped in to join the battle. A Thuranin heavy cruiser and two destroyers emerged from twisted spacetime above the Bosphuraq. The Thuranin ships had been lurking in stealth, keeping a close eye on their asshole supposed allies. When the Legion invasion force arrived so unexpectedly, the Thuranin had observed with curiosity and alarm, but took no action for the simple reason that they did not know which side they should support. On the one hand, a mercenary group of their own client species was acting in coordination with the Ruhar, and that could not be good for the Kristang or the Thuranin. On the other hand, the Achakai were attacking the Wurgalan, and that could not be good for the Bosphuraq. Having no orders regarding whether to interfere, the Thuranin commander had been patiently watching and waiting, until the signature of an Elder device was detected. The Thuranin could have launched their own dropships and engaged in a chaotic battle on the ground, but, with the Bosphuraq offering convenient and free same-day delivery to low orbit, why bother?

The two pairs of destroyers engaged each other in a running battle that carried them arcing over the horizon, while the two cruisers slugged it out at a rapidly-decreasing distance, the more-powerful guns and shields of the heavier Thuranin ship quickly knocked out the normal-space propulsion system of their allied ship. Soon the cruisers were pounding each other at point-blank range, blasting away armor plating until the guns and missile launchers of the Bosphuraq ship fell silent, and the Thuranin systematically destroyed the allied ship's point-defense systems. The way was then clear for the Thuranin to launch dropships stuffed with heavily-armored boarding parties and remotely-operated combots. The dropships latched on, soldiers raced out to place blasting charges and blow holes in the disabled ship's hull, then the armor-suited figures followed the combots inside.

Three lightseconds away, where they had been concealed in stealth since shortly after the invasion began, the five ships of Captain Scorandum's Ethics and Compliance Office task force keenly watched the battle with passive sensors. The task force was unofficial, in fact they were not supposed to be there at all, but Scorandum was burning with curiosity to see what Emily Perkins had planned. Sadly, three of his ships had developed serious engineering flaws, the exact nature of which could be decided later, so they had been forced to delay their next assignment.

Whatever Scorandum expected, an *Elder freakin' power tap* was not on the list.

"What do you think?" He asked the captain of the *It Was Like That When We Got Here*.

"Looks good," the other captain responded over the encrypted tightbeam. "We are detecting fewer explosions and gunfire from inside the hull, I think our Thuranin friends have done the hard work for us. The artifact might be damaged if we wait much longer."

"Agreed. Very well, you go in with the *Plausible Deniability* and the *Out On Bail*, my ship will provide high cover along with the *Parole Violation*. Bring back our prize."

An encouragingly short time later, Sublieutenant Kinsta called from inside the Bosphuraq light cruiser. "Captain Scorandum, we have eliminated all organized opposition, taken control of the ship and secured the artifact. We have no casualties and the artifact is undamaged."

"Excellent." Scorandum could not believe his luck. His task force had been trying to think of an excuse for intervening directly to assure the invasion succeeded, mostly because they had wagered in favor of success, but no one had been able to think up an excuse that wouldn't result in pissing off both the Maxolhx and Rindhalu. Now he not only had a solid excuse for direct intervention, he had a priceless Elder power tap. While boarding parties had gone aboard the light cruiser to secure the artifact, the *Out On Bail* had reduced the Thuranin heavy cruiser to scrap, and all four enemy destroyers had damaged each other to the point where none of them could move under their own power. It was an amazing success, far better than he could have hoped for. The only issue nagging at the back of his mind was the thought that aboard one of the ECO ships, there was almost certainly some lucky jackass who had drunkenly placed a wager on the extremely unlikely possibility of an Elder artifact being found on Stiglord, and now could not believe the nearly-forgotten wager would pay off handsomely. "Tell Captain Windevon to bring the artifact aboard the *It Was Like That* as soon as possible, and prepare to jump with us."

"We're not leaving a force here?" Kinsta asked, surprised.

"No, the artifact is too important. We need to report to Admiral Gasoghe and let her deal with it." Gasoghe commanded the four star carriers that were waiting outside the star system. "The Bosphuraq here certainly aren't going to cause any more trouble."

"Yes, Sir. One moment while I relay your orders to Captain Windevon."
There were a few moments of silence, then "Acknowledged. Sir, it was very nice
of the Bosphuraq and Thuranin to do all the work for us, so Captain Windevon has
a question for you."
"Oh? What is that?"
"Are we supposed to leave a tip?"

# CHAPTER THIRTY FIVE

The Jeraptha ECO ship *Will Do Sketchy Things* backed away from the star carrier, the crew exulting about another job well done, when the ship's commander announced they weren't done yet. Admiral Gasoghe knew that her superiors in Fleet Headquarters would be enormously pleased when she brought a priceless Elder power tap home with her ships. She also knew they would have questions about how such a supremely rare and precious item just happened to be found on a backwater world. They would want answers. So, the admiral demanded answers from Scorandum, and the ECO task force was going back to question the surviving Bosphuraq about what they knew of the incident. It was a waste of time, and Scorandum knew it, and the admiral knew it. If the Bosphuraq knew how the power tap got there, they would have known it was there, and it would not have *been* there when the invasion force arrived. The Bosphuraq were clueless like everyone else.

Well, Scorandum thought privately, not *everyone* was clueless about it.

Before he could do anything remotely useful, he had to go through the motions, and that meant jumping back into orbit near the still-smoking wreck of the Bosphuraq ship. Signaling the four other ships of the task force to accompany him, he ordered his ship to jump.

When the ECO ships returned to Stiglord, Scorandum sent a brief message to Admiral Kune, instructing the client species to stay out of the way, and then waited for a boarding team from the *Parole Violation* to secure the battered light cruiser again. No trouble was expected from the subdued Bosphuraq and indeed the enemy did not resist, except for a moderate amount of gunfire. Plus two grenades. And one call for supporting fire from the *Plausible Deniability*, which blew out twenty meters of the Bosphuraq ship's hull. When the All Clear was received, Scorandum's dropship flew across the short distance, and he personally supervised the tedious process of interviewing the clueless Bosphuraq on the bridge of the powerless ship, while his boarding teams checked the ship for booby traps, and for aliens who might be trying to hide in the nooks and crannies of the hull.

He was on the bridge of the busted light cruiser when the leader of the boarding team called him. Scorandum actually welcomed the interruption, as a break from the tedium of listening to various Bosphuraq denying any knowledge of how the power tap got to Stiglord.

"Captain, I am terribly sorry to bother you like this," Sublieutenant Kinsta said.

"Kinsta," Scorandum twitched his antennas in the Jeraptha equivalent of an eyeroll. The lieutenant was nervous about something, and based on Scorandum's experience, he guessed that Kinsta was worried about getting into trouble. "*What* is the problem?"

"I- Er, you," Kinsta sputtered. "It's best if you see for yourself."

What his subordinate meant, Scorandum interpreted, was that there was a mess, and the operative wanted to pass responsibility onto someone else. "We're on a tight schedule. Give me a hint, please."

"Er, um, well, when we left this ship, because we were in a hurry, you understand, we had to, well-"

"Get to the point, Kinsta."

"We had to leave the survivors of the Thuranin boarding crew in the custody of the Bosphuraq."

"You *what*?" Scorandum did not remember the boarding team informing him that they had captured Thuranin during the operation to seize the power tap. They had not told him, and he had not asked. At the time, he had more important concerns.

"We didn't have time to take the Thuranin with us, and, this *is* a Bosphuraq ship, so-"

"Please do *not* tell me that the prisoners got out and caused problems."

"No, they didn't cause any trouble. Sir, it is really best if you-"

"This had better be good. I'll be right there," Scorandum snapped, imagining all sorts of complications that he really did not want to deal with right then.

Whatever he imagined, it was not what he found. "What the hell happened here?" He bellowed, his antennas standing on end.

It was, indeed, a mess. He was in the section of the ship the Bosphuraq used as a brig, an oval-shaped central hub around which were seven holding cells that had energy fields, electrified bars and doors, and automated laser guns to prevent prisoner escapes. Four of the cells were empty. One contained four Thuranin who were gesturing wildly and shouting, though with the energy field engaged, he fortunately couldn't hear them.

The cell nearest the entry corridor had its energy field deactivated and the cell door was open. Kinsta was standing over the body of a Thuranin. Or, it *might* have been the body of a Thuranin, it was hard to tell.

"Damn it," Scorandum groaned. The situation had become complicated. He hated complications. "What the hell is going on?"

Kinsta stared down at the mangled body of what had apparently been a Thuranin. "The Bosphuraq guards here told me they think it was a boating accident?"

Scorandum gaped at the pair of Bosphuraq standing meekly up against the far wall of the hub. "*Boating*?"

The pair of Bosphuraq heard the translation and bobbed their heads vigorously, doing their best to play the part of innocent bystanders.

Turning back to the body on the floor, Scorandum crouched down. "Looks more like this guy got into an argument with a trash compactor."

"Let's go with that," Kinsta muttered with relief, tapping on his tablet. All he cared about was that *he* wasn't getting blamed for the mess.

Scorandum straightened, looking around. "What else?"

"This guy," Kinsta pointed to the adjacent cell, which contained another Thuranin body. "Apparently got access to a weapon, and killed himself."

"He killed himself, huh?" Scorandum stepped into the cell, avoiding the pools of blood on the floor. The body did exhibit signs of gunshot wounds, and the unlucky Thuranin did have a pistol clutched in one hand. "Kinsta, I count eleven bullet holes."

"So?"

Scorandum bent down to pry the pistol from the dead cyborg's hand. "*So*, this pistol holds only nine rounds." He looked at the Bosphuraq. "Would one of you care to explain that?"

The Bosphuraq looked at the deck or the ceiling, and one of the aliens ventured a guess. "He reloaded?"

"Good enough for *me*," Kinsta tapped again on his tablet.

"Oh, *hell*," Scorandum sighed. "Is that all?"

"Yes," Kinsta brightened, relieved to have dodged a bullet more skillfully than the dead Thuranin had.

Scorandum studied the four still-living Thuranin in the other cell, who were silently shouting outage at him, because the energy field absorbed all sound. "Kinsta, are those surviving prisoners trying to tell me that their fellows did *not* die by accident and suicide?"

Kinsta peered at the prisoners. "I can't hear them, Sir. They might be trying to order lunch."

"*Lunch?*"

"Well, *I'm* hungry," Kinsta said with a blank look on his face.

"I would like to pretend this never happened." Seeing that his subordinate was still tapping on a tablet, he asked "How are you listing the second dead Thuranin?"

"Um, I tagged it as 'Assisted Suicide'?"

"That is not remotely believable," Scorandum complained. "We need a better story."

"You're right." He tapped the tablet again. "I'm changing it to '*Involuntary Assisted Suicide*'."

"Kinsta, please, just don't tell me any more about this. What do you propose we do now?"

Kinsta looked up at the ceiling, considering his options. "We could ask the Bosphuraq to care for the remaining prisoners, until a Thuranin ship arrives to repatriate them."

"Care for them," Scorandum stared at his subordinate. "You trust the Bosphuraq to do that?"

"We could ask them very nicely?" Kinsta suggested.

"I don't believe this."

"Sir," Kinsta lowered his voice. "Do we actually care?"

"About these assholes?" Scorandum pointed an antenna at the four cyborg prisoners, who were silently screaming at him, making rude gestures and almost foaming at the mouth. "No, *I* don't care. But somebody above me does, so that makes it my problem."

"If we don't trust the Bosphuraq to keep them here, we could put them someplace safe."

Scorandum glanced around the brig, wondering what area of the ship could be more secure. "Like where?"

"An airlock?"

Back aboard the *Will Do Sketchy Things*, Captain Scorandum first dispatched the *I'm As Shocked As You Are* to report to Admiral Gasoghe that the surviving Bosphuraq had not a single clue about how an Elder power tap came to be on Stiglord, and that the ECO task force would remain in the area to search the planet for additional artifacts. Hearing that news would please the admiral, for Scorandum knew she had placed a significant wager on the success of the invasion.

The second thing he did was to signal the Ruhar admiral that it was advisable for that commander to commence landing the second wave of the invasion force as soon as possible, because the Jeraptha could justify remaining in orbit for only a limited time. Admiral Kune took the hint, and the assault carriers of the second wave began popping into orbit within half an hour.

The *third* thing Scorandum did was go aboard a dropship and fly down to the surface, so he could meet with a human named Emily Perkins, to have a little heart-to-heart chat about just how unlikely certain recent events were.

Perkins strode into the tent, wiping sweat from her forehead and trying to untangle the knots in her hair. From wearing a skinsuit helmet almost continuously since before the landing, her hair was sweat-stained and plastered to her head, a fact that the Jeraptha waiting for her did not care about at all. "Captain Scorandum, I am pleased to see you again."

"Pleased, yes," the Jeraptha said grumpily. "But not, I think, *surprised.*"

"Excuse me?"

"Colonel, if an Elder power tap had not gone active on this world a short time ago, we would not be having this conversation. Your forces on the surface would slowly be overwhelmed by the Wurgalan, and my ships would have remained in stealth while we monitored the situation, unable to intervene. Instead, the second wave of your invasion force has landed, and Admiral Kune expects to bring the third wave in before the end of the day. With my ships conveniently in orbit to provide cover, the Bosphuraq are unable to prevent this world from falling to the Achakai. You will have achieved all of your stated objectives, and perhaps some objectives that you failed to tell anyone about."

"Captain Scorandum, I have no idea what you mean. Surely you cannot be unhappy to have obtained a functioning Elder power tap?"

"I am thrilled about *that*. What I am less than thrilled about is being used for someone else's purpose."

She set her helmet down on a folding table, and picked up a water bottle, downing half of it in one thirsty gulp. Wiping her mouth on the sleeve of her skinsuit, she cocked her head at the alien. "Used? That is only true if we do not share the same purpose."

Scorandum clacked his mandibles together. "That would be easier to determine, if I knew what your true purpose is. You," he waggled a claw at her accusingly. "Are a devious little human."

"I'm not *little*," she stood tall, the skinsuit's elastic motors helping support her own weary muscles. "My people have a saying: 'All's well that ends well'."

"*My* people have a saying: 'If it seems too good to be true, it is'."

"Don't look a gift horse in the mouth," she countered.

"You *should* look, if it is a Trojan horse." Seeing her surprise, he added "Yes, I have studied some of your history. It seemed prudent to gain understanding of your species, unimportant though you are."

"I have plenty more clichés. We could go on all day like this, if you'd like."

"I would *not* like," he sighed. "Colonel Perkins, while I find it difficult to believe that you had an Elder power tap in your possession before you arrived here, I find it *more* difficult to believe that you just got incredibly lucky."

"My people have a saying: 'Shit happens'. Sometimes, it happens to the assholes on the other side of the fight," she made an exaggerated shrug. "I'm not going to argue with that."

Scorandum knew the conversation wasn't going anywhere. "Fine. Could you give me a hint whether my people are likely to find anything valuable on this world?"

"You *will* find our eternal esteem and gratitude. That's got to be worth something, right?"

He hid his eyes behind claws and shook his head slowly. "Oh, I am getting too old for this shit."

Dave Czajka enjoyed being able to run a hand through his hair, especially since as a civilian, he didn't have to keep his hair trimmed to regulation length. Emily had hinted she wanted him to grow his hair longer, but he hated feeling it brush his collar, and shaggy hair and a beard made it seem like he was pretending to be a special forces operator. So, he let it grow just long enough to annoy NCOs who assumed he was in uniform.

The best part of running a hand through his hair was that he *could*, because he wasn't wearing a skinsuit helmet twenty-four seven. The ceasefire with the Wurgalan was holding with both sides honoring both the letter and spirit of the agreement, a fact that was pleasantly surprising to everyone. The squids not only were being cooperative in preparing to surrender their planet, they were generally less bitter and resentful than expected. The lack of hard feelings might have been due to the fact that the new status of the Achakai would cause serious headaches for the Kristang, who were the hated rivals of the Wurgalan. And from the gleeful knowledge that the Bosphuraq, who were even more hated, were getting their asses kicked by the Jeraptha. Knowing that the loss of Stiglord caused pain to their rivals and patrons helped soothe the humiliation felt by the Wurgalan.

With the Wurgalan being quiet and cooperative, the only significant violence on Squidworld was between the Achakai and the Verd-kris, with the human troops caught in the middle and taking no shit from the ninjas. As far as Dave was concerned, the sooner the Legion evaced from Squidworld, the better, and good riddance to the assassin's guild.

The relative peace and tranquility on the planet meant that off-duty personnel did not need to stay sealed up in skinsuits all the time, as long as they had their gear close by for ready use. The first thing Dave had done when he took off his powered armor was to dump a bucket of water over his head, rinsing away the caked-on grime that the suit's internal cleaning mechanisms just never seemed to take care of.

"Hey," he waved to the group. Derek and Jesse had dragged crates into a rough semicircle and set up a tarp as an awning, a place to sit around and do nothing during their off-duty hours. "Sir," he nodded to Derek. Hanging out with officers could be awkward.

"Czajka," Derek said with a smile, sitting up to tossing a chocolate bar to Dave. It wasn't real chocolate of course, and the version created by the Ruhar always had a caramel aftertaste. Still, it was sweet and the only chocolate within a thousand lightyears.

"Thanks," Dave unwrapped the treat and bit into it. "What's up?"

"Nothin' much," Jesse was laying back on a stack of crates, drinking from a canteen. He rubbed his forehead, where he had a rash from the helmet liner digging into his skin. Reaching into a pocket, he got out a compass that had a mirror under the lid, so he could check the irritated area.

"Forget it, 'Pone," Dave laughed. "No matter how many times you ask that mirror, you are *not* the fairest in the land."

Derek offered a high five to Dave. "Good one."

"Hey," Jesse closed the lid and tucked the compass back in a pocket. "I never said I was Goldi freakin' locks."

"Uh, I think that mirror thing was Snow White," Dave said.

"You sure about that?" Jesse frowned. "I get that one mixed up with Sleeping Beauty."

"They were both poisoned and fell asleep," Derek said. "Kind of the same thing."

"You know what I wonder?" Dave took another bite of chocolate. "That Snow White chick lived with the Seven Dwarves, right?"

"Yeah, so?" Jesse wished he hadn't already eaten his own chocolate bar.

"So," Dave asked, "how many of those Dwarves you think wanted to bang her?"

"Well, they're guys, so, seven," Jesse answered, and they all had a good laugh.

"Got to be," Derek agreed. "Unless one of the dwarves was gay," he added.

"If one of them was," Jesse motioned for chocolate, and Dave broke off a piece and tossed it to him. "I'll bet it was Grumpy."

Derek sat up again. "Grumpy? Why's that?"

"Think about it. If you were the *only* gay guy around, you'd be awful lonely," Jesse explained. "That would make *me* grumpy."

"Ah," Derek nodded. "makes sense."

"Oh. My. God." Shauna exclaimed as she, Perkins and Striebich walked under the makeshift awning. "Is *this* what you guys talk about when we're not around?"

"Not all the time," Derek swung his legs over the crate. "We had a long conversation about the philosophy of existentialism."

"Really?" Irene laughed. "What do *you* know about that?"

"I know that most of the people who use that term have no clue what it means," Derek winked at her. "Colonel, you don't look happy. What's up?"

Perkins slammed a fist down on a crate. "This operation was a complete disaster. We didn't do *anything* we planned!"

"Come on, Em, uh, Ma'am," Dave's cheeked reddened at his mistake. "We did some good things that-"

"None of it was planned!" She threw up her hands, refusing to be comforted. "We didn't plan for our ships to be shot out of orbit, we didn't plan to crash in the middle of nowhere. We didn't plan to find and capture a plasma cannon site."

"Yeah, but that was a damned good thing," Jesse noted. "Cause we also didn't plan on Bosphuraq ships jumping in to spoil the party."

"Fine, sure," Perkins shook her head. "That was *one* good thing. The rest of the op for us was pulling two Verd platoons out of a city where they shouldn't have been in the first place. What a clusterfuck! We didn't accomplish anything we had in the plan. The worst part is, we gave away our toy," she used the code word for the Elder power tap.

"It's not a *complete* disaster," Irene mumbled through a mouthful of a chewy ration bar. "The ninjas own this rock now. We *did* accomplish our main goal, Ma'am. The Achakai have a homeworld, they can qualify to be recognized as a clan, and that will keep the lizards so busy fighting each other that they won't be going on the offensive against the Ruhar for years, maybe longer."

"You're right, Striebich. Somehow, we pulled a rabbit out of hat. Again."

"What I want to know," Irene pulled the wrapper down further, but didn't bite into the bar. It tasted like sawdust flavored with cocoa powder, and she decided she wasn't *that* hungry yet. "Is what's the end game, Ma'am?"

"Striebich, that's above my pay grade."

"Excuse me, Ma'am," Irene tucked the ration bar away in a pocket. "But that's bullshit, and we all know it."

"It is above *your* pay grade."

Irene shrugged. "Yes, Ma'am. It would be easier for us to help, if we knew what the hell we're trying to accomplish out here."

Perkins saw that everyone, including and maybe most especially Dave Czajka, were nodding agreement. "Ok," she took a breath. "Not now. You have to trust me on this."

"We do," Shauna agreed, though she looked hurt.

"All I can say is, there are a whole lot of moving pieces, so the next step depends on what the aliens do."

"Which aliens?" Irene wasn't going to let it go so easily. "The lizards? Or the Ruhar?"

"Both. Maybe both. It depends," Perkins said. "Listen, people, that's all I'm going to say on the subject. That's all I *can* say. When I know what the hell we're doing next, you'll be the first to know. That's a promise."

"Ma'am?" Shauna asked. "Surgun Jates, and Nert, they're not being read in on this?"

"No," Perkins shook her head. "We can't put them in that position. They might have divided loyalties, and that's not fair to them. Everyone," she looked at each member of her team one by one, searching their eyes. "That's as far as this discussion goes for now. Drop the subject. We have plenty of immediate issues to deal with."

Irene knew their leader was looking at her. "Yes, Ma'am," she agreed.

Dave followed the Mavericks leader when she walked away. "Em? Hey, Em, wait. You know this wasn't your fault. Why are you so pissed off?"

Before answering, she looked around to see if anyone was close enough to overhear. "Dave, we gave up the *toy*, for nothing."

"It wasn't nothing. We *won*. The Torgalau gave us bad intel, the hamsters missed an entire layer of SD satellites and a bunch of Bosphuraq warships. This was never going to be easy."

"I know that."

"We agreed that I wouldn't ask you about things you shouldn't tell me. So, I won't ask what your plans are. Cashing in the toy for a ride to Earth wasn't ever going to happen. We brought the toy here in case we needed it, and we *did*. Bad shit happened, we survived. All we can do is learn from it, and hope that we don't need a toy next time, 'cause we won't have one."

"Understanding all that doesn't make me any less pissed off. We had to rely on the beetles to bail us out twice now."

"Yeah, so? In combat, you utilize all available resources," he reminded her. "Besides, the beetles were looking for an excuse to kick ass here."

"I should have thought of something better than giving up the best asset we have."

Dave tapped her gently on the forehead. "The best asset we have is right here. When you think of something better you could have done, *then* you can get pissed at yourself. And hey, maybe next time we *plan* for the beetles to bring in the cavalry? Hopefully *before* I have to ride a cargo container down from orbit," he added with a wink.

"I'll do my best." She leaned forward and kissed him, not caring who saw the public display of affection. "I have to talk with the Achakai again. I'll see you at dinner?"

"Count on it."

# CHAPTER THIRTY SIX

Emily Perkins woke immediately to the sound of a soft *thump* on the dirt floor of her tent. The floor wasn't actually dirt, there were sort of rubber pads keeping the surface from churning into mud and dust, but the floor wasn't solid. She didn't mind the primitive conditions, because sleeping in a tent assured her the situation *was* temporary, and that she would someday soon be leaving Squidworld behind forever.

Any thump in the middle of the night was not a good thing, nor was it good that anything could have made a *thump* in her tent without her first being alerted by the motion-detector, infrared or other sensors that were supposed to be watching over her. Or the guards who patrolled the camp.

She was instantly awake, as much from a surge of adrenaline as from long practice in the military. Her mouth opened to draw a deep breath when a dry, rough hand covered her face and she felt the cold composite barrel of a rifle or pistol pressed to her left temple.

"Colonel Perkins," the harsh voice of a lizard hissed to her. "Do not attempt to call for help."

Silently, in the darkness, she nodded with as little movement as she thought necessary.

"Good. You understand." The cold muzzle was still against her skin, but the hand lifted from her mouth. A dim light shone, only enough for her to see the shadowy outline of a figure leaning over her. And, on the floor, another figure, prone and unmoving. That must have been the thump she heard.

What the *hell* was going on? The figure standing over her was Kristang, but not wearing the uniform of a Verd-kris soldier. The lizard also was speaking to her in English, bypassing the need for a translator. She recognized the accent.

He was an Achakai.

Screwing up her courage, she licked her dry lips and spoke in a whisper. "What's with the dead guy?"

There was a soft sound like a sigh, or a snort of derision. "He was sent here by a rival House."

"Sent here to kill me?"

"Yes. *My* House wishes to have the honor of fulfilling that contract. You would not understand." The pressure of the pistol pressed against her skin had not relented.

She was going to die. There was anger, but mostly there was regret. Regret for tasks not yet completed. Regret for things she had not said. "Your people had plenty of opportunity before this. Why now?"

"Because my leadership wished to wait, until our mission here was completed. We now control this world, and yesterday, the Swift Arrows formally recognized my people as a clan of the Kristang." It may have been her imagination, but it seemed like the assassin stood a bit taller when saying those words.

"I know," she raised her voice slightly, and the pistol pressed harder against her. Lowering her voice, she added "I know that, because I set up those negotiations between your people and the Swift Arrows. *I* got the Swift Arrows to appoint Admiral Kekrando as their representative."

"Yes. I, and my House, all of my people, are grateful to you."

"*This* is how you show gratitude?"

"Colonel Perkins, my people have been accused of being without honor, yet we have never failed to fulfill a legitimate contract. It is not possible for my House to back out of a contract. Honor must be satisfied."

*This*, she told herself, is what happens when you ally yourself with a group of assassins. Really, she was not surprised, only sad. "Then there isn't anything more to say. Go on," she settled back into the pillow. "Do it. Get it over with."

To her surprise, the pressure of the pistol at her temple went away, and the figure stood up, drawing to his full height, nearly scraping the roof of the tent. "My people have fulfilled a dream held for millennia. On behalf of all Achakai, I thank you."

"What? I-" While she watched, wide-eyed in terror, the assassin raised the pistol to his own temple.

"Honor *must* be satisfied." And pulled the trigger.

Lizard blood and brain matter splattered the roof and side of the tent, and the body slumped to the floor, the pistol clattering off the side of her cot as an alarm sounded outside and she heard human voices shouting.

"Well," she shuddered, coming down off her adrenaline high. "Ain't that some shit?"

Dave Czajka burst through the tent flap as she swung her legs over to sit on the cot, feeling pleased that she hadn't peed herself even a little. It is odd, she reflected, what your mind focuses on in times of stress.

"Em!" He shouted, stumbling as he stepped unexpectedly on a bulky object in the darkness. "What happ-"

"It's fine." She reached up and touched his forearm. It almost made her laugh that he was wearing only boxer shorts and one sock. "Dave, I'm Ok, really."

"Holy *shit*," he shone the light of his rifle onto the floor, illuminating the two bodies there. "You killed these guys?"

"No. They- I guess it was a murder-suicide?" She was too tired to explain further, then more soldiers burst into the tent and her night became a *major* pain in the ass.

Seven hours later, worn out emotionally not from fear or excitement but from the grinding *boredom* of being asked the same questions over and over, she stumbled back to her tent. No, not her tent, that was taped off as a crime scene, with the UNEF MPs going through the motions of their jobs, even though everyone already knew the full story. She went into a tent that had just been set up, supposedly for the purpose of getting a couple hours of sleep before her next meeting. In reality, there was no way she could fall asleep at that point, all she wanted was to get away from well-meaning people expressing their shock and concern. Yes, it was terrifying, she had responded over and over. No, I'll never get over the shock. Yes, we still have to treat the Achakai as allies or at least as customers. I am still alive, no harm done, see?

It was exhausting. There really was only one person in the world, in *any* of the worlds she had been on, who gave her energy instead of making her tired of interacting with other people. Only one person with whom she could be one hundred percent *herself*, and realizing that prompted her to make a decision.

She pinged Dave Czajka.

"Hey," he said softly as he closed the tent flap behind himself. "You should be sleeping."

"Like I can sleep with all that going on," she pointed toward the roof of the tent, which echoed with the sound of gunships circling as they patrolled the camp, watching for intruders. Human voices, shouting or just talking too loudly, surrounded the tent, soldiers determined not to allow another assassin in their midst. The voices were all human, because the few Verd-kris who had been in the camp had been politely but firmly escorted elsewhere, for the simple reason that no one could tell a Verd male from an Achakai. She put a thumb near her chin and pointed it upward. "Lift your faceplate."

Dave hesitated. "I'm on duty," he told her.

"Please. I want to *see* you."

He knew what she meant. Helmet faceplates could be set to be completely transparent, yet there was always a bit of a reflection, and with the faceplate closed the wearer of the suit had to talk through the helmet's external speakers. Dave hesitated. He was carrying a rifle in camp because the area was clearly not safe, and regulations required suits to be sealed for protection against chemical and biological weapons.

"I can make it an order, if you like."

"I'm a civilian now, remember?" He broke the seal and lifted the faceplate. "Is this better?"

"Much." She stood up off the cot and kissed him, awkward because the helmet's chin projected forward. "You know what the scariest part was?"

"Having a master assassin holding a gun to your head?" He guessed, forcing a grin.

"No. It was the thought that if I died, there would be so much left that I didn't do."

"Is this about windsurfing again?" That time, the grin was genuine. They had talked about taking leave to go windsurfing along one of the tropical beaches of Lemuria, where enterprising former soldiers had set up resorts for humans. Neither of them had ever so much as taken a single windsurfing lesson, and the subject had become an inside joke between them.

"It's about a lot more than windsurfing."

His grin turned to a frown. "Em, listen, you've got to stop with this shit about feeling the weight of the galaxy is on your shoulders." He pointed to the tent flap with one hand, and cradled her chin with the other. "The Legion has a whole *army* of people. It's not all on you."

"That's not what I meant," she shook her head, searching his eyes for understanding. He was in combat mode, she knew that, and he wasn't able to focus on anything else. All he wanted was to protect her, because he hadn't been able to protect her before. Dropping to one knee, she saw not surprise but concern in his eyes, thinking something was wrong with her. "I'm fine," she waved him away when he offered to pull her up. She took a breath. This is not easy, she thought. Taking one of his hands in hers, she looked up at him. "David Jakob Czajka, will you marry me?"

"*Damn* it," he exclaimed.

She cocked her head, not knowing whether to be amused or hurt. "That was *not* exactly the response I was hoping for."

"Sorry," he mumbled and dropped to his knees, bending forward so he wasn't looking down at her. "It's just, I had a whole *speech* planned. We were going to dinner at that beach bar we like. Instead, we're in a tent, after my girlfriend almost got assassinated by a lizard."

"Anyone can get engaged at the beach," she laughed. "*We* have a great story."

"Em, I got a ring and everything."

"You did?"

"Yeah," he kissed her and pulled away. "I was going to wait until we got back to Paradise, you know? We don't need any distractions on this rock, especially not you."

"You got a ring for me. I don't have anything for you."

Pursing his lips, he considered. "I don't think guys wear engagement rings?"

She rolled her eyes. "We're a thousand lightyears from Earth. On an alien planet. I'm ten years older than you. You think traditions really matter?"

She was ten years older than him, a fact that neither of them mentioned or cared much about. "Giving the girl a ring is a tradition. You don't want one?"

"Of course I want one," she blushed.

"Good, because this one is really special," he explained with enthusiasm. "I had it made from a fragment that came from an Elder starship, the one that crashed on Paradise."

"*What?*" She gasped. "How could you afford that?"

"The brewery," he said casually. "We're making a *lot* of money, you didn't know that?"

"We never talk about business."

"Maybe we should."

"Before that, can we talk about something else?" She tapped his armored chest. "You didn't give me an answer, Mister."

"Will *you* marry *me*?" he asked.

"Yes."

"Oh, *hell* yes," he grinned, before he rolled his eyes and groaned.

"What's wrong?"

"Now I have to plan all the place settings and get a dress and invite bridesmaids and select a cake. Weddings are *so* much work for the man."

"Oh, bullshit," she laughed. "The only thing *you* will do is show up at the last minute, hopefully not to hungover and in a suit that isn't too wrinkled."

"Well, sure, if you insist," he winked.

General Ross had been dreading the call. He was prepared for it, had rehearsed what he would say, had facts and figures ready to back up his argument, and knew that nothing he said would make a difference. Admiral Kune also knew the facts, had access to most or all of the same numbers, and nothing he thought would make much of a difference. Kune had his orders, and his ability to be flexible was limited.

The conversation began well. Ross opened by congratulating the Ruhar leader on successfully landing the invasion force, which they both knew had nearly been a disaster. Kune then praised Ross's leadership of the force on the ground, which they both knew had nearly been overwhelmed and defeated. After exchanging pleasantries for an appropriate amount of time, they both expressed their disgust with the unorthodox and surprisingly undisciplined infantry tactics of the Achakai.

"It was hell until the Wurgalan surrendered," Ross admitted. "Now I'm glad that the ninjas don't know shit about organized warfare. We're outnumbered down here, I won't sleep well until we get our last set of boots off the ground. I'm having to deploy all my human troops to keep the Achakai and the Verds separated, that leaves me spread thin. If the ninjas continue abusing the Wurgalan, the ceasefire could break down, and," he let out a long breath. "Well, you know what's going on down here."

"As we discussed, the priority for spacelift will be getting the Verds off the ground first. We will extract them through your territory."

"That's going to be tricky, but we'll manage. Any progress on the squids sending transport to pull their own people off this rock?"

"The ship that brought the surrender agreement to their central government only arrived there yesterday, if it was on schedule. I would not expect a reply for another three, four weeks. General Ross, the Wurgalan will be very alarmed by this development, I do not think they will easily accept loss of this world."

"Yeah, well, they can argue with the facts all they want. The Swift Arrows have recognized the Achakai as a clan, and the two major clans allied with the Swift Arrows have offered recognition also."

"At a price," Kune noted with a frown.

"That isn't our problem. It's nice to have *something* that is not our problem."

"Indeed." Kune cleared his throat, and got to the part of the conversation they both knew was coming. "General, the operation to extract the Verd-kris will commence at eleven hundred hours tomorrow. My battleship squadron will be departing once the majority of the Legion ground force has been pulled off the surface."

"Yeah. Admiral, I wish we could talk about that. The Jeraptha aren't providing cover anymore. If the birds come back, we will be awfully exposed out here. I'm not worried about the squids trying to take back this rock, the Achakai can handle it with help from the Swift-"

Kune interrupted, his eyebrows lifted with surprise. "You haven't heard?"

"Heard what?" Ross hated being surprised, especially by something his staff was supposed to keep him informed about.

"The official communication had not gone out yet, I just thought you might have heard the news from a back channel."

"Come on," Ross pleaded. "Don't keep me in suspense down here."

Kune's face broke into a broad grin, exposing his incisors. "The Bosphuraq will not be causing trouble for this world, not for a significant time. Without transport resources and support from their patrons, the Wurgalan are unlikely to mount a serious effort to take back this planet."

"Uh, Ok? What is going on?"

"The Bosphuraq were *very* naughty. You know they attacked those two ships the Maxolhx were sending to Earth?"

"Of course," Ross acknowledged, mildly surprised the Ruhar admiral mentioned it. He had to know that any reference to their lost homeworld was painful for humans to hear. "That's why we are out here, it cleared the way for us to take action against a client of the Bosphuraq."

"That's not all the birds did. We only learned about it this morning, when the courier ship arrived. The assumption was the Bosphuraq would take their punishment like good, obedient little clients. Keep their heads down, at least pretend they are cooperating with the investigation, ride it out until the Maxolhx got tired of using bird planets for target practice."

"If they're smart," Ross mused, "they'll play the long game. Their government plays for time while they try to identify the rogue group who attacked their patrons, get access to the technology. Maybe trade it in exchange for a measure of forgiveness, while keeping a copy of the tech for themselves."

"That would be smart. Maybe their government is doing that, but in the meantime, the rogue group isn't just keeping their heads down. They're hitting back."

"Holy shit. Hitting back how?"

"Some kind of ghost ship is out there, conducting hit-and-run attacks against Maxolhx ships. The ghost ship crew leaves messages, identifying themselves as Bosphuraq freedom fighters, or some nonsense like that," Kune snorted. "The ghost ship vows to continue attacks until their oppressors cease their unlawful actions against the peace-loving Bosphuraq people. The Maxolhx have been chasing the ghost ship all over the sector and beyond, with no result. The intel we received lists seven attacks, and the losses have all been on the Maxolhx side. The reason we care about this is the Maxolhx have predictably not backed down to the ghost ship's threats, they are striking the birds harder than ever. For now, and the foreseeable future, the Bosphuraq will not be able to send warships here, or provide transport to the Wurgalan."

"Whooo," Ross exhaled. "This is a game-changer."

"It is. General Ross, the situation appears to be a positive development for us in the short term, but it is *dangerous*. If the rogue faction of Bosphuraq are able to deploy their advanced technology with more than one ship, they could become rivals of the two apex species. That would upset the balance of power that has kept the galaxy from blowing up."

"The galaxy hasn't exactly been *peaceful*."

"An all-out war between the Maxolhx and Rindhalu could devastate the entire galaxy."

"I can see that. Admiral, that's above my pay grade. There's nothing humans can do to affect the outcome, one way or another."

"I do not see there is anything my people could do either," Kune lamented. "The result of this new information is I am being ordered to accelerate the extraction from this world. Our fleet is pulling back to a defensive posture, to prepare for trouble. Your people will be on the sidelines until this shakes out."

"Hmm," Ross grunted. Privately, he thought the Ruhar pulling back to a defensive posture would mean *more* work for the Alien Legion, not less. There would still be a need for fighting, and the Ruhar would especially not want to get their own Federal Army tied down in stamping out fires. They would rely on the Legion, because those troops were considered expendable. "I'm sure you're right about that," he lied. "You're telling me this, because you think we don't need to worry about any Bosphuraq warships crashing the party here?'

"Yes."

"I'd like to see the intel-"

"It was just transmitted to your command."

"Thank you. I'll need to look at it, but, it sure sounds like the birds have to worry about their own problems. I will get my staff to dust off the contingency plans to accelerate the evac. Like we agreed, we pull the Verds off this rock first. Admiral? I would like you to keep a couple of destroyer squadrons in orbit, until the last Legion boot steps off the ground. The Achakai have their own ships overhead, and their leaders must be considering that it would be useful to have Legion soldiers as hostages."

Kune's laugh was bitter, but sounded comical because of his slightly-squeaky voice. "If the Achakai are not looking for an opportunity to take hostages, I would be very disappointed with them. General, I have already planned to keep one destroyer squadron plus three cruisers here, until the evacuation is complete. That does not include any sort of liaison team you plan to retain here."

"We are not planning to leave a single human, or Verd, on this rock."

"I wasn't talking about *your* plans," Kune explained. "I do not know what Colonel Perkins intends to do next."

"Shit. Neither do I. Thank you, I'll get the revised schedule to you ASAP."

Getting his command staff up to speed, then quickly reviewing the existing contingency plan and ordering changes, took nearly an hour. Perkins was not able to speak privately for another twenty minutes, during which time Ross wondered what to say. By the time she called on a secure channel, he still had nothing. "I suppose you've heard the big news," he opened.

"Yes, Sir. Holy *shit*."

"That was my reaction."

"Have the birdbrains lost their fucking *minds*?" She asked.

"Either that, or they think they can win the fight, in the long run."

"Wow," she whistled. "That is one *hell* of a gamble."

"Maybe not. The Bosphuraq have had the boots of the Maxolhx on their necks for a long time, they've got to be sick of taking shit from their patrons. Somebody in their society decided that hitting their overlords directly is worth the risk. You understand this is an extremely dangerous development? The Maxolhx can't back down or they would look weak, and whatever group is flying that ghost ship sounds like true-believer fanatics. *They* won't back down."

"I wonder about that."

"What?"

"Did you read any of the messages from the ghost ship?"

"Some of it. Typically bomb-throwing revolutionary bullshit, why?"

"It sounds familiar. A little *too* typical, you know what I mean? It's like whoever wrote those messages wants us to *think* they are irrational fanatics."

"Hmm. I see what you mean," he said as he made a note to ask his intel people to look at the ghost ship's messages.

"Sir, does this all seem a bit too convenient?"

"I'm not following you, Perkins. It is convenient for our evac plan, but-"

"No, I meant, my bullshit detector went off when I read the original report, about the birds destroying the two ships headed for Earth. We are supposed to believe the Bosphuraq miraculously developed technology that neither the Maxolhx nor Rindhalu have? The birdbrains suddenly made a game-changing discovery, created a weapon neither of the apex species thought of over thousands of years? Do you think that happened, or it is more likely the tech came from the spiders?"

"Colonel?" Ross's head was spinning.

"Sir, think about it. It is a hell of a lot more likely this magical tech belongs to the *Rindhalu*, but of course, they can't use it directly without triggering all-out war with the Maxolhx. So, maybe they gave a piece of their tech to the birdbrains, to use against their patrons. The Rindhalu sit back and watch their enemy's coalition fall apart, while they get to deny any involvement. The Bosphuraq don't actually understand how the tech works, so there is no risk it can spread and threaten the Rindhalu."

"Shit. Perkins, the inside of your head must be a scary place."

"I can't be the only person who thinks the scenario in the official report smells like BS. Either we believe that Bosphuraq scientists pulled off the greatest Hail Mary play in the history of the galaxy, *or*, we try to imagine who benefits from us thinking the Bosphuraq developed the tech on their own."

"Oh, damn it, Perkins. I had a headache when I got out of the sack this morning, I don't need you making it worse. It doesn't matter what *we* think. What matters is the Maxolhx think their clients did it."

"*Officially* they think that way, yes. They're not stupid."

Ross knew that Perkins's inventive mind would spin with a dozen scenarios, none of which helped with his immediate task of pulling the Legion off the planet. "Let's put that aside. Our hamster overlords are accelerating the schedule for pulling us off this rock. They will cover the evac, but, they aren't providing a permanent presence here. What I'm saying is, if you have any plans to remain here

as a liaison, or to advance whatever devious plan you have cooked up, you need to-
"

"No, Sir. I'm as eager to get off this rock as everyone else. The Swift Arrows recognized the Achakai as a clan, our mission is done here. All we could do is get caught in the middle while lizards kill each other."

Ross leaned back in the chair, relieved. His fear was that Perkins had been given secret orders by UNEF-HQ, or had plans to go off on her own. "That's good to hear. The Ruhar plan to pull back their forces into a defensive posture, all across their territory."

"Makes sense. That means more work for *us*."

"Agreed. Admiral Kune thinks the opposite," he chuckled.

"The fighting isn't going to stop, and *somebody* has to be the trigger-pullers. Sir, actually, I was going to contact you, even before we got word about this ghost ship nonsense. I need to request permission to leave the theater."

"Leave? To go where?"

"Uh, that depends. The *Sure Thing* is waiting for me, so I don't need to arrange transport."

"Is this more secret-squirrel crap you can't tell me about?" He hated that aspect of his job. He hated it even worse when Perkins did something that not even UNEF-HQ knew about in advance, because HQ then asked Ross what the hell was going on. Technically, he was her commanding officer only for the current mission, but his leadership didn't see it that way.

"Sir, all I can say is, we stirred up a lot of trouble here. Poked a hornet's nest with a stick. The Kristang are in disarray and that is nothing but good for us, and our allies. I'd like to keep that momentum going."

"Very well," he didn't feel like putting energy into a useless argument. "You're looking for targets of opportunity?"

"Yes. UNEF-HQ gave me broad authority for the next phase of the operation."

"Hmmph," he snorted. "They didn't tell *me* about the next step."

"Don't you have enough shit to worry about already?"

"It's the shit I *don't* know about that gives me a headache. All right, Perkins, permission granted. Do me a favor?"

"Sir?"

"If you visit Lizardville, bring back a vintage bottle of that *shaze* crap they drink."

"We can't drink it," she cautioned. "It's incompatible with human-"

"It's not for *me*. I want it for the next time we accept the surrender of a group of lizard assholes."

"Oh," she laughed. "Got it. Will do."

# CHAPTER THIRTY SEVEN

The lizards came aboard the *Sure Thing*, rather than her taking a dropship to one of their ships. Mostly that was because she was safer aboard a Jeraptha ship, even if it was an old star carrier that had been converted into a shady merchant-slash-smuggler vessel. But also because making the lizards come to *her* made a statement about who had the power in the relationship, and also because, well, fuck them.

When the chief lizards of the Fire Dragon clan walked down the ramp of their gleamingly-clean dropship and stepped on the deck of the *Sure Thing*, they started to launch into an achingly dull ceremonial greeting, which was cut short by her security detail pointing rifles at the ugly lizards, demanding they stand still to be scanned to verify they weren't carrying weapons.

"Colonel Perkins," said a lizard who had a bearing a bit more diplomatic than his pissed-off companions. "We have complied with your terms, and are not carrying weapons. Surely it is not best to begin negotiations with a gesture of mistrust that-"

Perkins held up a hand. "You can stop right there. I don't care whether you trust me, and I sure as hell don't trust *you*. As far as I know, one of *you*," she glared from one lizard face to the next, "hired the Achakai to kill me. *You* requested this meeting, I didn't. If you're going to waste my time, I have better things to do."

"Ah," the lizard nodded sagely. "Your reputation for diplomacy is justified."

Captain Gumbano looked up from the scanner he had used. "They are clean, Colonel."

Perkins acknowledged that with a curt nod. "Fine, then. I'll try being diplomatic. What do you want?"

The talking lizard looked to the most gaudily dressed of the group, who made a hand gesture, apparently telling his spokesman to get on with it. "We do not wish to insult your intelligence," the lizard spokesman said, with an expression like he could not stomach speaking to a human, to a female. "The recent alliance between the Swift Arrow clan and the dishonored ones is-"

"Between the Swift Arrow clan and the Shining Dagger clan," she corrected him, using the name the Achakai had chosen for themselves. "They are a *clan* now recognized by more than enough clans to represent a majority in your governing council."

"Er, yes," the lizard looked stricken. "Quite so. This alliance," he could not bring himself to say the name of the newest Kristang clan, "is disruptive and dangerous. With the, the former Achakai," he decided on a compromise, "allied with them, the Swift Arrows now present a threat to all major non-allied clans."

What she wanted to say was '*Boo freakin' hoo*', but instead she settled for keeping the lizards pissed off and off balance. "Yup. Sure sounds like *you* have a major problem. Why should I care?"

"Because," the spokesman closed his eyes painfully, avoiding the murderous glare of his leaders. "My clan is threatened. We wish to restore the balance of power."

Bullshit, Perkins thought to herself. They wanted to tip the balance of power in their favor. "Interesting. Why are you here, rather than trying to negotiate alliances with other clans?"

"Because the clans with significant military power have all declared for one of the existing alliances. There are a few subclans who might be persuaded to change sides for a price, but we do not feel they could be trusted. Colonel Perkins, the *rules* which have governed our society quite effectively for millennia have been discarded by the rise of the, the former Achakai. We hope you appreciate the great damage this has caused to our society."

"You are here to *lecture* me?"

"No," the spokesman closed his eyes again. "We only wish for you to understand the seriousness of the situation."

"I am terribly sorry about that. You haven't answered my question. Why are you *here*?"

"Because," the lizard swallowed hard, choking on his own words. "To restore the balance of power, we wish to conclude an agreement with you." He looked away, unable to look her in the eyes. "We wish to hire the Alien Legion."

*There* it is, Perkins kept her very satisfied smile from showing. "*Hire* the Legion? To fight for you, against other clans?"

"Yes."

"Huh," she pretended to be thinking about the shocking proposal. Pretending to be shocked at all. "I have to say, your timing isn't the best."

The spokeslizard looked at his leaders, then ventured a question. "We do not understand."

She snorted, allowing the grin to break onto her face. "You need to get in line, pal. The Black Trees and two other clans already contacted the Legion," she lied. "All I can say is, you had better make a *very* tempting offer, or you are out of luck."

The lizards murmured amongst themselves angrily, until the most gaudily-dressed one turned to glare at her, less with hatred than with resignation. "Colonel Perkins, please." He looked at his fellow clan leaders, who gestured for him to continue. "Name your price."

THE END


**Author's note:**

Thank you for reading one of my books! It took years to write my first three books, I had a job as a business manager for an IT company so I wrote at night, on weekends and during vacations. While I had many ideas for books over the years, the first one I ever completed was 'Aces' and I sort of wrote that book for my at-the-time teenage nieces. If you read 'Aces', you can see some early elements of the Expeditionary Force stories; impossible situations, problem-solving, clever thinking and some sarcastic humor.

Next I wrote a book about humanity's program to develop faster-than-light spaceflight, it was an adventure story about astronauts stranded on an alien planet and trying to warn Earth about a dangerous flaw in the FTL drive. It was a good story, and I submitted it to traditional publishers back in the mid-2000s. And I got rejections. My writing was 'solid', which I have since learned means publishers can't think of anything else to say but don't want to insult aspiring writers. The story was too long, they wanted me to cut it to a novella and change just about everything. Instead of essentially scrapping the story and starting over, I threw it out and tried something else.

Columbus Day and Ascendant were written together starting around 2011, I switched back and forth between writing those two books. The idea for Ascendant came to me after watching the first Harry Potter movie, one of my nieces asked what would have happened to Harry Potter if no one ever told him he is a wizard? Hmm, I thought, that is a very good question.... So, I wrote Ascendant.

In the original, very early version of Columbus Day, Skippy was a cute little robot who stowed away on a ship when the Kristang invade Earth, and he helps Joe defeat the aliens. After a year trying to write that version, I decided it sounded too much like a Disney Channel movie of the week, and it, well, it sucked. Although it hurt to waste a year's worth of writing, I threw away that version and started over. This time I wrote an outline for the entire Expeditionary Force story arc first, so I would know where the overall story is going. That was a great idea and I have stuck to that outline (with minor detours along the way).

With Aces, Columbus Day and Ascendant finished by the summer of 2015 and no publisher interested, my wife suggested that I:

1) Try self-publishing the books in Amazon
2) For the love of God please shut up about not being able to get my books published
3) Clean out the garage

It took six months of research and revisions to get the three books ready for upload to Amazon. In addition to reformatting the books to Amazon's standards, I had to buy covers and set up an Amazon account as a writer. When I clicked the 'Upload' button on January 10th 2016 my greatest hope was that somebody, anybody out there would buy ONE of my books because then I could be a published author. After selling one of each book, my goal was to make enough money to pay for the cover art I bought online (about $35 for each book).

For that first half-month of January 2016, Amazon sent us a check for $410.09 and we used part of the money for a nice dinner. I think the rest of the money went toward buying new tires for my car.

At the time I uploaded Columbus Day, I had the second book in the series SpecOps about halfway done, and I kept writing at night and on weekends. By April, the sales of Columbus Day were at the point where my wife and I said "Whoa, this could be more than just a hobby". At that point, I took a week of vacation to stay home and write SpecOps 12 hours a day for nine days. Truly fun-filled vacation! Doing that gave me a jump-start on the schedule, and SpecOps was published at the beginning of June 2016. In the middle of that July, to our complete amazement, we were discussing whether I should quit my job to write full-time. That August I had a "life is too short" moment when a family friend died and then my grandmother died, and we decided I should try this writing thing full-time. Before I gave notice at my job, I showed my wife a business plan listing the books I planned to write for the next three years, with plot outlines and publication dates. This assured my wife that quitting my real job was not an excuse to sit around in shorts and T-shirts watching sci fi movies 'for research'.

During the summer of 2016, R.C. Bray was offered Columbus Day to narrate, and I'm sure his first thought was "A book about a talking beer can? Riiiight. No." Fortunately, he thought about it again, or was on heavy-duty medication for a bad cold, or if he wasn't busy recording the book his wife expected him to repaint the house. Anyway, RC recorded Columbus Day, went back to his fabulous life of hanging out with movie stars and hitting golf balls off his yacht, and probably forgot all about the talking beer can.

When I heard RC Bray would be narrating Columbus Day, my reaction was "THE RC Bray? The guy who narrated The Martian? Winner of an Audie Award for best sci fi narrator? Ha ha, that is a good one. Ok, who is really narrating the book?"

Then the Columbus Day audiobook became a huge hit. And is a finalist for an 'Audie' Award as Audiobook of the Year!

When I got an offer to create audio versions of the Ascendant series, I was told the narrator would be Tim Gerard Reynolds. My reaction was "You mean some other guy named Tim Gerard Reynolds? Not the TGR who narrated the Red Rising audiobooks, right?"

Clearly, I have been very fortunate with narrators for my audiobooks. To be clear, they chose to work with me, I did not 'choose' them. If I had contacted Bob or Tim directly, I would have gone into super fan-boy mode and they would have filed for a restraining order. So, again, I am lucky they signed onto the projects.

So far, there is no deal for Expeditionary Force to become a movie or TV show, although I have had inquiries from producers and studios about the 'entertainment rights'. From what people in the industry have told me, even if a studio or network options the rights, it will be a looooooooong time before anything actually happens. I will get all excited for nothing, and years will go by with the project going through endless cycles with producers and directors coming aboard and disappearing, and just when I have totally given up and sunk into the Pit of Despair, a miracle will happen and the project gets financing! Whoo-hoo. I am not counting on it. On the other hand, Disney is pulling their content off Netflix next year, so Netflix will be looking for new original content...

Again, Thank YOU for reading one of my books. Writing gives me a great excuse to avoid cleaning out the garage.

Contact the author at craigalanson@gmail.com
https://www.facebook.com/Craig.Alanson.Author/
https://twitter.com/CraigAlanson?lang=en

Go to craigalanson.com for blogs and ExForce logo merchandise including T-shirts, patches, stickers, hats, and coffee mugs

Printed in Great Britain
by Amazon